A Million Tears II

The Tears of War and Peace

By Paul Henke

A MILLION TEARS

From the Files of TIFAT
(The International Force Against Terrorism)

DÉBÂCLE
MAYHEM

Also by Paul Henke

NEVER A WINNER

A Million Tears II

The Tears of War and Peace

Paul Henke

GOOD READ PUBLISHING

First published in 1999 by Good Read Publishing
A Good Read Publishing paperback

10 9 8 7 6 5 4 3 2 1

A CIP catalogue record for this title is available from the British Library

ISBN 1 902483 03 0

Typeset by Palimpsest Book Production Limited,
Polmont, Stirlingshire
Printed and bound in Great Britain by
Caledonian International Book Manufacturing Ltd, Glasgow

Good Read Publishing Ltd
Auchleshie House
Kelty Bridge
Callander FK17 8LS

This book is dedicated to my wife Dorothy.

Acknowledgements

I would like to acknowledge the help and support of my wife Dorothy, without whom my books would never get written. Also I must thank Joy McKellen for her wonderful job, yet again, in editing the manuscript. Finally, I want to say a special thanks to Charles Gallacher who did such a great job of final proof reading.

A Million Tears II

The Tears of War and Peace

Prologue

SIR DAVID GRIFFITHS had recovered from his recent bout of bronchitis and, now allowed out by his doctor, was sitting in the wheelhouse of his motor sailer, *My Joy II.* Various members of the family were aboard, preparing to get the boat underway. The *Time* magazine reporter appeared on the jetty, threw a holdall onto the deck and climbed nimbly aboard.

'Morning, Sir David. It's a beautiful day,' he greeted the octogenarian.

'It is that. A pleasant cruise into the Channel, lunch and a leisurely journey back is called for. I'm glad you decided to come.'

'I wouldn't have missed it for the world, sir,' he replied, casting an admiring glance at Sian, Sir David's granddaughter. Sir David chose to ignore the look, but as usual, had missed nothing.

Sian, a beautiful, black-haired girl in her early twenties was adroitly coiling up a berthing rope and slinging it down the forward hatch. She was dressed in snugly fitting jeans and a warm jumper; the clothes she wore left little to the imagination.

'Perhaps you could give Sian a hand?' Sir David suggested. 'As soon as Madelaine gets here we'll cast off and head out to sea.'

The young man nodded and went out on deck to be given instructions to get the boat ready. Contentedly, he leapt to the jetty and removed the forward spring passing it up to Sian. They exchanged shy smiles, both of them remembering the previous evening. It might be the swinging sixties, he thought, but there were still conventions to follow. Dinner in a nearby restaurant had been followed by a brief tussle in the front of Sian's MG Midget. After a suitable display of reluctance on her part, a certain amount of intimacy had taken place but they had not actually made love. Sian seemed to be reading his mind because she looked at him, blushed, and then giggled. His heart soared; in his fevered imagination that giggle held a great deal of promise.

'Here are my mother and grandma,' Sian said, looking along the jetty.

Walking towards them were two striking-looking women, one a red-haired, elderly lady, with streaks of grey in her shoulder length hair. In her seventies, Madelaine looked ten years younger. Beside her was her step-daughter, Susan. Slim, black-haired with streaks of grey, there could be no mistaking whose daughter Sian was. Both women were laden down with baskets, and the reporter stopped what he was doing to rush forward and give a helping hand.

'Take Madelaine's,' said Susan. 'I can manage.'

'Thank you,' Madelaine said, handing the two baskets over. 'David, darling, it's a wonderful day to go sailing,' she called to her husband, who waved in acknowledgement.

A short while later the last line was cast off and Sir David moved the gear lever into reverse. The boat, a sixty footer and single screw, needed an expert to handle her properly and Sir David had years of experience. Once clear of the jetty he put the lever into neutral, paused and pushed it forward. The boat slowly moved ahead. Changing too quickly from reverse to forward there was always the danger that the engine would stall and result in an embarrassing situation or even a dangerous one. He smiled to himself, remembering a time when he had done just that and ended up jammed against another boat, held there by a strong wind. That had been a long time ago.

Once clear of Shoreham Harbour he handed the wheel over to Sian and went below for a cup of coffee. Sir David's brother, Sion, was sitting at the table in the wood-lined saloon, his hands wrapped around a cup of fresh coffee. His face was haggard, the ravages of the cancer that was killing him etched in his face.

'Well, bro',' Sion said with a smile, 'a last trip.' He coughed but stopped after a few seconds and sipped his drink.

Sir David shook his head. 'Not the last. We'll have some more.'

Sion shook his head. 'No, I don't think so. I've lived too long. It's time to go. My God, but it's been a great life. I've been sitting here remembering it all. There's a lot of sadness but a great deal of happiness as well.' A spasm of pain passed through him which left him gasping.

'Can I get you anything?' Sir David asked, worry lining his face.

His brother shook his head. 'No, it's all right. I've had enough painkillers for an hour or two. Where's this reporter you were telling me about?'

'He's in the wheelhouse with Sian. Shall I send him down?'

Sion nodded. 'If he wants to talk to me he'd better do it quickly, before it's too late.'

David was about to argue but thought better of it. It was an insult to both men's intelligence not to recognise the fact that Sion had only a short while to live.

Sir David poured himself a coffee from the jug sitting on the coal-fired stove, added milk, and went up to the wheelhouse. The reporter was sitting on the stool at the chart table, plotting their course. He looked up when Sir David appeared.

'Do you know what you're doing, young man?' Sir David asked.

'Sure, sir,' was the laconic reply.

'Gramps, you aren't going to believe it but Tim has spent half his life at sea. His father owned a fishing boat and fished the seas around Newfoundland. He was practically born with sea-water in his veins, not blood,' Sian smiled at the reporter.

'Oh? So how did you end up in Boston as a reporter for *Time* magazine?'

'My father died at sea in a storm fifteen years ago.'

'That's really sad,' said Sian.

The reporter shrugged. 'That's life, I guess. Anyway, my mother went back to Boston where we lived with my maternal grandparents. I took a degree in English and drifted into reporting. But I've still spent as much time as I could playing with boats, sailing and racing. I love it.'

Sir David nodded. There was more to the man than he had first imagined. 'Could you go below and talk to my brother, Sion? He wants to tell you what he can remember – before it's too late.'

Tim Hunter nodded. He knew about the cancer. He smiled at Sian and, notebook in hand, went down into the saloon. Sir David was looking out to sea, aware of the glances his granddaughter had been casting at the reporter.

'Seems a nice enough young man,' he said.

Sian made no reply but looked down at the compass and swung the wheel a few degrees to port. Sir David noted her deep blush and smiled. She could do worse, he thought and then mentally shook himself. They had only just met and here he was already marrying them off. It must be, he thought to himself, a factor of age. So little time left and so much to do.

He went below to find his wife. He needed a hug.

BOOK 1

David's Story

1

Spring 1912

I HAD BEEN IN South Wales for over six months and I was bored. After the initial delight in seeing the family – my uncles, aunts and cousins – and catching up on all their news I was left at something of a loose end. I made my base in Cardiff and for a while travelled by train up the valley to Llanbeddas. I called in to see my old friends and at first, had been excited at the prospect of seeing Cliff, my boyhood best friend. But the meeting had been fraught with embarrassment: we had nothing in common now. Cliff was a coal-miner working in the local pit as he had done from the age of thirteen, two years after we had left for America. He was married to a pleasant girl from one of the neighbouring villages and had two children. He already had the beginning of a miner's cough. I played down my family's success, not wanting to appear too boastful but at the same time itching to tell him all about it. I did describe some of the places I had seen and the people I had met. I found his lack of interest off-putting and, to some extent, insulting. After my first three visits I went back to Llanbeddas only to stand at my sister's grave. Sion and Sian had been twins; she had been killed when a slag heap had swept down onto the village school. I liked to stand next to her head-stone in order to talk to her and tell her all that had happened to us. I had heard my aunt telling my uncle that it was morbid but I didn't think so. Sian's death had been the beginning of it all.

I was sitting in the lounge of the Angel Hotel in Cardiff when my Uncle William entered. 'David, I thought I'd find you here,' he greeted me. 'This arrived in the second post.'

I took the letter and eagerly scanned the envelope. It was from America and I recognised Dad's writing. I ripped it open and began to read. As I finished each page I handed it to Uncle William, knowing that he was as eager as I to receive news from America.

According to the letter all was well and the business was going from strength to strength. Sion was working too hard but was also spending even more of his spare time on his hobby. Originally this had involved a fascination with kites, but now it had developed into an obsession with flying. So far he had crashed twice but had walked away without serious injury. Dad said that he was using up his lives faster than the proverbial cat with nine; needless to say Mam worried herself sick. Dad's time in Congress was becoming more demanding and he and Mam were in the process of buying a house in Washington DC.

The last part of the letter contained an instruction to me to contact John Buchanan in London at an address in Mayfair. I was to telegraph John to tell him when I would be going to see him.

'I wonder what John wants?' I asked my uncle, who shrugged in reply. 'Well, there's no time like the present to find out. I see from the letter that John's in London now.' I looked round the large, luxurious room and waved to a button boy standing next to the door. He marched smartly to where we were sitting and I asked for a telegraph pad and the *Railway Gazette*. I thought for a moment and then said, 'Do you mind if I go tomorrow?'

He shook his head. 'You've surprised us by staying so long.'

I was handed the railway timetable and I checked the time of trains from Cardiff to London. I wrote a brief telegram to John, telling him that I would be arriving the following evening. 'Where shall I meet him?' I asked my uncle.

'The United Services Club,' he replied promptly. 'He's bound to be a member.' I added the suggestion we meet at the USC for dinner. I gave the button boy a half crown and asked him to send it immediately.

'I take it that's the same John Buchanan who was the captain of the liner when you travelled to America?'

I nodded. 'He's been a family friend ever since. He's quit the sea and is now on the board of directors that runs the shipping line.' I grinned. 'Though, as he's the first to admit, inheriting the majority of the shares in the company from his father did help him to become a board member.' John now spent his time between England and America overseeing his considerable shipping interests. Although he had married a few years earlier they still had no children.

I waved over a waiter and ordered two whiskies and sodas. I asked my uncle, 'What did you think about that Frenchman Henri Seimet flying non-stop from London to Paris, yesterday?' I was referring to the news that was in all the papers on that day in March 1912. There was talk about flying around the world but I couldn't see that happening for a few years yet.

'It's amazing, if you think about it. Only a few short years ago aeroplanes were crashing left, right and centre,' Uncle William stated with a fine sense of exaggeration, 'and now they're flying between two of the greatest capital cities in the world.'

I grinned. 'Don't let the Germans hear you say that. They think Berlin is the greatest capital in Europe.'

'I know, but we have the greatest empire the world has ever known and the French have the most beautiful city,' replied my uncle. 'Berlin is drab, claustrophobic and, worst of all, full of Germans.'

My grin widened. My uncle had been abroad on numerous occasions, mainly to France, but one summer a few years previously, he and my aunt had taken a grand tour through the Continental Lowlands, Germany, Switzerland and south to Italy. He had come back with a deep seated dislike of foreigners in general and Germans in particular. Although he had been successful in business he was essentially a modest man and the arrogance he found in the Germans he met was more than he could stand. He maintained that one day we would have to take them down a peg or two. When I pressed him as to what he meant by that he had looked despondent and said, 'War. I mean war.'

Naturally I thought he was talking nonsense. He was a very presentable man, my uncle, a few inches shorter than my six feet two and with just the beginnings of a pot-belly straining at his waistcoat. His hair was grey, swept back from his forehead and hanging over the back of his collar. My aunt was forever nagging him to get it cut, but he did not. It was his one touch of vanity.

After we left the hotel we hailed a taxi and went to my uncle's house in Rhiwbina, a small hamlet on the outskirts of Cardiff. While I packed my trunk, my uncle sat in my room idly chatting about the political situation in Europe. His great fear was that Germany and the Austro-Hungarian Empire would agree on a treaty that threatened the stability of Europe. I was surprised at his knowledge and his understanding of the events that were taking place and, I have to admit, I learned a great deal from him. Most of it was interesting although I still considered it fantasy gleaned from reading too many newspapers.

The next morning I said goodbye to my uncle and aunt and caught the train for London. I travelled first class and enjoyed the panoramic scenery that unfolded as we made our way through the Welsh countryside. We stopped at Newport, Caerleon and Caldicot before entering the Severn Tunnel. It was an odd feeling to be travelling nearly three miles underground, a good part of it with water over our heads. As it was a fine, warm day I had the window open and as we entered the tunnel the smoke and soot from the engine suddenly engulfed the train and filled the carriage. With an oath I leapt to my feet and shut the window, coughing and spluttering in the noxious fumes. After a few moments the air cleared and I was able to breathe properly again. I was very happy when we re-emerged into the sunlight and pulled in to the small station at Almondsbury, in the county of Gloucester.

My aunt had provided me with a picnic basket and I now opened its contents whilst I sat and gazed out of the window. I enjoyed a very good lunch of chicken, baked potatoes and pickles, washed down with a fine Chardonney. As I did so I reflected on the differences between my family in Cardiff and those who had stayed behind in Llanbeddas. They were worlds apart yet separated by less than fifteen miles as the river Taff flowed.

The rest of the day saw me passing through the gentle farming countryside of southern England. I had never travelled that way before, and I found it fascinating to see the different towns and villages. People joined and left the train at various stops but nobody entered my compartment. I didn't mind as I was too busy wondering why I was to see John Buchanan. I had no wish to engage in small talk with a stranger.

It was exactly seven in the evening when the train pulled into Paddington station. It was huge, with a high domed roof stretching over the whole station. I was aware that Cardiff station had the world's longest island platform but I was unprepared for the grandeur, bustle and noise that greeted me in London. It was my first time in the capital and I was hungry to see as much of the city as possible.

My instructions had been to take a cab to the United Services Club along the Mall. I had a porter take my trunk while I carried my overnight bag to the cab rank. Although there were still horse drawn hansoms in use I was directed to one of the new cabs which I recognised from America as a black, Ford Model T.

I climbed up beside the driver and asked, 'Where on earth did this car come from? The last time I saw one of these was in America.'

He grinned, showing tobacco stained teeth at me through a walrus moustache and replied, 'Why, sir, you're not from around these parts I can tell. This car was made in Manchester last year, the first to be made by Mr Ford outside of America. A wonderful invention it is too. It cost £105 and has the new lowered chassis. I'm going to have a starter and a lighting set added as soon as I save £15 to pay for them.'

I nodded, enjoying the ride and seeing for the first time the sights and sounds of London. People were everywhere, hawkers on every corner and, here and there, match and boot-lace sellers scraping a living of sorts. The journey down Park Lane and along Constitution Hill took a pleasant fifteen minutes. Once we had passed Buckingham Palace and travelled a few hundred yards along The Mall the traffic came to a halt. The road was jammed with cars, omnibuses, horse-drawn hansoms and drays loaded with barrels of beer. People were milling about but we were not moving forward an inch.

'What on earth's happening?' I asked.

'Sorry, sir,' the driver spoke in his Cockney accent. 'I think it must be them suffragettes protesting again. A bleeding nuisance they are and no mistake.'

Damnation, this was the last thing I needed. Although I had enjoyed the journey so far I was eager to see John. 'Listen driver. If I leave you here will you bring my bags through and I'll meet you at the club? Here's a sixpence, with another when you get there.'

'Why, sir, that's very kind of you.' He touched his forepeak on his hat by way of a salute. 'I'll do it and no mistake.'

I jumped down from the cab and shouldered my way through the jostling crowd to see what I could of the protest. I had read a good deal about the suffragettes and I had to confess that not only did I have a sneaking regard for what they were trying to achieve, but I wholeheartedly endorsed their right to have a vote. It seemed to me a nonsense that half the adult population was denied the vote simply because of being female.

I reached the edge of the pavement about fifty yards along the Mall and looked at the marchers. Though the crowd was predominantly made up of women, I could see a number of men. At its head was Emmeline Pankhurst, the founder of the Women's Political and Social Union and walking next to her was her daughter Christabel. They were both recognisable not only from photographs which appeared frequently in the newspapers but also from the encouraging yells they received from some of the crowd. However, for every one who yelled encouragement, two yelled abuse.

As the protesters reached Marlborough Road, policemen poured out of the side roads and another contingent of police marched up from Buckingham Gate to confront the women, things turned ugly. Somebody near me threw what appeared to be an apple at the marchers which struck a placard. Suddenly missiles were raining down, thrown from all sections of the crowd lining the pavements and I could see the marchers trying to use their banners and placards for protection. I heard loud screams, and suddenly the air was filled with the sound of police whistles. To my horror I saw the police line up and baton charge the protesters.

Without thinking I pushed my way onto the road with the intention of helping the women. I reached one policeman who had his arm raised with a baton ready to strike down on the unprotected head of a young lady. I grabbed his arm, bent it back and tore the baton from his grasp.

'Pick on someone your own size,' I yelled at him, and for good measure poked him in the stomach with his own baton. He doubled up in pain and fell backwards. However, two other constables saw what had happened and leapt at me with their batons raised ready to hit me. I did the unexpected and stepped towards them, side-swiped one on the head and followed through with the baton to block the other's swing at me. I was only just in time. If the blow had landed I would have been badly injured. As it was the force sent a jarring shudder up my arm and I smashed my fist into the constable's nose. He crashed backwards and sent a number of his colleagues sprawling. A hand grabbed my arm and I turned, ready to fight, when I realised it was the girl I had saved from attack.

'Quickly, we must go. It will get a lot worse now this has started.'

I looked about me and saw that she was right. Women were laid out on the street, many of them bleeding. Some were being carried away, still struggling, while others were leaping at the police, in an attempt to rescue their friends.

I didn't need any further urging. I took her hand and pushed and shoved my way through the crowd, down The Mall, with the young lady right behind me, and away from the trouble. After a few minutes our progress became easier. Then we broke free from the crowds and were able to run down the street.

'Stop! Stop!' She pulled at my hand and I stopped running. 'That's better,' she panted, 'I couldn't keep up.'

'Sorry,' I ran my fingers through my hair, as I took a good look at her. 'Are you all right?'

She was about five feet three inches tall, was slim built with auburn hair, curls from which were showing under her hat. She had a pretty face with a determined chin, brown eyes and a wide mouth.

'Yes, thank you. And . . . and thank you for saving me back there.'

'That's okay. I wasn't going to stand around and let any rozzer lay into you. My God, that was appalling. All those women hurt . . . and arrested.'

She nodded sadly. 'We were only trying to march to the Palace to protest peacefully before the King. He's due there later on, coming from the Guildhall, and we wanted him to see the depth of feeling there is for votes for women.'

'I'm sure he knows that already. But why stop you like that? It's barbaric.'

'It always happens that way.' She spoke in a cultured, educated voice. 'Mr Asquith has said that as long as he is Prime Minister these protests will not be tolerated and they are to be stopped at all costs.'

I knew that. However, it wasn't all one-sided. On March 1 that year militant suffragettes had caused havoc when they had rampaged through the West End of London. They had been carrying stones and hammers hidden in their muffs and pockets, to smash windows and property. More than one hundred and twenty of them had been arrested. Some had broken through to Downing Street and hurled stones at Number 10, shattering windows on both sides of the famous door. Groups of women had struck in co-ordinated attacks without warning and within twenty minutes the trail of destruction had stretched from Oxford Street to the Strand via Piccadilly and Whitehall. No, I didn't agree with what I had just witnessed, but it was definitely not all one-sided.

'Look, can I escort you somewhere? See you safely home?'

'That's very kind of you but I'll have to find out where they've taken Emmeline and try and get her bail.'

'It's too soon for that. You need to give them an hour or two to settle down first. Then we can see about bail.'

'We? You mean you'll help me?'

'Why not? I've come this far, so I may as well see it through.'

'This isn't a game, you know,' she said with some asperity. 'We have the right to vote and we are determined to establish it.'

'I know, and I agree,' I said, giving her my warmest smile. 'But believe me, I know what I'm talking about. Where I come from I practice law. I'm a lawyer,' I added in explanation.

'A lawyer? Oh, a solicitor. You're American,' she said, her eyes opening wide, giving her a slightly startled look.

'Welsh by birth, American by adoption,' I explained. 'I'm going to the United Services Club, which I believe is further along The Mall. If you care to accompany me I'll see about getting you a cup of tea, perhaps something to eat and then we'll go and see about your friends.'

She hesitated a moment and then smiled. 'I'll be delighted to.' She put her hand on my arm and we strolled together along the street. From the corner of my eye I could see that she was surreptitiously looking up at me, trying to weigh me up. I guessed her age to be about twenty-one or twenty-two and I had noticed that there were no rings on her left hand.

The door to the club was high and imposing. We entered to a salute from the doorman and walked to the reception desk.

'Yes, sir?' asked the elderly man, who managed somehow to smile at me and scowl at the young lady.

'I'm meeting Mr John Buchanan. My name is Griffiths.'

'Ah, yes, sir. The Commodore is expecting you. He is in the members' lounge. However, erm, the young lady cannot enter. She may only use the ladies' lounge.'

I looked quizzically at him and he added, 'It's at the top of the stairs, sir.'

I nodded my thanks and led her past the marble bust of The Duke of Wellington and another of Caesar. They seemed to scowl at the idea of a woman walking in their hallowed halls.

'I still don't know your name,' I said.

'I know yours is Griffiths,' she smiled. 'What's your first name?'

'David. And yours?'

She seemed to be thinking about it for a moment and then she gave a gentle shrug. 'It's Emily, Emily Watson.'

'Nice to meet you, Emily,' I said as we walked up the wide stairway and into the ladies' lounge. Inside it was pleasant enough, with chintz covered chairs and sofas with occasional tables next to them. A few tables were occupied by ladies sitting with pots of tea and plates of cakes and sandwiches.

'Emily, you sit here,' I indicated a seat, 'while I see about some tea. Unless you'd rather something stronger?'

She looked up at me with a sudden start and a wide grin. 'Good grief, if I took anything stronger than a cup of tea I'd be the talk of the town,' she said. 'You'd better go and find John.'

I was a little surprised at her familiarity with his name, but I left her and went downstairs where I ordered tea for Emily and then went to find the members' lounge. In fact it was a well-appointed bar and I quickly spotted John Buchanan standing at the bar in conversation with two other gentlemen. He didn't appear to have changed much. He was still tough and athletic looking, a bit greyer around the ears perhaps, but his back was as straight as ever and there was hardly any paunch showing.

I tapped his shoulder and he swung round to me. 'David, my boy, it's wonderful to see you.' He grabbed my hand and shook it warmly. 'Allow me to introduce you to Lord Stockdale,' he indicated a slight, stooped, grey haired man, 'and Sir Angus Frazer.' I shook hands with Frazer and guessed from the name and accent that he was Scottish. Frazer was about my age, thick set, very fit looking and very alert.

'Can I have a word?' I asked, indicating that we should move away from the other two for a little privacy.

'Don't worry, you can speak freely in front of these two. In fact they're the reason I asked you here. Or rather, asked Evan to write to you.'

Intrigued, I nodded. I briefly told them what had happened and about the young lady sitting upstairs waiting for me. The reactions of the three men were comical in their diversity. John looked bland, Frazer laughed and Stockdale scowled.

'I couldn't let the police attack her,' I protested.

'Why not?' said Stockdale. 'Serves them right. It's a load of nonsense if you ask me. Votes for women, indeed. I ask you. They'll be wanting equal property rights next. Too many of the country's resources are being wasted on containing these blasted women and not enough on the important issues. Which is why we want you,' he said.

I was taken aback by his words but before I could ask any questions John said, 'That can wait. Let us go and see to the welfare of this young lady before we go for dinner.'

'I'll leave you to it,' said Lord Stockdale. 'You know what's required and I won't take no for an answer.' With that he nodded a curt goodbye and left us.

'Considering the old man must be pushing eighty, he's like a human hurricane,' said Frazer.

I looked from one to the other and said, 'Will someone please tell me what's going on?'

'Later. Come on,' said John and led the way up to the ladies lounge.

As we entered I saw Emily pouring a cup of tea. She looked up, smiled and said, 'Hullo, Uncle John. Hullo, Angus.'

She looked at me and suddenly giggled. 'If only I could capture that look on your face, I'd make a mint.'

I pulled myself together and smiled. No wonder she had felt free to be familiar with John's name.

'Hullo, Emily,' said Frazer. 'Does your keeper know you've escaped?' Which was sufficient to send her into peals of laughter.

'Your faces; all three of you.' She laughed again and abruptly stopped as the laugh turned to hiccups.

'Uncle John?' I asked quizzically.

'My sister's youngest daughter and the bane of my life,' said John, sighing and smiling at the same time.

'Now, Uncle John, you know that's not true. I'm your favourite niece, as well as the bane of your life.'

John smiled and sat down on the sofa next to his niece. 'Tell me all about it,' he took her hand and held it for a few seconds, the warmth and concern evident.

Emily more or less repeated what I had told him. When she had finished John shook his head and said, 'Emily, do you know what could have happened? If a baton hits you too hard you could be maimed for life, or worse, dead. You must stop this silliness.'

At his words she withdrew her hand and sat up straighter. 'It isn't silliness, Uncle John. It's time we had the vote and a say in what happens in our country. We contribute as much as any man, some of us more. We're better educated than many others who have the vote simply because they're men,' she snorted, scornfully. 'What's more, most of them don't know why they vote, nor why they vote for any particular candidate. At least we all have an idea of the issues. The things that really matter.'

'Some of you do, my dear, it's true. But your disdain for the uneducated man applies equally to uneducated women. And there's a lot more of them,' he added.

'That's why we need the vote. To make life better for all women. To free them from drudgery and . . . and slavery. That's why we educated women need to lead the way.

'I give up,' said John with a shake of his head. 'You talk some sense to her, Angus.'

'Me? She hasn't listened to me since she was knee high to a grasshopper and wore pigtails,' said Angus, a grin hinting at the corner of his mouth.

Emily, very unladylike for a moment, poked her tongue out at him and picked up her cup. 'I shall finish this and then go to the police station and find my friends,' she announced, calmly.

'You'll do no such thing,' said John, firmly. 'You will go home and I will find out all I can. When I know where they are and what's to be done, I'll do it.'

Emily smiled over her teacup at him. 'Thank you, Uncle John.'

It was obvious to me that she knew he would make the offer. Looking at John I saw that he knew it too. This was a scene they had played out before.

John stood up and looked down at his niece. 'Do as I tell you, Emily. Go home and I'll sort it out. I'll come over later and tell you how I've got on. Come on you two, we've a dinner to eat and, more importantly, a drink is needed.' With that we left Emily sitting with her tea and we retired back to the bar.

Once we each had large whiskies and sodas in our hands we took a corner table out of earshot of anybody else, and I was at last able to ask John what was going on.

'What's going on? You mean with regards to Emily?'

I shook my head. 'No. I mean why am I here?'

'Ahh, that's easy. We want you to go to Europe for us. Germany, Austria and Yugoslavia to name but three countries.'

Whatever I had been expecting it wasn't that. I had half thought that the summons had something to do with business. I didn't understand this.

'Why?'

'You tell him, Angus. I need to get hold of Parker and send him ferreting around the police stations to find out what he can for Emily.' With that he got up and left the room.

'Parker?' I enquired of Frazer.

'A sort of private detective. Used to be a peeler until he was shot by a Bolshevik during a siege in the Old Kent Road.' I nodded, remembering reading something about this a few years earlier. 'Now John uses him whenever he, em, needs certain things done.' He offered no further explanation and I dropped the matter.

'So what's this all about? Me and Europe?'

'How much do you know about the political situation across Europe?'

I shrugged and remembered what my uncle had told me. I repeated what he had said and at the end Frazer nodded. 'Good. Very good. In effect Europe is in turmoil. The Germans are arming as fast as they can. They have also signed a treaty with Austro-Hungary and are currently trying to persuade Italy to join their unholy alliance. If that happens we are fearful for the safety of Russia or even France and the Lowlands,' said Frazer, referring to Belgium, Holland and Luxembourg.

'I still don't understand what you want me to do,' I said, starting to get annoyed.

'We want you to visit a few places, meet a few people and gauge what's happening over there. Then we want you to report back on a regular basis and tell us what's going on.'

'You've got to be joking,' I said. 'Anyway, I haven't got time for that. I'm planning to return to the States shortly. I've even booked my passage for next month, on the maiden voyage of the Titanic. That's an event I don't want to miss. It'll be historic.'

'I'm sure it will but there'll be plenty of opportunities for you to sail on the Titanic in the future,' replied Frazer. 'We want you to attend a gathering at a private house in Bavaria. The Kaiser will be there along with half the German Cabinet. So will Archduke Franz Ferdinand, heir to the Austro-Hungarian throne. If that isn't enough the Italian Premier Antonio Salandra will be there and we want you to have a private word with him.'

'Look, this doesn't make any sense. Why me?'

'There are many reasons, which I'll let John tell you about.'

'Let me ask you a different question. What's all this to do with you? Why are you talking to me and who's Lord Stockdale? And what's it got to do with him?' I added.

Frazer grinned. 'That's more than one question but I'll try and answer them. Lord Stockdale is responsible for the safety of the United Kingdom and all her dominions. By that I mean he sits in the House of Lords and collects information from all over the world which he then passes on to a committee who report to the Prime Minister. You can imagine, I'm sure, how much information has to be sifted through, so that our, shall we say rulers, can make valid judgements regarding all manner of things.'

'Such as?'

'Such as, should the people in German East Africa attack Northern Rhodesia, who do we blame and what do we do about it? Such as if Serbia attacks Albania what should we do and what will the Italians do? And so it goes on. Masses of knowledge is needed to enable us to make decisions to protect not only our Empire but also parts of Europe. Turkey and the Dardanelles are a point in question. What if Turkey were to join with Germany and . . .'

'Wait a moment. You've just said what if Italy joins an alliance with Germany and Austro-Hungary.'

'I know I did. But don't you see, that's precisely my point. The whole lot is a big cauldron of supposition which could drag us into a war we not only don't want but aren't yet ready for. Why is Germany arming at the rate it is? Why are they building so many battleships and other craft? We need to know.'

I shrugged. 'Ask them,' I suggested. 'Let me get you another drink.' I stood up but Frazer told me to sit again.

'You can't buy drinks as you're not a member.' He waved to a passing waiter and ordered refills. While he was doing so, I was thinking. This was a preposterous idea. There was nothing for me to do but to return to America and get on with my life, perhaps join the business with Sion or even start my own legal practice.

'We've tried asking them,' Frazer said when he had taken a sip of his drink. 'We asked politely and then not so politely. They used diplomatic words to tell us to mind our own business. Nothing that is happening there right now makes sense and we need to make sense of it. If we don't, we could be in serious trouble.'

'I still don't understand why you want me to go,' I argued.

At that point John rejoined us and answered for Frazer. 'It's simple. You travel as an American, a wealthy one at that, who is committed to the neutrality of the United States. Which is their official line anyway. I know you speak excellent German because of Gunhild.'

I nodded bleakly at him. I didn't need reminding. The pain of losing Gunhild could still hurt. I remembered all the happy times we'd had together and the pleasure my family and hers felt at our intended marriage. I also had a fair smattering of French as well as German. For some reason I seemed able to learn a new language at the drop of a hat if I put my mind to it. This was a talent I knew John to be fully aware of.

'We want you to travel around Europe, visiting certain places and attending selected events. Basically you'll be eavesdropping. We'll spend the next four or five weeks grounding you in European affairs and at the same time we'll teach you one or two more languages. I take it your German's up to scratch?'

I nodded. 'Fluent to all intents and purposes. My Welsh is fluent also if you'd like me to infiltrate that part of Europe,' I said with a spark of humour.

John smiled and shook his head. 'Not yet. We might if the nationalists get too uppity. We'll arrange for you to have a cramming course in Italian and Hungarian. It won't be perfect but at least it will give you a head start when you get there.'

'Wait a second. I haven't said I'm going yet,' I protested. 'Anyway, I've set my heart on the Titanic voyage and I've paid for a stateroom. Do you know how difficult it was to get passage?'

'I should,' replied John, 'seeing I'm in the business. Don't worry, you can sell your ticket at a premium and make a profit. You'll double your money easily.'

'I don't want to double my money,' I retorted. 'I want to take part in an historic voyage. It'll be something to tell my grandchildren.'

'Look, David,' said John with a flash of annoyance. 'We need you and that's final. All we're . . . I'm asking is for six months of your time. Travel around and find out what's going on. Act the dumb American, say nothing but listen a lot.'

'Where does Frazer fit in to all this?' I asked, changing tack for a moment.

'He'll be your contact. He'll be near you at all times, somewhere available if you need him. You and he can work out the details between you. Incidentally, he's a major in the Black Watch.'

I nodded, impressed. It was not only an elite and famous regiment, it was also reputed to be a tough one. I still didn't like it.

'John, I need to think about it. I've got a career or a business to build. I've spent the last, what, eight months, doing nothing! The holiday's over. I've got to get back.'

John Buchanan nodded his understanding. 'I'll make you an offer. Help us and I'll help you to establish the name of Griffiths back here in England.'

'How?'

'I've an idea that I've already spoken to your father about. It's for he and I, as partners, to open a bank here in London. You will run it along with one of my people.'

'I know nothing about banking,' I pointed out the obvious. 'And anyway, I'm not sure that's what I want to do.'

'You don't need to know much. My man does. You're a quick

learner and you'll soon get to know what you need to know. Remember, we can hire cashiers, assistants and accountants. What we need is a driving force finding the deals, making it happen. That will be your job. My man will run the bank on a day-to-day basis.'

'Who's your man?'

John grinned, wolfishly. 'Angus's brother. His name is Hamish and he's currently working in a bank in Edinburgh. He's indicated that if he got an offer he'd accept it. We'll make an offer shortly. While you do your, shall we say spying, around Europe on our behalf, he'll begin to make things happen here. By the time you return you'll have a bank to run.'

I looked at John for a few moments as the idea percolated through my brain. The more I thought about it the more I liked it. I still hadn't met up with Jake, which had been my intention, and I wanted to see Estella and her brother Dominic, as well as the baby, before I went back to America. I could lead my hedonistic life for a little longer before I had to knuckle down to some hard work.

'I'll think about it,' I said, by way of a compromise. 'I don't promise, but I'm not ruling it out.'

'Good enough,' said John, while Frazer scowled at me.

'Away laddie,' he said. 'Your country needs you for a while. That's all. It's the least you can do.'

I was about to retort that my country as he called it had done nothing for me or my family and that we owed everything to America, when I caught John's slight shake of the head and I shut up. There was nothing to be gained by antagonising Frazer.

'Let's go in for dinner,' announced John. We drained our drinks and moved to the dining room.

We had finished our main course, the three of us eating well hung and gamy pheasant, when we were approached by a gentleman wearing a tweed cape over a grey suit and carrying a deerstalker hat.

'Parker,' greeted John Buchanan, 'please sit down.'

Parker drew up a chair and sat at our table while John poured him a glass of fine Tokay wine. 'Here's mud in you eye,' Parker lifted the glass and drained it, unaware that a bottle of vintage Tokay cost as much as a working man earned in a week.

'Well?' asked Frazer, impatiently.

'Well, sir,' said Parker, taking out a grubby handkerchief and wiping his mouth, 'they're at Bow Street.'

'What? All of them?' I asked.

'Most of them. Some are at Marlborough Street. Mrs Pankhurst is definitely at Bow Street and is locked up for the night. She will be seeing the magistrate in the morning. There's no bail and none will be set.'

'I expected as much,' said John, thoughtfully. 'All right, thank you, Parker. Here are five guineas for your trouble. I'll send for you when I need you again.' He handed Parker five guinea coins and Parker left, happily.

'Another bottle of this wine,' said John, 'and we'll go home and tell Emily what we know.'

A short while later Frazer left us and John and I walked out of the club. He hailed a taxi which quickly took us along Piccadilly and into Mayfair. We stopped at an imposing residence and John let us in through the front door using his key. 'Welcome to my humble abode,' he said, dryly.

His "humble" abode had four rooms on the ground floor, seven bedrooms, three bathrooms and servants quarters. It had been the Buchanan town house for nearly fifty years and had been continuously modernised as new inventions and, in particular, better plumbing had been installed.

Once in his study he pushed a button next to the fireplace and a few moments later a butler appeared. John ordered whisky and sodas for us and asked him to invite Emily to join us. We exchanged talk about business while I perused the titles of the books lining his walls and studied some of the paintings hanging there. After a short wait, Emily walked in carrying a silver tray with our whiskies.

'I thought I would save Beech the trouble,' she said. 'Have you found out anything about the Pankhursts and the others?'

John told her what we had learned and she hurried towards the door. 'I must go down there at once. To see if I can help.'

'Emily you will do no such . . . thing,' the last word was spoken to the closed door. 'David, go with her, will you? She's so headstrong I fear she'll do something rash.'

'Like what?' I asked as I stood and drained my glass. I was delighted to be told to follow the delectable Emily.

'Like brain the desk sergeant if he doesn't let her friends go. And all that will achieve is that she'll spend the night in jail and get her name in the papers in the morning.'

'Right. I'll see you later.' I hurried after Emily and caught her at the door.

'Where do you think you're going?' she asked, evidently displeased to see me.

'With you,' I replied, smiling at her.

'You will most certainly not,' she replied. 'I don't need a nursemaid, thank you.'

'Oh? Like you didn't need a nursemaid earlier on,' I reminded her.

'That was different. Now it's not necessary. All I shall do is go to the station to reason with the police for the release of my friends.'

I shook my head, sadly. Her naiveté was refreshing but misplaced.

'Don't patronise me with that look,' she said. 'I know what I'm doing.'

She stalked out of the house with me at her heels. She hailed a taxi and as she was closing the door on me I grabbed the handle and climbed in after her.

'Bow Street Police Station,' I told the driver as I settled down besides her.

'Stop,' she said and the taxi came to an abrupt halt. 'This gentleman is leaving.'

'No, I'm not. Drive on.'

The taxi started again and Emily called, crossly, 'I said stop. This gentleman is leaving.'

The car stopped and I said, 'No, I'm not. Just drive to Bow Street Police Station, please.'

The man turned in his seat and looked at each of us in turn. 'Make up your minds. I'll take both of you, one of you or none of you. Now which is it to be?'

'I'm coming with you,' I said to Emily. 'Your uncle ordered it.'

'Oh, very well,' she said crossly. 'Drive on.'

We sat in silence, she in petulance, me with enjoyment. All too soon we drew up outside the police station, climbed out of the taxi and I paid the driver off. We went inside to the smell of sweat, the noise of people vying for attention and the sight of green painted, drab walls.

Emily marched boldly to the front of the queue and said, 'My good man, I insist you take me to see Mrs Pankhurst immediately.'

What did she think she was playing at? The sergeant behind the desk sighed, put down the pen he was writing laboriously with and said, 'Listen, go to the back of the queue and when I've dealt with all these others I'll deal with you.'

Emily looked at the other people as though seeing them for the first time. I was fascinated. She had been born to riches, servants and dealing with ordinary people as though they were serfs. I don't think it even occurred to her that the other men and women there had the right to be attended to first. I could see she was about to argue so I grabbed her arm and pulled her away from the desk.

'Look, Emily, you can't do that. If that's how you and your friends normally behave then it's no wonder there are riots and virtual anarchy in the streets.'

'What? Don't talk nonsense,' she pulled her arm from my hand. 'I shall behave just as I like.' She made no effort to keep her voice down and one or two of the drunks and prostitutes began to take notice.

She turned to go back to the desk but was yelled at to get back and wait her turn. She took no notice. Things were beginning to turn ugly when two constables appeared and started towards her. With alarm I recognised one of the men we had confronted earlier that day. I hurried forward, grabbed her by the arm again, and dragged her towards the door.

'Hey, you. Stop,' said the constable, hurrying forward. He grabbed Emily by her other arm, she pulled away from me and before I could stop her she hit the constable on the nose. He gave a yell, more of surprise than pain and let go. I grabbed her again and pulled her towards the door. She needed no urging as she realised her position and together we rushed outside. There were more yells from behind as a police whistle was blown. We rushed down the steps and onto the pavement just as the door opened behind us and a number of policemen ran out.

'Run, Emily, run,' I urged.

2

SHE DIDN'T NEED telling twice. To my surprise she kicked off her shoes and ran as fast as she could down the street with me close behind her. We quickly outstripped the police who gave the impression of not trying very hard and soon they faded away and we were able to stop and catch our breath.

'Emily,' I said between gasps, 'where did you learn to run like that?'

'At school. We were taught the necessity of running away from amorous men,' she said and giggled. 'It also comes in handy when running from the police.'

I shook my head in despair. 'Don't you realise how close you were to getting yourself locked up for the night?'

'Of course I do. But we sisters must stick together if we are to get what we want.'

I looked at her and realised that I was completely captivated. She was beautiful, resourceful and courageous.

I stayed with John for the next week and stuck closely to Emily. She was fascinating to be with. The advantages of her wealth and position were as natural to her as breathing. She treated ordinary people such as shopkeepers, taxi drivers and costermongers as her social inferiors. She wasn't impolite to them, she just didn't see them as people, somehow. When I told her how she behaved she looked at me as though I had lost my senses. I even talked to John about it who nodded and said, 'I know. It's disconcerting to watch her. She seems totally unable to relate to people she considers her inferiors. If she isn't careful, she'll get into hot water one of these days. It's been troubling me and her mother for a number of years. Still,' he added, optimistically, 'she'll probably grow out of it.'

He and I did not speak of this again.

When I asked John about his wife he told me that she was taking the cure at the spa waters in Bath. She went four or five times a year in the belief that it did her good and cured, as John put it, one imagined ailment or another.

John waylaid me as I was about to leave the house to meet Emily. 'David, we need to know your answer. Are you going to help or not?'

I hesitated a second or two. If I said yes I would be able to spend longer in London and see more of Emily. If I said no I would need to catch the ship as planned. I nodded. 'Yes, of course I will.'

John strode forward and took my hand. 'Good man. I knew I could count on you. We need to . . .'

I interrupted him. 'Hold it a moment. Can this wait until I get back? I'm meeting Emily in Regent's Park and then going for tea.'

He looked shrewdly at me for a few moments and said, 'Of course, my dear fellow, of course. Meet me back here for dinner tonight. We have a lot to do.'

On that note I hurried along the pavement to my rendezvous. I hadn't fooled John for a moment but that was of no importance. I could now press my suit with Emily. I smiled to myself. The upper classes of England had a quaint way of expressing themselves. I was finding it irksome to act in a manner that I considered a charade. What I wanted to do was take Emily to a quiet place, whisper sweet words in her ear and hope for the best. This was proving harder than my courtship with Gunhild had been all those years ago.

I waited at the bandstand and after a few minutes Emily appeared, a little breathless.

'You needn't hurry on my account,' I said, smiling. 'I've been listening to the band warming up.' I indicated the men behind me, all tuning their instruments and creating a cacophony of sound.

She smiled back. 'I hate being late,' she said and tucked her arm in mine. We began to stroll aimlessly through the park, away from the noise.

Emily looked beautiful in her long skirt and a white blouse with a large bow through the collar and around her neck. Over this she wore an open coat which also reached the ground.

'What have you been up to today?' I asked. In the background I could hear the band begin to play a rendition of Jerusalem whilst around us horse-drawn buggies passed at a leisurely pace and cyclists weaved in and out of the horse droppings. It was very peaceful and enjoyable.

'Oh, nothing much. I went to court to stand bail for some of the sisters,' she spoke airily, as though going to court was a regular occurrence. Then she dropped her careless manner and said, 'It was awful. They were treated like common criminals. The judge should be shot for what he said,' she added, fiercely.

'What did he say?'

'He went on about a woman's place being in the home and added other patronising homilies. He had the nerve to tell Mrs Pankhurst that she did not understand the intricacies of government and that women could not be trusted with the vote. I ask you, have you ever heard such nonsense?'

I was not going to point out that what the judge had said was a regular theme in all the newspapers. If I did, I knew that Emily was capable of venting her anger on me and that was the last thing I wanted that afternoon.

We arrived at the Savoy in good time for five o'clock tea. A number of her friends were there and we ended up forming one large party. As was often the case I took a good deal of friendly leg pulling about my accent – the mixture of Welsh and what they termed Yankee and, as usual, I took it in good part. However, it did make me more determined than ever to change the way I spoke and from that day on I took care to drop many of the idiosyncratic words used in Wales and America for the words and manners of Edwardian England. I was rapidly blending in to their way of life.

We were returning through the park in the early evening dusk and had reached the bandstand. I took Emily's hand and drew her into the shadows and, for the first time, I kissed her. I did not know what to expect but was pleasantly surprised at the result. Instead of her haughtily drawing back and slapping my face she returned my kiss with passion. After a few seconds we pulled apart and gazed into each other's eyes.

'It took you long enough,' she said with an impish smile on her face.

'Long enough?' I asked stupidly.

'Yes. I've been longing for days for you to do that.'

'What? This?' I asked and I kissed her again.

'Yes, that. Now we need to get away from London for a while without anyone knowing about it.'

I couldn't believe my ears. Did she mean what I thought she meant? If she did she was very matter of fact about it and I was a little bit disconcerted. All the young ladies I had met were so demure that it was painful sometimes to watch them. It was, without doubt, a way of behaviour that I found unusual after having been brought up in the relative freedom of America.

'What do you mean?' I asked, sounding stupid even to my ears.

'Oh, David,' she said exasperatedly. 'What do you think I mean? We can't meet anywhere in London in private and we definitely cannot book into a hotel together. So we have to go away.'

'Where do you suggest?' I asked, dryly. Then added, petulantly, 'Where do you usually go?'

'What? How dare you,' she stepped back from me. Before I could move she slapped me across my cheek, hard and marched away. Her back was ramrod straight and though I called after her she kept walking. Ruefully I stroked my cheek where she had hit me and told myself that I had deserved it. The matter of fact way that she had spoken had made me assume she must have done something like it before. I was obviously wrong. Now I needed to make it up to her. I suspected that I would have to do a lot of grovelling before she forgave me.

I arrived back at the house in time to change for dinner. Dressed in a dinner suit and bow tie I went down to the library for a pre-dinner drink. John Buchanan was already there with Frazer. I was greeted by a hearty handshake from Frazer and a whisky and soda from John.

'Right,' said John, 'let's make a few plans.'

Frazer nodded and said, 'David, we want you to spend a few weeks at a country house brushing up on your German and learning Hungarian and Italian. Do you think you can do it?'

'Learn Hungarian and Italian?' I asked.

'Yes,' replied Frazer.

'I suppose I can,' I said doubtfully, 'given a year or two.'

'You haven't got a year or two,' said John. 'You've got six weeks to learn enough to get you by. After that you can hone your skills in the field, as it were.'

'Six weeks?' I repeated, aghast. 'I don't see me learning much in that time.'

'Don't worry,' said Angus. 'You'll be surprised how much you will learn. It will be an intensive six weeks, believe me. I've done two courses there and I can speak and understand both French and Italian. You'll find the same thing happens to you.'

I nodded doubtfully. 'When do I go?'

'Tomorrow,' said John, much to my surprise and chagrin.

I was about to protest that it was too soon when I paused. If I left, would absence make the heart grow fonder? Or would the heart I had in mind forget me? I made up my mind.

'All right. Tomorrow; say a ten o'clock departure?' I suggested.

Frazer nodded. 'I'll pick you up and drive you to Brampton Hall.'

'Brampton Hall?'

'Yes. It's the Duke of Northumberland's place. He let's us use it for, em, our purposes. We get staff in from the Royal Military Academy at Camberley and send his own staff to his house in the north. It suits them and it suits us.'

I nodded. 'How far is it?'

'Not far. It'll take us an hour or so, that's all.'

Frazer was at the door at ten sharp the next morning. He picked me up in a 1911 Nash, the Cross Country model Rambler which, I discovered, he had imported from America. It had been named after completing a 320 mile tour from Chicago to Toledo in record time. The car was famous for it's fifth wheel, attached to the side of the bodywork, next to the passenger seat. It was possible to change a wheel in under three minutes by removing six nuts. So far, according to Frazer, it had not been necessary to prove the claim. I persuaded him to stop at a flower shop on the way out of town and arranged to send most of the contents of the shop to Emily. Frazer had the tact not to ask who the flowers were for but I suspected that he knew.

Brampton Hall was an imposing residence. It was set in a few hundred acres of cultivated land with another few hundred acres of woods. It was at least three hundred years old, seeped in history. We were met by a butler and shown to our rooms. I was unpacking when there came a knock on the door and Frazer entered.

'Leave that, old boy. We've got work to do.'

I followed him downstairs and into the library. There we were greeted by a small, wizened man who introduced himself as Professor Schlester. He spoke English with no trace of an accent but explained that he was actually German with Hungarian parents.

'I propose to speak to you only in German, Mr Griffiths, for the next three days. During that time I will correct your speech at every opportunity. I will also explain something of the methods that I have developed to help you master the language you are learning more quickly. After three days we will start on Hungarian and Italian, both of which I speak fluently. Sir Angus will be joining us. He already has a smattering of Italian and no Hungarian.'

Out of the corner of my eye I saw Frazer bridle at the word smattering but he said nothing. Wisely, as it turned out.

We began right away. Because I had an ear for languages I enjoyed the lessons and found them relatively easy. The professor was a very clever teacher; he made us try and think in the language we were using and not to translate the words into English first. This was particularly important when he spoke German to me and, at the same time, teaching me Hungarian. If I had not been able to visualise what he said in German I would have been translating into English and then into Hungarian. It was a very interesting period and I quickly mastered the language. However, it soon became obvious that poor Frazer did not have my ability.

After a fortnight in the school I was becoming restless and tackled Frazer about going up to town. I wanted to see Emily as soon as possible. Absence making the heart grow fonder was one thing; complete abandonment, another.

'Orders, old chap. I'm afraid we can't leave until we've completed the bally course.'

'Blow orders,' I retorted. 'I'm a volunteer for this and not under anybody's orders. Now, either we go out for an evening, preferably in the West End, or I quit.'

He looked pensively at me. 'I suppose if you put it like that then we'd better see about a spot of leave. Can't have you going AWOL, can we?'

'Good.' Our conversation was in English and I realised that I hadn't spoken the language in days. After less than a fortnight's tuition I was thinking in Hungarian. The professor was correct. If you wanted to speak a second language, it was important to think in that language.

We escaped from Brampton Hall at 4 p.m. on Saturday. As it was a pleasant day we travelled with the roof folded down and the wind whistling around the car.

At the United Services Club we ordered drinks and I went to phone Emily. I got through quickly enough and then had to wait an age until she finally came to the telephone.

'Emily? Hullo, it's me, David.'

'I know it's you,' she said, frostily. 'You told Beech.' Beech had answered the phone.

'Look, I'm really sorry I left when I did but I had to go. Your uncle needed me.'

'Huh, a likely story. What did he need you for? And anyway, you could have rung me or sent a telegram, or something,' she said.

'No, I couldn't. Believe me, please. I didn't have access to a phone where I was. Look, I'm at the US Club with Angus. He's been with me the whole time. He can tell you. Why not meet us at the Savoy Grill for a spot of dinner?'

'Well . . . No . . . I can't. I've made other arrangements.' With that she hung up. I was about to telephone her back when I thought better of it. If that's how she wanted it then to hell with her.

I stalked back to the bar, gulped down a whisky and soda and ordered another one. Having been put up for membership by John while I was away, I could now order as much as I liked.

'What's up with you, old chap?' asked Frazer. 'We've a long night ahead of us.'

'Blasted woman,' I replied.

'Any in particular? Or do you mean just women in general?'

I looked at him over the rim of my replenished drink and retorted, 'You know damn well which one in particular. Emily. I just phoned her and asked her to join us for dinner and she hung up on me.'

He nodded. 'I thought that's what it might be. You've a bit of a thing for her, haven't you?'

I hesitated, took a mouthful of my drink and nodded. 'I love her,' I admitted.

He pursed his lips. 'That's serious. And how does she feel about you?'

'I thought she reciprocated my feelings but now I'm not so sure,' I admitted. 'Oh, hell. Forget it. Let's drink too much, have a good dinner and get back.'

An hour later we wandered out of the club and made our way to the Savoy. We had another drink at the bar while a table was made ready. There were numerous acquaintances sitting at various tables in the dining room whom we nodded to or exchanged greetings with.

Finally, we sat at our table and ordered our meal. A wine waiter had just poured a fine claret into our glasses and I was taking an appreciative sip when out of the corner of my eye I saw someone bearing down on us and looking up I saw Emily approaching. She had a beaming smile and was looking absolutely ravishing.

We both scrambled to our feet and I pulled out a chair for her. A waiter quickly appeared, put a place setting in front of her and poured her a glass of wine.

Frazer said, 'I say, old chap, will you kindly wipe that inane grin from your face? You too, Emily.'

'You came,' I said, stating the obvious.

'Naturally. I hope I punished you enough by letting you think that I wasn't going to meet you,' she said, her hand reaching across the table and touching mine.

'I was in agony,' I replied.

'Good. That'll teach you to go off without telling me. Now what's all this nonsense about Uncle John?'

I told her as much as I could about it and with Frazer's help convinced her it was the truth, though we both refused to tell her where we were staying. It had been impressed upon me that no one was to know our whereabouts. To me it seemed a lot of rubbish but Frazer and John Buchanan had been adamant.

She accepted that we could not tell her any more, and we settled to a very pleasant meal. I learned all sorts of facts about Emily's childhood, mainly from Frazer and though Emily made a pretence of horror at every revelation it was obvious she didn't mind me knowing. I also revealed more of my history, telling them about my time on the desert island, but tactfully avoiding the subject of Gunhild and our daughter.

After dinner we went to the theatre to watch Oscar Wilde's, *The Importance of Being Earnest.* It was a riot and an appreciative audience laughed in all the right places. Afterwards we went for a night-cap before it was time to say goodbye to Emily with a promise that I would see her soon. In London I felt it was best to have a chaperone and Frazer fitted the bill very neatly. He left us for a few moments, ostensibly to fetch the car, and I took the opportunity to kiss Emily goodnight.

By the time we had worked for a month I was speaking very good Hungarian and I could also converse well in Italian. I was also restless, but we had a message from John telling us that we were not to leave again until the course was complete. The professor had reported to him that being back amongst English speaking people had probably put our tuition back three or four days. I disagreed but got nowhere with my arguments. I was in a foul mood but there was nothing I could do.

One morning I received a telegram. It came as a complete surprise and for a moment I thought it was from John. When I opened it however there was a cryptic message inside which read -

LEAVE LIGHT ON AT MIDNIGHT. ARRANGE INGRESS.

There was no name and for a few seconds I was baffled. Then hope flared like a beacon to be replaced with commonsense. It had to be from Emily and what she was intending was to visit me at Brampton Hall. I wondered how she knew where I was. But that could wait. If she was discovered then she would be ruined. Her reputation would be in tatters and, in the claustrophobic world of the society she lived in, she could well be shunned. I needed to prevent her getting to my room at all costs. The easiest way was to ignore the telegram and neither arrange for my light to be on, nor a ladder for her to climb to my room. But there was also the danger that she could be found in the grounds and, though perhaps not as dangerous, it would still be very embarrassing. And what was worse I would be abandoning her to her fate.

At midnight I was pacing the grounds looking for Emily. I had left the light on in my bedroom and stood in the shadow of a huge beech tree keeping watch. There was a three-quarters moon bathing the landscape, but scudding clouds obscured its light from time to time. Just before midnight I heard a slight rustling noise and looked around the tree to see Emily darting quickly across the lawn. My heart skipped a beat at the sight of her.

'Emily, Emily,' I whispered. She hadn't heard me so I called a little louder.

'Oh,' she stopped, startled. 'You frightened the life out of me.' She hurried across to where I stood and put her arms around me, kissing me. 'Why are you here? I wanted to meet you in your room.'

'You silly goose,' I said softly in her ear, my arms clasped tightly around her. 'We can't risk it. What if you're seen? Your reputation will be shot to pieces.'

'I don't care about my reputation,' she retorted. 'I just want to be with you for a while.

I kissed her again and then said, 'Let's walk across the lawn and into the woods. It'll be safer there.' We waited until the moon was hidden behind a dark cloud and then quickly made our way to the edge of the woods. A path took us to a small, highly decorated gazebo about two hundred yards into the trees. I had already left some cushions and a blanket there, just in case.

We sat down and made ourselves as comfortable as possible. 'Now,' I said, 'what's this all about? How did you find me and, more to the point, why did you come?'

She giggled, wriggled a bit closer to me and put her arms around my neck drawing me down onto the blanket. 'I inveigled your whereabouts out of Uncle John. It doesn't matter how; just let me say that I finally wore him down. He made me promise not to come here, which I did. But of course, he couldn't know that I had my fingers crossed.'

We embraced for a while and I had the devil's own job keeping my hands off her. Finally, I broke away and said, 'Darling, I love you but you have your reputation to think of. I'm out of here in another two weeks, and then we can do what you suggested earlier and go away for a weekend.'

She sighed and said, 'David, I want you now. I don't want to wait.'

I smiled, wanting her just as much. 'I feel the same way. But think of the anticipation, the joy, of being in a bedroom. Doing things slowly and properly.'

She put her hand on my thigh and said softly in my ear, 'I know.

But I've never done it and I want to so much. I've read books which makes it all seem so exciting and I can't wait.'

I took her hand in mine and from somewhere found the will power to croak, 'I know how you feel. Believe me, it'll be all the better for waiting. Two weeks, that's all my love, I promise.'

She pretended otherwise but I could see that she was convinced and perhaps relieved. A short while later I walked her through the grounds and down to a lane where she had parked her car. We said a passionate goodnight and she finally drove away. I returned to the hall where I passed a fitful night.

That Wednesday an event occurred that shook the nation and took away all thoughts of passion with Emily. It was April 12th 1912. The Titanic hit an iceberg and sank with the loss of over 1500 souls. The great ship, the pride of the White Star line, considered unsinkable because of its sixteen watertight compartments, had sunk within hours. The rest of the week the newspapers consisted of nothing else. They analysed the event *ad nauseam* until the minutest detail had been explained.

We followed the story as avidly as anybody else but our discussions took place in German, Italian and Hungarian. I counted my lucky stars that I had not sailed on her. John had been right, I had sold my stateroom ticket for four times what I had paid for it.

On the last day that had been scheduled for our tuition the professor called Frazer and I into the library where we were greeted by John Buchanan and Lord Stockdale.

'I understand that you have shown a remarkable aptitude for languages,' said Lord Stockdale, without any preamble.

The professor answered for me. 'Indeed he has, my Lord. His German is fluent, and he could pass as a native of one of the northern regions like Schleswig-Holstein. His Hungarian is good enough for him to understand most conversations and what words he doesn't know he will be able to infer. The same goes for his Italian.'

'And Frazer?' Stockdale nodded at my companion.

The professor shook his head. 'His Italian has improved considerably but his Hungarian leaves a lot to be desired. He has worked hard but young Griffiths here is in a class of his own. He has a natural ability that cannot be taught. However, I have done my best and, I have to say, Frazer has tried hard.'

Lord Stockdale nodded, apparently satisfied with the reply. He looked at me, 'We want you to go to Berlin. There is another extremely important gathering taking place later in the year that will involve most of the ruling class of Germany. Not only will the Kaiser himself be there but just about every important politician and industrialist in Europe. We want you to join the gathering and find out all you can.'

'Is this the meeting you told me about? With Archduke Ferdinand and, what's his name? Antonio Salandra from Italy.'

Lord Stockdale shook his head. 'No. It's a different meeting. There will be far more dignitaries than in the other one.'

I frowned at Stockdale. 'I don't get it. Surely our own people will be there. They can learn far more than I . . . we can,' I added hastily.

John shook his head. 'That's the point. Those who have been invited either have no knowledge of other languages or, even more significantly, nothing of significance will be said in front of them. You, on the other hand, will be there as an American guest. You will be unable to speak or understand any other language and you will show no interest in European politics. You will make it clear that you are completely neutral in all matters European. But you must try and learn as much as you can. Do you understand?'

I nodded. My instructions were simple and clear enough. 'How do I pass back anything that I learn to you?'

'You will keep in contact with Frazer,' replied Stockdale. 'He will not be far away. You need to arrange various codes that will enable you to meet whenever it's necessary. Mr Griffiths, I must emphasise that we are entering a dark period in Europe. Winston agrees with me, which is why he is working so hard to build up our fleet. Unfortunately, too many people disagree and believe that our problems are with the colonies, but they aren't. At the speed Germany is arming something will happen, probably quite soon, and we need to be prepared for it.' Lord Stockdale was referring to Winston Churchill, First Lord of the Admiralty, who had made numerous speeches about the need for Britain to build bigger and better warships to counter the building programme embarked upon by Germany. He considered it a race for power in Europe.

I nodded. 'When do I go?'

'Tomorrow.'

3

'TOMORROW?' I REPEATED, aghast. 'I can't; not tomorrow. I have other things planned that I have to see to.'

'Such as?' Asked Lord Stockdale, icily.

'Such as private matters. Now look, I'm prepared to go on a wild goose trip around Europe on your behalf but I can't go until a week on Monday, and that's final. When is this gathering taking place, anyway?'

John looked at Stockdale, shrugged and replied, 'Not for months.'

'Months?' I cried, aghast.

'Hear me out,' said John. 'We need to plant you into the highest society in Europe. We'll only be able to do so by getting you accepted, and that won't be easy. We can get you into Italian society without difficulty. We want you to start there. It will be good practice for when you get to Germany. It won't be wasted, believe me. We'll be working to, shall we say, push you up the social ladder. However, the target is always Germany and don't forget it.'

'I still don't see why you want me to leave so soon,' I protested.

'I repeat, to give you time to establish your *bona fides*,' said John.

'In that case you can give me another week.'

'I'm sure we can, David,' said Frazer. 'Gentlemen, shall we adjourn to the study? David, there's a letter for you in the hallway.'

Frazer led the other two men from the room, whilst I collected the letter. The stamps showed it had been posted in America and I recognised the handwriting as that of my brother Sion. I settled down in a comfortable armchair to catch up on the news from home.

Dear David,

Can you imagine the mixture of emotions we felt when we learnt that you were not coming home on the Titanic and the relief we felt in view of subsequent events? You have a charmed life, my dear brother, and you should thank God for it. Only joking! Look you know I hate letter writing and so I've thought up a good way of tackling the chore. I will break down my news by subject and not give it in chronological order.

First, Mam and Dad. They are both doing well. They have settled in to what is known as a brownstone house, in a fashionable part of Washington. Mam entertains a great deal and, from what Dad tells me, is not shy in giving her views about world events. Some like her for it but others think she should be the silent support of Congressman Griffiths. (I ask you, can you imagine Mam being silent on any subject?) She will be writing soon to tell you her news herself. However, I can't resist in telling you that there is talk afoot about Dad being invited to stand for the Senate next time round! I'm left alone, more or less, to run things my way, which is why I had hoped you'd be back soon to help. I have just opened our sixth warehouse! I seem to spend most of my time hiring and firing people. Getting good management in senior positions is the most difficult job imaginable. I've had to sack two people for dishonesty – for theft, to be more precise – when we are paying them not only a good salary but bonuses too. I hope to have a place opened in Washington by the end of the year. After that I think we'll consolidate for a while before we expand any further.

I walked away from my fourth crash yesterday. According to Sonny I have only five of my nine lives left! However, if you think of the time you rescued me from those breeds and my flight off that mesa then I think he's exaggerating.

Luckily, this time, I walked away with a sprained ankle. Actually, I'm laid up for a day or two, hence the time to write. A month ago I flew a biplane built by the Gage-McClay company and reached a speed of over ninety miles an hour. Did you read about Captain Albert Berry? On March 1, this year, he jumped out of an airplane from 1,500 feet and used a parachute to land safely. I'm still working on the design of my own airplane. That was my latest crash when I sprained my ankle. I'm copying and learning as much as I can from everybody else and I'm especially interested in anything the French are up to. So if you can learn anything during your travels I'll be very grateful. I'd particularly like you to photograph any airplanes you see and if you can purloin any designs, a brother's undying gratitude will be heaped upon you. At present I'm working on a design that is not made of a wooden frame covered with canvas but something called stressed plywood which should be a lot stronger than current designs. I gather that the engineer Louis Bechereau is working on the same thing, though he appears to be ahead of me right now. Actually, to be honest, I walked away from my latest crash because of the airplane's construction. If it had been made of wood and canvas I think my next stop would have been into a wooden overcoat!

As for Gunhild, what can I say? Nothing has changed except to say that she appears to be ageing by the day. When you think what a vital and beautiful woman she was, it is a tragedy to see her old before her time. Her life is too hard and I pointed this out to Mam. But she said it was nonsense. Mam says that Gunhild's ageing is from within. She has become a self-righteous, bible thumping old biddy twenty years too soon. Susan though, is a precious little gem, so far untainted by everything around her, though I don't suppose this will last. She needs you big brother, though what you'd be able to do I don't know! As you know I've been sending Gunhild money on a regular basis but from what I can gather she's promptly paid it all to the church. I think it's a waste of money and so I've decided to pay the money into a trust fund for Susan. It may not be too late for her if she receives a suitable sum when she comes of age and can escape the life she is now leading. Am I playing God?

I think that's about all the news for now. If anything happens I'll let you know. In the meantime, please find time to write to us all and let us know how you're getting on. And don't forget – airplane plans will be well received!

The very best and a brother's love,

Sion.

I smiled at his salutation and frowned at the news about Gunhild and Susan. I had wanted Gunhild to come away with me, to a better life. Unfortunately, she had found a God who was a harsh and demanding God, punishing her for her sins. Caught up in that punishment was our young daughter, Susan. Gunhild had married a German farmer who was dirt poor. I hung my head in sorrow as the thoughts kaleidoscoped across my mind. "If only" are the two most powerful words in any language. If only I hadn't gone away. If only we hadn't been shipwrecked. If only . . . I shook my head and got my thoughts back in order. Sion was right to pay the money into a trust for Susan. One day she would understand that I had done what I could. Now I was moving on.

Thank goodness Frazer had persuaded Lord Stockdale and John to delay our departure. All that week, back in the civilised society of London, I saw Emily every day. We walked in the park, had dinner and went to the theatre. Someone always chaperoned us.

On Thursday, as I said goodnight, I whispered, 'Is everything arranged?'

'Yes, oh yes,' she replied, excitedly. 'We'll be at the Hotel Grand in Brighton. I'll be there because the sisters are going to march, and I'll be marching with them. I've arranged adjoining rooms. Oh, I can't wait.'

I grinned. 'Neither can I. You're a clever little minx for thinking up a wheeze like this.'

'I know,' she said, impishly.

'Come on, you two,' said Frazer. 'We've been waiting long enough.'

Emily and I strolled around the corner to rejoin Frazer and the young lady he was escorting for the evening, a friend of Emily's. They had appeared to have hit it off and plans were being made for further meetings.

Saturday couldn't come quickly enough.

After saying goodnight to the ladies Frazer and I repaired to the United Services Club to discuss plans for our journey to Berlin. On the face of it everything appeared simple and in order. Cynically I wondered what the reality would be.

On Saturday morning I was at Waterloo railway station bright and early. I took a first class seat and settled down with *The Times* to enjoy the journey through Sussex. It was pleasant enough, the day warm for spring. Halfway to Brighton the door opened and a young lady walked in and shoved a leaflet into my hand. 'Votes for Women,' she said, loudly, and departed. I looked at the leaflet. It was the usual exhortation for women's rights, inviting people to support them by cheering them on as they walked along the Parade at Brighton. I smiled. I'd be there.

I booked into the Grand Hotel and left my bag with the porter. I tipped him sixpence to take it to my room and left the hotel to find a place from which to watch the march. Unlike the event in London there was a festive air about the place. Whether that was due to Brighton being a seaside town, or the fine weather, I couldn't tell. Maybe, I thought, it was due to more support or more tolerance of the movement.

Just before 11.30 things began to happen. The pavements were packed with people, young and old, men and women. Many of them carried banners supporting the suffragettes, although a few booed and yelled obscenities. A band struck up, and from the distance I could see the marchers coming down the Parade. Within minutes they were passing by. In the front, alongside Mrs Pankhurst and her daughter, was Emily. She didn't see me, though I could see that she was searching for me. I yelled her name but it was drowned in the sea of noise. The tail end of the marchers had gone past when suddenly we heard the sound of whistles. The cheers turned to screams and suddenly people were running in all directions.

I stepped down into the road and began to push my way through the marchers who were now running back the way they had come. Placards had been discarded, bonnets were lying in the road, and one or two people were being trampled on. However, I pushed my way forward, praying fervently that Emily was safe. The crowd was beginning to thin as I neared the marchers at the front. There were dozens of policemen, all holding truncheons, who had formed a square around a dozen or so of the front marchers. I walked up to one of the officers and said, 'What's going on? Why have you surrounded those women?'

'None of your business. Now clear off.' He waved his truncheon under my nose, which was like a red rag to a bull and I stepped up close to the man.

'Now listen. I just asked you a civil question. If you don't answer me I'll take that truncheon off you and use it to put you in hospital. Do I make myself clear? Now tell me what's going on.'

Whether it was my tone or the words, I don't know. All I do know was that he wilted under my gaze and replied, sullenly, 'They're under arrest. That's all I know. Now clear off,' he added with a touch of his original belligerence.

I looked over the shoulders of the men in front of me and saw the women cowering from other officers who were waving their truncheons over them. It was then that I saw Emily. She was kneeling next to an inert form, cradling a head covered with blonde curls. I could see the bright crimson of blood discolouring the gold of the hair. Emily was weeping. An officer leant over her and she turned on him with venom. In the noise I only caught the word *bastard*. He stepped back, looked about him and raised his stick, his intention obvious. Emily hunched lower, an arm up to protect her head.

I didn't hesitate. I barged through the cordon, shouldering the two constables before me out of the way. I roared 'No!' at the top of my lungs, making sufficient noise for those around me to pause and look in my direction. The officer who was about to strike Emily paused and looked at me. He must have recognised something in my face because he turned away from Emily and faced me. For him, it was too late.

I ducked under his uplifted arm and hit him in the stomach with all the power I could muster. He doubled over. Knowing what damage he could have done to my beautiful Emily I lost control, and went berserk. I towered over the man. I had not only inherited my father's natural strength I had also inherited his temper when it came to protecting those whom we loved.

I picked the man up by his collar and hit him again and then again. I knew he was unconscious but I felt a primeval instinct to do more. I straightened him up and hit him with a pile-driver of a blow in the middle of the face and at the same time I let him go. He went flying across the artificial enclosure created by the uniformed officers and landed in a heap, unmoving.

At that point I realised I was in serious trouble. A number of officers were taking an interest in me and when their colleague landed on the ground they attacked me.

After that it was a blur. I landed a number of powerful punches but I didn't stand much of a chance. A blow to my head left me groggy, I heard Emily scream my name and then blackness descended.

I didn't wake up the way you do from a good night's sleep. Consciousness came in waves, full awareness getting closer with each one. Each time I was aware of pain in another part of my body. When I finally opened my eyes it was to the sight of Frazer sitting next to me, clean linen sheets and the smell of disinfectant. The smell associated with hospitals.

'What day is it?' I croaked, trying to sit up.

'Take it easy, old chap,' he said, leaning forward and putting a hand on my shoulder to stop me from moving. I winced at the contact. 'Sorry, but there are hardly any places where I can touch you which aren't bruised.'

'What day is it?' I repeated.

'Same day. About,' he looked at his watch, 'eight hours since the fracas.'

I groaned. 'What happened?'

'Let me see. It seems you tried to take on the whole Sussex constabulary single handed.'

Then I remembered. 'Emily? Is she all right?'

'Not physically hurt, thanks to you.'

'What do you mean, not physically?'

'Can you remember anything about the incident?'

I nodded and then winced, my head hurting like hell. 'Everything. Some swine of a policeman was about to brain her. She was holding a . . . a blonde lady in her arms.'

Frazer nodded. 'The person she was cradling died. Emily's in a bad way about it as you can imagine.'

'My God! Poor Emily! Where is she?'

'In prison.'

'What!' I was outraged and struggled to sit up, demanding my clothes. Frazer easily pushed me back as nausea swept through me and pain seared my back and legs.

'Stay where you are. There's nothing you can do until she's been seen by a magistrate and that won't be before Monday.'

'Angus, I was there. I saw it all. It was bloody disgraceful.

The police attacked defenceless women who had been protesting peacefully.'

'That's not the way the police are telling it, old boy. They say that Pankhurst and her cronies began the trouble by throwing stones at them.'

'Bloody rubbish, I tell you. I watched them go past. They were in good humour and I didn't see them carrying anything that could be construed as stones . . . or rocks . . . or anything.' Indignation swept through me, I sat up and sank back again, in pain.

'Listen, David. I'm telling you this for your own good. The government are dead set against the suffragettes. They've instructed the police to break them up with maximum publicity and as much mayhem as they can cause.'

'But why?'

'Because the idiots think that this is all women's foolishness and the little women will give up eventually. They think of them as the weaker sex and have decided that they have no stomach for a long fight.'

'Angus, you know that's completely the wrong reading of the situation. These women are determined. And rightly so,' I added.

'Rightly so? You've been listening to Emily.'

I glared at Frazer for a few seconds and then said, 'Not so, Angus. Women play an equal but different part in our society and they deserve to be recognised for it. It'll come one day and the sooner the better. In the meantime I want to press charges.'

'Against whom?' he asked in surprise.

'Why, the police of course,' I replied, equally surprised at the stupidity of the question.

He shook his head sadly. 'My dear chap, you don't know the mess you are in. Or, I should say,' he added hastily, 'the mess you were in until Lord Stockdale intervened on your behalf.'

'What are you talking about?' I stifled a groan. 'I've been done over, and done over properly.'

'David, first of all, after what you did to that policeman you're lucky to be alive and secondly if you weren't wanted by the government for a job considered to be of national importance you'd be deported as soon as you are able to walk as an undesirable alien.'

'What! That's preposterous. He was going to brain Emily, probably kill her. I saved her from the swine.'

'David, you half killed the swine and I know you're telling the truth but you aren't listening. The government doesn't want to know. They're backing the police to the hilt. You can't win a battle against them and if you try then even Stockdale might not be able to save you again.'

'Then sod them. As soon as I can I'm getting out of here, getting Emily and leaving for America.'

'No you aren't,' Frazer said softly. 'Stockdale thought you might take this attitude and so he gave me a message for you.'

I raised an eyebrow, about the only part of me that didn't hurt.

'Either you're on the boat train to Rome no later than Tuesday or Emily goes down for six months and you get deported back to the States.'

'He can't do that,' I said, aghast.

Frazer puckered his lips and raised his eyebrows but said nothing. The message sank in.

'He'd do that?'

Frazer nodded.

'What about John? Emily's his niece for God's sake. Doesn't he care?'

'It's because he does care that he'd do nothing to stop Stockdale having his way. Look at it from John's point of view. Emily could be dead or maimed right now if you hadn't been there. And don't forget, that's the second time you've been on hand to save her. She might not be so lucky a third time. If she gets locked up for six months it might not be very pleasant but it might save her life and bring her to her senses.'

'But prison! For Emily,' I cried, aghast.

'Oh, it won't be so bad. Stockdale and John will ensure she's looked after. It won't be pleasant but she'll survive.'

I could see he meant it and it made a certain sense to me, even in my addled state. 'Get me my clothes. I'm getting out of here.' I threw back the bedclothes and tentatively sat up. Pain swept through me but I gritted my teeth, sat on the edge of the bed and gasped, 'Get me my clothes, damn you.'

'Where are you going?' Frazer asked, unperturbed as he stood, opened a wardrobe and handed me my clothes. They were the worse for wear but would suffice, for now.

'I'm going to see Emily. Make sure she's all right. Any objections?'

'None, my dear fellow. But the police might have.'

I paused and then looked Frazer in the eyes. 'No, they won't. I'll co-operate but at a price. You come with me and make sure I get in to see her. You don't want to see me get really angry.'

Though this was something of an empty threat he treated it seriously. A short while later I had hobbled out of the hospital and he was driving me to the police station. Whatever he said to the Desk Sergeant worked because a few minutes after our arrival I was at the bars with my face pressed up to them calling to Emily.

She was lying curled up on her side, her back to us. At the sound of my voice she jerked round, startled, and I could see she had been crying. She leapt up, laughing and crying at the same time. 'Oh, David, David. I was so worried. Oh, you're safe. You're all right.' She stood at the bars and clutched my hands in hers. I smiled down at her, sheer will-power stopping me from grimacing in pain.

'I saw them,' she said, tremulously. 'I saw them hitting and kicking you and there was nothing I could do about it. The pigs. They killed that girl I was holding.'

I nodded. 'Angus told me.'

'I saw them beating you. Are you really all right?'

I dredged up a smile, nodded and replied, 'I'm only sorry that our night of passion has been ruined,' I whispered. 'It seems our love will have to wait a little longer.'

She smiled tentatively at me. 'I'm so sorry. Another time, another place,' she whispered back.

I nodded and then said in a normal voice, 'When will you be getting out of here?'

'Not before Monday. There are eighteen of us in all. I expect we'll keep the court clogged up all day. I should be back in London by Tuesday at the latest. Will I see you then?'

I shook my head. 'I'm going to the continent on the boat train on Monday. Italy,' I added by way of explanation.

'Oh, that means I won't see you. When will you be back?'

'According to your uncle, sometime in the autumn!'

'What! He can't do this! Why I'll . . . I'll . . .' Emily spluttered in indignation.

'You'll wait for me,' I said. 'I love you. So please wait.'

Her indignation suddenly melted away. ‘Oh, David. I love you, too. Of course I’ll wait for you.’

Just then a constable entered and ordered us out. Frazer had been keeping a discreet distance next to the door, trying not to overhear us. We left, me reluctantly and Frazer with relief.

‘Right, we’re for London, a last briefing and then we get ready for the boat train,’ he announced as we emerged from the police station.

4

WE CAUGHT THE eleven o'clock boat train from Victoria to Dover Harbour. There we disembarked and strolled along the pier to the ferry. In keeping with my status as a wealthy, carefree American, I had brought enough luggage to last me six months. Frazer was travelling light in comparison and had all his paraphernalia in two cases. We had agreed that we would travel together to Italy and there, to all intents and purposes, we would separate.

The ferry trip was calm and uneventful. At tea time that afternoon we were aboard the train for Rome. First class sleeper compartments had been booked and, while a valet unpacked a few things, Frazer and I sat in the restaurant and ordered tea and toast. My lessons as a spy were to continue. Frazer handed me what seemed to be a spectacle case.

'What's this?' I asked opening it and looking at an odd set of picks and probes the like of which I had never seen before.

'It's a set of locksmith's tools. I'm going to teach you the basics of lock picking and after that you need to practice at every opportunity. It's easy once you know what you're doing. All locks have a set of tumblers. The most common set has three, the most difficult has seven. Three tumblers are easy and you ought to be able to open that kind of lock in under a minute. Seven is nigh impossible and will take you a month of Sundays to learn to pick. If you get to five tumblers in five minutes you'll be doing well.'

'How will I tell the difference? To me a lock is just a lock. Either it has a key or it hasn't.'

'Don't worry, I'll show you. I've got a few locks in my case and you'll practice on them whenever you can. Use a pick on the lock on your hotel room whenever you get the chance. It's all a question of feel, and you'll understand as you try it. The different probes and picks are for different types of locks. I'll explain.' I was fascinated by what he told me and listened attentively. I was determined to master the skill of opening locked doors!

The train rapidly filled up and soon there was a noisy, bustling crowd demanding food and drink. Frazer and I sat at a table which accommodated only two people. At the table across from us sat four boisterous Germans, talking too loudly, demanding too much. Frazer gave a slight incline of his head in their direction to draw them to my attention and I nodded in understanding. I would begin not to understand German, Italian or Hungarian.

'*Sie da, reichen Sie das Salz "rüber"!*' the German sitting across from me said, rudely. I was about to reach for the salt when I realised I was not supposed to understand what he had said.

'Sorry, old chap. I'm an American. I don't speak German.'

'Ach, so. Pass me the salt,' he repeated, smiling.

Frazer was looking out of the window, ignoring us. The man then asked Frazer if he spoke German but Frazer ignored him. He repeated the question in English and I said, 'Frazer.' He looked round, pretending to be surprised. 'This chap is asking if you speak German.'

'Oh! What? No, I don't. Only English, I'm afraid.'

The man nodded and turned to his companions. He said in a loud, over-bearing voice, 'These two are nitwits. They only speak English. The one next to me is a dumb American.'

'What does it matter, Karl. Ignore them. They may not speak our language but they look as though they can take care of themselves.'

'Oh, I'm not so sure,' replied the man we now knew as Karl. 'I think I shall have some fun with them.'

The last thing that we wanted was to draw attention to ourselves especially because of a stupid, loudmouthed youth. I looked across at their table and deliberately looked at each in turn. One of the youths flushed and said, 'Don't, Karl. He may not understand us but I don't like the look of him or the other one. We aren't in Germany now, you know.'

I didn't understand what was meant by that statement, but it was sufficient for Karl to back off and merely make disparaging remarks about Frazer and me until we had finished our tea and left the compartment.

The train was luxurious. The sleeping compartments were more than adequate and the dinner served to us that evening would have done the Savoy Grill proud. The wines we had with the meal were of the finest vintages and the port afterwards would, according to Frazer, have done his Black Watch Regiment proud, even at a Royal dinner.

The train left on time and I was looking forward to three days of quiet, good food and drink, and the company of Frazer who had lived an interesting and varied life. It would also give my body time to heal. The pain had subsided to an ache with a searing twinge from time to time. However, the doctor had assured me that nothing was broken and that time would heal me.

At lunch the following day we had a spot of bother. We had passed through German customs at Saarbrucken an hour earlier and were on our way to Strasbourg. At lunch we found the table next to us again occupied by the four Germans who had been so tiresome the day before. They now indulged in the same type of petty remarks, made in loud voices, which brought sniggers from some of the other passengers. That seemed to egg the Germans on, and the one we knew as Karl became more personal. Unfortunately, if we indicated that we knew they were talking about us they would know that we spoke and understood German. It was galling, to say the least, and I could see that Frazer was having the same difficulty as I was in keeping his temper.

We sat and smiled at them, as each pointed remark was made. After lunch we adjourned to the lounge. Frazer said, 'The little bastards. It's taking all my will-power not to do or say something.'

I grinned at him. 'Don't let them rile you. You heard, they'll be getting off at Freiburg. We can ignore them until then.'

'You may but I'm telling you, David, I don't think I'll be able hold my temper much longer.'

'I don't mind, in that case. Say the word and we tip our hands.'

He looked as though he was about to agree to my suggestion when he shook his head and smiled ruefully. 'No, you're right. There are too many people on the train, anyone of whom we may meet again in different circumstances. We can't give our linguistic abilities away just yet.'

I nodded. 'I'll arrange with our sleeping car attendant to serve us dinner in your compartment before he makes the beds up. That way we can stay out of their way.'

'A good idea. You know they are the most arrogant people imaginable. Have you noticed the scars that three of them carry on their faces?'

I nodded. I had been intrigued by the similarity of their small disfigurements.

'Those are fencing scars. It proves that they have fenced to a very high standard, with a master swordsman, who has marked them with the sword. They will have stood and accepted the scar as a sign of their manhood. Only certain elite members of their upper class have that honour bestowed upon them. If,' he added, 'you can call it an honour.'

We had a pleasant dinner followed by a game of whist. I then made the error of saying that I wanted to stretch my legs and that I would walk along to the bar and pick up a couple of drinks.

I was walking back with the drinks when the four Germans appeared in the doorway ahead of me. Rather than create a fuss I stepped to one side to let them pass, which the first two did. Unfortunately, the third one, known as Karl, deliberately knocked my hands and spilled the drinks.

'You clumsy oaf,' he said in his thick, guttural accent. 'Look vat you have done. I shall thrash you for that.'

The other two had stopped and turned and before I could do anything Karl hit me in the stomach. It wasn't a very powerful blow because there was so little room, but on top of my other bruises it was enough to make me gasp, totter backwards and gasp again as my back hit the wall. Before I could do anything the fourth man hustled Karl away and I could hear him protesting that he wanted to teach me a lesson. I went slowly back to the compartment.

'Where are the drinks?' Frazer greeted me.

I told him what had happened. 'Look, Angus, I'm sorry but I'm getting off at Freiburg. The train stops for half an hour and I'm saying farewell to Karl.'

Frazer nodded. 'I agree. Honour is at stake. I'll come with you to make sure none of the others interfere.'

The train pulled into Freiburg at half past three in the morning. There was a great deal of noise, steam blowing from engines, passengers calling to one another and porters hurrying about with luggage. I stepped down from the train into the path of Karl and his friends with Frazer at my shoulder.

I didn't give him a chance. I hit him a pile-driver of a blow into his stomach and as he doubled up I hit him with my other fist in the side of the head. He went sprawling across the platform. The other three made a move towards me but Frazer said, 'Enough. Stay out of it. Your friend started it and my friend will finish it.' He had his hand across his chest and tucked under his arm, for all the world as though he had a gun hidden there.

The three men hesitated as Karl, gasping for breath, got groggily to his feet and said, 'Stay out of this. I need no help with this American wog.'

I figured that my old injuries and the ones I had inflicted on Karl left us more or less even in the fitness stakes. I wasn't so sure when he held his hands in front of him in the way I had seen bare knuckle boxers do and start to move around on his toes.

One of the others said, 'Karl was the champion boxer at Berlin University. I'll enjoy this.'

Karl grinned and danced towards me. His problem was that we weren't in a boxing ring. I stepped forward and kicked him, hard, in the right knee. His leg buckled and he stopped dancing around. His guard also slipped and as it did I hit him on the side of the head with my right fist. I hit him so hard that I damn near broke my knuckles. All the pent up anger at him, my frustration at the beating I had taken from the police and the stupidity of the situation was in that punch. He went down and made no attempt to get up.

'You do not fight fair,' hissed one of the others, seeing their champion laid out cold.

'No. I fight to win,' I retorted. 'Now get him out of here.'

We stood and watched as Karl was carried away. We climbed back aboard the train and stood at our carriage window until we moved away. I would not have put it beyond the four men to have sent for the police and caused us further trouble. And after what had happened in Brighton, I wasn't too keen to place any more trust in the German police than in ours when it came to believing us or believing members of their aristocracy. Luckily, nothing happened and an hour later we passed through the border into Switzerland.

We arrived in Rome the following afternoon. It was very warm with hardly any breeze. It was my first time in Rome and I was eager to see the sights and sample the city's delights.

Frazer and I now separated. We had worked out our various methods of making contact and had agreed on our codes and secret messages. I booked into a hotel on the Via delle Fornaci, a road that leads straight to the Vatican. Frazer booked into another hotel a few hundred yards from mine.

I began to inveigle my way into Italian society. It wasn't difficult. Appearing to be rich and unattached I had a great deal of attention showered on me. It was fascinating to pretend to speak only English and it was astonishing how careless people became in my presence. I attended a wide variety of events; dinner parties, weekends in country estates, outings to the opera. Much of Italian society was more than fascinated by the crass but extremely rich American. I also mixed with politicians and with the senior commanders of the navy and army.

On one occasion I deduced that Belgium and Germany had agreed that, should the Germans attack Northern Rhodesia from German East Africa, no protest would be made and no help offered to the British. I learned that the attack would take place later that year. I was later told that acting on the information I had supplied, two British regiments moved swiftly to the border between Northern Rhodesia and German East Africa and diplomatic notes were exchanged. The crisis passed without incident. On another occasion I discovered that Germany was sending arms to Ireland to support the nationalists. Three destroyers intercepted two trawlers filled to the gunwales with guns and explosives. The trawlers had been supplied at sea from a German battleship. They were sunk with all hands and more diplomatic notes were exchanged. I discovered that the Italians were very well disposed to the Bulgarians and that a large proportion of the Bulgarian army was being secretly poised to strike at Adrianople on the direct railway line to Constantinople, which would put the Turks and the Bulgarians at war with each other. I was also able to warn Britain that the Serbs would join the Bulgarians and demand independence for Macedonia. The message I received back from Frazer was that we were delighted with the way things were hotting up in the Balkans, provided Germany, Austro-Hungary and Italy kept out of it. We wanted Turkey's influence in Europe ended once and for all. I was able to assure Frazer, who passed the information back to Lord Stockdale, that the three major powers would stay out. Later in the year Turkey was smashed in the Balkans, tens of thousands of Turkish troops perished and large slices of its European holdings were annexed. Turkey's once feared army was left in total disarray. There were other minor successes, which enabled Britain to act before matters got out of hand.

Lord Stockdale took the trouble to send a message of congratulations to Frazer but with the caveat that Italy was child's play compared to Germany and Austro-Hungary.

Five weeks after arriving in Italy I received the most important invitation to date. Not only did it mean that I was now accepted by the highest in society, it was also an event I was eager to attend. I was to go the villa of Count Rotondo on the Piazza d. Popolo when the king would visit the Count. I had been expecting it.

Dressed in tails and white tie I alighted from a horse drawn buggy at the address on the invitation. It was a small palace. Police held back the crowds as dignitaries and famous people arrived and were cheered. John had shown me newspaper photographs of those I needed to become acquainted with and given as much detail about them as he had been able to obtain. I showed my invitation and went through the police cordon and up the steps and through the portal.

The injuries I had sustained had stopped aching and the bruises on my body had faded from dark blue and purple to a light tan and yellow. I was feeling in fine fettle as I moved along the line to greet my hosts. As I neared the end of the line there was a sudden commotion and I heard the words, 'The King.'

The line broke up and our hosts rushed forward as a huge cheer came from outside. A few moments later King Victor Emmanuel III entered with his entourage. I recognised General Alberto Pollio amongst them – the man I had come to see.

In the excitement of the king's visit all else was forgotten and I wandered through to mingle with the other guests. I kept up my pretence of not understanding Italian and was getting better at not reacting when spoken to. Many of the others spoke English, as it was the one language that most had in common.

Later that evening I had insinuated myself into a group of statesmen that included General Pollio and Helmut Weisman, the Vice Chancellor.

The conversation was in English to begin with and was about world matters in general. Having established that I spoke no German or Italian the General and Weisman quickly exchanged a few words. I understood that they and a number of others were to meet in the upper library at midnight.

A short while later we had broken up into smaller groups and I noticed Weisman working his way to certain people, presumably giving the same message.

I learned that the upper library was on the third floor, in the private quarters of the Count and not open to the guests that evening.

The main library was on the second floor and was available to guests. I wandered in with a glass of champagne in my hand to find that it was empty apart from an elderly gentleman sitting in a wing-backed chair near the balcony.

'Good evening, sir,' I greeted him.

'Good evening, Griffiths,' the British Ambassador greeted me. 'What have you discovered?'

'Only that there will be a meeting in the upper library in,' I looked at my watch, 'twenty minutes.'

He nodded. 'We must try and break up this damn triple alliance before it's too late. What are you proposing to do?'

'I was going to see if I can climb up the outside wall and get into the room where the meeting is being held, sir,' I replied.

The Ambassador nodded. 'I know the room. There's an alcove that has a heavy curtain across it. You can hide in there. Good luck. Don't forget that we need to know how strong the alliance is. I believe that Italy is the weak link but we must know for certain.'

I nodded and made to step out on the balcony. 'Incidentally, young man,' I paused to listen to the Ambassador. 'If you are caught they could easily shoot you and say it was a mistake, that they thought you were a burglar.'

I paused, his words giving me food for thought. Up to that point I had assumed that if I was found out the worst that would happen was that I would be deported or even just ostracised by high society for displaying bad manners. Suddenly I wasn't so sure that I wanted to go on with what I was doing.

My indecision must have shown because he added, 'I understand that you are Welsh and you are now living in America. Please believe me when I say that a great deal hangs on what we can learn. I, like many others, fear the worst. Not to put too fine a point on it, your country needs you.'

I was about to point out that my country was now America but decided not to bother. I looked around the room, spied a bottle of whisky and slipped it into my pocket. 'It might come in useful,' I said, not bothering to explain. I gave a half salute and went outside, onto the balcony which overlooked a small, dark courtyard. Even when I strained my eyes and ears, I could neither see nor sense anybody below. Looking up I saw, about twenty feet above me, another balcony like the one on which I stood. The stonework stretching before me was uneven, with gaps in the cement and niches and ledges all the way up. I began to climb. It was an easy ascent and I made rapid progress. I had just put my hand onto a ledge when there was a sudden squawk, a flurry of wings and a pigeon flew past my face. My feet slipped, I jerked my left hand away from the ledge and I was left hanging from my right hand, which was wrapped around the head of a small gargoyle. Fear left my mouth parchment dry. I grabbed the ledge again and scrambled around with my feet until I was firmly clamped back to the wall. I waited for a few seconds until I got my breath back and my heart stopped pounding.

I continued upwards, though this time exercising a little more caution. There were no further surprises and I clambered onto the balcony. The doors were open and I carefully looked in. The room was empty. Just as the Ambassador had told me, there was a curtain on one side of the room. I quickly stepped across the carpet and slipped behind the curtain just as I heard the door to the corridor opening and people, speaking German, enter.

As I peered through the curtains I caught a glimpse of some of them. Those I saw I knew to be either senior political figures or military leaders of Germany, Italy and Austro-Hungary. I had a ringside seat at their discussions and, because of their language differences, I heard the same thing being repeated in all three languages so there could be no misunderstanding. In a nutshell, the triple alliance was to hold tight, though I thought that the Italians needed coercing. Germany was going to invade Belgium and after annexing it, which would take less than two months, Germany would turn its attention to supporting Austro-Hungary against Russia. Austro-Hungary would also invade

Serbia, where there was already a great deal of internal support for such a move. Italy was to be supported in her adventures in Africa. Countries colonised by the French were to be the targets. Italy was to take Libya once and for all and thus end the dispute with Turkey over who controlled the country. Next Italy would sweep through Tunisia, Algeria and finally Morocco. While that was going on Germany would threaten France from the north. After that, there was nothing to stop Italy working her way east into Egypt, the Sudan and Ethiopia.

What I was listening to was unbelievable. It was a rewriting of the geography of most of Europe and chunks of Africa. Whilst I absorbed what I was hearing I realised that one of the occupants of the room kept looking across at where I was hidden. I saw him whisper to the man sitting next to him and they both looked in my direction. Quickly I slipped into the armchair and put my feet on the stool. I opened the bottle of whisky, swilled some around my mouth, looked to spit it out, saw nowhere to put it and swallowed a mouthful, nearly choking on the stuff. I laid back my head, dropped my arm over the chair rest and placed the bottle next to my fingertips. My other hand was within inches of my gun. I had no intention of being arrested as a spy.

I heard the curtain being thrown roughly aside and a voice exclaiming in German, 'I was right. Someone is here. You, you, come here. Damn it. What is wrong with the man?' I heard a number of people approaching and sensed rather than saw that someone was standing in front of me. Suddenly the stool was whipped away and my feet dropped to the floor.

5

'WHAT? WHAT?' I ASKED, blearily, hoping that I looked and sounded drunk. 'What's the matter, old chap?' I asked loudly, looking around at the grim faces staring at me. 'I say, I'm most frightfully sorry. Is there something amiss?' What I was apologising for I didn't know, but it was all I could think of to say at that moment.

'He has heard everything,' said a German general whom I knew to be Albert von Guttenburg, the Chief of General Staff.

'I am sure he was listening at the curtains. I saw him.'

Another man agreed.

'I don't think so,' said another, in Hungarian. I looked from one to the other. 'I know this man. He is an American who speaks no other language except English. Even that he speaks badly.' A few of the men tittered though most just glared at me. I was in the devil of a situation and more than a little scared. For the moment I decided to continue acting as if I were drunk and disorientated.

'We should take him out and shoot him,' someone said in German.

'Don't be ridiculous,' said an Italian. 'If you do we will have all sorts of problems with the Americans.'

'What can they do?' The German sneered. 'They are neutral in all things, have no army and no navy. They might send a diplomatic protest, but that will be all.'

'Even so,' continued the Italian, 'I do not think it will be wise. His father, I understand, is a member of Congress. We do not want any trouble.'

The arguments continued back and forth for a few minutes longer, and it seemed to me that those who were after my blood were beginning to win. I decided it was time I took a hand in the proceedings.

I stood up, the bottle in my hand, staggered to the curtain and put the bottle down on an occasional table. I looked back at the group of men who hadn't moved, surprised by my actions. 'Well, goodnight,' I slurred and weaved my way out of there. Nobody tried to stop me; by direct action, pretending to be the innocent, I had taken them by surprise. Luckily, no one thought to ask me how I had got into the room. I wanted to get away before this occurred to any of them. I decided my meeting with General Pollio could wait for another day.

I slipped back into the main part of the house, mingled with the other guests for a few minutes and then made my way out through the front door with some of them.

There were still crowds thronging the street with the police holding them back. The King had not left and I was committing a serious breach of etiquette by leaving before him. But, I reasoned, better to flout etiquette than be killed.

I had worked my way through the crowd, and looked back in time to see some of the men who had been in the upper library rush out of the door. They stood there indecisively, looking around. Looking for me.

I turned my head away and looked down, hunching my shoulders. I walked away as quickly as I dared and once around the nearest corner I strode out, covering a lot of ground rapidly without breaking into a run and risking drawing attention to myself.

I was well enough known, had been invited to enough social gatherings, to be found easily and quickly. Back at the hotel I packed a travel bag and went down to the lobby to speak to the concierge. I had been in the habit of paying my bill every week and so the outstanding amount was quite small. I also paid for a week in advance.

'I shall be back within the week,' I said. I smiled, 'A lady awaits me. I would appreciate it if you told no one that I have left. It is, shall we say, a little delicate? Her husband . . .' I let the inference hang between us and gave the man a tip of ten thousand lire. I estimated it was the equivalent of a week's wages.

He palmed it with alacrity and said, 'Ah, *Señor*, you can count on me. I say nothing. Nothing,' he added again for good measure.

I thanked him and left, using a side entrance.

I debated with myself whether or not to go to the Embassy, but I knew that if I did I would have to talk my way past the Italian police and the British soldiers standing guard, and neither appealed to me at that moment. I heard footsteps rushing down the street and quickly hid behind a wall near to the hotel. I saw three men, all from the group on whom I had eavesdropped, enter the hotel. A few moments later they rushed back out again. So much, I thought cynically, for saying nothing. Promises, indeed.

I decided that I needed to see Frazer as a matter of urgency, not only because of the information I now had but as a source of ideas for saving my skin. As I watched the three men disappear in the opposite direction I walked rapidly away, intending to lose myself in the more crowded streets.

I tapped on Frazer's door twice, paused, and tapped three times more. The door opened and I was looking down the barrel of a Webley 45. Frazer gestured me in, looked up and down the corridor and closed the door. As succinctly as I could I explained the position to him while he poured me a much needed whisky and soda.

'We have to get this information to London as quickly as possible,' he said when I had finished. 'We also need to get you out of Rome. I think this city has become too hot for you.'

I raised my glass to him and nodded in concurrence with his decisions. 'Have you left anything in the hotel that you'll need?'

I thought for a few moments and then shook my head. 'I don't think so. Apart from my clothes I've left nothing of value behind. My money, passport and important papers are all in my body belt. The gun I left behind in the chair in the upper library. If it hasn't been found yet it will be soon. That'll put the cat amongst the pigeons.'

'Was it the Bodeo you left?'

I nodded. The Italian gun had been in service since 1889 and there were tens of thousands of them throughout the Mediterranean and Balkan regions. It carried six 10.4mm bullets, a calibre unique to Italy.

'That's something. At least they can't tie it in to you. Do you think they'll try hard to find you?'

I thought about that for a few moments and then, reluctantly, I nodded. 'I think the fact that I've done a bunk will tip them off that I heard their discussion. I can always claim that I didn't understand what was going on but was just, em, frightened. Which, quite frankly, was true.'

'Good. A spot of fear helps keep you alive. And don't forget it, young Griffiths.' As he could only have been about two or three years older than I was, calling me young was a cheek, but I let it pass.

'So what do we do now?'

'Now, my dear chap, we pack up here, pay the bill, and quietly depart. I've a suitable black steed outside and we can be in Switzerland by tomorrow night.

He was as good as his word. Half an hour later we had left Rome, crossed the Tiber and were on the road for Civitavecchia. The car was a two seater Bugatti with no hood; designed to be driven in fine weather only. Its lights left much to be desired, but luckily there was almost a full moon and we could make the road out without too much difficulty. Once out of the suburbs the road deteriorated but at least it was tarred. We passed through small villages but no towns, arrived at the port of Civitavecchia an hour after dawn and drove down to the docks. We topped up the petrol tank at a garage near them and bought an additional three jerry cans of petrol, which would, we hoped get us to the Swiss border.

We also bought food, bottles of wine and some local lemonade. I took over the driving whilst Frazer made himself as comfortable as possible and in spite of bouncing over potholes and lurching round bends soon fell sound asleep. At lunchtime he woke, we stopped for a natural break as he called it, grabbed a mouthful of food and drink and were soon on our way again.

'Speed is what will save us,' he said, now driving with his foot firmly on the accelerator and the needle on the speedometer hovering between seventy and eighty kilometres an hour. I agreed. I settled down and promptly fell asleep. It was dusk when I awoke.

'Where are we?'

'Approaching Leghorn. My estimate that we would reach Switzerland by tonight was overoptimistic. We're only half way there.'

I pulled out a map and measured off the distances. 'Actually, this is better. We'll get to the border at dawn tomorrow when the guards will be at their lowest ebb. In fact, I can see from this map that if we go to Turin and then to Grenoble we can get to France quicker.'

'I know. However, all the roads between Italy and France have customs posts. Because of the close association between Italy and Switzerland many roads on their borders have no customs posts and so we can get in unobserved.'

'How do you know?'

'I've used the route before. Don't forget that the Swiss supply the guard for the Vatican, and a large part of Switzerland is Italian speaking. Believe me, going into Switzerland will be the safest route.'

I nodded. That sounded reasonable to me. From Leghorn we headed for Pisa and soon we passed through the town whose main claim to fame was a tower that was leaning over because of subsidence.

A while later we emptied the last of the remaining petrol from the jerry cans into the tank, ate some stale bread and cheese, drank a mouthful or two of tepid wine and set off on the last hurdle.

The road climbed steadily and soon we were surrounded by white, snow covered mountains. We were still on a main road and although we hit the odd patch of ice we encountered no problems. The temperature dropped sharply and in spite of putting on a few layers of clothes under our coats we were soon bitterly cold. We passed through Breno and Edolo without mishap and had left Aprica behind when the car stopped

'What's happened?' I asked groggily, the change in noise and lack of movement waking me from a shallow doze.

'Out of petrol, I think.' Frazer clambered out of the car, unscrewed the petrol cap and lifted out the dipstick. 'I thought so. Dry as a bone.'

'What do we do now?'

'We're not on any map but I can tell you we're about twenty-five kilometres from Tirano. We turn off just before there and travel about two kilometres to the Swiss border. We cross at a little place called Brusio. The last time I passed through it was unmanned. I suspect it still is. We can hike it in about five hours,' this thought gave me no pleasure, 'or,' he added, 'we go back about two or three kilometres and see if there is any petrol to be found in the last village we passed through.'

'Was there a garage?' I asked and then added, naively. 'And anyway, if there was it won't be open.'

'David, you slay me, you really do. We're on the run and you're bothering about the niceties of opening hours of garages! No, there was no garage but I had in mind that we find a truck or car, syphon off some petrol and get back here as fast as we can.'

Suitably chastised I agreed.

'Help me push the car up that track so that it's out of sight. I know the likelihood of anybody coming along at this hour is remote but we daren't take a chance, just in case. We must get the information we have back to John; we should never take chances. That way we might live to fight another day.'

It was a good lesson to learn and I took it to heart. After straining every sinew we managed to shove the car out of sight behind some boulders and, taking a jerry can each we began to walk back the way we had come.

In less than fifteen minutes we had returned to Aprica. There were about two dozen ramshackle houses scattered on each side of the road, many with large outhouses. We sneaked along like the thieves in the night we were, one on either side of the road, looking in the windows of the larger outhouses and searching for a petrol driven vehicle.

The night was utterly silent, there was no wind and the slightest sound carried far and wide. I heard three snaps of his fingers and knew that Frazer had found what we were looking for. I crossed the road and helped him to open the door. Inside was a brand new Fiat truck. Frazer was about to open the petrol cap when I tapped him on the shoulder. I indicated a large tank sitting in the corner. I cracked open the tap and as the liquid dripped out the stench of petrol assailed our noses.

We placed a jerry can underneath the tap and quickly filled it. While Frazer changed cans I wandered into the back of the shed to see if there was anything else that could prove of use.

The sing-song words, 'Hands up,' in Italian took us both by surprise.

6

I STOOD STILL AND looked across the shed. A young boy was pointing a shotgun at Frazer. In the gloom I could see the end of the gun shaking.

Frazer lifted his hands and said, in English, 'Don't shoot. I mean no harm.'

The lad was distracted and I was able to step behind him, put my arms around and jam my thumb across the two cocked hammers, effectively preventing the trigger from being pulled. The boy struggled for a few seconds until, in Italian, I told him to hold still or be hurt. 'If I let you go, will you keep quiet?' He agreed and I let him go, taking the shotgun from him.

'We need petrol. We are not stealing it.' Before he could contradict me, I added, 'Here is five thousand lire. That is three or four times more than the petrol is worth. We just want to leave as quietly as we arrived. Do you agree?'

He nodded warily and then held out his hand for the money. I handed it over to him. Frazer picked up the cans and walked to the doors and looked out. 'All clear. Ready?'

'Yes,' I said. I broke open the gun and removed the cartridges before handing the weapon back to the boy. I bade him goodbye and followed Frazer. We hadn't gone fifty yards when the doors burst open and the boy started yelling at the top of his voice.

'Stop thieves! Stop thieves! Rich thieves have robbed us! Help!'

Frazer and I didn't wait to argue but took to our heels, our progress hampered by the heavy jerry can we each carried. 'What the hell was that all about?' he gasped. 'I thought the boy would just have let us go, quietly.'

'Money,' I said. 'I think he's after our money. If I was prepared to pay so much for a drop of petrol how much more are we carrying? You saw how poor that place is. They could rob us blind and leave our bodies for the crows and nobody would be any the wiser. He must have figured that we've also got a car and that would be worth something to them, too.'

'I think you're right. Listen!' Frazer stopped and we both turned back the way we had come to listen in the stillness.

We could hear excited voices and yells and then we heard the gutsy roar of an engine starting up. 'That truck. We should have disabled it,' I said.

By way of reply Frazer turned and started running once more, with me close on his heels.

'They're gaining,' I said, looking back as the looms of light from the truck got brighter. 'We aren't going to make it.'

'Take the cans. I'll stop them,' he gasped giving his can to me.

'We'll stop them together,' I replied, putting both cans down in the road.

'Don't be so bloody stupid,' he said, harshly. 'We haven't come this far to blow it now. What you carry in your head is too valuable to lose. We must get the information back to Britain. So you do as I tell you and go,' he gave me a rough shove pushing me towards where we had left the car. 'Grab those cans and run.'

He tore off his over-coat to aid movement and took his revolver out from under his jacket. 'Go on, damn you. I'll hold them off for as long as I can.

I hesitated then grabbed the cans. 'I'll be back as quickly as I can,' I said, running and stumbling down the road. I went round a corner just as the headlights of the lorry lit up Frazer standing in the middle of the road. I heard the shot, the sound propelling me faster. There was a screech of brakes and a loud crash and then I heard more shots followed by the sound of the shotgun being fired.

I was gasping for breath when I reached the car. I poured the petrol from one can, slopping a lot of it down the paintwork. I was careful not to get any on me.

The car had an electric starter but I needed to prime the engine first. I undid the straps holding down the bonnet and found the petrol pump. I located the thumb press on the side of the pump and began squeezing.

At first it moved easily as air was pumped through the system. Then, as the petrol began to fill the void it got harder until I couldn't move it. The motor was primed. I jumped into the driver's seat, said a prayer and pressed the starter. The engine groaned and turned over. I pressed again and this time it burst into life with a throaty roar. While I had been busy I had been listening to what was happening back up the road. After the initial fusillade there had only been an occasional shot. At least, I hoped that it was an indication that Frazer was still alive.

I drove back on to the road and reversed carefully along it, back the way I had ran. I wanted to be ready for a fast getaway. When I got to the bend where I had last seen Frazer I stopped the car and placed the other can of petrol by the side of the road.

'Angus! Angus!' I said in a loud whisper.

'Over here. Keep your head down, you fool. I told you to get away.'

'Shut up. Where are they and how many of them?'

'I'm guessing but about a dozen. I shot one of them. Killed him, I think. The others are crawling over the hillside, coming this way.'

I opened the boot of the car and took out the Lee-Enfield Mark III, short magazine rifle. It held ten rounds of .303 calibre bullets and had the smoothest bolt action ever made.

I saw Frazer about ten yards away and even as I did I saw a figure loom up behind him. I dropped to one knee, aimed and fired. The figure behind Frazer jerked backwards, a wicked looking knife flying through the air as its owner landed in a heap. Two more figures suddenly materialised, one of whom I shot while Frazer shot the other. There was more firing but no bullets came near me.

'Are you all right?'

'Yes. Grazed that's all.'

'Can you move?'

'Yes. No problem.'

'Wait until I say so then run. I'll have the car ready.' I uncapped the jerry can, still full of petrol, which I had placed on the side of the road, threw it as far as I could and waited while the petrol gurgled out. 'Get ready, Frazer,' I said.

As the petrol trickled down I yelled, 'Now! Run like hell!' He needed no second bidding and as he left his cover I threw a lighted match into the petrol. It flared up in a blinding flash of heat and light.

As it did a number of figures stood up and began firing at Frazer. I returned the fire as rapidly as I could and had the satisfaction of seeing our attackers dive for cover. I heard Frazer grunt but he was still moving when I dived back into the car and engaged the gears.

He jumped in beside me and I accelerated away as quickly as I could. More shots fired but none seemed to come near us and we rapidly made our escape.

'Are you all right?'

Frazer was slouched down in his seat. He put a hand under his jacket and when he removed it I saw, in the moonlight, the blackness of blood. 'My left side. Low. I think I'll survive.' He twisted around and gasped in pain. 'Exit wound. Just need to stop the bleeding.'

'Can you hold on for a bit? Until we get further away?'

'Bloody well have to, won't I? You shouldn't have come back, David. I told you to leave me.'

'Sure, like you would have left me, right?'

'If I'd had to, I would've,' he said, without conviction.

I didn't argue but concentrated on the road. We were descending around dangerous hairpin bends and more than once the wheels skidded dangerously close to the sheer drop falling away on our right.

'Slow down,' said Frazer, 'before you accomplish what those bandits didn't.'

I needed no further urging and slowed right down. A few minutes later we reached another hamlet called Tresenda and a cross-roads where the sign pointed left for Sondrio and right for Tirano. I turned right. This road was an improvement on the one we had just left and I was able to pick up speed.

'About ten kilometres along you'll see a turning to the left. It's a dirt track, not a road. Take it. We'll be less than a kilometre from the border then.'

We reached the turning in less than ten minutes and I pulled off the road. I stopped the car and said, 'Right, old chap. Let me look at this wound of yours.' When I got his clothes off, I saw that there were two. One was a slight graze to his upper arm around which I wrapped a handkerchief but the other was more serious. The bullet had entered his left lower side and exited out the back. I bandaged him up as best I could, relieved to see that the blood had reduced to a trickle out of the exit wound. 'You've been damned lucky,' I said. 'Another inch to the right or upwards and you'd be a goner.'

'Funny, I don't feel lucky,' he gasped. 'But then all these things are relative.'

I grinned. Frazer was getting his sense of humour back which was a good sign. We climbed back into the car and we started forward. The track looked as though it was used only by animals, and in the beam of the headlights I saw no sign that other motorised vehicles had been that way.

'It's a smuggling route,' said Frazer. 'And the peasants take their sheep and cows along here looking for pasture higher up once the snows are melted. The border is an imaginary line which has never, to my knowledge, been fixed. When we get to Brusio we're in Switzerland.'

He lapsed into silence and I concentrated on the track. The snow was patchy on the hills around us, though in the near distance I could see the brooding menace of the Alps. The moon set and all I could see was what was in front, showing up in the headlights. Frazer had drifted off to sleep and for a few minutes I enjoyed the tranquillity of the journey which was such a contrast with the fear of the previous few hours. We crested the brow of a hill just as the sun broke over the horizon and the dawn was with us. I had not even noticed the changing light until that moment. I switched off the headlights and drove down into the hamlet of Brusio.

It was a poor place of about a dozen hovels and we kept going. A few people stopped to look but otherwise ignored us. I was beginning to worry again about the petrol situation when we arrived at Poschiavo, a town of reasonable size with a garage that sold petrol, much to our relief. I left Frazer in the car, filled up the tank and the two remaining jerry cans and bought some food and drink. We still had a long way to go before we could relax.

Later that day we abandoned the car at Chur and took a train for Bern, needing to get to the British Embassy as quickly as possible. We arrived in Bern that evening. We had cleaned ourselves up on the train and looked reasonably respectable when we booked into the Bahnhof Hotel at the railway station. We had decided to rest and go to the embassy in the morning.

Frazer had slept for hours on the train and went out like a light when he went to bed. I sat for a while pondering my fate and thinking about Emily. It was six weeks since I had seen her and I wondered what she was doing and whether she was thinking about me. The thoughts of her prompted me to write letters home and one to Emily. I also spent an hour writing down all I had learned in Italy.

The next morning Frazer lay in bed unable or unwilling to get up. I took a look at the wound, which was already healing. Only the merest hint of blood had seeped out during the night. 'It looks pretty good to me,' I said, 'but I'll ask the embassy doctor if he'll come and take a look. You stay here.'

He nodded. 'When you get to the embassy ask for Major Curtis. He's the military attaché. You'll be told he's not available. In reply say that you understand but that you have a message from his cousin, twice removed. You got that?'

'Seems simple enough. Then what?'

'Then you'll be ushered into him as quickly as they can manage. It's the code for dire emergency.'

I took a tram, changed once and soon found myself outside the British Embassy. It was an imposing building; a Union Jack fluttered above it in the breeze. A soldier saluted when I walked through the gates and up the front steps. I paused and looked along the street. It was ironic to see the embassies of all our enemies within a few hundred yards of where I stood.

Everything was precisely as Frazer had said and within minutes I was seated opposite Curtis, a cup of coffee in my hand. I handed him the report I had compiled and watched as he read it.

'Good Lord. This is serious. We have a great deal to do. Including, I may add, having you debriefed.'

'I've written down all that I can remember,' I said, tartly. 'Now all I want to do is have Frazer seen by a doctor and go back to England.'

'The former is no problem, the latter I'm not so sure.' Curtis drew his right index finger over his pencil line moustache and added, 'I know something about you and Frazer. The information you've sent back to Britain to date has been invaluable. I'll send Doctor Albright to look at Frazer. You can stay here for a day or two until I get instructions about what to do next. In the meantime I want to go over your story again, bit by bit. You'll be surprised how easy it is to have forgotten something or, equally importantly, dismissed something from your mind which you consider to be irrelevant.'

I didn't like it, but I had to admit that it made a certain amount of sense. I spent the day in the embassy with Curtis, at the end of which I had grown to like the man. He was dapper, precise and highly knowledgeable about the situation in Central Europe. Finally, he said, 'I think that'll do. I'll get this away by messenger tonight and wait for a reply.'

He picked up a telephone and dialled a single digit number. A brief conversation took place at the end of which, a grey haired, stocky gentleman entered the room.

'Let me introduce you. This is Captain Carruthers. He's a King's Messenger and will take our dispatches to London tonight. Can you do this, Captain?'

Carruthers looked at his watch and then replied, 'Yes, sir. I can be in time to catch the twenty two hundred hours from Basle. I'll be in London tomorrow evening.'

'Good man. Take these to Lord Stockdale and wait for a reply. He will see that we need instructions urgently.'

Carruthers nodded, took the papers and left.

'What's a King's Messenger?' I asked.

'Exactly what it sounds like. We have a small army of them across the world who carry diplomatic pouches between embassies and our government. All of them are ex-army or ex-marines and live on inadequate pensions. Their pay as Messengers gives them a reasonable income and, of course they have virtually no expenses. Ludicrously, the pouches they carry are sacrosanct in that they have diplomatic immunity and so no foreign power should open them, but the Messengers don't have the same protection. They can be arrested, shot, harassed but the pouches get delivered. It's a funny old world, isn't it?'

On that note we left the Embassy to return to the hotel to check on Frazer. He was asleep and so we went to a restaurant for dinner. It was an enjoyable evening and when I went to bed that night it was with the thought in mind that I would soon be returning to England and Emily.

We kicked our heels in Switzerland for another ten days. All the time I was becoming more impatient, although the delay gave Frazer time to recover. On the tenth day Curtis arrived at the hotel with a letter which he handed to Frazer.

Frazer tore it open, read its contents and then gave it to me.

We were instructed to go to Austro-Hungary immediately. The embassy there would have further instructions for us.

7

IN THE AUTUMN I complained to John Buchanan. He had journeyed to Budapest to brief Frazer and me personally. When I pointed out, reasonably enough I thought, that I was supposed to do this work for only a few months and that I had now been spying in Europe for nearly seven months he had answered that it was common for members of the army and navy to be separated from loved ones, or away from home, for up to three years at a time. I countered this with the obvious statement that I was not a member of any military force and that I wanted to return to England. I may as well have saved my breath. We did cross examine Buchanan about the gathering in Germany we were supposed to have attended – the original reason given for us being where we were. To our surprise he told us that the meeting would be taking place at Christmas time. He handed me an invitation to a grand ball to be held on December 24th 1912, at the Hayermeyer Palace, Berlin.

'This is the big one, David,' said John. 'We need to find out why the German's are arming as fast and as furiously as they are. What are they intending? We keep matching them Dreadnought for Dreadnought, battle cruiser for battle cruiser, man for man. It's an endless expense and we don't want it. We need to get off the treadmill, but we need to know what's happening before we do.'

Sick at heart I nodded. 'But after this I want to come home. I want to see Emily, dash it all.'

'I understand, but you must realise how precarious matters are. Thanks to you and Frazer we've managed to stop a good deal of our European neighbours' adventurism. Italy is now wavering in her alliance and Germany was prevented from invading Belgium. The

Balkans continue to be a problem but now it's contained. And it's all due to the efforts of you two. We've been able to nip in the bud many of the hair-brained schemes the Kaiser and his cronies have dreamt up. We have to stay ahead of them at all costs. And frankly, if that cost is you not seeing Emily for a while then,' he shrugged, 'too bad.'

It was true that Frazer and I had passed a mountain of information to Lord Stockdale. We rarely found out what was done with it except from time to time we would read a newspaper article and put two and two together to understand why certain things had happened and what they were. It was obvious to us that Europe was on a powder keg and that it would take very little for it to explode.

In December Frazer and I moved ourselves to Berlin, which proved to be as drab a city as its reputation suggested. The architecture was Teutonic, just like a certain type of German – staid, arrogant, overbearing and militarist. The city reflected the character of its people.

As usual I booked into one hotel and Frazer into another close by. Walking around the city I noticed a surprising number of men in uniform, both army and navy. We had found the same in Budapest and Vienna but the military presence hadn't been as intense as it was in Berlin.

Frazer and I met in a small bar on Klingelhofer Strasse two nights after we had arrived. Over a plum schnapps and beer chaser I said, 'With so many men in uniform and under arms, Germany has to do something with them. Either they'll start trouble here in Europe or, more likely, out in the colonies; somewhere like Africa.'

Frazer nodded. 'Perhaps. I think Europe is the favourite, though. There are vast tracts of land in Russia that Germany and Austro-Hungary would love to get their hands on. Now Belgium has been let off the hook there's nothing stopping them going East. Especially with Russia tied up with Japan and the altercation over the islands off their eastern seaboard. Russia has taken her eye off the western ball and it could prove disastrous as a result.'

'Maybe. You know, I'm sick of all this intrigue. I just want to return to America and forget the rest of the world even exists. There's a lot to be said for isolationism.'

'The world's too small to forget any part of it. That's something I've learnt during the last ten years. An event takes place in the Far East and the consequences are felt in England and France. Events taking place now, in this city, will affect us all, for better or worse. And we need to know what they are, just as John Buchanan said. Isolationism isn't an option.'

'I'm not convinced. Once this one job is over I'm going back, and that's the end of it.'

I ordered a plate of goulash and black bread, which I washed down with German beer and followed with a cup of coffee. 'I've done nothing I planned, like visiting Jake in Spain,' I said. 'I haven't seen Emily in nearly seven months . . .'

'David, stop whingeing will you? Finish this job and then have a break. Don't think it'll be longer than a break, though, because you'll be back.'

'No, I won't,' I exploded. 'And I'm not whingeing, as you put it. I'm just stating facts.'

'Be that as it may, give it a rest. Have you received your invitation yet?'

I shook my head. 'Not yet. I gathered from Lord Stockdale that it's proving more difficult then he expected. He's got Lady Aster and Lord Rotherhime working on my behalf. Apparently they're related to the Kaiser somehow. Anyway, palms are being greased, favours called in, etcetera, etcetera.'

'You'll get an invitation. The only problem is that we don't want it to draw too much attention to you.'

'It's a bit late for that. What I gather is that my name is being bandied all over the shop as a rich, eligible bachelor looking for a German wife because of my pro-German sympathies. Fortunately they appear to have bought the story that I'd run off with a married lady after that fracas in Italy, that she'd had second thoughts and returned to her husband. John did an excellent job of planting that story.'

'You'd have thought that after all the work we did in Italy, Austria and Hungary, your acceptance would have been far easier.'

I shrugged. 'It appears that the Germans do their own thing, even socially. However, we did put together a lot of useful information. I'm just surprised at how long the benefits have lasted.'

An hour later I returned to my hotel. There was an invitation waiting for me at reception. I was to join Baron von Ribbentrop and other guests for a weekend at his castle in Bavaria, exactly what we had been hoping for.

The following morning found me in the main railway station enquiring about trains to Munich. From there I needed to go to Tutzing on the Starnberger See, a lake thirty kilometres south of Munich. I had two choices, leave first thing in the morning and arrive at Munich at 9 pm or take the overnight sleeper, leaving at midnight and arriving at 8 am. That would give me the day to get to Tutzing. I decided on the latter. I booked two berths for the following week. I left a note for Frazer at his hotel detailing our travel arrangements and asking him to meet me at the restaurant in the station on the evening of departure.

At dinner, before I left, I said to Frazer, 'I see that we got what we wanted in the Balkans.'

Frazer nodded. 'We got exactly what we wanted and in large part thanks to us. Greece, Bulgaria and Serbia have attacked Turkey, but Germany has announced that the Great Powers will not engage in a Balkan war.'

'The only place we've failed in is Libya,' I said. I was referring to the fact that the Sultan of Turkey had finally ceded Libya to Italy in a peace treaty signed at Ouchy, Switzerland. In return, Italy agreed to remove its forces from Turkish islands in the Aegean Sea, which would release more Turkish forces for the Balkans.

'Not so,' said Frazer. 'What you don't know is that I've had a letter from Stockdale.' He looked around to make sure nobody was within listening range but still lowered his voice and leaned closer to me. 'We backed Italy by sending a note to Turkey. The triple alliance is in danger of crumbling. We are trying to persuade Italy to declare that it will be neutral should anything happen.'

'How does sending a note to the Turks help?'

'We are, shall we say, proving who Italy's friends are. The Germans and the Austro-Hungarians are obsessed with Russia and Western Europe. It's a ploy that appears to be working. One of our tasks is to try and find out whether or not the Great Powers will intervene in the Balkans.'

'I thought that they wouldn't. The German Foreign Minister said so as recently as October.'

'Things change, David, as you well know. Now that Constantinople itself is threatened there's a real fear that the war will engulf the rest of Europe. The Balkan League now senses victory. Look how dramatic the changes have been over the last month. Albania has declared its independence from Turkey, the Serbs have occupied Durazzo and the Bulgarians are besieging Adrianople and are at the gates of Constantinople. Turkey lost forty thousand men at the Battle of Lule Burgas in Thrace in just a few days, which shows the depth of fear of a general conflagration in Europe. Modern weaponry means the deaths of tens of thousands, not like previous wars when a death toll of a couple of thousand in one battle was considered excessive. No, modern warfare means annihilation. We must prevent that at all costs.'

I agreed with Frazer and felt the call of duty for the first time since I had started this adventure. It was possible that he and I could make a difference.

This was a sobering thought to take with us on the journey south.

Aboard the train we went our separate ways. I had a first class sleeping compartment to myself whilst he had elected to sit up in second class all night. He wanted to see who was travelling to the same destination as we were. It was unlikely that we would be followed but we were taking no chances.

I got off at Munich and set about finding a means of getting to Tutzing. At the station I learned that there was a stopping train to Starnberg and there I would need to hire local transport. I pondered my options for a few seconds, looked about until I saw Frazer, scratched the side of my nose and my ear lobe and went into the nearest bar. I stood at the counter and ordered a coffee as Frazer joined me.

'I'll buy a car,' I said quietly, as I lifted the cup to my lips. 'We might need it later. Meet me south of Starnberg.' I paid and left.

Finding a garage presented no problem in a city as wealthy as Munich. I haggled over the price of a Mercedes-Benz tourer and secured one for the equivalent of one hundred and twenty pounds. By lunchtime I was driving along Otto Strasse, a map open on the seat next to me and directions clear in my mind. Even so, I got lost twice before I finally got clear of the city and found myself on the right road. By the middle of the afternoon I had passed through Gauting and half an hour later was in the village of Starnberg. Dusk had fallen and night was approaching rapidly when I saw the two crossed poles lying by the side of the road. I stopped the car and Frazer jumped out from a hedgerow and climbed in. Working together, we had developed a sophisticated series of signals which covered almost every eventuality and had so far stood us in good stead.

'Thank God for a heater,' said Frazer with feeling. 'It's damnably cold out there. I think there's snow in the air.'

'Did you learn anything about where we're going?'

'Yes, I asked in the local village. They all seemed eager to talk. Proud of the fact that the Kaiser will be passing through in two days time. Tutzing is about twenty kilometres away. The castle is on a rise just before we get to the village and overlooks the lake. We are currently driving on land owned by the Baron. In effect, he owns the lake and the land surrounding it which amounts to hundreds of thousands of hectares. He's considered a kind and thoughtful landlord.'

'That's not what I'd heard,' I replied.

'You should learn to recognise sarcasm when you hear it,' was the rejoinder.

Soon we could see the lights of Tutzing ahead of us but they were insignificant compared to the blaze of glory we encountered on our right hand side. The Schloss was illuminated with searchlights and covered with coloured bulbs in their thousands. It was an overwhelming sight of grandeur, wealth and power. Frazer and I lapsed into silence, overawed, in spite of ourselves.

We turned off the road and drove deep into the surrounding forest before we stopped. We wanted to reconnoitre the area before I walked into the lion's den.

Two days later we had circumnavigated the lake, made as many contingency plans as possible and seen as much as we could. We discussed many different options for my escape if I needed to get away in a hurry. However, we both hoped that all I would need do was bid farewell at the end of my stay.

I abandoned Frazer to the discomfort of a wooden hut we had found on the lake shore, about a kilometre from the castle, and drove to the main gates where I was called upon to present my invitation which a guard compared to the names on his list. After a few seconds he waved me through and turned to the car behind me. In my mirror I noticed it was a Rolls Royce, made in Britain and the latest in expensive automobiles for the wealthy and famous.

I pulled up at the front door, in effect joining a queue of other cars, many chauffeur driven. I climbed out and removed my bag which was promptly taken from me by a liveried flunkey. My car keys were taken by another and I followed my bag inside.

The hall was huge and thronged with people. I was taken to a trestle table and there I gave my name to another servant. An envelope was handed to me and the wish was expressed that I would enjoy my stay. As this was in German I merely nodded, aware that I needed to act the part of ignoramus to the hilt. A typed message on blue crested note paper welcomed me to the castle, giving details about my stay, including sleeping arrangements, dining times and activities to amuse myself during the day. It pointed out that over a hundred guests were visiting the Schloss that weekend and that my host, the Baron, would appreciate my endeavours to be punctual and not to ask too much of the servants. The note was in German and so I pretended not to understand.

I returned to the flunkey who had handed me the note and said, with a great deal of meaningless mime, 'No understand. Scusi. What say this?' I waved the envelope under his nose.

Before he could reply another servant stepped forward and said, 'If you will permit me, *mein Herr*, I will be pleased to translate it for you.' He took the envelope, translated it and handed it back to me with a slight bow.

I thanked him in English for his kindness and he called a young lad over and instructed him to show me my room. While all this had been going on I had been looking at the other guests. Many I recognised from other similar gatherings and some I knew only from their photographs in the press. I exchanged greetings with those I had met as I followed the servant upstairs. My room, reached after a long walk down a dark corridor, was a small bedroom overlooking the forest at the back of the Schloss. I gave the boy ten reichmarks and waited until he left and closed the door behind him.

I knew I wasn't an important guest but the tiny room spoke of a contempt that I had not expected. Alarm bells began to ring in my head.

I quickly unpacked, hung my dinner jacket up in the tiny wardrobe and decided to explore. In the envelope I had been given was a map of the public rooms and, from it, I gathered that there were at least a hundred bedrooms for the guests as well as servants' quarters. My room was at the end of a corridor; a solid door blocked the way beyond. I tried it; it was locked. I looked behind me to ensure there was nobody in sight and took out my spectacle case. In it were the picks and other tools that successful burglars and spies needed.

It took me less than twenty seconds to open the three tumbler lock. I opened the door very carefully, listened, heard nothing and stepped through into another world. That this was the servants' quarters there could be no doubt. The floor was stone, the walls poorly painted and the corridor narrow. There were doors at frequent intervals, indicating that the rooms behind were small and, I suspected, mean. The change from one side of the Schloss to the other was extreme. I walked along the corridor as silently as possible until I reached the end, there I threw open a casement window and looked out onto the lake. I was at the northern end of the castle, furthest from the entrance. Ten feet above me was a stone gutter, and sixty feet below this was a stone courtyard.

I returned the way I came without encountering anybody and locked the door to the corridor behind me once more. I decided that I needed to take a few precautions, but before I did so I wanted to explore further.

I wandered through the remainder of the Schloss, identifying the rooms on the map and orientating myself between the public rooms and the other bedrooms and corridors. The place was a maze and one could easily get lost in its vastness. I met other guests being shown to their rooms and exchanged greetings with a number of them. Down in the main hall I mingled with the throng until I worked my way outside and walked around the grounds.

I spoke to the man who had taken my car keys. 'Excuse me. I've left something in my car. Can you tell me where it is?' I wondered if the man spoke English.

'*Ach, so*. What kind of car is it?' he asked, politely.

I told him and he explained where he had parked it. I found it around the back of the stable block, the keys in the ignition. I thought of taking the keys with me but then thought better of it. I didn't want to draw attention to myself by doing anything differently from the other guests. I took a coat from the back of the car and walked away, towards the lake.

I followed a path through the trees for the hundred yards or so it took me to get to the water's edge. There was nobody in sight and so I stood facing the water and lifted my arms up and down, slowly, as though I was doing some gentle exercise, hoping that Frazer would recognise the signal. After a few minutes a flash of light came from the shed on the other side of the water. Satisfied, I went back into the trees and, making sure nobody could see me or sneak up on me, I wrote a note to Frazer. I went back to the lake side and began picking up flat stones and skimming them on the water. As I did I surreptitiously made a small mound of stones at the water's edge covering my note. I went back up to the tree line and broke a small sapling, leaving it hanging in half.

I made my leisurely way back to the Schloss. In the hall I was greeted by a flunkey who told me that afternoon tea and coffee was being served in the library. I pretended not to understand his German, and he repeated the message in English. I went into the library where a couple of dozen of the other guests were already seated. It was a vast room. One wall was lined with books, and another had so many trophy heads of dead animals that I couldn't count them. Some I recognised, like a moose, a tiger and a stag, others I didn't and I spent a few minutes comparing the heads on the wall with a key that lay on a nearby table, naming the animals.

On one of the other walls there was a huge fire place, on either side of which stood a stuffed rampant bear; on the left was the black bear of Germany and on the right the white polar bear of Alaska and Canada. On the wall hung various swords, pikestaffs and clubs. It was overwhelmingly a masculine room, and I found it distasteful.

As I was looking at a head of a gazelle I became aware of somebody standing at my shoulder. 'Quite an eyeful, aren't they?'

I hid my surprise and said, 'Hullo, John. What are you doing here?'

'As chairman of a major shipping line I received an invitation. There are some people here who wish to discuss a joint venture with me – to build the greatest liner of all time.'

'I thought she had just sunk,' I replied.

'There were interesting design faults on the Titanic which we won't repeat,' he said.

'Such as?'

'Such as bulkheads that go all the way to the deck and don't stop short. Such as an engine room which is one huge space and not compartmentalised. Such as enough life boats for everybody,' he replied, dryly.

'Is that the only reason you're here?'

'Primarily, yes. Also to act as chaperone.'

'Hullo, David,' Emily had sneaked up behind me as I was talking to John.

'Hullo, Emily,' I grinned suddenly. 'How nice to see you.'

'Nice? Nice? Is that all you can say when I've travelled all this way to be with the man I love?'

'That's enough, Emily,' said John, sharply. 'You will act with complete decorum while you're here. David has an important job to do and you mustn't forget it.' John looked at me, grinned and shrugged. 'I had no choice; she found out you'd be here and insisted on coming. I figured that at least I can keep her out of mischief.'

'How did you find out?' I asked her.

'I saw a letter from you to Uncle John and I read it,' she said, totally unabashed.

We took a seat at an occasional table and Emily ordered tea and crumpets from a waiter in idiomatic German.

John said, 'Once this is over I want you back in England. It's time to get working with the bank.'

'You mean after this week-end?'

He nodded. 'You've done enough. You and Frazer have done a sterling job but it's time to quit while you're ahead. Have you been giving any thought to the future?'

'Naturally. In between, em, duty, I've been doing a great deal of thinking. I backed it up by action.'

'Action? What sort?' asked John.

I grinned. 'I've been in the unique position of being able to hear a great deal more than just political tittle tattle. I heard about business, mergers, take-overs and the like. I bought into Krupps, Thyssons and Marconi. I sold General Electric in August and bought again last week. I bought Rotherham Steel before they announced that they had the order to supply the iron and steel for the six new Dreadnoughts Churchill announced in Parliament. There are a few dozen other deals Frazer and I have pulled off. All in all, it's been highly lucrative.'

John pursed his lips and said, 'As government employees I'm not sure I can condone your actions, but,' he grinned, 'as a future partner I heartily endorse them. How big are the profits you've made?'

'Uncle John,' chimed in Emily, 'you can't ask a gentleman such a question. But I can ask my fiancé,' she smiled sweetly.

'Fiancé?' I choked on the word. 'I don't remember asking you to marry me.'

'Do you remember that part in The Importance of Being Earnest? I'm paraphrasing but it must have slipped your memory. Important things you never remember without writing them down, the unimportant you do.'

I remembered some such nonsense and nodded. 'You mean I forgot that I asked you to marry me?'

'Exactly. So how much profit did you make?' she asked eagerly.

'Where's the ring?' I teased her.

'David,' she said in mock vexation, 'I'll smash you over the head with this cup if you don't answer Uncle John.'

I shrugged. Truth to tell, I was rather pleased with myself. I took out a small note book and pencil and made a few rapid calculations. 'In total just over ten thousand nine hundred and seventy three pounds.'

They both gasped. Neither needed telling that it was a fortune. 'How did you manage it?' asked John.

'Shortly after we arrived in Rome I realised that I was hearing a great deal about business. I took a gamble on one piece of information and found a stock broker to buy me one hundred pounds' worth of shares in a new car manufacturer called Fiat. I doubled my money in a week. I told Frazer what had happened, he matched my two hundred pounds and we got started. With Marconi and Krupps as well, we trebled our money in another week.

'Where did you learn about General Electric?'

'In Vienna. Hartley was at a reception talking to one of the Kaiser's entourage.' Hartley was the Assistant Minister of Works in Britain. 'I heard him say that General Electric was not getting the contract to fit the battleships in Glasgow.'

'So you sold. Why did you buy?'

'Because,' I said with a laugh, 'I heard the man he was talking to say that they were getting the contract to supply generators and engines for German ships, and that the announcement was to be made in two months time. We had,' I consulted my notebook, 'four hundred shares bought at three shillings and nine pence each which now are at nineteen shillings and eleven pence. I sold them. They then dropped like the proverbial stone to less than five bob, and I bought the lot back again. Not a bad day's work altogether.'

'I lost a packet on General Electric,' said John. 'If you get any more tips, how about wiring me? I'll set up an account for the bank and really get to work.'

'I thought this was my last job?'

'It is. But perhaps we could use you as,' he lowered his voice and said, 'an economic spy.'

'Thanks, but no thanks. After this weekend it's back home to . . . em, a wedding.'

'Oh, David. When can we get married? Soon. A New Year's wedding. How romantic.'

'Not so fast. I'd like to invite my parents and brother. I want Jake and his family. Then there's the Welsh lot to consider. No, we can arrange matters for an April wedding without any difficulty, but not before.'

Emily pouted prettily and John said, 'Quite right too. It'll do you good to wait my girl. You're too used to getting your own way.' He stood up. 'Come on, let's go for a walk. David, we'll leave you to circulate.'

By now I had developed the art of greeting people and joining in their conversations with such finesse that it seemed to me they hardly noticed me until I was somehow in their midst. I spent the next half an hour talking to different groups but learned nothing. I hadn't really expected to, as it was only over a good dinner and wine-loosened tongues that the real nuggets of information could be gleaned. Mostly they spoke their own language but many, out of courtesy to me, spoke English. However, some solid gold nuggets of information came my way when the odd sentence was made in their own language, be it German, Italian, Hungarian and even French.

I returned to my room. As soon as I entered I knew that it had been searched. I had been taught by Frazer to place my clothes so that if they were disturbed it would be obvious. It was not the slight disturbance of a good servant ensuring a guest is comfortable and his suitcases unpacked, but a systematic search of all my belongings. Luckily there had been nothing to find.

I had a bath in the bathroom at the other end of the corridor and changed into my dinner suit. That evening was to be a cold buffet, cards and charades. The dinner and ball would not be held until the following evening after the Kaiser arrived. Drinks were to be served in the library from seven onwards. Promptly at seven I went down.

I took a glass of champagne and wandered over to the fireplace. I was the first person there, as I had intended to be. Within minutes others arrived and joined me where I was standing in the most pleasant place in the vast room. Conversation started, halted as I professed an ignorance of any language but English and picked up again as others joined us. The talk was mainly about the arms build-up, the arrival of the Kaiser and the economics of the world powers. At that time there were three, Britain, Germany and Austro-Hungary. I picked up some useful tips for share dealing, but I learned nothing I did not already know about the world political situation. Serbia, Greece, Albania and Turkey still presented huge problems and the fervent wish of the gentlemen I spoke to that evening was that the problems in the Balkans didn't spill over to the rest of Europe.

The buffet was superb. There were dozens of different types of salami and other cooked meats, pots of potatoes, some in their skins, others coated in melted cheese and yet others with a creamy, tangy sauce. There was an unlimited supply of pastries and tarts and it was all washed down with the finest wines, all German.

Later the men settled down to games of cards, from whist to poker to twenty-one. The ladies adjourned to a smaller room and there indulged in small talk; some entered into the spirit of the evening by playing charades.

Over the cards I was learning many interesting and important facts. I was careful not to drink any alcohol as I needed my wits about me. It was very taxing to listen to a language I understood almost as well as English and yet to pretend total ignorance. At midnight the party began to break up. There was to be a wild boar shoot the following morning and breakfast was to be served promptly at nine o'clock for a ten o'clock start.

I had said goodnight to the last few stragglers and professed a desire to take a walk in the grounds, for some fresh air before turning in. I was at the door when I heard a commotion outside. Suddenly the door burst open and an excited servant rushed in and yelled, 'It's him. The Kaiser has arrived. The Kaiser,' he ran through the house, rousing as many people as he could.

Within moments people were pouring down the stairs, servants were hurrying in, still dressing, and the doors were thrown wide open. A retinue of men and women wearing outdoor clothing streamed through the door. Then I saw him. He was a slight bird of a man, barely five feet six in height, thin with dark hair and a bushy, upturned moustache. He was wearing army uniform with a helmet covered in gold which added about four inches to his height. I stepped into the shadows to watch the proceedings.

The household was thrown into uproar which gave me an immense, childish pleasure. Bedrooms had to be vacated for more senior members of the party, linen needed changing, people who had slept through the turmoil of the Kaiser's arrival needed waking. In short, chaos reigned supreme.

I returned to the library, safe in the knowledge that my tiny bedroom would remain mine. I poured myself a well earned whisky and water and settled by the fire to wait for the fuss to die down. I still wanted to go for a walk, hoping to find something that Frazer had left for me.

The household soon settled down again and about thirty minutes later I was about to try to get out for my walk when the door was thrown open and eight or ten men entered, all speaking jovially and loudly in German. I stood with my face to the fire, unsure what to do. Should I stay and listen to what could be vital small talk, or should I return to the lake?

'Ah, Herr Griffiths, allow me to introduce Karl von Ludwig,' even as I turned I felt the hairs on the nape of my neck stand on end. I looked into the unsmiling face of my adversary all those months ago on the train.

He looked at me for a few seconds and then pulled his mouth back in a rictus of a grin, and gave a stiff, Teutonic bow. 'We meet again. How fortunate.'

I inclined my head and said, 'Indeed it is. What a pleasure.'

He looked me in the eye and said, 'No, sir. The pleasure is, no, it will be, all mine. I have hoped to meet you again. And here you are.'

'Yes, here we are. Well, goodnight gentlemen.' The decision of whether or not I was to stay and listen to their conversation had been made for me. I walked out of the room, feeling their eyes on me. The tension between von Ludwig and myself was palpable, and was not missed by the others. The weekend was becoming more interesting than I had intended or desired.

I walked into the hall, made sure nobody was following, and went out through the front door. I sauntered down the steps and headed across the lawn towards the lake. I had nearly got to the cover of the forest when I sensed a change in the light at the castle. I looked over my shoulder and saw four men hurrying out, one of whom was von Ludwig. I heard one of them yell and point in my direction. They began running in my direction and I took to my heels. One or even two of them I could cope with, four would be impossible.

Within seconds I was out of their view. It was bitterly cold and I wished that I had brought an overcoat. I also wished that I was armed. I stepped off the path and moved as silently as I could through the trees. I could hear my pursuers blundering around, calling to each other. I moved away and soon the sounds of them receded. I arrived back at the lawn about a hundred yards along from where I had entered the forest, saw there was nobody around and ran for the door of the Schloss. I paused at the entrance, pushed my hand through my hair and straightened my jacket. There was no angry yell from behind me when I went in.

I crossed the hall, climbed the stairs and paused as the front door burst open. I was about to call down a cheery goodnight or equally inane quip when I thought better of it. I stepped into the shadows and watched the four men. They stalked into the library and slammed the door behind them. I hurried up to my room, closed the door behind me and locked it. I then placed a chest of drawers against the door and moved the bed so that it was between the chest and the opposite wall. It was a tight fit and meant that the door would have to be broken into match wood before anybody could enter. I slept soundly in spite of the excitement and awoke refreshed and eager for the day. At that moment I acknowledged a perversity in my nature – I liked, no I relished – adversity.

8

AFTER BREAKFAST EVERYONE who wished to take part in the hunt was asked to go around to the stables. Overnight there had been a light fall of snow, and the landscape was now white. I found John at the stables and quietly told him what had happened.

'In that case, stay close to me. I wouldn't trust von Ludwig not to arrange an accident.'

'You know him?'

'No, but I know his father; and if his son is anything like him then he's a nasty piece of work.'

'Who is he? I mean, after all he's travelling with the Kaiser.'

'You don't know?' John asked in surprise. 'Von Ludwig's family owns iron and steel factories all over Germany. Hell, half the Ruhr belongs to them. They've now branched out into automobile manufacturing and I hear they are negotiating to purchase a dockyard at Bremen. In the world of international commerce, they are huge.'

I nodded, I could place the von Ludwigs now. I had heard about them and indeed I'd even bought and sold some of their shares. There was talk that they were interested in acquiring an aircraft company in France. 'Here he comes now,' I said, as Karl von Ludwig and five others came round the corner and approached the stables, near which we were standing. Karl appeared not to notice me.

A man dressed in red, like an English Master of Fox Hunting, appeared. He was accompanied by the Baron and half a dozen other men carrying rifle cases.

The Baron addressed all of us. 'My friends, the Kaiser will be joining us in a few minutes. It was to participate in this shoot that we had the unexpected pleasure of his arrival last night. You will all be armed with Mauser Gewehr 98s. For those of you who are not familiar with the gun let me instruct you.' He nodded and a case was opened and a rifle handed to him. 'This gun was first manufactured by my own company in 1898. You may be aware that it is now used throughout the German army. I can tell you that it is robust, well-made, accurate and reliable. This gun we call the Gew 98 as it has a third locking lug beneath the bolt,' he showed us, 'which locks into a recess in the left action sidewall. It takes 7.92 by 57 mm cartridges and the magazine carries five rounds. There is a manual safety catch on the rear of the bolt. If this is turned to the left, the rifle is ready to fire. If it is turned to the right the rifle is safe.' Again the Baron demonstrated. 'To unload, place the safety catch to fire and open the bolt to extract any round in the chamber. Examine the magazine aperture and if there is any ammunition in the magazine, press the magazine floor-plate catch in the front end of the trigger guard. This allows the magazine floor-plate to hinge at its front end, open, and dump the contents of the magazine. Examine the chamber and magazine aperture again, close the bolt, press the trigger, and then close the magazine floor-plate.' He continued the demonstration and then added, 'Please be careful with this, as it is easy to have an accident.'

I don't know why but I looked at von Ludwig at that moment and caught him looking at me. He moved his right hand in a parody of a gun, pointed it at me and moved his thumb like a hammer firing. I understood the message loud and clear, but I was flabbergasted at his cocksureness in making such a gesture. He had to realise that I would be on my guard. Or perhaps that was part of his pleasure, I thought.

'One more thing, gentlemen,' the Baron added as his men moved amongst us, handing out weapons and rounds of ammunition. 'We have a family of wild boar in the forest. I wish the Kaiser to kill the boar.' There were a few laughs. Just then the little man himself arrived with a flunkey who carried a rifle case. There were respectful greetings from the group before half a dozen waiters appeared, carrying trays with hot mulled wine. A few minutes later we set out. There were about thirty of us with guns and at least fifty beaters, and following behind came a small army of servants carrying stools, baskets of food and drink. They were accompanied by a few ladies, presumably out for the fresh air.

I had never been on a boar shoot, but I recognised the fact that there was a protocol I would need to follow. John gave me some hints as we began to spread out. We were on the right hand side of the guns, the Kaiser was near the centre and a little ahead of the others. Between the Kaiser and us were about fifteen guns, the five closest being von Ludwig and friends. As we walked along von Ludwig gradually edged us further right, away from the main party. After we had gone about half a mile we were a good hundred yards or more from the main party when a stentorian voice yelled at us to close up in case the boars tried to pass between us. Reluctantly von Ludwig and his friends moved further to the left along with John and me.

'Over the next rise we come to the beginning of the woods. It's cultivated but after a few hundred yards it becomes thicker and eventually turns to forest,' said John, thoughtfully. 'I know because I've done this before. That's when we could start having problems; I expect the shooting will start then.'

I nodded. 'Makes sense. Any ideas?'

John thought for a moment or two and then replied, 'If we shoot any of them we can be charged with murder or, at best, manslaughter. Our chances of justice in a German court are, frankly, zero. We can't claim that they started it as we have no proof.'

'Unless,' I said, dryly, 'one of us is killed first.'

'Precisely my own thoughts, old boy. Are you volunteering?'

'No, are you?'

He didn't bother to answer. 'When the shooting starts – usually within a hundred yards of entering the woods – drop to the ground.'

'How do you know?'

'I told you, I've been here before. And anyway, it's fixed. The boars are held in a pen and will be released and will be driven down onto the Kaiser's rifle. Nobody is fooled, but the Kaiser kills a wild boar and there is rejoicing and laughter in the land,' he said sarcastically.

I couldn't help grinning. 'Okay, we duck and run. What if they come after us?'

'They won't,' said John, grimly. 'Because you and I will fire a fusillade over their heads. They'll be too busy ducking.'

'We hope.'

'We, as you so rightly say old boy, hope.'

'Are you up to this?' I asked, concerned now that danger was getting so close. I looked at his solid, middle aged bulk; the streaks of grey in the neatly cut hair. He had to be fifty-five or more and, though he was in good condition for his age, what we were about to do was hardly conducive to a long life.

'Don't worry about me, David. Just worry about yourself. If anything happens to you Emily will never forgive me.' He changed the subject. 'See how they are talking together?' I looked over his shoulder to the half dozen men who were now nearly thirty yards away. John and I had been moving away from them for the last five minutes.

We were nearing the trees when we heard a shout. A shot was fired and the men suddenly moved closer. John and I darted into the trees, ducked low and practically crawled away deeper into the woods. On John's word we stopped, hiding behind a tree each, and as they came into view fired as rapidly as we could. We had the satisfaction of watching our pursuers dive for cover, and then we ran like the wind back into the open and towards the servants who were still behind us. We were half way to them when there was a yell and they all looked towards us. Some stopped and put down their burdens whilst others continued walking. When we got near them, panting, I pretended we had a wager and demanded John give me five pounds for losing the race. With a smile he took out his wallet and handed me a fiver.

I promptly handed it to one of the servants and said, 'A bottle of Tokay, for God's sake. I need it after that run.' There were a few laughs and some applause as we opened the bottle and took a drink. I had given the man the equivalent of at least a fortnight's wages. I added, 'Please share it with your friends and when we get back to the castle I'll give you another. But you'll have to remind me.' At this there was another laugh.

John and I toasted one another as we continued walking towards the guns which were now firing regularly. I saw von Ludwig and his friends rejoin the main part of the hunt whilst John and I stayed with the servants.

A picnic was set up at the edge of the woods and all the guns were soon back to enjoy the food and drink. The Kaiser had shot his boar and was in fine spirits, laughing and joking with all and sundry. I managed to join the group around him and listened avidly to what was said.

Unfortunately I learned nothing of interest apart from one thing. The Kaiser let it be known that he had written that very morning to Count Franz von Hotzendorf of Austro-Hungary and General Alberto Pollio of Italy. I wondered if the letters were still in the Schloss, and if so could I find them?

John and I exchanged glare for glare with von Ludwig and his friends until it was time to return to the castle. We stayed close to the main body as we went. We handed in our guns and walked into the Schloss. I followed John up to his room.

'Von Ludwig and company are a nuisance we could have done without,' said John, without preamble, pouring me a whisky and soda from the well stocked cabinet in his room. If I needed further proof that I was a second class or even third class citizen in the Schloss it came as I saw the opulence of John's quarters.

I told him about my room to which he said, 'That doesn't surprise me. We used a bit of, em, coercion shall we say, to get you invited. You have proved too valuable an asset for us not to have you here. Perhaps,' he said thoughtfully, 'we over played our hand. If we did it could mean you're in serious trouble.'

'You mean with Karl and his friends?'

'No. I mean with the Baron. It would explain a few things to me; a few statements I've heard which didn't make sense. But if I put it in the context that you are, shall we say, *persona non grata*, then there could be some real trouble ahead. David, I think it's time we cut our losses and you got to hell out of here.'

I shook my head. 'Not yet. I'll go tonight, after the dinner, or during the ball. Tell me, where are the Kaiser's rooms?'

'The Kaiser? Why?'

'He's written some letters I would dearly love to read,' I replied.

'How? Are you going to break in?'

'Probably. Now where are the rooms?'

We argued back and forth until he gave in. But then, after telling me where the rooms were, he added, 'You won't be able to enter them anyway. There are two guards on the doors and only trusted servants are allowed to enter.'

I nodded, an idea already taking shape in my mind.

By six o'clock that evening I had rested for a couple of hours, had a bath and changed into my evening attire. As it was a formal ball, the ladies would be wearing evening gowns and the gentlemen tails and white tie. Knowing that the other guests would be getting ready I slipped out of a side door and hurried along to the lake shore. It took only moments to find the equipment hidden there by Frazer. I lit the small miner's lamp he had left for me and began flashing it across the lake in the general direction of the hut where I hoped Frazer would be watching. Every minute I flashed twice and at the end of ten minutes I was about to give up when I received an answering flash. I flashed three times and received two back. I put out the lamp and sat down to wait for him. A few minutes later there was the creak of an oar-lock and a small wooden dinghy appeared. As Frazer reached the shore I helped him to clamber out. We exchanged greetings, information and plans. All was set for the evening.

I was wearing an evening cloak that swept down to my knees and under which I was able to carry the canvas bag that Frazer had given me. I returned to my room without being stopped or hailed.

I worked the small holster on my belt around to my left side. Into it I inserted a German Sauer M1912 and although it was one of the smallest pistols in the world, it carried seven rounds of 7.65mm Browning ammunition. Like most pistols it wasn't particularly accurate but at the distance at which I would be using it that was not relevant. Under my coat it was impossible to detect and I felt better to be armed again.

I opened the door, made sure that nobody was about and, carrying my canvas bag, slipped into the servants' corridor. There was nobody there either, as it was now approaching seven o'clock and they would all be on duty, getting everything ready for the evening. I pushed up the window at the end of the corridor and climbed on to the ledge outside. I closed the window, careful not to lock it. The ledge was about a foot wide and I inched along it, my back to the wall, until I reached the corner of the building. Working my way around the corner was tricky but not impossible. Finally I reached my goal. I unslung the bag from my shoulder and extracted a grappling iron which I threw over my head and at the second try it caught in the concrete guttering and held. I then sat down on the ledge and resigned myself to waiting. While I was sitting there I clung grimly to the rope which was attached to the grappling iron and contemplated the next few hours.

As the time approached eight o'clock I was beginning to freeze, my behind was numb and I was wondering whether or not to get off the ridge when the light below me was extinguished. I slithered over the edge and lowered myself down the rope. The balcony doors were locked, but they took less than ten seconds to open. I stepped into the huge quarters that the Kaiser had the privilege of occupying and looked to begin my search. It wasn't difficult. In a corner stood an ornate desk and I quickly went over it searching for any useful papers. I struck gold almost immediately. In a locked drawer – which I opened in seconds – I found copies of the letters he had sent to Austro–Hungary and Italy. I found some paper and as quickly as possible copied them word for word. I had returned the letters to the drawer when I heard a key in the door. I dropped down behind the desk, tied a black silk handkerchief over my mouth and waited.

The Kaiser and the Baron, along with a few of his inner circle, entered the room.

9

THE DESK WAS at least six feet deep, with drawers either side and I could easily hide in the space. One man, whom I assumed to be the Kaiser, sat at the desk and the others remained in front of it.

'That blasted window is open,' said the Kaiser. 'Somebody close it.'

I waited with bated breath for whoever went to close the window to look out and see the rope dangling there. Nothing happened and I sighed, silently, with relief.

'That's better. Now, to business. We have only a short time before we must join the other guests. Please make your reports,' said the Kaiser.

A voice I did not recognise replied. 'We have sent a message to the Italians that we expect them to fulfil their obligations under the renewed triple alliance treaty and reminded them that it is an obligation which lasts another six years. We have warned them not to vacillate or else we will stop their expansionist plans in Africa.'

'Good. Very good,' said the Kaiser. 'Otto?'

I assumed that he was talking to the Baron and recognised the voice in reply. 'We have spoken in private to the Serbs and Albanians. Although we are allied to the Turks in this matter we have made it clear that we will not interfere under any circumstances in their little Balkan difficulty and as a gesture of goodwill we have sent them ten thousand guns and a million rounds of ammunition.'

'Excellent. I want the Turks to think that we are supporting them while we ensure their power base in Europe is broken once and for all. General?'

'We have finished the invasion plans for Belgium, Holland and

France. We will begin to move our forces into position over the next year. We will then need a reason to attack.'

'A reason? Why?' asked a voice I didn't recognise.

'So that we can keep the damned British out of it,' replied the Kaiser. 'They have the only army and navy that will present us with any problems. The others will collapse like a pack of cards. Once we have occupied the lowlands we will conscript millions of their men into a German army and attack Poland and Russia. Agreed Johannes?' Now I could put a name to the voice.

'We agree. The Emperor is in full accord. He has also requested that once matters get underway that we also take Serbia and Albania.'

'I have no objection. Gentlemen?'

There was a chorus of agreement. It was the kind of meeting where nobody would disagree with the Kaiser.

'Right? No other matters to discuss? Good. Then I suggest we rejoin our guests before we are missed.'

'There is one other matter, your Excellency.' I recognised the voice of Karl von Ludwig. 'I have been making enquiries about one of the guests. An American by the name of David Griffiths.'

The sound of his voice startled me, the sound of my name sent a frisson of shock through me.

'It appears that Herr Griffiths is not all that he seems. He has turned up in a number of places over the last six months and has insinuated himself into our society. I believe him to be a spy.'

'Have you any proof?' some one asked.

'No, but there has been too many coincidences for my liking. I would like your permission to arrange a suitable accident. Just in case.

There was a silence that lasted for a few seconds and then the Kaiser said, 'Very well. There is too much at risk. Ensure he is silenced before he leaves.'

'Thank you, your Excellency,' von Ludwig replied.

With that there was a scraping of chairs, an exchange of polite words and the men left the room. I crawled out from under the desk, stretched my cramped limbs and went across to the balcony doors. I needed to get what I had learned into Lord Stockdale's hands as soon as possible. I opened the doors and was about to step onto the balcony when the door to the corridor was thrown open and I heard a voice say, 'I am sure my cigars . . .'

He got no further because he saw me and yelled, 'An intruder. A burglar. Guards come quickly.' The Kaiser rushed across the room at me. I hit him a glancing blow on the head with my pistol, dived out of the window, grabbed the rope and slid as quickly as I dared for the ground. Luckily I still had the handkerchief across my face.

I landed awkwardly and fell into the snow. I looked back and saw a number of men on the balcony. Somebody pointed at me and yelled 'Stop thief!' and next I heard the sound of a gun being fired. I had already made a dash for the corner of the stables and the bullet came nowhere near me. There was pandemonium in the house. I hesitated. My instinct was to run, and run as fast as I could. My common sense told me that I needed to pass the letters I had copied to John and to tell him about the conversation I had heard. If I was captured and killed before I passed on the information then my efforts would have been in vain.

I found a side door, which was locked. It took me less than thirty seconds to open it but even as I was picking the lock I could hear shouted instructions behind me and the sound of running footsteps. I stepped into a dark hall, closing and locking the door behind me. I wasn't a moment too soon as I heard somebody try the door only a few seconds later. I was in the servants' part of the castle and I hurried along the corridor, looking for a way into the main part where I could mingle with the guests and find John. I took the handkerchief off, put the gun I was carrying back into its holster and spent a few moments tidying myself up.

I arrived at the other end of the corridor without mishap and stepped through the door into the kitchen. It was a hive of activity with chefs and waiters busily finishing off their arrangements for the dinner. I paused and walked straight through, nodding politely to the staff as I did. I reached the other end of the huge kitchen without mishap and stepped into the main dining room. Huge tables were covered in gleaming white clothes, candelabra stood every few feet and the candlelight flickered off the vast array of silverware and glasses. Waiters were busy putting the finishing touches to the setting and pulling the corks from the bottles of wine. I sauntered over to the other side of the room and let myself into the hall where pandemonium reigned.

I found John standing with Emily. I pulled them to one side and quickly told them what had happened. John was phlegmatic, Emily agog and excited. I handed the letters to John.

'What are you gong to do now?' he asked.

'I'm not sure. They don't know it was me in that room and they can't be sure that I was there during their meeting or that I had just arrived when the Kaiser walked in. I know that they will come for me so I think my best course of action is to wait until the excitement dies down and try and get away later. If I attempt to go now I don't think I'll get five yards. If they want to take me without any fuss it will have to be in the middle of the night, so I think I'll be safe until then.'

'Right. You have been with us for the last twenty minutes or more. Understand, Emily?'

'Yes, Uncle.' She looked across the room and said, 'Oh, oh. Here comes trouble.'

I looked to see von Ludwig and some of his cronies bearing down on us.

'Herr Griffiths, we would like to speak to you in private. If you will come with me,' said von Ludwig and turned away, expecting me to follow.

I ignored him and continued my pretence of small talk with John and Emily.

He had only taken a pace or two when he realised I was not following and turned back and took hold of me by my arm. 'I advise you to come . . .'

He got no further as I shoved my elbow into his stomach and said, 'Go away von Ludwig or I will break your arm.'

'I say,' said John. 'This is deplorable, young fellow. Kindly leave us to our discussion and do not interfere.' He spoke in a voice loud enough to attract attention and other guests were looking at us, speculating on the fuss. I caught a sign from the Baron, aimed at von Ludwig who gave a stiff bow and departed.

'That was close,' said Emily. 'What do we do now?'

'We do nothing,' I said. 'But I do a great deal. I don't want either of you involved so that you can't either talk your way out of it or bluff your way through. Therefore, leave it to Frazer and me.'

'What are you going to do?' asked John.

I grinned, wolfishly. 'I don't know yet, but I'm thinking of something.'

A short while later dinner was announced and we went in to our allotted seat. Unfortunately, mine was not at the same table as John and Emily and so I was forced to make small talk with a fat Italian Countess who had a moustache that could only have been to honour the Kaiser and a small tubby Hungarian who turned out to be the editor of an important newspaper printed in Budapest. It would have been fascinating to talk to him but he spoke no English and I was maintaining the fiction that I spoke nothing but English. The next two hours passed painfully slowly on one level and yet on another the time flew by. All too soon the port was being passed, cigars were being lit and the women were leaving.

I was seated near the door to the kitchen, without doubt one of the poorest tables in the room. Now that the ladies had withdrawn the idea was that we would move closer into the room and mingle with some of the other guests. As we stood to do so I stepped two paces away from the table, pushed open the door to the kitchen and walked rapidly towards the door through which I had entered earlier. Nobody tried to stop me and I had reached the door to the corridor when I heard a commotion behind me. Looking back I saw von Ludwig and two of his companions rush into the kitchen. Luckily they managed to bump into a couple of waiters who were laden down with trays of glasses and sent the lot smashing to the floor. There was great deal of fuss and noise going on but I didn't stop to enjoy it. I went into the corridor and ran along it as fast as possible until I reached the door to the outside. I unlocked it in under ten seconds and quickly relocked it behind me.

I was halfway to the trees when I heard the noise of my pursuers pounding on the door. I continued to walk at an even pace, in case there was anyone about. Just as I reached the trees I heard a shout and a shot was fired in my direction. The bullet hit a tree next to my right shoulder and I took to my heels.

I was halfway to the lake when I heard the dogs. I had hoped to make my getaway without too many problems, but now I knew I was in serious trouble. The woods thickened and the sound of the hounds grew louder. Knowing that I couldn't escape them I quickly climbed a tree. As soon as I was clear of the ground I began to climb from tree to tree, making my way at right angles to my original direction. I had probably gone about fifty yards when I heard yelling behind me and a voice saying, 'We have him now. He's treed.'

I dropped to the ground and continued as silently as possible away from the hounds and the tree they had surrounded. I was in a dilemma. Should I continue to try and escape or do the unexpected? I chose the latter. I returned to the Schloss, found another side entrance and let myself in. Ten minutes later I was back in my room, sitting in an armchair, wondering what my next move should be.

I must have dozed because the next thing I was aware of was a cramped neck and a stiff leg. I stretched, stood up, and changed my clothes for ordinary day wear. I thought it was time once again to try and escape. I carefully opened the door, heard nothing, saw nothing, and crept along the corridor. I had the canvas bag with a few belongings slung over my shoulder and my gun in its holster at my side. The house was in darkness, which was only to be expected at three o'clock in the morning. I had reached the main hall when I heard voices at the front door and I darted into the library to hide.

I was about to hide behind a sofa when the door was thrown open, the light switched on and an oath escaped the lips of von Ludwig as he stood staring at me in shock. I was better prepared than he was, and took a run at him, hitting him across the head when I swung the canvas bag at him. Too late I realised there were three others with him but I managed to kick one in the knee before I turned and ran back into the room. I tripped over a stool, fell flat on my face and scrambled back to my feet before they could reach me.

'Wait! Don't touch him,' said von Ludwig. 'He's mine.'

I reached under my coat for my gun, found an empty holster and looked at where I had fallen. Mocking me was the revolver, its handle protruding from underneath a settee.

I warily stepped back, edging closer to the trophy wall containing the mediaeval weapons I had admired earlier. The four men closed in on me, von Ludwig in front, the other three just behind.

'I don't want him killed,' said von Ludwig, 'just crippled. I want him to talk.'

I grabbed a sword, wrenched it from the wall, and jabbed it at von Ludwig. He was as fast as lightning. He stepped back, turned, and armed himself with another sword before I could get my balance.

The other three stepped back to give us more room, gleefully encouraging von Ludwig. I moved closer to my adversary and exchanged parries. Among the sports I had tried at university had been fencing; for the whole of two terms I learnt to parry and thrust. It took about fifteen seconds to realise that my opponent was a master with the sword and within half a minute I was desperately defending myself. After a few minutes I realised that I was being toyed with. Von Ludwig paused and said, 'You know that this is an unfair competition, Herr Griffiths. I have been selected to represent Germany at the next Olympics and as you know, we are a nation famed for its fencing prowess.'

At that moment I knew I had serious problems. The only way out was to use every conceivable means of cheating that I could. I took the first one by stepping to the wall and pulling down a pikestaff which I promptly threw at von Ludwig. He stepped aside but not fast enough and the cruel point on the end of the blade sliced through his upper right arm. He dropped his sword but before I could do anything he grabbed it with his left hand and with added ferocity attacked me. I fell back, realising that he was almost as good with his left hand as he was with his right. He snarled an instruction to the other three, telling them not to interfere. I could barely keep up with him as he cut left and right, thrust deeply at me, missing me by fractions of an inch. He used his sword like the master he was. I was beginning to sweat, the sword heavy in my grasp, fear gnawing at my guts. I parried one last time, my sword was sent flying from my grasp and von Ludwig stood with his sword at my throat. We stared with hatred at each other.

'Go on,' I said. 'Finish it.'

He grinned mirthlessly at me. 'I think not, Herr Griffiths, I shall cut a few pieces off you, starting with you ears and nose, but I shall not kill you. Not yet, anyway. We have need of a great deal of information, including what you have told the British authorities and who your accomplices are.'

'That is easily answered,' came a gentle voice from behind the four men. I had been so intent on watching von Ludwig that I had not noticed Emily enter the room.

I looked at her, as did the other three, but von Ludwig stood staring at me, the sword pricking my throat.

'I believe that we now have the lovely Miss Emily in our presence,' he spoke with sarcasm. 'Have you come to see your lover mutilated? I suggest you leave immediately before you see too much blood.'

'If I do it will be yours,' she said, drawing back the hammer on my gun which she must have recovered from under the settee, with a loud click.

That got everybody's attention, including von Ludwig's. He glanced over his shoulder and said, nonchalantly, 'I think not, Emily. One thrust from me and your lover is dead. And I don't think you will fire that gun. So I suggest you hand it over to one of my friends. Dietrich, take it off . . .'

The noise of the shot was deafening in the enclosed room. Von Ludwig screamed and collapsed, holding his right knee and Emily calmly waved the gun at the other three. 'Don't move or I shall kill you. I just shot Karl in the knee and I won't hesitate to shoot you. David, come here.'

I kept out of her line of fire and stood next to her. 'Would you like me to take that?' I asked, tentatively.

'Will you do a better job?' Emily asked, tartly.

'Em, no. I just thought . . . em, nothing.'

'Good. Shut up Karl, you're making too much noise.' She waved the gun in his direction and I could see the effort he was making to stifle his moans. 'You three, don't move. David, walk us towards the door.' I put a hand on her shoulder and guided her backwards. I was wondering whether the sound of the shot would bring others to the scene but then we reached the door, threw it open and rushed out.

'Quick. The car is outside,' she cried.

We hurried down the steps and clambered into the car. I started the engine, rammed the gear stick into first and drove away with a spinning of the wheels and a roar of the engine. No shots were fired and nobody came after us.

'That was close,' I said. 'Thanks.'

'I couldn't let them kill the man I love, now, could I?' she said flippantly and then gave a low moan and a sob, covering her face with her hands.

'Hey, take it easy. If you hadn't intervened I'd be dead now. Or worse, a prisoner maimed for life by that thug von Ludwig. Where did you learn to handle a gun, anyway?' I asked.

She snuffled, took out a handkerchief and blew her nose then replied. 'With the movement. Many of us have learnt in case we need to man – or should I say woman – the barricades,' she said with a touch of her normal flippancy. 'That's better. I'm all right now. So where to? Germany is going to be too hot for us in about half an hour.'

'Are you saying you learnt to shoot with the suffragettes?' I asked, aghast.

'That and a few other things.'

'Such as?'

'Such as how to make bombs. Now shut up and concentrate on getting where we're going. And where is that, anyway?'

'First we need to pick up Frazer. They'll scour the area and are bound to find him. Then we need to get into a big city and lie low, or perhaps we should make a mad dash for it like we did when we got out of Italy.' I threw the car around the corner, found the track I was looking for and bounced into the forest where I slowed down. The last thing we needed was a puncture or for me to break the low slung differential drive which connected the motor to the back axle.

After about ten minutes we reached the hut. I climbed out and called for Frazer. He stepped out of the trees behind me with a gun in his hand. I quickly told him what had happened. He had his gear ready for immediate departure and within minutes I had turned the car and we were going back the way we had come. When we reached the road I turned right and headed towards the north of the lake.

'OK,' said Emily, leaning over the back of our seats to talk to us, 'what do we do? Where do we go? Oh! What about John?'

'He'll be all right, he's travelling with diplomatic immunity. The Germans may be barbarians but carrying a diplomatic passport still counts for a lot in Europe. With me, it's different. I suspect the word has already gone out to stop us at the border. Army units will be rushing to join the border police and customs and believe me, the Kaiser will do everything to get David, especially if he believes that he's the one who hit him. Germany will be sealed tighter than a duck's behind, and that's water tight.' Frazer tried injecting a little levity into our situation but neither Emily nor I felt like raising even a smile.

'So what are our options?'

'We hole up in the country,' was the prompt reply. 'I'll debrief you, write everything down and Emily can take it out of the country. Then you and I can get out, separately.'

'How? How will Emily get out of the country?'

'Easily. I'll get her a new passport and she can alter her appearance.'

'How?' I asked.

'We cut her hair. Dress her in a dowdy manner, put glasses on her and send her on her way with her new passport. Believe me, she'll get out all right. With you and me it's different. They'll be stopping everybody between twenty and sixty and double checking their *bona fides*.'

'Why don't we make a rush for Switzerland again, or France?' I asked.

'David, those'll be the first borders they shut. We'll never make it. No, our best bet is to do the unexpected and that's to head north, right through the middle of Germany. They can shut off the borders but they can't shut down the rest of Germany. We're entering Starnberg, keep an eye out for any problems.'

There were none and an hour later we were approaching Munich. It was now nearly five o'clock and we decided to head for the railway station to see what time the first train would leave the city. As we approached the station we noticed a number of truckloads of troops going in the same direction and decided that we were too late to catch a train – any train.

We turned away and headed north for Ingolstadt, a small town about eighty kilometres away. By the time we arrived the shops were open and we were able to buy food and drink. We also bought German clothes and accessories, deciding that it was safer to be German than English right then. We found a garage where we filled up with petrol and, remembering our flight from Italy, we also filled up four jerry cans each with fifty litres of petrol.

'Right, I think I have it,' said Frazer.

'Have what?' asked Emily and then, with a flash of her old self, added, 'Whatever it is you can keep it.'

Frazer grinned and said, 'We drive non-stop for Denmark. It's straight north, about five hundred miles.'

'Five hundred miles,' said Emily, aghast. 'That'll take a week.'

'No it won't. We'll stop in Nürnberg. You can take a train while I try and contact our man in Berlin. I'll tell him to meet you in Berlin and supply you with papers in a different name. He can escort you to Hamburg and put you on the ferry to Ipswich. In fact, he can escort you all the way back. He has a diplomatic passport and you can be his sister. Yes, that's the best course of events.'

'What will you two do?'

'We'll drive to Rostock or Kiel and pinch a boat. We can be in Denmark a few hours later. They can stop the usual routes out of Germany but they can't stop them all. Any objections?'

There were none. I was relieved at the idea of sending Emily out with a suitable escort though I was not so sure that Frazer and I would get away so easily. As I drove Frazer cross-examined me about what I had heard and Emily took notes. There were details that I had forgotten when I had spoken to John Buchanan, and Emily duly wrote them down. It was not an easy task as the car jolted along but she did her best. We arrived at Nürnberg without mishap and I dropped Frazer off at the post office. Emily and I drove back out of the city and found a quiet spot. There, with my help, she cut her hair and changed her clothes. The latter took a little longer than usual as we embraced and kissed during the process. However, she resisted my advances with the coy suggestion that now we were to be married I could wait. Considering her previous ardour I thought that was rich but I let it go. I could wait; she was right.

Her appearance was transformed now. With her hair cut short, old fashioned clothes and shoes and a pince-nez perched on her nose she looked twenty years older and forty years out of date.

'I feel a frump,' she said, looking in a mirror.

'You don't look it,' I said gallantly. 'Your beauty shines through. Which is only to be expected.'

She hit my shoulder playfully and then gave me a longing kiss. We returned to the city centre where we parked the car and walked to the station. I spent a few minutes checking the train times and bought a ticket for Emily. We had discussed whether or not she should travel first or second class and much to her disgust Frazer and I agreed it should be second as there would be more people to mingle with and so it would therefore be easier to hide.

Back at the car we found Frazer. He had not managed to get through to Berlin as there was a delay of at least another two hours and he had been forced to book the call. We decided that it would be safer if Emily went back to the station to wait for her train while we left the city for an hour or two. We said farewell to Emily and she left us. We headed north for about twenty kilometres to reconnoitre the road and then returned to the post office. Frazer went in and I went around the corner to park the car. In spite of booking the call it was still nearly an hour before he rejoined me. He climbed into the car and we set off.

'All right?' I asked.

'No problems except for the interminable wait to get a line. The attaché will meet her train. He'll have papers for her, describing her as his sister. They'll travel by train to Hamburg and take one of the ships heading for England. She should be in London within three days.'

'Let's hope so. I filled up with petrol while I was waiting so we should make Magdeburg before we need any more.' As we drove north the weather deteriorated until we were travelling through a fully fledged snow storm. The roads were treacherous, darkness fell early and the heater in the car proved to be inadequate. The only thing in our favour was that we saw no other car, truck or passer-by. The populace of Germany had enough sense to hide when the weather was as bad as it was.

We used more petrol than we had expected and on two occasions had to fill up using the jerry cans. Our speed was cut right back as any accident would be a disaster, and so it took us until the following morning to get as far as Leipzig. We agreed that it would be madness to continue and so we found a country hotel on the outskirts of the city and, posing as two German businessmen, booked in. We holed up there for three fretful days. Finally it stopped snowing and we were able to venture out into a landscape that had almost been transformed because so much snow had fallen. The skies had cleared, the sun shone, but the road was now buried under four feet of snow.

'What do we do now?' I asked.

Frazer shrugged. 'We know the railway lines will be kept clear by using the train ploughs so with any luck Emily will have made it. We can go into Leipzig and take a train north and take our chances, or we can battle across the country by road.'

'It's about a hundred and twenty kilometres to Magdeburg. We need to fill up with petrol in Leipzig before we go any further and there's every danger of our breaking down and being stranded before we get to Magdeburg. If we break down in the middle of nowhere we could freeze to death.'

'If we get caught on a train we get shot instead,' said Frazer, with a grim humour.

'The roads will be hellish. Another storm could be fatal, and we've got a very long way to go.'

It was a difficult decision to make. Heads we don't win, tails we lose. 'Let's get some petrol while we think about the situation,' he offered as compromise.

We were ten kilometres from the centre of Leipzig, and even that short journey was a nightmare. To go any further wasn't even worth considering and so the decision was made for us. We abandoned the car in the town centre and trudged through the snow to the railway station. As we had expected the railway lines had been kept free in spite of the heavy snowfall and we bought two second-class return tickets to Rostock on the first train out of Leipzig that afternoon.

In the evening we pulled into Berlin Hauptbahnhoff, the main station. We were due to be there for at least forty-five minutes and we both alighted to stretch our legs and buy some food and drink. The station was crawling with troops and people were being stopped and asked to show their papers. We saw numerous men being hauled away, protesting their innocence. We hastily climbed back on to the train and waited for it to leave. Two women and their six children entered our compartment and I immediately struck up a conversation with them, in German. I soon learned that they were travelling to Rostock to visit their husbands, seamen who were due to arrive there the next day after six months at sea, ploughing the eastern seaboard of America. In keeping with our cover we pretended to be travelling salesmen representing Krupps and on our way to one of the shipyards in Rostock to discuss the laying down of a new ship. That tenuous connection to the sea ensured a friendly atmosphere and I was able to persuade the women to send the two oldest boys to purchase food and drink for us all. I would pay for this as the firm could pay me back.

By the time the train started we were one big happy family, enjoying a picnic on the train. A short while later when the ticket collector threw open the door he had two troopers with him. I held him in conversation while Frazer made a pretence of collecting the tickets from the women.

When we passed over the tickets we were, to all intents and purposes, a family group travelling together. The ticket collector punched the tickets, exchanged a few more words with us and carried on up the train, the guards in tow. They didn't so much as look back at us.

We didn't arrive in Rostock until the following morning. In keeping with our new cover we helped the women with their bags and harried the children like any father would. We left the station without any trouble in spite of the fact that it was crawling with troopers and policemen. Nobody as much as looked at us and no one asked us to show our papers.

We said farewell at the tram stop outside and Frazer and I walked to a nearby hotel. We booked in and spent the rest of the day quietly in our room, getting some rest for the busy night ahead. Rostock being on the Baltic Sea was relatively free of snow and though the city was prone to blizzards and freezing winds the snow rarely stayed for any length of time.

That evening we left the hotel to look for the docks and find a suitable boat to steal.

10

THE PAVEMENTS WERE wet with slush and soon my feet were freezing in spite of the extra pairs of socks I was wearing. We left the centre of the city and ventured into the mean streets surrounding the docks. We passed numerous bars and many ladies of the night plying their trade with the sailors and troopers in the area.

At the docks themselves we found nothing but large cargo ships, troop carriers and a number of warships, but there was nothing suitable for our purposes. We eventually found ourselves in a mean dive of a bar having snifters of brandy to warm us. We spoke Italian, not wanting to be overheard and not wanting to give away the fact that we were English.

'What now?' I asked.

'Now we go and find the fishing fleet,' said Frazer. 'A small fishing smack will be ideal for our needs and I reckon we'll find them in the inner harbour.'

'How do you know there's an inner harbour?'

He grinned, wolfishly, 'I asked the barman. He's Italian and was keen to help.'

Ten minutes later we were back out in the cold and wet. By now a light snow had began to fall, adding to our woes. We walked for about three or four kilometres until we found the inner harbour. There we found dozens of boats, ranging from ocean going trawlers to inshore lobster pot layers. The former were three hundred tonnes and with a crew of at least twenty, the latter were small dinghies with sails requiring only one or two men to sail them.

We wandered around, looking at everything and discussing our options. Finally we returned to the hotel, cold, wet and footsore. But at least we were optimistic.

The next morning we had an early breakfast and returned to the harbour. In the bright sunlight the snow crunched underfoot; it was easier to walk on than the slush of the night before. At the harbour we spent some time walking around, ignored by the few people who were about at that time on such a cold day. The fact that Christmas was upon us meant that the fishing fleet would be in for some time, so this was a good time to steal a boat.

'You're the sailor,' Frazer said to me, referring to my exploits in the Caribbean. 'Do we go for something with an engine or just with sails?'

I looked at the weather, gauged the wind and thought about it. 'A sailboat will be silent but slow. Do we need stealth or speed?' I asked.

'I don't know. What's the best option?'

'It'll hardly be speed,' I replied. 'These things will be lucky to do six or seven knots. And we'll have to flash up the engines for a few hours if we need to build up a head of steam. We'll need oil and diesel as well as everything else that we need to get away.'

'All right, you've answered your own question. We sail out.'

'In that case we should take that thirty foot boat, the one that's tied up to the outer wall. Its got a small cabin for shelter and is next to the harbour entrance.'

'I know the one. I noticed it as well. When shall we go?'

'Tonight. There's nothing to wait for and everything to gain by getting away quickly.'

'How long will it take us to get to Denmark in that thing?' Frazer asked.

'It depends on too many factors from the wind direction and strength to how well the boat sails. However, assuming our navigation holds, we should be there mid-morning tomorrow.'

We returned to the town and began to buy clothing and stores we would need for the journey. We kitted ourselves out in sou'westers and bought heavy canvas trousers and warm shirts and jumpers. We purchased food and drink to last for at least three days, and gutting knives for added protection in case we needed it. By six o'clock we had returned to our hotel to be greeted by the receptionist with the information that the police had been in looking for two strange men. She hoped we didn't mind but she had given them our names and room numbers. The police had said that they would return later that evening.

We thanked her, gave her a ten reichmark note and went up to our rooms. We quickly packed our bags and were in the process of returning to the front desk when we heard voices and the heavy tread of officialdom on the stairs.

We found a back stairs used by the staff and rushed down, heavily laden with our bags. Once in the street we hailed a passing taxi and climbed aboard. A short while later we were dropped at the docks, near to the boat we were going to use.

Luckily it was already dark, and we climbed aboard. I left Frazer to stow our belongings while I went to the forepeak and into the sail hold. As I had expected, all the gear I needed to sail the boat was neatly stowed there. I sorted out the tackle, ropes and sails and began to hand them up to Frazer. A short while later I was running ropes and tackle and getting ready to hoist the foresail when we heard a loud commotion ashore.

'I let them off here. They walked down there.'

We heard boots marching, raised voices giving orders and the sound of rifle bolts being opened and slammed home.

Frazer and I cut the lines and dragged the boat along the wall and into the ebbing tidal stream. We moved silently in the night, the still air echoing to the sounds of the men on the shore. There was hardly any wind and I sat in the stern, steering the boat away from the sounds. We weren't moving fast enough for my liking but there was nothing I could do about it. We had at least four kilometres of docks to pass before we reached the open sea and the ebbing tide was our only means of propulsion. As the noise of the men faded I breathed more easily. We had been floating along for about half an hour, past hull after hull when we reached the warships. The merchant ships had been empty, an air of abandonment about them but now we saw men walking along the decks, each gangway had a guard and there were sailors coming and going all the time.

I decided it was time to hoist the foresail and I left Frazer to steer whilst I saw to it. Immediately I felt the canvas stiffen in the wind and the bow of the boat lifted a few degrees as she picked up a little speed. Even in the light easterly winds she was responding. She may have been an old fishing boat but she handled well. The harbour lights were in sight and the open sea less than half a kilometre away when we were challenged.

A naval cutter came out from behind a huge battleship and headed straight for us. Within moments it had closed to less than ten metres and three rifles were levelled at us. We were ordered to turn round and follow them back to the shore. I pushed over the tiller as if I were going to obey and as the boat came round Frazer opened fire with the rifle he had ready in case of an emergency. It was so unexpected that the coxswain of the cutter did nothing as the three riflemen were hit but then he came to his senses, ducked down and turned away from us.

I turned the boat again and we headed back towards the entrance, the open sea only a few hundred yards away.

'Angus, take the tiller,' I yelled. 'I'm going to raise as much sail as I can.' Frazer took over the tiller and I began to hoist the mainsail. There were more yells from behind us and shots were fired in our direction. Once we were through the entrance and out of the lee of the dockside wall the wind picked up and filled our sails. The boat heeled over to port and we were flying along, at something between six and eight knots; the wind was from the south east and we held a steady northerly course. Behind us we heard the sound of more boats starting up, their throaty engines a raucous roar in the night.

The hunt was on.

For the next hour we kept our course. Even as we did we saw dozens of boats streaming out of the harbour entrance, all carrying their lights and, we guessed, all carrying armed men determined to stop us. Or, because of what we had done, to kill us.

The water was becoming choppy, a swell building up from the east. The sky was also becoming overcast and I prayed for rain. Visibility was poor and I knew we would be difficult to see against the backdrop of a cloudy night sky. I took over the tiller and tried to draw every fraction of a knot from the boat. My memory flooded back and I became more adept with every passing minute. I fine tuned her until she was racing, but it did no good.

The chasing boats had spread out and were covering five or more kilometres of water behind us, fast. They were closing inexorably and it couldn't be long before we were spotted. However, I failed to realise our good fortune: we were heeled over, presenting a low profile and were sailing towards a dark shore about fifteen kilometres away. Looking back the boats were as clear as lights on a Christmas tree. They must have been going at about ten knots because soon the nearest boat was less than a hundred yards behind us and still they hadn't seen us.

'Angus, we'll need to shoot a few more,' I said reluctantly.

'They'll hang or shoot us anyway,' said Frazer, 'so a few more won't matter. But will it be enough to keep them away?'

'It will for a while, but they'll regroup and come after us. I'm surprised we haven't been spotted already.' The words were hardly out of my mouth when there was a shout from the boat behind us. Frazer immediately opened up with a barrage of fire and the boat behind veered away.

There were more shouts from the other boats and I saw two turn to converge on the boat Frazer had been shooting at.

Just then a squall hit, rain started to fall and then, within seconds, we were enclosed by a snow storm. I turned further to port, let out the main sheet and let out the jib sheet as well. The boat came more upright and we began to run before the wind, picking up speed. The lights on the boats behind dimmed as the visibility became poorer and were soon extinguished altogether. I knew that in that weather the naval cutters would have to give up and return to harbour. Our craft could sail in a lot worse, but the cutters would be in danger of being swamped. The sea was picking up as well and now we were pitching uncomfortably. I relished it but poor Frazer suddenly leaned over the side and was as sick as a dog.

That night the weather saved us. We had no charts or maps, and what we had brought with us was of little use, showing only an outline of the Danish coast – though Germany was shown in great detail. Even so, it was sufficient for our purposes as it showed that if we continued heading north west we would pass between Danish Lolland to starboard and German Fehmarn to port. I held our course all night.

In the light of dawn the land was hinted at on the starboard horizon and I turned further to starboard to get closer. I wanted to get Denmark within closing distance, just in case. The wind freshened, the snow stopped and the sky cleared. We could see no sign of pursuit, and we were becoming hopeful that we would escape.

At ten o'clock Frazer pointed to the entrance to a small harbour and we decided to land, to get our bearings and make more plans. We were both dog-tired, freezing cold and curious as to where we were. I changed tack, drew closer to the harbour entrance and then just as we passed through the entrance, dropped the main sail. I put the tiller hard over, came into the wind and we stopped dead in the water. There were only a dozen or more fishing boats in the harbour, nothing else. We saw no sign of life as we tied up to the wall and climbed ashore. A short walk brought us into the hamlet of Rodby, a small Danish fishing port with nothing evident to redeem it.

We eventually found an old man who spoke German, although with an almost incomprehensible accent, who told us we were in Rodbyhavn and that Rodby town was two kilometres away. A train service ran from there northwards, connecting with other services which would eventually get us to Odense. We thanked him and were about to walk on when I had the sense to ask when the next train was due. The answer – it was four days away – nearly floored us. But the old man pointed out that as it was Christmas Eve nothing would be running anywhere for the next three or four days anyway.

We returned to the boat, in a dilemma as to what we should do. In the small cabin we lit the primus stove for warmth and to boil some water. We made ourselves something to eat and warmed up some soup.

'If we carry on we need to hug the coast, sail around the island and north to Odense. We can be there in about two days. We gain probably two days, freeze half to death and, if we're lucky we won't hit another storm. Alternatively . . .'

'Alternatively,' interrupted Frazer, 'we get into town, even if we have to walk, find an inn or a hotel and get drunk for a few days until a train arrives. We travel in comfort to Odense, and then to Esbjerg. There we get a ship for England. There's no contest, David.'

'What about money?'

'Gold guineas are good anywhere in the world,' was the reply.

I agreed and it was precisely what happened. We arrived back in Harwich on New Year's Eve where we caught a train for London.

When we arrived at John's house there was no welcome: everybody had left for a ball at The Dorchester Hotel on Park Lane. Frazer went home to change and I had a bath and climbed into my dinner jacket and black tie. When Frazer returned, we set off at a brisk walk to Park Lane. Ten minutes later we were at the door being denied entry.

'I'm sorry, gentlemen, but it's tickets only. I can't let you in,' said a large doorman, with no hint of regret in his voice. He waved through a couple who didn't show a ticket and I challenged him about it. 'Her Ladyship and her escort don't need a ticket,' was the reply.

I was about to argue when Frazer grabbed my arm. 'Come on, David. Think of the delicious irony of going in and out of the Schloss at will and then escaping from Germany, and here we are unable to get into a hotel in England.' He dragged me away. 'Let's go round to the back.'

Frazer had picked the lock of one of the entrances in fifteen seconds and we were amongst the revellers a few minutes later. The place was packed, the noise was raucous and the laughter loud. We tried to find John and Emily but it was impossible. So instead we settled for buying a couple of bottles of bubbly at the bar and mixing with a few cronies we knew.

Suddenly midnight was upon us and there was the usual countdown. Balloons were released as the men began to shake hands and the ladies started to kiss everybody. It was then that I saw my love, standing alone next to a pillar in the corner of the room.

I sneaked up behind her and said, softly in her ear, 'Thinking of anyone in particular?'

'David! David! Oh, David!' She whirled round, laughing and crying at the same time, her arms wrapped around my neck, raining kisses on my lips, cheeks, wherever she could find.

I was grinning hugely, my arms wrapped tightly around her. 'Happy New Year, my darling,' I said.

'Oh, David! I do so love you! Where have you been? How did you get away? Oh, there's so much to talk about. Come on, we must find Uncle John. He's been desperately worried about you. He's been sending coded messages all over Europe trying to find you.'

We tracked John down talking to Lord Stockdale. There were handshakes all round and an instruction from Stockdale for Frazer and I to report to his office in the morning. I pointed out that it was New Year's Eve and the next day, although a Wednesday, was a holiday. He gave in with bad grace and demanded that we appear on Thursday 2 January 1913 at nine in the morning. I wanted to know how John had got out of Germany but it turned out to be simplicity itself. His diplomatic passport had been honoured in the punctilious manner for which the Germans were renowned. Frazer and I, with John, duly presented ourselves at Lord Stockdale's office in the House of Lords at the appointed time and date. We were shown into an anteroom and kept waiting for a few moments before being ushered into Stockdale's inner sanctum. To our surprise we were greeted not just by Stockdale but also by Winston Churchill, First Lord of the Admiralty and David Lloyd George, the Chancellor of the Exchequer.

Chairs had already been arranged and we sat down. Churchill immediately dominated the conversation. In his gravely voice, between puffs on his foul smelling cigar, he said, 'We need to get a feel for what is happening in Europe. We have amassed a good deal of information from agents all over the continent but you two are the only ones to have operated in Italy, Austro-Hungary and Germany. And what's more important, you've been rubbing shoulders with leaders of every segment of the ruling-classes. That's military, political and, not to be underestimated, social leaders.'

'I haven't, sir, with all due respect,' said Frazer. 'Mr Griffiths here has. I've just been keeping his escape routes open, so to speak.'

'I am aware of that,' said Churchill. 'And, from what I can gather, Mr Griffiths wouldn't be here today if it hadn't been for the assistance you were able to render him over the months. We have a serious dilemma. Do we continue arming, or do we spend our money on social aid to the underprivileged in this country? I think the former, the Chancellor isn't so sure.'

'I can speak for myself, thank you, Winston,' Lloyd George said, his Welsh accent prominent as he spoke. 'I am not a pacifist as you well know, but I do have difficulty in, shall we say, balancing the books. We have huge deprivation problems in this country and I could spend four million pounds doing a lot of good and not waste it all on a new Dreadnought. But I am also aware of the fact that Germany is posing a serious threat in Europe which could spill over into something we cannot control or even contain. I want your views, your impressions, so that I can make a more balanced decision.'

I looked at Frazer in some surprise. It was hardly our position to advise the Government; we could only present the facts as we knew them. It was up to the politicians to interpret the information we supplied. I told them so.

'Yes, yes, Griffiths,' Lord Stockdale said testily. 'That's all well and good but we do not have your feel for what is happening. You listened to the Germans. Are they belligerent? Cocksure? Aggressive? What?'

'Sir, with all due respect, the Germans are all of those things and always have been.' My response caused a guffaw from Churchill and a smile from Lloyd George.

'What Lord Stockdale is getting at, David,' said John, 'is do you have the impression they want war or are they just making the right noises for the benefit of their Chiefs of Staff and the Kaiser? Do you think the politicians are ready to commit to an act of aggression which could plunge Europe into war, which we believe would be a catastrophe?'

I thought for a few moments, but I already knew the answer. Frazer and I had spoken at some length about what was happening in Europe and where it was heading.

'In my opinion, and it's Angus's as well, Germany will go to war sometime in the next two years. We believe that they are currently looking for an excuse to start something and that it is inevitable.'

'Why do you say that?' asked the Chancellor.

'Sir, the Germans are building up their fleets and have more men in uniform than ever before in their history. There is a pressure building up, a boil which can only be lanced in one way. The Germans cannot suddenly announce that they are demobbing hundreds of thousands of men. It would lead to civil unrest in the country simply because there is nothing for the men to do. Germany has created a wild tiger in their army and navy and their politicians are holding grimly to its tail to keep it in check. Frazer and I believe the tiger is about to turn and that it will attack.'

'Frazer?' Stockdale said.

'I agree with Griffiths, sir. I've never seen so many men in uniform walking around the towns and cities. What happens when you train a man, get him fit and put a gun in his hand? He wants, no, he needs to show his prowess. He wants a fight. A war.'

Churchill nodded, puffed on his cigar and sat back in his chair, a satisfied look on his face.

Lloyd George frowned, took out a cigarette, struck a match, lit it and inhaled deeply before replying. 'When we built HMS Dreadnought in 1906 she cost three million pounds and some change. Now it costs over four million per ship. If we lay down six at a time we can get the price down to three and a half million. For that sum I can give every man over the age of sixty-five a pension that will see out his life in relative security. I can build enough hospitals to eradicate some of the diseases we are fighting such as rickets and consumption. So I have to convince the House of Commons and the general populace that we need to spend our money on even more armaments and on the men to use them. It's an almost impossible task, and yet,' he held up his hand as Churchill was about to interrupt, 'and yet,' he repeated, 'I know that if we don't head off the danger posed by the triple alliance we could end up paying a far higher cost in the future.'

'Can't we find some sort of compromise?' I asked, hesitantly.

The Chancellor gave me a pitying look, 'We've been compromising for years. Germany has three times as many men under arms as we do. We have more, bigger and better ships but they are catching up. If, as we expect, Austro-Hungary sides with Germany in a European conflict then they will have – and mark my words – five times as many men as we can muster.'

'But we won't be alone,' protested John. 'We'll have Belgium and France on our side.'

'Not necessarily,' said Stockdale. 'According to our agents in France we can only expect support from Paris if France herself is threatened.'

'But surely, sir,' I argued, 'that is precisely what will happen. Germany isn't going to invade Britain. The Kaiser has made his intentions clear. He wants Belgium and France before he turns his attention to the east and Russia.'

'That is so. That is so,' nodded Stockdale, repeating himself. 'Yet it is a situation fraught with danger. The Chancellor is right. We will have the devil's own job selling the idea that more money is needed for our armed forces to either the Lords or the Commons. Gentlemen, we thank you for your help. I gather from Mr Buchanan that you are about to enter into commerce, Mr Griffiths?'

I nodded. 'Yes, sir. Banking.'

'An honourable profession. And you Frazer? What are your plans?'

'As you know, sir, I can return to my regiment, but I have decided to resign my commission. I also am entering into the field of commerce,' he grinned suddenly. 'With Mr Griffiths.'

I kept a straight face. I had been trying to persuade him to join me for some time but so far he had resisted my overtures. Now it seemed that he had changed his mind.

We left the distinguished company and went to the United Services Club to discuss our future plans. John ordered drinks while I asked Frazer when he had made his decision to join me.

'This morning, when I was listening to our political masters. War is inevitable and they'll sit on their hands and hope it doesn't happen. I don't want to be involved unless I'm given the tools for the job. And anyway,' he grinned, 'you'll need me to get you out of the holes you dig for yourself.'

Our plans were made. Frazer resigned his commission; his resignation was accepted immediately and together we found the premises we wanted for our bank. Within a month Griffiths, Buchanan & Co was open for business. The order in which our names appeared over the door had been settled by the simple expedient of tossing a coin. We hired a dozen tellers and a secretary, a man named Albert Witherspoon to manage what we termed the retail end of the banking. Frazer and I were to work in the commercial or private banking sector. There was a great deal of publicity for the new venture, aided by the fact that John announced that he was moving all the shipping line's business to the bank and so was Lord Stockdale. It seemed that I had, according to John, made a bigger hit with the old curmudgeon than I had thought. We acquired a few more wealthy clients, mostly contacts of John's and then, unexpectedly, we hit the jackpot.

The government had decided to build the warships it needed but would not be using it's own funds. It wanted to borrow twenty million pounds at an interest rate of 4%, fixed for five years. At the end of that term the capital would be repaid or the interest rate recalculated. Griffiths, Buchanan & Co was given the task of raising the money.

Frazer and I wrote or called on every wealthy person we knew. At the end of a month we had pledges for less than three million pounds. Concerned at our lack of progress I went to John's offices to see if we could work out what to do.

'The problem we're facing is that this government is not liked by the wealthy. The interest rate is fair, the return and the capital is guaranteed and yet only thirty people have taken up the offer. So I doubt you will raise the money, at least not in the way you're going about it. You need to find another way,' was John's helpful suggestion.

'I appreciate that,' I replied. 'But what? If I can't raise the money from a few subscribers I shall have to . . .' I trailed off, deep in thought.

'Have to what?' asked John.

I suddenly grinned. 'Do what my father did back in St Louis.' I stood up, eager to get on with my plan. 'Thanks, John. Talking to you helped a lot.'

'But I didn't say anything constructive,' he protested.

'No,' I agreed. 'But it was the way you didn't say it that helped,' I joked and hurried from the room. I paused at the threshold and turned back to him. 'One question. How did we manage to get this deal?'

'For services rendered. This is the way a grateful government is repaying you and Frazer for what you did last year. You two really did help avert a number of major incidents which could have been catastrophic.'

I nodded my understanding and left. Back at the bank I went into Frazer's office. 'Any more joy?' I asked.

'Some,' he admitted. 'I have another half million or so pledged. You?'

'No but I've got an idea.' I explained to him what it was and after his initial scepticism he agreed it was worth a try.

Two days later we had advertisements and editorial copy in as many newspapers as we could contact. We were offering an investment in a guaranteed fund with 4% return per annum and the capital to be returned in 5 years. It was open to anybody and amounts as small as one pound would be acceptable. Each year the investor could take his dividend by applying to his local Post Office. The post office would then redeem the money paid from the treasury. The scheme was enthusiastically reported in the "gutter press" whilst the broadsheets denounced it. Investing would start one week after our advertisements appeared.

The day that we began to take the investment I was walking towards the bank and was astonished to find a queue of people stretching past Threadneedle Street and down towards the Thames. I was also amazed to see sacks of mail in the entrance.

I entered the main door to find Witherspoon in a dither until I got him to calm down and start business for the day. At exactly nine o'clock the doors opened and the customers streamed in. It was non-stop, with tellers grabbing only a few minutes a break, and most of them eating their lunches at their stations. Frazer and I helped out but most of the time we had to be on the telephone and answering calls.

The amount that came in from the general public was pitiful when you considered our objective was to raise twenty million pounds. The largest investment we received was ten thousand, but mostly it was in the £5 to £100 range. Even the sums that came through the post didn't amount to much. What it did do was create a huge amount of publicity and Frazer and I found investors who had turned up their noses at us a week or two earlier now keen to jump on the band wagon. 'Buy now while stocks last' was the cry.

Within three weeks of the launch we had raised a few thousand over the needed twenty million and earned £100,000 in fees or commission. We had also helped to put the bank on the map, and we were now in a position to look at other ventures. We were asked to finance a factory in Manchester, a hotel in Bath and a block of offices in London, all of which we did. We issued cheque books and savings accounts and paid 2.5% interest on cash on deposit. We lent money at base rate plus 3% which at that time meant 6.5% per annum.

In March Emily and I announced our intention to marry on 1 June.

Between business and the wedding plans I hardly knew what day it was. Invitations had to be sent out to the hundreds of guests we could expect and, of course, special arrangements had to be made for Mam, Da and Sion.

The suffragettes still played a large part in Emily's life and she had spent days in the Old Bailey giving moral support to Emmeline Pankhurst at her trial for bombing Lloyd George's £2,000 golf villa at Walton Heath, Surrey.

Asquith, who was then Home Secretary, introduced a Bill at the end of March allowing hunger striking suffragette prisoners out of prison if their health was at risk. It would be a temporary discharge and they would have to go back to prison once they were well again. Needless to say the women protested vehemently. Emily continued to be in the forefront of the protest but now, thank goodness, her activities were tempered by her involvement in planning for the wedding.

I received a letter from Mam saying that they would all be coming over in April and staying at least until July. The legislative commitment for my father was negligible, and it would not be increasing again until the Fall term. Sion wanted to spend some time in Europe visiting aircraft manufacturers and pilots. He had been in constant touch with many of them and was looking forward to meeting and exchanging ideas.

We were already so busy at the bank that we had hired more people to help with the day-to-day running. We were also considering starting a stockbroking arm which would manage people's investments as a portfolio.

'My idea,' I said to Frazer, over a mid-morning coffee, 'is that we actively manage the investments instead of just acting upon instructions we're given.'

'You mean that we buy and sell shares for our investors without referring to them?'

'Exactly. We can send them valuations every three or six months and charge a fee. If the funds do well it'll encourage more investments.'

'Surely that's the rub. We have to do a good job, and how do we pick the right shares?'

'We didn't do such a bad job last year,' I reminded him.

'That was different. We had a lot of inside knowledge. Hell, it was like picking apples in an overabundant orchard.'

'What were we told last night in the Club?'

'To buy shares in the Ford company as it is about to announce record profits.'

'Exactly. We're always getting insider tips. We know when things are going to happen sometimes before the directors and do you know why?' I answered my own question. 'Because we know the people with the money.'

He thought about it for a few seconds, his natural Scottish caution at odds with the possibilities. He nodded. 'I agree. How much will we charge for the service?'

I shrugged. 'I've no idea. At the moment its at the fruition stage. The next step is to work out a detailed plan. I think we'll also combine it with a stock broking department giving our clients the option of instructing us to act or leaving us to manage their money. We can also use the same department to buy and sell shares for our funds.'

He grinned. 'David, you're a Welsh wizard. I think it's a marvellous idea. We'll need somebody to oversee the whole thing.'

'Why not you or me?'

He shook his head. 'Don't talk daft, man. We don't have the expertise to run something like that. Thinking up ideas and the logistics of putting them into action are two different things. No, we must play to our strengths. Whilst we are capable of acquiring insider knowledge to give our fund managers the edge, we have to leave the paperwork to others.'

It made sense to me. 'Fund managers?'

'What?'

'You said fund managers, plural. You're already thinking big when I was thinking of a single manager for a single fund.' I grinned at him.

'Did I?' Then he grinned back. 'Actually, I did and the reason is simple. We have two or even three funds. How about a British fund and a European fund? Or some other specialist fund? What about,' Frazer was getting excited as the idea took hold and flourished in his fertile mind, 'a specialist fund for high risk or new start up businesses? Instead of just borrowing money from a bank on a loan basis, why not allow investors in to the company right at the start? At present you can only invest in companies quoted on the stock market.' Frazer was now pacing the room as the ideas began to flow.

A short while later we adjourned to the Club to begin to put some meat on the bones of the venture. Frazer scribbled notes while we tossed ideas back and forth.

It was while we were at lunch that Jake Kirkpatrick walked in.

11

WHAT A REUNION! Frazer was a little flummoxed by it all at first, but as Jake and I reminisced about our time in the Caribbean and our adventures on the *Lucky Lady* he soon became eager to learn what had happened. He and Jake also hit it off which meant we sent a message back to the bank telling the staff we would not be returning that afternoon; important business had cropped up.

'Where's Estelle?' I asked as we started on our second bottle of champagne.

'In the hotel. She sends her love. She understood that we'd need some time together. Before, as she put it, she brought some civilisation to the company.'

I nodded. 'And Dominic?'

'He's with her. They'll both see you tomorrow. David, do you remember when we met in the Gut to Throaters?' He laughed. 'By God, you were going to get your throat cut that night and no mistake.' And we were off, swapping stories back and forth, out of sequence but full of meaning to us.

I had been due to meet Emily for dinner but I sent her a message that I was unavoidably detained. A message came back in the form of John and Emily. We were well into our cups by that stage. John joined us while Emily went off to find Estelle, Dominic and the baby. She intended to move them all to John's house. Jake protested but Emily would not take no for an answer.

When she left us, with a disdainful shake of her head at the state we were getting into and at John's stated intention of catching up with us, Jake said, 'Wow! Some woman, amigo. You're going to have trouble with that one. I can tell.'

'You mean like you do with Estelle?'

He suddenly laughed uproariously. 'Thank a benign God for strong women.'

'Amen to that,' said Frazer and set us off laughing again.

Somehow we got home but I don't know how. A homing instinct was at work, according to John. It had been a long time since any of us had been as roaring drunk as we were that evening.

Jake had prospered in Spain. He owned a large ranch on the south coast and bred prize cattle and grew enough grapes to justify having his own vineyard. The combination of his hard work and Estelle's financial acumen assured their success. Dominic was proving to be something of a success as a vintner, and was now selling some of their fine Riojas to London restaurants and hotels. Our wedding gift from them was twelve dozen bottles of vintage red wine to be laid down for five year before being opened. Ideal, as Jake put it, to wet the baby's head. When I pointed out there were one or two preliminaries before a baby came along he hit me on my shoulder and said, 'That, my dear friend, will be the least of your concerns.'

Jake had been such an important part of my life only a few years earlier that I had forgotten that Mam, Dad and Sion had not met him.

They had arrived in Cardiff aboard a luxury liner two weeks earlier. They had spent this time in Cardiff and Llanbeddas, visiting friends from the past; after an absence of thirteen years there was a great deal of news to catch up on. It was a very emotional time for them; I remembered how I had felt standing over Sian's grave.

Emily and I waited nervously at Paddington railway station to meet them. 'I hope they'll like me,' she said. 'It's daunting to meet your mother-in-law for the first time.'

'Don't worry. Mam is a peach. Very strong minded, I suppose, but very protective of her family.' I paused and thought for a moment. 'We all are really.' I grinned, 'Cross one Griffiths and you cross us all.'

I paced up and down the platform with Emily on my arm. In only three weeks we were to be married in Westminster Cathedral followed by a honeymoon aboard one of John's ships, the SS Montrose, the newest and best of the fleet. We would be travelling to Cape Town in South Africa where we would remain for eight days while the ship's cargo of automobiles was landed. The ship would then take on a cargo of fruit and return to Britain. The passenger facilities on the SS Montrose were second to none and I was looking forward to the journey. Apart from anything else, I wanted to see Africa!

As I turned at the end of the platform I bumped into a beggar. I apologised and put my hand in my pocket to give him some change when he suddenly turned and limped away.

'Poor devil,' I remarked to Emily. 'Probably wounded in the Boer War. I've noticed quite a number of our lads begging for a living now that they are no longer of any use to the Army or Navy.'

'What?' said Emily. 'Oh, them. They're just trash; ignore them. I know I do and I think it's by far the best way.'

'Hmm,' I patted her hand, thoughtfully, not really listening to her. There had been something vaguely familiar about the figure but I couldn't think what it was. Just then the train pulled in and we hurried along the platform find my parents. We had yet another joyful reunion, though this time without the copious amounts of alcohol.

Mam immediately walked away with Emily, deep in conversation. Soon Emily gave a loud squeal of laughter and looked over her shoulder at me. I didn't need to be a mind-reader to know who was the topic of their conversation. Later that day Mam gave me her blessing and her complete approval of my choice of wife.

In the meantime Dad, Sion and I exchanged news and ideas about business and what we should do next. I hadn't seen either of them in nearly two years, but they hadn't changed much. Dad had grey in his hair which made him look distinguished and Sion had filled out with solid muscle. He was about two inches shorter than me but had broader shoulders and granite-like strength in his hands and arms. He had already made arrangements to visit the airfield at Biggin Hill and the new one at Heathrow and to meet a number of aircraft companies. One of the men he was planning to meet was Thomas Sopwith. We discussed the proposed loan of five thousand pounds to build a seaplane. Our shares in his company were later to be worth hundreds of thousands of pounds.

With Jake and his family staying with John, there was not sufficient room for us and so I had rented a large town house in South Audley Street for myself and the rest of my family. There would be plenty of room when the other Griffithses came from Wales, just before our wedding day.

We had dinner that night in a private room at the Savoy. John's wife was proving to be as elusive as ever and had, that morning, gone to Llandridnod Wells. If John was annoyed he didn't show it as he enjoyed a mild flirtation with my mother, much to my father's amusement.

Over port later that evening my father said, 'I want to know what's going on over here. I've been given the task to report back to Congress on the situation in Europe. How likely is war? How will it come about? Who'll start it? Can it be stopped? And I've got a million other questions. We have a very powerful lobby in America who are set on neutrality. Many of them care nothing for the old order of things and, truth to tell, would like nothing better than to see the ruling classes in Europe swept away. After all, many of them went to America in the first place to escape the tyranny of Europe. So who's going to tell me what's going on?'

We looked at John as our spokesman. 'You have to understand, Evan, that it's devilishly complex. A whole raft of attitudes and events are conspiring to create a powderkeg which can be ignited with one spark. What that spark is nobody yet knows. We're working like hell to prevent it but it seems almost as though Europe is hell-bent on a war.'

'As I understand it,' said my father, 'we have the five powers of Britain, France, Germany, Austro-Hungary and Russia at loggerheads.'

John shook his head. 'Not quite. We have the Triple Alliance on one hand and The Triple Entente on the other.'

'This is news to me. Perhaps you will be good enough to explain it?'

'Let me go through what we consider to be the position of each power and why we foresee a problem. First of all, let's take Britain. We have a treaty with Belgium that goes back to 1839. Next, we wish to preserve our naval supremacy. We're obligated to support France, of course; we have a naval agreement whereby Britain will protect the English Channel and the North Sea zones so that France can operate her fleet almost exclusively in the Mediterranean. And finally, we have a desire not to see the balance of power shift in Europe.'

'That makes sense,' said Dad, helping himself to more port. 'But none of that, none of those aims, will cause a war, surely?'

'True. But now look at Germany. She has a treaty with Austro-Hungary which she will honour whatever it costs. The Kaiser is terrified of being encircled by Britain, France and Russia – the Triple Entente. But bear in mind, that the alliance only came about because of the treaties of Germany, Austro-Hungary and Italy with each other. Each of us have been feeding off the fears and paranoia of the others. Germany also wishes to become a world power and is jealous of Britain. That should not be underestimated. The Kaiser wants to take Germany out of being only a continental power, and we believe he has ideas of world domination.'

'That's nonsense. It's too late. The world has already been carved up and nobody is going to change things,' replied Dad.

'That's not what the Kaiser and his immediate staff believe. They think that there's a lot of the world still available. Let me finish. Austro-Hungary wish to crush the Pan-Serb movement and effectively to take over Serbia once and for all. They think that will remove a huge thorn from their side. So far they've done nothing but foment unrest in the Balkans but, I have to add, they've done it extremely well. If they can dominate the Balkans by crushing Serbia they will secure Austrian control of the routes to the Aegean, which has been a long cherished ambition of theirs. It would open up their way to Africa.'

'And where does France fit in all this?'

'That's a difficult one. She is the smaller of the players in Europe, in spite of her overseas territories. She is fearful of Germany, has treaty obligations with Russia and wishes to regain Alsace and Lorraine which they lost to Germany following the Franco-Prussian wars of 1870 and 1871.'

'It sounds a real mess to me,' said Dad, shaking his head. 'How I'm going to explain it all to the folks back home I just don't know. All right, finally, what about Russia? As far as we can tell she has huge internal problems with the Bolsheviks fighting the Czarists, the Cossacks fighting everybody and the Ukrainians wanting independence.'

'That's the whole point, of course. The position of the Tsar is somewhat tenuous right now. There are semi-revolutionary murmurs sweeping the country and a good foreign war would be just the thing to avoid internal strife. Anyway, Russia doesn't want Serbia taken by the Austro-Hungarians and Russia wishes to dominate the Balkans themselves. That gives the Russians access to the Mediterranean, something they are desperate to achieve.'

'What's your prognosis?'

'We're staring disaster in the face and seem unable to prevent it. The warmongers on all sides seem determined to start a conflict and we seem to be powerless to stop it.'

'Do you want to?' asked Dad, going to the heart of the matter.

John Buchanan smiled and shook his head in mock resignation. 'Ah, Evan, that's the big question. Do we really want to prevent it happening? What if we had a war that once and for all established Britain as the major power in the world? What if we could dominate Europe like we do the rest of the world? We could establish an Empire, that will last longer than the Roman Empire did nearly two thousand years ago. We could civilise the world in our own image. English would be the dominant language and the pound sterling the currency of the civilised world.'

'John, do you believe that?'

He grinned. 'Of course I don't. I'm telling you what's being said in the corridors of power by men who should know better. People want the right to decide their own destinies. Look at Ireland. There'll be war there soon, mark my words. Better dead than slaves is the cry. No, there's a Pandora's box waiting to be opened and when it is open it will take more than we've got to get the ills of the world back in.'

Just then the ladies rejoined us, which was just as well as the conversation was taking a sombre turn. We talked in generalities and made plans to visit the theatre to see Isadora Duncan dance.

A few days later we were sitting in the bank and going through various business ideas. We were all there – myself, Dad, Sion, Angus, John and Jake. Dad turned the conversation back to the possibility of war. 'Am I out of order to suggest that if there is going to be trouble we want to ensure we don't lose out by it?'

'How do you mean?' asked Sion.

'What's going to be needed? Arms, ships, machinery of all sorts.'

'Food,' said Jake. 'If war breaks out there'll be no one to work the land. If it's Europe wide who's going to feed and clothe the people?'

'Good point,' said John. 'You know, there's a great deal we could profit from. Look at some of the banking dynasties that were established, in part at least because of the Napoleonic wars.'

We all nodded in agreement, the possibilities beginning to grow in our minds. The ideas came thick and fast and after a couple of hours we had homed in on a few. Jake was going to find as much land as possible to expand his beef herds and wheat growing operations which our bank would finance for a forty nine percent shareholding. Sion was going to look at factories making cars and trucks with the intention of offering enough cash to carry out any expansion plans they might have. Austin's in Oxford was where he was going to start.

We had hired three managers to establish investment funds, in Britain, in Europe and a third as a high risk/high reward fund. Money was beginning to trickle in as a result of our advertisements, but if we were to carry out our plans we needed it to become a flood. Angus and I would start applying ourselves to the task.

John and Dad were going to look at shipyards. 'We operate ships all over the world. If there is a war we're going to need more than we've got and more than we're producing. So why don't we build our own?'

'It'll take a great deal of money to buy a shipyard,' I said. 'Too much, if we carry out all our other plans.'

'No, it won't,' said Sion. 'Not if we do it my way.'

'And what's your way, pray?' said John.

'Not prayer, Uncle John, that's for sure,' he retorted, raising a few laughs. 'No. We find a yard that's in trouble. Start along the Medway. There are dozens of small yards, many in trouble.'

'How do you know?' I asked. 'You've only been here five minutes and you seem to know it all, little brother,' I said, acidly.

Sion grinned, taking no umbrage and unfolded that day's copy of the *Times*. 'It says so, right here.' He had the paper open at an article about the plight of dock workers in the Medway towns of Chatham, Rochester and Gillingham.

'That says nothing about the dockyards,' I said.

'Of course not. But it talks about short time working, lay-offs and a lack of orders at some yards. That's ridiculous at this time, with what's going on. The orders are all going north, to Liverpool and Glasgow. So what's their problem? I'll tell you, lack of investment. They can't compete but they do have something that's invaluable.'

'What's that?' asked John, intrigued.

'Water frontage. We need water frontage and locks. Two, maybe three locks at least. I reckon we can pick up the yard cheaply but we'll need to spend a lot on the plant. We also bring in American working practices.'

That made sense. As usual, Sion had got it in one. Like me, the others were suitably impressed with his acumen and business sense; Sion had an instinct and a flair that was remarkable.

The following day Sion asked me to go to Biggin Hill with him. As I had never been to an aerodrome before I agreed. We set off before lunch and took the road to Croydon. From there it was a short distance to Biggin Hill, the biggest aerodrome in Britain, if not the world.

As we drove across the grass Sion identified Sopwiths, Spads, Voisins and a Farman. Most of them were in different stages of construction, engines out, wings off. In one or two cases an engine was being run up and here and there a plane would be moving across the grass. Nowhere was there an aeroplane taking off or landing. I pointed this out to Sion.

He laughed. 'Of course not. They'll spend days getting the planes ready just for one short flight. We're making a lot of progress but we've still got a long way to go yet. I know we've set speed records, endurance records and flown across not only the English Channel but also the Mediterranean. But they're all one-offs.'

'We, bro'?'

'Sure, we. I'm a part of all this. I love it. I've flown a hundred times. Maybe more. I've designed and built five different planes so far.'

'You have?' I asked, surprised.

'Sure I have. The only trouble is, only one didn't break,' and he laughed.

'Which one was that?' I joined in his laughter but choked on it a few seconds later.

'That one,' he pointed. 'I call it the Griffin.'

12

'THE GRIFFIN?' I repeated, walking around the plane.

'Yes. Named after the Griffiths family, more or less. She's my own design. I took the best from all the others and put her together. Here, let me show you. We went into a nearby tent where I was introduced to two men, Peter Cazorla and his son Raphael. 'Peter was Pedro when he lived in Mexico,' explained Sion. 'I met him there a year ago when I was down on business. It turns out that he's a genius with engines. I persuaded him to move his family to St. Louis to help me with the planes.'

'It was a good move, Sion,' said Peter Cazorla. 'My family likes America and Raphael likes aeroplanes, along with me.'

The father was squat, thickset and had fingers like sausages. His son was a younger replica. Both smiled continually as though they found life one huge joke and both were brilliant mechanics as I learned with time.

'Come, let me show you what we've done,' he went on.

It turned out that after they had landed in Wales, Sion had sent them both directly to Biggin Hill and they had been there for weeks getting things ready.

Later we sat down and Sion explained. 'The best four-stroke engine in the world is probably a Ford. We've adapted it to run the propeller which effectively drags us through the air. Understand?'

I nodded. It wasn't exactly difficult.

'Good. Now we've also taken the best design in body frames. There have been dozens of different attempts to make a robust but light body. But if you analyse the best of them they haven't been.'

'Haven't been what?' I asked stupidly.

'Light. They haven't been light. What they have been is robust, but with under-powered engines for their weight, and so the results have been disappointing to say the least.'

'So what have you done?'

'The body and wings have been made of plywood and we've covered them with canvas which has been soaked in a type of glue and resin mix we call dope. I found Pedro using it to repair a hole in a truck and he told me all about the stuff.' He rapped his knuckles on the taut wing covering and then pulled at the wire struts that criss crossed between the upper and lower wings. They twanged like a bow string. 'The other important factor is smoothness. Rub your hand along this.' He was stroking the edge of the wing and I did likewise. 'See. Smooth as a baby's bottom. A Frenchman made the connection between lift and smoothness. In a paper he wrote, he said that the smooth airflow over the wings shouldn't be disrupted to give maximum lift to the plane at minimum speed. It's why we are trying to reduce the number of vertical struts between wings. We have far fewer than any other aeroplane and I think it's a reason for our success.'

'What success?' I asked, intrigued.

'Come and have a cup of coffee and I'll tell you.' At the back of the work tent was another tent, used as living quarters by the Cazorlas. 'It's safer for them both to stay here to guard the plane,' explained Sion.

'Guard the plane?' I asked, stupidly. 'What from?'

'The competition, of course. Listen David, air travel and aeroplanes are the next big business after automobiles and ships. I'm not saying they'll take the place of ships, of course I'm not. But for those people who need to be somewhere fast, or have a package or letter delivered the next day, then aeroplanes will be the way. And I want us to be at the forefront of it.'

'I see. And how do you propose achieving that?'

'Look around you. This is the most important aerodrome outside of Paris and I'm telling you we have the best plane in the world. We can reach speeds of 110 mph and easily fly to 10,000 feet. More importantly we've done something the others are still playing catch-up on.'

'And what's that?' I asked, intrigued in spite of my scepticism.

'Our maintenance costs are about ten percent of every other manufacturer. We can land and take off as often as we like. We de-coke the engine every twenty landings as opposed to five or six for the others, and we don't have anything like the breakage problems that the others do.'

'You mean engine breakdowns?'

'No I mean bits breaking off. The trouble is they aren't small bits. You'll see if you hang around long enough. Planes bounce as they are taxiing and undercarriage struts break, or they land awkwardly and a wing will tear. We've solved those problems.'

'How?'

'I've already shown you. It's in the dope. When it sets it's like a hard shell. A . . . a tortoise shell if you like. The trouble is it's brittle but the wood underneath gives it a compressive strength to complement the shear strength.' He handed me a piece of wood, like a pick axe handle, coated in the same stuff as the plane. 'Try and break that.'

I tapped it with my knuckles, pulled it against my knee and then stood up to put all my weight down on it. All that time the three of them were grinning like Cheshire cats who had got the cream. 'All right, I'm impressed,' I said, sitting down and helping myself to another coffee.

'Not half as much as you'll be when we go for a flight,' Sion said, nonchalantly.

He said it just as I put the cup to my lips. I swallowed, spluttered and spat the coffee which only added to the amusement of the others.

Sion threw me a leather hat with goggles. 'Here, put these on. I've also got a leather coat your size, specially bought for the occasion.'

Young Cazorla went into the tent, returned and handed me a brown, knee length, leather coat.

'Come on, Sion, you've got to be kidding. I'm not going up in that thing. It's not safe.'

'Yes, it is. I've flown it dozens and dozens of times.'

I allowed myself to be taken to the plane and in something of a daze I climbed in. Sion explained it all to me but I found it hard to listen. He climbed in behind me while Peter Cazorla leant in to tie up my straps.

I came out of my daze and asked him, 'What's it like? Flying?'

He shrugged. 'I have no idea, Señor.'

'No idea?'

'No, Señor. I have never been up. If God had meant us to fly surely he would have given us wings.' He laughed aloud at his joke, jumped to the ground and went round the front of the fuselage.

He swung the propeller and yelled, 'Contact.'

'Contact,' Sion yelled.

'Ignition,' he yelled.

'Ignition,' repeated Sion and Cazorla swung the propeller. There was a mighty roar, the engine caught and settled down to a deep throated roar. Young Cazorla pulled some blocks of wood out from under the wheels and he and his father took a wing each and swung us around to face down the field. We moved out, slowly.

Men all over the field stopped what they were doing to watch us. I looked back over my shoulder to see Sion grinning wildly in the seat behind me, clearly enjoying himself. He waved his hand, the two Cazorlas stepped away and suddenly we were racing along the field, bouncing over each hummock as we picked up speed. The bouncing grew more intermittent until there was a final thump and we literally bounced into the air. I was flying!

It was an unforgettable experience. We headed south to the coast, turned left and flew low along the edge of the sea. I recognised Brighton pier and then we turned left once more and headed inland. Everywhere we flew people stopped and stared, many waving. I had lost my fear and was thoroughly enjoying the experience, appreciating for the first time Sion's love of it all. A short while later we were approaching the airfield. Sion circumnavigated the field a couple of times, lined up on an imaginary line and took us down. Just before we hit the ground the engine stopped. At the time it felt as though my heart had stopped with it.

We landed with a few bounces and came to a stop after a couple of hundred yards. I sat there until young Cazorla undid my straps and I climbed stiffly out.

'What, what happened to the engine?' I croaked.

'Nothing. I switched it off,' Sion replied.

'What! In heavens name why did you do such a stupid thing?' I yelled. 'You almost gave me a coronary.'

'It's not stupid,' Sion said, stiffly. 'It's a precaution. Look, let me show you.' He pointed to different parts of the plane. 'Petrol is highly inflammable. It's gravity fed from here to the engine, here. If we crash the petrol can spill onto the hot engine and cause a fire. By turning off the tap here,' he pointed again, 'we use up the petrol in this pipe and, in the event of a crash, no petrol can get to the engine. So, no fire,' he finished.

'You could have warned me,' I protested.

Sion grinned. 'What and spoiled our fun? Incidentally, I heard what Peter said to you. About his not flying. He's got almost as many hours as I have in this thing, and Raphael's not far behind us.'

The Cazorlas were doing their Cheshire cat act again and then Peter burst out laughing, so did his son and so did Sion. Although I was the butt of their joke, I saw the funny side and began to laugh as loudly as they were.

A number of the other workers gathered around the plane and soon they were all in a deep technical discussion about the plane. Sion and his two mechanics said a great deal without imparting any useful information.

Later that day we were making our way back to London when we stopped in a country pub for something to eat. 'What you haven't seen and what I can't show you is how we fit guns to the plane.'

'Guns?' I asked, stupidly.

'You know, those things that kill people.'

'I know what a gun is, you fool. But I don't get it. Why would you put a gun on an aeroplane?'

'Think about it, David. A moving platform in the sky able to fire down on troops; even to drop bombs on them. It will be the ultimate killing machine. And if war comes to Europe then the aeroplane will play a big part in it.'

'I'm not so sure. You said yourself that they're unreliable, can't carry much and can't stay in the air for very long. I think you're overestimating their usefulness.'

'Rubbish. Mark my words, they'll be used for all sorts of things – reconnaissance, shooting, bombing, message carrying. Hell, loads of things. I've spent some time looking at war and technology.'

'War and what?'

'Technology. Throughout the ages inventions and developments have suddenly blossomed at times of war. Desperation spurs people onwards to achieve things they never thought possible. Money is no longer the issue.'

'What is, then?'

'Killing your enemies as quickly as possible,' was the sober reply.

I thought about it and was forced to agree. 'So what are you suggesting?'

'I'm suggesting we form a company to develop the Griffin and then manufacture the plane, so it'll be ready for war. I've got a load of ideas which I'd like to try out and though I could do it all using my own money it'll take me years as opposed to months if we applied some business acumen.'

'Not forgetting business money,' I added, dryly.

'That too,' Sion grinned.

'Let me think about it.' Sion began to protest but I raised my hand and he stopped to listen. 'I think it merits a discussion at the bank.'

We arrived back in London and I parked the car outside the house. As I closed the door and walked around the car I bumped into a scruffily dressed man, apologised and watched him limp away.

The day before the wedding came sooner than I had expected. I had hardly seen Emily, what with the pressure of business and her involvement with the preparations. Luckily, she, Mam and Estelle had everything under control and we men were merely given instructions. It suited everyone.

My stag night was enjoyable though certainly not riotous. We had dinner at the United Services Club while the women stayed at home. The situation in Europe and our businesses dominated the conversation. More plans were laid and I was able to tell Sion that the bank had agreed to use the money in the high risk investment fund to finance the new company. Sion was excited about the future and we eagerly discussed the new company.

'What's it to be called?' asked Dad.

'Griffiths Aviation,' Sion replied.

'What does aviation mean?' Jake asked.

Sion smiled and said, 'It means flying heavier-than-air aircraft. Which is appropriate, don't you think?'

The rest of the evening passed convivially; business and finance was not mentioned again.

As I had promised Emily I was in bed shortly after eleven o'clock that night. I was dozing when the door opened and a ghostly figure entered the room. It sat on the side of my bed and caressed my cheek with soft lips. My eyes flew open, my senses came pounding back to me and a voice whispered, 'My darling, I couldn't wait.'

Emily stayed with me until nearly five o'clock before she went back to her own room. I hadn't even been aware that she was staying in the house but she had made some excuse or other and, as was so often the way, she got what she wanted.

It was after ten o'clock when Sion woke me to tell me that we were being banished round the corner to John's place as Emily was on the premises. 'According to Mam it's bad luck to see your bride before the ceremony. So we go out the back way and meet them at the church or, I should say, Abbey.'

By ten minutes to midday we were standing at the alter. The Abbey was packed with relations and friends from all over the world. At exactly one minute to the hour the organ struck up the wedding march and Emily started down the aisle on John's arm. She looked breathtaking in her white dress, her train carried by four young cousins in matching lilac dresses. Preceding her were two page boys, embarrassed and clearly wishing they were elsewhere. Seeing the costumes they were wearing I couldn't say that I blamed them.

Emily stopped at my side and the ceremony began. Sion handed me the ring and thirty minutes later we were walking out into the bright sunlight of a beautiful June day. The photographer took an age but finally he said he had finished. We had a horse-drawn carriage to take us to the Savoy whilst the remainder of our guests followed in taxis and cars.

When we arrived there were dozens of street urchins waiting for us and as was customary I threw handfuls of small coins. I noticed a handful land at the feet of a beggar but he made no attempt to pick any up whilst the children scampered here and there for the farthings and half pennies.

After the champagne reception we sat down to a superb seven course meal that went on late into the afternoon. Speeches were made, innumerable toasts were drunk and then it was time for us to leave.

Emily and I had our clothes ready in rooms upstairs. Together we left the dining room and went to get changed, hurrying when we noticed the time. The ship had a departure time and would wait for no one. Our luggage had already been sent on and all that was required was to take a taxi to Waterloo station and catch the train for Southampton.

Emily wore a grey travelling suit with mother of pearl buttons and a pert hat on one side of her head. She looked beautiful as we returned to the dining room to say goodbye. Outside on the pavement the sea of urchins was still there, as we expected, and whilst Emily swept past them I paused to throw more money.

Suddenly, the sound of gunfire was loud in my ears. I fell to the pavement in shock, blood pouring from me. I crawled to Emily while screams and yells abounded around me. She was lying in a pool of blood, her hat still perched on her head. I cradled her in my arms, tenderly.

'Emily, Emily, darling.'

'David, oh David,' she whispered. 'I'm sorry to spoil our day. Look, even the weather is turning against us. See how the sky is darkening.' I looked up at the clear blue sky, the sun still shining brightly. When I looked back down she was gone. Von Ludwig I thought, and then I fainted.

BOOK 2

Sion's Story

13

SION WAS STANDING just behind his brother when the shots were fired. He saw David and Emily fall and knew the others would look after them. He saw the beggar with the gun and yelled. The beggar turned and began to run away, his limp obvious for all to see. Sion chased after him, shouting at him to stop. An open touring car was parked along the street with three other men in it.

'Stop him,' yelled Sion. 'He shot my brother.' To Sion's astonishment the beggar leapt into the car, which pulled away with a loud roar. Nonplussed, Sion stopped and looked for a taxi. Anything. A car screeched to a halt beside him and it took Sion a second to realise it was Frazer's. He leaped into the car and Frazer shot off, his foot pressing the accelerator hard down to the floorboards.

'Go left. They just went left.'

'I see them,' said Frazer. 'Keep them in sight if you can while I concentrate on the road. Don't take your eyes off them. The last thing we need is to hit an innocent bystander and get stopped by the police.'

Sion glanced at the speedometer as they raced along Park Lane. It was showing over sixty miles an hour. 'What's the speed limit?'

'Ten miles per hour. Don't let me lose them, Sion.'

'Turn left at the top.'

'They're going through the park,' Frazer replied.

In the park the car in front was scattering strollers and children in all directions. A policeman, alerted by the first car, stepped into the path of the car in which Frazer and Sion were travelling and held up his hand. Frazer put his hand to the horn and held it there. Lucky for the policeman he jumped out of the way with nothing injured other than his pride. Behind them they could hear the sound of whistles.

'How are David and Emily?' yelled Sion.

'Don't know. I didn't stop to look. I figured there were enough people to look after them. I need to catch those swine.'

'Me too. Who did this? Why?'

Frazer shook his head slowly. 'I don't know. There's nobody . . .' he trailed off.

'There's nobody what?' prompted Sion.

'I know who it is. In the car. The man who fired the shots. It has to be Karl von Ludwig.'

'Who?'

While driving like a madman Frazer told Sion about their escapades in Europe and how Emily had shot von Ludwig in the leg. 'That's why he was limping. It was von Ludwig.'

'They're pulling away,' yelled Sion. 'Faster.'

'Sion, I can keep up with them on the bends but not on the straight. Their car's faster than this one. Here, can you use this?' Frazer handed Sion his Webley 45.

Expertly, Sion checked the magazine and said, 'Get me close enough for a clear shot and you'll see how well I can use it.' Grimly, he held on to the dashboard as the car swerved round corners, narrowly missing other road users and gaining not an inch on the car they were chasing. And so it went on, mile after mile. It was the aeroplane in the sky that alerted Sion to where they were.

'Angus,' yelled Sion, 'up ahead there's a turning into a field. Go in there.'

'What? Don't be crazy man. We'll lose them for definite.'

'I haven't time to argue. Just do as I say. Pull in here. Now.' He screamed the last word and Frazer swerved into the field and slowed down. 'Don't slow down. Faster. Down there,' he gestured with the gun. 'And don't hit anybody or smash into any planes.'

They stopped next to the Griffin. Sion leapt out and yelled, 'Peter, Raphael come here. I need you.'

Father and son ran round from behind the tent. 'The plane. Quick. I want to be airborne in two minutes.'

The two men rushed to the plane and pulled away the chocks. While they turned her around Sion ran into the tent and rummaged through his belongings. He hauled out a gun case and handed it to Frazer. 'Can you use this?'

Frazer opened the case and hefted the rifle. 'American made Springfield M1903A4, a sniper's rifle. Sure, I know it well.'

'Good. You'll need it. The scope is in this box,' Sion handed Frazer another box, 'and is zeroed in. We're trying to adapt the gun and sight for the plane but we haven't managed it yet. Here, you'll need this.' Sion threw him the leather coat worn by David while he shrugged into his own. 'Here's a box of shells. Come on.'

They rushed round to the plane. Peter had the engine running and was climbing out of the cockpit when Sion climbed up the other side. 'Peter, once we're airborne, I want you to go and find a telephone. Ring the Savoy Hotel in London. Get hold of my father. Tell him we're in pursuit of the men who shot David and Emily and that we're using the Griffin. Tell him the culprit is . . . who?'

'A man named von Ludwig,' said Frazer.

'You got that?' Sion asked.

'I got it, Sion. Good hunting.'

While Sion strapped himself in Raphael helped Frazer.

Five minutes after turning into the field they were in the air. Sion quickly gained height and turned towards the road. He tapped Frazer on the shoulder and handed him a pair of binoculars. From the air everything looked different but it took only a few minutes to spot the car they were after in the distance.

Frazer could see that the car was now approaching Westerham; it was only a short distance to Sevenoaks. If the men in the car realised their pursuers were in an aeroplane then all they would need do was stop in Sevenoaks and wait for the plane to land due to lack of fuel before continuing their journey. Or wait in the town until nightfall, now less than an hour away.

Sion understood the problem and yelled at Frazer above the noise of the engine. 'We'll go for them now. I'll fly right alongside them, waggle my wings. You wave to them. Lull them into a false sense of security. Understand?'

Frazer nodded. Sion dropped out of the sky and swooped over the car. Frazer waved like a mad thing at what he saw was four men who, hesitatingly at first, but then enthusiastically waved back.

As he swooped back into the sky Sion yelled, 'I'm going to drop down by them and fly alongside. Wave and, as soon as you think you can, shoot them.'

Frazer held up his thumb. He realised that he would get an opportunity for a clear shot if the men thought that they were on an innocent flying jaunt. Frazer had no doubt that the men would be armed and that a fusillade of shots at the aeroplane, before he could fire, could have dire consequences. Sion flew back down and throttled right back. The aeroplane was just above stalling speed, less than thirty yards from the car. Frazer had loaded the weapon with five rounds and had fixed the scope. The driver was concentrating on the road but the other three were looking at them, pointing. Suddenly Frazer lifted the rifle, took aim and fired all in one smooth movement. Pandemonium broke out in the car. The bullet hit the driver in the head, killing him instantly. Frazer had already quickly and smoothly changed his aim and shot another of the men before the car swerved out of control and smashed into a tree. Sion increased speed, flew round three sides of a square and turned to land on the road.

He taxied up to the crashed car, stopped the engine and he and Frazer leapt out. Carefully they approached the car, which was now lying on its side. The four bodies had been flung from the wreckage, the two with bullet wounds were dead. The other two were injured and unconscious.

Frazer stirred one of the bodies with his foot. 'This is him. Von Ludwig. Do you recognise him?'

'Sure. He's the one who shot them. Help me search them,' said Sion.

Apart from bundles of cash and weapons the only other thing they found of interest were the passports belonging to the four men. 'Oh, hell,' said Frazer, looking at one of the documents.

'What is it?'

'All four men are army officers. Two lieutenants and two captains.'

'So? Who cares? They're murdering scum.'

'I agree. The only problem is von Ludwig is the military attaché at the German embassy.'

'I don't care. He can hang just the same.'

'No he can't, Sion. He's got diplomatic immunity. He won't even stand trial.'

'What! Rubbish! After what he did he deserves to hang.'

'He might deserve it but he won't. I can't imagine von Ludwig or his government waiving his immunity rights to stand trial. Believe me, where he comes from von Ludwig will be considered a hero. Hell, David knocked down the Kaiser and Emily crippled von Ludwig. Justice will have been done, according to the Germans.'

'We'll see about that,' said Sion, lifting Frazer's Webley, cocking it and aiming it at von Ludwig's head. He hesitated while Frazer looked on with interest, making no attempt to stop him. Still Sion hesitated.

'It's easy to kill a man when in hot pursuit; but in cold blood it's a different thing altogether,' said Frazer, with compassion.

They both heard a car pull up and two policemen climbed out. It took some time to explain what had happened, but once they had done so they were allowed to leave on condition that they reported to the police station in Sevenoaks. A short while later Frazer and Sion were back in the air and returning to the airfield.

At the airfield the two men rushed to find Peter Cazorla, wanting to know the situation with David and Emily but all he could tell them was that they were in the hospital. Sion went over to the lit brazier and began to throw papers onto the hot coals.

'What's that you're burning?' asked Frazer.

'Their papers. Passports and other things I found on them. The money's in my pocket.'

'What good do you think that will do?'

Sion looked at Frazer and said heavily, 'Not a lot. But it's all I can do right now. It'll make their lives a little more difficult, that's all. Of course,' he added, with a bitter smile, 'it may not be necessary if the scum die from the accident.'

'I don't think so, somehow. Come on, we'd better get to Sevenoaks and find a phone.'

They bade farewell to the Cazorlas and drove to the police station. Once they were there they discovered that the two Germans were recovering in a cell and demanding that the police contact their embassy. Sion left Frazer to talk to the police and went to the cells.

Looking through the bars of the cell he said, 'Good evening, von Ludwig.'

'So you know who I am. I demand to be let out of this prison immediately. I have diplomatic immunity. I demand you release me.'

'You do? But I thought you were a homeless beggar. Look at your clothes. Where are your papers?'

Von Ludwig made the mistake of coming too close to the bars and snarling at Sion. 'I don't care for your tone and I don't care who you are. But you are making a grave error. I will make so much trouble for you your head will swim.'

Sion reached through the bars and grabbed von Ludwig by the head and pulled it with all his strength against the bars. His grip tightened as von Ludwig struggled to break free. 'My name is Griffiths, you scum. That was my brother and sister-in-law you shot. You may be able to prove you have diplomatic immunity, but your friend can't. You should be hanged for your crimes and he should go to prison for a long time. As it is, I don't know what will happen.' Von Ludwig had stopped struggling when Sion told him his name. 'But mark my words. I'll kill you if my brother dies. I had you in my sights but I couldn't do it. Now I know I can, you filth.' With that he thrust von Ludwig away from the bars and he went sprawling onto the floor.

Von Ludwig glared, his face filled with hate, at Sion, 'Neither you nor your family worry me. I hope the bitch is dead. And your brother. I was to represent my country in the next Olympic games but she left me lame. And it was the fault of your accursed brother. I spent a long time plotting my revenge and, with the Kaiser's help I have had it. I will be out of here and back in Germany before you know it Griffiths.'

'I don't think so, somehow,' said Frazer, joining Sion. 'You cannot prove who you are. We choose not to believe you. A trial will be held soon and after it you will hang.' Unfortunately, Sion knew it was not as easy as that. If the embassy discovered where von Ludwig was, he would be identified and released.

Sion and Frazer walked out of the cell block. A sergeant greeted them, giving each of them a cup of tea, and invited them to join him in a small office.

'Well, gentlemen, I must say this is a pretty kettle of fish you've landed me with. The Police Commissioner himself is giving instructions. I gather those swine killed a friend of yours?'

To Sion's horror Frazer nodded and then saw Sion's face. 'Not David, Sion. I phoned John. David's alive, Emily is dead. David is in hospital with two bullet wounds neither of which are life threatening.

He lost a lot of blood but some rest and good food and he'll be up and about in no time.'

'Poor David,' said Sion, sadly. 'He never seems to get much luck with his choice of women. What's to happen to those two?'

'Interesting situation that.' Frazer looked at the sergeant and decided he had better not say anything else. 'Sergeant, did you understand your orders?'

'Yes, sir. My men are out there now clearing up. The two dead bodies will be buried in unmarked graves. Don't worry, sir. When I explain that they are German spies and that they shot dead a lady they'll keep mum all right. What about those two?'

'A wagon will appear for them tomorrow. They'll be taken to London where they will stand trial as spies. With luck, they shall hang sooner rather than later.'

The two men left the police station and found a local hotel. It was a very sombre dinner they had, followed by too many drinks in the bar.

The next morning after breakfast they returned to the Police Station. The sergeant who had been on duty the night before greeted them. 'They are demanding to have their embassy told where they are. The one with the scar on his face is claiming diplomatic immunity.'

'That doesn't surprise me,' said Frazer. 'We're going back to the cells. Please call us when the wagon gets here.'

Frazer and Sean stood at the bars and looked at the two men, huddled under blankets, their heads bent.

'I demand that my embassy be told where I am,' said von Ludwig, looking up at the implacable faces staring in at them.

'Your embassy will not be told of your whereabouts,' said Sion. 'We've come to tell you that the young lady, Emily, is dead. But my brother lives.'

Von Ludwig looked back at Sion and said, 'What a pity. Next time I will get him as well.'

'There won't be a next time,' said Frazer. 'You are both going to London where you will stand trial. You will then be hanged.'

'You fools. You cannot hang me. I keep telling you that I have diplomatic immunity. Let me out now, before this farce goes too far.'

Sion shook his head in mock sorrow. 'Von Ludwig, you're not listening. We don't believe you are who you say you are. You are a tramp, a hobo, who killed a lady. You smuggled yourself to Britain from Germany for some reason. You're a spy, pretending to be a tramp – and so on, and so on. You're going to be hanged and I'll be there to see it,' said Sion.

Within the hour the two Germans were thrown unceremoniously into the back of a police wagon and taken back to London. Sion left Frazer to deal with them while he went to find his family.

Four days later David was allowed out of hospital. He attended Emily's funeral in a wheel chair but recovered quickly and was able to walk when he went to see von Ludwig in his cell. Before he did he gave some instructions that were promptly carried out.

Sion stood behind his brother as they stared at von Ludwig in his cell.

'I won't be here long, Griffiths. As soon as my government knows I am here I will be released.'

Without a word David handed over a newspaper folded to the third page. Von Ludwig took it, read it, and let out a howl of rage. 'You won't get away with this.' Von Ludwig was shaking with fear and rage.

'I already have,' said David quietly.

'As soon as the body is examined they will know it's not me. They'll know. The leg. They'll be able to tell from the leg.'

Mirthlessly David grinned and drew a gun the cocking of which made a sinister sound in the enclosed cell. He pointed it at von Ludwig's leg and pulled the trigger. The hammer smashed down on an empty chamber and von Ludwig collapsed in terror, holding his knee. 'You swine,' he whispered. 'You filthy swine.'

'At least I am not a lady killer. So you see, you will stand trial, and you will be hanged. Both of you. Good day to you both.' David touched the rim of his hat in a mock salute and he and his brother walked out into the fresh air of a late June day.

'I enjoyed that almost as much as I would have if I'd had a bullet in the chamber.'

'How did you manage to pull it off?' asked Sion.

'What? Oh, sorry, Sion, I should have told you. I called in the biggest favour I could. The two dead Germans weren't buried. They were still in the morgue. Angus arranged an artistic accident with the car and the bodies were burnt beyond recognition. There were a few papers in a case at the side of the road identifying the two bodies as those two in there.'

'And the real bodies?'

'Who cares? They're dead and gone to hell. Maybe somebody will mourn them but not me.'

'And the leg?'

'Frazer thought of it. He fired a shot into one of the legs of the corpse. The coroner's report identified the bodies on the evidence supplied and the bodies were shipped to the German Embassy to be sent home.'

'What's going to happen next?'

'Next? There'll be a military trial before an army provost. Then they'll be taken to Dover Castle and hanged.'

'Why Dover?' asked Sion, intrigued.

'It's where these things are done,' replied his brother dryly. 'Right, I have other things to do. That was my entertainment for the day.'

'Are you all right?' asked Sion, concern for his brother etched in his face and voice.

David shrugged. 'I feel empty inside. So,' he clapped his brother on the shoulder, 'I shall work as hard as you and build an empire. And destroy another.'

'What do you mean by that?'

'The Kaiser made a mistake sending von Ludwig after us. I am now declaring my own war on Germany and, believe me, I shan't rest until I have my revenge.'

'Don't be daft, man,' said Sion. 'How can you declare war on Germany?'

'Economic war. I already have a few ideas I mean to put into action. As they say in the newspapers, watch this space.'

'Can I give you a lift? I'm going back to the office.'

'What? Oh, no, thanks. I'm going to Biggin Hill. I'll tell Peter and Raphael about our plans and then I'll go looking for a site. By the way, how have Dad and John got on with finding a shipyard?'

'Like you said, there's plenty of opportunities along the Medway. In reality, we're spoilt for choice. Where are you going to look?'

Sion grinned. 'Nowhere.' Then seeing the look on his brother's face he added, 'I don't need to. I've already found a place.'

'Already? Where?'

'Pretty obvious really. A farm next to Biggin Hill. It's got the farmhouse and a number of outbuildings and about one hundred acres of land. It's to the north of the present site and it's exactly what I want.'

'That was a bit of luck, wasn't it?'

'Luck my foot,' retorted Sion, 'I knew I could buy it.' Seeing the scepticism on David's face he explained. 'I went around the area talking to the farmers about milk yields.'

'About what?'

'Milk yields. Believe it or not, that's the amount of milk a cow will produce in a day. There was a little local difficulty in Pittsburgh about the effect the aeroplanes were having on the cows. The noise frightens them half to death and they react by not producing milk. Okay, for most of the States it doesn't matter as most cows are raised for beef, but for the dairy herds it's different. Anyway, at the Hill, as it's called, the planes usually take off to the west or north because of the prevailing wind. So that's where I went. There are a dozen farms in the area all they are all complaining about the drop in milk production. One of the farms is owned by a couple who wish to retire. Hence the luck I told you about. They wanted to sell it as a going concern as they wanted their animals looked after. However, I was able to strike a deal with them that suits everybody.'

'What's the deal?'

'We'll pay the rate for a working farm. They keep the animals and sell them separately to other farmers in the area which will increase their profits by nearly twenty percent. They're happy and we're happy. The site's ideal for what we want. The land is well drained which is very important as it stops the ground being churned into mud too easily and we'll have access to trained labour when the time comes.'

David nodded, impressed. As often happened, his younger brother had taught him a new trick. 'Sounds good. Has the contract been signed yet?'

'No. It'll be signed tomorrow at Sevenoaks, at the solicitors. I'll need a cheque.'

'Don't worry, you'll have one drawn on the bank's account. Anything else you need?'

'Nope, that's it. Just one thing. What are we going to do about America?'

'I don't understand. What needs doing?'

'Dad and Mam will be returning soon. They're going to Washington. We've a very good and very substantial business in the States. I know, I built it up. Neither of us is interested in wholesale distribution, but we are interested in what we're doing here,' he explained and went on, 'So what's to be done? Are you going to go back? Do I go back? Do we leave it all to somebody else? If we do how do we control it? David, there're a few hundred more questions like that.'

David nodded, thoughtfully. He'd been away for so long he hadn't given much thought to the American business. He was suddenly aware of the substantial income he received for doing nothing, an income which had allowed him to subsidise his life-style in London. 'Is Sonny up to the job?' David was referring to one of their senior managers.

'I think so, on a day-to-day basis. We've got two people who seem to be able to keep the books, one in St. Louis and the other in New York. We could promote one of them to be, what's it called, Financial Director?'

David nodded, thinking furiously. 'Which one would we promote?'

'Emily would have loved this,' said Sion. 'A Miss Judith Harte. Oh, sorry, I didn't mean . . .' Sion lapsed into embarrassed silence.

David smiled sadly at his brother. 'It's all right. You can mention her all you like. I need to mention her, I need to talk about her. Somehow it keeps her alive in my head, and I need that right now. And you're right, she would have loved it.'

'Well, anyway, I think Judith's got what it takes. She's a suffragette in New York, tough minded, in her thirties and single.'

They discussed other aspects of the business as they strolled back to their respective cars. 'Okay, we're agreed,' said Sion. 'Now all we need do is persuade Mam and Dad.'

To Sion's surprise David shook his head. 'No, we don't. We need to persuade John, who can persuade Mam and Dad. Leave that to me. Dad can then sort it out when he returns to America, and we can concentrate on what we're doing here.'

Sion laughed. 'A great idea. Okay, I'll see you later.' Sion climbed into his car and headed for Biggin Hill, his mind flitting between ideas he planned to implement and worries about the design of the Griffin.

At the airfield he found the two Cazorlas in a foul mood. During the night somebody had tried to sneak into their tent and steal their supply of the dope they used on the plane. It was only due to the fact that Raphael had answered a call of nature that the theft had been prevented. The thief had escaped across the fields but they were sure he was one of the men from a contingent of French aviators who were based on the other side of the aerodrome. Father and son had spent the night armed and patrolling their area.

'Don't worry about it,' said Sion, 'we're moving soon.'

'Moving, Señor? Moving where?' asked Raphael.

Sion explained what he had done. The two men became excited and began to tell Sion some additional ideas they had. For the remainder of that day and well into the night the three of them worked on their plans.

The following morning a messenger arrived from the bank with a cheque and Sion left for Sevenoaks, where he drew up outside the solicitor's offices.

The farmer and his wife were already there, as eager as he to conclude the deal. The documents were signed, the cheque handed over and, after a glass of sherry they parted, the farmer to organise the sale of his livestock and his wife to start packing. The farm had been in the family for two hundred years and it had always been their intention to hand the farm down to their son. Unfortunately, he had been killed in the Boer war at Mafeking and the couple's heart had gone out of farming. They planned to take it easy for what was left of their lives and retire to a cottage in Sevenoaks near the wife's sister.

Satisfied with his morning's work Sion returned to the field and twenty minutes later was flying south towards the English Channel. He revelled in the freedom that flight seemed to impart and began to put the plane through its paces. After diving down to sea level and climbing in an almost vertical line to eight thousand feet he levelled off and headed out to sea. When he was away from the land, his heart in his mouth, Sion put the plane into a shallow dive. As it picked up speed to one hundred and thirty knots he pulled back on the stick.

The plane soared upwards like a bird. Sion sagged heavily into the straps holding him in, the weight on his shoulders eased as he continued round in a circle and then he was flying straight and level. He had looped the loop! He was the first pilot ever to have done so and he let out a whoop of delight. It worked! The petrol was held in a tank behind the pilot's head, and was fed to the engine by gravity. When the plane manoeuvred violently, particularly when pilots tried to loop the loop, petrol failed to reach the engine and it cut out. Restarting was difficult, often did not work and the plane usually crashed. Sion and the Cazorlas had been working on a small pump which cut in when air and not petrol flowed to the engine. The engine hadn't even stuttered as he had gone round.

When Sion landed back at the airfield an anxious Cazorla snr. asked, 'Well? Did it work?'

Sion grinned and danced a short war-dance. 'It was brilliant, just like we said it would be. A shallow dive then whoom, up and over.'

The two Cazorlas joined in Sion's war dance.

14

THE NEXT FEW months were a busy time for Sion. He moved into the farmhouse and started to redesign the outbuildings. The old milking parlour housed the offices and the barn became the hangar. After a week of trying to make it all fit together efficiently Sion pulled the lot down and started with a cleared site.

While that was being done he redesigned the house to include two bathrooms as well as three bedrooms. But then he had a problem with Peter Cazorla.

'Sion, you know we were happy to follow you here, but I have not seen my wife and the other children for months. I need to know how long we will be staying, before we return to St. Louis.'

Sion looked at his right hand man, aghast. In his single-minded quest to build a first class plane it simply hadn't occurred to him that Peter would want, no, would need, his wife. It was a huge problem and he needed to sort it out quickly.

'Would they come here to live?' he asked.

'I don't know. Probably. Possibly. I will have to ask my wife. But when you say *here* what do you mean? In England, in this house, with us, what?'

'I'll tell you what I'll do. You have the house for you and your family. I can arrange something for me next to the offices or in the hangar. We have the workmen here now, so we can do what we like. You'll have three bedrooms, two bathrooms, a dining room, lounge, kitchen and a garden. You'll be able to persuade her to come for all this, won't you?'

'And the weather?'

'That I can't arrange. It's colder and wetter than back home but,' Sion shrugged, 'a lot more interesting.'

'Okay. I'll go and fetch her.'

In spite of trying to persuade him otherwise, Peter Cazorla was not to be moved. Sion arranged for him to leave a few days later, hoping to see him within six or eight weeks. In the meantime he and Raphael got on with the alterations to the house and with supervising the erection of the new building. They also spent some time trying to work out a means of fitting the plane with a gun that could be fired when the plane was pointed at a target. The first thing they did was build another fuselage with an engine and propeller fitted but without wings. This was to be the platform from which they would fire the gun.

The original design was to fit a sight along the top and point the gun out of the bottom of the fuselage on a long tripod, so when the gun was fired it would miss the propeller. They worked out a system so that at one hundred yards a bullet would hit its target.

After the gun was first fired, Sion looked at the small hole in the target and remarked, 'Raphael, that's about as much use as a hole in the head. In fact, it's only of any use if it makes a hole in the head of the enemy pilot. We need to fit a machine gun. I'm going to the armaments depot at Chatham and see if they've got anything we can use.'

Before he went to Chatham Sion drove to London to see David and Angus Frazer. At the bank he found that David was abroad but that Frazer was available. Sion was shown into his office where he waited, accepting a cup of coffee while Frazer finished a phone call.

'Where's David gone?' asked Sean.

'Chasing after von Ludwig,' was the astonishing reply which caused Sion to jerk forward and spill his coffee.

'Damn. What the hell did you say?'

'Haven't you read the papers?'

'Not for weeks. I've been stuck down in Kent getting things sorted. What do you mean he's chasing von Ludwig?'

'Von Ludwig escaped three days ago.'

'How in the name of all that's precious did that happen?'

Frazer shrugged. 'I think I'll have the proof I'm looking for later this afternoon. The papers got most of it wrong, needless to say, but they got enough of it right to be very worrying. How much do you know about the trial and everything?'

'Nothing. Like I told you, I've been busy. I did think that I might be called as a witness to identify the killer as von Ludwig but I heard nothing.'

Frazer nodded. 'It wasn't necessary. Von Ludwig admitted the shooting and tried to justify it on the grounds of being shot by Emily and the attack by David on the Kaiser. He described it as besmirching the honour of Germany. Anyway, with his admittance of the offence he was found guilty and sentenced to be hanged.'

'When was that?'

Frazer looked at a calendar on the wall behind him and said, 'Exactly ten days ago.'

'So what happened?'

'I believe he bribed one of the guards to contact the German embassy. After the trial the two men were taken back to prison and then a few days later taken by sealed truck to Dover. Or rather, that was their destination but they didn't arrive. The truck was ambushed within three miles of their destination, one policeman was killed and another seriously injured and von Ludwig escaped. The injured man is in hospital. I'm going to see him this afternoon. You can come with me, if you like.' Sion nodded. 'Good. We might learn more. The other man with von Ludwig was killed, I think by the policeman who is now in the hospital.'

'So where does David fit into all of this?'

'As soon as we heard what happened, which was within hours of the event, he was off chasing von Ludwig.'

'Where's he gone?' asked Sion, showing his anxiety.

'I don't know. Germany, I presume, but I haven't heard from him since he left.'

'The bloody fool,' Sion exploded. 'He should have just let it be, not gone off half-cocked. Right, let's go and see this policeman and find out what he has to say.'

At St. Swithin's Hospital they found the constable sitting up in bed, a bandage round his head and another round his shoulder.

'How are you feeling?' asked Frazer.

'Bloody awful, sir. Me head hurts and me arm. I can't lift it. I'll probably lose me job now and then what will me and the wife do?'

Frazer nodded and then said, 'I may be able to help you there. Do you feel up to talking?'

'Yes, sir. But I told that other one all about it. The old gent.'

'The old gent? Do you mean Mr Buchanan?'

'Yes, that's him, sir. He came in with the Commissioner. I told him all I could remember.'

'We appreciate that. It's just you may have recalled some more that might help us find the man who escaped.'

'Right, sir. Well, it was like this. Me and Brown saw the prisoners safely into the truck and made sure they were shackled. After we left Brown was real nervous. He kept fiddling with his gun and night stick and looking all over the place. I kept telling him to relax, he made me so nervous.' Sion nodded. 'Anyways, we had instructions not to stop before we got to Dover, so we didn't.' Sion looked at Frazer as the invalid continued. 'Then, about four or five miles from the town a car came out of a side street and tried to ram us. Well, I could see what they were trying to do and I swerved and they missed.'

'Good. Well done,' said Frazer.

'I then started going like the clappers with the car chasing behind us. That was when Brown shoved his gun in my face and told me to stop or else. I asked him what he thought he was playing at and not to be so bloody stupid. And he said it's too late for that. He'd taken the money and we had to stop. I said I wouldn't and that was when he hit me. Left me groggy like,' the constable put his hand up to his head, grimacing. 'So anyways I stop. The car comes up with three men in it all with guns. They force us out. Not that it was difficult to do,' he said bitterly. 'Not with Brown on their side. Anyways, they takes me keys and opens the doors and they let those two Germans out.'

Sion nodded. 'There was nothing else you could do,' he said.

'Just as they are rushing away I pulls me own gun which they seem to have forgot about. I hit one of them. Killed him, I'm told. It was one of the prisoners.' He paused, shaking his head at the memory. 'Brown shoots me and I shoots him dead. Only he'd shot me in the arm and I fall down. The Germans don't wait to see what's happened. They jumps in the car and drives away. We was late and so a patrol comes looking for us later. Guess I was lucky, otherwise I'd be dead now.'

'I see,' said Frazer. 'That's very interesting. Thank you. I have to say you were very brave.'

'Thank you, sir. Just doing me duty, that's all,' he mumbled.

'I think not,' said Frazer, his tone suddenly changed, 'because you have told us a complete pack of lies from beginning to end. You see, there are certain facts you don't know about.'

'What! Rubbish! I'm telling you the truth, sir. Honest I am.' The man pushed himself back in his pillows, fear etched in his face.

Frazer shook his head. 'While you were unconscious I have had a doctor look at your wounds and the wounds of the dead constable and the dead German. You did kill Brown, there's no doubt about that. You were driving and you could have stopped as soon as the car appeared. Brown tried to make you drive on, which was when he hit your head with his gun. Then he jumped out of the truck and fired on the Germans at least six times. I know because his gun was empty. He had a Webley .455 WG model. They don't make them anymore but there's a lot of them about and it makes a very big hole if it hits anybody. The Germans got the keys from you and let the two prisoners out. Brown killed one of them, blew half his head away in fact. You on the other hand had a French Lebel which is used by the French police and fires only .32 ammunition. Most of the metropolitan police force now use it. The bullet makes a much smaller hole than the Webley, and you used it to shoot Brown in the back. Indeed, it seems you only fired one shot. Your bullet wound is consistent with a shot fired from a German Arminus pistol of which we found quite a few spent cartridge cases.'

'It's lies. All lies,' the constable cringed back in the bed, fear now etched across his face. 'I tell you I tried to stop them. You can't fit me up like this. That's what you're doing. Fitting me up for something I didn't do.'

There was something close to pity in Frazer's voice when he said, 'I think not. You see, in spite of the lateness of the hour there was a witness, a farmer seeing to one of his cattle. He saw it all. When the firing started he hid behind a tree and watched it all.'

The fight went out of the man and he turned ashen. 'Oh, my God. Oh, my God. They'll hang me for this.'

'Probably,' said Frazer. 'Why did you do it?'

'For the money. They paid me two thousand nicker. Two thousand! Me and the wife, we could go away, retire to Bognor like we always wanted. Now it won't happen.'

'Your wife will. She's got the money I take it.'

The constable nodded his head.

Frazer continued, saying, 'You'll hang. A constable will be outside the door from now on. Don't try and escape.'

Sion and Frazer left. Outside they paused before entering the car and Sion asked, 'Do you really have a witness?'

'No. But I was with some of the men from the new division they've formed at Scotland Yard where the idea is they apply science to detective work. They put it all together and told me what they thought. One of the men had been a doctor in the army and had made a study of bullet wounds. It was really amazing,' he shook his head in wonder.

Back in the office, Frazer took a message which he quickly read.

'What happens now? And I still don't know where David is,' said Sion.

'He's already in Germany, that I know because I've just received this message. He's using the same system of contacting me as we had when we were operating together.'

Sion took the paper and read it. 'Can you arrange for me to visit the armoury at Chatham?' he asked.

Frazer nodded. 'I should think so. Let me find out who's the Officer in Command and give you a letter of introduction. The old boy network is far better than official channels. Why do you want to go?'

'I need to find a gun to fit my plane. A single shot from a rifle at an exact distance to the target is useless in the air. I need to be able to fill an enemy plane with holes so that it falls out of the sky or kills the pilot, or preferably, both.'

'You don't need to go to Chatham for that,' said Frazer. 'You can talk to me. I am, or at least I was, an arms expert before I was a banker. You've got two choices. The Lewis machine gun or the Hotchkiss M1909. We have them both here in London.'

As Frazer drove them back to the bank he began lecturing Sion. 'The Lewis Mark 1 was designed by a man named MacLean and refined and perfected by an American called Colonel Lewis. The Yanks didn't want to know and Lewis brought the design over to Belgium. The Belgium Army accepted it and he started manufacturing there. I was one of the officers who tried out the gun and recommended it to our army. The result was that the BSA – British Small Arms – company now manufactures it here under licence. It's gas operated, fires five hundred and fifty rounds a minute and weighs about twenty five pounds. You can use two different drums of forty seven or ninety seven rounds.'

'What are drums?'

'You know how a machine gun is fed by a belt of bullets? Well, with the Lewis, the bullets are contained in a round drum which sits on top of the barrel. It's very easy to handle and reloading is quick and simple.'

'And the Hotchkiss?'

'The Hotchkiss is French, weighs about thirty pounds, has a rate of fire of five hundred rounds a minute and is fed by metal strips of thirty rounds a time. It's proven very reliable and extremely accurate. It's been used by us since production in 1909 and so has been around four years longer than the Lewis. The Lewis is yet to be used in war but so far in trials it's proved to be a good weapon. All in all I think the Lewis is the better gun provided it works as well as the Hotchkiss in real combat.'

'Is there any chance of me seeing both, or better still getting my hands on them? So that I see how to fit them to the plane and test them out.'

'That may be more difficult,' Frazer said, thoughtfully. 'I tell you what though, let's talk to John. If we can get a contractor's licence for the company then anything's possible.'

'A contractor's licence? What's that?'

'It's to allow the company to supply the army. We'll need one soon anyway so we might as well get it now. Then I can arrange for you to meet people who can get you some of the equipment you'll need.'

While arrangements were being made for the company to get its licence Sion learned about the development of a new engine called the V8 by Hispano-Suiza, the only company in the world that had started as a designer and builder of engines specifically for use in aeroplanes. The new engine had eight pistons and developed over two hundred and forty brake horse power. When it had been fitted to a car, it had taken the car up to a speed of eighty miles per hour. Although the company was Spanish it now had a factory in France because that was where most of the interest and many of the developments in aviation were taking place.

Sion took the train to Paris. From there he travelled west to the outskirts of the city where the factory had been established next to an airfield. His name was already known to many of the people there; they had been exchanging correspondence and ideas for some years. The V8 had been kept a secret until it was shown to the press as a car engine; at that point there were no plans to put it into a plane. Sion had other ideas. He bought a car with the engine in it and drove it back to Biggin Hill. He also bought a spare engine, which he carried in the back of the car.

The roads north of Paris were small and winding, connecting every hamlet, village and town. Eventually he arrived at Calais and put up at an inn for the night. The next morning he drove on to a ferry and enjoyed a relaxing journey across the Channel.

By midday he was back at Biggin Hill and working with the new engines. Soon after that Peter Cazorla left to return to America to fetch his wife.

During the weeks that followed Sion heard from Angus Frazer about David from time to time. He was apparently criss-crossing Germany looking for von Ludwig but so far, to no avail. However, in his guise as a wealthy German, nobody recognised him as the American David Griffiths, and he was picking up a lot of useful information and passing it all back to Frazer. The information was mainly to do with business, and enabled Frazer and the fund managers to make some profitable investment decisions. They were steadily building up an impressive portfolio of shares which was showing a greater rate of return than normal. The spread of risk appealed to many people and money was pouring into the funds. Sion was able to tap into the "high risk fund" for more cash with which to build up the aeroplane business.

Six weeks after leaving England Peter Cazorla returned with his wife, Maria, and their three other children. The boy, Juan, was soon up to his elbows in grease working alongside his father and brother, while the two girls, aged thirteen and fourteen, helped their mother look after the house, the garden and the men. Originally the house was to have contained offices but now it held only the family. There were three spare bedrooms so that visitors like Frazer and John Buchanan had somewhere to stay when they visited the works.

In the autumn Sion asked Frazer to meet him at Biggin Hill to discuss demonstrating the Griffin to the army.

'We need to show the army why they should buy Griffins and not Spads or Farmans,' Frazer pointed out.

'That's easy,' replied Sion. They were standing next to the plane, now fully armed and fitted with the new engine. 'Let me ask you something, since you know the army and their attitude.'

'Sion, if it's an efficient killing machine the army will buy it. But they'll buy others as well because they can't be sure which is the best machine and they won't know until war breaks out and the planes are really tested.'

'That's a sobering thought,' said Sion. 'Right, let's look at the technical side. At present the aeroplanes are mainly pushers, with the propellers in the back, shoving the plane. This allows the gunner in the front to use machine guns. Right?'

'Sure,' said Frazer. 'That's the way most of the fighting planes are going. Even Sopwith has pushers, though he's working on a design with the propeller in the front.'

'Right. But we know we get more power, more speed, hell more everything with the propeller pulling instead of pushing. The problem is we can't fire our guns forward through the prop. Right? So this is what we've done.' Sion reached up and swung a machine gun, mounted on the side of the plane, through an arc. 'The gunner sits in front, as usual, and he can fire to port with this gun and to starboard with another. We did consider having just one gun mounted with a quick release to move it from one side to the other but it's too difficult. These pins here prevent the gun from firing outside its arc, so it will shoot from the tip of the prop around and along the side to end up next to the tail. It's a firing arc of nearly one hundred and fifty degrees.'

'I see you've mounted the Lewis. Hang on, it looks different.'

Sion nodded. 'It's a better gun for what we want and we've been able to remove the cooling cover from the barrel.'

'Won't it overheat?'

'No, that's the beauty of it. It makes the gun three pounds lighter and the air passing over the barrel keeps it cool. It was Raphael who pointed this out and he was right.'

At the sound of his name Raphael looked up from the work bench where he was busy and gave a grin. Sion waved a hand in his direction and said to Frazer, 'The boy's a genius. His father is very clever but

Raphael has the gift to see further than what exists and to think up new ideas.'

'Right, that's the armament. But what about the plane itself?' asked Frazer.

'At present the average engine throws out eighty to one hundred and twenty horsepower which directly relates to the plane's speed, lift and so on. Agreed?'

'Sure. That's pretty obvious.'

'Right. Well the V8 was designed to produce one hundred and sixty horsepower, twenty by each of the eight pistons. We've modified it to shove out twenty five hp per piston; that's two hundred horsepower.'

'How did you do that?'

'We increased the petrol supply using a small pump which forces petrol into the engine instead of it being gravity fed.'

'How does that translate into speed, lift, manoeuvrability?'

'Take-off speed is around forty-five miles per hour for the average plane, if there is such a thing. Top speed is currently eighty to ninety and shallow dives take it up to about a hundred and ten. The limiting factor is two fold – the engine and the wings. Right?'

Frazer nodded, enjoying the lecture from this expert.

'Our limiting factor is the wings. If we had a better construction we could easily reach one hundred and eighty miles per hour but if we did the wings would rip off.' We're working on a mono-wing design right now, but it's going to take a long time before we're able to get the lift and weight ratio right.'

'I thought the Deperdussin had solved that.' Frazer was referring to an aircraft designed by a French engineer named Louis Bechereau. His floatplane had a single wing and the engine was enclosed in a cover and air cooled by using vents. It was the most aerodynamically designed and fastest plane in existence. Using a 160 horsepower Gnome engine it had achieved a record speed of 100 miles per hour.

'It's solved a lot of problems, but it has others. It needs a long runway to take off and the engine torque makes it very difficult to fly. It's got the speed, but I think manoeuvrability is at least equally important.'

'Yes, I'd go along with that.'

'Well, we can reach a hundred miles per hour and we can manoeuvre to our hearts content.' Sion threw a flying helmet and goggles to Frazer and said, 'Climb aboard and I'll show you.'

Frazer grinned and put the helmet on with alacrity. This was something he wanted to experience. A short while later they were taxiing across the field and at forty two miles per hour they lifted into the air. Sion flew them south and over the Channel. Once there he got Frazer to swing the machine guns through their arcs, showing how they were free to fire. They flew for nearly an hour before Sion turned back to Biggin Hill. When they landed they were met by all three Cazorlas, anxiously waiting to learn what Frazer had thought of the plane.

He stood for a few moments looking at the beautiful machine and then nodded. 'It's absolutely fantastic. This has to be one of the best planes in existence.'

Sion and the others grinned. 'What do you mean, one of the best,' said Sion. 'It is the best.' There was laughter all round and the four men went to the house to discuss their next steps and to enjoy a celebratory drink.

'I'll arrange for you to see Lord Stockdale and the Secretary of State for War. If we can get them on our side we can get the Generals to take a look. Leave it with me,' said Frazer, over a glass of malt whisky.

'Any word on David?' asked Sion.

'Plenty. He's still alive and still looking for von Ludwig who appears to have vanished off the face of the earth. David thinks he's in Austria and so he's on his way there. In the meantime he's sent us back some useful information which I've been able to pass on to Stockdale. David's more convinced than ever that we're hurtling headlong into war.' He paused and then continued, 'The Gatling machine gun used during the American Civil War was considered the foretaste of modern warfare. I hate to think what devastation will be caused this time with the guns we have now. Have you ever heard of Rourke's Drift?' Frazer asked.

Sion shook his head. 'No. What is it?'

'It's a place in South Africa. Using modern weapons against natives armed only with spears a small number of our soldiers held out against overwhelming odds, but the natives were massacred. If we have two opposing sides equally well armed what will be the result? Horrendous losses on both sides.' He suddenly smiled, lifting the gloom, 'Still,

I am sure that in army messes all over Britain tonight they will be raising their glasses and toasting to a Bloody War and a Sickly Season.'

'Why?' asked Sion.

'It improves the survivors' chances of promotion,' was the cynical reply.

Two weeks later they were visited by Lord Stockdale, the War Minister Lord Kitchener, and the Minister of Munitions, David Lloyd George. Sion took an instant dislike to Kitchener, finding him arrogant, self opinionated and, in Sion's book the worst sin of all, stupid. However, Lloyd George was none of these and, with their Welsh background in common, he and Sion got on well. At the end of four hours of the plane being put through its paces the three men held a brief discussion and, much to the surprise of Sion and the others announced an order for twenty planes to be delivered as soon as possible.

'When can we have them?' asked Lloyd George. 'We need to start training pilots as quickly as we can.'

'It's now October,' said Sion. 'We ought to be able to fill the order by, say, April.'

'That's no good, man,' retorted Lloyd George. 'If you can't manage it in six weeks you can keep your planes. There's a war coming and we need to be ready. Well? What do you say? Can you manage it?'

Sion nodded weakly and said, 'We'll do our best.'

15

AFTER THE MAN had left Sion sat with Peter, Raphael and Juan in gloomy silence. It was all very well saying they'd do it, but it was quite another to achieve.

'What are we to do?' asked Juan.

'Pour a large whisky in this glass,' said Sion, holding it out to the youngster, 'and plan.'

Frazer came in from saying goodbye to their guests and replenished his own glass. 'If we fulfil the order then this company is made,' he said. 'If we don't then we're finished.'

'Finished?' queried Sion.

'Kitchener said he'll ensure no plane is ever bought from us. The man's an idiot and a bully, but he can and will carry out his threat.'

'Right. In that case we get started right away,' said Sion, galvanised by the possibility of losing everything he had worked to create. 'Tomorrow Pete, I want you and Raphael to talk to as many mechanics as you can here at the Hill. Find out what they're earning and pay them fifty percent more.'

'Twenty,' interrupted Frazer. 'That'll be enough.'

Sion grinned sheepishly. 'Twenty it is.'

Peter Cazorla shook his head slowly.

'You've got a problem with that?' asked Sion.

The older man shrugged his shoulders. 'Not in itself, but money won't bring any man here. They work for the love of it; for the creation of something unique. Money they need, yes, but as long as they have enough they're satisfied. What will bring them here in droves is to discover what we are doing. Already we are the talk of the aerodrome. We have been careful not to let them see too much, which is why we do so much of our flying out to sea, but there are plenty of rumours. Share some of our vision and we'll have no difficulty in finding men.'

Sion thought about it for a few seconds and then reluctantly nodded. 'Okay. But tell them the minimum you have to – enough to get them here and no more. What next?'

'Next,' said Raphael, 'we need to have some sort of assembly line, like the pictures we were shown of the Ford motor factory. If we try and build the aeroplanes one at a time we'll never make it. We get a man to do the same job for each plane so that he's fast and competent at it. We break down each part of the work into a fixed pattern, the one following on the other. Understand?'

Sion nodded. 'I think so. What else do we need?'

'The obvious,' said Frazer, dryly. 'And that's a place to build them. Winter is coming and soon it'll be cold and wet.'

'It gets colder and wetter than this?' wailed Juan in mock despair that had them all laughing.

'Aye, that's a problem,' said Sion who suddenly grinned. 'I've been around Frazer too much, saying aye. We need to expand the hangar as quickly as possible. Any ideas?'

'Tents?' suggested Juan.

'No use,' replied Frazer. 'We need something more substantial than that. Leave it with me and I'll try and think of a solution.'

They continued talking about their plans for the rest of the evening, and the conversation continued during the evening meal. The following morning when Frazer returned to London, everything had been worked out. Now all that was necessary was for them each to implement the plan.

Two days later the problem of building the premises was solved in a most unexpected way.

Frazer was sitting in his office and going through his mail when he came across a letter from a man in Sheffield. Its contents were sufficient to send Frazer racing home to pack a bag and then to the train station. By the evening he was in Sheffield.

After an uncomfortable night in a mediocre hotel and an indifferent breakfast Frazer took a taxi to his final destination, a small factory near the centre of the city.

He introduced himself to the writer of the letter, Clive Smithson, the owner of the factory. 'I understood from your letter that you've designed a technique to manufacture sheets of metal which can be nailed together to form buildings which are ready for use immediately. Is this true?'

'Aye, it is. Though the last thing I expected was a visit from you. At best I hoped you might want to see a sample of what we do.' He was a large, friendly man, ruddy cheeked with startlingly blue eyes.

'Will you show me round?'

'Aye. Come this way.' He led Frazer onto the factory floor. There were a dozen men working at different jobs. 'This is where we flatten the iron until it's wafer thin,' said Smithson, stopping next to a huge press. 'You can see as it goes through it gets thinner and thinner until it's so thin it bends like paper. Next we cut it here and then we run it though this press. See, now it's corrugated and lengthways it's fairly inflexible. Here,' he moved further along the factory floor, 'this is where we add the zinc which stops it from rusting . . .'

An hour after they had started the tour Frazer and Smithson were back in the office each holding a mug of tea. 'As I understand it,' began Frazer, 'you can make a wooden frame and nail the sheets to it, creating a building which is wind, and water, tight. Right?'

'More or less. Once the frame is up and the sheeting on you can line the inside with wood to make it warmer or just leave it as it is. Most factories have fires and so tend to be warm enough without any more insulation. Add a concrete floor, and Bob's your uncle.'

Frazer nodded. 'You wrote asking for a loan of one thousand pounds. I have to tell you that's a small sum for us to bother with. What do you want the money for?'

Smithson took his time in replying. 'I'm not sure whether to be encouraged or disappointed with your idea of what's a small sum. To me it sounds a fortune.'

Frazer shrugged. 'I suppose it is to some but, believe me, to us it's small change. We're used to much larger investments. I repeat what do you need the money for?'

'We've been told by the Council that we have to leave. They want the site to build houses – compulsory purchase they call it. Aye, and we're being paid a fraction of what the site is worth. The bloody councillors in this city are bloody corrupt,' he said vehemently.

'When do you have to move?'

'I'm told the meeting's next week,' the big man slumped into his chair. 'After that it'll be all over. I can't afford to move. I've invested everything getting this far. I'll have no choice but to close down. What'll happen to my men then, hey? Somebody tell me that,' he said bitterly.

'Your men? What about you?'

'I'll manage. I was a blacksmith,' he held up his hands. 'I can go back to being a 'smith somewhere. My men have families to feed and need the work but I can manage.'

'I won't lend you one thousand pounds,' began Frazer but before he could go on he was interrupted.

Smithson stood up suddenly. 'Right. Thank you for your time. I've wasted enough of mine and need to try other avenues. There's always the Jews.'

'Please sit down, Mr Smithson,' said Frazer, politely. 'No loan; I propose an equity investment. Furthermore I shall ensure that you won't have to move off your site. You can leave that to me. Now, if the bank invests, say five thousand pounds, will you be prepared to part with forty nine percent of the shares. You'll still retain control of the business . . .'

Smithson had sat down so heavily the chair shook under him, his jaw had dropped open and he was staring at Frazer. 'Hold it a second,' he held up a big hand. 'Are you telling me you're willing to lend me five thousand pounds?'

Frazer shook his head. 'Not lend. Let me explain it to you.' Half an hour later Smithson understood what Frazer was proposing and had shaken hands on the deal.

'What did you mean by me not having to move?' Smithson was grinning from ear to ear as he asked the question. If possible the grin widened when Frazer told him the answer.

'There is just one thing,' added Frazer.

'Damn it, I knew there had to be a catch,' Smithson said warily.

'No catch. You need to produce sufficient sheets of corrugated iron to build a hangar about thirty feet high, sixty feet wide and at least a hundred and fifty feet long. Preferably two hundred feet,' he added.

'What's a hangar?' asked Smithson as he picked up a pencil and made some rapid calculations on a piece of paper.

'It's where aeroplanes are kept, except that in this case it will be where they are built.'

While he listened to the answer Smithson made his calculations. 'We need one thousand eight hundred sheets which will take,' he paused and finally looked up, 'fifty six days.'

Frazer shook his head. 'We have six weeks to build the planes and we need a factory to do it in. You have two weeks to build the factory while we get ready to begin assembling the planes. If you can't do that then I'm afraid we can't have a deal. I hadn't realised it would take so long to manufacture the sheets.'

Smithson looked at Frazer, aghast. His problems had been solved and now they were back as quickly as they had vanished. 'I'm sorry, Mr Frazer, I really am. It just can't be done. The process takes fifteen minutes a sheet once we start. Eight hours a day is fifty six days. The mathematics is that simple.'

Frazer laughed aloud, relieved at what the problem was. 'Mr Smithson, is that all? I thought it was something serious that was preventing you from doing the job in time.'

'Something serious? Isn't this serious enough? It can't be done.'

'Yes it can. Look, I hope I haven't overestimated your abilities,' Frazer said. 'The money is to double your plant size and gives you enough to pay your workers overtime to fill the order. There are twenty-four hours in the day and seven days in a week. I expect you to use all of them. I expect you to get started right away and while your foreman or manager or whatever you call him gets on with producing the sheets you can be installing the new machinery. You've got plenty of room out there.'

'There isn't a manager or foreman. I look after everything, like I always have.'

Frazer wondered for a moment if he had made a serious mistake in his assessment of the burly man sitting opposite him who was now stroking his chin in thought. He was about to speak when Smithson looked keenly at Frazer and gave a smile of delight, 'My God, but it'll be a great challenge though. Young Hopkins can run the place. I know where I can get what I need and finding men won't be difficult. We only need one machine and that's a new press. One of those modern ones which works faster. I've loads of capacity in the other machinery to cope. Aye, this could be a bigger adventure than it seemed when we started. But I have to be honest with you, Mr Frazer, we don't need five thousand for what we need to do. I reckon three will be more than enough.'

Frazer shook his head. 'No, it won't. There's a war coming and we're going to need all the huts, factories and hangars we can supply.'

'A war? What war? You mean in Africa again? Or Ireland?'

Frazer shook his head. 'No, Mr Smithson, there'll be war in Europe soon and we're going to be needed, believe me. You fill the order for Biggin Hill and make plans to quadruple the size of this place. In the meantime leave me to deal with the compulsory purchase order.'

Frazer stayed in Sheffield for another two days whilst the solicitors drew up the necessary papers. By the time he returned to London the factory was working twenty four hours a day and the new press was about to be delivered. He sent a telegram to Sion, explaining what he had done and made suggestions as to what was needed next.

Frazer's meeting with Lloyd George was short and sweet. Within twenty four hours an instruction went out from Whitehall that no compulsory purchase order was to be imposed on the Smithson Factory Limited and that all help was to be given when plans to extend the factory were submitted.

One week after he had agreed to build the aeroplanes Sion met with Frazer and Smithson at Biggin Hill.

'I thought I ought to come down myself,' said Smithson, 'and tell you what to do.'

They were standing by the sheds, each of which was large enough to hold two aeroplanes. So far eight mechanics had been persuaded to join them from within the close knit flying community, and another five had promised to think about it. Peter Cazorla had also poached a man from a garage in Sevenoaks who had jumped at the chance to work with aeroplanes and was glad of the extra money. They were still desperately short of skilled men and were now advertising in the local newspapers.

If we use the retaining wall there,' Smithson pointed, 'we can build straight on from there in no time. Lay out your floor area and get the concrete mixed and laid straight away. I'll get the timbers cut at a local yard. While we're doing that you try and find some labourers to do the donkey work and I'll get a couple of joiners and carpenters to supervise it. I've made a drawing which only needs slight modification now that I've seen the site, and I reckon it'll be good enough for any joiner to follow. I can then get back and crack the whip over my lads, not that I need to. With the money they're being paid most of them want to work eighteen hours a day, seven days a week, but that's no good. If they get too tired they'll make mistakes and that's dangerous and unproductive. Right, do we all know what we're doing?'

Frazer was relieved that his first instinct about Smithson had been the right one. He was proving to be a human dynamo.

'We need more pilots,' Sion said to Frazer over dinner that night. 'We need men who can fly – who can put the plane through its paces so that we can test each one before we sell it to the army.'

Frazer nodded. 'That's your part of ship, old chap,' he said. 'We've got enough on our plates right now. And anyway I couldn't tell a good pilot from a bad one.'

'There are quite a few pilots out there who are on the breadline and fly for the sheer love of it. If I find two or three I could put them on the payroll and use them on the design work as well. Most of them have a lot of ideas worth tapping into. Then they could be the ones to train the army on the planes,' he paused as a huge problem suddenly came to light. 'Training the army! How in the world are we going to train the army if they can't fly already? How many pilots are there?' he directed the question at Frazer who shrugged in reply. 'That's what I thought. We could have planes and nobody to fly them at this rate. You'd better take that problem back to London with you. Lloyd George mentioned it when he was here but has he done anything about it?'

Frazer shook his head. 'Not that I know of. I'll prompt him when I get back. What's happening about the engines?'

'I have twenty-five on the way – I ordered extra just in case. I tried to get a discount for the bulk purchase but didn't get much joy there, I'm afraid.'

Frazer grinned. 'Once a market trader always a market trader,' he said.

'I did get a decent discount on the plywood and canvas. I've hundreds of yards of wire coming and plenty of copper tubing. Here's the plan for production once we get started. I don't intend using the existing buildings at all, only the new one that Clive builds.'

'Why not?' asked Frazer.

'Because we'll need to continue with our development of new planes. We'll use the sheds and keep anything we do private. Peter and the family,' he nodded at the men sitting round the table, 'can cope with the production side while I work on a few new ideas.'

What's the point?' asked Frazer. 'We need to get the Griffin sold to the army before we start anything new.'

Sion shook his head in disagreement. 'Not if we're to stay ahead of the game. One off, yes. A long term viable business, no. We need to stay ahead of the competition. I need to figure out how to manufacture a single wing plane that will do all that the Griffin can. If we manage that I think we'll be able to achieve greater speed because the plane will be a lot more streamlined.

The planning went on. Within a fortnight the hangar was built; production started immediately. Some of the work on the wings had already began and while carpenters shaped and fitted the plywood bodies, mechanics modified the engines to power planes instead of cars. Throughout the process ideas were discussed, some implemented but most discarded.

Sion and his men were trying to achieve the impossible: nobody had ever built a plane in six weeks. They worked round the clock, grabbing sleep whenever they could or when they were too tired to function properly.

Sion had installed a new telephone line in order to keep in contact with Frazer, and on the Monday of week five he received a phone call from him. 'It's the last week, Sion, are we going to make it?'

'No,' was the disappointing reply.

16

'WHY EVER NOT?' Frazer demanded, facing Sion across the table that served as a desk.

'It's just that the time scale was unrealistic. We could do it now. In fact we could do it in three weeks now we've sorted out all the problems. As it is, the first plane will be finished in the middle of next week which is three days beyond the deadline with another being ready about every four hours after that. We'd finish by Friday and be five days late.'

Frazer leaned back in his chair, put his feet on the battered table and scowled. 'All right, I think I can work it. If we are able to produce aeroplanes in three weeks after this, I can sell the fact to Lloyd George. As long as that pompous ass Kitchener isn't there I think we'll get away with it. What about pilots?'

'I found two who are willing to work for us. They'll test fly the planes and deliver them to the army as each one is finished. Do you know where they have to go?'

'Yes. The army have a place at Hendon. Do you know it?'

Sion nodded. 'Yes. It's north west of London. An hour from here. I landed there once.'

'That's the place. Apparently a new operation called the Army Flying Corps is being set up there, to train pilots ready for war.'

Sion snorted in derision. 'How can they train pilots for war when they don't know what form the warfare is going to take? What are they going to do? Shoot at troops, drop bombs or shoot down airships?'

Frazer shrugged. 'No idea, but at this time it's not our problem. What is our problem is to get these planes finished and to get a further contract for another twenty. I take it that the planes will be ready to be fitted with the Lewis machine guns and that an army armourer can do the job?'

'Yes. We've made it as simple as possible. All he needs to do is slot the stock into the clamp and rest the barrel on a rod we've added and tighten the clamp. It's rock solid and foolproof.'

'It may be foolproof but is it army proof?' asked Frazer with a flash of humour.

'Probably not,' came the reply. 'Any news about David?'

'Yes, plenty. He'll be back in about ten days.'

'Where is he?'

'He was in Hungary but now he's on his way to Bosnia. He reckons von Ludwig is headed there.'

'How do you know so much?'

Frazer looked surprised and asked, 'Don't you know how we keep in touch?'

'No. I just know you get information from him regularly while I hear nothing unless I talk to you.'

'We use pigeons.'

Sion looked at Frazer in astonishment. Whatever reply he had expected it wasn't that. 'Pigeons?' he repeated, stupidly.

'He has access to our embassies and consulates all over Europe. He gets a coded message to them and they forward it. I'm the only one who has the code to understand what he sends. I then act on what he tells me. Either it's to do with business or it's for Lord Stockdale.'

'And he's coming back?'

'Yes. He needs to get out for a rest. He said that if he doesn't find von Ludwig this time he'll go back. He's convinced the Germans are up to something in Bosnia.'

'I look forward to his return and I'm relieved he's all right. Come on, let me show you what we've achieved around here.'

Sion took Frazer on a guided tour. In spite of the fact that the planes weren't ready what had been achieved was impressive and Frazer told Sion so. 'You can see that if we need to we can build at least the same again and double the hangar area. That's why I've had the concrete laid to twice the size we needed. I reckon that if we were in production we could be churning out a plane every day on average. You've been dealing with the financial side of the equation; will we make a profit after our setting up costs?'

Frazer grinned. 'Yes. After all costs, including the building and the tooling we'll still make a healthy profit.' He suddenly became grim. 'It's true to say that at a time of war somebody makes money at the expense of other peoples' lives. Well, I've been responsible for others making a lot of money and now it's my turn. Along with you, John and David of course.'

'What will you do if there is a war? Will you fight?'

Frazer shrugged. 'We're all hoping it won't come to that. But the news David has sent back isn't encouraging. The Germans are arming at a phenomenal rate and we're lagging seriously behind.'

'What's David's opinion?'

'Really pessimistic is the best description. One thing we've done is secured a deal with the Turks to exploit the oil in Arabia, Mesopotamia and Syria. Churchill is particularly pleased because it secures the Royal Navy with a safe supply of crude. We've invested with Lord Inchcape in a company that owns the monopoly on navigating the Tigris and Euphrates. We also have two representatives on the board of the Baghdad Railway. So we're in great shape, thanks to David.'

'David? What's he had to do with it?'

'He tells us what's going on and makes recommendations as to where to invest. We're well on our way to making a fortune.'

David was back in time for Christmas. He was impressed with what Sion had achieved and pleased with the continuing orders for the plane. They spent a dismal Christmas in London with neither of them looking forward to the new year. That was until Frazer browbeat them into joining him in Edinburgh.

They caught the train at Kings Cross on December 31st 1913. The journey was long and peaceful and gave the brothers time to chat and exchange their news. Their parents had been disappointed that neither of them were in America but had written saying they understood the reasons that had kept them away.

'I haven't had a chance to ask you, but what do you think is going on in Bosnia that's so important?' asked Sion as he unpacked some turkey sandwiches for their lunch.

David was busy with the cork in a bottle of claret. He poured them each a glass and after a few moments replied, 'I don't know. I do know that von Ludwig is there and that he's made contact with a Serbian secret society known as the Black Hand.'

'The Black Hand? Is that some sort of joke?'

'No. They really do exist. They're a group of army officers who believe the Serbs are oppressed by the Austrians. I can't understand why von Ludwig has contacted them but if he has it can't be for anything other than a sinister reason. I'm trying to find out what it is. If he's trying to foment a war I don't see what he can do in Bosnia or, more particularly, in Sarajevo. I'll go back soon and continue to search.'

'Why don't you give it up?' Sion asked, concern etched in his voice. 'Leave von Ludwig alone. You'll come across him again and you can deal with him then.'

David was about to retort angrily but bit back his words. 'I can't do that. Not just for Emily's sake – she's dead and there's nothing to be done about it. No, something is happening and I want to find out what it is. I might be able to prevent a catastrophe that could plunge Europe into war.'

Sion shook his head. 'From what you've been telling me and from what John was saying over Christmas, I also think it's inevitable. Churchill is going to make a major policy speech in the new year. Ah, we've arrived at Darlington.' He looked at his watch. 'Exactly on time.'

They arrived at Waverly station in Edinburgh at seven o'clock to be met by the snow, falling gently, and by a cold Frazer pacing the station.

'I'm glad you made it. We're staying at the Grand Hotel on Princes Street, overlooked by the castle. Tomorrow we're going north to Perth and the family seat. We're going on a deer hunt.'

David grinned and said, 'The last hunt I was on, John and I were the target. Remember?'

'Yes. That boar hunt with the Kaiser.' That started them off, reminiscing, and telling Sion of their adventures.

When they arrived at the hotel they were surprised to be advised by Frazer to get some rest as it would be a long night. They had expected to be changing and to go to a party somewhere. It came as a shock to discover that the party wouldn't be starting until nearly midnight. They were to be in the bar at eleven forty five.

They duly arrived, dressed in their dinner jackets. The place was filling up and by midnight it was mobbed. They were each given a glass of whisky, and then the party started.

The next morning they were much the worse for wear. They made their way to the station to catch the train to Perth. The cold, crisp air helped to inject some life into them, but not a lot. Large malt whiskies poured by Frazer as they settled in their carriage helped them more.

'We'll be passing over the Forth Bridge,' he explained. 'A really wonderful sight.'

So it proved to be. The journey passed quickly as the train penetrated the Scottish Highlands. In the middle of the afternoon they arrived at Perth to be met by a chauffeur driven car, a new Napier 30-hp shooting-brake, the boot an integral part of the car. Frazer scowled at the car as they climbed aboard. A five mile drive took them to what Frazer referred to as the family seat, a huge mansion at Kinfauns on the Firth of Tay.

'My father's the Laird. The fact is he's got so many titles I can't keep up with them all,' said Frazer, showing them round the baronial hall. There were glass-eyed deer heads intermingled with ancestral portraits that caused Sion to say, 'Which are the ancestors? The stuffed heads, or the paintings?'

They met Frazer's father in the library where they were greeted with a large malt produced in a local distillery which was owned by the family. He was a friendly and convivial man, obviously delighted to have his eldest son back home.

'And when pray, Angus, are you coming home for good?'

Frazer shrugged and looked sheepish. 'Not for a while, father. I have a lot to do in London.'

'Aye, a lot of women you mean. It's time you married and settled down and gave me and your mother grandchildren, so that when I go, I can go in the peaceful knowledge that the line is secured. You know we've been here for nearly six hundred years.'

'Yes, father. I know and appreciate it. Where did you get the money to buy the car?' he changed the subject.

Frazer's father looked a little sheepish before replying. 'I didn't. I told the garage that I wanted to try out the new Napier and could I borrow it for a few days.'

'Father, you know only too well we can't afford it. It'll have to go back in the morning.'

'I'd rather not discuss our private matters in front of guests, if you don't mind Angus. Especially friends of yours.'

'These are friends and business colleagues,' said Frazer, a hint of tiredness in his voice, as though he was engaged in a common argument with his father. 'And they've been instrumental in allowing me to make sufficient money to send to you to keep the bailiffs away.'

David was becoming uncomfortable at the turn of conversation while Sion was staring at his drink as though it gave him inspiration.

'How much of this do you make?' Sion asked suddenly, holding up the cut glass beaker.

'What? Oh, about two hundred bottles a year,' replied Frazer. Though irritated at the question he didn't show it.

'Why so few?'

'We use it ourselves and give the odd bottle to friends as a present. Why do you ask?' Frazer was now intrigued, aware that Sion wasn't indulging in idle gossip.

'How much could you make?' Sion countered.

'Thousands of bottles if we wanted. Now why are you asking?' Frazer's irritation began to show in spite of himself.

'Sell it,' was Sion's reply.

'What do you mean? Sell the distillery?' Frazer was puzzled.

David had cottoned on to Sion's idea and said, 'Angus, you're too close to the problem. I gather you need money and a lot of money to keep this place going. Right?'

'Look fellows, I didn't invite you here to talk about the family cash problems. I invited you here to enjoy yourselves. We've got a shoot that'll last a few days, we'll enjoy venison steaks and drink too many drams. After that we'll all three of us return to London.'

'Angus, listen to me,' said Sion. 'This is excellent whisky. Full of flavour with a hint of peat in it. It'll sell a bomb in London. We get this place producing commercial quantities of whisky and you solve your problems.'

Frazer laughed while his father looked on perplexed. 'Sion, nice try but it can't be done.'

'Why not?' asked David.

'Because it takes eight years to create a masterpiece like the whisky you're holding. We have some vats that are up to twenty years old. Which is this father?'

'That? Oh, that's the eight years old from the port barrels.'

'Port barrels? What has port got to do with it?' asked Sion.

'We age the whisky in barrels that have been imported into the country from Spain and Portugal full of sherry or port wine,' the Laird replied. 'It adds to the flavour of the whisky. If you try a glass that has been stored in a sherry barrel you will notice a subtle difference in the flavour.'

'Interesting,' said Sion. 'What's the shortest time it takes to ferment whisky?'

'You don't ferment whisky, you distil it,' said Frazer. 'And the shortest time would be three years but it wouldn't be particularly palatable.'

'What if it was then mixed with a quality malt like one of these?' Sion asked, holding up his glass.

Frazer shook his head. 'Whisky is a delicate drink. You could easily smother or spoil a first class malt with an inferior blend. It happens all the time. Come on, let me show you to your rooms and give you a guided tour.'

They were standing on the banks of the river Tay when Sion said, 'Let me get this right. You have one hundred and forty five thousand acres of land, more or less, hundreds of deer, grow oats by the ton, enough carrots, onions and swedes, sorry what you call turnips, to feed towns. You also distil sufficient whisky to keep London drunk for a day or two,' he paused while Frazer nodded. 'Yet you're broke.'

'That's about it. Except you forgot the salmon,' he waved a hand at the river. 'We have a hundred and fifteen people living off our land, we only use the whisky locally, nobody eats venison except us and the vegetables are sold in the markets of Perth, Dundee and Edinburgh to bring in enough money to pay wages for the staff. The oats and barley gives us a surplus but we need a lot of it to feed the cows in the winter. The milk we produce also goes to market. The wood is shipped from that landing there,' he pointed to a wooden dock, 'and sent down to Dundee for the saw mills. There it's dressed – that is, it's made ready for use as timber – and often ends up as the decks of ships. After all that we run at a deficit of seven thousand pounds a year and owe the banks nearly a hundred thousand secured on the land. And,' he finished heavily, 'I see no way out.'

David and Sion looked at each other, both recognising that the same thoughts were coursing through the other's head. Suddenly they burst out laughing and clapped each other on the back. Frazer was affronted as he thought they were laughing at his predicament and hurt that two people he considered his best friends could act like that. He was about to stalk off angrily when David and Sion stopped and each clapped him on the shoulder.

'We have good news,' said David.

'And very good news,' finished Sion. 'Which do you want first?'

'What are you talking about?' asked Frazer in some bewilderment.

'Angus, Sir Angus,' said David, 'you're too close to the problem to see the solution. I can see it and so can Sion. Now, we need to think about everything we need to do and get started. It'll take a while but we can turn this place around in what?' He looked at his brother. 'Two years?'

'At the most. Break even in a year, in profit from then on.'

'Look chaps, I don't know what you're talking about but we don't have a year. Unless I can sell at least thirty thousand acres we can't stop the banks from foreclosing on the mortgage. Even that doesn't get rid of the problem but only gives us another year whilst the haemorrhaging of money continues. We need a new roof on the house and that'll cost at least fifteen thousand. So it goes on. The best solution is to sell off as much as possible, in fact all of it, keep the house and life style until my parents are dead and then sell that off too. The money I'm earning at the bank and the investments we have can do that easily. After that I'll move to London permanently.' He suddenly grinned. 'I could sell the titles as well, including the Earldom.'

'Is that what you want to do?' asked David.

'No. We've been here too many generations to leave but we've no choice. It was because of this place that I resigned my commission with such alacrity and joined you. There's no money to be made as an army officer – usually quite the reverse. It costs a monstrous amount to hold a commission in a regiment like the Black Watch. My mess bills alone were eating up over fifty percent of the pittance of a salary I was paid. Acting on the information we were getting in Europe enabled me to clear my overdraft, but it also allowed me to watch the rest of it evaporate like water in the desert that is this place. Look, I invited you here for a good time and now I've added to your woes. Let's forget it and I'll show you the distillery.'

'Listen Angus, we Griffiths make good friends and lousy enemies,' said David, thinking of von Ludwig. 'And as we said, you're too close to the problem.' The three men were walking away from the river, towards a building perched on a low hillock a few hundred yards away.

'And you're our friend. Don't you see you have enough here to solve your problems? The only problem is you aren't utilising it.'

'Actually,' interrupted David, 'what Sion means is you are aren't utilising it fully. You're doing the hard work of making produce that's wanted all over Britain and giving away the lion's share of the profits. Let's take the whisky as an example. What does it cost to make a gallon of the stuff?'

'A gallon?' Frazer repeated in bewilderment. 'Why . . . why it's so small an amount I couldn't tell you. It's not even pence. The problem we have is to store the liquid for years while the process continues.'

'So where do all the profits on a bottle of whisky go then?' asked Sion, intrigued.

'I don't know. I've never thought about it,' was the reply.

They were shown the huge vats where the fermenting process took place and the cellars where the barrels were stored. They were in date order, ranging from that autumn to before the turn of the century.

'These are called hogsheads,' said Frazer and each one contains about fifty imperial gallons.' He noticed Sion counting them and added, 'There's twenty.'

Sion pointed to a small room at the end of the cellar and said, 'What's in here?'

'Frazer shrugged. 'I don't know. Don't forget I've been away for nearly twelve years and before that I was at boarding school. I only came home on weekends and holidays and not very often then. Let's take a look.'

The lock was rusty but yielded to a few twists of the handle. The hinges were rusted solid but they were soon able to pull open the door and step inside. In the guttering light of a candle held by Frazer they saw that they were in a low room along one side of which were racks of small barrels.

'These,' said Frazer, continuing his lecture, 'are called kilderkins or pins. They hold about three gallons.'

'I wonder what's in them?' asked Sion, giving the nearest a tap with his knuckles. 'It sounds full, whatever it is.'

David and Sion lifted a barrel to the ground and Frazer took hold of the spigot that blocked up the bunghole. He pulled at it for a few seconds, trying to work it loose. 'It's no good. It's swollen inside. I'll get the pincers to remove it.'

He left the two brothers standing there and while he was away Sion walked the length of the room tapping on each barrel and counting as he went along. The barrels were stacked five deep in rows twenty long. 'A hundred,' announced Sion.

Frazer returned with a long handled pair of pincers that fitted neatly over the bung. He had the barrel opened in seconds and the pungent aroma of whisky filled the air.

'I think we'd better take this out and see what we've got,' said Frazer.

'What do you mean?' asked David. 'It's whisky.' He stated the obvious.

'I know, but is it drinkable?' countered Frazer. 'That's what we need to know. My guess is it's old, fine and highly palatable. But we need to check it.'

Frazer proved to be correct. It was a superb malt that had lain there for over twenty years

'Look, we need to think this all out,' said David. 'I can think of half a dozen ways to make money here.'

They were now sitting in the dining room, the barrel on a chair near them, a tapped bung now in place. Each man had a glass of the amber liquid in front of him and was staring at it, fascinated. The liquid was a light brown colour with a smoky after-taste. It was highly drinkable, magnificently so in fact.

'Only half a dozen?' retorted Sion. 'You're slipping, bro.'

'What do you have in mind? Look, I have to tell you we're running out of time rapidly,' said Frazer. 'I need a small, no . . . a large fortune, soon.'

'How much do you need?' asked David.

'Let me see,' Frazer rested his head back on the chair and contemplated the ceiling for a few seconds. 'Fifty thousand to get the bank off our backs, twenty thousand to do the place up and the same again to carry out a few improvements we need just to keep going. After that we won't be able to pay the interest so we'll go bankrupt even faster.'

'Not enough,' said Sion. 'You need five thousand for the saw works, the same again for the bottling plant and the feed producing factory.'

'We need the abattoir,' added David, 'and the new piggery.'

'I hadn't thought of that one,' said Sion, both brothers enjoying themselves, pretending to ignore Frazer's open mouth. 'We need to ship in the oil for the briquettes, crude will do, and we need to increase the milk herd.'

David nodded. They ignored Frazer's feeble attempt to interrupt them and continued to talk as though he wasn't there. Finally David looked at him and said, 'Right, Angus, that'll do for a start. You got all that?' Then he and Sion burst out laughing.

'Will you two clowns behave yourselves for a minute and tell me what the hell you're talking about.'

'It's simple,' said Sion. 'David and I have been in this situation before, in America. We've seen what can be done, what should be done,' he corrected himself, 'in a situation like this. Our father worked closely with the German farmers in St. Louis, and don't forget we've spent years in the wholesale and distribution markets of America. We know where the profit is and it's not in what you're doing. In America they've got a term for it. Sion, you were telling me about it.'

Sion nodded. 'It's what they call "value added" to the goods. Angus, you're supplying too much raw material. You need to finish it off. Bottle the whisky, stick a label on it and sell it to shops in London. Produce more milk, get it into churns and deliver to Edinburgh. Cut down the trees and make the planks here.'

'And the oil?' asked Frazer.

'Keep the sawdust and soak it in oil. Make briquettes which you sell to ironmongers to light fires with. The abattoir is self evident although you'll need to hire a few butchers to handle it all. You should include venison, beef, pork and lamb. Sell to the shops and keep a great deal more of the profit. That'll do for a start.'

'Forget it,' said Frazer. 'We've no money to get started.'

'Yes you have,' said David, 'it's in the Griffiths & Buchanan Bank.'

'I can't take that. It's charity. I won't have it. I've never mentioned this place and the problems before because . . . because . . .' he spluttered.

'Because you were too embarrassed,' said Sion, kindly. 'Let's work out the deal, get the papers signed and the money in place. We need a manager for each project and an overseer to control the lot. Any ideas?' Sion looked meaningfully at Frazer.

'What deal?' he asked.

'The usual. Not a loan,' said David, 'a shareholding. Turn the whole place into a limited company and the bank takes forty nine percent. We supply all the capital that's needed and get things moving. The bank then takes responsibility for cash flow and lets you get on with things. We've done it enough times in the past.'

'Maybe so, but isn't this a hell of a big gamble?' asked Frazer.

'Of course it's not,' replied Sion. 'Angus, you're too close to it all, I keep telling you. Every penny the bank invests is covered by the value of the land and its assets. You're problem is that you're asset rich and cash poor, a common problem for landowners. You've done things in the same fashion for so long that you're unable to see beyond what you're doing.'

'I can't deny that,' said Frazer thoughtfully, lifting his glass and taking a sip. 'There's a great deal of merit in what you say but I need to think about it.'

'What is there to think about? You led us to believe that the bailiffs are about ready to knock on the door and yet you've got the solution staring you in the face. It's a good deal for you and a good deal for us.'

'I agree.'

'So what's your problem?' asked David.

'My father,' said Frazer. 'I don't think he'll like the idea of giving away nearly half the estate.'

'It's either that or lose the lot,' replied David. 'Why don't we put it to him?'

'Put what to whom?' asked the Laird, walking through the door at that moment.

The three men explained it all to Frazer's father who listened attentively, an untouched glass of whisky in his hands. When they had finished he sat there in contemplation for a few seconds.

'You see,' cried Frazer, 'I told you he wouldn't go for it.'

'Why do you jump to that conclusion, laddie?' he asked his eldest son. 'You youngsters think that because a man is over fifty he's incapable of clear thought. If you want to know it'll be a great relief to do as you've suggested. Your mother and I have been going out of our minds trying to find a solution. The nearest we could come up with is to find you a rich heiress to marry and neither of us wanted that forced on you. There's a great deal of merit in what you've proposed and I can tell you one or two have already occurred to me. The problem has been to find the capital to make it work. More loans are no good, it's just a cycle that can't be broken then. This is ideal. However, I would want a clause . . . no, two clauses in the contract. One will be to the effect that I can buy back the estate at valuation and the other that you will not sell the shares to anybody until I get first refusal. Actually,' he added, 'not only that but if I need it you will lend me the money to buy the shares. In that way I can stop the bank selling to someone I don't think is suitable.'

David smiled at the older man and held out his hand. 'You, sir, have a deal.'

The deer shoot didn't take place; there wasn't enough time. Instead, they worked on the plans to make the "family seat of the Frazer" as David put it, a profitable business. The scope of what they intended to do was huge. Initially, six new businesses, all of which needed new buildings and plant, had to be started. David travelled to Edinburgh with the Laird to visit his solicitors and then the bank.

At the Bank of Edinburgh a secretary announced the two men to the manager, 'The Earl of Strathperth and colleague, sir,' she said.

Once they were seated the manager began without preamble, 'You've saved me having to write to you on a most distasteful subject,' he began, ponderously, evidently enjoying every moment. 'But I am afraid that the bank is calling in its loans.'

The Earl nodded. 'For how much?'

The manager made a show of consulting a folder in front of him, 'For one hundred and two thousand, six hundred and seventy pounds, four shillings and eleven pence.'

'Have you got that, David?'

'Yes, sir,' David was busy writing. He handed the paper across the desk to the manager. 'You will see that's a cashier's cheque. Kindly have the deeds sent round to the Earl's solicitors at your earliest convenience. No, not at your convenience,' David changed his mind. 'Immediately.' He stood up and looked enquiringly at the Earl, 'I think that will be all, won't it, sir?'

Strathperth stood as well. 'I believe so, David. It's been a pleasure,' he scowled at the manager, his expression making a lie of his words, 'to deal with you. Good day.' He stalked from the room, leaving the door open, the shocked expression on the manager's face providing some consolation for the petty humiliations he had suffered at the man's hands over the years.

That night over a celebratory dinner back home he recounted the meeting word for word. They were half way through the meal when the door was thrown open and two young men in their early teens rushed in followed by a middle-aged lady.

The lady was Frazer's mother and the two boys his brothers. They had been visiting friends in Inverness and had returned a day earlier than they had planned, much to the pleasure of the Earl and his son. Introductions were made, places were set at the table and the evening was spent explaining all that had happened. It was a happy and convivial party that went up to bed.

17

'WHAT WE NEED urgently is someone to oversee everything,' said Frazer a few days later.

'I know,' replied Sion, 'but we haven't thought of anybody that's suitable. Unless we advertise for the job and begin interviewing candidates. Or . . . or we could try and find someone from your old regiment. You must know scores of men who would take the job if they had the chance.'

'That's possible. Let me think about it. I'll discuss it with my father later on.'

'I thought he was set on you doing it,' said David.

'He was, but I've dissuaded him of that idea. I've a lot to do in London and he seems to accept the fact that I'll be going south soon.'

'Not without a management structure here, you're not,' said David. 'We now have a major investment that needs nurturing for a while. I've got to get back to Serbia . . .'

'You aren't going until I'm back in London,' said Frazer, sharply. 'If anything goes wrong at least I can try and pull your irons out of the fire even from that distance. From up here I won't even know what's going on. Leave it for now. What's happening about the building plans?'

'I've an architect working on a few things,' replied Sion. 'Three sheds will be built using corrugated iron from the factory in Sheffield. That's for the pigs, the cows and a new milk parlour. The bottling plant will be built next to the distillery. I've got an agent looking at different plants in Birmingham where so many beers are bottled nowadays. That idea of yours to buy in whisky from other distilleries is a corker. I've done some preliminary figures and with what we've got here he could be producing ten thousand bottles a year which will take care of the next eight years. After that we should have enough of our own whisky without buying more in.'

They went over the projections in detail. Next they went through the plans for the sawmill which was already under construction. They had bought all the equipment they needed from Dundee and would soon be able to start cutting up their own trees into wooden planks.

'Hamish McDougal,' said Frazer aloud, apropos of nothing.

'Hamish who?' asked David.

'McDougal. Hell, what an idiot I am. He's the son of one of our crofters. He's a very bright fellow whose father helped him to go to university. He took a degree in engineering a few years back and is now working in Leith, I think, at one of the shipyards. I'm sure his mother told me last summer that he'd like to come back if there was work available. Leave that to me. I'll go and see the family this evening. What's next?'

They spent the afternoon working out detail after detail. Frazer left the brothers still at it and went to visit Hamish McDougal's family and didn't return until dinner was finished.

'I ate with the McDougals,' he announced on his return. 'We had the most amazing luck. Hamish was there. He was returning to the yard tomorrow.'

'And?' queried David.

'He's still going back to the yard tomorrow but only to resign and collect his belongings. That's why I've been so long. When I told him what we're doing he jumped at the chance to be involved. I brought him up to date with events and he threw in a few ideas for good measure. He is an engineer but he took a second degree in chemistry, which I hadn't known about. He's just the man to take charge. He's also about to get married to a girl from Perth, so all in all everything's come at the right time for him.'

'We still need more qualified help,' said Sion. 'What about some of the other men working the estate?'

Frazer shrugged. 'I suppose there's the odd one or two but on the whole they're an uneducated lot who have more brawn than brains.'

His father had come into the room as he was speaking and remonstrated with his son. 'They are the salt of the earth, Angus, and don't you forget it. They might not have had much education but they still have a great deal of intelligence. Perhaps we should find a way to train our own people instead of finding newcomers.'

The argument that ensued was one-sided as David and Sion agreed with the Laird. The result was that the next morning the Earl of Strathperth called his factor to a meeting and began to work his way through a list of likely men who could work at some of the new jobs being created on the estate.

The following day Sion announced his intention to return to Biggin Hill. 'I can't stay any longer, there's a lot to do down there. Anyway, you don't need me now. Hamish arrives in the morning and he can soon get to grips with what's needed. You two can phone me when you get back to London.'

It was agreed and early that afternoon Sion was driven to Perth to take a train to Edinburgh. There he would catch the new night sleeper service to London. He'd be back at Biggin Hill the following lunchtime. It didn't work out like that but he did get to Biggin Hill.

In Edinburgh he found he had four hours to kill before his train was due to leave and so decided to have an early dinner at the hotel next to Waverly Station. He left his luggage with the station master and walked briskly up the ramp and headed for Princes Street. He was about to enter the hotel when a slight figure bumped into him, uttered the word sorry and began to walk away. Sion leapt after the boy and grabbed him by the arm.

'No you don't. Give me my wallet back,' said Sion, angrily.

'I don't know what you're talking about,' was the reply. 'Let me go. You're hurting me,'

Sion felt in the boy's pocket and retrieved his wallet. 'What's this then?'

'All right. Call the police if you like. Only let me go, please, you're hurting me.'

'Good grief. You're a girl,' said Sion in disbelief.

The girl shook off Sion's hand and said, 'I won't run away. Believe me, I'm tired of running. Now call the police.'

Sion looked at the girl and felt pity well up within him. She was skin and bone and under the grime might even be pretty. He opened his wallet and took out a fiver. 'Take this,' he thrust it into her hands.'

'Here? What's the catch? I'm not like that you know. You can't buy me for your rotten ends.'

'There's no catch. Just take it before I change my mind. Only answer me one thing. What did you mean by being tired of running?'

'I ran away from my stepfather. He was beginning to look at me in a way I didn't like. And my mother's no good. She won't stand up to him and he hits her. So I ran away.'

'Where are you from?'

'Are you after my life story or what? If you must know I'm from Glasgow,' the girl said reluctantly.

Sion thought about his niece, Susan, David's daughter and what her life was like, and knew that he couldn't abandon the girl.

'There's no catch in what I'm going to suggest. I promise I won't hurt you,' Sion said gently. 'Why don't you come with me and get something to eat while we decide what to do with you?'

'You aren't deciding anything,' was the rejoinder. 'I'm going to London to make my fortune and you won't stop me.'

'I like your courage and I'll help. I'm going to London and you can come with me,' said Sion.

'I told you, I'm not like that,' she said fiercely. 'I ran away to escape that.'

'I know. I understand and I wouldn't dream of touching you. I'm on the sleeper tonight. I'll pay for a third class ticket for you and you can travel on the same train. Unless you want to stay here in the snow and cold of Edinburgh, that is.'

She thought for a moment and then shook her head. 'Thank you. I appreciate your kind offer and accept.' She looked down at her clothes and said, 'If you're going in there they won't let me in dressed like this.'

Sion was puzzled. The girl spoke in an educated manner which belayed her appearance. But about her entering the hotel she was right. They would have to find somewhere else. At the top of Leith Walk was a pub which sold sandwiches and the girl led Sion there. He tried to press her for more information about herself but got nothing of any interest from her except that she came from Hillhead in Glasgow. She was obviously ravenous and quickly devoured two rounds of beef and pickle sandwiches washed down with lemonade. Sion did likewise except that he drank a bottle of locally brewed stout.

They walked back to the station, where Sion bought a ticket for the girl. He still hadn't learnt her name and had decided that it would be better not to keep at her until she was ready to talk. He handed her the ticket.

'This is our train,' he said. 'I'm in the front while you're in these carriages here. My coach is A and I'm in berth four. If you have any problems with the ticket collector, the guard or anybody else then come and get me. All right?'

The girl looked up at Sion's face and said, 'You're very kind. Thank you.' There were tears in her eyes as she walked away from him and climbed up into the carriage.

Sion walked pensively to his own sleeper where his luggage had already been deposited by a porter. Pensively he wondered what he was to do about her once they got to London.

He had an undisturbed night and when he awoke the train was pulling into Kings Cross Station. He thought about the girl and still hadn't decided what to do when he alighted from the train and waited there for her to walk along the platform. He didn't have long to wait before she came skipping along, excitement written large on her face.

'Do you still have that fiver I gave you?' he asked.

'Of course? Why shouldn't I?' she replied. 'Oh, this is so exciting. London at last! I can't wait to go and see what it's like. I've read so much about it. The grandeur, the riches; the King and Queen and Parliament.'

'It's like any other big city,' said Sion. 'It's full of wealth and squalor, plenty and nothing, those that have and those that don't. Good luck.' He turned away and was about to leave her standing there when he thought better of it. 'Here's where I can be found. I'm at a place called Biggin Hill about fifteen miles from here. If you need help you can telephone me at this number. Or better still,' he paused and thought . . . what the hell. 'If you get into trouble go to this address. It's a bank. Ask for David Griffiths or Angus Frazer. Have you got that? Tell them that Sion said you were to be helped.'

'Who's Sion?' asked the girl.

'Me. What's your name, by the way?'

The girl thought for a moment and then replied. 'It's Kirsty. Kirsty Murray.'

Sion held out his hand to her. 'Well, Kirsty Murray, good luck to you. I hope you find whatever it is you're searching for.' He shook her hand and walked away, leaving her standing there.

Two hours later he was immersed by the problems at the aerodrome.

Sion and Raphael were working on a new design for a plane which they told nobody about. Sion had doodled drawings which were in his head but which were proving difficult to translate onto paper. He could see what he needed to do but was it possible? He knew that it wasn't the lightness of the materials that the plane was built from that allowed it to fly. It was true that the airship flew as a result of hydrogen lifting the craft whereas a plane flew because of the air pressure under its wings forcing it up. So why not build a plane of metal, not wood and canvas? It was to this idea, now becoming an obsession, that he turned all his energies.

David was now back in Bosnia. Sion had heard from Frazer that David was hot on the trail of von Ludwig and was sending back information about Europe that was proving invaluable to the rearmament efforts of the government. In March the First Lord of the Admiralty, Winston Churchill, presented a new navy budget to the Commons which he admitted was bigger than ever before. He stated that it was the government's intention to put eight squadrons into service before the Germans could build five. A Labour spokesman declared that Churchill's attitude represented a danger to the security of the country and to world peace. Churchill had also requested an additional budget of two and a half million pounds for the Royal Navy to boost its oil reserves and to speed up the battleship and aircraft building programme. That month the German Admiral Alfred von Tirpitz admitted that his navy was expanding with fourteen new major warships entering service that year.

In Austro-Hungary the army was given precedence in the budget, and Russia announced it intended to quadruple the size of its own army for a final show-down with Pan-Germanism. However, in Berlin a French Cabinet Minister told a pacifist group that there was no innate hostility between their countries and war was unnecessary. Unfortunately, Europe was now galloping towards the precipice and there seemed nothing that anyone could do about it.

That was when Sion got the phone call.

'Sion? It's Angus. Look something odd's come up. A young lady has sent a message asking for my help. She claims to be a friend. The only trouble is she's in Marylebone Road Jail.'

'Name of Kirsty Murray?'

'That's right. So you do know her.'

'We've met. What's she supposed to have done?'

'Stole some money. Errm, what do you know about her?'

'Nothing. I helped her out, that's all. Why?'

'She was working as a prostitute in the West End. She went up to a room with some man and tried to sneak off with his wallet.'

'Oh, God,' said Sion, sick at the thought. 'Leave it to me. I'll go and see what I can do. And Angus, thanks.'

Sion drove up to town and to the police station. At the desk he asked what was to happen to the girl and was told that she would be appearing before a magistrate the following morning. Sion was not allowed in to see her and had no choice but to appear in court the next day.

He was there early and sat around, watching the procession of sad and pathetic people who were being brought up on petty charges from theft to the odd affray to prostitution. The latter were all dealt with in the same way. A ten pound fine or a month in prison. As the women had no money in the first place (which was why they plied the trade they did) they inevitably ended up going down for a month. He didn't recognise Kirsty when she was called. She was using the name of Elizabeth Browning and was dressed entirely differently from when Sion had last seen here. It was only the sound of her voice that drew his attention to her.

The magistrate banged his gavel and, in a bored voice announced, 'A ten pounds fine or one month. No money.' Bang, 'Right . . .'

'Wait,' said Sion leaping to his feet. 'I'll pay the fine for her.'

'What? How dare you interrupt these proceedings, sir,' the magistrate said ponderously. 'You should have told the Clerk to the Court of your intentions to pay.'

'How could I? Nobody asked me. I said I'll pay, so let the lady go.'

There was laughter in the court at Sion's description of the girl as a lady and Sion blushed. 'Silence! Silence in Court,' said the magistrate, banging his gavel hard. 'Now look what you've done, sir. Made a mockery of my court; a laughing stock. I shall fine you for contempt. What is your name?'

Inspiration visited Sion at that point. 'My name is Sir Angus Frazer. There has been some mistake as I happen to know that this young lady is the granddaughter of a very important person.' That caused a stir and Sion told himself to tread carefully. He didn't want too much interest in her. 'You only have to speak to her to know that she's well educated. Now, can I pay the fine or do you want trouble?'

The magistrate was not used to being spoken back to in his court, but there was something about Sion and the way he spoke that warned him to be careful. He made up his mind and brought his gavel down again. 'Fined twenty-five pounds,' he looked at Sion defiantly as the people in the public gallery gasped at such a heavy fine.

Sion paid the fine with alacrity and escorted Kirsty from the court. A number of newspaper men had gathered to try and talk to them but Sion shouldered past them and led Kirsty to his car. Luckily there were no photographers about. He said nothing as he drove away and she sat huddled in a corner, as silent as the grave. When he looked at her Sion realised with a shock that she was crying. He handed her a handkerchief and said gently, 'Do you want to talk about it?'

'What's there to say? You must think me a harlot. You can stop and let me off when ever you like. And thank you.'

Sion ignored her and kept driving. After a few minutes she said, 'Drop me off. You don't want me in your car, I can look after myself.' She began to cry again.

'No, you can't, and you still haven't told me what happened.'

'You won't believe me even if I did tell you,' she said, fiercely wiping her eyes. Anger made them sparkle.

'Yes I will. Nothing surprises or shocks me and to discover you were in jail on a charge of prostitution came as no surprise.' He shook his head.

'I used the money you gave me sparingly. I tried everywhere for a proper job but it was hopeless. Then,' she faltered. 'Then I allowed this man to take me to his room. God,' she shuddered, 'it was awful. He tried to kiss me. He had a little bristly moustache. And he tried to touch me. I wouldn't let him. I broke free and ran from his room.'

'Taking his wallet with you.'

'No I didn't. That was a lie. He ran after me and yelled at me to stop, that I was a thief. A policeman caught me. The man put his hand in my coat pocket and took out his wallet. Said I had stolen it. I swear, I didn't take it. He must have had it in his hand when he put it in my pocket. The policeman didn't believe me and I was arrested. It was awful. That was when I thought about what you had said. I used my last shilling to send a message to you. When I heard nothing I thought either that you hadn't received the message and the person I asked had just taken my money or that you had received it and didn't want to help.'

'I came as soon as I heard. Is that the truth?'

'Yes. Look will you stop the car and let me out? I don't need any of this. Especially to be treated as a liar after what I've been through.'

'I believe you and I'm not stopping. You've no money, no prospects, nowhere to live, nothing. So you may as well come with me.'

'I told you I'm not that sort of girl. I . . . I couldn't go through with it and I won't. I'll find something.'

'Do you want to go home? I can arrange it if you like.'

'No! I don't want to go home. Not with my tail between my legs, like a whipped dog.' Kirsty showed a fighting spirit that Sion liked. 'Anyway, you lied in court. You said you were Sir Angus Frazer and yet you told me your name was Sion.'

'It is Sion. Angus is a friend of mine and I borrowed his name and title for a few minutes, that's all. I figured it would impress the magistrate more than Sion Griffiths, which is my real name.'

'It did that. Twenty-five pounds of impression,' she laughed, the sound sending a shiver along Sion's spine.

Sion grinned back at her. For the first time Sion noticed that she was beautiful. She had large brown eyes in a heart-shaped face, brown hair framing an intelligent smile and a high brow, at the moment wrinkled in thought. 'Where are we going?'

'Biggin Hill, to my aeroplane factory,' said Sion.

'Aye, that'll be right. An aeroplane factory. Pull the other one, it's got bells on it.'

Sion shrugged, 'As you like. But we'll be there soon enough.'

As they neared the Hill aeroplanes began to appear in the sky and Kirsty sat up and took notice. She kept casting glances at Sion, evidently wondering whether he was telling the truth or not.

The sign GRIFFITHS AVIATION LTD at the entrance to the factory convinced her he wasn't lying and she lapsed into silence, intrigued as to what was before her.

What she found was a warm welcome from Mrs Cazorla and her daughters. Sion told them that she was an addition to the household and that he would be finding her a job in the factory. With that he left her to settle in, while he went back to work.

In the evening Kirsty wandered into what was thought of as the experimental shop. There she found Sion and Raphael pouring over their plans. 'What's this?' she asked, picking up a sheet of paper.

Sion looked at what she was holding and replied, 'It's a drawing of that engine there,' he nodded at the V8. 'Connected to a pump and an ignition switch.'

Kirsty nodded, picked up a pencil and a fresh piece of paper and swiftly drew the engine. Sion looked at it with interest and then with astonishment. In just a few minutes she had drawn an exact replica of the picture of the engine.

'That's a talent,' said Sion. 'Why didn't you use it? This is amazing. Look, Raphael,' he showed it to the young man on the other side of the work bench.

'That's very good, Miss,' he smiled at her and then turned back to what he was doing.

'Why didn't you do people's portraits or . . . or anything. You could have made money doing that. You still can.'

She shook her head. 'I . . . No, let me show you.' She deftly drew a picture of Sion and showed it to him.

'He looked at it, smiled and then burst out laughing. He handed the paper to Raphael who had the same response.

'You see, I can't help it. I can draw inanimate objects as I see them but as soon as I try and draw a portrait something happens and I make a, what do you call it? Cari . . . cari something or other.'

'Caricature. Cartoonists do it in the newspapers all the time when they're lampooning politicians.'

'Yes. I see the funny side of people and it comes out like that. It's not even deliberate. I can't help it. A lot of people don't see it as funny though. They're insulted and I don't mean them to be.'

'I think you're going to be a great help,' said Sion. 'Our difficulty is creating the drawings we need to work things out on. Look, let me show you.'

Kirsty became absorbed in the detail of what the two men were doing and it came as a surprise when Raphael's mother called them to dinner. From then on Kirsty helped anywhere she could, happy to turn her hand to anything. She cleaned up with the two Cazorla girls, helped with the cooking and made the drawings that Sion needed. She proved to be as educated as Sion had first thought, witty in an inoffensive way and, with good food in her, she was becoming prettier by the day.

The orders for aeroplanes continued as Europe continued on its mad rush to war. The problems of Ulster and the suffragettes were both becoming insurmountable as confrontation followed confrontation. In May Frazer received a long report from David that led him to go to see Sion to tell him what his brother was up to.

'David's in Sarajevo, in Bosnia,' he said. 'According to David, von Ludwig's in the city plotting something. He doesn't know what it is except that it involves the Black Hand gang and some student radicals. A young man by the name of Princip is involved and seems to have a lot to do with it. He also thinks that Archduke Franz Ferdinand is the target and wants us to warn the Archduke.'

'Why? Anyway, that doesn't make sense. We know that von Ludwig is a part of the German establishment. The Archduke is heir to the throne of Austro-Hungary and is Germany's staunchest ally. No, it doesn't make sense.'

'That's what I thought,' said Frazer. 'By the way what do you think of the whisky?'

'Excellent. I like the label as well,' said Sion, hefting the bottle in his hand and staring at the design. The label showed a drawing of the house in light grey on a yellow background. Across the top was the heading THE STRATHPERTH, and below the picture was the legend, SINGLE MALT WHISKY, aged 8 years. 'How are sales going?'

'It's early days yet but Harrods have taken a dozen cases so that's a good start. Anyway, it does make sense if you have a mind as warped as von Ludwig's.'

'How?' The two men were sitting in the room attached to the workplace where Sion was designing his new aeroplane, enjoying an early evening whisky. In the room was a table, two arm chairs and Sion's bed.

'If the Germans get the Black Hand to kill Ferdinand the Austrians will attack Serbia and take the Hungarians with them. Germany will side with their allies and before we know it the war that they have been wanting all this time will happen. It makes a great deal of sense to me but before I passed my crack-brained idea on to anyone else, even John, I thought I ought to put it past you first.'

'You may be right. It could just be the kind of excuse they want. What are you going to do?'

'Tell Lord Stockdale and let them decide. The problem is that Austro-Hungary is virtually our enemy, even though we pay diplomatic lip service to the contrary. They may not believe us even if we do tell them. It's a hell of a problem.'

The door opened and Kirsty came in. 'Let me introduce the two of you,' said Sion. 'This is the young lady I rescued from prison and this, Kirsty, is the gentleman who's name I took in vain in the court.'

'I'm very pleased to meet you, my dear,' said Frazer, somehow managing to be captivated and patronising at the same time. 'What do you mean about my name in vain?' he asked Sion.

Sion told him and after an initial flash of annoyance Frazer laughed out loud. 'You cheeky young pup,' he said.

On June 28th 1914 Archduke Franz Ferdinand and his morganatic wife, the Duchess of Hohenburg, were assassinated in Sarajevo, killed by a nineteen year old student named Gavrilo Princip. David was standing six feet away when it happened, but he had been unable to prevent the killing. War was now only a matter of weeks away.

18

DAVID RETURNED TO London a few days later. He sat with Frazer and Lord Stockdale at the bank, being debriefed. 'Serbia wasn't alone,' he said. 'There were no police or soldiers lining the street and at one time a bomb was thrown which landed in the car. The Archduke calmly picked it up and threw it back. The Bosnians are involved up to their collective necks. So's von Ludwig. He met with Princip two days before the Archduke arrived at Sarajevo. I missed him by minutes. If I could have got to him maybe I could have prevented this catastrophe. What's going to happen now?'

'Now we wait and see,' answered Stockdale. 'It all depends how Austria reacts. So far it doesn't bode well.'

He was interrupted by the appearance of a secretary. 'Sir, you asked me to bring in the afternoon copy of the Chronicle. I have it here.'

'Thank you, Mary. No more interruptions, please, but we could do with more coffee.'

Frazer perused the paper briefly and handed it to Lord Stockdale. 'Not good, I'm afraid.'

Stockdale read it and passed it to David. 'Well, they've certainly made the most of this. They talk of a "clap of thunder" over Europe. In Rome Pope Pius X, admittedly a sick man, fainted on hearing the news and in Vienna the Emperor, Franz Josef broke down and cried out, "No sorrow is spared me". Things are hotting up. Students are burning the Serbian flag and demonstrating against the Serbs and demanding action. I don't like what's being said in Sarajevo. The press there is happy, for God's sake, about the crime. And why haven't the authorities made any mention of the Black Hand Secret Society. You did pass the information I gleaned back to the relative ministers, didn't you, sir?' David looked enquiringly at Stockdale.

'I passed it to the appropriate authorities for onward transmission. I was told that the warning had been passed back to Belgrade. The problem is we don't know how deep this secret society spreads its tentacles. Perhaps the information didn't get to where it could have done any good. I just don't know. All we can do is be ready for war. What do you think will happen, Griffiths? You've been remarkably accurate about these matters to date.'

David no longer felt uncomfortable at being put on the spot and paused a few seconds before replying. 'Austria will break off diplomatic ties with Serbia and Serbia will mobilise. Russia will side with Serbia, Austria will invade and Russia will mobilise.' David shrugged and thought for a few seconds. 'After that Germany will warn Russia to back down and when it doesn't the Kaiser will declare war, ironically, on his cousin the Czar.'

In spite of himself Lord Stockdale was fascinated by David's analysis; it more or less coincided with his own. 'What'll happen then?'

David took the opportunity of pouring coffee for the three men to think about his reply. 'It will all depend on what the other chancelleries in Europe do. If they act together war can be averted, if they don't war is inevitable. Because of the Russian/French agreement Germany will declare war against France, which will drag us in.' He shrugged. 'Italy will stay neutral in spite of her pact with Austro-Hungary and Germany, as will Spain. As for the remainder of western Europe, I believe Holland, Denmark, Sweden and Norway will remain neutral.'

'What about the Swiss?' asked Frazer.

'They'll stay in their chalets counting the gold they'll make from the rest of Europe. They can't be counted on to do anything either constructive or destructive. And I have to say that I can't really blame them, stuck in the middle like they are.'

'Thank you, Griffiths. What plans do you have now?' asked Lord Stockdale.

'I'm travelling to Scotland, sir, to look at some investments we have near Perth. Then, on my return I shall see. If there is a war then one commodity will be vital in the winning of it.'

'What? Oil? Coal? Steel?' suggested Stockdale.

'Money,' was the laconic reply.

* * *

Sion was overjoyed when David arrived at Biggin Hill. He showed his brother what progress had already been achieved in the short time they had been in production.

'Who drew all these cartoons?' David asked, looking at the pencil drawings of various employees adorning the walls

'Kirsty did,' Sion replied.

By far the most drawings were of Sion in various poses and guises. David laughed out loud at some of them and cast a thoughtful look at Kirsty. She's sweet on him, he thought.

'How's production going?' David asked his brother.

'We've had some problems, but not many. We keep coming up with ideas to improve things and so we keep changing everything around. Remember that idea we had back in St. Louis, paying the men for any improvements? Well, I've implemented the same idea here. There's one lad who keeps coming up with suggestions most of which we can use. This all helps me to improve production and at the same time shows me who's bright enough for promotion when the time comes. Which, from what you've been saying, will be quite soon now.'

David nodded soberly. 'When the balloon does go up what will you do?'

Sion looked startled. 'Me? I hadn't thought about it. Join the Army Flying Corps I should think. What about you?'

'The Army.'

By the time David left half a dozen drawings of him had been added to the walls.

Unknown to Sion, David called in to see John Buchanan on his way to Scotland. Sion was considered too important to the war effort to be allowed to join any of the armed forces. David thanked John for his help and continued north, satisfied that he had kept his brother out of harm's way.

Events in Europe moved rapidly. Britain ignored what was happening up until 31 July. For the previous two months the British cabinet had been wholly occupied with the Irish problem until, on 28 July 1914 the Foreign Secretary, Sir Edward Grey, announced that Austria had given an ultimatum to Serbia demanding that Austrian officials be allowed to help investigate the matter of Serbian involvement in the assassination of the Archduke and his wife. Unfortunately, at the same time, the Kaiser left for a yachting holiday in Norway, General von Moltke, head of the German army, was taking his cure in a foreign spa and the French President was on a state visit to Russia. The Serbian Prime Minister was away from Belgrade preparing for an election campaign and the Russian Ambassador to Vienna was absent on leave. Europe was totally unprepared for the forty-eight hour ultimatum.

Austria invaded Serbia and declared war the next day. The Czar mobilised over a million men and the following day was told by the Kaiser that unless Russia ceased the mobilisation, Germany would also mobilise. Italy declared her neutrality, the Kaiser declared war on the Czar and the Royal Navy was mobilised.

Then, just as David had predicted, Germany declared war on France which caused the British government to tell the Kaiser that it would stand by the 1839 Treaty of London guaranteeing Belgium neutrality and protection of the French coasts. Twenty four hours later Germany invaded Belgium. That was in the first four days of August. After that Austria declared war on Russia and Serbia declared war on Germany. Germany and Austria threatened Italy if it refused to renounce its neutrality; Liege in Belgium fell to the Germans and a British Expeditionary Force (BEF) landed in France. German troops took Brussels and the Japanese Emperor declared war on Germany. The Germans were fighting along a 150-mile front from Mons to Luxembourg as Russian troops penetrated 50 miles into Prussia.

August ended with Europe entering a bloodbath of unprecedented proportions. The war to end all wars had started.

Britain's declaration of war against Germany sent cheering crowds through the streets of London, converging on Downing Street and Buckingham Palace. Field Marshal Sir John French, who was in command of the BEF declared that it would all be over by Christmas. Most of the cabinet and press agreed with him. Surprisingly, the one dissenting voice was the newly appointed Secretary of War, Lord Kitchener. In his opinion the struggle would be a long and bloody one and he mounted a campaign to find at least one hundred thousand volunteers for the army. The remainder of the British Empire was rallying to the call to arms and expeditionary forces were offered by

New Zealand, Australia, Canada and Chief Lewanika of the Barotse tribe of Northern Rhodesia. By the end of the year there was deadlock on every front in Europe.

Sion was test flying a Griffin on Christmas Eve with Raphael in the front seat. At first he had been angry at being told he could not fight because of his war work but had eventually accepted the situation. Instead he flung himself into work, developing and improving the planes as quickly as possible. Sion was now working on converting the Griffin to perform a dual role as a bomber and a fighter. To date the plane had proved to be popular with its pilots; it was fast, manoeuvrable and reliable. He had been sickened to read in the papers that morning that the Germans had taken 578,000 Allied prisoners and anger surged through him as he gripped the flying control wheel. It was nearly three o'clock on a cloudless, crisp winter's day. They had fired their guns over the Channel, looped the loop and were turning back to Biggin Hill when Raphael yelled and pointed to the east. Six, no eight, aeroplanes were approaching England.

Sion climbed rapidly to eight thousand feet, at least four thousand above the advancing planes. He waited until they had passed beneath him and turned to take a better look. Immediately he recognised the German crosses on the wings of the Jeannin fighters. He still had plenty of petrol and although unsure of their intentions he guessed the Germans were up to no good. He mentally went through what he knew about the planes he was about to attack. At least thirty miles per hour slower than the Griffin, each had one gun carried on the starboard side and pigs to manoeuvre. All the advantage was with him.

Nobody had worked out aerial tactics, nor how the aiming of guns was affected by a plane travelling at nearly 100mph aimed at another travelling at 60mph. The planes he was swooping down on were over Dover when Sion saw that bombs were being dropped on the town. He opened the throttle to close on the enemy more quickly and yelled at Raphael to begin shooting. Raphael aimed the port gun and pulled the trigger to emit a long burst of gunfire. The shots went wild until Sion saw what was happening and jinked the Griffin to port. The bullets cut a swathe across the wing of one of the planes, which turned on its side and plunged towards the earth.

Sion was now among the planes and the pilots finally woke up to the fact that he was there. Guns were fired at the Griffin but no shots came near. The enemy turned away from the town and began to flee back across the Channel. Sion gave chase, trying to get another clear shot at the enemy. Raphael turned back and forth between the guns as the opportunity presented itself, but missed his target every time. The rapid rate of crossing made it almost impossible to aim a gun at another moving target. The enemy scattered and were soon near France. Sion realised that petrol was now becoming a problem and reluctantly turned back towards England. Anger was surging through his veins.

Then he saw there was another Jeannin, low and to his left. He dived and yelled at Raphael to fire. He did, missing by yards. In his frustration Sion threw the Griffin into a tight turn and came behind the enemy. He throttled back, aimed at the plane below him and dropped the Griffin on to the German. The wheels of the Griffin smashed into the weak canvas-covered wings and broke them off. The German plane began to drop out of the sky with Sion's plane firmly embedded in its wings.

In spite of the cold, sweat stood out in beads on Sion's forehead as he pulled pack on the column and opened up the throttles to maximum power. The headlong plunge from the sky slowed but their rate of fall still meant certain death when they hit the freezing water beneath them. They were at two thousand feet and still plunging when Sion gave the wings a hard waggle to port, then to starboard. But still they were locked in a death throes with only a thousand feet to go.

Desperately, Sion pushed the column wheel forward to increase their rate of descent and watched as the speedometer wound up to 140mph, past any speed he had achieved before. The wings on the German plane tore away from the fuselage just as the Griffin's wings were strained to breaking point. Sion pulled back hard on the column wheel as the water rushed up to meet them, trying to loop the loop. The other plane fell away, and with only feet to spare the Griffin soared into the air.

Sion flipped out of the loop at the top and headed towards the white cliffs near Dover. That had been close!

He approached Biggin Hill and was lining up to land when he saw Peter Cazorla waving at him. He waggled his wings in salute and continued down. At the moment when he expected the front wheels to hit the ground the nose of the plane continued down, and the underside of the fuselage landed on the grass. Thankfully it had been a cold and frosty day – the ground was rock hard and the grass already white with an early frost. The back wheel held the tail up as the plane ploughed on, the speed dropping off only slowly.

They had landed at 54mph and would normally have stopped in just over a hundred yards after Sion had applied a hand brake to the forward wheels. But now they skidded on the grass, the speed still over 40mph and the side of the hangar looming large in front of them. If they smashed into it there was no telling how much damage they would do.

Peter Cazorla had not been waving a greeting when he saw the plane. He had been trying to warn Sion that something was wrong – that the undercarriage was missing. When he saw the plane line up he knew he wouldn't be able stop Sion landing, so he ran as fast as he could to the tractor and trailer holding bales of straw parked nearby. The straw was used in the wet months to trample into the mud to make the field firmer for the take-offs and landings.

He drove the trailer into the path of the oncoming plane, a few yards in front of the hanger. He scrambled up onto the straw and began to throw the bales off, dropping them between the trailer and the plane. It was a Herculean effort as he frantically tried to make a barrier that would absorb the weight of the plane hurtling towards him.

The plane ploughed into the first bale, shuddering at the impact, its speed slowing further. Then it hit a second and a third bale with bone-jarring crashes, still moving but slowing rapidly. Sion and Raphael were thrown against their harnesses as the plane hit the trailer. Peter Cazorla was thrown clear, the plane came to a halt and overturned the trailer just feet from the hangar. Fire was the problem now as petrol dripped from a ruptured pipe onto the hot engine.

19

SCREAMS AND YELLS penetrated consciousness as he began to come round. Then the stench of smoke and the pilot's fear of fire jerked him back to full alertness. Peter Cazorla was sitting on the ground, dazedly shaking his head. Kirsty was at his shoulder calling his name, telling him to wake up.

Raphael was screaming as the flames licked towards him.

Sion snatched up the knife carried in a sheath strapped to the side of the plane and hacked at the straps holding him in. It sliced through them and he was able to pull himself to his feet and leaned over the cockpit. The flames seared his head and face, his hair was on the point of catching fire and the skin on his hands began to cook.

He cut the straps holding Raphael, grabbed him under his arms and, with an effort that equalled that of Raphael's father when he dispersed the bales of straw, he heaved Raphael out of the cockpit in one swift movement. With no wheels the plane was only two and a half feet off the ground but even so Raphael landed with a heavy thump. Sion jumped out, staggered a few paces to a water butt and plunged his head and hands into the ice cold water, smashing through the coating of thin ice covering the top. The relief was fantastic, he thought as he slid back into unconsciousness.

When Sion came round next, he was in his own bed, the pain seeming to fill every part of his body. He tried to sit up but was firmly pushed back by a gentle hand. He looked to his side and focused on the frowning face of Kirsty. 'Don't move. The doctor said you need to rest.'

'Raphael,' he croaked. He coughed and said, 'Water . . . please.'

Kirsty handed him a glass of water which he tried to take but couldn't grip because of the bandages wrapped around his hands. He looked at them in surprise as Kirsty held the glass to his mouth and tilted the cooling liquid between his parched lips. He greedily emptied the glass and then sank back onto the pillows with a sigh.

'God, that feels better. Raphael, how is he?'

'He was lucky. He only hurt his shoulder when you threw him out.'

'What? How? I mean, he was screaming. The fire was all over the cockpit. Wasn't he burned?'

Kirsty shook her head. 'Not much. The flames weren't actually on him; he was being roasted not burnt and it was the terror of what was happening that scared him into screaming. The flames were on you, over the whole of the cockpit. You were burned cutting him free and lifting him out. His legs are a bit sore but nothing much. You'll see when he comes and talks to you later.' She smiled tenderly at him. 'How are you feeling?'

'It hurts,' he replied and lifted his bandaged hands to his head. 'Ouch. My face is tender as well.' He put his hands to his hair but he couldn't tell if he still had any through the layers of bandage. 'Has my hair burned away?'

'Only a bit. It's singed badly but it should grow back again. The doctor has treated quite a few pilots; his practice is only a mile or two up the road.'

'Dr Grainger, yes, I've met him. He's patched up a few of us in his time.'

'Well, he's seen worse burn cases who've made a full recovery. He told me to tell you not to worry, your good looks will return one day.'

Sion tried to grin but grimaced with the pain. Good looking, he thought. She thinks I'm good looking!

He slept for over twenty-four hours and when he woke it was to a darkened room. Night had fallen and he struggled to sit up. The pressure in his bladder needed relieving, urgently. As his feet swung off the bed a voice whispered sleepily, 'Where do you think you're going?'

'Kirsty!' Sion whispered back, 'You gave me the fright of my life. I didn't expect you to be here.'

'Well, I am. Where are you going?'

'To the water closet,' he used the euphemism for toilet, embarrassed.

'Oh, right. Can you manage?'

Sion grinned, the pain of stretching his mouth not as bad as it had been. 'I guess I'll have to.

Awkwardly he sat on the toilet and as he did so a thought came to him. He returned to the bedroom and asked, suspiciously, 'Who put my pyjamas on?'

In the moon light Sion saw Kirsty suddenly grin. 'I did,' and she burst into giggles.

Sion's recovery was reasonably rapid. He missed Christmas but on the last day of the year he had a visit from John Buchanan and Angus Frazer. By this time he was up and dressed, the bandages on his hands were on each individual finger so that he could use his hands more easily, though clumsily, and Kirsty had cut his hair so that the frizzled ends had disappeared. His brows and lashes were growing back and the skin on his face looked like raw ham, but even that was healing. According to the doctor, when Sion had plunged his head and hands into cold water he had stopped the cooking of his flesh instantly, and that had helped.

'I understand you got two of the Boche,' said Buchanan after the pleasantries and health enquiries.

Sion nodded. 'Shot one, crashed the other.' He paused, remembering. 'It doesn't work,' he announced, sadly.

'What doesn't?' asked Frazer.

'Shooting sideways from a moving platform at a moving target. It's impossible. I've been thinking about grouse shooting.' The two men looked at Sion questioningly. 'Think about it. A grouse flies up, left to right,' he held an imaginary gun and aimed, twisting round, 'and at the same time you move, right, left, up, down.' He weaved around. 'The plane is jerking all over the place. The gun fires a thin stream of bullets and,' he shrugged, lowering his arms, 'it inevitably misses. It's an impossible shot.'

'So what's the solution?' asked Buchanan, a worried frown creasing his forehead. 'I have to tell you that things aren't going well. So far three quarters of a million men have died or been captured. It's unheard of – it's unprecedented in the annals of war. We need an edge and we don't have one.'

'An edge?' Frazer was shocked to the core. 'We need more than an edge. We need a miracle. We've got men bogged down in a network of trenches shooting at each other, charging each other to be machine gunned to death without achieving one single objective. Much as I loathe the man I have to admit that Kitchener was right. This is going to be a long war of attrition. An awful lot of men are going to die. The Germans carried out a Naval bombardment of the east coast of England and killed hundreds of men, women and children, and then there was the aerial attack on Dover you intercepted. We need more ideas, more machines, if we're to end this war sooner rather than later.'

'How can we fire from the planes effectively, Sion? I gather there's no problem strafing troops or shooting down observation balloons and airships, but what about other planes?'

'Troops are virtually stationary as is the airship so, like firing on grouse, there's only one moving target.' Sion walked over to a blackboard, awkwardly took a piece of chalk in his hand and drew an outline of a plane. Above and behind it, swooping down out of the sky, he drew another one. From the nose of the second plane he drew an intermittent line and said, 'Ratatatat. If the firing plane was moving in a straight line towards the target the effect is the same as if it was stationary in terms of the firing solution.'

'That's why the pushers fly like they do. So the gunner can fire forward,' said Frazer.

'Yes, we know that but at what an expense in speed and manoeuvrability! No, we need to find a way to fire through the propeller.'

'That's impossible,' said Buchanan, 'we all know that. When the prop is turning it's like a solid wall. No bullet can penetrate it without chopping it to pieces.'

Sion nodded. 'I agree but we need to find an answer and I have something working in the back of my head which could do it.'

'Are you going to tell us?' asked Frazer, intrigued.

'Not yet, but I will soon. Ah, here's Kirsty. Can you bring us some tea please? It's been a long afternoon.'

Kirsty had entered as Sion was speaking, concern for her patient, etched on her frowning brow. 'All right. But you mustn't tire yourself. One cup of tea and then they'll have to go.' She flounced out of the room.

'She's sweet on you,' announced Frazer, a grin on his face.

'What? Kirsty? Don't be daft. She's just looking after me,' replied Sion, blushing.

Frazer and Buchanan glanced at each other, both managed to keep straight faces as they nodded their agreement with Sion's statement.

'What's the word on David?'

'David is in Austria sowing seeds of mistrust and doubt,' replied Buchanan, enigmatically. 'I received a request that he be allowed to join a regiment, with Frazer, to fight in the trenches. I told him he couldn't and to stop asking.'

'I didn't know he had asked,' said Sion, surprised at the news. 'Why don't you let him go? And what's this? You're joining up, Angus?'

Frazer nodded.

'He can't join up,' said Buchanan, 'on the orders of Stockdale who had it from Churchill. David's work is worth a battalion at least. He has caused enemy regiments to be deployed uselessly and others to be taken out when they're most wanted. No, he'll continue doing what's he's proved to be good at.'

'What happens if the Germans catch him?' asked Sion. 'A soldier is put into a prisoner of war camp. What happens to David?'

'They'll shoot him,' was the abrupt reply. 'Which proves his worth to us, and proves how dangerous he is to the enemy.'

After their tea the two men left to return to London and Sion went outside to join Raphael.

'How's it going?' he asked him.

The reply was a shrug.

'Come on, Raphael, cheer up. It's over, forget about it.'

'I can't, Sion. I remember it all the time. The heat, the fear. I was paralysed. I knew I needed to grab the knife and cut myself out but I couldn't get my hands to work. I just sat there. I was waiting to die.'

'Raphael, you're sixteen years old – hardly more than a boy, but you're doing a man's job. You did well when we attacked the Boche, and we survived. I couldn't and, indeed, I can't manage without you, so please, forget about it and let's get on with the job. Now, have you made the sheath?'

Raphael showed Sion what he was doing. He had made a metal sheath which would fit round the base of the propeller and part of the way along each blade. When the gun was fired some of the bullets would be deflected as the wooden propeller swept round while others would pass through. Sion knew that John Buchanan's misconception was a commonly held one. When the propeller was spinning there wasn't a solid wall, it only appeared to be one. At the speed a bullet travelled, Sion estimated seventy to eighty percent of the rounds fired would pass through in a straight line.

'When will it be finished? A few days?'

'About that,' replied Raphael.

Sion clapped the younger man on his shoulder, wincing with the pain in his hand. 'Cheer up. I'm going to get some rest. I'll see you at dinner.' He turned away and then stopped at the sound of his name..

'Sion . . . Sion . . . I want to thank you for what you did. If it hadn't been for you . . .'

Sion interrupted the youngster fiercely, 'If it hadn't been for me none of it would have happened. I got us into the mess by doing what I did. It was stupid, unprofessional and dangerous. We got out of it by the skin of our teeth. We were in danger from the time I hit that Boche plane and we plunged towards the sea to the time we climbed from the plane. If your father hadn't been so quick thinking, hadn't done such a brave thing, we'd either be dead or a damn sight worse off than we are. So if there's anybody to thank it's your father, not me. Now, stop feeling sorry for yourself, buck up and get on with your work.'

For the first time in days the boy smiled and then squared his shoulders and nodded.

Over dinner that night, Sion said, 'Peter, I want to thank you for what you did. You saved our lives.' The older man shrugged and looked modestly down at his plate, clearly embarrassed. 'All right, no speeches. Just to say that you are officially the works director and as such get a pay rise of two hundred pounds a year.'

There was a lot of excited chatter around the table, and their heartfelt thanks were expressed by the two Cazorlas. It transpired that Mrs Cazorla was pregnant again, which nobody else had known. So it turned in to an evening of celebration.

A week later Sion and Raphael fitted a machine gun behind the propeller of their test engine, tied a piece of string to the trigger and retired around the corner of a nearby building.

'You can have the pleasure of pulling it,' said Sion to Raphael. The youngster did so and the gun fired a few dozen rounds. Mixed with the sound of the shots was the occasional clang of a bullet on metal. The engine didn't falter.

They returned to look at the results of the test firing. The target they had erected a few yards in front of the gun had been made of bales of hay, to absorb the bullets. Some of the shots had fired straight and true. Others had been deflected in all directions as evidenced by the marks in the bales surrounding the engine There was one huge problem, and Sion and Raphael stood considering it for a few seconds.

'That gouge mark in the cowling means the bullet came straight back. It would have killed either you or me,' said Sion.

'Me,' was Raphael's monosyllabic reply.

'Any ideas?' Sion asked.

'Nope. We need to go back to the drawing board,' said Raphael.

'I wouldn't say quite that far back. What if we built an armoured deflector around the gun to stop the bullets?'

'But then I won't be able to aim the gun,' pointed out Raphael, reasonably.

'No, so you won't,' said Sion, thoughtfully, a new idea taking root. 'Right, let's leave this for now. The army can work on it. After all it's more their problem than ours. Let's go and work on the X'plane.'

Three weeks later Sion took the bandages off his hands for the last time and flexed his fingers, trying to get the dexterity back in them. They were stiff and clumsy still but, to his relief and in the fresh air, they continued to improve quickly.

On 24 January he flew a Griffin for the first time since the accident. He headed east and north and found himself at the estuary to the Thames. He was about to head west towards London when he changed his mind and continued along the coast. After a further twenty minutes flying time, he turned east with the intention of returning to Biggin Hill. The flight had been intended to test the additional fuel tanks they had installed, thereby increasing the range of the plane to nearly two hundred miles. So far it was proving a success. It was then, out of the mist, he saw the ships.

The ship in front was the largest Sion had ever seen and the three behind weren't much smaller. He recognised them as German battle cruisers. He flew lower to take a closer look, sure they were heading for the east coast to shoot the towns up again. As he turned away the last ship in line opened fire and the plane began to buck.

Sion dived, gathered speed and, as the enemy gunners got his range, pulled back on the column and looped the loop, throwing the enemy off. His heart in his mouth, he dived for a localised fog bank and vanished out of sight. The firing ceased and he again made the plane climb, gaining altitude. He headed south, worried, frantically wondering how to warn the British about what he had seen.

Ten minutes later he saw a British squadron of cruisers. Flying low, waggling his wings to show he was friendly, he flew parallel with *HMS Lion*, astern of which was *HMS Tiger*, followed by *HMS Princess Royal.*

The Griffin he was in was due for delivery to the army. As these planes were often used for spotting, either troop deployments or troop movements, they carried a naval signalling light in their cockpits. It was operated by the pilot and powered by a wet cell battery stowed under his seat. As he flew near the ship he recognised the flag flying at the masthead as belonging to an Admiral. Sion didn't know it, but Vice Admiral Sir David Beatty was aboard and in command of the squadron.

Awkwardly Sion lifted the signalling lamp and aimed it at the bridge. He flashed Bravo Tango, a dash followed by three dots, a pause and a dash. He received an answering dash of light. Ponderously Sion sent the message :- GERMAN BATTLE CRUISERS AHEAD. TARGET EAST COAST. SPEED TWELVE TO FIFTEEN KNOTS.

The signal was acknowledged and Sion had the satisfaction of seeing smoke belch out of *HMS Lion's* smoke stacks as her speed was suddenly increased. Aware that he was getting low on petrol, in spite of the extra tanks he had installed, Sion turned back to the coast. He still had to get to Biggin Hill.

The next day the newspapers reported what had happened. The British squadron had caught up with the Germans cruisers just off Yarmouth. They had not been spotted until they opened fire on the German cruiser *Blücher*, acknowledged as the most powerful battle cruiser in the world. A fast running sea battle had ensued which had resulted in the sinking of the *Blücher*, most of the damage being inflicted by *HMS Lion's* 13.5 inch guns. She had sunk on the Dogger

Bank and was the largest warship destroyed to date. Three other cruisers, the *Derfflinger*, the *Seydlitz* and the *Moltke* were badly mauled and escaped only by entering their own minefields. The British losses were light, the *Lion* suffering just eleven wounded. In a postscript to the story was a short sentence which read, "Finding the Germans was no accident. Admiral Beatty acknowledged the help of an unknown flier who had sent him and his squadron into battle. Whoever you are, sir, this newspaper salutes you."

Sion smiled quietly to himself.

20

IT TOOK UNTIL March to get the gun firing through the propeller without endangering the life of the pilot. It had occurred to Sion that if he aimed the aeroplane like a gun at the target and pulled the trigger himself he wouldn't need to carry an additional person in the form of the gunner. That in turn would give the plane a greater range because it would be able to carry more petrol. That was how he had been able to fly so far from his base when he had warned the fleet.

He and Raphael now had armoured deflectors protecting the propeller which were designed in such a way as to push the bullets to one side by no more than twenty degrees. Eight out of ten bullets fired straight and true.

When Sion showed his design to John Buchanan it was agreed with alacrity that his other planes had to be fitted with the same capability as soon as possible.

'That explains a lot,' was the enigmatic statement from his friend.

Sion looked at Buchanan in surprise. 'What explains a lot?' Sion asked.

'Do you remember a man named Roland Garros?'

Sion nodded. 'Of course. He was the first pilot to fly the Mediterranean. I think it was about two years ago.'

'That's him. He's been shooting a lot of Germans down and the information we had was that he was able to shoot through his prop. He was flying a Morane-Saulnier Type L monoplane and had suggested to the French that his design be taken up.'

'You talk about him in the past tense. Is he dead?'

'The Germans captured him and his plane last week. If they use his design and it works then we're no further ahead but at least we aren't lagging behind.'

'Damn it,' said Sion, angrily. 'How are we going to win if we don't pool our knowledge and information? If we keep thinking of the same things but each of us jealously guarding his secrets we'll never get ahead of the Boche.'

'You mean like the secret you have in the shed over there?' Buchanan suggested slyly.

'That's different,' replied Sion, hotly.

'Is it? How?'

'It . . . it just is,' Sion paused. 'Hell, no it isn't. I'm trying to do something no-one's done before, that's all. And I don't want to make a laughing stock of myself by failing.'

'What is it?' Buchanan asked.

'Come on and I'll show you,' said Sion, walking towards the shed and taking a key from his pocket. 'As you know, one of the problems we have is in the construction of the planes. Wood covered in canvas and caked in dope is highly inflammable, which means a lot. The armies on both sides are using incendiary bullets which, if they strike almost any part of the plane, start a fire. The petrol behind the pilot ignites at the merest hint of a spark and the planes go up so quickly there's nothing a pilot can do to save himself. If he jumps he falls to his death, but if he stays where he is, he's burnt to death. As you know, that's why they all carry pistols so they can kill themselves and avoid a painful and horrible death. However you look at it they're still lost to us. It's one of the main reasons that we and the Boche lose as much as seventy percent of our aeroplanes and pilots once an engagement starts.'

Sion pulled open the door to the shed and said, 'Voilà. My solution.'

Inside sat a low, gleaming monoplane. It was like nothing that Buchanan had ever seen before. In spite of himself he gave a low whistle of appreciation, walked into the shed and ran a hand over the metal wing. 'Does it fly?'

Sion shrugged. 'I don't know,' was the honest reply.

'You don't know?' Buchanan repeated in amazement.

'In theory it should. A similar design has flown recently, but it crashed. I've made some alterations which should make all the difference, but I haven't tried it out yet.'

'I don't remember seeing anything about a crashed, all-metal plane,' said Buchanan, continuing to wander round the wings and tail.

'You wouldn't have. It happened in Germany.'

'What?!'

Sion laughed at Buchanan's expression of surprised incredulity. 'Don't worry, I'm not collaborating with the enemy. David stole a design from a man named Hugo Junkers who is working along the same lines. We had both designed the cantilever wing and developed the planes as single-wing completely independently of each other. He had a few refinements I hadn't thought of and, I can tell you, I've got some that he doesn't have. He was ahead of me in that he flew a prototype but as I said it crashed. The pilot walked away with minor injuries.'

'How do you know all this?'

'Actually, David was there and saw the whole thing. That was when he decided to pinch the drawings. Anyway, I think the plane crashed due to fuel starvation and I'm also sure that Junkers hasn't worked that out yet. He's gone back to the drawing board to start again. I don't think he needs to do that. I also think he's got the wrong engine. He's using a Benz V4 and it's too underpowered for a machine of this weight. I've changed the V8 we use by increasing the piston size and letting more petrol get through. This gives a lot more power, but that's needed if the plane is to get off the ground. In theory it should work, in practice . . .' he shrugged.

'What's left to be done? How soon can you try?' Buchanan asked eagerly.

'I still have to work on the controls. I need to figure out how to operate so many moving parts with only two hands. I've tried combining the tail fin flap with the cantilevers on the wings but it doesn't work. It's a problem but not insurmountable. That's what I'm working on and when I've got the problems solved I'll share it with Gabriel and Charles Voisin, Tommy Sopwith and Uncle Tom Cobbley and all.' The Voisins and Sopwith were amongst the leaders in aeroplane design at the time and highly regarded by everyone connected to the industry. 'What's the news on David? Where is he and what's he doing?'

'Somewhere between Belgium and Germany, the last I heard. He has learnt that the Germans have developed a new weapon. Apparently it is hideous in its effect, silent in use and about to be launched at us. As yet nobody knows what it is. Lord Stockdale thinks that David's been operating behind enemy lines too long and is going gaga.'

'I don't think so,' said Sion, loyally, 'not David.'

'I agree with you. If David says something is afoot, then you can count on it. The only problem is what, where and when.'

'That's three problems. Anyway, as there's nothing I can do about that I'll carry on working on the X-plane. That's what I've called it until I get it working properly.'

A short while later Sion drove them to the nearest pub for dinner, a few miles along the road. He was busy changing gear for the umpteenth time when he allowed the car to drift to a halt, a puzzled look on his face.

'What's wrong?' asked his passenger.

'That's it. Of course,' said Sion, excitedly.

'What is?' asked a puzzled Buchanan.

'The solution. I, in common with all other pilots, have only two hands,' he said, jokingly, 'but we also have two feet.'

'What's your point?' asked Buchanan as Sion drove on.

'I'm going about the controls for the plane in the wrong way. I need to incorporate a way of using the feet to fly as well as the hands. And I think I know how to do it. Right, let's forget about that and discuss more interesting matters. How's Angus getting on?'

'He's been given the rank of major and seconded to Stockdale, much to his disgust. He wants to get into the front line and lead his regiment but he's too valuable. We've used him and his techniques to run other agents like David albeit not with as much success. But then it's early days. We're effectively setting up a separate corps within the army called military intelligence.'

'That's a contradiction in terms; military and intelligence,' Sion said with a grin.

'True. The way they're fighting this war is proof of that. Hundreds of thousands of men killed and wounded for yards of waste land won first by one side and then the other,' Buchanan shook his head. 'It's nonsensical. Have you heard from your parents recently?'

'Yes. Mam wrote saying that Dad is lobbying Washington to get involved in the war. But it's proving very difficult to get anyone to agree with him. On the personal side, our business continues to do well and we may be opening another warehouse, this time in San Francisco.'

'That's on the West Coast, isn't it? I haven't been there.'

And so they spoke of more pleasant things, each man forgetting the war for an hour or two. Later that evening they parted, John Buchanan to return to London and Sion to "fiddle with his plane". At 5 am he finally went to bed, convinced that he had solved one of his biggest problems.

Two nights later he started up the engine, Raphael helped him to manoeuvre the plane out of the shed, and he taxied over the grass. He did that a few times, going back and forth, building up the speed. Finally he opened up the throttle and began to accelerate. The speedometer increased quickly and the needle passed through fifty miles an hour, fifty five miles and hour and . . . a few moments later the bouncing ceased and the plane was flying. It quickly gained altitude to three thousand feet and Sion started turning port and starboard, up and down. The plane ran sweet and smooth, to Sion it was as graceful as a pigeon. No, he thought, that wasn't the right analogy. Pigeons were fat, satisfied and cowardly. His X plane was a falcon; elegant, fast and deadly. The Griffiths Falcon had appeared at last.

He returned to the airfield and landed in the darkness, guided down by the lights Raphael had placed along the ground. Even so the landing was very difficult, and Sion came down more heavily than he had intended. He taxied back to the shed and they quickly put the plane under cover, away from prying eyes.

The following morning Sion was woken by a hammering on his bedroom door. The door was flung open and John Buchanan rushed in with Frazer on his heels.

'What? What is it?' Sion sat up groggily, trying to get his sleep-filled mind into some semblance of order. 'What time is it?'

'Five-thirty. Get up Sion, David's in trouble and needs your help. Desperately.

Sion dressed rapidly and followed the men into the kitchen where he found Peter and Maria. She was busy making coffee while Peter tied his bootlaces and rushed out to wake up Raphael.

'What's this about David? Where is he?'

'He's in France or maybe Belgium,' answered Frazer. 'He's on the run. The Germans are hot on his heels and if we don't do something quickly he'll get caught.' He broke off to accept a cup of coffee into which he ladled three teaspoons of sugar.

John Buchanan took out a sheath of maps and laid them on the kitchen table. 'This is the position along the front at the moment. It's called Joffre's Wall and stretches along this line,' he pointed at a position midway between Ostend and Nieuport and drew his finger south, past Lille and then south to Noyon, then east to Rheims and Verdun before continuing south to Belfort. 'Angus received a message from David a few hours ago. It's two days old. He was on the run from Mons and heading for Lille. He's on foot and the Germans are right behind him.'

Frazer opened a briefcase and extracted papers of his own. 'One of the contingency plans we had was a series of what we call extract points across Europe. Different places need different ways to escape. We've had plans for David to get out using boats, cars, trucks and in Hungary, a raft. Along here it's always been our intention to use an aeroplane if we could. Without saying so or asking I think David always assumed you'd go and get him.'

Sion nodded while he helped himself to more coffee. It went without saying. There was nothing on this earth that would stop him from trying.

'From the information we received I believe David is heading for this particular field.' Frazer referred to a French map showing a place where two rivers met. 'This is the confluence of the rivers Schelde and Scarpe. I believe he'll be there waiting for a plane.'

'When will he get there?' asked Sion, his mind already busy working out distances and fuel and speed.

Frazer replied, 'At dawn.'

'When? Today?' Sion was aghast.

'Yes. In about one and a half hours. That's why we came at this ungodly hour.'

'What happens if I don't get there in time?'

'If he's still alive he'll be there tomorrow. After that he'll try and make it through the lines on foot. I don't hold out much hope of him surviving but there's a more important consideration.'

'What's more important than David's life?' Sion asked.

'He says that the Germans are going to unleash their secret weapon shortly. We need to know what it is, urgently. We need to get David out this morning and we need you to do it.'

'I'm on my way as fast as I can get there.' He was pulling on his flying boots and reaching for his jacket when Raphael entered the kitchen. 'Rafe,' Sion said, 'tell your father I want the X-plane made ready to go. Full fuel, guns loaded and the Lee-Enfield with the scope in its holder. I'm away in ten minutes.'

'Okay, Sion,' said Raphael, hurrying out the door.

'What else do I need to know?' asked Sion, as he accepted a bacon sandwich from Mrs Cazorla.

'Nothing,' replied Frazer. 'I want to reiterate that the Boche could be on his heels, so be careful. Will the new plane do the job?'

'It's his only hope. It's the fastest thing in the skies. If the Germans are right behind him we could survive the incendiary bullets as long as they don't hit the petrol tank or engine. In the Griffin we wouldn't stand a chance.' Sion grinned, 'This is our secret weapon.'

Outside it was still dark. A heavy dew had fallen and Sion shivered at the prospect of what lay ahead. He became aware of the person standing right next to him, an arm going around his waist. He looked down at Kirsty and returned her hug.

'Please be careful, Sion. I couldn't stand it if anything happened to you,' she said softly and then rushed back into the house to hide her tears.

Sion was disconcerted for a moment and then the roar of the engine on the X-plane brought his mind back to the job in hand.

The Cazorlas wheeled the plane out of the hangar and Peter Cazorla said, 'The Falcon is ready, Sion. She will fly like the bird she's named after. Good luck.' He held out his hand.

Sion shook it energetically and said, 'I'll be back.' He zipped up his leather fur-lined jacket and climbed into the cockpit.

Frazer stood next to him and yelled, 'Where will David sit?'

'On my lap,' and with that Sion gave a cheery wave and taxied away. He lined up on the field and gunned the engine. The Falcon accelerated rapidly, eager to rise into the air. Sion kept her steady and as the speed passed 55 mph he pulled the column control back and the plane sailed smoothly up into the dark sky. At seven thousand feet

Sion levelled off and headed towards the sliver of oyster white that was the dawn breaking far ahead of him.

His biggest problem was navigation. How did he land on a particular small field in the middle of nowhere in territory occupied by the enemy?

The big V8 engine purred and the stream-lined plane flew through the air at a speed never achieved before – 152 mph made the Falcon the fastest plane in existence. Sion had mapped out way points, which he knew he had to hit if he was to find David. The white cliffs were the first and the easiest to find. He left the English coast behind and aimed straight at Calais, the lights of which he could see clearly in the night.

At Calais he adjusted his heading to 145 degrees true and prayed he would hit Lille. He could only work on a navigation method known as dead reckoning, which meant that he had to keep a steady speed and course for a given time. If he did this right he would hit his target; if he didn't he'd get lost. The problem was that he couldn't account for any drift to port or starboard caused by the wind. The sky was lightening rapidly now as dawn approached. Although it was freezing cold in the open cockpit Sion didn't notice, his mind was completely taken up with the problem of finding David.

He could see the trenches and the heads of hundreds of thousands of men facing each other with weapons of mass destruction unlike anything else in the history of warfare. He flew lower, flashing by too fast for the men below to react, either to wave, if they were British or to shoot at him if they were the Boche. A town appeared ahead. He dropped even lower, heading straight down the road. Then he saw it. The roadside sign said Lille and, with heartfelt relief, he headed back up into the sky. He turned five degrees to port and looked for the river. He could not see it but he knew it had to be ahead of him; he should reach it any second.

As the light strengthened the silver ribbon of what he hoped was the river Schelde appeared about a mile ahead. He turned sharply to starboard and put the plane into a shallow dive, increasing speed to 165 mph. Then he saw it. The river Scarpe was ahead. The confluence of the two rivers was clearly visible in the dawn light.

He flashed past, turned steeply to starboard and then swept round to aim at the field where his brother ought to be. To the right he saw a copse of trees and to his left open fields could be seen. Beyond the copse he could see a line of soldiers advancing slowly. From the shape of their helmets he knew they were Germans, now less than a mile away. In the middle of the line two lorries were keeping pace with the soldiers. He throttled back, lined up on the middle of the field and headed in to land, praying that David was there.

He touched down and eased back on the throttle, setting the engine to idle. He looked frantically left and right but saw no one. He turned the plane, ready to take off and itching to go. His pulse was racing but he forced himself to stay calm. He took up his rifle and levered a round into the breech. Then he saw movement. A figure staggering from the trees. It was David.

Sion stood up in the cockpit and yelled to his brother, 'David! David. Come on! The Boche are right behind you.'

David was all in. He had been on the run for fifty hours, been unable to rest and also unable to steal any transport. Since killing von Ludwig the Germans had hounded him mercilessly. They wanted him for von Ludwig's death but they wanted him even more for what he knew. He stumbled in his exhaustion, determined not to go quietly but to take as many of them with him as he could manage before they killed him.

He was now in a daze, unable to think clearly. He knew he was hallucinating because he had heard a plane and then his brother call his name. No, there it was again, a figure standing up in a silver winged plane the like of which he had never seen before.

Sion! It was Sion. 'Come on bro', get a move on. They're right behind you.' Sion stood up and took careful aim with his rifle. He fired and a German soldier who had been about to shoot David in the back collapsed with a cry.

From the depths of his being the joy of seeing his brother surged through David and brought the last of his adrenaline with it. His exhaustion was temporarily swept away and he ran faster than he had ever run. Sion was firing steadily, shooting any German who was stupid enough to show his head. The sight on the rifle ensured he didn't waste a bullet and the Germans suddenly dived for cover, returning fire.

David reached the plane and clambered aboard. Sion sat down on

David's lap and gave him the rifle. 'Fire a few more rounds at them while I try to get us airborne,' he said.

Gasping for breath, the rifle unsteady in his hands, his movements awkward in the cramped cockpit, David fired the rest of the rounds in the magazine. Sion opened up the throttle and the aeroplane gathered speed, heading away from the Boche.

Out of the corner of his eye Sion saw one of the lorries speed out from behind a copse of trees and race across the field towards him. The Falcon had now reached a speed of 35 mph, and the lorry was almost in their path. He couldn't turn for he was committed to the take-off. The lorry stopped directly in their path and soldiers poured out of the back. Sion fired the machine gun mounted on the front of the plane and was gratified to see the lorry being shredded to pieces and enemy soldiers being flung in all directions as the bullets hit.

He looked at the speedometer for a moment – 48 mph and they weren't going to make it. They would hit the lorry before they could take off and it would all be over. But he could brake hard, slew the plane around and with luck they would miss the lorry.

He gunned the engine, slamming the throttle wide open. They were thirty yards away from the lorry and travelling at 50 mph. He pulled back hard on the stick, the plane lifted a few feet, then he slammed it forward and the plane smashed down onto the field. As it did he pulled back with all his might and the Falcon bounced into the air, the undercarriage missing the now burning truck by fractions of an inch. Bullets smashed into the plane as they gracefully attained height, the Boche left far behind them.

Sion turned towards the north west and yelled to David. 'That was close, bro'. Next time don't leave it so late.'

David's reply was to pat Sion on the shoulder. David closed his eyes and let his head fall forward onto his brother's back. He collapsed into an exhausted sleep, the last surge of his energy used up. Half an hour later they were nearing the English Channel. Sion eased his cramped body, trying not to disturb David too much. As a matter of course he looked at the fuel gauge and frowned. It was almost on empty. In a mild panic he tapped the glass. It didn't move. By his estimation there should have been at least a quarter of a tank of fuel left, if not more. He tapped again and then looked around him.

There were bullet holes all over the plane. If they had been flying in the more usually constructed wood and canvas biplane such as the Griffin they would have been dead long before they reached the Channel. As it was, the metal plane had been punched full of holes but neither the petrol tanks (there were three of them), nor a vital part of the engine or controls had been hit. So they had flown straight and smooth. Except that a fuel pipe had been ruptured and they were losing petrol. Sion prayed there was enough to get them home.

They were halfway between France and England when the engine stuttered. Sion flew lower now, only a few feet above the sea. A squadron of British destroyers were ahead of them, perhaps three miles away and steaming across their path. The engine stuttered again and the change in its noise woke David.

'What's happening?' he yelled in Sion's ear.

'We're about to get our feet wet. We're out of petrol. A ruptured feed somewhere,' Sion yelled back. 'The plane will sink like a stone so be ready to get out as soon as we hit the water.'

'The wheels,' yelled David. 'The wheels will hit the water first and we'll flip over. I've seen it before.'

'I know,' Sion said to himself as he throttled back hard and brought the Falcon down on its tail with a bone-breaking jar. The rear of the plane dropped into the calm water of the English Channel.

21

THE FALCON, LIKE all aeroplanes, rested on three wheels, one at the tail and one under each wing. When the planes had been forced down onto water, the front wheels dug in and the plane flipped over, usually killing the pilot. When he had designed the Falcon, Sion had added something new, intended to solve this problem. Around the rear wheel he had placed a cleverly designed cover, shaped like a kedge anchor. The aerodynamic shape did not hinder the Falcon's flight – on the contrary, it helped it as the air passed more smoothly over the wheel. However, when the tail hit the water, the cover dug in and pulled the plane down, tail first. When the front wheels hit a second later the plane did not flip over but came to a rapid stop.

It worked was the thought that flashed through Sion. Both brothers were thrown forward the few inches it took for them to hit against the edge of the cockpit. For Sion it was painful, for David less so as his head hit Sion's back. The plane immediately began to sink and the water was lapping at the edge of the cockpit when the natural buoyancy of the plane, mostly in the wings, kept her afloat.

The water was freezing cold and both brothers were beginning to shiver. They had lost a great deal of heat already due to the flight and neither of them had much in the way of reserves.

'What now, bro?' Sion asked laconically, as he stood up, the water now up to his knees.

David also stood up. Fatigue was etched in his face and he flopped back down immediately to sit on the edge of the cockpit. The water lapped the seat of his trousers but he didn't care, too exhausted to try and stand.

'Thanks for coming,' he said, looking up at Sion. 'I knew you would. Sorry it's ended like this.'

'It hasn't ended yet,' said Sion. He watched as the grey hull of one of the British destroyers bore down on them. He waved his arms over his head causing the plane to rock alarmingly. 'Here comes the Navy.' The words were hardly out of his mouth when they both heard the hoot of the ship's siren and the plane sank gently beneath the water.

It was so unexpected David and Sion were spluttering and swallowing sea water, unable to prevent themselves. They both floundered on the surface until one then the other was dragged down. Kicking furiously they managed to come up for air, gasping.

They began to kick off their boots and drag at their clothes to try and remove them before the weight dragged them down forever. The destroyer was closing on them and a boat was being lowered into the water even as they removed their coats. David was tiring rapidly, his movements becoming more and more feeble. Sion grabbed his shoulder and kicked furiously, trying to keep them both afloat. David was rapidly losing consciousness, the last vestiges of his strength now gone. Sion was tiring, the weight of his brother pulling them both under.

It never entered Sion's head to let him go and so they both began to sink together.

Sion regained consciousness coughing up water, and found himself dangling over the side of a whaler, the sea-boat used by the Royal Navy when going to the rescue of a man who has fallen overboard. Next to him David was doing the same; cheery voices encouraged them as they both coughed and spluttered. Sion heard the order, 'Oars!' Followed by, 'Give way, together.'

They were helped up the jumping ladder that dangled down the side of the destroyer and were met on the deck by an officer and a number of sailors, all armed, all pointing their guns at them.

'We're British,' said Sion. 'Thanks for rescuing us.'

David managed to nod his thanks before he collapsed. He was carried to the sick bay, Sion walking next to him, where they were examined. David was left to sleep while Sion was fitted out with some spare clothing and taken to the bridge.

He was introduced to the captain, Captain Williamson, known as

Captain “D” because he had command of a squadron of six destroyers. Sion learned that the ships were en route to Portsmouth from Rosyth, in Scotland. From Portsmouth they would be going to join the huge naval force already deployed in the Dardanelles. Allied losses had been substantial in the previous month and the offensive had been called off. The destroyers were to meet up with a virtual armada of other ships to restart the offensive. 75,000 troops and 200 ships would be taking part.

‘What was that strange looking aeroplane we saw?’ asked the captain.

Sion sighed heavily. The loss of the Falcon was only just beginning to sink home. All that work, all those months, gone. He would have to start again.

‘Sir, it’s a new design I’ve been working on. Can anybody tell me what happened? The last thing I remember is being in the water, and then we were hanging over the side of the boat.’

‘You have Leading Mechanic Ellis to thank,’ replied the captain. ‘It seems that as the whaler approached you both drifted down into the water. He dived in and grabbed you. When he got to the surface he found that you had a tight grip on the other man and so both of you were saved.’

‘I must thank Ellis. But in the meantime I have a request to make. Do you have any way of contacting the shore?’

‘Yes. We can send signals to the Admiralty. Why?’

‘It’s vital that a message is sent to Lord Stockdale telling him that we’re all right. Actually, to be more specific, that my brother is safe.’

‘Your brother?’ The captain repeated.

‘Yes. The man in the sick bay. He has important information for Lord Stockdale. We must get it to him as quickly as possible. Or at least let Stockdale know he’s alive and will be told what the information is when we arrive at Portsmouth.’

‘He must be important, your brother. I know who Lord Stockdale is, of course, but I’m not sure I’ll be able to get a message to him.’

‘Will you try?’

‘Yes, of course. Tell me what you want sent and I’ll get the radio operator to code it and send it to London.’

The message was despatched. The signal was sent by flashing

light to the signalling tower at Beachy Head and then by telephone to the Admiralty at the Arches in London. It was not considered an operational matter in spite of the emphasis that it was urgent and so it was not passed to Lord Stockdale or his committee.

At lunch time at Biggin Hill everyone knew that David and Sion wouldn't be returning.

David slept like a dead man until the middle of the afternoon while Sion napped in the wardroom. After a hot meal Sion had regained his strength and energy and had been on the bridge as the squadron approached Spithead. They passed the round forts, those beacons in the sea built during the Napoleonic wars to warn England of an approaching enemy and to fire on any men of war that tried to land. They were manned now, and signals were hoisted to pass between the ships and the forts.

When David awoke he climbed out of the bunk and dressed in his own clothes; they had been dried in the engine room. He wandered through the ship until he found the galley. The cooks knew he was one of the men rescued that morning and fed him copious cups of tea and wedges of cheese and bread. The food released energy in his body and the weariness rolled away. He went looking for his brother and found him talking to one of the sailors out on the deck.

'Are you okay?' David asked him.

'Sure, bro. Let me introduce Robert Ellis. He saved our lives. He's just been telling me that he was a mechanic before he joined and that he's worked on planes before. He wants to become a pilot.'

David shook the man's hand, thanking him profusely. Ellis was a slight, diffident individual, with fair hair going prematurely bald. His grip was firm and he had a steely look to his eyes that came alive when he talked about flying. Like a lot of men he had been bitten by the flying bug.

Just then over the tannoy came the announcement 'Special Sea Dutymen close up. Prepare to enter harbour. Everyone out of the rig of the day clear off the upper deck.'

'That's me, gentlemen,' said Ellis. 'I need to go to the engine room. I suggest you go to the wardroom as you aren't dressed in the right rig for entering harbour before the Jimmy sees you.'

'The Jimmy?' queried Sion.

'The First Lieutenant. He's a tartar for correct procedures which, now we're at war, is irksome to say the least. So I'd go below if I were you.' With that he left them and the two brothers took his advice and went down to the wardroom.

'You're quiet,' said David to Sion after a while.

'Just thinking what I need to do to rebuild the Falcon. It's going to take a long time, I'm afraid. Still,' he shrugged, 'it was worth it. I was also thinking that I'll have a word with John and see if we can help to get Ellis into the Army Flying Corps. So what happened to you in Germany?'

David thought for a moment, getting the events of the past month into sequence in his mind. 'I followed von Ludwig into Germany. There's a town in southern Bavaria practically owned by his family. Anyway, there I found a factory which was being used to produce mustard gas. To be honest I don't think I would have found it if there hadn't been a terrible accident which I witnessed. A number of women from the town were gassed. I followed a truckload of the stuff towards the front and realised it was meant for use against our troops. Actually, that's not quite true. I followed the truck to a factory on the Belgian and German border that was manufacturing gas masks. That's when I realised what the gas was to be used for.'

'What made you follow the gas in the first place?'

'Actually, I wasn't. I was following von Ludwig who was travelling in the convoy escorting the gas.'

'Why didn't you just shoot him and forget about him?' asked Sion.

'I'd thought about doing it a few times. But I wanted to be up close. I wanted to look him in the eyes when he died,' was the whispered reply. David cleared his throat. 'Then I saw the gas masks and overheard some of the German soldiers talking. I found out that they were going to release the gas a day later, after the masks had been distributed. I knew where the lorry was and sneaked into the garage that it was housed in. I slashed the tyres of the lorry and damaged the engine beyond repair so that the lorry couldn't be moved. I then prepared a fire using a knife to slash a hole in the fuel tank. As the petrol spread I was about to set it alight when I had some good luck.'

'Oh? What was that?'

'Von Ludwig walked in on me. I heard him coming; he hadn't been expecting anyone to be there and so did not trouble to be quiet. I was behind the door when he entered, alone. I held my knife to his throat and told him not to shout. He almost fainted when he saw it was me. I said "Hullo, von Ludwig. Goodbye von Ludwig," and thrust the knife through his throat into his brain. The satisfaction of the act lasted about two seconds as he fell dead at my feet. I lit the fire and got the hell out of there. I watched the garage go up and I'd run about a hundred yards when I realised I was downwind of the gas and ran like hell in the opposite direction. That was when I was seen. From then until you picked me up I was on the run.'

'How did you get the message to Angus?'

'I eluded the Boche for two days and got to one of our agents. I compiled my report and escape plan and sent it by pigeon and then I kept running. You arrived in the nick of time.

'How bad is this gas?'

'Pretty terrible. When I saw the accident I saw women choking and frothing at the mouth before they died. It's green; a deadly shade of green.'

'If it was that important to tell Stockdale, why didn't you send the message by pigeon.?'

'I did,' David looked surprised and then shrugged. 'The pigeons couldn't have made it, I guess. I let loose three pigeons, two with a message about the gas and one with my escape plan. It seems the gods were smiling on me if Angus only received the one with the escape route on it. It's been more and more usual for pigeons not to arrive and we suspect it's because the Boche are shooting down any that are flying west, in the same way that we shoot any flying east. I hope that the message has been passed on and that gas masks are being distributed to the troops.'

'I'll be surprised if we have any available. What do they look like? How do they work?'

'No idea. Someone in Whitehall will know,' said David.

After they docked at Portsmouth the two brothers quickly went ashore to find a telephone to call Lord Stockdale. But he was in the House of Lords and Frazer was not in the office. David left a message and then they took a taxi to Portsmouth Harbour railway station. It was nearly midnight when they arrived in London. They made their way to John Buchanan's house to find that he wasn't there either and so, feeling they'd reached something of an anti-climax they borrowed one of John's cars to drive to Biggin Hill.

They were surprised to find all the lights still on and even more surprised when they walked into the kitchen. The place was full, people sitting round the large table, on stools and leaning against the walls. There was a palpable gloom in the air, cigarette smoke permeated the kitchen along with the smell of whisky.

Pandemonium broke out when the two brothers walked in.

When order was restored and glasses of whisky thrust into their hands a babble of voices broke into questions. David quietened them and briefly told them what had happened.

'The Falcon?' asked Cazorla Snr.

'Gone I'm afraid,' replied Sion. 'We'll have to build another one as soon as we can. We . . .' he got no further as the door to the corridor opened and a whirlwind rushed in, throwing itself into his arms and raining kisses on him. Sion was momentarily surprised and then, under the gaze of his friends and colleagues, returned the kiss. The catcalls brought them to their senses and Kirsty moved away and looked adoringly at him while he grinned at her.

Sion put his arm around her waist and continued talking. 'We'll have to start again. Now, if you'll excuse me I need to talk to Kirsty about something.' There was more laughter and ribald commentary as he led her outside into the quiet night.

'I'm too old,' he said, without preamble. 'And you're too young.'

'I'm nearly nineteen,' was the rejoinder, as she added a year to her age, 'and you're not too old. 'I love you and I think I always have.'

'I . . . I love you too,' said Sion, finally putting into words what he had thought for months. He had been afraid to say anything, unsure how he would handle rejection, terrified of making a fool of himself. 'But that's not enough. The age gap is too much. You're too young,' he repeated himself.

'Sion, women of my age are married with children. The war is accelerating marriages all over the country. People are grabbing happiness while they can. I was sick with grief when you hadn't returned. We were sure you were dead. We all knew that you would die in an attempt to rescue David and . . .' she paused. 'It's not that, is it?' Distress filled her voice. 'It . . . it's because of my past. Sion, I never did it. It was the first time when I took the wallet and ran. I . . . I . . .' She whirled round and ran into the darkness.

Sion sprinted after her, grabbed her arm, turned her round and clasped her to him. He kissed her passionately and then took a handkerchief from his pocket to wipe away her tears. 'All right, I give up. I love you. I have never thought about your past, not for an instant. As long as you know what you're taking on. I live for flying and I'll keep doing it, in spite of the dangers. Can you live with that?'

'I have been, every day I've been here. I love you so much Sion. I want you as you are. I don't want you to change.'

Sion led Kirsty to his office and into the back to his room. He sat her on the bed and began kissing her again, his hands roaming until she pushed them away. 'I'm a virgin, Sion. And I want to remain so until my wedding night.'

Sion sighed. 'I'll get a special licence tomorrow.' He sat back, frustrated and wild for her. He hadn't realised that she had blossomed so much, filling out into a curvaceous beauty, who made his mouth dry with desire.

'Will you?'

'Will I what?' he asked in bewilderment.

'Will you get the licence? Can we get married soon?'

Sion hesitated; he hadn't really planned to get married for years yet. But here he was . . . 'I'll sort it tomorrow. Let's see if the vicar can fix us up on Saturday.'

Kirsty tightened her grip around him, happy for the first time in a long while. A contented peace washed over her. She'd be a good wife and mother, she resolved, unlike her own had been.

On April 22nd, as dusk fell on the Western Front, both the French Zouaves and the Canadians saw an amazing sight. Across the German lines swirled a yellowish-green vapour. Moments later the Zouaves were fleeing their trenches and dugouts, blinded, coughing and panic stricken. Behind the cloud marched the Germans wearing gas-proof helmets. They made a four-mile gap in the Allied front, but were stopped by the Canadians who were not stricken by the gas.

In spite of David's efforts and warning no gas masks had been produced for the Allies and the troops had been advised to go into battle with wet cloths and towels tied around their faces. This was yet another scandal, paralleled by the lack of guns and ammunition now affecting the Allied troops.

It had taken longer than Sion had hoped to get the marriage licence and the wedding did not take place until 2 p.m. on 8 May.

At 2.12 p.m. a German submarine sank the Cunard liner *Lusitania* off the Old Head of Kinsale in Ireland.

At 2.30 p.m. Kirsty, looking radiant in white, threw her bouquet of flowers which was caught by Mary Cazorla, the eldest of the daughters and head bridesmaid.

At 2.33 p.m. the Lusitania vanished beneath the waves, leaving nearly 1,978 men, women and children struggling for their lives.

At 3.15 p.m. the wedding guests were sitting down to a meal, prepared by the Cazorla women and served in the main hangar, now transformed by the judicious use of coloured bunting and flags.

At 4.35 p.m. the first of the rescue boats began to arrive off Ireland, in a desperate attempt to save lives.

At 4.55 p.m. Sion led his bride in a slow waltz around the temporary dance floor to the joyous handclapping of his friends.

At 8.00 p.m. off the coast of Ireland all those who were still alive had either been picked up or were safe in lifeboats.

At 8.45 p.m. Sion and Kirsty left for a brief honeymoon while the first of the passengers rescued from the treacherous waters off Ireland were landed ashore.

A few weeks earlier Italy's Premier, Antonio Salandra, authorised the signing of a secret treaty with Britain, Russia and France. Italy was no longer honouring the Triple Alliance and would now fight on the side of the Allies on condition that her territorial claims against Austria would be honoured. On May 23rd Italy declared war on Austria and David returned to Italy to find out how matters were progressing and to gauge the attitude of the people to the war.

Sion started to redesign the Falcon but unfortunately he was hampered by the need to build a house for him and Kirsty. The loss of the original Falcon had taken the heart out of him and he decided to continue working to improve the design he had used for the Griffin. He hoped that within six months the Griffin would be a monoplane but still built out of wood and canvas.

In the meantime he drew up plans for their new home. It would have four bedrooms, two lounges, a dining room and a huge kitchen. The latter had been at the insistence of Mrs Cazorla, and would make it the heart of the house. A separate bath house and toilet was to be built a short distance from the main house.

Millions died as the war continued. Conscription was established and taxation increased to pay for the war effort. Discontent with Asquith and his government continued, especially over the dreadful situation of the serious lack of munitions at the front. When Lord Kitchener died at sea, travelling to Russia aboard the cruiser *HMS Hampshire*, which struck a mine off the Orkneys, the country went into mourning. The people had considered him a hero but those who knew kept secure the fact that he was a butcher, as indeed were the other generals on both sides in the war.

In September 1916 a British secret weapon was unleashed on the Germans. For the first time a vehicle built under the strictest secrecy and codenamed "Tank" went into action. It proved to be a highly effective weapon but there were not enough tanks to do anything other than win a few local battles.

At the end of that year Lloyd George became Prime Minister and John Buchanan purchased a baronetcy for £20,000. It was a hereditary title but unfortunately he had no heirs.

On April 6, 1917, America entered the war on the side of the Allies and Kirsty gave birth to a boy named Alexander Evan Griffiths.

22

EUROPE WAS WAR-WEARY with millions dead and the continent unable to supply food for its people. Due to the mayhem and losses caused by the German U-boats, Britain and the Allies were in serious trouble and in danger of being forced to surrender due to the lack of food and of raw materials. A solution was found by the use of convoys, and soon supplies were streaming in from America. By the end of 1917 American soldiers, known as Doughboys, were arriving in France at the rate of 50,000 per month. Sion received a message from David that the German aircraft designers Hugo Junkers and Claudius Dornier had developed an all-metal, semi-monocoque plane that was the most advanced in the world.

Sion immediately began work on the Falcon II, aided by his own designs and those of the two Germans that David had stolen. He hoped to have a prototype ready within three months.

'You're working too hard, Sion,' Kirsty said to him, one evening just before Christmas. 'Why don't we take time off over the holiday and go away for a few days, to the coast. Let's get away from it all and forget this beastly war just for a short while.'

Sion smiled at his beautiful wife, beamed at his son and nodded. 'Why not? I think we deserve a break. We've been turning out aeroplanes by the hundreds and a rest will do us good. Here, let me hold him' He took his son in his hands and sat making silly noises, completely content with his life and his love for Kirsty. He was the rarest of people in that terrible year, a happy man. 'We'll go to Torquay on Christmas Eve,' he announced. 'Shall we go alone, or should we invite a few others to join us.'

'Like who?' asked Kirsty, jealous of the time she had alone with her husband.

'Like John, Angus, David . . . to name but a few.'

'If you like,' she spoke with a touch of petulance, wanting to be alone with him and Alexander.

Sensing her mood Sion said, 'No. Let's go away by ourselves for a change. We'll go and we won't tell anyone where we are so they can't come after us or demand an answer on some trivial matter that they ought to be able to solve for themselves.'

Kirsty sighed. 'That'll be lovely, only we can't go. It's too selfish. I know that, really. I just wished for a second . . . Never mind, wait till the war's over.'

Sion shook his head. 'No, we've been saying "when the war is over" for years. At the rate things are going, it'll be even more years before it ends, and we should grab what happiness we can when we can. I'll tell you what, we'll fly down.'

Kirsty looked as Sion aghast. 'You can't be serious,' she gasped. 'It's far too dangerous to fly anywhere. Especially with the baby and in this freezing weather. You are joking Sion, aren't you? Tell me you're joking.'

Sion was about to deny that he was joking when he saw how upset she was and smiled. 'Of course I'm joking. Though one day we'll all be flying all over the world and not even think twice about it.'

Kirsty nodded sceptically, happy to go along with her husband's madcap ideas even if they were idiotic. The very idea that people would be flying anywhere was stupid. Except, of course, to fight battles and drop bombs on towns and cities.

Raphael knocked on the door and walked in. 'Sion, we're ready now.'

Sion nodded and stood up, handing the baby back to Kirsty. 'Take care,' she said, fearfully.

'I'll be all right. It's only a test flight.'

The Griffin II was ready. It was a monoplane with some of the refinements of the Falcon and it promised to be fast, manoeuvrable and deadly. The Griffin and the Sopwith Camel had proven to be two of the best aircraft in the skies. Sion hoped that the new design would surpass Sopwith's; they had now become Britain's leading aircraft manufacturer.

The Griffin II was still using the V8 Hispano-Suiza engine. Sion calculated that the reduced drag of the single wings would compensate for the reduction in lift given by two wings and that a higher speed would still leave the plane flying efficiently, as it had done with the Falcon.

He climbed into the cockpit and checked the plane over. Everything appeared to be in order and he gave the thumbs-up sign to Raphael, who removed the chocks from the wheels. Sion taxied to the end of the field, turned into the wind and increased speed. The plane lifted into the air at fifty-eight miles an hour, the same speed as that of the Falcon Sion noted with interest. Sion circled Biggin Hill, gradually increasing his height and moving slowly further afield. He was nearing the coast when he saw the three huge and unmistakable German bombers approaching.

The Riesenflugzeug was Germany's answer to the failure of the Zeppelin airship's bombing campaign. These planes were giants with a wingspan of 138 feet. They carried a crew of seven and eighteen 220-pound bombs. Normally they flew only at night and after twenty-eight sorties over Britain there had been no casualties amongst the Zeppelin Staaken R. 1Vs.

Sion, on a test flight, was unarmed.

He executed a tight turn and raced back to Biggin Hill. Where could they be going in daylight, approaching Beachy Head? It took him a few moments to understand. The airfield! Biggin Hill with the factories and repair facilities was an obvious target. He opened up the throttle, sent the plane into a shallow dive and raced home, praying the wings would take the strain. He noted that the Griffin II reached 128 mph with the wings still attached. At that point in time he was grateful for small mercies.

As he approached the airfield he took out the Very pistol and fired a red rocket across the field, then lined up to land. Biggin Hill came to life like an ants' nest after being kicked over. Thornycroft 3-Ton "J" Type lorries were deployed around the field. On the backs were 3-inch anti-aircraft guns, each weighing 12,500 lbs. and firing shells weighing 12.5 lbs. They had a vertical range of 18,000 feet, a horizontal range of 31,000 feet and a rate of fire of 15 rounds per minute. Hurriedly the gun crews parked up and extended the stabilising jacks in the four corners of the lorry. In the meantime, all non-essential personnel hurried to the underground bunkers that had been built during the previous year. So far the bombing raids of the Germans had been concentrated on London and the surrounding area, this was a new departure for them.

Sion stopped at the hangar and leaped out of the cockpit. 'Get the ammunition and fill her up,' he ordered Raphael, rushing away to check that Kirsty and the baby were safe. They had already gone down into the basement in the house, designed to be used if ever there was an air-raid on Biggin Hill.

Sion ran back to the plane and said, 'How's it going, Rafe? Are we ready to fly?'

'Sure, Sion. The ammunition's aboard and twenty gallons of petrol has refilled the tanks. What's coming?'

Just then the roar of the quadruple engined planes were heard and Raphael blanched. 'Sion, you can't. It's suicide. You won't stand a chance against those things. No one has shot one down yet.'

'That's because they've never come over in daylight before. Now's the opportunity to find out what they can do.' He climbed into the plane and accelerated rapidly away. The Griffin II rose gracefully into the air. He realised as he raced for height that to date he had used up eight of his nine lives.

Sion had no illusions about the enemy target. The giant bomber had four engines, two pulling and two pushing. It was 72 feet long, had a span of 138 feet and a ceiling of 14,200 feet. It's endurance was eight to ten hours and it's only Achilles heel was its maximum speed of 84 mph. All engines were accessible during flight and an extra engine operated a wireless transmitter. There was inter-communication between the crew and dual control in the event of the death of the pilot. The plane carried a second, fully qualified co-pilot. It had a separate bomb-aimer's position and, irony of all ironies, its main armament consisted of two British Lewis guns.

Sion had one Lewis machine gun, his Lee-Enfield with scope and his Webley pistol. The latter he could throw at the enemy for all the damage it could do. He also had speed and manoeuvrability on his side.

The three enemy aircraft were coming in low, convinced of their own invincibility. Dropping bombs from 14,200 was a difficult task, hampered by the need to wear cumbersome oxygen masks and by the inaccuracy of the aiming gear; they were more likely to blow up a cow than an aeroplane or do any serious damage to the factory and other maintenance sheds scattered around the area. The sun was over Sion's left shoulder; he was at 8,000 feet with the targets around 4,000 feet below him. They were a mile away from the field when he started his dive.

The bombers were flying in a V formation, the lead aeroplane about five hundred yards ahead of the other two, themselves separated by a further thousand yards. The aeroplanes were the first to be designed specifically as bombers and so most of their machine gun fire was directed aft in defence. For that reason Sion decided to go for the lead plane. Only two machine guns could be brought to bear on him as he swooped down on his target.

From the complacent way they were flying on a steady course and speed, it was obvious that the enemy had no hint of danger. When Sion opened fire his bullets smashed into the four men sitting in the stern cockpit. All four died under the lethal shower without even knowing they were under attack. Even as he worked the Griffin along the length of the Staaken R. 1V, hosing the great plane from left to right at the same time, it was beginning to climb, clawing the sky for its safest defence position – maximum height. The two bombers at the rear of the formation were already turning, one to port and the other to starboard and climbing at the same time. They expected an attack at any second, not believing for a moment that they were under attack by one lone madman.

Sion turned to port and headed down in a steep dive, wanting to get away before the gunners in the other planes fired at him. He was over the airfield and swooping back into the sky, throttle wide open, as he tried to catch up with the behemoths now circling upwards like vultures, striving to gain height. At 14,000 feet their only danger would be from the notoriously inaccurate anti-aircraft guns; they could drop their bombs and go home, mission accomplished even if it was hit or miss.

The plane he had damaged was still flying. Sion aimed at the underbelly and climbed as fast as the Griffin would go. His speed advantage would continue until about 10,000 feet and then his smaller plane would find it difficult to speed ever higher whilst the huge wing span of the bomber would take it serenely upwards.

Up to 8,000 feet, 9,000 feet, 9,500 feet and then Sion began firing. He strafed the underbelly of the bomber, saw its port engine catch fire and then was past the target, flying up through 10,000 feet. He began to feel the effects of oxygen starvation and his thinking became a little hazy, distances more difficult to gauge. He flipped over to starboard and the Griffin dropped lower just as the anti-aircraft guns opened fire.

He flew away from the field and at 8,000 feet turned back and up to observe the damage. The bomber he had strafed was on fire and heading straight down to earth. He watched it for a few moments, awe-struck by its majestic beauty and strength. In spite of the fire on the port wing it was still gliding, but even as he watched the wing broke away and the plane tumbled from the sky.

Sion was not carrying any oxygen but he went streaking back, the Griffin again clawing for height. The other two planes were above him, dropping their bombs when he began to fire into the underbelly of the nearest one. He was 1,000 feet below and slightly behind it when he began shooting. Again the lack of oxygen began to affect him but he willed himself to stay focused, to keep at the target. His bullets smashed through the bomber's forward cockpit, killing both pilots and the second bomber began to swoop elegantly down from the sky. Lack of oxygen prevented Sion from thinking straight; his own plane continued upwards. At 11,500 feet the second bomber and the Griffin passed each other and Sion was in the sights of the rear gunners who were flying down to certain death. Both Lewis machine guns opened up and the Griffin was shredded. The wings fell apart within seconds and the plane turned over and dropped towards the earth.

Sion quickly regained full consciousness, realised what was happening and, upside down, clambered out of the cockpit. He pushed himself away from the wreckage and looked down to see the ploughed fields of the farms and the airfield itself racing up to him. The first recorded parachute jump from an aeroplane had been on March 1st 1912, by an American named Captain Albert Berry, 1,500 feet above Jefferson Barracks in St. Louis, Sion's home town. The parachute had been stored in a container attached to the aircraft. Sion had helped the captain with the design after Sion had explained about the time he had thrown himself off a butte, dangling on the end of a home made kite. Since then Sion had been interested in the idea of escaping from an aircraft using a parachute but had never previously had the opportunity or desire to try it. Now was the moment. Now or never, he thought.

The bag containing the parachute was tied to his waist by a short length of rope. Although he seemed to be hurtling towards certain death he kept calm, grabbed the knife he carried in a sheath strapped to his right leg and cut the cords holding the bag closed. The huge cotton sheet began to open when he was 4,250 feet above the ground. His fingers were numb with cold as he scrabbled to pull the 'chute free. Fear and panic welled up within him and he swallowed both; they tasted like bile.

The parachute began to fill with air and the cotton went racing through his hands. It blossomed open above his head and the rope tied to his waist brought him up with a sickening jerk that made him yell in agony, the breath squeezed out of his lungs. The rope slid up to his armpits, scraping the skin off his back at the same time. He was dangling underneath the lines, only semi-conscious, when he passed through 1,500 feet. Pain brought him back to life and he looked up to see the canopy open above his head and the ground gently moving beneath his swaying feet. The rope was biting into him. He reached up and grabbed two of the ropes connected to the cotton and pulled at them, trying to ease the pressure under his arms and around his chest. He breathed more easily for a few seconds but then the effort became too much to sustain and he let the ropes go. He realised that he was drifting towards the airfield and that the guns had fallen silent. He looked to the north and saw the second bomber still floating down. It hit the ground seconds before he lost sight of it and then he too was about to land. He braced his feet together, hit with a bone-jarring thud and fell backwards, smashing his head into a ploughed furrow.

Pain brought him around. His mind contained the thought that he was too old for this; then a second thought struck him: he had now used up all nine lives but still he lived. As he lay there, his eyes closed, he counted the crashes he had walked away from. He counted them again, and then knew why he had still lived. His early count had been wrong: this had been his eighth time.

He lay in the field, unable to move, listening to his name being called. Finally, wearily, he struggled to sit up. He turned over, lost his strength and collapsed, his mouth filling with earth. He spat it out and this time managed to get to his feet. He stood there for a few seconds, still winded, his body aching, unable to put one foot in front of the other. When he tried to do so, his leg buckled under him and he nearly fell, feeling acute pain shooting up from his right ankle. Tentatively he tried again, this time with a little more success, and he began to hobble towards the figures running his way. His ribs ached, his left eye was swollen closed and his right foot was on fire. Sion felt great.

Peter Cazorla was the first to reach him and put his shoulder under Sion's arm to help take the weight. Others rushed up yelling their congratulations, happy to see him still alive. Kirsty ran up close, paused, burst into tears and fled back to the house, half a mile away.

'What the hell?' asked Sion.

'Take no notice,' said Peter Cazorla, 'she's just happy you're alive.'

'Well she's got a funny way of showing it,' replied Sion.

In the house Kirsty had the bed turned down and a bath ready. She took charge of him as soon as he was helped through the door and sent Raphael for the doctor. She busied herself until he was lying in the warm water and said, 'When I saw the plane break up I nearly died. Then I saw you climb out and then that . . . that thing opening, and you floating down to earth. I was terrified, elated and angry all in a matter of seconds.'

'And now?' Sion asked.

'Now I'm just relieved. And, yes, happy.' She shook her head at him. 'I suppose it'll always be like this? Not knowing whether or not you're walking away from the next flight. But you warned me, so I can't complain,' she said philosophically.

'Sure you can,' said Sion with a grin, 'and you will.' He reached up for her and pulled her, squealing, to him.

'No, Sion. You're hurt too badly and the doctor will be here any minute. So get out of the bath and get into bed until he's seen to you.' She looked down into the water, 'I'll see to *him*, later,' she promised.

Sion had a fractured ankle, a broken rib and a black eye. He was told to rest and not get out of bed for a few days at least.

John Buchanan, now Baron Guilford, came to visit him, bringing the news that Sion had been awarded the Military Cross, the medal that had recently been designed for the war and introduced on January 1st 1915.

'Any news about David?' asked Sion, easing himself in his bed, chafing to get up.

'Yes. He's in France with Foch and his senior aides. He has information that he thinks will shorten the war, but I've no idea what it is.'

'Doesn't Angus know?'

'Angus has gone to the front with his old regiment, the Black Watch. He was promoted to Lieutenant Colonel and he insisted he wanted to be with his men.' Buchanan shrugged and added, 'May God have mercy on them. You might like to know that from April 1st the Royal Flying Corps and the Royal Naval Air Service are merging.'

'Oh? Why?' Sion asked.

'A number of reasons. Last year's air raids on London killed hundreds of civilians and dented our national pride. That led to an enquiry by General Smuts into the lack of co-operation between the RFC and RNAS. He made it clear that the rivalries and wastefulness between the services were jeopardising pilots and planes. The only irony is that the new Chief of Air Staff, Lord Trenchard, has told the army commanders in France that our ministers are quite off their heads to think that aeronautics will help to end the war. Still, we shall see.'

Two days later Sion got out of bed and went down to the kitchen. He over-rode Kirsty's protests and continued working on his design of the Falcon II.

He was still hobbling around a few days later when David walked in.

BOOK 3

John's Story

23

October 1918

I LOOKED ACROSS THE breakfast table at the woman I had come to hate and resignedly asked, 'What did you say?'

She looked up from her newspaper and said, 'I intend going to Bath again. I'm sure you won't mind.'

'Delighted,' I said, ironically, glad to see the back of her. I had stayed with Helen because it wasn't entirely her fault. It was, if I was honest, mostly mine. I had known that I could never marry the woman I loved, so I had married Helen to fill the void that was in my life.

I'd had a highly successful career as a seaman, rising meteorically to become Captain of a transatlantic liner. I will admit that as my family owned the shipping line my promotion had never been in doubt. Still, without false modesty, I can say that I had been a good captain, considerate of my men and the passengers and always with the motto "safety first" uppermost in my mind.

I had never been in love, though I had enjoyed many shipboard liaisons as we sailed from Britain to America and back. That was, until my life was saved by the most beautiful, spirited and intelligent woman I had ever met. The problem was that I could never tell her as she was married to a man I admired. He became, with the fullness of time, my best friend.

So I had married Helen, left the sea and became a director of the shipping line, The Buchanan Shipping Company. On my father's death I had inherited sufficient shares to take control, and I was now the Chairman of the Board. The remainder of the Board was made up of quarrelsome cousins and sundry others to whom I paid lip service, before doing what I wished.

The war had proved a curse on mankind and a blessing to certain individuals. I was one of those individuals – if blessings were counted in cash. When the war had started we had eight liners, twenty-eight cargo carriers of various sizes and ages, forty-eight coastal traders and a yacht; the latter was my personal property. David had been aboard with me on numerous occasions, seeming to take to sailing like a duck to water, or more aptly, like Sion to flying.

If I'd had children I'd have wanted them to be like the two Griffiths boys. Meg's children, the woman I loved and the wife of Evan, my best friend.

To date, over the last four years, we'd lost all our cargo ships, one liner and fifteen coastal boats to enemy attacks. Now, as the tide of war turned in our favour in Europe, we had ten liners, thirty-five cargo carriers and a hundred and fifteen coastal traders. All had been paid for by the government as we desperately tried to keep Britain fed.

Apart from the heavy losses in shipping and the waste of manufactured goods that had bled Europe dry, there had been a death toll of between nine and ten million, the final tally probably never to be known. On top of that, if that wasn't bad enough, Spanish 'flu was sweeping the globe. Millions of people had already died and so far no vaccine had been developed that could combat the disease. Although called Spanish 'flu it was by no means clear that the virus had started in Spain. China and India had been the hardest hit to date with millions reported dead. Now it was spreading through Europe and America, to people who had been weakened by the privations and hardships of war. The US Federal Bureau of Health had, only a few days before, announced that more American servicemen had died of influenza than of wounds suffered on the field of battle.

Helen had been obsessed with her health for almost as long as I could remember and was always away taking one cure or another. I was relieved that she was going to Bath. She loved being the Lady Guildford and used her title whenever she could. In her eyes, purchasing the baronetcy was the one redeeming thing I had done in years. That had been Lloyd George's idea. At first he had proposed the idea to raise money for the war effort, but that had changed quickly as the political infighting continued. He had needed money to finance the Liberal party and had let it be known to selected people that should a large contribution be made to party funds an honour would follow. The precise terms were shrouded in secrecy and I suppose depended on who was buying the property and how wealthy they were. I was extremely wealthy and paid over the odds, but I didn't care. I couldn't take the stuff with me and it had silenced Helen's carping for a while. I just hoped the novelty of the title wouldn't wear off too quickly.

'When are you leaving?' I asked, more for something to say than out of any genuine interest.

'In an hour. I shall be away for a week. Perhaps longer.' She spoke icily; there was no love lost on her side either.

She had been a vivacious and pretty thing when I had first met her. A natural blonde, tall and willowy, she had a sharp tongue which substituted for intelligence. If I had to describe her in one word it would be superficial. Still, I had married her for better or worse and in my case it was the latter. Life still had its compensations and as long as she left me alone I was prepared to leave her to her own devices. I was looking forward to the evening as I was meeting David at the United Services Club for a few drinks followed by dinner. I wanted to quiz him about his meeting with General Foch, the French Commander in Chief of the army at the western front. He had come up with an idea that he wanted to implement and I had made the necessary arrangements for his interview with the high command.

Helen left and I got down to some work. I had a board meeting in the morning and I wanted to be prepared for it. I made sure I was fully briefed and had all the facts at my fingertips before dressing for dinner. As I tied my bow tie I looked critically at myself in the mirror. Not bad, I thought, considering my age. At fifty-five I was still able to look down and see my feet, without having to suck in my belly. I had a full head of hair, albeit grey at the sides. My hooked nose had been the result of a fracture when I was a young man on a sailing ship, fighting for my virtue shortly after we'd left Cape Town. I grinned at the memory. Because of my background, three sailors thought I would be easy. They learned differently. I was six feet tall and stood out in a crowd.

I got to the club early and enjoyed bantering a few words with some of my cronies before David arrived.

When he came, it was with a bounce in his step and an air of belonging that to me at any rate spoke volumes. I knew him to have been brought up in a tiny house in the valleys of Wales and to have suffered a great deal over the years. But always he fought his way through and came bounding back, sure, intelligent and undoubtedly one of the bravest men I'd ever known. He was the spit of Evan, his father.

We always met as though the last time had been hours before and not months. A quick hello, how are you and what'll you have were sufficient for us both. I noticed him eyeing me up and sucked my stomach in a few tenths of an inch and then grinned at him, letting it out again. I wasn't in such bad shape for a man of fifty-five. Though I was big and heavy I was not fat. I could still pack a punch should I ever need it. Or so I thought.

We retired to a corner of the room, taking our drinks with us, and I was able to cross-examine him about what had been happening.

David rubbed a weary hand across his brow and replied, 'I've just spent time with Stockdale, bringing him up to date. Where should I start? Errm, the morale of all of Europe probably reached its nadir last winter, when the death toll reached its peak. You agree?'

I nodded. 'People were rebelling all across the continent. The redcaps began shooting soldiers for desertion, the Russians hung a lot of their own people for the same reason and the German fleet talked openly of mutiny.'

'They hung a dozen of the ringleaders in Flensburg last Christmas and the mutiny fizzled out,' said David. 'There was widespread disaffection in Austro-Hungary which was accentuated by conflicts between the nationalities, and, in effect I think we were witnessing the beginning of the end of their Empire.'

I nodded. That was my assessment also, if they and Germany lost the war.

'In view of all that it became vitally important for Hindenburg and Ludendorff to achieve a rapid military victory on the western front before too many Americans arrived. They used vast numbers of troop trains to bring men from the Russian front to the west. You know that Lloyd George and Clemenceau,' David was referring to the French Prime Minister, 'anticipated a big push. But even they were staggered at the size of it. What did the Germans take? Forty, fifty miles of front and again Ludendorff was threatening Paris. I was all over the front at the time trying to get a picture. And then I had a realisation. It's the only way I can explain it. Here we had two huge armies, exhausted and driven to a standstill pounding each other to pieces. Agreed?'

I nodded, intrigued.

'We are all agreed that so many deaths are a complete waste. Were a complete waste, I should say, as we can never bring those boys back. Yet for all these years nothing has changed. And one of the biggest problems has been each country's commander has had his own agenda. There was no unified command until this year when Foch was entrusted with defeating the Germans. That was my chance. I saw Foch and convinced him that he should have a flexible front.'

'A flexible front,' I repeated. 'How?'

'If we allowed the Germans to extend their lines of supply, which as you know were stretched thin, we could attack from the rear. Look, let me show you.' David took an envelope from a pocket and quickly sketched what he meant.

'We have a thin line here, the Germans attack, we retreat or let them break through. The Germans gallop into our lines as fast as they can move. We come in from behind in a pincer movement and cut them off. And we bite chunks off like that all along the front. The Germans, just like us, are so used to charging and taking useless land that they'll just keep going. I had a hard job convincing him but he eventually agreed to try. It was General Petain who tried it first at the Marne. We call it the tactic of elastic defence. It's worked in that we stopped the Germans and have been moving forward in short bursts ever since. The Germans are now in full retreat trying to salvage what they can from the rout that's taking place. Do we stop at the German border or do we occupy Berlin? It's a difficult question and, thank God, not one for me to answer.'

'Will they retreat as far back as their old borders?' I asked.

'Yes. When I was in Matthias Erzberger's study a few months ago he assured me they would.'

My jaw dropped open in astonishment and, I confess, I spluttered at the news, whilst David guffawed with laughter. When I had finally recovered my equilibrium I said, 'You were with Erzberger?'

'Yes, just before he asked the Reichstag to sue for peace. It was partly due to the message I delivered to him that he asked them to try for peace under their terms. I was there at the behest of Lloyd George, under diplomatic protection. It didn't achieve anything of course, but the meeting did establish certain, shall we say, parameters that allow us to decide whether to accept an offer for peace or at what point they will surrender unconditionally. Bulgaria has surrendered and Hungary has declared independence from the Habsburg Empire. Germany will collapse but as yet we can't be sure when.' David drained his glass and beckoned a waiter for a refill for both of us. 'The Germans have made it clear that if the terms of their surrender are too harsh they will fight on to the bitter end. I'm not so sure. The people are as tired of war as we are.'

I nodded, accepting what David said completely. 'We're routing the enemy all over the middle east and, as Lloyd George predicted, by knocking away the props we can get at Germany. That's worked and now . . .' I trailed off, David looked at me quizzically and then I made a number of connections. 'It was you. That's what the Welsh Windbag,' I was referring to the Prime Minister, 'meant when he said he'd taken advice from a man who really knew what was happening in Europe. We all thought he was talking about the Minister of War. But it can't have been. Tell me I'm right, David.'

'You're right, David,' he joked.

'That's why we concentrated our efforts so much in Italy. We got the Bulgarians to capitulate whilst at the same time we forced the Austrians to sue for peace. Is that what you told the PM would happen?'

'In a nutshell,' David replied. 'We'd have spent the next ten years battering Europe to death, needlessly, along the iron front of the west. The underbelly was exposed and I suggested to the PM we take advantage of that fact. I have to be honest and say that it didn't take much to persuade him. His biggest problem has been lack of munitions and weapons which, as we both know, was caused by our lack of money, which was always the most important commodity required. He and I knew that. Then with my help in other matters we've been able to grab the lion's share of raising funds for the government.'

I nodded. It was true that the Griffiths & Buchanan Bank was going from strength to strength as a result of the war. 'What'll happen next, do you think?'

David shrugged. 'The Germans will want an armistice as soon as possible. Half of Belgium has been retaken and Foch is preparing for a huge push into Germany itself. The Germans have been surrendering by the hundreds of thousands, we've a million Americans in Europe with almost as many still to come. If Germany doesn't surrender soon, her armies will be smashed to smithereens. I think that'll be a grave mistake. We need to let them keep their dignity and honour.'

'You're joking,' I said, aghast at the idea. 'They've cost us millions of pounds, millions of lives and misery that cannot be calculated. They have to be made to pay.' I was surprised at David's attitude. He knew as much as anybody what the war had cost.

'The people of Germany have suffered as much as the rest of Europe. They didn't start it, they were led into it. I'm not saying they didn't go into it with, shall we say alacrity? But it was the leaders that caused it. The egomaniacs who own most of the continent are the guilty ones. We should not make the ordinary man and woman suffer further.'

I didn't necessarily agree but I let it rest. 'You're just back from Foch's headquarters. What's going to happen now?'

'About five million armed and vengeful men are about to walk across the remainder of Belgium and into Germany, and they won't stop until they reach Russia. Germany will be a bloodbath which can only be prevented by the Central Powers making peace within the next week. After that it'll be too late.' He paused, taking a sip of his drink. 'Enough talk of war. What's happening here? How's Sion and the family? What's the latest news from Mam and Dad?'

'One thing at a time,' I slowed him down. Like his father, David was a passionate supporter of his family. I had always recognised that it was the source of their amazing strength and I envied them for it.

We went into dinner while I brought him up to date about what was happening with the family and the business. Our tentacles were now spread far and wide as we took shares in more and more companies.

'We need Angus back, to be honest,' I said. 'The management we have at present are all well and good for the day-to-day running of the bank but we need a leader to get things through and, you have to admit, Angus was very good at it.'

David nodded. 'I agree. I thought I could do it but it's not what I want. I enjoy roaming around, putting together the deals and ideas. So what's the situation with Angus? Is he all right?'

'The last I heard he was. He's received the MM, the GM and has been mentioned in despatches twice. He was gassed once, and was also slightly wounded. He's at Marne now, waiting for the big push that Foch has been planning for. I could get him back tomorrow but he won't come. He said he wants to stay with the regiment until the end, seeing he's missed most of it. I think he's mad but the decision is his to make. I just hope he survives, that's all.'

'He's bound to,' replied David. 'I don't think there will be a big push. I think that it'll all be over in November. Damn, we're doing it again! Talking about the blasted war!'

'It's inevitable. It feels as though it has dominated our lives for years and will continue to dominate them for a lot longer yet. The end of the war will not end the suffering. We have a country to rebuild. No, a continent and that will take a lot of work. I fear that we also have a bigger world-wide problem.'

'What's that?' David asked.

'America.'

'Why America? They've just pulled our irons out of the fire. If it hadn't been for them the war could have continued to be in stalemate for years. You said it yourself.'

'That isn't the problem,' I replied. 'America will now try to become a world power like Britain is and Germany was. The Americans have flexed their muscles and said, hey, I like this. This is fun. That's going to cause us serious problems all over the world. Don't forget the sun literally doesn't set on the British Empire.'

David was silent for a few moments absorbing what I had said and then he nodded. 'I agree. They have the potential to be the most powerful nation in the world but do they have the will? They could well sink back into apathy and isolationism as soon as the war ends.'

'If President Wilson forms the association of nations like he suggested in January then America will be forced to play a major role. It's the only country left in the world that still has the strength to achieve anything on a world-wide basis. The world that we know is tired . . . exhausted is a better description. America can step into the breach left by Europe and conquer the world. Not militarily, I agree, but ideologically.'

'How will that affect Britain?' David asked me.

'America will want to impose their view of freedom and justice and equality which, you have to admit, isn't ours.'

David grinned. 'That's for sure. You mean a meritocracy instead of a nation built on privilege and wealth?'

I grinned back. 'That's exactly what I do mean.' I reached into a pocket and withdrew a sheet of paper. I wrote down Woodrow Wilson's fourteen point plan. 'Summarised, this plan amounts to free trade, open diplomacy, national self determination, armaments to be reduced world-wide to the lowest point consistent with national defence and the association of nations to be formed to guarantee independence and territorial integrity. The rest of the points all apply to specifics in Europe to end the war. But let's take one point alone. National Self Determination, or NSD as the newspapers are calling it. What does that mean?'

David shrugged and poured us each a glass of claret before cutting a piece of the horse steak we were trying to eat. 'NSD means independence for all nations and if we go down that route it means the break-up of the Empire at the time when we can least afford it. We need the natural resources of Australia, New Zealand, South Africa, Canada, India and so on. Britain needs to rebuild.'

'Agreed, but we won't be able to do so if America gets its way. Look at what's happened at home because of the war. Women now have the vote, or at least they have if they're over thirty and married, the Trade Unions have increased powers and better wages and Ireland is going to hell in a basket. All these are advantages taken as a result of the last four years. And that's just the domestic advantages. Think what the world will do. What better time to kick your enemy that when he's down?'

'So what do you think America will do?'

'I think the Empire is in for a period of sustained unrest which will result in its break-up.' I shrugged before continuing, 'Which means a great deal of change, and that means that if we're ready for it we can profit by it.'

'How?' David asked as the waiter appeared at our table and began clearing away the dishes. He shook his head when offered the menu for a further course and ordered coffees.

'I don't know yet. New companies will be formed to take advantage of any change and countries will need cash to rebuild their infrastructures either because of the past four years or because they get independence. We could make a fortune lending to the affected countries provided we have, or can find, the cash. I even have a name for the fund we create – The Sovereign Fund for lending Sovereign Loans which are backed by the entire resources of a country. We lend millions at a time and make millions as a result.'

David thought about it for a moment and then smiled at me. 'I like it,' he broke off, glancing at the door. He raised a hand and the paper boy came in with the first copies of the next day's papers. The headline carried the news that 2,225 people in London alone had died that week from influenza.

'This influenza problem is as bad as the war,' I said, heavily. 'Thousands of prisoners of war have died from it already.'

From the club David and I returned home for a night-cap. The following morning he and I were summoned to Number 10 Downing Street.

24

THE PRIME MINISTER began in his ebullient Welsh manner, without preamble, 'Good of you to come. I thought I should tell you that we have received word that the Austrian Emperor Karl is seeking an armistice. I want you two to get there as quickly as possible and represent this government.'

He had taken us by surprise, but then he often did.

'Surely, sir, there are plenty of others who can represent the government at these talks?' David asked. 'Why us?'

'Because you two have the best grasp of European politics of anybody I know. The Habsburg empire is crumbling and new countries will be springing up all over that part of Europe. I want Britain to be at the forefront of helping them develop. That way we will retain some influence in the area which may help us in the future.'

'But we've nothing to help them with,' I protested. 'Britain needs all the help we can give her.'

Lloyd George nodded his head and stroked his grey moustache. 'We need raw materials to build up Britain, but we can print money. That's something we have plenty of.'

'Won't that lead to inflation?' David asked.

'Some. But a small dose of inflation won't hurt. It helps make the people feel better as they feel they're getting wealthier. Now, I want you to make it clear at the talks that we'll do all that we can to recognise and help the new governments.'

Then I understood. The wily old fox! 'You mean you want us to have private talks with them as representatives of the Griffiths & Buchanan Bank. You don't want the others to know that we're there with your blessing. That way you'll keep the Allies sweet and perhaps even steal a march on them.' I nodded as I pondered the implications. 'It makes sense.'

'Good, I think so too. Especially with a general election coming up. I want to be able to announce some good news before we go to the polls. After that I want you to go to Germany.'

That took the wind from my sails. Germany! 'Whatever for?'

'They'll be surrendering soon. You will be given diplomatic papers which I want you to present to the Kaiser. I want you to try and convince him that it would be in his best interests to abdicate. Not only his interests but those of Germany as a whole, too. Only if he does this will he prevent a bloodbath across the country. Now that Ludendorff has been discredited and replaced by General Groener there's a good chance that reason will prevail.'

Lloyd George continued with his instructions for a further half hour and then we left. 'I need a drink,' I said to David.

'So do I but there's no time. The boat train leaves in an hour and a half. As we were leaving the PM gave me these,' David waved an envelope under my nose. 'It contains our diplomatic passports and letters of introduction. We have only days to get to Vienna.'

I protested to David but he overruled my objections and hustled me into a taxi. We dashed home and I gave instructions to have my trunks and cases packed with clothes to last at least two weeks. David did his own packing, wryly commentating that he was so used to it he could complete the task in ten minutes. He wasn't far out with this boast.

We were at Waterloo in time to catch the boat train. We were on the train and settled into our seats when David suddenly stood with an oath and exclaimed, 'John, grab the trunks and cases. This is hopeless. We'll never get to Vienna.'

I looked at him in puzzlement. 'Why won't we?' I asked stupidly.

'Across a war torn Europe? How will we get there? It's impossible and I'm surprised Lloyd George hadn't thought of it. If we had a fortnight maybe, but not in a few days.'

I saw the sense of what he was saying and hurriedly grabbed the cases and manhandled the trunks out of the carriage and onto the railway platform.

'What do we do now?' I asked.

'Drive to Biggin Hill,' was the surprising reply.

We took a taxi back to the house and then David got his car.

We were on our way when I said, 'Show me the papers the PM gave you.'

David handed me the envelope and I took out the various documents. 'Have you looked at these?'

'I did as we got on the train and I realised we'd been set up.'

I threw back my head in laughter, as pleased as Punch.

'What's so funny?'

'Because I realised the same thing about ten minutes ago. We get a summons at the last minute, get briefed and get bounced onto a train. It's only when we . . .' I noticed his grin. 'All right, all right, I admit it – when you point out the obvious that I begin thinking straight. The irony is, of course, all the pointers were there at the meeting.'

'I agree. We arrive after the armistice has been signed. And it won't be hours after, it'll be days or even weeks. We'll find that Czechoslovakia, Hungary, Poland, Romania and Yugoslavia and some parts of other Balkan countries will have been forced to agree to terms that are, probably, despotic and we say we're really sorry but we did want to help. Sorry, there's nothing we can do about it now but we are your friends. If there's something in the future that's mutually beneficial perhaps . . . and so on. God! I can hear it now.'

'Exactly. We pointed out to Lloyd George that we've nothing to help with and he said cash. That's a nonsense and we both know it. If we print money, all it will do is trigger inflation. Britain needs to get vast amounts of supplies from the colonies. We'll bleed them white until we're solvent again. But in the meantime we're seen as the white knights of Europe fending off the capricious and greedy victorious allies who are out to punish the people who started the war.'

'You described the PM as a wily fox. I'd say he's more like a conniving, duplicitous bastard.'

'I know, thank the Lord.' I caught David looking sidelong at me. 'Don't forget, he's on our side.'

David laughed uproariously.

'I take it you plan to get us there by aeroplane,' I spoke nonchalantly, managing, somehow, to keep the terror out of my voice.

'No choice, if we want to get there. I take it we do want to get there?'

'That's a very interesting question which leads us to a very interesting dilemma. If we arrive on time we're doing as requested by the Prime Minister but we know it's not what he really wants. And do you know something?' I asked rhetorically, 'I'm really annoyed. I don't like being taken for a fool, especially by a Welshman – present company excepted of course. If he'd told us his intentions we'd have gone along with it; I can see the merits in his idea. Political obligations without cost and available to be bargained with in the future. As it is, I think the Griffiths & Buchanan Bank will give its own help. At a price, of course.'

We arrived in Biggin Hill to a warm welcome. The factory now employed over two hundred men, turning out aircraft for the war effort. The Griffin and Griffin II had become amongst the most successful planes of the war, probably as popular to fly and as robust as the Sopwith Camel. The Falcon had gone into production and had been successful against the German metal planes which had taken to the air only months earlier. Both of them – the Junkers J1 and Dornier D1 – had flown successfully and were far harder to shoot down than their wooden counterparts. The Falcon had been the solution and whenever one of the German metal planes appeared in the air a Falcon went after it. The result was that few of the new planes were seen flying over France or Belgium though they were used on the Eastern Front where no Falcons had been deployed.

David played with Sion's son Alex while we explained the problem.

'I've good news and bad news,' was his response, grinning at us.

'What's the good news?' I asked, fully aware of Sion's wicked sense of humour.

'We've been working on a new aeroplane; twin engined, single wing, seating for eight and space for luggage. Range of at least 1,500 miles and with a capability to carry more fuel if we carry fewer passengers.'

'So we can get to Vienna?' David asked.

Sion nodded. 'In theory,' he stroked his chin, which made David laugh at a joke I couldn't see.

'What's so funny?' I queried.

'The bad news,' said David, shaking his head and laughing again, much to wee Alex's amusement because he joined in the joke as well.

'Well?' I asked exasperatedly, 'What is it and how do you know what it is?'

'I know because I know my brother. And the bad news is the plane hasn't been flown before. Right, bro?'

'Right, bro,' replied Sion and he laughed again. 'Still, this is an ideal test and maiden flight. Do you want to see her? She's called The Griffin Carrier.'

'Lead on McDuff,' said David, standing with Alex comfortably sitting on his shoulder.

We went into a new, enlarged hangar. The Griffin Carrier rested in the middle of a concrete floor and even to my layman's eyes looked a thing of beauty.

'Twin modified V8 Hispano-Suizas, full metal body, a wing span of fifty two feet and an enclosed body for the passengers to sit in. The pilots sit behind the windscreen and fly from inside the open cockpit.'

'Why didn't you have the pilots sitting in an enclosed cockpit?' I asked.

'As a pilot I think it's more important to get a feel for what's happening in the air. I can't explain it except to say it's like sailing a dinghy, which you'll understand. You need to feel the wind, feel the sea and feel the boat.'

'I agree, except you don't need to do that in an ocean going liner. You navigate by observation, you dock using tugs and you no longer sail a boat by the seat of your pants. Can't you do the same with an aeroplane?' I asked.

Sion thought for a moment or two and said, 'I think you may have something there. I'll look at that when we return. In the meantime we've made life more comfortable for the pilots by directing warm air through pipes over the engines and into the cockpit. There are panels in the passengers' part that can be opened and warm air gets blown in there as well. Here, let me show you.'

He proceeded to do so. While we were talking Raphael and his father topped up the petrol tanks, Mrs Cazorla appeared with a picnic hamper and Kirsty presented us with a cartoon of us standing beside the plane. I thought she appreciated the terror showing in my face perfectly, and I told her so.

All too soon it was time to leave. I had assumed that David would fly in the front with Sion but instead Raphael climbed aboard and David joined me in the passenger cabin. There were doors on either side of the cabin and three small slots in the floor. I was wondering what they were for but my curiosity was soon satisfied. Peter Cazorla began fitting a tripod to the slots and then he screwed a Lewis Mark 2 machine gun onto it.

He shrugged his shoulders at me. 'Sion says we're still at war and you'd better be prepared,' was his explanation.

David and I sat on either side of a narrow aisle, on seats which were not particularly comfortable but would do. Sion put his head through a door and said, 'You can talk to me through that speaking tube,' he pointed, 'and you can hear me by putting the tube to your ear. If I need to contact you I'll blow a whistle and you can pick it up and listen. In an emergency I'll blow three sharp blasts. That means strap your harnesses on and get ready for a fight.'

With that cheery thought he grinned, closed the door and clambered into the cockpit alongside Rafe.

The engines started with a mighty roar and a belch of blue smoke and we taxied out of the hangar. After about ten minutes waiting on the runway, during which I was beginning to think nothing was going to happen we heard the blast of a whistle and I picked up the speaking tube and put it to my ear.

'Strap yourselves in,' yelled Sion. 'We're about to go.'

I repeated the message to David and we buckled our harnesses. The noise inside the plane was loud but not unbearable and David and I could converse without having to shout to each other. We bounced over the field and turned to face the wind. After a short delay we began to accelerate, bouncing over the field as we did so. After what seemed an eternity we bounced one last time and we were airborne. I willed myself to unclench my knuckles from the seat rest and as I let go we hit an air pocket and dropped a few feet before continuing the climb. My knuckles continued white as my grip intensified. David was nonchalantly looking out of the porthole, watching England rush by, as we turned towards the White Cliffs of Dover and the Channel.

At one point David turned to me and pointed out of his porthole, 'Those puffs of cloud are gunfire. There's a battle going on over there.' Even as he spoke the plane banked sharply to starboard and the whistle sounded, once, mercifully.

'John? Are you two all right?' Sion asked.

I put the speaker to my mouth and yelled. 'Yes. No problem.

We saw the puffs of smoke and then you turned.' I put the tube to ear.

'We're going south of Paris to an airfield I know. We should be able to get a bed for the night and take on more fuel. We'll only be about another two hours. You might like to know the plane's running as smoothly as I dared hope.'

'You cannot imagine,' I yelled back, though I think the sarcasm was lost in the noise, 'how happy that makes me.'

We landed on the outskirts of Vitry le Francois near the River Marne. It was a bustling airfield from where aircraft flew into the war. As the evening was approaching there was far less happening and we were able to land without too much undue attention. Sion went to find a mechanic to help us find some petrol and we stretched our aching limbs, glad that the noise of the plane was no longer assaulting our ears. When he came back he had a volume of good news.

'One of the squadrons operating on the other side of the field fly Griffins. When they learnt who we are they agreed to give us all the petrol we need. There's a hotel in the town about a mile away where we can stay, the squadron CO will arrange a guard and the Adjutant will drive us to town. Not bad for ten minutes work.'

An hour later we were in the hotel and I had enjoyed a hot bath which eased my aching limbs before I went downstairs. I was in the bar drinking a Pernod when the other three joined me.

'Where do we go from here?' I asked Sion.

'We need to go round the Alps so I think we go north about, just inside Switzerland, skirting Germany. We're effectively doing a shallow dog's leg south, touching Liechtenstein and then east to Vienna. The total journey is 650 miles as near as I can tell. We averaged 120 mph today so if we do the same we'll take five hours and forty minutes. Add in a fudge factor then six hours should see us there. If we leave about 8 am we could be in Vienna by 2 p.m.

It was the first time that air travel had been put into perspective for me. A journey lasting days was going to be completed in hours. I found this absolutely mind blowing. For the first time I began to understand Sion's passion. Maybe it was to be the travelling method of the future, after all. For a shipping man I found the thought depressing.

The inn was good enough, just, the food was awful and the wine thin and watery. It was all blamed on the war which was also used to justify the exorbitant price we paid. However, the bed was comfortable and as far as I could tell, bug free, so an early night and a good rest did me a world of good.

We were away early and lifted off from the airfield a few minutes before 8 am. It was another calm, fine day, hardly a cloud in the sky and with patches of mist across the valley. It was terrible to imagine that only a few miles from where we stood two huge armies faced each other, still needlessly killing and injuring the life blood of Europe – its men.

The Germans were surrendering in droves, often hundreds of men yielding to a lone soldier or a patrol. But even so, some of the die-hards were continuing to fight, insistent that there was need for a greater Germany and that it was within their grasp. There was no longer room in their minds for reality.

The plane continued to function perfectly and we crossed into Switzerland two hours later. We skirted south past Lake Constance and north, past Liechtenstein. Sion announced we were on time and on track and so it proved to be. We landed on the outskirts of Vienna, in a field covered with planes. They belonged, mainly, to the Italians, but there were a few Austrian biplanes amongst them. Our arrival caused quite a stir, but luckily our diplomatic papers stood us in good stead with the commanding officer of the Italian Flying Corps. As I had seen so often in the past, amongst pilots and the flying fraternity Sion's name was all he needed. We left him and Rafe at the field, discussing aircraft with their new-found friends while David and I made our way into the city. Luckily I was able to rent a car and a driver to take us around, albeit at an exorbitant price.

We went straight to the British Embassy where our letters and papers ensured that we were given an audience with the Ambassador. He turned out to be a pompous, arrogant fat man to whom I took an instant dislike.

'I was led to believe,' he said, ponderously, 'that you would not be arriving for some time, in days if not weeks.'

'We were sent yesterday. In fact we were in 10 Downing Street yesterday morning,' I replied, convinced now that David and I had been right.

'How is that possible? You cannot have crossed Europe so quickly.

Why even before the war it took days and now I should think it would take even longer.'

'That's what we thought,' I said, politely, 'which is why we flew.'

He looked at us as though we had suddenly grown second heads, his mouth agape. 'Flew?' he spluttered. 'Why, that . . . that's impossible. How could you do that?'

'By aeroplane,' I replied, facetiously. 'Now, where's the meeting taking place?'

'Meeting? What meeting?' The Ambassador was so blatantly prevaricating that I nearly laughed in his face.

'Ambassador,' I said, 'we have been sent to attend the armistice meeting between the Austrians, the Hungarians and the allies. There will be representatives from each of the countries that have broken away from the Habsburg Empire, each trying to ensure that they are not held accountable and not required to pay reparations to the allies. Our task is to offer help to the representatives and to pledge the support of the British government.'

The Ambassador coughed and squirmed, a sight I thoroughly enjoyed, and said, 'Errm, quite so. However, I don't think you should be too eager to, errm, offer too much in the way of, shall we say, succour to our former enemies?'

I nodded, pursed my lips as though cogitating on what he had said and then asked, 'Where is the meeting taking place?'

'At the palace. It will be tomorrow at 10 a.m. There is no formal list of those who will be attending but I gather that it will include, as you surmised, the leaders of the breakaway republics and one or two, shall we say, aspirants to high office. As you know Czechoslovakia and Hungary have declared independence from the Habsburg Empire and are in desperate need of aid. They claim that they've been bled to death by Franz Josef and his successor Emperor Karl. King Ferdinand of Bulgaria has abdicated in favour of his son Boris hoping to stave off the imposition of a republic but the unrest continues so whether his ploy will succeed or not I can't tell. All together it's a mess and, I must tell you, I have recommended to the government at home that we stay clear of it all. Let them stew in their own juices for a while and then we'll see.'

'I can see that's a possibility,' I pontificated, 'but we need to assess the situation for ourselves. My instructions by Lloyd George are quite clear, to offer what assistance we can.'

He coughed, squirmed and then, apparently remembering the dignity of his office, said, 'Look, I know what your instructions are. Only . . . don't take them too literally. The PM, errm, that is to say, the PM doesn't want to give too much, errm, that is . . .'

I must be getting soft in my old age because I didn't let him squirm any longer. 'We understand the position. Britain has suffered a great deal over the last four and a half years and can't afford to be too generous. It's gesture politics, as I'm sure you'll agree.'

He nodded, relief flooding his face. He would have made a rotten bridge player and a worse poker player. 'That's so. Yes . . . quite. So what do you propose?'

'I propose that we, that is to say David and I, attend the meeting and assess the situation for ourselves. If it's possible I would like to speak to anybody you consider to be an expert on the countries that may be involved. We need to know about their natural resources, industries, assets and so on, to decide whether or not we can lend money to them.'

The Ambassador nodded as if he understood what I was talking about but I could see from the expression on his face that he was lost outside the rarefied atmosphere of diplomacy. 'Let me get Miss Villiers to speak to you. She joined us recently from London. We have been forced to recruit women due to the shortage of men . . . the war, you know.' He let the sentence hang in the air between us while he sent for a secretary to find Miss Villiers. David and I exchanged glances which spoke volumes.

A few minutes later an attractive redhead entered and was introduced as Madelaine Villiers. I wished I was at least twenty years younger; Madelaine was tall, slim and beautiful. She had a ready smile and for me, exuded an intelligent warmth that I found appealing.

David looked as though he had been hit with a thunderbolt.

25

WE LEFT THE Embassy in the company of Miss Villiers. There was a hotel not far away which, surprisingly, sold decent coffee. I remarked on the fact to which she smiled and said, 'The war has passed Vienna by. The fronts are a long way from here and the government has done its best to keep the Viennese happy . . . No, that's the wrong word, content is probably better.' She smiled a devastating smile and glanced at David. 'He doesn't say much, does he?'

I smiled back at her. Since she had walked into the room David had been struck dumb, had been giving the impression of a deaf mute and managing only monosyllabic replies to direct questions. At that moment he appeared to shake himself out of it and said, 'I'm sorry. I've been thinking about what we need to do. I do apologise. Can we get down to business?' Smoothly he dominated the discussion, asking probing questions about the countries we could have an interest in. After nearly an hour I could see that Madelaine was beginning to wilt from the verbal probing David was subjecting her to and I suggested we stop there and order more coffee.

With a sigh of relief Madelaine sank back in her chair and said, 'Wow, that took some thinking. I'd forgotten that I knew so much, if you see what I mean.'

I nodded, 'Your memory is remarkable,' I said. 'One question we haven't asked you which I think is significant is where did you come by all this information?'

'It started at University. I read European history and modern economics. I know it seems an odd choice but it actually helps in what I do now. I can also speak French and German fluently so a job in the Foreign Office was relatively easy to come by. The war has helped a great deal of course,' she said sadly, 'but there's an inevitability to the changes which will sweep aside the current working patterns of all the classes. Without being too melodramatic about it we have lost a generation. Most of them were the best any country had to offer and that vast gap will be filled by women.'

'You aren't a suffragette too, are you?' asked David, sharply. The suffragettes were now fighting for the same rights as men. Women could now vote if they were thirty years old and married; men could vote from the age of twenty-one irrespective of their marriage status.

'A suffragette? Me? Why, no. And why do you say "too"?'

'Nothing. It doesn't matter. I'll go and see if we can book a room for us in this hotel,' he said, standing and striding away.

'What was that all about?'

I hesitated about explaining and then said, 'Nothing. It's just his way. You can't tell me,' I continued, 'that the information you've given us all comes from your studies.'

'No, of course not. Since I've been here I've been gathering as many facts as I can. I've had contact with other embassies and their officials, and I've used the local library. It's wonderful, with a modern index system that makes finding any piece of information easy. I anticipated a need for a detailed knowledge of the whole of eastern Europe and so I've spent time putting it all together. Hungary and Poland have vast coal deposits, Bulgaria has very little in the way of natural resources and what is there to say about Austria?' She shrugged her elegant shoulders. 'Switzerland without the cuckoo clock?'

I burst out laughing just as David returned. I repeated what Madelaine had said and he laughed as well. It was a pleasant sound and not one that I had heard much of since his wife's death. Madelaine joined us for dinner during which we kept probing her for information although not as harshly as earlier.

During the evening David discovered that Madelaine had been engaged but her fiancé had been killed at Mons, she had no current beau and her father was a vicar in Surrey. At the end of the evening we agreed to meet after breakfast, when Madelaine would go with us to the palace. David volunteered to walk her home but she would have none of it. She said goodnight and briskly walked down the street without a backwards glance. David stood and watched her go.

The following morning we met Madelaine and the three of us took a taxi to the palace. There we were met by chaos. Men in uniform and officials in civilian clothes were everywhere. There were at least five different languages being spoken, all in raised voices. It was a biblical, modern day version of Bedlam, where nobody spoke the same language but where everybody spoke at the same time.

The three of us made our way to various groups, identifying their interests and the country they represented. Eventually, some semblance of order reigned and on Sunday 3rd November 1918 Austria signed the armistice with the Allies. We had appointments with eight different groups, the most important being with Tomas Masaryk of Czechoslovakia and Michael Karolyi of Hungary. By the end of the day I felt that we had done a good job.

Dinner was the same as the previous night except that I decided to have my night cap in my room and leave David and Madelaine alone. I could tell when two was company and three was definitely a large crowd.

Two days later we met again with Tomas Masaryk and his colleague Eduard Benes. Masaryk was known for his lofty ideals and had served in the Austrian government. He was popular in his own country but had huge difficulties holding together the troublesome mixture of Czechs and Slovaks. He was also married to an American and I thought that the injection of new world ideas could do no harm to a politician who had lived in an empire which had existed beyond its time.

We met in a run-down cafe on the edge of the city. I liked what I saw of both men and thought them intelligent and, rarest of qualities in a politician, honest. We sat over cold lagers and plates of indifferent sliced cold meats, none of which were to my liking.

'My government,' I began ponderously, 'has empowered me to offer help to the emerging nations. Reparations have been surprisingly light, I think you'll agree but that's been because of the break-up of the whole of the east of Europe. There's nobody to demand payment from.'

Masaryk nodded his head. 'This terrible war has resulted in certain . . . benefits is the wrong word. Changes is better, perhaps, that were unforeseen.' As was usual for politicians and statesmen in Europe he spoke fluent English, albeit in a pedantic style that immediately identified him as a foreigner. His colleague, Eduard Benes, spoke

German and Hungarian only and so we had a mish-mash of languages between the four of us with David and Masaryk translating when necessary. My linguistic prowess ran only to English and schoolboy French.

'So what are you proposing?' Masaryk asked.

'You need cash to rebuild your industries. I understand that you have certain natural resources which could be, shall we say, exploited? For the benefit of your people. You have huge forests, superb farmlands and the high grade iron ore to be found in the Slovak Ore Mountains.'

Masaryk nodded. 'The Slovenske Rudohorie has a number of ores, one of which is iron. The war caused some of the area to be developed but there is still much to do. Do not forget that we also have rice and hops for our breweries. Our beers are sent all over Europe, particularly to France and Germany.'

I nodded while David translated for Benes' benefit.

'We propose a partnership with the bank and your government. We supply the money as a loan to your government at an agreed rate of interest, secured by guarantee. We also have a share in the companies we invest in, and take dividends along with other investors or even yourselves.'

'You have a saying in English, heads you win and tails you can't lose. Correct?'

I nodded. 'Something like that. We also have another saying that goes something like being held by the short and curlies. Nobody else is going to come forward to help you. The remainder of Europe is too busy looking after its own interests. We also have a huge commitment within Britain but our industries have not been demolished. In fact, it's the reverse. We have had to expand all of our industry to fight the war. Business is booming while the government is bankrupt. The loans they have taken to pay for the war are a huge debt to Britain. Britain therefore needs to import capital and export goods. That is a concept that our politicians are unable to comprehend. We do, which is why our efforts are going to be concentrated overseas, and not just in Europe. We will issue Sovereign loans to stable governments of countries who will guarantee the money. We will raise the money in different ways, none of which need concern you. Are you empowered to act for the Czechoslovakian government or aren't you?'

He shrugged. 'I can only recommend, I cannot issue a decree. I need time to think about your proposal. I think it has merit and is of interest. Can I speak to you later?'

'How much later?' David asked.

'Three days?' was tentatively suggested.

David and I exchanged glances and nodded. Three days was reasonable. 'Is that long enough?' I asked, wanting to be reasonable as well.

'In a fledgling democracy three days is more than ample. Do you intend making this offer to any others?'

The question took me by surprise but I hope I didn't show it. David didn't even blink. He answered for us. 'Perhaps. We have still to decide. I am sure you won't be offended if I say that this information is confidential. A great deal depends on what happens over the next few months. The upheaval throughout Europe is colossal. We intend to help to stabilise the continent in any way we can.'

'That is very philanthropic of you, Mr Griffiths.'

'No it isn't, Mr Masaryk. It is very businesslike of us.'

Masaryk laughed, translated for Benes who also laughed. I smiled, showing that we all enjoyed a good joke.

We left the two men sitting there and wandered into the sunlight. 'Why didn't you let them know that you could understand Hungarian?' I asked David.

'Because there was the odd snippet I learned which was useful. I can tell you now that they are agreed. They need help desperately if they are to keep both factions in the country working together. It's agreed to all intents and purposes. Where next?'

'Next we meet the Polish delegation.'

'What on earth do the Polacks have to offer?'

'Coal,' I replied.

The brutal Slavic features of the two Poles with unpronounceable names glowered across the table at us. They both spoke German but no English. David did the talking while he and I conferred in English. They spoke to each in Polish and after ten minutes I'd had enough.

'David, thank them for coming,' I stood. 'I don't trust them and I won't do business with them.' I put my hat on, touched the brim in a farewell gesture and walked out, David at my heels. The two Poles sat where they were looking astonished.

'Why did you do that?'

'As I said, I don't trust them. They'll cheat and connive for all they're worth, and it just isn't worth the trouble. We need to meet the Hungarians in four days time and then go to Germany. '

'We need to go to Compiègne,' David corrected me. 'That's where the signing of the armistice will take place. I think we should go on to Germany after we see what the terms are. Otherwise we won't know what we're talking about.'

'Nothing new then,' I joked. David grinned back and nodded in agreement.

We had dinner without Madelaine that evening, much to David's chagrin. I had made enquiries and found that Compiègne was fifty kilometres north of Paris and as a small provincial village in France was totally unremarkable; except that it was the place where the armistice was to be signed.

I saw little of David for the next two days. Apparently he was wining and dining Madelaine, the lucky devil. However, a day late, we met with the Czechoslovakians and agreed terms in principle. In exchange for our financial support they would take one of our new Sovereign loans and we would participate in the profits of their various industries. Direct investment in some businesses was needed and encouraged. All in all I was extremely satisfied.

The Czechs and the Hungarians hated each other. That was made obvious when we met with Michael Karolyi, the new leader and a liberal aristocrat of Hungary. I discovered that the Hungarians thought the Czechs were traitors to the old Empire and the Czechs thought of the Hungarians as their oppressors. The Hungarians, or Magyars as they were also known, had enjoyed equal status with the Austrians within the old Empire since 1867 and now it came as something of a shock to find that they had had been relegated to a new role and were now no longer part of the Austro-Hungarian Empire. Already there were factions within the Parliament; the capital, Budapest, actually consisted of two historic towns; Buda on the west bank of the Danube and Pest on the east which held the parliament building.

However, the pressure was on for Hungary to reconstruct itself and in order to do so the Hungarians needed money. Hungary had a huge farming community, growing cereals and grapes and rearing vast numbers of cattle and pigs. Britain had a need for food products and Hungary needed help with their engineering and selling their finished goods. A mutually satisfactory deal was struck but had not yet been signed and sealed. Karolyi needed to get approval from his parliament. However, I was satisfied that we had done all that we had intended and I suggested we leave.

'Where to?' David asked.

'Near Compiègne. Angus is there. I thought we could see him before we go to the meeting.'

David nodded. 'I'd like that. I haven't seen him in ages. We need to find Sion and see if he can get us there.'

We went out to the airfield and to our surprise learnt that Sion had returned to England. Neither of us had thought to speak to him to ask him to stay longer.

'What do we do now?' I asked David.

He shrugged and said, 'Take a train or a car. The first may never get there and the latter could run out of petrol. But either way we need to get going if we're to arrive on time.'

I agreed. We spent two hours attempting to buy a car, but there was nothing suitable. Finally, fed up to our back teeth, we returned to the city to see about train times and availability. We met Madelaine for lunch and told her our problem and as was so often the case in life, help came from an unexpected quarter.

'You can have my car,' she said.

'You have a car?' I asked, incredulous.

'Of course. I've had to travel all over the country and the only way has been by car. It's not much,' she spoke doubtfully, 'but it's proven fairly reliable.'

'What's fairly reliable?' David asked.

She pursed her lips in thought and said, 'Agnes only breaks down every hundred miles or so.'

'Agnes?' I said. 'You've given a car a name?'

'Of course. She's a pretty, temperamental wee thing and I love her to bits. So I had to give her a name.'

The car was a Calcott open tourer. There was enough room to fit us and one small case into it. It had a folding roof which, when it was up, meant we had to bend our heads. It was a small car, highly popular at that time, reliable on the whole and capable of speeds of nearly 60 mph. David filled the tank with petrol at the Embassy, while I sat on my mound of luggage and waited to see what he was going to suggest we do with it all.

He ignored me, put his holdall in the space behind the driving seat, climbed in behind the steering wheel and started the engine. I sat where I was, waiting. I caught his wink to Madelaine when he said, 'Are you coming or not?'

'What about this lot?' I waved a hand around me.

He couldn't keep his face straight any longer and burst out laughing. 'Sorry, John, but you can't take it with you.' He climbed back out of the car and he and Madelaine helped me sort out what I needed. David's idea of what was necessary in a civilised society and mine were somewhat at opposite ends of the spectrum but we finally got it down to a holdall and a suitcase which we strapped to the back of the car. Finally, we were ready to leave.

'You will take care of Agnes, won't you?' said Madelaine, unsure, now that the time to part had come, that she had done the right thing in offering the car to us.

'Of course,' David said. 'I haven't wrecked a car in weeks.'

'What?' she was aghast until she realised that David was joking. 'Oh, you,' she gave him a gentle tap on the arm. As she did so, David took hold of her and kissed her. In return she put her arms around his neck whereupon I had the good grace to look away.

After a minute or two I looked back but they were still in a tight embrace and I coughed and said, 'All right, all right. Both of you come up for air and let's go.'

Madelaine stepped back half a pace and said to David, 'You took your time. I thought you'd never kiss me.' She turned to me as she added, 'Take care of yourselves as well as the car.' With that she spun on her heels and ran into the Embassy.

David grinned sheepishly at me, I shrugged back and we climbed into the little car. Moments later we were on our way.

Vienna is in the eastern corner of Austria and we needed to drive all the way across Austria to Switzerland and then into France. It was going to be a long journey. The roads varied from reasonable to diabolical, the car performed well and occasionally we managed speeds up to forty or forty five miles per hour. We had 900 miles or thereabouts to go.

The journey was a nightmare and took three days. Petrol was scarce but, more by luck than judgement, we never ran out. The car broke down only once but David was able to fix it. I did some driving but he did the lion's share. An adventurous ride across Europe became a slog and I was glad to get to into France. On the third evening we arrived at Verdun, on the western front.

We dined that night in the mess with Angus, Brigadier Sir Angus Frazer, to give him his full title, second-in-command of the Black Watch Regiment in Germany. He seemed to have aged ten years since I had last seen him, only a few months earlier. We sat in a marquee, surrounded by the Regiment's silver and trophies and discussed the end of the war. Frazer was continually wracked by a rasping cough, courtesy of a leaking gas mask.

'When do you think it will be over?' I asked.

Frazer still had a small spark of life left in him, even after all the horrors he had seen and managed a smile. 'Soon, I hope. We all hope,' he waved a hand indicating the other members of the mess. There were thirty to forty officers in mess dress, the first semi-formal dinner they had had in six months. It was a subdued affair with very little laughter. If I had to describe the attitude of the men in a single word I would have said it was exhaustion. And these were the victors!

David seemed to sense it too and, unusually for him, had very little to say.

'I understand that the delegation from Germany arrives tomorrow,' I said. 'The intended big push planned by Foch for 14th. November is now delayed. Kaiser Wilhelm appointed Prince Max of Baden as Chancellor and he's appealed to President Wilson for an armistice.'

'But look what happened,' David said with some bitterness. 'The terms were the immediate cessation of all U-boat operations, but they're still sinking allied shipping. They sank the transporter *Leinster* with six hundred civilians on board as well as our cruiser *Britannia.* If Foch attacks we can wipe out German resistance once and for all. If the front gives way, which I think it will, then we can be in Berlin as fast as we can walk.'

Frazer shook his head. 'We don't have the strength to crawl anymore, never mind walk. I have never understood what total exhaustion was before now. It's not being tired in body, it's in the spirit too. These men have been asked to give their all and they have. Many of them have given more than they had to give. And do you know what thanks they get for it?'

I shook my head, intrigued by the bitterness in Frazer's voice.

'Redcaps. Butchers and the scum of the earth. I saw three off them off myself.'

'What on earth are you talking about?' I asked. 'I thought that they were a new regiment of army police to keep order and investigate petty crimes.'

'That was the propaganda put out by the war office. They stand behind our men in the trenches and when the whistles blow for the charge they make sure you go. If you don't, then they have the authority to shoot you.'

'What?' I was scandalised. I'd read of the occasional court martial and execution of soldiers for cowardice but not the summary shooting of soldiers without a fair hearing.

'That's the latest idea from those butchers in the high command,' Frazer kept his voice low, aware that if he was heard he could be tried for sedition and put in front of a firing squad. 'We had redcaps turn up here last week, under the command of a captain. He told me that they were there to ensure we charged the enemy when we were ordered over the top on the fourteenth. We've never had any problems here, these men are brave beyond words and I didn't want their morale damaged more than it is already. I took the captain behind the latrines and pulled a gun on him.'

'You did what?' I was aghast. Haig had issued an order that anyone threatening a redcap would be shot.

'I rammed my pistol into his mouth and cocked the trigger. I told him that if he and his men weren't gone by noon I'd shoot him and hang the consequences. They're all cowards, that's why they volunteer to become redcaps; that and instant promotion by at least one rank. We'd gone this long without them threatening us and I figured we could go the rest of the war.'

'What happened?'

'Oh, they left in a hurry. I received a summons this morning to appear before a tribunal to explain my conduct.'

'Good God, man, what on earth are you going to do?' I asked.

Frazer shrugged, looking at me with hollow eyes, the spark extinguished by the telling of his tale. 'Answer the summons.'

'What'll happen then?' David asked.

'Then they'll shoot me,' Frazer replied, laconically. 'So tonight we eat, drink and be merry for tomorrow we die. Messman! Messman! Another bottle of the finest claret for my friends and guests.'

The meal was deplorable but the wines were excellent. The conversation picked up and Frazer was more like his old, irrepressible self. Before we left for the night to retire in the abandoned farmhouse where we had been billeted I saw Frazer and David in deep conversation.

As we walked away I asked him, 'What was that all about?'

'What was what all about?' David asked, playing the innocent.

'You know damn well. What were you talking to Angus about?'

'Nothing. Only this and that.'

'He seemed angry, shaking his head like that. What did you say to upset him so much?'

'Forget it, John. It was nothing. Now, goodnight.' Abruptly he stalked off to his room, leaving me to wonder what was happening. As I hadn't a clue I gave a mental shrug and retired to my camp-bed.

We were roused before seven o'clock. Frazer had promised us breakfast before we travelled to Compiègne and after a shave in cold water I walked over to the mess. David was nowhere to be seen. Frazer was already eating and I joined him.

'Have you seen David?' I asked.

Frazer looked at me sharply. 'No. Isn't he in his room?'

I shook my head. 'Not when I looked. Strange, it's not like him to go off without telling me. We need to get moving. I want to be at the signing of the armistice.'

'The blasted fool,' said Frazer, with some heat, and then he smiled.

'What's so funny?'

'Nothing,' he replied, quickly wiping the grin from his face. 'It's just David up to his old tricks.'

At that moment David walked in, slightly dishevelled and in need of a shave. 'I'm starving,' he rubbed his hands together and sat at the table. A few moments later he had a plate full of bacon and eggs before him and began tucking in. I said nothing, just watched him as he handed a folded sheet of paper to Frazer. Frazer read it, nodded and handed it to me.

It was from a Captain Derek Scudamore to Frazer apologising for any embarrassment he might have caused when he had falsely accused Frazer of threatening him. He had put in a report rescinding his original statement. I looked up from the sheet of paper and said, 'How did you manage this?'

David shrugged and replied, 'Persuasion. It's amazing how a little reasonable chat can help.'

Frazer laughed, it quickly turning to a cough and said, 'You'll be the death of me yet,' and wiped the tears from his eyes. The spark was back. Frazer was more like his old self again.

We left with an escort of a sergeant and three men. We had a hundred miles to travel and as it was just 10am, and the signing was in the morning, we had plenty of time to get there. The car proved to be a faster vehicle than the one used by the four man patrol and so we stopped and I told them to go back to Verdun. We then stopped worrying about our escort and travelled as quickly as we could. David was driving and we had travelled over forty miles in an hour.

'Are you going to tell me what happened?'

David grinned, looked sideways at me and said, 'Sure. I told the good captain that if he didn't retract his statement I'd cut his balls off.'

'What?' I was shocked. 'What made him think you would?'

'The fact that I had a knife to them. Like in New Orleans that time with Jake. Remember?'

I thought for a few seconds trying to recall the incident and then I it came to me. 'You wanted your money back. Cat Ball was killed by his own men. No, a woman, wasn't it?'

'Exactly. It's amazing how focused a man becomes when a flick of the wrist loses him his wedding tackle. He saw the error of his ways and withdrew his allegation against Angus.'

'You can't go round doing that sort of thing,' I said, half heartedly.

'Yes I can. Angus didn't deserve what was happening to him. He's one of the best people I know and the country owes him a great deal. What's more, I owe him my life. You know very well that, when it comes to family and friends, nothing is too much trouble.'

I nodded and smiled to myself. Like father like son, I thought.

We arrived at Compiègne in the evening. I made a few enquiries to discover that the meeting was to take place in a railway carriage hidden in the forest. I learnt that the Germans would be arriving early the following morning. The papers I carried ensured we got through to the train. It was ringed by soldiers, French, British and American. Inside the carriage was Marshal Foch and the British Admiral Wemyss representing the Allies.

Neither man was happy to see us. They insisted that all they were going to do was to end the war; the question of reparations would come later. I read the initial terms of the armistice and thought that it was fair. The Germans had to evacuate all territory west of the Rhine and the Allies would establish three bridgeheads over the river; the British at Cologne, the Americans at Koblenz and the French at Mainz. The Germans would be required to hand over thousands of tons of goods, surrender their lands in East Africa and annul various treaties including the important Bucharest treaty. Considering all that had happened in the previous four years I thought the Boche were getting off lightly. The only paragraph I had trouble with was the one covering the need for damages to be assessed later and for compensation to be agreed.

The German delegation arrived at 5 am and was a surprise. I had at least expected Hindenburg or Ludendorff to be there but instead there was a politician, Matthias Erzberger, head of the Catholic Centrists, two junior army officers and a civilian. They carried a white flag. The armistice treaty was signed after a few moments by Erzberger, after he had read it, and the message was sent out to the troops standing guard.

The war was over.

26

THE ELEVENTH HOUR of the eleventh day of the eleventh month was to go down in history as one of the most important dates in Europe. All over Europe national flags were flown, rejoicing was rampant and exhausted men smiled for the first time in years. In Germany soldiers walked away from their guns and started to go home, leaving behind their regiments and comrades. In defeat they were zombies, broken in spirit as well as body. The Allies were little better off, only discipline keeping the men at their posts.

David and I decided that there was no point in going to Germany. As the leadership was in so much upheaval nothing could be done for months. In any case I was too dispirited to continue. I had a fit of the blues and wanted to get away from the squalor and destruction that surrounded us. I wanted to sort out the problems of my shipping line before I helped sort out the problems of Germany. I was tired and too old.

The final cost of the war was never to be known. Estimates were made, and they were staggering. The Allies had spent six trillion pounds of which America had contributed six billion. The enemy had spent a similar amount. The Allies had mobilised forty-two million men, of whom five million had been killed. The Central Powers had mobilised twenty-three million men, of whom three and a half million had been killed. In all twenty-three million men had been wounded, excluding civilians. The same number as had been mobilised by the Central Powers.

In my opinion the real cost was not just financial but was the obliteration of an entire generation of young men. How many mathematicians, playwrights, scholars, poets and scientists were lost? How many sons, fathers, brothers? That was the real incalculable cost of the war.

Back in London I was busier than I had ever been in my life. I often thought longingly of my years as a ship's master, when the problems and decisions were so much simpler and immediate. Now I had to think in the long term about the company and make decisions that affected thousands of my staff.

At the same time Spanish 'flu was sweeping the world.

Helen was a hopeless hypochondriac who drove me to distraction and anger. At dinner just before Christmas she sneezed, shivered and announced, 'I think I have a cold. I shall go to Harrowgate for the cure.'

I nodded happily. I would be glad to see the back of her. 'When?' I asked, pausing with a glass of port to my mouth.

'Tomorrow. I don't wish to stay long in London where so many people are falling ill and dying.' She shivered again, this time alarm registering on her face. 'My goodness, I do feel ill. I shall retire immediately.' She rose from the table and said, 'Goodnight, John.'

'Goodnight, Helen.' I rose courteously and watched her depart. I drained my glass and wandered over to the sideboard to pour myself a malt whisky, one of our own. As I sipped at the drink I thought fondly of Frazer. He had received his discharge only days after the war had ended and had returned immediately to London. Within a week he announced that he was returning to Scotland and would stay there, to run the estate and look after his family interests. As those interests coincided with those of the bank, neither David or I made any objection. We both figured that after a few months of rest he would be raring to go again and would be returning to London to be in the thick of the business action.

I nonchalantly picked up the *Times* newspaper and began to read about world affairs in particular the flu epidemic. Millions had already died and it was estimated that one in every four people in the world had come down with the life-threatening illness. The Stock Exchange had been closed for a few days, and other public buildings were also shut. Quack remedies were being touted at inflated prices as fear struck at the populace. Hundreds of children were being taken into care by the local authorities as their parents died more quickly than the men on the western front.

I frowned at a noise in the hall and was startled to see the door burst open. To my joy and delight a figure stood in the doorway, a portmanteau in one hand and a cane in the other.

'Evan,' I cried, smiling, leaping to my feet. 'My dear fellow, what a wonderful surprise. Come in, come in. Don't just stand there. What on earth are you doing here?' He had not changed much from the last time I had seen him. He was ramrod straight, tall, good looking and elegant. In his fifties, he had achieved much in his life, from Welsh coal miner to American politician in twenty years was something to be proud of.

Evan grinned at me, dropped his bag and shook my hand. 'John, it's good to see you. Why don't you pour me a drink and I'll tell you all about it.'

Seated, and with a large malt in his hand he said, 'I'm over with President Wilson. He's in Paris right now talking to President Poincaré about the peace agreement. You've heard his ideas for a League of Nations?'

I nodded. 'Yes, it's brilliant. Far reaching, forward thinking, and so doomed to failure.'

'You old cynic,' replied Evan, 'It's an idea that's reached its time. Imagine an international organisation formed and dedicated to peace and wealth around the globe. It would consist of every nation, each having an equal vote.'

'That's a problem in itself,' I interrupted. 'We believe that we are all equal, but some of us are more equal than others.'

Evan shook his head. 'We must find a formula to prevent further wars like the one we have just been through. If all members agreed to turn over to a Council within the league any dispute that could lead to war to be arbitrated by the council, then all future wars could be abolished.'

'And who would be on the Council or League, whatever it's called?' I asked.

'The Council would consist of five small nations who would be voted on as well as standing members of the United States, Britain, France, Italy and Japan. Any member who refused the recommendations of the Council would be open to economic sanctions and, if necessary, military action by the Council. That's what Wilson's come to discuss with the French and the British. He's getting opposition for the idea in the States from the Republicans led by my old sparring partner Senator Henry Cabot Lodge, but the President could still bring it off. Anyway, enough of politics. I'm not here to talk world matters but to get personal and family news. I want to know everything that's going on.'

I smiled at Evan, seeing so much of David in him. 'Where should I begin? You got the letters telling you about our adventures in Europe. Since then it's been fairly quiet. Sion's aeroplane business is now well established and he's churning out fighters for the Allies to be used for keeping the peace. Angus is back in Scotland recuperating and David is in Austria.'

'What's he doing there?' Evan asked in surprise.

I grinned at Evan. 'What any young man who's in love does. Chasing a beautiful girl.'

Evan grinned back and asked, 'And who is she? Not Austrian, I hope.'

I shook my head. 'No. A true blue British girl. We met her at the Embassy and she was a great help to us. She's intelligent and resourceful and if matters go further then I think that it's true to say that he'll have a handful in future years.'

'Sounds just what he needs. Meg and I have been very worried about him since Emily died. What's the girl's name?'

'Madelaine. I'm sure you'll both like her when you meet her. Talking of Meg, how is she? Is she over with you?' I kept my enquiry nonchalant, hiding my real interest.

To my disappointment he shook his head. 'No, she had to stay in America. She's dealing with the purchase of a new building in New York. She sends her love and says that next time she will be over, come hell or high water. I had to come, as the President asked for my help.'

'He did? How were you to help? I mean, why you specifically? I didn't think you were a particular crony of Wilson's.'

'I'm not, but I'm the only member of his party and the Senate who knows at first hand what's been going on and who had such a large vested interest in the war, what with Sion and David and so on. So he thought I could be of use. I've probably been chosen as his so-called advisers are singularly misinformed.'

'Singularly misinformed? What a wonderful, quaint phrase. You mean they're talking rubbish?'

Evan nodded. 'Exactly. The phrase I borrowed from the President. Heck, we're back to politics again.'

I stood, took Evan's glass and refilled it. 'How long are you staying?'

'A few weeks anyway. I want to see Sion and, if I can, David as well. I also want to see my grandson.' He shook his head in wonder. 'I'm too young to be a grandfather.'

I laughed at his rueful expression. 'That may be so but you're not too young to drink too much with an old friend. Far too much I think is the order of the day.'

'Delighted,' he said. 'Incidentally, how's Helen?'

I grimaced. I had never kept the facts of my marriage secret from Evan but at the same time I didn't broadcast the situation either. 'You know. She's in bed claiming to have influenza. She's going to Bath or Harrogate or somewhere, to take the cure. If she'd had half the illnesses she claims then she needs to leave her body to medical science so that after she's dead they can find out how she managed it. She'll outlive the lot of us,' I said with some bitterness.

'That's always the way. I see you've eaten. Do you propose we go out or stay here?'

'Are you hungry? I can get something rustled up in the kitchen if you like.'

'No thanks. I ate on the ferry crossing the Channel. But if you've eaten I thought we could go out on the town for an hour or two.'

'Why not?' I drained my glass. 'Just give me five minutes to change and we can go.' I left Evan whilst I changed my smoking jacket for a coat and found my shoes. I didn't bother looking in on Helen as her self pity was more than I could stomach.

We went down the West End and found a busy pub. We bought large drinks and stood in a corner watching the festive mood of the victorious allies. Behind it I detected an anger that I thought would spill over in the future into violence.

'I don't like it,' said Evan. 'Something's wrong. We've won the war but there seems to be an underlying bitterness that I can't fathom.'

'You've been living too long in the States,' I spoke loudly, above the hubbub. 'This land fit for heroes is virtually bankrupt. There's little work and no money. The government are now refusing to print more notes in case it leads to inflation and so the economy is drying up as the oil it needs to keep it turning vanishes.'

'Oil? Oh! You mean cash. Liquidity. Just like in a company.'

'Exactly. If they don't act soon then there'll be riots and strikes. Red Rosa Luxemburg has been sending her treasonous rubbish across the Channel, calling on the workers to unite and rise up across Europe. There's virtual open warfare in the streets of Berlin and Russia is in turmoil. Their poison is spreading here and if we're not careful it will engulf us.'

Evan nodded. 'I agree but at the same time we need to offer the people something to work and live for. If we don't then they'll take it. If that happens, God alone knows what the result will be.'

We replenished our glasses and continued with our discussion, shouting to each other over the noise. I thoroughly enjoyed myself as Evan had a sagacious wit that was refreshing and original. At closing time we left to walk back to the house.

The streets were busy with people spilling out of the pubs, most of whom were the worse for drink. We had walked as far as South Audley Street when I realised that we were being followed. I looked over my shoulder to see half a dozen men lurching behind us, at least two of whom were carrying staves.

'It looks like we're in for trouble,' I said to Evan, glancing at his profile.

He grinned wolfishly in the gas light from the street. 'I know. We'll stop at the next corner and sort it out, okay?'

I returned the grin, relishing what was about to happen. 'Okay.'

We turned the corner and stopped in the shadows. We heard the men suddenly shout and come running after us. Evan and I both carried stout walking sticks, mine in reality a sword stick that I had never drawn in anger. However, I did have my Blue from Oxford for fencing as well as another one for boxing, to draw on when I needed to.

I smashed the first man across the knees with my stick and he went down heavily with a shriek. The crack sounded as though I had broken something. Evan's blow caught one of the gang on the elbow and he also fell out of the fight with a scream. The other four had stopped, breathing heavily, eyeing us with caution but still determined to get us. They spread out, one of them carried a stick and another made a sudden lunge to pick up a stave dropped by the man I had hit. They were all fighting drunk and vicious.

The one who tried to pick up the fallen stave never reached it. Evan kicked him in the face so hard that he flew halfway across the street before landing in a broken heap. The other three charged at us, drink giving them a false courage combined with stupidity. The one with the stick took a swipe at my head. I ducked under the blow, stepped in close and hit him with a solid upper-cut to the chin. He fell as though he was pole-axed and I turned in time to see Evan do the same to one of the others. That only left one of them and in spite of the drink inside him he hesitated. Then bravado took hold and he squared up to me in a boxing stance.

'Come on then,' he said in a slur, 'I'll take you on. We licked the Boche and I can lick you.'

I was appalled. 'Stop it! Stand up straight,' I said in a harsh voice. 'Call yourself a soldier when you behave like this? How dare you attack a superior officer.'

The man sprang to attention, years of ingrained obedience to orders working through his fuddled brain.

'What is your name and regiment?' I demanded.

'Royal Fusiliers, Sir. Sergeant Major O'Donnell, number D136054. Sir!'

'O'Donnell?' I frowned. 'Not the O'Donnell who won the VC at Amiens?'

His shoulders sagged. 'Yes, sir.' He seemed to come to his senses. 'For all the good it's done me.'

'Good God, man,' I said. 'What on earth do you think you're up to? You're a hero acting like the worst kind of scum. Where's your pride?'

'In the pawn shop with me medal,' he replied, a spark of anger flaring within him and he hunched his shoulders and prepared to throw a punch.

'My name is Sir John Buchanan and this is my friend Evan Griffiths. I want you to come to my house at ten o'clock tomorrow morning,' I gave him my address.

'What for?' He asked sullenly, his belligerence replaced by curiosity.

'Because, Sergeant Major O'Donnell, I think you should explain yourself. Perhaps I can help.'

By this time his friends were coming round, groaning and trying to stand up. One was being sick and another was holding his arm claiming it was broken, which it probably was.

'Who are these other men?' Evan asked.

'Others like me,' O'Donnell replied. 'Good men thrown on the scrap heap now that the war is over and won. It's only six weeks since it finished and already there's nothing for us to do. After what we suffered and all.'

Unfortunately, I couldn't find a counter-argument to his bitterness. 'Right, here's five pounds,' I handed him the white note. 'I want you to get your men seen to by a doctor and you will be on parade at my house tomorrow at ten ack emma sharp. Do I make myself clear?'

'Yes, sir. Thank you, sir,' he saluted.

'Do you remember my address?'

He grinned at me and repeated it. 'Drunk I may be, sir, stupid I ain't.'

Evan and I watched them help each other to their feet and stagger away. We turned to continue the journey but before we could walk away a man stepped into our path. I eyed him cautiously, in no mood for any further trouble.

'Very impressive, gentlemen. We were tempted to give a hand but thought no, we'd let the older generation manage without us.' Behind the man who spoke stood Sion, a grin on his face. David's grin was just as broad.

'See, David. I told you they'd be able to take care of it.'

It got a bit silly after that, with the four of us dancing around the street, our arms around each other, laughing and yelling for all we were worth. At that point a police whistle blew and we calmed down and continued home.

It seemed that both of them had been to the house, arriving only minutes after we had left. They had assumed that we had gone to the club and went after us. Rather than wander London looking for us they had stayed at the club for a few drinks before walking home. They'd seen us coming and were hiding, intending to jump out and surprise us. Instead, they had seen the attack and were ready to come to our aid but decided to let us deal with it unless matters got out of hand.

'I have to say,' said Sion, 'that for a couple of old men you did fairly well.'

'Old men? You cheeky young whippersnapper, I'll have you know that I was an Oxford Blue at boxing and fencing and can still take care of myself.'

'And I learned in the school of hard knocks,' said Evan. 'You youngsters should remember that.'

Sion put an arm affectionately around his father's shoulders, 'So you did, Dad. So you did.'

Back in the house I poured a drink for us all and then asked, 'What are you doing here, anyway?'

'We came to see you, John. David's just returned from Austria and I have a meeting at the Ministry tomorrow, early. So we came up from Biggin Hill tonight.'

We exchanged our news, the boys obviously delighted to see their father once more. It turned out that Madelaine was returning to London shortly and David had come on ahead to see about somewhere for them to stay. I was surprised, unaware that things had progressed that far between them.

David had shrugged and said, 'It was the war. It makes you realise how short and precious life is. You have to grab every minute you can before it's too late.'

Both Evan and I agreed with his sentiment and nodded. The war had changed, and was still changing, many entrenched ideas and attitudes. It was very late when we finally went to our beds.

I was woken by the housekeeper just after six o'clock. I was askance; it was her job to look after my wife and run the house, the butler saw to my needs.

'Please sir, wake up. I'm so sorry but it's Mrs Buchanan, Lady Helen. She's right poorly.'

'Mrs Carstairs,' I said, struggling to get my wits about me, 'kindly send Beech to me and remove yourself from my room.'

'I'm sorry, sir but your wife is really ill this time.'

I looked at her distraught yet kindly features and sighed, 'How often do we go through this?' I asked.

'I know, sir. But this time I think it's for real. She's not pretending like she usually does. I think . . . I think it really is this flu that's getting everybody, sir. Really I do.'

'All right. Send for the doctor and send Beech up with a cup of tea. I shall get dressed and go and see for myself.'

The woman hurried from the room. Mrs Carstairs was the salt of the earth, not prone to panic or exaggeration. I lay back on my pillows with a sigh, trying to keep the thoughts I was having from my mind. I didn't really wish her dead, did I?

Beech appeared with a cup of tea which he placed on the table at the side of my bed. 'Run a bath for me and call me when the doctor gets here,' I ordered.

I took a sip of tea and promptly fell asleep again. I was awakened a while later by Beech announcing the arrival of the doctor. I bathed and went downstairs to the dining room. Breakfast was already laid out on the sideboard and I helped myself to bacon, eggs and devilled kidneys. The doctor entered the room and without a word helped himself to some food. He sat down opposite me and began to eat.

'Well?' I asked impatiently.

He looked at me through red rimmed and exhausted eyes. 'She's got the flu. What can I tell you?' He shrugged. 'I don't know what the outcome will be. She may live and she may die. There's no real reason for one or the other to happen. We doctors don't know, that's for sure. We have no cure and no way of preventing the fever. So far more people have died from it than were killed during the war. The poor and the rich live and the poor and the rich die.' The doctor was blue-eyed, young and very good at what he did, but he looked about fifty just then. 'I've been at it non-stop for weeks. I've been working in the clinic with Sedgebourne trying to find a cure, but we haven't got one yet. As well as my own patients I've picked up dozens more as other doctors succumb to the illness. It's only luck that's stopped me getting it so far.' He tucked into the meal in front of him. 'This is the first hot meal I've had in days.'

I nodded, sympathetic to his problems. 'How bad is Helen?'

He paused with a fork full of food halfway to his mouth and said, 'Pretty poorly. The problem is I can't really tell. She's been playing us up for years and now that it's real I just don't know how much of it is an act and how ill she really is?' He paused, chewing thoughtfully. 'I'd say she's very ill. The next twenty four hours will tell. In my experience that's the make or break time. She will get worse, sweating and hot one moment, freezing cold the next. She will shake and shiver, throw off her bedclothes one moment and demand more covers the next. She needs constant care and I suppose it's true to say that if she's to survive then staying here gives her the best chance she'll have. There's nothing I can give her that will help except perhaps for the odd prayer or two.' He dabbed his mouth with a napkin and stood up. 'I need to go. Thank you for breakfast. I want to spend an hour or two at the clinic trying to find a cure.'

'Are you near to one?' I asked, intrigued.

He paused at the door and looked at me for a few moments. 'We think so. If we find what we're looking for can I bring it to you?'

I nodded. 'Certainly. A cure would be worth a fortune to the man that finds it.'

'That's what I thought,' he said with a tilt of his head.

When he'd left I pondered on the idea of investing in a company manufacturing medicines. The idea appealed to me immensely and I made a mental note to look at other patent medicines. I was trying to remember what I had heard about a tablet called aspirin. It was new and stopped headaches and other aches and pains. I needed to discuss it with David whenever I had the chance. Just then the housekeeper entered the room.

'Sorry, sir. It's just to say that I don't think Mrs Buchanan is any better. She's worse if you ask me.'

I nodded. 'Apparently there's nothing we can do except wait and see what happens. If the fever breaks she will live, if it doesn't then I fear that she won't.' I couldn't bring myself to say that she would die.

I finished my tea and stood up. 'I'll come with you to her room.'

The curtains were drawn and there was an oppressive feel to the room. I walked over to the bed and looked down at my wife. She stirred and then opened her eyes. 'Is that you, John?' She murmured.

'Yes, it is,' I replied, sitting on a chair next to her. Dear Lord, but I tried. I looked for pity, for a vestige of love, for any feeling of affection but felt nothing. I sat there and wished her dead and I hated myself for it.

'John, I'm . . . I'm sorry.' Tears rolled slowly down her cheeks and she tried ineffectively to wipe them away with the back of her hand. I gave her my handkerchief and sat watching her. 'John, I'm scared. I don't want to die.'

'You aren't going to,' I replied, wishing that she was. What a mess I'd made of my life when I'd married her. It was wonderful for a period that could be measured in days not years. The constant claims of headaches, the lack of warmth and normal husband and wife relations. I'd accepted years ago that Helen was frigid and that there was nothing to be done about it.

'John, I want you to know something. It wasn't you. It was all men. I . . . I,' her voice faltered and went on more strongly, 'I don't like men, any men. I . . . I prefer the company of women.'

I nodded, 'I know. That's why you go to your bridge clubs and guild meetings. And let's not forget the suffragettes,' I said with some bitterness.

'No, John. I'm dying and I want you to know that I prefer women in that way,' she emphasised the word *that*, and even then it took a few moments for her meaning to sink in. And then I realised what she meant. And then all the little things, events, comments, looks . . . suddenly they all made sense. I recoiled in loathing and then took a grip of myself. What a fool I'd been! Me, John Buchanan, ex-ship's master and world traveller hadn't seen it. My wife loved other women!

'I always have done,' Helen continued, as though it was a death-bed confession. Perhaps in her mind it was. 'I tried to love you. I tried to make it all right when you touched me. At first I could do it but after a short while I found it impossible. It disgusted me. It filled me with loathing for you and for it!'

I was dumbfounded. It filled her with loathing? The most natural act in the world filled her with loathing, yet what she did she found normal?

'Helen, I don't think you should say any more. We can discuss this when you are better.' I stood up and turned to leave the room when I became aware of Mrs Carstairs still standing in the room, a look of horror on her face. I indicated the door and we both left.

'You heard?' I asked her.

Mrs Carstairs nodded, miserably. 'I didn't want to, sir. I didn't mean to, neither,' she said, biting her lip, worry, even fear in her eyes.

'Mrs Carstairs, if my wife dies then that is the end of the matter. If she lives then you are a witness and I may call upon you for testimony when I seek a divorce.'

'Oh no, sir. I couldn't do that. Not to the mistress. She's been good to me, she has. Generous and kind and never demanding like some that I've known.'

'Oh?' I looked down at her, straightening my back and frowning. 'And I have, is that it?'

'Oh no, sir. The very idea! You've been kindness itself.'

'Then do not forget who pays your wages,' I said, more harshly than I had intended. She wilted under my gaze and tongue and I felt like a bully. 'Mrs Carstairs, if my wife lives all well and good. Arrangements will be made that enables me to have my freedom. If she does not give it willingly then you will be my witness to the distressing scene you have just em, witnessed. You can either stay here as housekeeper or make other arrangements to suit yourself. Do you understand?'

She nodded and walked away, her head bowed.

I went back to the dining room and sent for Beech to bring a pot of coffee while I cogitated on what I had learned. Whatever the outcome of her illness I would be set free. Suddenly I no longer wished her dead, which I found eased my conscience a great deal. While I sat there Evan came in and we exchanged pleasantries. He helped himself to breakfast off the hot dishes on the sideboard and sat opposite me. It took me a second to decide to tell him and a few minutes to unburden myself. His food went cold on the plate.

27

AT TEN THIRTY later that morning the men we had fought the night before arrived at our door. Beech came for me and in a supercilious voice said, 'I have to announce some errm, gentlemen to see you, sir. I told them that you were too busy to see anyone but they insisted that you had an appointment. I take it that is not correct, sir?'

'You take it wrongly, Beech,' I said, hiding a grin. Looking at Evan nearly caused me to explode with mirth. Beech was a pompous ass but he did a good job. 'Please show the, erm, gentlemen in.'

Evan and I stood side by side at the fireplace as our assailants from the night before were shown in. They looked a sheepish lot, shuffling their feet and clearly embarrassed. They were scruffily dressed and it seemed to me that there was hunger in their eyes. 'Beech,' I called out to the retreating figure.

'Sir?' He looked back, disdain evident in his bearing.

'Tell cook I want last night's roast and the vegetables warmed up and brought in as quickly as possible.'

Beech hesitated at the door, and I said, 'Is that clear?'

He nodded and left the room.

'There's no need for that, sir,' said O'Donnell, who appeared to be their spokesman as he stood in front of the others.

'I'll be the judge of that, Sergeant Major. All of you, sit down.'

They shuffled around the table to take seats as far from Evan and me as possible while O'Donnell stood where he was. 'It's plain mister, now, sir,' he said with bitterness. 'Not sergeant major.'

'Thank you, Mr O'Donnell, for reminding me.'

At that moment David came in with Sion, who strode over to me and placed a box in my hand, nodding at me. I handed it to O'Donnell and said, 'Yours, I think, Mr O'Donnell.'

He took the box tentatively, as though it would bite him or explode in his hand. He opened the lid to gaze down on the gun metal cross and crimson ribbon. The cross was embossed with the words FOR VALOUR. It was dull looking, made from the bronze metal of Russian guns captured during the Crimean War. When he looked at me there were tears in his eyes.

'I don't,' he cleared his throat. 'I don't know what to say.'

'Say nothing, O'Donnell. No man should have to sell his medals, particularly the Victoria Cross. They are only awarded to a rare breed of men.'

He offered the package to me.' I can't accept this,' he said. 'I'll only pawn it again when I need money, which will be about ten minutes after I leave here. You'd better keep it, sir. But thank you for letting me hold it again. It was a proud moment when I met the King and he gave it to me with his own hands, so he did. It was a day to be proud of.'

'You shall keep it,' I said. 'The reason I have asked you all here is to discuss the plight you're in and what can be done about it.'

'There's nothing to be done, sir. We need and want jobs. A land fit for heroes is what we were promised and what do we come home to? Nothing, that's what! A land fit for heroes, be blowed. We all lost something out there.' I learned that the Western Front was called "out there" by all those who had been in the trenches as though it was another world.

'We need men to help in our enterprises,' Evan said, 'and you six can be the start.'

'Doing what?' asked one of those seated at the table. Before either Evan or myself could reply the door opened and food was brought in. It was placed on the table, along with plates, knives and forks. Beech's manner annoyed me and I called him over.

I held out my hand and said, 'Beech, do you know what this is?'

He looked at the cross and suddenly looked up at me. He nodded wordlessly. I pointed at O'Donnell. 'It's his.'

Beech's mouth fell open. He then did a very strange thing. He drew himself up to his full height and saluted O'Donnell. With a ramrod straight back he walked from the room while I stood there with my mouth agape. But for me it also summed up what the Victoria Cross meant. It was the ultimate accolade our nation could pay a soldier, sailor or airman for outstanding heroism. Along with it came a certain protocol that was ingrained. A senior officer saluted the man who wore the medal, irrespective of rank. I had already thought that O'Donnell deserved help; now with that gesture by Beech I knew beyond doubt that he did. And so did the rest of them!

Nobody had touched any of the food and no-one made a move towards it until Sion sat down, announced he was hungry and told them to help themselves. They fell on the food like starving wolves.

'O'Donnell, we need to find work for you and your men,' said Evan. 'Do any of you have any skills? Engineers, mechanics and so forth?'

O'Donnell paused with a fork full of roast beef half way to his lips and said, 'I'm a mechanic. Joe's also a time served mechanic, Mack's a time served printer, Fred's a fitter, Bert's a carpenter and Stan's a . . . Stan . . . What are you?'

'Blooming hungry,' was the reply which made a few of them laugh and we smiled. 'I was articled to a solicitor's office.'

I couldn't have been more surprised if he had said that he was a cook.

I turned to Evan and said, 'These are highly skilled and intelligent men. What the hell is happening?'

Evan had a worried frown on his face and shook his head. 'I don't know. Surely there's more work than we have men to fill the jobs?'

'Not blooming likely,' said O'Donnell. 'We're coming home in the thousands and there's nothing here when we arrive. The promise of jobs being held for when we returned has long been forgotten. The bosses argue that new ways of doing things means we can't fill our old jobs. A lot of woman have taken our places, especially on the land and in some of the factories. I heard there's going to be a general strike in Glasgow and if there is and the Riot Act is read then there'll be trouble; real trouble. Like blood on the streets.'

I nodded, my heart heavy. What on earth could we do?

'Any suggestions?' I asked, aiming my question at Evan and his sons.

'We need to invest more in Britain than we plan to overseas,' said David. 'To be honest I had no idea it was as bad as this. If something isn't done then we could end up going down the same road as the socialists in Germany. What do they call themselves? Spartacists?'

'That's right. Red Rosa and her lot. They're communists who believe that all wealth should be state owned,' I said. 'I'll go and see the PM and see what he has to say. In the meantime we need to find these men jobs. Any ideas?'

'I can use mechanics,' said Sion. 'Provided they're good. Are you any good?' He asked O'Donnell.

O'Donnell grinned ruefully. The smile lit up his face and changed his whole persona. 'I think so. But then that's for you to find out.'

Sion nodded. 'Fair enough. I can also use a fitter and a carpenter.'

O'Donnell said suddenly, 'We don't want no charity.' He stood up. 'I want a job that's meaningful, not a handout from rich folks.'

The other men nodded in agreement.

'I run Griffiths Aviation and we all,' Sion indicated the rest of us, 'own the company. We make aeroplanes like the Griffin. Does that mean anything to you?'

O'Donnell sat down in surprise. 'Good Lord. I'd no idea. Well I'm blowed. You mean the jobs are real?'

'Of course they're real,' said Evan. 'You should also know that I was a coal miner in South Wales and know what it is to work hard. What about our printer and articled clerk?'

'We can use an articled clerk at the bank,' said David. 'As for a printer well, I'm not so sure. We don't own a newspaper.' Then he added as an afterthought, 'Yet.'

'Leave it to me. I'll get on to Rothermere at the *Daily Mail*,' I said. 'Right, gentlemen. I think that about settles that. Any questions?'

There were plenty and I left the two boys to deal with them. Evan and I collected our coats and I ordered Beech to whistle up a taxi to take us to Number 10. We would not be interrupting the Prime Minister as neither I nor Evan carried sufficient political clout to demand an audience. But Evan already had an appointment to discuss the arrangements for President Wilson's arrival.

David Lloyd George was his usual ebullient self and listened attentively to what we had to say. The matter of the American President's visit was dealt with in minutes. Another hour was taken up with the problems of post-war Britain and the demands of the unions. It was a depressing discussion.

Afterwards Evan and I went to the club to discuss matters. We met with Lord Rothermere and he agreed to give a job to Mack, working on the *Daily Mail* in Fleet Street. We had fulfilled our obligations to six men yet we knew we had an obligation to hundreds of thousands, if not millions.

When we returned home David and Sion had left with the men. Beech knew where they had gone, so I sent a message to Mack about his new job in Fleet Street. While Evan sat in the library writing a letter to Meg I went upstairs to see how Helen was faring. She was still the same, alternating between the heat of fever and shivering cold. I left her to her misery, unwilling and unable to stay in the same room.

Twenty-four hours later her fever broke and she began to get better. I left her to convalesce and joined Evan and the boys at Biggin Hill for Christmas.

On Friday, 27th. December 1918, there was a state banquet at Buckingham Palace for President Wilson. Evan managed to get me an invitation, for which I was extremely grateful. Both of us had one regret that night, and that was Meg's absence.

Early in the New Year I made an appointment to see my solicitor, Richard Witherspoon of Witherspoon and Mandrake. Richard's father had been my father's solicitor and the relationship had continued when I had taken over the business. I hadn't kept Richard on for sentimental reasons but because he had a first class legal brain and could get things done. Usually.

'Two years!' I was aghast.

'About that. The courts don't like divorces. They maintain that you each took a sacred vow. You remember, don't you? Forsaking all others, until death do you part, and all that.'

'Of course I remember. Which is why I've stayed with her for so long. But now it's time to part. I've had enough.'

'Is there another woman?' Richard's big hands fiddled with a pencil on his desk as he looked enquiringly at me.

'Probably,' I retorted. I didn't want to tell Richard what had brought this about. I regretted having told Evan but I knew him to be as silent as the Sphinx when he needed to.

'Probably? Don't you know if you've got another woman?' Richard smiled while I just looked at him, silently. Like I said, Richard is very sharp and after a few seconds the penny dropped. 'Oh! Ah! I see. Good Lord. You mean Helen, erm, with other women?'

I nodded. 'I just found out. I want a divorce and I want it now. I'm too old to wait two years. Hell, Henry the Eighth managed it a lot more quickly and that was a few hundred years ago.'

'He was a king,' Richard replied, dryly. 'The fact of the matter is that you'll go on a low priority waiting list. It'll take a year to get to court, six months for the judge to grant a decree nisi and another six months for a decree absolute. Then you'll be divorced.'

'Damnation, Richard, that's too long to wait. I want to get rid of her now. Tomorrow. I want her out of my house physically and I want her out of my thoughts forever.' I sat there thinking for a few moments. 'Do you know Judge Jeffries?'

He nodded in surprise. 'Of course. He's nicknamed the hanging judge after his namesake, though to my knowledge he's never hanged anyone.'

'Get hold of Jeffries and tell him I want a favour repaid. He'll fit us in within weeks, not months.'

'I can't do that!' Richard was scandalised. In his legal domain judges walked with God and their every utterance had to be listened to. You didn't ask judges for favours. Only I wasn't in the mood to play legal niceties.

'You can and you will, Richard. Jeffries owes me a great deal and said some years ago that if I ever needed anything I had only to ask. Well, I'm asking now. So please speak to the Judge and explain what I want. I would prefer that none of the details be made public, just that it happens.' I stood up, shrugged on my overcoat and picked up my hat and walking cane. I pointed the cane at him. 'I don't wish to get heavy with you, Richard, but I will if I have to. I expect to hear from you by tomorrow lunchtime. I'll be at the club. Good day.'

I returned home in a thoughtful mood. I'd made up my mind and it was time to finish with Helen once and for all. I found her sitting in her private sitting room off her bedroom, reading a book. When I entered the room she looked up at me fearfully. For a moment I felt sorry for her. It was only for a moment.

'I've been to see Richard,' I began without preamble. 'He's arranging the divorce.'

Before I could go on she said, 'I don't want one. I refuse to divorce you. I like being Lady Buchanan.' There was a spark of defiance in her which I was surprised to see.

'Your wishes are irrelevant, Helen. You will leave this house tomorrow morning and not come back.'

'I will do no such thing,' she exploded, leaping to her feet, the spark having been blown into a full fired rage. 'You can't order me around like a . . . a servant. I've just told you, John, I will not divorce you.'

I looked at her in disgust. All the anger and loathing welled up in me and I fought to control my temper. She did not know how close she was to being hit across her face. 'You disgust me,' I said, my voice quivering with surpressed rage. 'I have spent years blaming myself for my failed marriage. Yet it wasn't me, not all of it. You . . . You and what you do disgusts me. Men with feelings like yours usually have the good grace to shoot themselves; I suggest you do so too.'

'Why should I?' she retorted. 'What you do is equally disgusting. The love of a beautiful woman is far sweeter, cleaner than the degradation you put me through.'

I looked at her in utter surprise. The act between us had only ever been done in one position and each time it was unsatisfactory as far as I was concerned. When I thought back to some of the women I had known when I was Master of the different liners I had sailed on and remembered their natural liking for making love and compared them with Helen, I could have wept in frustration.

'You will retire to the cottage in Tavistock,' I said. 'You will receive a small annuity for the rest of your life. It will be sufficient to live on but not sufficient for you to be extravagant. If I ever hear from you again apart from whatever is necessary to complete the divorce I shall stop the money. If I ever see you in London or hear that you have been in contact with any of my friends I shall stop your money. If you try to stop the divorce or contest it in any way I shall stop your money.' By this time she had gone ashen, her hand to her throat.

'I have told Beech that you can leave with all your personal belongings and nothing else. You brought nothing to the marriage and you will take nothing away apart from what I give you. Do I make myself clear?'

She stepped towards me and swung her open palm at my face, hard. It stung my cheek like the devil but I did not give her the satisfaction of seeing me so much as wince. She tried it again but this time I was ready for her. I grabbed her arm as she swung it at me and I twisted it viciously, forcing her to her knees. She gasped in pain and shock.

'Listen to me, Helen, you've spoilt enough of my life. You can now get out of it. If I killed you now I'd probably get away with it. Go quietly and nobody need ever know that you're a lesbian. Make any difficulties and I will make sure that every editor in Fleet Street learns the story. I despise you and your kind.' I pulled her to her feet and looked at the hate in her eyes. 'Don't be in this house tomorrow lunchtime.' I let go of her and went over to the door. 'Beech will ensure you take nothing that doesn't belong to you.'

The last time I saw her she was standing there, rubbing her arm, tears of anger and hate glistening in her eyes.

I went below to the library and sent for Beech. I issued my instructions and told him to book me a room at the Ritz. If he was surprised he didn't show it.

I saw Evan at the club and told him what was happening. He was leaving that afternoon to accompany the President to Italy before returning to America. I was going to miss him.

Bright and early the next morning I was in the offices of The Buchanan Shipping Company, sipping coffee and going over the reports that had accumulated on my desk during the Christmas holiday. When I had first become Chairman I had known every ship, where it was and what cargo it was carrying. Now, the line was far too large for one man to know everything in such detail. During the war we had lost a great number of our vessels, some old but many new. I had lost many friends and shipmates and most painful of all I had lost the *SS Cardiff* when she was torpedoed off New York in the summer of 1917.

The one fact stood out starkly from the information in front of me and that was that we needed even more ships. Britain desperately needed raw materials and foodstuffs from her colonies and they could only be brought in by ship. We had come near to starvation in 1917 but had somehow managed to survive. If we were to stop anarchy in the streets and more bloodshed then we needed to find work for the millions of men home from the front and to resurrect our manufacturing industries. We needed vast quantities of raw materials. It was, I thought, a good time to be in shipping. The only problem was that we didn't have enough cash in the company to finance an expansion programme.

When my secretary appeared at nine o'clock I ordered a fresh cup of coffee and told her that I didn't want to be disturbed. Ten minutes later the door opened and I was about to remonstrate with her when Ponsonby, director of the Far Eastern division, burst in. It could only mean one thing.

'Which ship and where?' I asked.

'The *Rosebud*, off Algeria,' he replied, sitting opposite me and helping himself to a coffee.

'Any reason?'

He shrugged. 'We don't know yet. She was two days overdue and then we heard that a Mayday had been sent from her during a storm. We think she's been sunk with all hands.'

'Who was the Captain?'

He looked glum and I knew it was more bad news, if that was possible. 'Jack Masters.'

'Jack? What the hell was he doing on the *Rosebud*?'

The *Rosebud* was, had been, an adequate ship of 3,000 tons, plying her trade from the west coast of Africa to Southampton and back. A captain of Jack's seniority would never be on board such a small ship.

'He was checking out the new Master. A short run to Freetown and back and then he was going on a month's leave. He was due to take over the *London* after the next trip.'

I nodded. The present Master was retiring and Jack was taking over the sister ship of the *SS Cardiff*, my last command. 'Is there any hope?'

'There's always hope, John, you know that.'

I nodded again. In keeping with the rest of the company, the divisional directors had all been ship's masters, and as such, felt rightly, that they could call me by my first name. The one exception was the Finance Director and he was an accountant, not a sailor. He called me Sir John. 'Anyone looking?'

'Yes. We have the *Daffodil* and the *Thistle* in the area now. So far there's been nothing.'

'All right, keep me informed. If there is any news, day or night, then call me. I'll be at the Ritz tonight and at home from then on.'

After Ponsonby left I sat for a while thinking about the *Rosebud* and Jack Masters. To have survived the war only to die in a storm was the saddest of ironies. I hoped I would not have to tell his wife that he was dead. I prayed to a benign and kindly God to spare him and the rest of the crew – then the thought came unbidden – the same benign and kindly God who had listened to the prayers of the millions who had died during the war and were now dying from Spanish Flu.

I was leaving the office at nine o'clock when the news arrived. Ponsonby burst in and said, 'It's all right. They're all safe. The *Daffodil* picked up four lifeboats about two hours ago. Every man safe.' He was practically doing a dance around the office floor.

I broke into a big beaming smile and poured two large malts for us. 'Thank God,' I said.

'Amen to that, John. Amen to that.'

We clinked glasses in happy reverence to a benign and kindly God.

The next day I returned to the house. Helen was gone, along with her personal belongings. There was a message from Richard telling me that the divorce hearing would be held in six weeks time at the court at Kingston-on-Thames. Judge Jeffries would be presiding. I'd had good news for twenty four hours and it was still coming in. Another letter had come from Sion, inviting me to travel by air from London to Paris on the first passenger flight on 9th February. In an expansive mood I foolishly accepted.

I arrived at Kenley airport at 11am, in plenty of time for the flight. Sion was already there, taking a good look at the Farman F60 Goliath that we would be flying in. It was a twin-engined biplane and would carry a dozen officers and ourselves. There was still a ban on civil flying, so all the passengers were military. I didn't ask Sion how he had wangled permission for us to accompany the flight.

We settled into comfortable seats just before midday and before we took off the officers were indulging in a game of cards and smoking. I was too interested in my discussion with Sion to wish to do either.

'How long will the flight take?' I asked.

'Between three and four hours. It all depends on the wind. Compare that to the usual eighteen hours, and you'll see why air travel is coming of age.'

'I grant you that,' I replied. 'But you're geared up to make fighters.'

'For now, that's true. But why don't we diversify into a passenger carrying plane that can be converted to a bomber in time of war?'

I thought about the idea before replying. 'I like it. It's an excellent idea. The only problem is, do we have enough cash to carry out the development?' I was thinking of my own requirements for the shipping line.

'Yes. We're sitting pretty right now. Every plane we can turn off the assembly line is being bought by Britain and we have an offer to manufacture the Griffin under licence in the States. I've sent Peter Cazorla and Rafe to look into it.'

'Who's the company that's interested?'

'I've never heard of them. It's a new small firm in California calling themselves Boeing, I think. We'll see what Peter and Rafe have to say when they get back in about a month.'

At 12.20 precisely we took to the air and three and a half hours later we landed at Versailles. We had averaged 97 miles an hour even though we'd hit some very strong head winds which had caused a delay. The journey was not uncomfortable and, thanks to some sort of sound proofing, it wasn't too noisy. At Versailles we found a local hotel and I spent an evening discussing passenger-carrying aircraft with Sion. It was obvious that he had given the matter a great deal of thought and had a lot of ideas that would enable me to ask the government for development funding.

'Incidentally,' Sion said, as we were preparing to leave the bar and go to our respective rooms, 'O'Donnell is proving a Godsend.'

'Oh? I'm delighted to hear. Is he such a good mechanic?'

Sion laughed. 'No. He's hopeless but,' he raised his finger to stop me interrupting him, 'his name opens doors.'

'What do you mean?'

'Just that. With VC after your name it seems everybody wants to know you. I am creating the job of sales manager and O'Donnell is getting the job. All and sundry want to shake the hand of a real hero and it appears that he's one. Not just the fact that he has the medal but how he earned it.'

'How was that?' I asked, for though I had known the name I didn't remember the story.

'His men were pinned down by three German machine gun nests. He charged each one, killed the Germans and saved the lives of his men. He was reticent to tell me but I persevered and eventually I got the story out of him. Some of the others had been with him and they elaborated on what had happened. I asked him why he had done it and his reply was very interesting.'

'Oh? What was that?'

'He said, if you've nothing to lose you may as well get on with it.'

'What did he mean by that?'

'Just that he was going to die if he stayed where he was. So he had nothing to lose and everything to gain. So he attacked and won. It's an interesting analogy, isn't it? The country is currently filled with despondent even desperate men. I believe the most dangerous creation of any society is the man who has nothing to lose. These battle weary millions need a purpose in life. If they don't see any hope then socialism or even anarchy will be the result.'

It was a thoughtful note to go to bed on.

28

IN SOUTHERN ENGLAND there is a famous cliff known as Lover's Leap. It's at Beachy Head, near Eastbourne. A few months after I got my divorce Helen and a Mrs Mathers jumped off the cliffs holding hands. In the letter they left behind they said that they could no longer live in such an intolerable society and that they were going to a better place. I felt a twinge of regret about the news but my predominant feeling was one of relief. I hoped for their sakes that it was indeed a better place they had gone to.

My status became far more acceptable to society now that I was a widower as opposed to being divorced. My social life took a turn for the better and I was continually being asked to one event or another. I declined most of these invitations, as business was taking up almost all of my attention and energy. I spent a great deal of time with David and Sion and, occasionally, Angus. Sion had developed an aeroplane that could take us easily and comfortably to Perthshire in a matter of three hours, carrying a dozen passengers and some cargo. The restriction on carrying civilian passengers was pan-European and did not apply to flights within Britain and so he was developing the idea of a regular flying service from London to Edinburgh. I wasn't so sure.

In June we flew to Scotland for a midsummer night's party. Kirsty and Alexander came with us, as did David and O'Donnell. I was surprised to see the latter with us but said nothing. It transpired that he was learning to fly and acted as Sion's assistant in the cockpit. Kirsty was six months pregnant and looked well with it. In my life I'd noticed that pregnancy suited some women and not others. Kirsty gave off a radiant glow, which not only reflected her happiness but made her look beautiful. Sion doted on her.

We left Biggin Hill just after nine o'clock in the morning, with a fine mist hanging in the valley and a gentle breeze blowing off the hillside. It promised to be a warm, sunny day. After we took off Sion came back and sat with us, explaining that O'Donnell could fly the plane easily, provided there were no problems. It was then that I realised how quiet it was.

'This is amazing,' I said, 'I can talk to you without having to yell. What on earth have you done?' I looked about me in bewilderment.

Sion grinned. 'Courtesy of Peter and Boeings,' he said, enigmatically.

'What do you mean by that?'

David poured a glass of lemonade for us all and replied, 'Peter has done a deal with Boeing to build the Griffin for the American Army, right?'

I nodded, I already knew that. I accepted the glass and said, 'So?'

'So Peter and Rafe managed to visit Boeing's secret development office and found that they were working on a means of reducing the noise levels in the cabins of passenger planes. They discovered they were using sheets of compressed cotton wool in a linen lining. By covering the whole of the body of the plane we are able to reduce the noise level by sixty to seventy percent. We're even walking on it in the cabin. As you see we've also lined the cabin with pine wood. The result is reasonably quiet comfort and safety. Ideal for a passenger service.'

I had my doubts but didn't argue. I needed to see the figures first.

'By the way, David. How are you getting on raising money to finance that new liner?' I asked.

David shrugged and then said, 'Not so good, I'm afraid. There doesn't seem to be as much money around as there was. But we're still trying.'

It didn't surprise me. Unemployment was rife, money was scarce and people were frightened. Those who had the most also had the most to fear. Sion's aviation company was doing well because every fighter he could build was being bought by both the army and the flying corps. In the last eight months we had seen military action in Amritsar in India, Egypt, Ireland, Afghanistan and at Archangel in northern Russia. Further afield we were busy in almost every country in Africa and had serious problems in the

Far East. Britain was having to fight hard to keep her crumbling Empire.

Sion returned to the cockpit with sandwiches for O'Donnell and himself and we had a picnic around the table, much to Alexander's joy. He was a dark, curly haired little boy, full of the joys of spring and the apple of his father's eye. I envied Sion and Kirsty their love and happiness and felt like an old man.

It was an uneventful and smooth flight and we landed in a field near Perth three hours and a few minutes later. Frazer was there to greet us.

I'd seen Frazer a few times since the war ended and I was happy to see that he had a bounce in his step and something akin to the old twinkle in his eye. I must be getting old, I thought when I heard David say, about ten seconds after we met with Frazer, 'Okay, Angus. What's her name?'

Frazer looked startled for a moment and then burst into laughter. It quickly turned into a cough but wasn't as bad as it had been in earlier months. After the smogs of London the fresh air of the Perthshire countryside was doing him a great deal of good.

'I said to Catriona that you would ask me that within five minutes. But I didn't expect it within seconds!' And he laughed again, as did David and Sion. Kirsty and I stood with wide grins while O'Donnell looked perplexed.

'So? Who's Catriona?' I asked.

'Och, a wonderful lass. And, if she'll have me, the girl I'm going to marry.'

'Is there any reason why she won't have you?' asked David. 'Apart from the fact that you snore, your feet smell and you pick your nose.'

'I do no such thing,' the Laird began, before he realised that David was pulling his leg. He stopped smiling and then . . . 'She thinks I'm too good for her,' were his surprising words.

We trundled across the field to the car with our few items of luggage. A number of farm hands had appeared to help with the plane and Sion went to show them what he wanted done.

David repeated the question. 'Why does she think that you're too good for her? That's impossible.'

Frazer shrugged and said, 'She's the cook. Which is how I came to meet her. She applied for a job at the house and I helped to interview her. Actually, I wasn't supposed to concern myself with the selection of the cook but I saw her from the window and wanted to meet her. God, but she's beautiful. We have to be careful. If anybody found out about us there would be a real scandal.'

'In this day and age?' David was aghast. My sympathies went out to Angus.

'This isn't London,' said Frazer, heavily. 'Here we still have a class structure that would do the Raj of India proud.'

'Well, that's blasted nonsense,' said Sion. 'Look where we come from and we're accepted into the highest society.'

'That's entirely different, Sion, believe me,' I said. 'I agree with Angus that it's a problem. However, let's look forward to meeting Catriona and make the most of our stay. What have you planned, Angus?'

'Well, I thought we could take a flight up to Scapa Flow in the Orkneys tomorrow, before the party, to see the German Fleet. There's seventy ships at berth there, waiting to be sold or taken into the British Fleet as part of the reparations settlement. Apparently it's a wonderful sight to see. Then we have a huge barbecue arranged for the evening. It's such a lovely day, and it promises to be the same tomorrow. I thought we'd steal the idea from our American friends,' he indicated Sion and David. 'Having heard so much about them I thought we should give it a try.'

'I don't feel very American any more,' said David. 'Europe has reasserted its hold.'

'Me neither,' said Sion, who gave a wistful sigh. 'It looks like I'm doomed to stay here for the rest of my life.'

'Oh? And why's that, may I ask?' Kirsty broke in, archly.

'Because, my Darling Girl,' replied Sion, 'I make the important decisions in our household.'

'Such as?' I asked, suckered into another of Sion's jokes.

'Such as who we should elect to Parliament and should we declare war. Kirsty makes the unimportant ones like where we live and what schools the kids will go to. So I guess we'll stay in England. For a while yet, anyway,' he added, as an afterthought.

We all burst out laughing and Kirsty went a delicate blushing pink. I continued to envy them their modern, shared marriage. Looking at

Angus I was sure that he felt the same. Well, I had a solution to his problems. But that could wait until I met Catriona.

That afternoon Frazer, David and I spent an hour going over the accounts of the estate. Frazer had worked wonders, in spite of having been back for such a short time. The sawmill was being expanded and was in operation almost continually, the bottling plant was now going twenty-three hours a day in three shifts, bottling for other distilleries as well as our own, and the deer and beef herds were expanding nicely.

'We're able to bring heavy barges along the Tay as far as the landing stage. We can then send the logs and wood down to Dundee. I gather the Buchanan Shipping Line has put in a bid for the contract,' said Angus with a wry smile.

'Funnily enough,' I said, with a straight face, 'their tender will be the lowest. Just.' The others nodded. It suited us all.

We had finished our discussion when Frazer rang the bell and ordered tea. A strikingly attractive woman entered carrying a tea tray. She was dressed in a clean, white cotton dress that was then the standard uniform for a cook. Her hands were red from washing and scrubbing pots and pans but she had an intelligence and warmth about her that was very attractive. I would not have thought it possible for Frazer to blush but he did.

'Ah, Catriona, thank you. I didn't expect you to bring the tray. Where's Mary?'

'I told her to wash some dishes,' she replied, quickly setting the tray down and dispensing cups and plates.

'Where are you from, Catriona?' I asked, unable to place her accent.

'Manchester, sir. I came to Scotland to be with my husband. He was a sergeant in the Scots Dragoons. He was killed at Passchendaele in October 1914. He was part of the Third Cavalry Division that attacked the German Fourth Army. Or so I understand.'

I nodded. 'You understand clearly. It was the first of the big wipe outs. Hundreds of thousands of men killed for valueless land. But it was a necessary sacrifice in the end.'

'Excuse me, sir, if I cannot agree with you,' she said, tartly. 'Will that be all, sir?' She turned to Frazer, clearly not liking my comment and not afraid to show it. I liked her for her spirit as well as her looks.

'Catriona, please sit down and join us,' said Frazer. 'These are my best friends. I've told you all about them. They'd be delighted if you joined us.'

'I'd better not, Angus,' she said gently. 'McBride is hovering outside. And you know what a gossip and tartar he is.'

'McBride can go hang,' said Frazer with passion. 'I'm the Laird and he had better not forget it.'

'He's the ghillie,' replied Catriona with a smile at Frazer.

'What's a ghillie?' Asked David.

'He runs the estates for me,' said Frazer. 'He's also my attendant as I am a Highland Chief. In reality he takes care of the herds and the fishing and shooting. I suppose it's true to say that he's number two up here and holds a lot of power.'

'Exactly,' said Catriona. 'So I had better leave you three alone.' She picked up the tray and walked smartly out. We heard her greet McBride as she closed the door behind her.

'It seems McBride is also keeper of your morals,' said David, dryly.

We had a superb dinner that night, just us, with no extra guests. Because there were so few of us Kirsty stayed when the port was passed and we made plans for the next day's flight. Kirsty decided not to join us. O'Donnell ate in the kitchen with the other staff at his own request.

'What are you going to do about Catriona?' I asked Frazer.

He shrugged miserably and replied, 'I don't know. If I married her she would never be accepted as mistress of the household, at least not for an awful long time. You know that, John. And I can't make her my mistress.'

'Why not?' I asked.

'She won't let me,' was the honest reply. Needless to say that caused a certain amount of mirth to David and Sion. They had no understanding of the hierarchical lifestyle of the upper classes in Britain having been brought up in the free and easy American West. Mind you, the Eastern seaboard of America, from Boston to New York, could teach even the British about snobbery. However, theirs was based on wealth, ours on breeding.

'How tied to this place are you?' I asked.

Frazer looked startled for a few seconds and then replied. 'I don't know. It's my home; always has been. I enjoy it here. I would like to remain.'

'I'm not sure you can if you want Catriona,' I replied. 'However, you could return to London, take up your post at the bank, marry Catriona and visit here regularly to keep an eye on the place. Catriona need never be subjected to any unpleasantness then, real or imagined.'

Frazer frowned in thought before he said, 'I suppose so. I'm just not sure.'

'The alternative is to sack every member of staff who's unpleasant to her, and you live here.'

'I couldn't do that!' Frazer was shocked. 'Why, most of these people have been here as long as we have. Their families go back generations. No I couldn't do that.'

'Well, it seems to me that the solution is in your hands.' I stood and wished them all a goodnight. I wanted peace to ponder Frazer's problem.

It was a pleasant evening, and though the sun had set it never really got dark at that time of year. I sat at the window of my bedroom looking down to the River Tay. I heard a noise below me and saw Frazer and Catriona walk out of the front door together. I watched as they vanished in the dusk towards the river, arm in arm. After all the sacrifices their generation had made you would have thought that a great deal of latitude would be given when it came to affairs of the heart. But it wasn't so.

We took off at 10 am. The plane carried Sion and O'Donnell in the cockpit, myself, Frazer and David in the cabin. Catriona had packed us a huge picnic lunch and the day was fine, with a slight breeze bringing warm weather from the south.

The journey north was uneventful and we took turns changing seats with O'Donnell to get a better view. We passed over the Ladder Hills and reached the Moray Firth in just over an hour. We could see the North of Scotland forty to fifty miles away and as we drew nearer Sion pointed out John o' Groats.

A few minutes later we could see the Orkneys and there in Scapa Flow was the German Fleet. It was an incredible sight, dozens of ships of all sorts and sizes, from battleships to cruisers and destroyers. Many of them had steam up, though they weren't going anywhere, and Frazer explained that the ships were manned by skeleton crews which were needed to keep the boilers lit for warmth and cooking. The ships had been valued at £50,000,000, and would form part of the reparations the Germans had to pay.

Sion flew lower and we passed through the fleet, so close that I could make out individuals standing watching. As we banked round the eastern end of the bay I exclaimed 'Look! They appear to be hoisting flags on all the ships.'

Sion turned his head to see and said, 'Good Lord. That's the German Eagle! What on earth can be happening? Look! The lifeboats are being lowered as well.'

Intrigued, we flew towards the west and then back over the fleet. 'That's odd,' David was standing behind me and said in my ear. 'Look how that destroyer has shifted.'

Sion had handed me a pair of binoculars and I focused them on the ship David was alluding to. 'My God! She's sinking!' I quickly scanned the other ships and thrust the glasses at David. 'So are the others. Take a look. The Germans have scuttled their fleet.'

I was aghast. Already ships were listing one way or another. A number were down by the bows and others by the stern. Lifeboats were all over the water and I could see men jumping off ships and into the sea. I looked at my watch. It was now 12.15 and I saw a destroyer turn turtle and sink beneath the water.

There were a few British ships and tugs afloat in the bay and we watched as they towed a number of cruisers and destroyers onto the nearby beaches.

It was a truly shocking sight and we were speechless at the wanton and wasted destruction. We stayed around for nearly an hour. We used the Aldis lamp to signal the British ships explaining who we were and asked if we could stay and watch. Permission was granted when we used the Laird's name.

We flew south just after 1pm and arrived back in Perthshire in plenty of time for tea. It was in sombre mood that we went back to the house to enjoy the evening's revelry.

A marquee had been erected on the front lawn during our absence and duckboards had been placed over the grass. The most pleasant surprise of all was to find that Madelaine had arrived from London on the overnight sleeper. David was delighted and set off to show her round the estate.

That evening I changed into my dinner jacket and looked critically at myself in the mirror. Not bad for my age, I thought. A bit overweight but certainly not fat. The grey that peppered my hair gave me a distinguished look and my eyes stared back steadily enough. All I wanted was a good woman and the one I wanted I couldn't have. Damn, but who said that life had to be fair?

Downstairs the garden and marquee were packed with people. An army of servants helped to keep glasses filled, the ladies drinking sherry and the gentlemen various malt whiskies. It was a jolly, friendly crowd who had come to see the Laird, now that he was back from the war and settled on the estate. I knew a number of the guests, as many Scottish landowners had interests and houses in London. Soon I was in deep discussion about world affairs with some of my old cronies. I related what we had seen at Scapa Flow that day.

At nine o'clock bagpipes started and the band of the Black Watch, Frazer's old regiment marched onto the lawn. Conversation stopped as we stood and listened with appreciation. After half a dozen tunes – reels and pibrochs – the band marched off again. A few minutes later half a dozen of them reappeared and set up in the marquee and began to play dance music. Soon many at the gathering were dancing an eightsome reel.

I attached myself to David and Madelaine but they ended up dancing with Kirsty and Sion. Frazer saved me from my gloomy thoughts.

'It seems everybody is having a good time except us,' he gestured for a refill and within moments a servant brought a tray of fresh malts.

I took one and tasted it. 'This is very, what should I say? Peaty?'

Frazer lifted the glass and looked at the colour and then sniffed it. 'It's from Islay. It has a unique flavour due to the local water. I like it, though it can be something of an acquired taste.'

'Why is it Catriona has a Scottish name yet she's from Manchester?' I asked, changing the subject but taking the conversation in a direction I thought he wanted.

'Her parents were from the borders. They'd been tenant farmers but were thrown off the land in the clearances at the end of the last century.'

'I remember. That was a terrible time. Are they still alive?'

'No. They both died a few years ago. She has a brother but hasn't spoken to him for years. He appears to be something of a waster from what I can gather. I wish she was standing here right this minute.'

'Listen, Angus,' I said with some ausperity. 'You're one of the most resourceful chaps I know. Find a good manager for this place and come back to London. Marry Catriona and enjoy your life once more. I wasted too much of my life on Helen and I do urge you not to make the same mistake. If you love her you can go anywhere and do anything. Go to America! Evan will make suitable arrangements and you can build up one of the businesses over there.'

'It's an idea, I suppose. I'll think about it.' He broke off as two ladies approached.

'Angus, I'd like to introduce my cousin Shona, she's been dying to meet you.'

I slipped away, not wanting to hear any more. As I wandered by the edge of the lawn I saw a movement near the hedge and saw O'Donnell talking to an army officer. They appeared furtive to me and I walked towards them, curiosity getting the better of me. I heard O'Donnell mention guns and the army officer mumbled a reply. He saw me coming for he gestured in my direction and O'Donnell spun round with an oath.

'Oh, it's you, sir. You gave me quite a start, I can tell you.'

'So I see, O'Donnell. Everything all right?'

'Yes, sir. Is there any reason that it shouldn't be?'

'No. None at all.' I introduced myself and was introduced to the officer who I could see now was a Captain in the Black Watch. I couldn't place his accent though it bothered me for some reason.

We exchanged pleasantries and I returned to the middle of the throng. Isobel Smith found me there.

'Hullo, Isobel, where's William?' I asked, looking round for her husband.

'He's had to get back to London. He's on tonight's sleeper south. Needed at the department, so he said. Wanting to see his mistress I say.' There was no bitterness in her voice, only resigned acceptance.

I looked closely at her. Isobel was about forty, very attractive, with the sort of full figure I liked. She had short, bobbed hair, very much the fashion and the bodice of her gown had lifted up her breasts to show them to best advantage. I was having thoughts I shouldn't have. However, she linked her arm in mine and walked with me to the bar.

'We've gone our separate ways for years. You know William, a stickler for doing the proper thing, although it's just his version. I don't mind. I stopped loving him a long time ago. I hear you did get divorced. Is that true?'

I nodded. 'Helen committed suicide with her lover.'

'Oh! How romantically stupid! Who was he?' Isobel asked, wide eyed.

'He was a she,' I replied, dryly. 'What would you like to drink?' I smiled at her wide open mouth and the stunned look on her face.

'But, but,' she paused and then burst out laughing. 'Oh my, I think I'll help you to make up for lost time. Champagne for me,' she added.

I hoped she meant what I thought she meant.

She did.

I awoke in the middle of the night, Isobel asleep beside me. The Captain's accent! It was Irish! I thought we might be in for trouble.

29

I FINALLY WENT BACK to sleep. Some early morning gymnastics with the lovely Isobel put me in a good mood and I went down for breakfast feeling ravenous. I felt like an eighteen year old but I tried to act my age. Nobody made any comments so I guessed that nobody had noticed what I'd been up to, or more importantly, who with.

When O'Donnell entered the room my worries of the night returned with a vengeance and I decided to talk to David. I was replenishing my plate at the sideboard when Frazer stepped up to me and spoke in a low voice, 'I've sent some scrambled eggs, toast and tea up for Isobel.'

'You knew?' I was incredulous.

He looked puzzled and then he smiled. 'We all knew,' he whispered and went and sat down.

After breakfast I sought David out and took him into the garden. I told him what I'd heard and what I thought. 'If he's Sinn Fein we can't have anything to do with the man,' I spoke earnestly. 'They're traitors, the whole damn lot of them.'

His response surprised me. No, more accurately, it shocked me. 'Of course he's Sinn Fein. He believes in a free Ireland.' David looked at me, hesitated and then said, 'So do I.'

'What!' I was askance. 'You can't be serious.'

'Never more so. John, I've never lied to you and I'm not about to start now. The British House of Commons is for an independent Ireland. The only reason it hasn't happened already is because the House of Lords is blocking it. And why are they blocking it?'

I shrugged, uncomfortable at hearing the truth when I just wanted to go by my instincts.

'Because the Lords own vast farms in Ireland. They are afraid that if Ireland is given its independence then their lands will be nationalised and they will lose them. That's in spite of the fact that the Irish have assured them it won't happen. The land will be bought at the market price from those who want to sell, and anybody wishing to keep their land can do so. The Lords don't trust the Irish and the Irish certainly don't trust their Lordships.'

'So what is O'Donnell up to? He was given a VC for God's sake. By the hand of the King himself. Now he's a traitor, conspiring with other traitors.'

'A traitor to whom? O'Donnell thinks of himself as an Irish patriot. He's done his bit for King and Country and now he wants what he thinks he's entitled to. If we don't give Ireland independence they'll take it for themselves. It will be at the price of a great deal of bloodshed and bad feeling but in the end they'll get it.'

'David, how can you possibly think such a thing? If we don't give it to them they'll never take it.'

'John, it's impossible to keep people as serfs. Not in the twentieth century. America wanted freedom and took it a long time ago. Ireland's time has come. Lloyd George has grappled with the Irish question throughout his time as Prime Minister. He's sick of it. It costs us vast sums of money, and we get nothing in return. We don't need more potatoes and we don't need any peat. Ireland has no natural wealth and the Irish are semi-educated peasants without any real industry. So why do we keep Ireland under our yoke?'

The question took me by surprise and I thought for a few seconds. Finally all I managed to say was, 'It's been ours for hundreds of years.'

'It's belonged to the Irish for thousands. We invaded and took their land. We've no moral and only a dubious legal claim to the country. The Irish will get it back and I think they should be given it without bloodshed.'

'What about O'Donnell and that Black Watch Captain? What should we do about them?'

'John, what do you suggest? Arrest a hero with a VC because you say so? I don't mean that disparagingly and certainly not offensively.'

'No offence taken,' I said.

'There's no proof either of them have done anything. You also need to remember something else. Many of the Irish who fought for us are considered to be enemies by those fighting for Irish freedom. Their lives are at risk if they return home and their liberty is at risk over here. I'd say they're between a rock and a hard place. Wouldn't you?'

I nodded, uncomfortable at thinking the unthinkable, at least as far as I and many of my class were concerned. It was true that I owned nothing in Ireland but it had always been there, a part of the Empire. The Irish always appeared to me to be ingrates for not appreciating how lucky they were to be part of the greatest Empire the world had ever known.

'We still need to do something about O'Donnell,' I said feebly.

'We will,' said David.

'Oh? What?' I was eager to learn what he proposed.

'We turn a Nelsonian eye to him. Leave him alone. Let Ireland sort itself out. If O'Donnell gets up to mischief and into trouble that's his look out. As long as he does nothing to bring trouble to us then let him connive and conspire as much as he likes.'

'Shouldn't we tell Scotland Yard, at least?' I protested. 'They could keep an eye on him.'

David thought for a second before replying. 'I suppose so,' he spoke hesitatingly. 'I'm just not sure. My natural sympathies are with him, but I don't want to see any more lives lost. Why don't you and I talk to him? Warn him off?'

'Surely all we'll do is succeed in putting him on his guard?'

'Or convince him that there's no point in carrying on with whatever he's plotting.'

'Do you think that'll be the case? The man isn't exactly a coward.'

'I know,' David shrugged. 'I just don't want to see him in any more trouble. I respect his beliefs and, as I said, I believe him to be right. And, as I also said, so does Lloyd George and most of the cabinet, if not parliament as a whole.'

'Ireland is a complete mess,' I said with feeling.

'Never a truer word spoken,' O'Donnell said from behind.

I spun round with an oath. 'How long have you been there, O'Donnell?' I demanded.

'I've just walked out to say that Sion was wondering what the programme is for today and I said I'd volunteer to find out. And then I heard your profound statement . . . Sir.'

The pause had been long enough to suggest insolence without causing offence. It was a good example of a typical soldier's attitude to authority when they wanted to convey a message without saying anything that would get them into trouble.

Sergeant Major O'Donnell had been in the British army for twelve years. To have reached this rank showed that he had brains as well as resourcefulness. Though the bloodiest war in history helped the survivors to attain a higher rank than they could normally have expected.

'If you like, sir, I'll debate Irish politics with you at any time. The true version, unlike the one taught in English public schools.'

I was about to riposte, but thought better of it. 'I shall look forward to that, some day,' I added. 'But not now. Our programme for today? I'm not sure. What did Sion have in mind?'

'A picnic. To take the steam yacht down the Tay and, depending on the weather, out into the Firth and back.'

'Sounds excellent,' said David. 'Tell Sion that's a grand idea.'

Much to Frazer's delight Catriona came with us. We had a full boat, with Sion, Kirsty and the toddler Alex, David and Madelaine, Isobel and myself, Frazer and O'Donnell. Frazer didn't allow any other servants to come. He wanted us to handle the boat ourselves, saying that it would be fun. I was sure he wanted to enjoy the Catriona's company without having other servants around.

The boat, the *Sea Spirit,* was a motor sailer, constructed by William Osborne of Brighton. She was forty feet long and ten feet wide, and we learnt from Frazer that she was built of rock pine on oak and was driven by a single, diesel driven propeller. She also had two masts, which carried a jib, a main sail and a mizzen. Below deck was a comfortable saloon, two cabins and the engine room.

'She'll do eight or nine knots,' Frazer announced, delighted with his new acquisition, having owned her for less than a month. 'She will take just about any sea thrown at her.'

David and I exchanged amused glances. We had both been in some pretty rough seas in our time, me aboard large ships while he had been marooned on an island in the Caribbean some years earlier.

While the ladies went below to sort out the huge packed lunch they had brought, we set about preparing for sea. Frazer had already arranged for the sails to be fitted, ready for hoisting and the engine had been started to allow it time to warm up. O'Donnell volunteered to look after the engine, I was going to take the helm and the others would pull on various ropes when I gave the orders. We were in a jolly, festive mood on the bright and breezy day.

We cast off and I turned the *Sea Spirit* downstream. She was a lovely little yacht, a real joy to handle. David had lit the stove in the saloon and soon cups of coffee and tea began to appear. The breeze was from the south east and she heeled over slightly as the sails filled. The engine chugged sweetly and the morning passed in a pleasant blur.

Soon the city of Dundee came into sight. It was amazing to think that this had been the first city in the world to have electricity. The Scots had pioneered more inventions than any other race, at least as far as I could see. They may have been a dour, surly lot, but they were also industrious, tough and intelligent.

With the stream behind us I estimated that we were doing twelve knots. The boat held a steady heel to port of a few degrees and the amount of required rope pulling and sail adjustment was negligible. It was my idea of sailing.

We passed the docks and had to change tack a number of times as we slipped past some of the large ships and ferries that continually plied across the Firth of Tay. As we passed the castle on the point to the east of Dundee, the swell began to pick up and we pitched gently and soporifically along. We helped ourselves to lunch as we approached Buddon Ness, the most easterly point of land and we decided to keep on our heading until we'd finished eating. Alexander was busy wandering about, the boat's movement sending him dropping on to his bottom every few minutes. We all sat on the foc'stle, on comfortable lounge chairs and cushions, while we ate.

Isobel and I exchanged a few meaningful glances. I was looking forward to bedtime with relish.

Frazer had the helm and Catriona sat with him in the wheel house. Now that we were away from the house Catriona had transformed into a bubbly, friendly personality whom Frazer was mad not to marry at the earliest opportunity. I forgot, when I described the Scots to mention one other trait: the lower orders were unmitigated snobs. But then, on reflection, that was also true of English servants.

Finally, it was time to go about and head back. Frazer called the orders, and we jibbed, everyone busy with their allotted tasks. As we turned through the wind and the boat heeled to starboard there was a loud scream.

Kirsty was on her feet. 'Alex! Alex has gone overboard.' She was pointing astern of us and I saw his small white face appear in the wash for a few seconds. Sion was below checking the engine, David was on the jib, Frazer was on the wheel and I was in front of the wheel house. O'Donnell was already diving into the sea. Frazer was no seaman, I was. Although he was turning the wheel I knew what was needed and rushed into the wheelhouse and grabbed the wheel from him.

'Get the sails down,' I yelled. Sion had appeared from below, and rushed to loosen the main sail while David released the jib and Frazer the mizzen. I held the wheel steady until we were sixty degrees off our track and then I threw the wheel the other way. When we had reversed course we were following the exact course we had just travelled. I saw O'Donnell ahead, swimming fast and furiously. There was no sign of Alexander. The woman were standing anxiously, scanning the water and suddenly there was a shriek.

'There he is! There!' A voice yelled and a finger pointed and then I saw him but only for a second. He vanished below the surface and as he did so O'Donnell also went under. A few seconds later he reappeared and to everybody's joy he had Alexander in his hands.

I stopped the boat alongside them and O'Donnell handed Alexander up to Sion. The little fellow was lying quite still, a sodden mass of clothes and a blob of a white face. It was Catriona who then took charge. To my astonishment she turned Alexander onto his stomach and began to pull back on his arms and push on his back. She appeared to be pumping air into him. She kept at it for a few seconds, the remainder of us watching, scared to say anything. O'Donnell clambered back on board over the stern and came forward to see what was happening.

Alex gave a shudder, water poured from his mouth and he began coughing and gulping in air. He stirred and Kirsty, in tears, swept him up and hurried below into the warmth. The other ladies followed her.

Sion held out his hand to O'Donnell and shook it warmly. The rest of us pummelled his back, shook his hand and laughed and chattered like magpies. My God, it had been a close run thing!

O'Donnell's teeth were chattering and he said, 'Let me go and find something to wrap round me. It's freezing in there.' He nodded at the water and went into the wheelhouse to go below. As he did so Sion stopped him.

'Mike, I owe you more than I can ever pay. If there's anything you want, anything at all, come to me first.' Sion held his hand out to O'Donnell. 'My word on it.' They shook briefly and then O'Donnell went below to find other clothes to wear.

We sorted the boat out, engaged the engine, turned back to our planned track and hoisted the sails. Soon we were serenely sailing back into the Firth of Tay.

Alexander was soon up and about and Kirsty had the devil's own job keeping him below decks. Finally she gave up and allowed him to join us on deck but this time he had a rope tied around his waist and secured to her wrist. He didn't like it but after a few grizzles and caterwauling he accepted the situation.

The journey up river was relatively peaceful though much slower. We had been helped on the outbound journey with about three knots of current going our way and now we were fighting that same current; we were effectively travelling at about half our earlier speed. I gave up trying to explain the facts to Isobel. As we neared the landing stage back at the house a subtle but distinct change settled over Catriona and she metamorphosised back from being a beautiful butterfly into a hard working cook. I was determined even more to get some sense into Frazer's dense skull.

The following morning we left to return to London. We had an extra passenger as Isobel decided to fly with us. I'd managed to have a quiet word with Frazer but I wasn't sure whether or not I'd made an impression. We flew into a headwind and the journey was not nearly as comfortable as our trip north had been. However, after some four hours and a few minutes we landed at Biggin Hill and clambered out of the plane. I was glad to get my feet back on solid ground.

'Well? What do you think?' asked Sion, after we were seated in his lounge at home.

'About what?' I asked, perplexed.

'About flying, of course. About carrying passengers long distances.'

'It'll never replace ships,' I retorted, 'ever.'

'It's not meant to. Flying is meant to add to travelling, not take anything away. Look what happened last week when Alcock and Brown flew non-stop from the US to Ireland. That's just the start. It took only 16 hours and 12 minutes to do the journey. By liner it would have taken four days.'

Sion's enthusiasm was one thing, his blind stupidity quite another. 'Sion, they flew a Vickers-Vimy biplane from Newfoundland to a bog on the Irish coast. You step onto a liner in a major city, sail halfway across the world, and step out into a major city. You don't get wet. You eat, drink and on the whole have a merry time and you arrive refreshed and ready for life. From what I read in the *Times*, Alcock said it had been a terrible journey, they flew through fog and storms and the two of them had only sandwiches, chocolate and coffee to keep them going. It might get better,' I added, 'but not for an awfully long time. I think you should stick to building bombers.' From the look on his face I guessed my words had fallen on deaf ears.

I returned to London with Isobel, leaving David with Madelaine at Biggin Hill. Isobel and I settled into a routine which suited me and, I assumed, Isobel, and which lasted for a number of months. Her husband took frequent trips away, ostensibly on business, and I was free to entertain her, discreetly, at home. Because of my conversation with O'Donnell I took a closer look at the Irish question so that I could have an educated, formed opinion rather than the one I had expressed in Scotland.

At the election in December 1918 Sinn Fein MPs had been elected to Westminster. They had set up a Dail Eireann or Irish Parliament, led by Eamon de Valera. This was in spite of the fact that the man had been imprisoned in Lincoln gaol only the year before and had only recently escaped. However, as a result of an amnesty Dev, as his followers called him, was back in Ireland. He had tried to take part in the Paris peace conference but had been kept out by Lloyd George. The PM had announced that the future of Ireland was an internal British affair and no concern of the rest of the world. At that time an uneasy peace had settled over Ireland which didn't last long. On September 11th. 1919 Britain declared the Dail Eireann illegal.

Soldiers and police surrounded the Mansion House in Dublin and tried to arrest Michael Collins. Collins was the "Minister of Finance" for the Irish Parliament and had escaped through a skylight in the roof. A warrant was issued for his arrest. Ireland and Irish politics was rapidly going to the dogs. Again!

Gradually my views had altered. I began to see Ireland through clearer eyes and was appalled at what I was learning. Far from being ungrateful clods the Irish seemed to me to be gifted writers and orators and had suffered a great deal under the British. It came as a complete shock to my system when I found that the prejudices and opinions I'd held all my life were so fundamentally flawed. David had been right in one thing. Far from contributing anything from our national coffers, Ireland was a huge drain, tolerated for the benefit of a few landowners.

My passion for Isobel was waning. My spirit may have been strong but the flesh was definitely getting weak. We took to chatting, reading together and occasionally, visiting a provincial theatre, rather than pursuing activities in the bedroom. Once or twice we had a half-hearted discussion about Isobel divorcing her husband and marrying me instead but it was never serious. Like many of these affairs ours just faded out and we stopped, by mutual consent, seeing one another. However, having been denied my creature comforts in the arms of an accommodating woman for so long, I was keen to find another.

In the meantime, apart from Ireland, another catastrophe was looming. Germany and the peace talks were in dire trouble and had been for some months. The treaty of Versailles was causing huge problems on the continent. The terms that had been agreed were so harsh that Lloyd George said in parliament, "Because of the treaty we shall have to fight another war in twenty five years time, at three times the cost".

Germany was called upon to pay twenty billion gold marks in reparations and to give up vast tracts of land. The Germans were also forced to pay the cost of the Allied occupation of the left bank of the Rhine for the next fifteen years. It was too much for the German cabinet who resigned en masse while the general population took to the streets and burned the French flag. The League of Nations, envisaged by President Wilson as a guardian of peace, was seen by the Germans as a self-serving alliance of the winners. David and I had looked at the possibility of aiding Germany with loans but decided that not only would it not be politic but Germany was on the verge of collapse and bankruptcy and we would end up losing our money.

In the meantime strikes were erupting all over Britain like a rash of boils. Even the police were going on strike, protesting against the Police Union being stopped by a new bill going through Parliament which would prevent them from taking part in normal union activities; instead they would have to join a new body called the Police Federation. However, I thought that the strike call was unlikely to succeed. Not only had the police been given a substantial pay rise but they were also to get a lump sum of £10, equivalent to ten weeks pay for an experienced policeman. I was wrong.

The police strike led to riots across most of Britain's towns as lawlessness gripped the nation. The army was called in and there were numerous deaths. A rail strike resulted in the rationing of all basic foodstuffs such as meat and sugar and it looked as if the postal, as well as dairy workers would join in the strike. Lloyd George made it clear that the army would be used, and the rail strike ended as quickly as it had began. There was a call by the unions to nationalise the coalmines but it was rejected by Lloyd George and the strike by the iron founders' union was settled. Most of Europe was gripped in a general strike or at least had vast numbers of workers withdrawing their labour. While all this was going on the government announced that the national debt had now risen to an all time high of £474 million, and six Sinn Fein prisoners escaped from Strangeways prison. The last piece of news we received while I was down at Biggin Hill.

We were sitting in Sion's kitchen when we heard the sound of gunfire and the door burst open. Mike O'Donnell rushed in followed by the six escaped men.

30

'WHAT IN THE name of God,' I began but shut up when I saw the gun O'Donnell was waving.

'Sorry, Sir John, but I had no choice. Sion, I'm calling in that favour. You said that any time I needed help I could rely on you.'

Sion nodded. 'Okay Mike. But there's one condition.'

O'Donnell bristled, 'I didn't make any conditions when I saved young Alex,' he said.

'Maybe, but I can't help that. I want your assurance that nobody's been killed.'

O'Donnell burst out laughing. 'Of course not. Do you think I'm completely mad? I don't want to hang, not even for the cause. I fired a few shots to discourage two coppers who were behind us. I think they've gone for help. There'll be no killing if we can get away now, tonight. Sion, I'm sorry,' there was desperation in his voice now, 'but I had no option.'

'Come on, O'Donnell,' said one of the six men. 'You said you could get us away. If you fail you know what'll happen.'

O'Donnell looked from Sion to me and shrugged, helplessly. 'They have my family,' he said, in a voice drained of emotion. 'The boyos didn't think I'd do it without some encouragement, on account of my VC and me going native, so to speak. So they've threatened my family. In Ireland,' he added by way of explanation.

I looked at the six men. They were all nondescript, shaven headed, and dirty. They looked as though they had walked from Strangeways.

'Right, there's no time to lose,' said Sion. 'If we take off now we can be in Ireland in three or four hours. The moon'll be up by then so we ought to be able to see to land. It's a clear night so there shouldn't be any problems. The Griffin III is ready, Mike. You've flown in her often enough, go and get her ready. You six, get yourselves in the back and strapped in. I'll be with you in a minute. Kirsty, will you be all right?'

Kirsty nodded, white faced, her hand holding her bulging stomach.

'I'm coming,' I announced, getting to my feet.

'No you aren't,' said one of the men. 'I don't trust you, Sir John,' he emphasised the Sir, caustically.

'Too bad. Sion can't fly there and back without navigational help. I know O'Donnell can fly but he knows next to nothing about navigation. I used to be a ship's Master and I know more about navigating by the stars than just about anybody alive. So if you want to get where you're going in one piece then you'll need me. I particularly want Sion to get back here alive, so that's another reason why I'm going.' I was standing, shrugging on my coat. 'Come on O'Donnell. Get a move on.'

O'Donnell nodded and gestured to the others to follow him. However, one of the men didn't move. 'How do you know that we can trust them? I reckon they'll send for the police the moment we leave the room.'

'You really are as stupid as they say, aren't you?' said Sion

'What do you mean? And less of your lip. Or else.'

'What are you going to do? Shoot me? Then you'll never get away. I'm the pilot. You need me.'

'But we don't need her,' he pulled a gun from his pocket and pointed it at Kirsty. Sion immediately stepped in front of his wife and a tense confrontation built up.

'What about the police?' the man repeated.

Sion looked at him with anger and disgust. 'I owe O'Donnell. Nobody will ring the police. Understand?'

One or two of the men nodded.

'That'll do,' said O'Donnell. 'Please, Sion. Can we go?'

Sion nodded, kissed his wife on the cheek and grabbed a coat. 'Let's go.'

'Sion! Be careful,' said Kirsty, tears glistening on her cheeks.

'I will love, don't worry.'

We went through the back door and into the hangar where the Griffin III was kept. Carefully, Sion swung open the two doors and peered out. All seemed quiet. Nobody shouted after us and there were no shots fired in out direction.

'Mike,' Sion hissed in a loud whisper, 'we'll start her in here and drive out.'

'Hell, Sion,' argued O'Donnell, 'we've never done that before. Is it possible?'

'The noise and movement might confuse the police long enough for us to get airborne. If we try and push her out they might realise what we're up to and start shooting. The plane could give us a few seconds grace.'

'Assuming there's anybody there,' I pointed out.

'Yes, there's always that,' replied Sion, 'but I don't want to risk it.'

O'Donnell had pulled the chocks away, Sion was in the pilot's seat and I was next to him, scrabbling about for the folio of maps I knew he carried in the cockpit. Using my cigarette lighter I was relieved to find naval charts covering the Irish Sea and the two coastlines.

'Okay, Mike,' said Sion. 'Hit it.'

O'Donnell swung the propeller on the port engine which coughed and he swung again. Another cough gave way to a deep throated roar and the engine burst into life. He did the same with the starboard engine and as O'Donnell scrambled on board Sion eased the plane forward. We inched into the starlit night, my nerves as taut as bowstrings. The clatter of the engine was a cacophonous scream that matched my mood. Suddenly I saw a light, and then another one. Then there were dozens of flashlights springing on across the field to our left. Sion turned right and opened up the throttle.

'Not that way!' yelled O'Donnell. 'My God, Sion, you'll kill us.'

The plane bounced across the field, the engine roared louder and a shot was fired behind us.

I suddenly understood what O'Donnell meant. In front of us loomed a long, low building, a series of sheds, each one holding a Griffin ready for sending to the new Royal Air Force. I glanced at Sion whose features showed only concentrated determination. He was willing that damn plane into the air.

'I've done this before,' he said.

I didn't know what he meant so I said nothing. My will was working alongside his, wishing the plane to get airborne. We bounced and a fusillade of shots rang out, some hitting the plane. There was a scream from behind and a moan. The plane bounced again and at the last minute bounced over the building.

'Hell, that was close,' said Sion, wiping the sweat away with the back of his hand. 'Try and shut him up, will you?'

'O'Donnell,' I looked back and yelled, 'shut him up. Or throw him out,' I said callously.

'Shut your face,' said the man I now took to be their leader, 'and do your navigating. We'll look after him.' The man who had been shot was moaning softly.

'Be quiet,' said O'Donnell, 'you're getting on my nerves. It's only a flesh wound. I've seen soldiers with worse stand up and fight.'

'It hurts, Mike,' whimpered the wounded man. 'God, it hurts.' But he lapsed into silence and I stopped listening, concentrating on where we were and how we were to get to Ireland.

'Sion, have you ever tried to navigate at night?'

'No! A compass doesn't work well in a plane. You know we always get about by following the signposts.'

I nodded. It was a wasted gesture as he couldn't see me in the gloom of the, thankfully, cloudless night. Sion was talking about the way pilots literally flew low, looking at the name on a signpost and working out which way to go. Often they just followed railway lines, roads or rivers.

'We've two choices,' I said. 'Either we follow the south coast to Land's End and head directly north following the pole star or we cut across country, follow the south coast of Wales and hit Ireland heading west.'

'I take it the second route is the shortest.'

'Correct. Significantly shorter. Like a hundred miles or more.'

'Can you navigate the shorter route?'

'Easily.'

'Then we'd better take it. I'd hate for us to get our feet wet.'

'What do you mean?' I asked, puzzled and then I understood. 'Oh, you mean landing on the sea.'

'Correct. We're full of fuel but I want to get across and back without hanging around in Ireland. I don't trust that lot behind us.'

'I agree. Okay, come right,' I peered into the sky. 'Steady, steady. Right. Look ahead. See that cluster of lights about ten miles away?

Aim for those. I'll keep giving you way points to aim at which, hopefully, will keep you on track.'

I studied the stars again and identified the North Star, Arcturus, Vega and Altair. I looked to my left and found Capella and the planet Jupiter. I looked ahead and saw a vast configuration of lights and said, 'That's Bristol. Head for it while I take a look at the map again.'

Suddenly the plane swooped down and my stomach hit the back of my teeth. There were cries and oaths from behind us.

'Sorry,' said Sion, 'Geese.'

'What?' I looked out of the cockpit window and back. Flying behind us, cutting off the stars, was a V-shaped flock of geese.

'They can knock out an engine. It's another reason we tend to fly during the day. Remember during the war we lost planes from night raids when no enemy action had been reported?'

'Certainly. Wasn't it put down to pilot error or engine failure, or something?'

'That's right. Except later, when enough pilots came back and were able to compare notes we discovered the planes had been brought down by birds. Usually geese,' he added as an afterthought.

'What happened?' O'Donnell was at our shoulders. 'The boyos are complaining.'

'Tell the boyos,' I began savagely and then thought better of it. 'Geese,' was all I then said.

'I'll explain.' O'Donnell hesitated and then added. 'Look, I'm really sorry. I had no choice, believe me. When we get back I'll explain it to you.'

I didn't know about Sion, but I was startled. 'You're coming back?'

'Sir John, if I don't they'll kill me,' he said, matter of factly.

I never had understood the Irish nor their politics. I understood them even less now.

I looked up at the stars again, found the ones I needed and said, 'Come left a few degrees. Aim for the bottom end of the lights of Bristol. We ought to see a dark expanse of nothing and then another mass of lights.'

Sion made the slight alteration and we settled on the new course. 'There's the Channel. And there's Cardiff. Good.' We were now travelling in an east-north-east direction following the line of the

Welsh coast on our right and the sea on our left. We'd been in the air for just over an hour.

We followed the same light hopping techniques until we reached the end of Wales and flew over St. George's Channel. There was nothing but sea beneath us and nothing else ahead. Now I was navigating by the stars, with the North Star ahead and to our right and Acturus almost dead ahead. I gave Sion occasional changes of direction as the wind drift moved us to the left. For nearly half an hour we saw nothing and I was beginning to wonder whether we'd really been much further south and heading too far to the west. If we had been we'd miss Ireland and fly out into the Atlantic. That was fanciful nonsense, of course, as after an hour all we had to do was head directly north and we'd hit Ireland. However, on a dark night, over the sea, one's imagination ran away with one. Then I saw lights and pointed.

'I see them,' said Sion, relief in his voice.

'Oh ye of little faith,' I said, the relief evident in my voice also.

Sion laughed.

O'Donnell came up behind us again. 'The boyos are getting restless,' he said. 'They want to know how much longer.'

Sion looked over his shoulder at the ex-sergeant major. 'Tell them it won't be long now. What do you want to do?'

'Sion, if I stay they'll kill me. I know that. I'm considered a traitor because of my time in the British army and the medal and everything. I need to come back with you and they want me to stay. Any ideas?'

Sion thought for a moment before be said, 'I want to land on a road, long and straight. As they get out, shout, and I'll go like a bat out of hell.'

'Right.' Mike left the cockpit.

We dropped gradually lower as the coast came up. There were lights ahead and to our right.

'I think that large group of lights in the distance is Waterford,' I said, after consulting the map. 'The lights to our right are Wexford. According to this army ordnance map there's a road inland of Loch Garman which heads north.' I scanned the dark mass of land ahead. 'That's the road. You can see it now the moon's risen.'

'Got it. Call Mike up here.'

I looked over my shoulder and yelled for O'Donnell who quickly joined us.

'Mike, don't tell them anything. I'm going to land and bounce a bit. Make a fuss. I'll roar "fire". Get them panicked and leaping out. As soon as the last one is out shout, and we'll be gone from here.'

Sion lined the plane up on the road and dropped lower. He throttled right back and the plane landed with a thump, bounced and landed a second time. A third bump followed and Sion yelled at the top of his voice. 'I can't hold her! Fire! Get out everybody.'

We came to a stop and the door was flung open. I looked back and saw men leaping out, the plane rocking on her springs. O'Donnell shouted that the men were out, and Sion opened the throttle wide. We shot off along the road and smoothly lifted into the air. Without the six men the plane was far lighter and much easier to fly. I saw that O'Donnell had shut the door. He came and stood behind our seats.

'Thanks, Sion,' he said, patting us both on our shoulders. I was looking forward to hearing what he had to say about it all.

I repeated the task of navigation and we were over Wales when Sion announced, 'We'll need to land soon. We need petrol. Is there anywhere on the maps showing an airfield?'

We were now flying between Swansea and Cardiff. I was exhausted so God alone knew how Sion must have felt. I scanned the maps, looking for some place to put down.

'There's a place shown here that's unpronounceable.' I spelt it out, 'L.L.A.N.T.R.I.S.A.N.T.'

Sion made a noise as though he was clearing his throat and pronounced the name.

'It's got a common behind the hill. There's a track across it and no sign of any wires or poles. That might be our best bet. Apart from that I can't see anywhere else.'

'Can you find it?' Sion asked.

I took another look at the map and identified a number of villages and towns. I saw a place I guessed and hoped was Bridgend and said, 'We need to head due east. Come left, steady. That's it. Now aim for those lights. I hope that's a place called Pontyclun. Sion, go lower. I want to see the silhouette of a hill on top of which is some sort of tower.'

We went lower and I saw a river ahead and the hill to my left. 'That's it. Come left and head for that hill we can see. Now right. There's the common.'

Sion flew over the hill, directly above the tower, and then the flat common was spread out in front of us. The moon was setting by now, but it still cast a bright light over the grass, which looked black in the starlight.

'I can't see the track,' Sion said. The starboard engine coughed and spluttered. 'That's it, we've got to land.'

The port engine coughed and then picked up again. We went lower and were now merely feet above the grass. It looked flat but I knew how deceptive that could be. If we hit a low hummock or a clump of reeds the plane could be flipped over and that would be curtains for all of us. Both engines spluttered and stopped together and we were gliding down with no options left.

Sion assured me later that it had been a text book landing until we hit the pony. When we did we slewed sharply round, skidded to one said and came to a halt, the starboard struts collapsed and we were sitting at an angle. Outside was pandemonium, horses milling about and neighing in terror. After a few moments peace fell and the horses settled down again.

'Are you all right?' I asked Sion.

He gave a loud sigh in the deathly quiet that now surrounded us and replied. 'I think so. Mike, you okay?'

'Bejesus, but I think so as well. That was some landing, Sion.'

We sat in the silence for a few moments and then I asked, 'What do we do now?'

'Nothing,' said Sion, 'until daybreak. Settle down and try and get a little sleep.' He slumped in his seat and a few moments later I was astonished to hear quiet snores emanating from him. O'Donnell had done the same. In spite of my own weariness I was unable to sleep and I carefully climbed out of the plane and onto terra firma once more.

The ponies had moved away and were quietly champing at the grass. The one we'd hit was lying still and I checked that it was dead. I looked about me but it was eerily still. Imperceptibly almost there was a gradual lightening of the sky and I realised that dawn couldn't be far away. I could tell that the land gradually rose ahead of me and I walked that way. I came to a track, the one I guessed that was shown on the map, and followed it. After a few moments I came to a proper road across which was a cattle grid. The land steepened sharply at this point and I could see houses to my left and right. I trudged along further and after a few hundred yards came to the brow of the hill. There, in front of me, was a horse trough and pump.

I worked the handle a few times and pumped up some fresh water and washed my head and took a drink. Refreshed, I looked around me. There were houses in front and on either side. The road to the left went downhill. I went right. I walked in between two rows of houses and came to an imposing church on my left. The light was getting stronger and when I looked ahead of me I could see the round tower we'd followed to our landing. The road now went left down the hill and I walked along hoping to find a garage or a smithy where we could get some help. I had seen no one but then it was still very early. Finally, I came to a row of small, neat houses, overlooking the valley. No, it was more than that. I could see for miles, a vale that almost reached the coast in front of me and farmland stretching left and right.

As the light strengthened I could see that there was a wonderful view practically all the way to the coast. Down the hill I saw another two rows of houses and down in the valley a small village. From the map I guessed that I was looking down on Talbot Green. I sat on the ground for a few minutes and must have dozed off. The next thing I was aware of was my shoulder being gently pushed.

'Are you all right?' I heard a man's voice ask.

I opened my eyes and blearily looked at the young man who was kneeling beside me. He had a worried frown, a hooked nose, black hair and a kindly face.

'Yes, thanks. I fell asleep. Been awake all night,' I said.

'Come on, let me help you.' The man put his hand under my arm and helped me to my feet. He took me into one of the houses. I remember it had a short passageway that led into a cosy room where a fire was lit in the grate. I sat down gratefully in the armchair and closed my eyes.

I heard him say, 'Beat! Beat! Can you come through here a minute?'

'What is it Bill? I'm just getting some bread and . . . Oh, who's this?'

'I don't know. He was sitting on the pavement against the railings. He looks tired out. Can we get him a cup of tea?'

'Give me a moment. The kettle's nearly boiled.'

I managed to open my eyes and protested. 'It's all right. Thanks. I need to get back to my friends.'

'Where are they?' asked the man.

'On the open ground behind the hill.' I gestured, vaguely. 'I was wandering around looking for a smithy or a garage.'

'What are you doing on the Common?' the young and obviously pregnant woman asked.

'Ran out of fuel. Oh, sorry, I should explain. We were travelling in an aeroplane. We ran out of fuel and had to land.'

'That's the Common,' said the man. 'I'm a freemen of Llantrisant and we're allowed to graze sheep and horses there if we wish.'

'Oh! Look, I'm truly sorry but we hit one of the ponies and killed it. We'll pay.'

I was having a great deal of trouble understanding his accent but I managed to follow what he and she were saying.

'My name, incidentally, is Buchanan, John Buchanan.' I offered my hand.

The man took it and said, 'Bill Whalley. I may be able to help with the smithying. I've got an anvil and a small fire and furnace up the back. Once you've had your tea we can go back to the Common. This is my wife. Beatrice. Everybody calls her Beat.'

I smiled at the pretty young woman and said, 'Thank you.'

'Oh, it's nothing. We're only too pleased to help, aren't we Bill? Let me get the tea and perhaps a round of bread and butter.'

After both I felt refreshed. I offered to pay them for their help as I could see there was little money about the place but they refused. A short while later Bill and I walked back over to the common.

He was astonished to see the plane and walked around it in wonder, touching it. Sion and O'Donnell climbed out, sleep tousled and grumpy. I made the introductions and left Sion and Bill to discuss what they were going to do. I climbed in to the back of the plane and promptly fell asleep.

It was the middle of the morning when I woke, stiff and short tempered as the others had been. I climbed out of the plane to be greeted by O'Donnell, Bill Whalley and a stranger.

'Sir John, you're awake,' said O'Donnell. 'We're needing your help. Bill took Sion back to the forge and left him there. We need to lever the plane up and unbolt this strut. This is Charlie Williams. He's come to help us.' He was a small, nattily dressed man who nodded a greeting.

'If you can help with this pole,' said Bill, 'errm, Sir John.'

'Just John will do, Bill. I was plain John Godfrey Buchanan long before I got a knighthood.'

He smiled hawkishly and took out a pair of round glasses which he slipped on. It made him look less predatory, more owlish. 'I need these for close work,' he said by way of explanation. 'Right, Charlie. Shove them two logs under there and give me a hand.'

We quickly levered the plane up and Bill and Charlie built a prop underneath the wing. Satisfied it was safe, O'Donnell crawled under and began to undo the bolts that held the wheel strut in place. In the meantime Bill Whalley and Charlie Williams stood apart and lit a cigarette each.

After he had removed the strut O'Donnell carefully checked every bit of the plane and said, 'I think that was the only damage. Once Sion gets back we'll be able to fit the strut and wheel and push the plane over to the track.'

'What about petrol?' I asked.

'There's a petrol pump on the corner of – where was it again?' He looked at the two men.

'The Ralt,' said Bill. 'It's not far. We can get as much as you'll need from there.'

Sion returned then, carrying the strut across his shoulder. They set to with a will, replacing the strut and the wheel. In the meantime, Bill Whalley and I walked back into the village to find the garage.

'How long have you been here, Bill?' I asked, more for something to say than out of any interest.

'Three years now. I came from Swansea, married Beat and settled here. Charlie's from her side of the family.' We were at the top of the road and he said, 'Over there is the castle that belonged to Edward, the Black Prince. He lived there for a long time in the thirteenth century. It's pretty much fallen down now but there's a lot of history around here.'

We found the garage and Bill spoke to the owner. He arranged for us to have six jerry cans of petrol, I paid and we began the trudge back to the common. I'd only gone a hundred yards when I put the cans down with a sigh.

'I'm getting too old for this. Let me take a breather.'

Bill nodded, put his own cans down and stepped away before he lit a cigarette. After a few seconds I indicated I was ready to continue and he carefully pinched out his cigarette, placed it behind an ear and picked up his two cans.

That was the pattern we followed for the next twenty minutes which was the time it took to retrace steps that had originally only taken six or seven. When we got back the repairs were finished and the plane had been shoved onto the track. We carefully emptied the petrol into the plane and the others left to get some more, leaving me to have a rest. I was sitting down when I became aware of a shadow in front of me and, looking up, saw Beatrice standing there.

'I've brought some food,' she said. 'It's not much. Just some cheese sandwiches. It's all I can spare.'

'That's very kind of you. Thank you.' To tell the truth I was ravenous and had been thinking of finding a local pub to get us something. 'The others have gone to fetch more petrol. With luck we'll get away before it's dark.'

She gave a shy smile. 'It's amazing to think of you all flying in one of these.'

'When is the baby due?' I asked.

'In about six weeks. If it's a boy I'm going to call him Raymond and if it's a girl, Barbara.'

'Nice names. I take it the building behind your house is the school?'

'That's right. This is a very nice place to live. So convenient.'

That was about all the small talk I could manage and luckily the others arrived back with the petrol and the garage owner. His curiosity had got the better of him and he wanted to see the plane. We poured the petrol in and Sion did his checks.

He climbed out of the cockpit and said, 'That's it. Time to go, I hope. Thanks very much for all your help,' he held out his hand to Bill and Charlie. He then bent down and gave Beatrice a kiss on the cheek. She blushed prettily.

I shook hands with Bill Whalley and slipped a white five pound note into his hand.

'There's no need,' he protested.

'Yes, there is,' I replied. 'With a baby on the way a few pounds will help.'

'Thanks. Beat, this is Sir John Godfrey Buchanan. Just think, we've had a Sir in our house.'

I smiled with embarrassment. 'I told you, just John will do.'

'Godfrey? I like that name,' said Beatrice. 'If we have a boy I'll name him Raymond Godfrey, after you.'

I was inordinately pleased at the suggestion and said in that case I hoped they'd have a boy.

We climbed into the plane, O'Donnell swung the propeller and after a few more turns the port engine burst into life. He did the same with the starboard engine and we sat there for a few moments while the engines warmed up.

We waved to the small group standing in a huddle beside the track. They waved back, Sion opened up the throttles and we accelerated down the gentle incline. After a few seconds Sion lifted the plane into the air and we turned back to buzz over the village.

The Whalleys, Charlie and the garage owner stood and waved. Sion waggled the wings of the Griffin and we roared off to the south, heading for the coast.

I directed us easily and quickly to Cardiff and we headed east for Bristol. My skills were no longer required as Sion was capable of navigating us back to Biggin Hill in the daylight. Throughout the journey O'Donnell stood behind us and told us what had happened and how he'd become involved. We also worked out what we were going to say.

When we landed the police were swarming all over the place and as we clambered out of the plane we noticed the guns steadily levelled in our direction.

31

Kirsty rushed out, shoved past the police cordon and threw herself at Sion.

'Are you all right?' Sion asked, wrapping his arms around her.

'Yes, I phoned David. He came right down. He told me not to say anything so I haven't. Not a word. It's been very difficult,' tears sprang to her eyes. 'David sat with me and finally told them to leave me alone, that you'd return. I don't think they believed me.'

Sion nodded. A policeman approached and said ponderously, 'I want a word with you, errm, gentlemen.'

'Certainly,' I took charge. This was for me to sort out. 'Do you know who I am?' I was at my most supercilious.

'Yes. You're Mr Buchanan.'

'Sir John Buchanan,' I corrected him, 'constable.'

'Inspector,' he corrected me, unimpressed by my title. 'And I still want a word. If you don't mind.'

'Actually, I do. We've had a horrendous time. We were held up at gun point, forced to fly to Ireland and we crashed in Wales on the way back. You can come back tomorrow and we'll give you the full story.' I walked away, the others following me.

'Wait a minute,' came the angry call from behind us. 'You're under arrest.'

'You might be an inspector now,' I retorted, 'but if you arrest us I'll make it my task to have you broken to constable. You know who I am and you know these people. I'm a personal friend of the Chief Constable and also the Commissioner in London. I can pick up a telephone and speak to the Prime Minister if I need to. Now, tell me, inspector, do you really want to go up against me?'

The officer hesitated and as he did I walked away. He called after us, 'I'll be back tomorrow when I must insist on speaking to you.'

I waved a hand airily in his direction and continued to the house. Inside I sat at the table and said, 'That was close. I'm not in a fit state to bandy words with the police just at this time.'

'Me neither,' said Sion. 'I'm in need of a week's sleep, at least.'

'I'm really sorry,' O'Donnell spoke to us both, 'for all the trouble I've caused.'

'Forget it, Mike,' said Sion. 'You saved my son's life and that's a debt hard to forget, or to repay. Why don't we all get some sleep and meet down here for supper? We can hear all about it then.'

When we reconvened after what had been, for me, a refreshing sleep, there was a feeling of a great deal more optimism about the place. I learned that David had not been inactive while we had been resting.

'I've spoken to the Chief Constable and the Home Secretary,' he said, after I had poured myself a large malt whisky and water.

'Nothing like going straight to the top, is there?' I said with a smile and a wave of my glass.

'Didn't somebody once say that was what the top was for?' he retorted.

'Quite right, David. So what did they say?'

'They promised to call off the dogs until we were ready to make a statement. However, it was pointed out that the statement must be made sooner, rather than later.'

'We'll do it tomorrow,' I said. 'We should use our friends, not ab-use them,' I emphasised, smiling at the pun.

'Right, O'Donnell, do you care to tell us what's been going on?'

'Sure, Sir John, sure. It's like this. You know that those of us who've been serving in the British army are, shall we say, disliked by the nationalists? Quite a few good soldiers have been killed when they've gone back to Ireland. Well, on account of my medal, I've been . . . targeted. So I've tried to do my bit but at the same time keeping it pretty much low-key. When you heard me talking to that captain in Scotland it was about me helping the breakout. He had the same problems as me. Our families have been threatened and believe me, if you ignore the threats they're carried out. As a lesson to the others. Clear so far?'

We all nodded. I felt sorry for the sergeant major.

'Anyway, I tried refusing. Then I got a letter from my Mam telling me that if I didn't help they'd kill me brother and sister. If I still refused then they'd kill me Mam and Dad. So what was I to do?'

'How did they get away?' Sion asked. 'Out of the prison I mean.'

'Same way. The prison officers let them out. It was either that or have their families killed. I picked them up about five miles from here with the police hot on their trail. We gave the police the slip and they didn't catch up with us until we were at the gates, so to speak.'

'What had you planned to do?' I asked.

'Take the plane myself. Get them away from here and let them out. I couldn't have got them to Ireland. Hell, I doubt I'd have survived the landing, wherever it was. If I'd been killed, well so be it. At least they'd have to leave my family alone after that.'

In a perverse way there was a certain logic in that.

'As it was, with the coppers on my tail I knew I needed Sion's help.'

'All right,' said David, 'Sion's told me some of the ideas you had. It's too complex to make up a story. Mike was here that evening with you all. The gang burst in and forced you at gunpoint to fly them out of here. That's the only bit of the story that you need to remember. The rest should be the truth, the whole truth and nothing but the truth.'

We debated that for a few more drams and picked at some light snacks, and then I was ready for my bed once again. I was definitely getting too old for all that running around.

The next morning I was up with the larks. My sleep pattern had been totally disrupted. I went downstairs for breakfast to find the rest of the household already gathered around the table. We were half-way through breakfast when the door was flung open and in walked the inspector from the previous day.

'I want a statement and I want it now,' he began without preamble.

'Do you know, inspector, you're really annoying me,' said David, leaning back in his chair and looking with disdain at the man. 'What's your name?'

'Eh? What?' The question took him by surprise. 'What do you mean?'

'I mean,' said David with heavy irony, 'what label do you use. Where I come from it's called a name. You might know it as something else. Now please enlighten me.'

The man drew himself up, and for the first time in my life I understood the idea that a moustache could bristle with indignation. 'It's Jackson. Inspector Jackson.'

'Well listen to me, Inspector Jackson,' said David, 'you can either sit down and have a civilised breakfast with us and we'll answer whatever questions you may have or you can leave. If it's the latter I'll phone the Chief Constable and have you removed from the case.' David leaned forward in his chair and added, 'I hope I make myself clear.'

Indecision was written large all over the man but then he seemed to realise that bluster was no good in the company in which he found himself. 'I'll have breakfast.' He sat down at the table with us.

He left in the middle of the morning. He didn't like it, but he had to accept the story we all stuck to. He tried to show that O'Donnell had been with the gang but, as we swore that he'd been there all evening, he had to accept it. We told him what had happened and how we had crashed in Wales. We gave him the address of the people who had aided us and he finally had to acknowledge that he was going to get nowhere. When he left I wished him good luck in finding the escaped men.

'We'll get them,' he said, 'one day.'

I returned to London with David. Soon the problems of Ireland and of the last two days receded into the background as we tackled the day-to-day problems connected with the bank and our various enterprises.

'The sovereign loans we've granted so far appear to be working well,' he said. 'Though I'm glad we didn't get involved in Germany or Poland.'

'Something more's happened?' I enquired.

'Strikes and more strikes. The Germans are up in arms about Versailles and the Polish, well, what can I say?'

'They're bovine and easily led,' I grinned at him.

'Exactly. There's a great deal of unrest, fermented by the Russian Communists. If the White Russians lose, I hate to think what could happen across Europe.'

'One of two things,' I told him. 'Either we allow a gradual change to some form of socialism, doling it out bit by bit or we have the same anarchy that's sweeping Russia right now. If we do the former, then it's controlled and contained, but if it's the latter, then we'll have the same bloody revolution that rocked France in the eighteenth century and Russia in this one. But we'll need to start making concessions and we need to start soon.'

'Will Lloyd George allow the changes?'

'He'll instigate them. Mark my words, he's the canniest politician we have. He knows the writing is on the wall. Some wealth and privilege has to be sacrificed for the greater good, but he understands that.' I paused and changed the subject. 'Any news from Angus?'

'Just to say that Catriona is getting more fed-up by the day. I think he'll do as you suggested and come south sooner rather than later. He'll either do that or he'll lose Catriona.'

'And she's far too good a cook to lose,' I said, deadpan. We both laughed.

Back in my own offices at the shipping line I had a dozen urgent tasks to complete before I could go home. Soon life slipped back into its usual, thankfully, humdrum pace.

A few weeks later I was relaxing at home in front of the fire, my feet up, a newspaper in one hand and a drink in the other, when I had the surprise of my life.

The door opened and I irritably was about to ask Beech what the devil he wanted when Meg walked in. I nearly dropped my glass but instead she took it from my hand and placed it on the occasional table next to my chair.

'You're probably drinking too much,' she said and leant down to give me a peck on the cheek.

'What on earth are you doing here? And where's Evan? Why didn't you say that you were coming?'

'One thing at a time, John. First a glass of sherry would be very nice.'

'What? Oh, yes. Dry?' I got her a drink while she removed her coat and elegantly sat in the chair opposite mine.

She took an appreciative sip and said, 'Lovely. Right, as to your other questions, Evan is in Southampton and will travel up tomorrow. I couldn't let you know as we came unexpectedly. We were in New York on business when he suggested we come over. Actually, the *SS Cardiff* was in harbour and on an impulse we decided to come. I must say, the ship's looking a little tired these days, but it was fun nonetheless. The journey this time was a little different to the first one.'

We both smiled at the memories. I owed this beautiful and courageous woman my life. By way of gratitude I'd given her my heart. Luckily, she wasn't aware of it.

'Why has Evan stayed in Southampton?'

'During the voyage, he found out that there's a large tract of land for sale on the edge of the city. He has some idea or other and decided to go and see it while he was there. I was impatient to see you and David and so came on. I went to David's house first but he was out somewhere with Madelaine. So I came here. What's been happening?'

I told her about our adventures and she took it all, as usual, in her stride. 'Thank goodness nothing worse happened. I don't know, I try not to worry about Sion and his flying but it's very difficult sometimes. I try not to think about it but it seems to me he's lived a charmed life ever since he began. Actually,' she added as an afterthought, 'ever since he flew off that cliff all those years ago.'

We spent an evening reminiscing, a friendly warmth between us. It was my greatest regret to know that if I made an untoward move my friendship with Meg and Evan would end. She was Evan's forever, nobody else's. I had to be content with just her friendship and luckily, as I saw her so rarely, it proved to be sufficient.

We had a cold buffet dinner served where we were sitting and had just finished eating when the door was again thrown open and David strode in, Madelaine right behind him, a huge grin on his face. After Meg provided more explanations as to why she was there we settled down to talk about family matters, helping Madelaine to realise what she was marrying into.

'When is the wedding?' Meg asked, naturally interested in the plans for her son and her future daughter-in-law.

'Soon,' said David. 'We've decided to have a quiet wedding – just family and a few, a very few, friends.'

'That's all very good, David,' said Meg, with a flash of irritation, 'but your father and I need to make plans if we're to be here. We can't just drop everything and come on a whim.'

'You just did,' protested David.

'Yes, but there was nothing to drop, so we could act on our whim. Oh, you know what I mean.' Slightly flustered, Meg waved an elegant hand and picked up her empty sherry glass and pretended to take a sip. She seemed to realise what she was doing because she handed the glass to David to refill. I guessed she was now about fifty-eight or even sixty. With the years, her natural beauty had matured.

Madelaine helped her out. 'Why don't we get married while you're here?'

David looked surprised, Meg was delighted and I was, I suppose, flabbergasted.

'Well, David?' prompted Meg. 'What do you say?'

'Oh? Yes. Well, I say yes! Can we fix it so quickly?'

Madelaine laughed. 'Mrs. Griffiths, I've enjoyed listening to the stories about the Griffiths family,' she began.

'Oh, my dear,' Meg interrupted her, 'please call me Meg. And I'm so sorry, how thoughtless of us to go on about . . . us,' she finished weakly.

Madelaine laughed again. 'Meg, please, I enjoyed it immensely. What I wanted to say was there are one or two skeletons in my own closet that I haven't told David about. Oh, nothing scandalous, I assure you.'

'What a pity,' David joked, 'I was looking forward to some juicy titbits.'

Madelaine gave him a nudge with her elbow.

'Ow,' he grimaced.

'Give him one from me, too,' said Meg, which Madelaine dutifully did.

'All I was about to say was we've never really talked much about my family, there have always been other things to occupy us,' she blushed prettily.

'It's just that I've a cousin who's a parson at a small village in Norfolk. If I twist his arm I'm sure we can arrange things quickly. And if, as we agreed, it's a small wedding then there's nothing to stop us.'

It was agreed and the next day when Evan arrived in London he was told the good news. Meg and Madelaine took charge and left us men to ourselves which, frankly, suited us all. Kirsty came up to London to help, promptly went into labour and delivered a baby girl at St. Bartholomew's Hospital. They named her Louise Sian and she was as pretty as a picture. The wedding was delayed another week to give Kirsty time to recover, as she was to stay in hospital for five days, and it would also give Jake Kirkpatrick and his family time to travel from Spain.

The wedding took place in a small church in Swaffham near Norfolk. Although it was a happy occasion I suddenly felt overwhelmed with grief. I held back the tears as I suddenly thought of Emily. She had been like a daughter to me and her marriage to David had been a defining and wonderful moment in my life. Her death had devastated me, but, as always, life went on. I didn't begrudge David his happiness with Madelaine it was just – well, that she wasn't Emily. Meg must have sensed something of my mood for her hand stole into mine and gave it a squeeze. I looked down at her with gratitude and saw the tears in her own eyes. I realised then that there could never be a similar event when she wouldn't think of her own, dead daughter, and live with the regret of what might have been.

It did not turn out to be such a small wedding after all. The Griffiths family was there in their droves and I have to confess that I lost track of uncles, aunts, cousins and all the rest. However, I did spend time with Evan's brothers, and I enjoyed listening to their views and ideas. They were all ambitious in their own way and I was impressed by the small businesses, mostly in hotels and shops, they now controlled. They had combined together in a single company, which was prospering throughout the Vale of Glamorgan and Pembrokeshire.

For a small wedding we still managed to have over a hundred and fifty guests. Jake was best man and made a very funny speech about the time he and David had been marooned on a desert island. I was also called upon to speak which, as usual, I enjoyed doing.

Then the day was over, the bride and groom departed and we had a party in the hotel in Norwich we had commandeered.

In the New Year's Honour's Lists I was made an hereditary peer and elevated to become the Earl of Guilford. However, I still had the same problem that I had as a baron. There was no son to inherit.

BOOK 4

Evan's Story

32

Summer 1921

EVAN STOOD TO speak. He was one of the most polished speakers in the Senate and was popular with the press who loved to quote him. Today it was a packed gallery of hacks representing most of the major newspapers in America.

'I know that the passage of the 19th Amendment to the Constitution of the United States still has a rocky time ahead of it. However, let me warn you that if we are to take our place in the twentieth century, as the greatest country in the world, rivalling Britain in particular, and other European countries in general, then we require this bill to pass. This is the first nation in the world to have a constitution based on freedom for all. This means, not,' Evan waved his right index finger in the air, 'just for fifty percent of us but for us all. Universal suffrage must become enshrined in law before this session ends.'

There was cheering from the public gallery and subdued clapping from the press gallery. The Speaker rapped his gavel to regain order to allow Evan to be heard. There were smiles on his side of the Senate and scowls from the Republican opposition.

'We Democrats must allow women the vote in order to have a balance of views across America.'

A voice yelled from the gallery, 'Is that what Meg reckons?' There were howls of laughter and the Speaker had to regain order once more, although with a grin on his face.

Not to be outdone, Evan grinned in return and said, 'I guess so. She wrote the speech.' Which brought the house down and it took some time before he could continue.

Later he sat in the Senate dining room, flushed from his success in the chamber. A number of senators came over to congratulate him on his speech until he was joined by Rutherford Hyams, the Senator for Illinois, Evan's neighbouring state.

'I could kill for a drink,' Evan said, with a grin.

'Prohibition is a terrible thing,' said the tall, gaunt Hyams sitting opposite him. 'Which is why I carry my cane.'

The second senator from Missouri looked quizzically at the other man. Hyams smiled, flipped open the top of his cane and pulled a cork stopper. He pushed the cane under Evan's nose and the tantalising smell of bourbon wafted out. 'No gentleman should travel without one,' he quipped.

Evan grinned. 'Where on earth did you get that? And where did you get the bourbon? I thought all stocks were destroyed and no more being produced.'

'There are still one or two states holding out. And Canada is a long border. And don't forget you can still get whisky for medicinal purposes.'

'Is that how you came by it?'

'No. I got it from a friend of a friend.'

'A hoodlum?' Evan asked.

Hyams shrugged, 'Probably. Would you like a sip?'

'Not here, man. Good God! This is where we should set the example.'

Hyams laughed. 'Evan, your constituents will vote you in forever. You're a rare politician. A completely honest man.'

Evan looked uncomfortable. 'Perhaps not completely. But I hope I am honest and tell it as it is.'

'Evan, look around you and tell me what you see.'

Evan looked about the luxuriously appointed dining room which was half full of men, all members of the senate, talking earnestly with one another.

'Do you notice the number who are carrying canes? Do you notice how they're tipping them into the cups they have on their table?'

Evan, who had considered himself to be observant of matters going on around him, looked again. He saw many walking sticks leaning against tables and chairs and he saw one or two being upended over a cup.

'Pour me a drink,' he told his friend. 'How in the world did we let this legislation through?'

Hyams shrugged. 'It was almost inevitable. I've been here a lot longer than you have and saw it coming a long time ago. We fought a delaying battle, that was all. I told the House that crooks and gangsters would take over and that Prohibition would lead to trouble. It's already happening although we only went dry on 16th. January. A man named Capone has become a millionaire in less than a year from supplying hard liquor and that's just the start.'

Evan picked up his cup and took an appreciative drink of the bourbon. 'Cheers. However, you didn't sit here to share a drink. What's on your mind?'

'As always, Evan, you miss nothing. We're very concerned.' By "we" Evan took Hyams to mean the Democratic Party. 'The President is not a well man. The breakdown he's suffered has meant his League of Nations idea has been stopped by Lodge and his cronies and we're in danger of becoming isolationist.' The Senator was referring to Henry Cabot Lodge, the Republican Senator for Massachusetts who had managed to defeat the motion to ratify the Versailles Treaty. 'The President is being blamed for the rejection of the pact. Europe is slipping into anarchy and the Republicans are fearful that socialism and communism will come here if we don't do something fundamental. There's widespread fear on the issue and my concern, along with others, is that the Republicans will sweep to power in November. If they do we're going to have a lot of trouble. A hell of a lot.'

Evan nodded. 'The President is no longer able to drive forward any of his ideas and I hear that even Mrs Wilson is deciding on some issues. It gives a whole new meaning to the term "kitchen cabinet", doesn't it?'

'It's no laughing matter, Evan.'

'No, I know. But what's to be done? The President may be nicknamed "the schoolmaster" but he's proven to be one of the greatest pioneering presidents this nation has had.'

'True, but his illness is proving to be a real millstone around the neck of the party. That's why we want you.'

'Eh?' Evan looked at his friend in surprise. 'What do you mean, you want me?'

'To lead the party. We have less than two months to the election. If

Harding wins then the Republicans will really crack down with their new Law and Order Bill. We can expect deportations and hangings to escalate out of all proportion. Wilson can't win, we know that. He's not been seen in public for eight months. The problem we have is that there is no means of replacing an incumbent unless he stands down voluntarily. I've been in to see Woodrow and he's adamant that he will lead the party in November. If he does we'll lose and I think we'll be out of power for a long time.'

'I agree,' said Evan, 'but what do you think I can do? I can't become President as I'm not American born.' That was one of the fundamentals of independence, as everyone present was aware.

'With the Citizens Bill being debated next week, should it pass you would become eligible,' replied Hyams. He took a sheet of paper from his jacket pocket and spread it on the table between them. 'I have here the actual wording of the Constitution. Let me read it to you.' He cleared his throat and began. 'This is Article two, section one. No person except a natural born Citizen, or a Citizen of the United States, at the time of the Adoption of this Constitution, shall be eligible to the Office of President; neither shall any Person be eligible to that Office who shall not have attained to the age of thirty five Years, and been fourteen Years a Resident within the United States.'

Evan nodded. 'I knew that. In the same way that a Senator needs to be thirty years of age, been a citizen for at least nine years and a resident of the State he represents.'

'Right. Only the position of President goes further. It says you have to be born an American. But,' Hyams held up his finger and waved it in the air, 'as a matter of expediency it allowed that the President could be elected if he was a resident for fourteen years. The reason was because few people fitted the criteria of being born American back in those days.'

Evan nodded. 'That makes sense, only I don't think anyone has ever been elected President who wasn't a natural born American.'

'That's true, but some of those who stood for office but did not get elected weren't born here,' Hyams shrugged. 'The fortunes of politics. The Republicans are arguing, with some justification, that by sticking to the letter of the Constitution, we are depriving this country of electing a person of high calibre solely on the grounds that he wasn't a native American. The Citizens Amendment Bill can change that. After all, it's been successfully argued often enough that the Constitution is not carved in rock but is a living set of rules by which we run our lives. We have to change as times change.'

Evan frowned. 'But I thought we were going to oppose the amendment.'

Hyams' smile was wolfish. 'We'll support it instead.'

The proposed amendment by the Republicans would bestow full citizenship on all naturalised Americans irrespective of their country of origin. It had already been agreed that should such a Bill pass into law then the current legislation prohibiting a person not born in America to become President would be superseded. The Bill was known to be a ploy by the Republicans to allow a rising star in their own party, a man born in Germany, to become leader in eight years time and to run for the Presidency.

Evan was in shock. He'd only been a Senator for five years and was coming to the end of his first term in office. He wasn't convinced he'd be elected next time although he was assured by his followers back in St. Louis that there would be no problem. And now they were offering him this? He was excited and appalled at the prospect yet at the same time his mind churned with unanswerable questions.

He tried a further argument. 'Even if the Bill goes through there are many Americans who believe that the President should be born here, to ensure his loyalties aren't divided. I'd be a liability rather than an asset.'

'We need a popular figure. One who can make speeches that will inflame the imagination of the populace and with whom the vast majority of Americans can identify. We've cast around the party and your name kept coming up. We want you to see the President and ask him to step aside and let you lead us into the next election. When we reselected Woodrow last year we had no idea he was going to be as ill as he is. We all recognise the fact that we need a year of electioneering at least but now there isn't enough time. We all hoped the President would have recovered but he hasn't. So we've no choice.'

Evan leaned back in his seat and smiled caustically. 'I get it. The caucus has decided that we need a fall guy and I'm elected. You know I can't win if the papers are to be believed. There's no time to get the message across. It takes at least six months just travelling back and forth across the country, speaking in every town and city we've got.'

'Evan, I swear you're not being used as the fall guy, though it may seem like that. And we agree on the time scale of things. However, if the Bill passes we can exploit radio for the first time to help to get the message across. We can get a campaign moving as soon as possible. All you need to do is say the word.'

'I need to think about it,' said Evan.

'And that's another thing. Your stand for the rights of women is well known. If nothing else you should get the woman's vote.'

Evan laughed out loud, much to Hyams surprise. 'Rutherford, for now and many years to come women will vote according to the dictum of their husbands. Believe me; it happened in Britain. They may have the vote but they have yet to gain the independence of thought that will allow them to act according to their own consciences. If, that is, they bother to vote at all.'

'That may be so. It still doesn't alter the fact that we need you.'

'Let me talk to Meg, all right?'

Hyams nodded.

'One other thing. I'll only agree if I get the President's blessing.'

Hyams was about to argue but thought better of it. 'I'll need to speak to the others about that. Anything else?'

'Yes. Where can I get a cane like yours?'

When Evan arrived home there was no sign of Meg. He wandered into their large and comfortable library and pulled a copy of the bible from a shelf. It was a large and ornate book, a recent gift from David and Sion. He opened the cover and took out the single malt whisky bottle that nestled there and looked at the almost empty bottle thoughtfully. If ever he needed a drink it was now. He poured the remainder of the bottle into a cut glass tumbler and took an appreciative sip. He needed to find a way to replenish his stock. Soon.

Meg arrived back a short while later and was surprised to find him slumped in front of an empty grate, a glass dangling from his hand, a frown etched on his face.

'What's wrong?'

'What? Oh, nothing. At least, I don't think it's anything. I've been asked to lead the party into the next election.'

'Good Lord.' Meg sat down heavily in the chair opposite her husband. Whatever she'd been expecting it hadn't been that. Then she frowned. 'Surely that's impossible. You can't become the President as you weren't born in America.'

Evan explained his conversation with Hyams and the Republican Bill that was to be debated and voted on during the following week.

'If the Bill goes through what will you do?'

'I've decided nothing and I told Rutherford that I needed to talk to you.'

'And what about Woodrow? What does he say?'

'He doesn't know yet.'

Meg digested the news in silence while she thought through the vast implications for her and Evan. It was bad enough being a Senator but what if, horror of horrors, he was to become the President of the United States of America? Their lives would never be their own again. They would spend the next four years living in the fishbowl called the White House. Evan's name would go down in history. The first non native born President of the United States. Suddenly, with an overwhelming desire, she wanted it more than anything else in the world.

'Can it be done?' she asked. She leaned across to her husband and took the glass from his hand. He was about to protest but then figured she needed it just as much as he did. She took a sip, coughed at the pungent, aromatic taste and handed the glass back to him. 'I need a sherry,' she announced.

Evan stood and took down a thick, large volume of Bradshaw's Guide to British Rail Times and opened the cover. The gift to Meg from her sons held a bottle of sherry. Empty. Evan lifted it out and jiggled the bottle in the air. Meg blushed and said, 'Oh, it's empty!'

Evan laughed and ruefully put the book away again. 'Prohibition is a nonsense,' he said for about the hundredth time that year.

'Roberts was telling me only this morning that he can get us what we want if we're willing to pay for it,' Meg said, referring to their general factotum who ran the large house for them.

'Trust Roberts. However, under the circumstances I don't think we'd better, until we see which way the wind blows with regards to my nomination.'

'President of the United States of America and the First Lady,' Meg murmured, startling Evan. 'I like it. I like it very much.'

'You do?' Evan asked, thoughtfully. 'What if Woodrow doesn't agree?'

Meg was about to say "so what", but thought better of it. 'Why shouldn't he?'

Evan shrugged. 'No idea, love. Perhaps I wouldn't be his first choice. After all, I'm not exactly a crony of his.'

'No, that's true. So why have they picked you?'

'No idea. I was flabbergasted. Unless,' Evan thought a few seconds and then continued what he had started to say. 'Unless they want me because I can't win! Yes! Think about it, Meg,' he said. 'They know Woodrow can't win. The country's in a hell of a mess with half of the population wanting isolationism. So they pick a relative unknown, me, shove me into it all and let me sink. Oh, they'll make all the right noises; they have to. But there's no expectation of winning. They'll regroup and come out fighting in four years time, blaming me for their failure. That leaves the party and its policies intact and . . .' he trailed off, Meg nodding in total agreement.

'I'm afraid that you're right, Evan. It makes more sense than choosing you because of your wonderful personality.'

'Cheek!' Evan grinned at her, not taking umbrage.

'So what do we do?'

She turned the question back on him. 'What would you like to do?'

His grinned widened. 'Stuff it to them.'

Meg laughed. 'Me too! We need help.'

'The boys.'

'Yes. Let me see now.' Meg picked up the *Washington Post* and turned to the shipping news. In there was the expected arrival and departure of all European ships and liners. 'I read something the other day. Ah, here it is. The competition for the Blue Ribbon Trophy hots up this week. The *SS Waterlooville* will attempt the crossing in under the current five days and six hours set by the holder of the prestigious award. Hang on. Got it. The ship departs in two days from Southampton. They could be here in a week.'

'The timing is fortuitous as that's when the Citizen's Bill will be voted on. Right, in that case let's get a telegram off.' Evan went over to his desk and picked up a sheet of paper and began writing. He paused and then announced he was satisfied. 'Need help as I am running for President. Both of you please sail on WATERLOOVILLE in two days. See you in one week. Dad.' Evan looked at Meg and asked. 'Too bossy? Should I dress it up a little?'

'Of course not. They'll know we'd only ask for their help if we needed it. We can expect a telegram tomorrow telling us they're on their way. I'll send for Roberts to take it to the Wells Fargo office.

The telegram was sent from Washington to New York, through Boston to Halifax in Nova Scotia. Halifax's claim to fame was the new radio station which had been established a few years earlier, to broadcast to Europe. The message was marked with an initial code word used internally by Wells Fargo. It meant it had priority because the sender was a member of the Senate. Less than thirty minutes after Evan wrote the message it was being transmitted from Halifax to Ballycroy, a small town in county Mayo, Ireland, where the radio mast and station was established. It then went by land line to Dublin and the Post Office. Undersea cable ran the message to Wales and then overland to London. There the Post Office received the message and had it delivered to David at the bank. The process had taken an hour and twenty minutes and was proof positive that the world was 'shrinking'. Unfortunately, David wasn't in.

Meg and Evan began making plans. A map of the country showed what a daunting task lay ahead of them. After a while Evan said, 'This is hopeless. It's too big a job and we're too far down the campaign trail. We should have planned this a year ago and started no more than six months later. We need a lot of help if we're going to make even a dent in the Republicans' lead.'

'What we need,' said Meg, 'is the blueprint that's been used for other elections. Find out how it's been done before. That way at least we won't be starting from the beginning. How's it described? Reinventing the wheel?'

Evan nodded. 'We're also going to need an army of helpers.'

'There's plenty of those, as we found out in St. Louis. It's finding the right ones that's the difficulty.'

'The press are bound to go on about the lame duck candidate, the no-hoper from Europe etcetera. I can just see it now,' said Evan, as the reality of the task before them hit home, plunging him into gloomy introspection. 'No. It's useless. Send another telegram telling the boys not to bother.'

Meg crossed the room and stood by Evan, placing her hand on his shoulder. 'Don't talk like that, love. We can do it. We can have a try and make the country take notice. If we fail, and I agree the likelihood is that we will, then let's give them a real run for their money. You're still young enough to have another go next time. Then they'll have to take serious notice of you. We can spend the next four years building up your position in the party so that you can win at the next Convention fair and square.' Evan still hesitated. 'Come on, where's your fighting spirit?'

He smiled. 'You're right, Meg. Listen to me complaining, and we haven't even started yet! I'll go into the meeting in a positive frame of mind. I'll take what we need and get to work.'

'I think you should go in knowing they aren't on your side; but play their game. What about Rutherford?'

'Yes, an interesting question. Whose side is he really on?'

'Oh, that's easy,' said Meg. 'Rutherford's of course. If it suits him he'll help, if it doesn't he won't. By the same token, I don't think he'll necessarily hinder you.'

'That gives me an idea. We need a list of those we think will be for me, those against and those who'll sit on the fence. Let's do it separately and we'll see how we compare.'

So it went on. They brainstormed Evan's assault on the presidency, looking at it from every angle they could. A cold supper went almost untouched, coffee was drunk by the pint until, at two o'clock in the morning Meg announced she was ready for bed.

The next morning they were both up bright and early. Whenever the door bell rang they reacted like cats on a hot tin roof waiting impatiently for a reply to their telegram. At lunchtime Rutherford Hyams arrived to take Evan to meet President Wilson.

Evan had been to the oval office on previous occasions although he hadn't seen Woodrow Wilson in many months. When he did, he was shocked at the change in the man. He was sixty five but looked eighty. The grind of the years had taken their toll and he was obviously not a well man.

The President's opening remarks startled Evan. 'So, Griffiths, having given my health for this country you now want me to give up the job too.'

'No, sir. It's not like that.'

'Then what is it like?' he asked, harshly.

'You can't win,' Evan replied, bluntly. 'The party would like us at least to have a chance this time.'

'Who says I can't win, eh? Eh? Who says?' The President became agitated and began coughing.

'Now, dear, don't exercise yourself so much.' The First Lady glared at Evan. 'Now see what you've done?'

When Evan had entered the room he had been in awe of the power emanating from there, but suddenly that was no longer the case. He saw a frail old man incapable of being the President of the United States of America, surrounded by toadies and helpers who were there solely for their own reasons. It was, he thought, a case of Nero fiddling while the Democratic Party burned.

Evan leaned forward and spoke to the two men and woman arraigned behind the President. 'With all due respect, this office needs a leader with vision and strength. Mr President, you had those in abundance and have proven it many times in the past. However, times have changed. It's time for a new vision and a new strength to drive this country forward. The party has asked me to be that person and I'll accept with or without your blessing. Sir, you can't and won't win. Maybe I can make a difference.'

Woodrow Wilson sank back in his chair. He had proven to be a highly intelligent and competent President who was also a realist. The truth was that he didn't want to carry on. He was exhausted and hoped that James Cox and Franklin Roosevelt would run on a joint ticket. Though he saw little hope of them winning. Cox had shown the good sense to decline and Roosevelt was still a young man who could make another bid later. But right then the party needed a standard bearer, one who would be no loss should he fail, thought the President; Griffiths appeared to be the man to do it.

'Why have you come here if you've made up your mind?' Wilson asked.

'I hadn't, before I arrived,' and Evan was surprised to discover that was the truth even as he spoke. 'Now I want it. The country needs a strong, honest leader. I think I'm both.'

Wilson chuckled without humour. 'Oh, you think so, do you? Whoever said power corrupts and absolute power corrupts absolutely knew what they were talking about. I don't doubt your sincerity and honesty, Griffiths. However, every day you'll need to compromise with this, give a bit with that, just to get things done. Then very soon you'll have to deal with your friends who think that because you're the President you can do them favours; or worse, that you should do them favours, that you owe them for their support. You've no idea what it's like. Nobody has until they sit at this desk.' He paused and added, 'I'll endorse your candidacy, Griffiths and announce my retirement.'

Both men stood to leave. Evan offered his hand and after a second's hesitation Woodrow Wilson shook it and wished him luck. 'I take it that this is conditional on the Citizen's Bill next week?' he asked.

'Yes, sir, it is,' Hyams replied.

Once they had left the White House Evan asked, 'Where to now?'

'Now we meet the boys and plan our campaign,' replied Hyams. After a few moments, as they walked along the drive towards the gates, he suddenly added, 'Evan, I have to tell you something.' Then he stopped.

'What?'

There was no reply for a few paces and then Hyams gave a heavy sigh. 'Oh, what the hell, you might as well know. The country is in a mess, we both know that. Europe is affecting us, socialism is rife and unrest is sweeping from north to south and east to west. Agreed?'

'Sure. That's why we want a strong leader. Someone who can sort out the mess, given time.'

'We don't think we have the time. We think the Republicans should take the chalice, heavily laced with poison, and drink from it. We think there will be serious problems ahead of us for the next decade which is when we'll want to make a serious bid for the Presidency. Let the Republicans take the blame for the mess. You were chosen because we want to keep some of our big guns, like Roosevelt, for later, when it really matters.' Hyams paused and added, 'I just wanted you to know, that's all.'

Much to Hyams' surprise Evan burst out laughing.

'What's so funny?' The man walking beside Evan was affronted. He had been fighting with his conscience for forty-eight hours. Was party loyalty more important than friendship, or at least Rutherford Hyams' version of friendship?

'Thank you for the information, Rutherford, but we knew. Meg and I figured it out last night. That's what makes it all the more interesting. What if we win?'

Hyams was startled. 'Win? You can't win. It's too late now; it's impossible. Somehow we've managed to get into a mess where the only option was to lose the election. That's why Roosevelt was unhappy at being asked to run as Vice-President. Even that was just so he could get experience at a national campaign. He's being groomed for the future. He's even been described as tomorrow's man.'

'While I'm yesterday's?' Evan asked, dryly.

Hyams shook his head. 'You weren't even that, I'm afraid,' he said.

'Good. Then there's nothing to lose and everything to gain. I relish a good fight.'

'Evan, you don't get it. We're paying lip service to the election. We don't want to win. The problems are too vast. We don't want the party to take responsibility for the mess we're drifting into. Hell, it's not even a drift, it's a headlong gallop.'

'But aren't we responsible? We've had power for eight years.'

'And the four Presidents before that were Republicans. Hell, politics is a dirty business.'

'Only if you let it be. There's a cab. Let's get downtown and get this over with.'

'What do you intend doing?' asked Hyams.

'Why, I intend winning of course.'

Two hours later he was back at the house, a dazed Hyams with him. Meg heard Evan calling her and joined them in the study. 'Meg, send Roberts out to get us a bottle of the hard stuff. Preferably a Scottish malt if he can find one, if not a decent bourbon.'

'Why? What's happened? Are we celebrating something or drowning our sorrows?'

'He's celebrating' said Hyams. 'I think I'm doing the other.'

'Why? What's happened?' she repeated.

Evan said, 'Pending the passage of the Bill I'm to be the democratic candidate for the presidency.'

'And, he,' Hyams jerked a thumb at Evan, 'has persuaded the caucus that I should be his running mate, not Roosevelt who has happily stood down. And, like a fool I accepted.'

Meg laughed, delighted. 'I love it!'

'Have you three glasses?' Hyams asked. Meg put out three whisky tumblers and was intrigued when he unscrewed the top of his cane and poured three drinks.

'We still haven't heard from the boys. I hope they get the telegram in time to catch tomorrow's boat.'

'Let's not worry about that now. Realistically we can expect a reply tonight or, more likely, tomorrow morning. Now, let's get down to work. We have here, love,' Evan opened his document case, 'the so called plan of action on how to become elected President. I've glanced through it and quite frankly it's a load of old rubbish. An eight year-old planning a birthday party could do better. So I'm afraid we need to start again.'

They worked into the night. They were continually interrupted by those who wished them well and the Press who demanded a statement. The latter were told the same thing each time. It all depended on the Bill due the following week. Hyams didn't leave until nearly midnight, although Meg and Evan continued working for another hour or two. Finally they went to bed, exhausted yet exhilarated.

The following morning they were down early for breakfast and sent out for as many newspapers as could be found. For most of them the story had come too late to reach anything but the stop press. What was written there was neither encouraging nor totally discouraging. What it all amounted to was "watch this space".

'When you talk to the Press,' said Meg, 'I think you should try something entirely different.'

'Such as?'

'Total honesty. Why not tell them that you're fully aware you're the underdogs? That way you'll get more attention, even if it's just to balance the American view of what's fair play.'

'Yes, why not? It might help and I'm certain it won't hinder us.'

'What's that commotion?' There were loud cries in the hall, doors banging and people calling out.

'It can't be,' said Meg. The door flew open. 'It is!' She jumped to her feet and rushed to greet her two sons, standing grinning in the doorway. O'Donnell stood behind them.

33

When the telegram had arrived in London David had been at Biggin Hill with Sion. David's instructions to his secretary was that any telegram, even if marked personal, was to be opened and read. If it was urgent David was to be tracked down and told the contents. His secretary had telephoned him at Biggin Hill and when they had received the message they had decided to fly across the Atlantic.

On hearing the news Meg gasped in horror. 'What if something had happened? You were mad. You shouldn't have done it!'

'Yes, we should and as you can see, nothing did happen. Anyway, what's all this about a Presidential race? Are you seriously going to run for the Presidency of the United States?'

Evan nodded. 'Yes, I am.' He briefly explained the situation to the three men.

'In that case, we need the plane if we're to criss-cross America canvassing,' replied Sion. 'Anyway, with Mike here it was easy. He and I took it in turns to pilot the plane while one of us slept. David sat in the back making plans and writing notes about what we need to do. I've had the actual trip planned for months, so it was too good a chance to miss. After all, it's not exactly pioneering stuff any more, the Atlantic has been crossed so often. Mam, don't look so worried. In two weeks time a gang I know are setting off to fly around the world and plan to do it in less then three weeks. This is a new era, planes, wirelesses – the modern age. We need to embrace it all and take a vision of the future to the people. I'm quoting.'

'Who are you quoting?' asked his father.

'You,' said David. 'It's part of the press release I've prepared for you. You haven't met with the press yet, have you?'

Evan shook his head and laughed, delighted to have his sons with him on this momentous adventure he'd embarked upon. 'Anything else I'm to be quoted on?'

'Lots, Dad. If we can have breakfast, I'll brief you,' said David.

A week later the Citizens' Bill passed rapidly and smoothly through the Senate and was signed by Woodrow Wilson. Evan was now eligible to become the President of the United States of America.

At a strategy meeting David said to his father, 'In particular I want to establish your nickname.'

'His what?' asked Meg.

'His nickname. Nearly every President since the original Father of his Country has had a nickname.' David was referring to George Washington, the first President. 'Some have been ludicrous. William Harrison was known as Old Tippecanoe and Franklin Pierce as Young Hickory of the Granite Hills.'

'So what are we calling your father?' Meg asked.

'The Welsh Wizard,' replied David, straight faced.

Meg and Evan burst out laughing.

'The Welsh what?' asked Evan.

'Wizard. Because you're going to wave a magic wand and make it all better.'

'Son, whatever I do I won't be able to do that.'

'I know, Dad, but it's perceptions that win elections, not reality.'

'I'm not so sure, David,' said Meg. 'Don't you think you're short-changing the people?'

David shook his head decisively. 'No, I don't. This country is built on optimism and dreams. I'm not saying that we pretend times aren't tough now, but we have to offer hope above all else. There are major problems we need to tackle but only some we need to make issues of before the election.'

'I'm not so sure about this nickname business, either,' said Meg. 'If we call him the Welsh Wizard we're emphasising the fact he's not American born.'

David nodded his head. 'Yes, there is that. But we turn it into a virtue. Emphasise his international knowledge and background. Okay, what about the Wizard of St. Louis? Or the Welsh Wizard of St. Louis? Yes, that's better.' The discussion went back and forth with neither

Meg nor Evan convinced of the need for a nickname. However, David was adamant, and finally won the argument. The Welsh Wizard of St. Louis it was to be.

'How will you make it stick?' asked Meg.

'By giving it to a few friendly reporters. Incidentally, Kirsty, Madelaine and the kids are coming over in a few weeks. To support Grandpa, the family man.'

'David,' gasped Meg, 'that's awful. How utterly cynical. Your father is a family man and everybody who knows us knows that as a fact.'

'I know, Mam, but not everybody knows us. Look, we've got a long way to go and no time to get there. So we have to use every trick we can. If we don't, then forget it; you're playing a game. Or are we in this to win?'

'We're in this to win, David. We think your father is the right man for the job.'

'Right, then we've a lot to do.' David became Evan's campaign manager by the simple expedient of issuing instructions. 'Senator,' he addressed Hyams, 'we need a list of wavering states. We haven't time to visit every city in America, never mind the towns and villages. So we stay away from the states we know will vote for us and we stay away from those where we have no chance. What we need to know are those states where the votes are either evenly divided or where the turnout in the past has been very low.'

'How will I do that?' Hyams asked, feeling overwhelmed.

'Easy. List the states where there's a democrat and republican senator to start with. Next take Congress and do the same. After that get the returns, from – where? The National Library?'

Hyams thought for a moment and then nodded. 'Yes, you're right. There's a breakdown county by county of how people voted. But, heck, it'll take a long time to collate that lot.'

'Agreed and you aren't the person to do it. So we need help. We'll hire a legion of assistants all from within the party. That's your job – to find the drones. There are many dedicated and intelligent people, particularly amongst the younger ones, who'd be delighted to assist and just work for pin money. And that's all we're offering mind – pin money. Expenses, unlimited donuts and coffee and a chance to work for and meet the future President of the United States of America. We need to know which states we're going to tackle first because Sion needs to get information about landing strips and airfields and so on. He knows what we need, don't you, bro?'

Sion nodded. 'Leave it to me and Mike. We'll get cracking straight away.'

'You're really going to use a plane? But presidential candidates use a train,' said Hyams.

'That's right. Which is precisely why we aren't going to. We need to create a stir and a buzz everywhere we go. Arriving by train won't achieve that as much as arriving by plane. Sion is going to change the seating arrangements as much as he can on the Griffin so that we can make maximum use of it. Instead of being on a train we arrive in a city, make a speech and get a good night's sleep. We can do more in a month than Harding and Coolidge achieved in six,' he paused. 'Any questions?'

There were dozens but David appeared to have the answers to them all. Both his parents and Hyams could not help but be impressed.

'Okay, this first press announcement is important,' said David. 'You have the statement we worked on?' he asked his father.

Evan took a sheet of paper from his pocket. 'Yes, it's all here.'

'Good. Now, I'll introduce you, just like we agreed. You make your speech and ask for questions. If the questioning becomes too difficult, I'll interrupt,' he paused, 'probably by announcing that drinks are available.'

'We can't,' said Meg, 'the country's dry.'

'Damnation! I forgot! So the cases of malt whisky we brought with us are no use?'

'Cases of malt?' Evan repeated. 'How did you get past customs?'

'The question never arose. We landed in Maine, refuelled and came on here. Nobody's been near us. I suppose because there's so little brought in by plane. How strict is the law?'

Evan grimaced. 'It depends on the state and it depends on the zealousness of local law enforcement officers. At present you can still buy a drink out West in most of the saloons, here in the East it's different. Hotels are refusing to sell hard liquor, and are even arguing about selling wine with food. Heck, son, it's a total mess. The government have recruited 1500 agents to enforce the law but as you'd expect in a country this size there's very little they can really achieve. I suppose once the courts impose heavy fines and prison sentences things might change but, quite frankly, I doubt it. No, this law is doomed to failure, it just depends when that'll be.'

'What if the press asks you about it? What will you say?'

'What I just said to you,' was the thoughtful reply.

'No good, Dad. That won't work. If you do, you'll alienate the temperance lobby on your first day. We need to work on issues like this so that you can be seen to have powerful convictions and yet appeal to everybody.'

'That's impossible,' said Meg.

'Sure it is, but we can try,' her son replied. 'Right, if the question of prohibition comes up then you say that it's early days. We live in a democracy and what the majority of the people want the politicians have to supply. If the experiment of prohibition works then all well and good. If it doesn't then it has to be rethought and replanned. Yes, that's the tack to take. Play it off the cuff but give answers you've obviously considered. Mam, can you arrange sandwiches, coffee and lemonade? At least if we feed and water them it might soften them up a bit.'

'If my experience of reporters is anything to go by,' said Hyams, 'I doubt it. But I have to say David, this plan of yours is in danger of working.'

They all laughed, happy with the way things had started.

Over thirty reporters turned up at the house and one of the first questions Evan was asked was whether he would have the interests of the country at heart considering he was not born an American. Evan was able to convince some of the hard-bitten reporters that his interests lay solely with America; others would need more persuasion.

Whenever a reporter began to probe too deeply, David moved the questioning on. Many topics were covered including prohibition, universal suffrage, jobs, wages and the depression, organised crime and immigration, the Ku Klux Klan and the future of national radio. It was a mammoth yet superficial interrogation covering all the issues that were then exercising Americans. Thanks to David's preparations Evan did brilliantly with his answers; right up to the end.

'Senator, Wilt Tyburn, *Washington Post*. What is your view on the 14th Amendment and should all minorities get the vote?'

'Yes. It's the law.'

'Even Negroes?'

'Certainly, why not?'

'Because, sir,' a reporter in a white Panama hat interrupted, 'most of them are too ill-educated and stupid to understand what they're doing.'

'And you are?' Evan asked.

'Tim Rice, *Memphis Chronicle*.'

'Well Mr Rice, perhaps we ought to give them more of a chance. Improve their education so that they do understand.'

'That, sir, is treason against white folk,' the reporter was turning puce, vitriol spluttering from his lips. 'The people of Tennessee and Mississippi don't like that sort of talk. Which is why we support the Republican Party. They know what's right and what's wrong.'

Evan was about to argue when David stepped forward. 'Okay, everybody, that's all for now. We hope you enjoyed the last couple of hours and that when you write your articles you'll give Dad a fair hearing. I'm in no way biased when I tell you that I think he's the best man for the job.'

There was great deal of good-natured laughter and banter and the force of the argument with Tim Rice was diffused.

Food and non-alcoholic drinks were served while David moved through the throng having a quiet word with a number of the reporters. Leaving his father and Hyams to circulate a few minutes longer, David went into the study where, within minutes, two reporters joined him.

'Where's this malt you were talking about?' asked the first, a small, skinny individual who reminded David of a ferret. Wilt Tyburn was supposed to be the best newshound in Washington.

The other man was a complete contrast, tall, well built and with a nose that had been broken once or twice. His name was Peter Garfield and worked for the *St Louis Times*. He and David had been at school together.

David poured the two men generous shots of malt whisky and raised his own glass in salute. 'To my father. May he win the election.'

Both men did the same and took appreciative sips of the amber liquid. 'My God,' said Tyburn, 'offer a bottle of this with every vote and your father'll walk it. So what can we do for you, Griffiths?'

'Simple. I want you to follow the Senator on his campaign trail.'

'What? Are you mad?' Tyburn put the glass down and stood up in horror. 'Travel day after day around the country getting cold, wet, miserable. Rotten food and worse hotel rooms and nothing to write about except the band playing and the crowds cheering in one hick town after the next. We let the stringers send in their pieces and pay ten cents a word we publish.'

'Who do you want to win the next election?' David asked.

Both reporters looked uncomfortable. Peter Garfield finally answered, 'I want your father in the White House.'

'And you, Wilt?' David asked.

Reluctantly the man nodded. 'I guess so. I don't like what those Republicans stand for. Civil liberties will go back to the ice age if they get in. At least your father will be pushing for more of the kind of reforms my editor and I would like to see.'

'Right. That's why we want you along on the trip. No overnight sleeping on hard train seats and no third-rate hotels.'

'How? What are we going to do? Sprout wings and fly?' Garfield joked.

'More or less,' said David, and explained his plan.

The following morning the *Washington Post* was headlined:-

THE WELSH WIZARD OF ST. LOUIS

and the *St Louis Times* was headlined:-

OUR OWN WELSH WIZARD!

Both articles were highly favourable about Evan's candidature and described Hyams as an inspired choice as running mate. The dropping of Roosevelt from the ticket wasn't mentioned.

Other papers weren't as kind but the consensus of opinion across the most important papers was Evan should be given an opportunity to put his case to the people.

David had achieved his first and most important objective – Evan was not going to be ignored and the Democrats were not going to be dismissed as a party with no future as they had been over the previous months.

'It's a start,' said David, cutting out another article and handing it to his mother. 'I think, Mam, you should be the keeper of the knowledge. We collate all the articles into different categories. The first is for and against. Then each one is colour coded as to whatever the main issue is. So if it's for Dad and about prohibition then do this,' he showed her what he had in mind, 'and if it's against Dad and about segregation or other racial matters we'll do this.' Again he showed her.

'Why?' Meg asked, reasonably.

'Because we'll tackle the issues being raised in the state we're visiting.We'll adjust Dad's replies to suit the audience that little bit better than if he stayed with the same message all the time.'

'Isn't that being, if not dishonest, at least slightly duplicitous?' she asked.

'No. Actually it was Dad and Rutherford who said that politics is the art of compromise. We can't be all things to all men but, by Golly, we'll have a good go at it.'

'Have they started their meeting yet?' David was referring to the fact that Evan and Hyams were talking to the men they wanted in senior government positions should they win the election. They were also explaining what they wanted in return. It was the political equivalent of quid pro quo.'Yes, half an hour ago. Why?'

'I wanted to go over a speech with him. Talking about the dynamics of the twenties in the twentieth century. The ever increasing pace of life and the need for America to adapt to a new world order in which we are amongst the leaders. I've also got a reference to our special relationship with Britain and how together, our two nations could be a force for good in this benighted world.'

Meg smiled. 'There are one or two words you'll need to explain to your father, like benighted,' she said.

'Benighted means to be ignorant or living in intellectual or moral darkness. I thought it an ideal word to describe our present situation.'

Meg shook her head. 'Your father was told, when he first entered politics, not to use two-syllable words where one will do. It'll confuse the masses. And he's right. Don't forget that the average school learning age for most adults across America is under twelve and vastly inferior to Europe. That's an issue he ought to speak out more on. Education.'

'Once a school teacher, always a school teacher, eh, Mam?'

Meg shook her head. 'That was a very, very long time ago. No, it's just a fact that education is woefully lacking across the States. Your father should start talking about it.'

'I take your point and I'll change some of this speech. Actually,' David said, thoughtfully, 'what I should do is use the same speech but altered for different audiences. I'll need to think about that.'

Sion came in, covered in oil stains and sucking a bleeding finger. 'I think we're about ready. We've changed the seating to six comfortable chairs and put two cots along one side. Mike's doing some more work on the sound proofing which I think'll help a lot. He's going to put up a partition and door between the cockpit and the cabin so that'll cut down even more noise, we think. And I've changed the tubing around the engine so more hot air can blow into the back. We're almost ready to go, bro'. Only I don't know where to.'

'We'll need to work that one out once we get the analysis of voting we need, otherwise we'll just rush around the country like headless chickens achieving a great deal less than we could. In the meantime I'll get things moving around Washington. What we should do,' David said, thoughtfully, 'is throw a ball. Like the inauguration ball but called something else. Any ideas?'

'A sort of Presidential Trail Ball,' said Sion.

'Yes. What do you think, Mam?'

'I think it's a lovely idea six months too late in announcing. Don't forget that people need to plan months in advance for something as grand as a ball.'

'True. Okay, then why don't we have a ball and call it a party instead,' Sion suggested with a laugh in which his brother joined. Meg smiled happily, overjoyed to listen to their banter and humour after having been apart from them for so long.

'If we could get something arranged for next Saturday when Madelaine and Kirsty are here, we could start on the campaign trail immediately afterward.'

'Aren't we leaving things a bit late to get started?' Meg asked.

'No, because we'll work Virginia, Pennsylvania and Maryland for the next few days. We have the party and then announce our itinerary in the weekend press. In the meantime we use the Party to contact all the regional offices we need to and send them a copy of the itinerary.

We also send copies of positive articles to every provincial newspaper in America.'

'What? When did you dream that one up?' Meg asked.

'About five minutes ago. We spoon-feed editors across the States with everything written that's favourable. If they wish they can repeat whatever's said under the bye-line of "Washington Correspondent" or whatever they decide. In that way we'll maximise the coverage created by one article. I'll arrange a team of three to deal with it. Right, the party. Where shall we hold it?'

'That's easily answered,' said Meg, 'The Connaught. I can think of one or two who'd kill for tickets even if it is only for a party – a black-tie party, of course.'

'Of course,' said Sion, winking at David. 'Can we leave you to make the arrangements?'

'I'll enjoy it. I also need to get things ready for Kirsty and the children. Madelaine will be in David's room so I don't need to change anything there. Is Kirsty bringing a maid?'

'A what?' Sion exploded in laughter. 'I shouldn't think so for one minute.' Then he seemed to change his mind. 'Unless of course Mrs Cazorla comes with her. But even if she does, Kirsty won't have her travelling as a maid.'

Meg nodded. 'Well, it's not a problem, she can stay here if she comes. Is Mr O'Donnell coming back?'

Sion shook his head. 'Not before tomorrow. He wants to test the engines once he's completed overhauling them. When will I get an idea of the itinerary, David? I'd like to look up some weather records to see what we can expect for the next six or eight weeks.'

'I'll try and get it to you tomorrow. But don't forget, nothing is cast in tablets of stone. We'll do what we have to when we have to, even if that means major changes as we go along.'

'Sure, bro', I've no problem with that. Right, I'm going for a bath.'

Sion left the room as Evan and Hyams entered. There were six other men with them and they were introduced to David and Meg. 'We've been carving up the jobs for after the election,' said Evan, 'and have agreed on most of them. We thought you might like to be Attorney General, David, seeing as you're a lawyer.'

David looked at his father in shocked amazement and then laughed. 'Dad, I don't want any job in the government. I mean it.' He saw the look of surprise and on one or two faces, relief, of the men in front of him. 'Dad, I really don't. I'm here to help get you elected and then I'm going to go back to England. I've a lot to do. While John was delighted that I was coming to help you, he wasn't happy about me being away so long. The businesses are growing like Topsy and to be honest I'd rather make money than be in government. Any government, I hasten to add. And anyway, nobody will be able to accuse you of nepotism if I don't take a job. In fact, I think I'll tell the press that neither Sion nor I want a job at the White House and that we're only working for you because we think you're the best man for the job.' He thought his strategy through for a few seconds and said, 'Yes, that's what I'll do. Now, can I get you gentlemen a drink?'

Sion finished his bath and was dressed in clean clothes. He was about to go downstairs when he decided to call the airfield and see how Mike was getting on. He lifted the receiver on the telephone situated in the hall on the first floor, an extension that was connected to four other telephones in the house. He put the receiver to his ear and was about to dial when he heard a vaguely familiar voice.

'Okay, I've got that. But remember, we want Griffiths to lose this election. If he wins we'll be left with the mess to carry for the next four years. Let the Republicans carry the can for a while and we'll come back later.'

'I know. I understand that.'

'Then do everything you can to ruin Griffiths' chances.' The phone went dead and Sion thoughtfully replaced the receiver.

34

SION WENT DOWN to join the others, eager to talk to David in private.

Evan had finished discussing plans and policies with the men who would run his government, should he win. He now sat with his family after the whirlwind of the last few days. 'I understand we're having a Presidential Trail Party,' he smiled.

'It seems a good idea to get started,' replied David, 'with a bang. Mam will do the organising and Kirsty and Madelaine can help when they get here. I had a telegram saying they were on the Waterlooville so should be here the day after tomorrow. That gives us time to get organised before you burst like a bright star on the presidential campaign, Dad.'

'Ugh,' said Evan. 'Don't say that. There's a limit to the eulogies and flowery language I can take.'

David smiled at his father. 'I know but I didn't make it up. I'm quoting a by-line in a Chicago newspaper.'

'Chicago? How on earth have they got on to it so fast?'

'I sent a wire to all the main newspapers across the States,' David said matter of factly, 'telling the editors what was going on and at the same time quoting a few phrases written here. I have an idea which will be interesting if it works.'

'What idea?' asked Sion.

'It seems to me that most newspaper editors can't leave things alone. They won't quote what they think everyone else is, or what I supply and so they embellish. If we send out statements from articles to newspapers supporting us, I think the editors will add to them. And so the myth will grow. If Dad's got lots of support already, he'll get more. Most papers, it seems to me, don't try to influence their readers' opinions, but reflect them. If we get on a roll we could ride it all the way to the White House!'

The rest of the evening was spent working at the itinerary, based on some of the information put together so far by assistants working in Evan's and Hyams's offices. Sion spent a great deal of time on the telephone using his aviation contacts to identify airfields and landing strips all over America while Meg started planning the party.

Evan paused in his work with David and looked around the room. He was a highly contented and happy man, exhilarated by the future and its prospects.

Madelaine, Kirsty and the children arrived two days later, much to everyone's joy, but especially Meg's. She set about winning over her three year old grandson who was initially quite shy. It didn't take long, for Meg had the knack of gaining the confidence of the young with ease. She found her heartstrings pulled by baby Louise who looked so much like Sian, her own, dead daughter. She told herself not to be so stupid at her age, but it didn't do much good. She loved her dearly yet, somehow, she couldn't bring herself to play with her – it brought back so many painful memories. She left it to Evan to coo over the baby girl, and cuddle her.

Evan worked on his speeches which were drafted by David and which were frequently changed by ideas from the rest of the Wizard's inner circle – the nickname given to the family and the election aides. David worked tirelessly on creating the legend – The Wizard was needed in the White House!

When the day of the party at the Connaught arrived Meg took charge and was like the eye of the storm. She was a calm centre while all around her mayhem and chaos appeared to reign. However, it all went according to plan and her two daughters-in-law proved to be towers of strength. Her sons had married well and for that she was grateful and happy. In her opinion if a man was to succeed then he needed a good woman by his side. She made sure that both Kirsty and Madelaine knew her views.

By the time Evan returned to the house to change into his black tie and dinner jacket it was nearly eight o'clock and he had made five speeches across Washington and the State. Far from being exhausted, he was buoyed up, the adrenaline keeping him on a high.

'Meg, you look ravishing,' he said to her, when she showed him her turquoise, floor length evening gown. 'Perhaps we can have an early night?'

'Evan! What would the boys think?'

'That I'm lucky to have such a beautiful wife and they such a beautiful mother.And that I'm,' he took her in his arms and kissed her, 'one of the luckiest men alive.'

A few minutes later they began to gather in the study where a drink was available, whisky for the men and sherry for the ladies. It was a sparkling and happy gathering that waited for Rutherford Hyams and his wife Elspeth so that they could arrive together at the Connaught Hotel. A short while later they appeared and a small convoy of cars left from the house. When they drew up at the hotel there was a large crowd waiting and when they saw Evan, with Meg alongside him and Rutherford with his wife, they burst into loud cheers.

Neither men heard David say softly to Madelaine, 'Rent-a-crowd worked.' Her response was to give him a sharp dig in his side.

When they entered the huge doorway a small band stopped playing and silence quickly fell on the waiting throng. A major-domo announced, 'Ladies and Gentlemen, please welcome the next President of the United States Of America and his Vice President.'

There was loud clapping and cheering and flash bulbs burst all around them. There were yells for speeches and Evan raised a hand for silence. 'I'm not sure that the announcement wasn't a little premature,' he said to loud laughs and cries of "No, not possible", 'but I thank you for it. We have a long way to go but I think it's a road we can travel together all the way,' he paused for effect, 'to the White House.' There was loud cheering and whistling and he and Meg led the way into the ballroom.

'It appears, my dear,' he said to her, 'that an awful lot of men in Washington these days have need of a walking cane.' He waved his own to a group of friends who lifted their own canes in salute. Some were already unscrewing the tops and spicing their fruit cups. A black, eight piece band began playing the latest music known as ragtime and soon there were couples dancing and others standing in groups to discuss – what else – The Presidential Race.

Evan and his party were given the American treatment equivalent to that dished up to European royalty, though normally to a crown prince rather than a king. Evan worked the room like the expert he was. He shook hands with dozens of people, exchanged words and pleasantries with dozens more and managed to create a stir wherever he and Meg went. He answered the occasional question on policy but mainly kept matters to inconsequential banter. It was a masterful performance which David appreciated more as the evening went on.

Surreptitious sips were taken from canes and hidden bottles and soon the noise reached a level where it was difficult to be heard. At that point David and Sion steered the group into the dining room where it was a lot quieter and where a huge buffet had been laid out. Bottles of red and white cordial were in evidence and David offered a glass to his father.

'Cordial?' Evan said. 'I hate the stuff. What sort is it, anyway?'

Somehow David managed to keep a straight face when his mother replied, 'Grape cordial and I'm sure you'll like it.' She took the glass from her son and shoved it into Evan's hand.

Evan lifted the glass to his mouth and grimaced. 'It's disgusting, I expect.' He took a gulp, spluttered and burst out laughing along with the others. 'I was wrong. This is one grape cordial I like.' He appreciated a glass of his favourite claret on such an occasion.

The dining room filled and many people came to the table to wish Evan and Hyams good luck. Many ladies congratulated Meg on her appearance and the wonderful party she had organised; she responded with a natural grace and dignity.

There was only one jarring note when Franklin Roosevelt lumbered over. He was the same age as Sion and had qualified as a lawyer fifteen years earlier. He had been drinking heavily.

'Griffiths, you're a charlatan. You're not the right man for the job. I should have been with you on this ticket or, better still, I should have run with Woodrow. For two pins I'd knock you down.'

Before Evan could reply, David and Sion appeared either side of Roosevelt and hustled him from the room. David's natural instinct was to throw him into the street but his political instinct told him to take care of the man. Sober, Roosevelt would owe him a favour.

Evan and Meg appeared untroubled by the incident though Hyams wasn't quite so nonchalant. When his sons returned, they told Evan that they had given Roosevelt some coffee and sent him home in a taxi. Evan nodded his appreciation. That was the right decision. There were enough enemies inside and outside the Party without making matters worse.

At midnight carriages were called and Evan and Meg, along with their entourage, left for home. They were both ready for bed, the amorous feelings earlier minimised by their fatigue. David and Madelaine travelled in the car with them.

'We'll have a party every week,' David announced after a few minutes of weary silence. 'We must make sure that we spend Saturdays in places where we can do this again. We'll get a team to work on it. Mam, you write a list of all that needs to be done and we'll copy tonight's success all across the country.'

'Son,' said Evan, with a groan, 'can't you give it a rest just for tonight? We'll talk about it in the morning.'

'All right,' said David. 'I want to see what the papers have to say but I think it's a good idea. Dad, you can rest tomorrow but on Monday we fly west.'

'Thanks, son, you're all heart,' Evan said, dryly.

On Monday morning at six o'clock, Evan, Rutherford Hyams, David and Sion arrived at the airfield. Mike O'Donnell had the plane ready and proudly indicated the steps to the group of men when they left the limousine. Sion was grinning broadly, pleased with what he and Mike had done to the plane.

David climbed aboard first and was followed by the others. The cabin had been completely changed. Now there were six leather armchairs instead of the original ten seats and along the port side were two cots, each with a curtain for privacy.

'Let me show you,' said Sion. He pulled a lever on the side of the chair and pushed at the back. The chair reclined while at the same time a footrest swung up along the front of the seat. 'These two can also swivel around and we can put that table,' he pointed at the cabin wall, 'into these slots and make an area for four to eat or work. At the back we've got a rest room with a wash basin. Make yourselves comfortable while I start the engines.'

Evan and the others were suitably impressed as they settled down in the comfortable chairs. David was busy swinging the two chairs around and putting the table in place. 'We can get to work straight away,' he announced.

Evan and Rutherford Hyams exchanged resigned glances but agreed with good grace. David began briefing them on what would be happening during the day. Like a general organising his forces, David had split his workers up into groups of three and had already sent them out to various destinations to prepare the way and to liaise with local Party activists. Each group knew where to be for the next four weeks and would travel there by train and automobile, always ahead of Evan and his party.

The engines started and the three men looked at each other in wonder. It was as quiet in the cabin as if they were sitting in a limousine. The noise of the engines increased and the plane begin to move, bumping over the grass to the recently laid concrete runway. They increased speed and a few minutes later they rose smoothly into the morning sky. Over the brow of a low hill they hit an air pocket and swooped down before regaining height. Rutherford Hyams was promptly airsick.

Although he fought it for the next twenty minutes or so Hyams finally gave in and crawled into one of the cots, leaving Evan and David to continue working. Luckily they were flying in a cloudless blue sky, with only light winds from the north west bringing cold, dry air across the country. It took just over two hours to fly to Columbus in Ohio, the first of the marginal states.

'I thought you'd arranged to have two reporters come with us,' said Evan.

'I did,' David shrugged, 'but unfortunately they chickened out. They intend travelling by train.'

'Sensible fellows,' Evan murmured.

Nearly two hours later the door between the cockpit and cabin opened, letting in O'Donnell's bulk and also the noise from the engines. The soundproofing that he and Sion had fitted had not extended to the cockpit. 'We're arriving in ten minutes, gentlemen. If you look out through the window you'll see a field full of people all waiting for you, sir,' he said to Evan. 'Sion is going to fly over it a couple of times so you can see them all and, at the same time, give them all something to cheer about.'

He closed the door and the noise immediately abated. There was a change in the pitch of the engines and the plane banked to port and circled the field. Looking out, Evan could see thousands of people below, looking up and waving.

'Damn it,' said David, 'we've missed a trick.'

'You, son? I don't believe it,' Evan smiled at David.

'Sure, Dad. We should have a means of streaming a sign behind which says "VOTE FOR THE WIZARD". I'll talk to Sion and see what we can manage.' He made a note on the pad in front of him and Evan shook his head in wonder. His son, no, both his sons, would make any man proud.

When they landed and the door opened a great cheer went up and it continued until Evan climbed on the rostrum, and waving his hands in the air, brought silence onto the field. 'This decade,' he began, 'is the decade when the heat of progress should be shared by all, when every man, woman and child in this great nation of ours should bask in the warmth of the wealth that is now being created thanks to that progress.' He paused and a huge cheer went up, orchestrated by David with the help of the local Democratic Party.

When he finished his speech David leaped onto the platform and said to the crowd, 'Ladies and Gentlemen, another round of applause for the next President and Vice-President of America!'

A band played, there was more cheering and the crowd stood respectfully aside to let the party return to the plane. Mike O'Donnell and Sion had refuelled and checked the engines and were ready to depart. An hour after arriving they were airborne once more and on the way to the next meeting. Behind them they left a field of people who were getting ready to enjoy a barbecue and a dance. The main topic of conversation would be what they had just seen and heard; arriving by aeroplane had been a huge success. In Columbus, the Democratic supporters had found new heart, the waverers had been converted and the Republicans had a good time. Reporters were already busy scribbling their articles, eager to phone or telegram in their stories. David's bandwagon was rolling, carrying Evan on the journey of a lifetime.

That day they landed at four different destinations in the state and Evan made, more or less, the same speech. Rutherford Hyams was airsick each time they took off but recovered as soon as the plane's wheels touched the ground. At the end of the day they settled into a comfortable hotel in Cincinnati and, over dinner, discussed what they had achieved. After dinner a group of local Party leaders joined them to be briefed by David on what was expected of them by way of support and what they could expect in return should Evan win. The group left happy men, hope fired within them that a Democratic President would yet again be in the White House. They were not reminded that there was still a very long way to go!

The next morning the plane took off in a blinding rain storm. It was uncomfortable and poor Hyams was violently ill. Evan and David just managed not to be sick but only with a lot of effort and willpower. Once they were in the air Sion turned south and a few minutes later they flew into clear, blue sky. They flew around the storm and reversed track, heading north for Cleveland.

They landed to a great welcome, just like the previous one, and this time both Evan and Hyams made a speech, though the latter took a little longer to recover from his airsickness this time. Cleveland had a thriving coal mining and oil producing community and Evan's speech went down a storm when he began, 'I was a coal miner; and let me tell you, once a coal miner always a coal miner.' That initial sentence got him an ovation that lasted ten minutes. After that he couldn't fail and by the time they left to climb back into the aeroplane he had converted hundreds to his cause.

On Saturday, after a week of flying from one venue to another, they arrived in Atlanta, Georgia, to a warm, blustery day and an ever warmer reception. As they flew over the field David released a banner that fluttered from the tail of the plane with the message THE WIZARD FOR PRESIDENT. Waiting for them were Meg, Madelaine, Kirsty and Elspeth. After the speeches David called the two older women onto the rostrum and introduced them as the Future First and Second Ladies of America. There was an even greater amount of cheering, clapping and flag waving. A band marched past followed by hundreds of school children all waving banners proclaiming "Evan for President".

'I don't know how it was done,' said Meg, 'but this event is marvellous. Whoever thought of getting the children to do that?'

'Thanks, Mam,' said David, 'I'm glad you approve. It was easy to arrange once I thought of it.'

'You?' said Meg and then added. 'But then, why am I surprised?'

'All I did was send telegrams. The kids are leaving here to have a party of their own, funded by us. It was no big deal, to be honest, but it's created a great deal of goodwill.'

And so it proved. That evening they held a party for the important people of the city and district which again was a roaring success. The local Democratic Congressman and a Senator came, as did a number of top businessmen and labour union leaders. Many photographs were taken and many fine speeches were made. They all had one theme in common – Evan for President. By midnight, copies of their speeches were being sent to every major newspaper in America.

David had created a blitz of interest and a raft of goodwill for his father which was proving to be unstoppable.

The following morning Rutherford Hyams told Evan that he did not want to fly anymore.

The men met after breakfast to discuss the week ahead. Later they were to attend a local church for a service before their departure.

'Evan, I'm sorry,' said Hyams, 'but the thought of the flight makes me ill. I just don't want to be sick again. I'd hoped that if I kept going I'd get used to it but it's not working, as you know.'

Evan was disappointed but said, 'I understand, Rutherford. To be honest I think you've shown a good deal of fortitude to have kept trying as long as you have. What do you want to do instead?'

'I thought I'd travel by train and do the same as you but in more localised areas. David, what do you think?'

'Actually, I think it's a good idea. We're wasting the resource represented by you. You should be working some of the areas we can't get to, areas that can only be done by train. What if you go out west and start in San Francisco? Work California, Oregon and Washington State. We'll be at least a month before we get there and we ought to be doing something to counter Harding and Coolidge. That's why we need to go to Massachusetts in about three weeks.'

'There's nothing like climbing into the lion's den for a really good fight,' said Evan, dryly. He was referring to the fact that Coolidge was the Governor of the State and that the Republicans had a strong base there, though by no means impregnable.

'Dad, I've been meaning to ask you, how dirty do you want to fight?'

Evan looked at David in puzzlement. 'I don't understand, son. What do you mean?'

David lowered his voice. 'I've just learnt some dirt on Harding which, should we make it public, will stop him in his tracks.'

'What dirt?' Evan asked.

David shrugged, uncomfortable. 'I'd rather not say.'

Evan looked at Hyams and then back to his son. Comprehension dawned and he said, 'You mean, about his mistress?'

David's jaw dropped open in surprise. 'You knew?'

Evan and Hyams exchanged amused glances and then burst out laughing.

'Of course we knew. Everybody in Washington knew. We just don't talk about it.'

'But if you knew,' David protested, 'why don't you use it?'

Evan shook his head. 'I'll not hound a man out of politics because he has a mistress. Half the senators and congressmen would be forced to leave and there'd be nobody left. Don't mix their morals with their ability to be good leaders. You don't know what their marriages are like and you don't know what arrangements they might have with their wives. If we hounded out every man for his infidelities we'd have no one suitable for President left.'

'Except you,' said Hyams.

Evan grinned. 'Except me. And you,' he added.

Hyams shook his head. 'I wouldn't like anybody to look too closely. However, that's all in the past.'

'What do you propose to do about travel arrangements for Rutherford?' Sion asked changing the subject.

'Hire a train,' said David. 'Money is pouring into the war chest so we can afford it. If we can't, I'll fund it through the bank. Will that suit you, Rutherford?'

The Senator nodded, relieved that he wouldn't have to fly again. 'I won't let you down, Evan, you know that. You can count on me.'

Evan nodded, 'Sure, I know. Boys, excuse us will you? I'd like to have a private word with Rutherford.'

David and Sion left the room, showing no surprise. When they'd gone Evan turned his steely blue gaze on Hyams. 'Can I really, Rutherford? I know what's been going on.'

'I don't know what you mean,' replied Hyams, who then shrugged and added, 'I'm sorry, of course I do. Originally, I was to somehow scupper your chances. We didn't want you to win. Heck, we didn't think you could win. The country's in a mess and it's going to get worse. We wanted the Republicans to take over and run things for a few years before we made a comeback. Over the last few weeks I've changed my mind and so have a lot of other people. Now we really want you as President.' Hyams held out his hand and Evan unhesitatingly shook it.

'I'm glad you feel that way,' said Evan. 'I hated the idea of ditching you as my running mate at this late stage.'

'You'd have done that?' Hyams asked in some surprise.

'Sure I would. I'm in this to win.'

Rutherford Hyams burst out laughing. When he finally got himself under control he said, 'I was right about you. You're a ruthless son of a bitch, which is what we need.'

Evan stood up and said, 'Only when I need to be. I'm a great friend, Rutherford, but a really rotten enemy.'

Hyams laughed again. 'I hope I'm the former.'

'So do I, Rutherford. So do I.'

When Evan told David and Sion about his conversation with Hyams, Sion told his father about the telephone call he'd overheard. 'I didn't know it was Rutherford, otherwise I'd have told you. David and I have been keeping an eye out in case we did discover who the traitor was.'

Evan grinned at his sons and surprised them by saying, 'I knew all along. Or at least, I had a very good idea. It was part of the Party's plan that I should lose. David, with your help,' he clapped Sion on the shoulder, 'changed all that.'

Rutherford Hyams's place on the plane was taken by an assistant David hired in Atlanta. He was a young man by the name of James Hay, a bright lawyer who had achieved the impossible. He had taken a degree and then qualified as a lawyer – he was black.

'Are you sure about this?' Evan asked David. 'You know I'm not racially prejudiced but is America ready for a high profile assistant who's black?'

David shrugged. 'It's a gamble but the liberal press will love it. It will also help win black votes.'

'Are there many of those?' Evan asked, cynically.

'We know the abuses that go on state by state to prevent blacks from voting but there are still an awful lot who do get to put their cross on a ballot paper.'

'I thought they were mainly democrats anyway,' argued Evan. 'So aren't we just giving something for nothing? If the blacks are going to vote for us why alienate a proportion of the white voters?'

'I'm hoping it will encourage more blacks to vote and that the increase in blacks voting for us will be greater, a lot greater, than the white votes we lose.'

'It's a hell of a gamble, son,' Evan said, heavily.

'I know, Dad. I'm sorry if you think I've overstepped the mark by hiring Jim. If you like I can fire him,' he paused. 'Or sideline him, if that'll make you happy.'

Evan suddenly smiled and said, 'Don't do either, son. I'll go with your decision. I've given you the task of spearheading this campaign and it's too late to interfere now. I trust your judgement and you haven't proven me wrong yet. So, introduce me to Jim and ask him how he feels about flying.'

Jim Hay proved to be a brilliant speech writer who took David's drafts and improved them beyond recognition. As a result Evan's storming campaign went up a notch. Not a single national newspaper said a bad word against Evan for hiring a black man. None dared as tolerance and liberalism was the order of the day in many states.

However, dozens of regional and local newspapers, particularly those south of the Mason-Dixon Line, castigated Evan for his decision to give the job to a negro.

That was when Evan received his first death threat.

35

THEY HAD BEEN campaigning for six weeks. They had covered thirty states and Evan had made over two hundred speeches. He was in every newspaper across America and his every utterance was reported. David made sure of that.

'Don't tell your mother about the death threat, son, she'll only worry.'

'Of course I won't, Dad. She already knows.'

'What? How does she? I've only just seen this.' Evan waved the piece of paper under David's nose.

'I know, Dad. I gave it to you. It arrived last night. I kept it until this morning not to worry you and let you get a good night's rest.'

'That's very thoughtful of you, David, but it still doesn't explain how your mother knows.'

David looked a little sheepish before replying. 'She'll read it in the newspapers. I've sent copies out with the rest of the press releases.'

'You did what? Without talking to me about it first? David, you've gone too far! I know I said that you could get on with things but this is too much! You should have cleared it with me first!'

'Wait a minute,' said Sion, 'it wasn't just David's decision. He talked to me, Mike and Jim about it first.' The other two men nodded.

'It's true, Mr Griffiths,' said O'Donnell. 'We need a strategy to protect you. One way is to let everybody in the world know you've been threatened. That may make any would-be assassin pause for thought before doing anything stupid like trying to get to you.'

'Like trying to kill me, you mean,' said Evan.

'Sure,' said O'Donnell. 'Like trying to kill you and anybody else in the way. David's also got agreement that for your protection we can carry guns across state lines.'

'Guns?' Evan was aghast.

'How else are we going to protect you?' Sion switched his coat aside to show the holster and gun, snugly tucked into his left side. 'The others have something similar. Do you want one?'

It was a reasonable question and Evan paused for a second or two before shaking his head. 'I don't think it's a good idea for a future President to shoot anybody, even if they deserve it. I'll leave it to you three stalwarts to protect my venerable body,' he quipped.

'If anybody shoots at you, Dad,' said Sion, 'I'll duck behind you before firing back.'

That broke the tension and they laughed. 'Okay,' said Evan. 'I think you called it right, David. The more people who know the better, I suppose.'

David did not point out just how much publicity the announcement had generated.

'I see from the itinerary that we're due in Denver, next week,' said Evan.

'Correct. Provided the weather isn't too bad. There have already been snowstorms in the Rockies, though nothing serious, so far.'

'Good, that's one visit I'm looking forward to. Sonny is there at the moment sorting out a business problem for us.'

'Sonny?' said Sion. 'That's great news. Heck, I haven't seen Sonny in half a life time. How's he doing?'

'Very well. He's the ideal man to build the business and look after the staff, but he needs somebody else to run the financial side. That's why we've hired the people we have done. Anyway, he's there for a few more weeks before he goes back to St. Louis.'

'I'll phone him,' said David, 'and see what he can do for us. I think the local caucus can use a shake up as they definitely haven't been all that forthcoming.'

'Perhaps we should by-pass them,' said Sion.

'It may not be good politics to do that,' pointed out Evan.

David shook his head. 'Dad, we're the makers of the politics for now. Some of the Party may have had their noses put out of joint as a result of you coming in at the end but that's the way it is. You've become a force in the Party, Dad and they have to listen. If they won't, we'll use our own resources.'

'What problems have you been having?' Evan asked.

'Nothing I can't handle. If I need a big gun – you – I'll yell for help. I prefer to try and solve any problems first.'

'So what's wrong in Denver?'

'I've been trying to get them to organise our Saturday night party but it seems it's impossible as everywhere is full. Which I don't believe,' David shrugged. 'It's nothing I can put a finger on, it's just there's a lack of co-operation. Sonny can find out what the problem is and sort it out for us.'

Evan nodded. 'If that's what you want. Or I can kick a few butts. The Democratic Party chairman has assured me of full backing across the country. If there are any problems I'm to let him know and he'll fix them.'

'If we do that we could create resentment against you in Denver which could easily turn into something worse, like active hindrance. Okay, it won't be to our faces but behind our backs; which is probably worse. Instead, why not use Sonny, make sure everybody we want is at the party and give the credit to the caucus. Sonny won't mind and we might create friends, not enemies. A carrot is often better than a stick.'

Evan thought about it for a few moments. 'I guess you're right. Your Mam and the others are going early so they can help as well. She can do some cajoling of the Party members while Sonny organises things.'

'Where can I get Sonny?' David asked.

Evan dug a notebook out of his pocket and scanned the well thumbed pages. 'Try the office. Here's the telephone number. If that doesn't work we can send a wire.'

'I'd rather not,' said David. 'I don't want everybody knowing what we're about.'

Evan shook his head. 'They won't. We've had a code working for years. We've had to, to stop others stealing any plans and ideas we've had.'

David and Sion looked at their father in surprise. Evan explained. 'On two occasions land we wanted to build on almost doubled in price. We couldn't understand it at first but then came to realise that the telegraph operator must have passed on the information about what we were up to. Ever since then we've had a code, known only to a few select individuals.'

Telephoning proved to be impossible and so they resorted to the code and a long, detailed telegram to Sonny McCabe, who had been with Evan from the beginning. He had shared many adventures with the family and had helped to build up their thriving wholesale business that now stretched from one side of the country to the other. He was also a significant, minority shareholder and, as a result, a wealthy man. There was nothing he would not do for Evan and he had proved that many times in the past. They knew that he could be relied on to carry out his instructions.

Three days later Sion groaned to O'Donnell, 'Today's Wednesday, so it must be Wichita.'

O'Donnell grinned. 'It's hard work but by God, Sion, we've had some of the most amazing flying experiences anybody can imagine.'

'It's been too much,' Sion said, running a hand over the struts and tyres of the plane. 'The engines are getting ready for a major service or we could end up in trouble.'

'I know. They're sounding harsher than I like. I was going to suggest that we need to do something, only I don't know what. If we strip them down and work on them we'll be out of action for a week. Somehow, I don't think David will like that.'

'He won't, but that's our decision at the end of the day. It's better than crashing, which is a realistic alternative.'

'It won't come to that, will it?'

Sion shrugged. 'I've been flying a lot longer than you have, Mike. I've seen it all and right now we're flying on borrowed time. We need to do something drastic if we're to carry on.'

'Such as?'

'Well, we could put in new engines. I've had four delivered to New York, to our warehouse there. If we have them shipped to Denver we could start work on Sunday. We could finish the job by Tuesday and continue the programme.' Sion looked at his watch. 'We're taking off in thirty minutes so I'd better send a telegram for the engines now. I know our manager in New York so I'm pretty sure we'll get them on time.'

'What about David?'

'Leave him to me,' was the nonchalant reply.

Sion and David had a blazing row which Evan had to stop.

'David, you know nothing about it, so leave it to Sion. You've done a great job to date but this is Sion's responsibility, not yours. Sion, do as you see fit. You're right when you say crashing will not help our cause one iota. David, stop scowling. We'll stay an extra day in Denver and rest up. Either cancel a day or rearrange matters as you see fit. Now that's the end of the matter.'

'But, Dad . . .'

'But me no buts, David. You're in charge but only up to a point. Some decisions stop with me and this is one of them. All right?'

David was about to argue again but then changed his mind. 'Sorry, you're right. Sorry, Sion. I won't interfere again. A day off won't harm us. We can recharge our batteries and work on some new speeches. Jim's had a few ideas that we should all go over.'

'Good. Now, shall we get this show on the road?'

Sion climbed into the cockpit and Mike swung the port propeller. The engine coughed, spluttered and burst into life. They repeated the process with the starboard engine and Sion let the engines idle while O'Donnell climbed onboard. He checked that his passengers were safely seated before trundling the aircraft onto the dirt track runway.

There were a number of well-wishers to wave them farewell and soon they were at five thousand feet and heading west. In the rear David adjusted the sliding flap that let hot air blow into the cabin and settled down to work with Jim and his father.

'Denver is a big one for us. It's so marginal that last election they had to have a recount of the votes. We, that is the Democrats, won by a whisker. We've three weeks to go to polling day and so now's the time to hit them hard. That's why having Sonny on the ground could be a great help. We're landing just outside the city and going in by car. A motorcade, in reality. Once we reach the town hall you'll give a speech on the steps before going in to a small reception. Then we'll be working the whole area before we have the party on Saturday. Jim's got some ideas he'd like to go over with you about the speech.'

'Mr Griffiths,' said James Hay in his deep, cultured voice, 'there's not a lot of industry in or around Denver. Colorado is mainly farming land for cattle and cereals. It's very sparsely populated and most of the industry found there is related to ranching. However, there is also a strong mining community.'

'Coal?' Evan asked.

Hay shook his handsome head. He was an imposing figure, tall, slim and with tight, black curls cut short. 'It started with gold in 1858 but now they mine lead and zinc as well. Gold is still one of their biggest mining projects and there's always friction between the ranchers and the miners. Old fashioned territorial wars still erupt from time to time.'

'Any going on at present?' David asked.

'Nope. All's quiet right now. There's been some trouble still with the reservations because gold was found on one of them less than ten years ago. There were also serious problems in the area in 1914 when National Guardsmen and security men hired by the Colorado Fuel and Iron Company set fire to the tents of striking miners.'

'What happened?' asked Evan.

'The miners and their families were shot at. A few men and women died but so did thirteen children. That was seven years ago but people have long memories. So we have the conservative ranching community on the one hand and the urban and mining democrats on the other. Senator, we don't need a lot more people coming to our cause to win easily. This is one area we can think of as a key state. Now, I propose we use two speeches, one when we arrive and the other when we go out to Wellington and Fort Garland.'

Hay fell silent as the plane suddenly swooped down and all three men grabbed at the table to steady themselves. The engines picked up speed and the plane climbed. Sion threw back the hatch and said, 'Sorry about that. We're hitting a lot of turbulence as we cross some of the peaks. We'll have to climb a bit as well, so it might get even more uncomfortable. Nothing to worry about, though.'

After a few more minutes they stopped trying to work and each of them looked out of a window, watching some of the grandeur unrolling beneath them. Once or twice an engine missed a beat but in the cabin it was hardly noticeable. In the cockpit it was different, and Sion and O'Donnell kept a careful eye on the fuel, temperature and oil pressure gauges. The port engine was running a bit hot and the starboard oil pressure was a few pounds low. Nothing to worry about, just indicators that the engines needed a serious overhaul. In the middle of the morning Denver came into sight, a sprawling metropolis surrounded by rolling hills of lush pasture set against the peaks of the Rocky Mountains in the distance. It was a truly awe-inspiring sight that greeted them.

As usual, Sion flew over the field, David let out the banner and they lined up to land. They touched down to a mighty cheer from the crowd when there was a loud bang and smoke poured out of the port engine. Sion quickly cut the petrol and luckily the smoke died away. None of the crowd realised anything unusual had happened.

When they came to a halt Sion leaned back in his seat and said, 'Heck, that was close.'

O'Donnell nodded and tried to speak but it came out as a croak until he cleared his throat. 'I thought our time had come, I really did. You weren't wrong when you said we were living on borrowed time. Anyway, David can't argue with us now.'

'We'll make a start as soon as possible. We can do all the preparation work and be ready to put in the new engines as soon they arrive. I'll see if we can find a couple of mechanics who can help. We can also take the time to check out a few other things. We've tightened the wires about as far as they'll go so we could replace a few of those, too.'

They sat in the cockpit and watched as Evan, David and Jim climbed down. A figure came out of the crowd and shook hands with Evan and Jim and gave a huge bearhug to David. Sion grinned and threw open the cockpit cover and yelled.

'Sonny! Sonny, you old son of a gun!' He clambered out glad to see his old friend.

'Sion? You drove that thing?' Sonny was all smiles, giving Sion the same friendly bearhug he'd given David.

'Sonny, let me look at you. You haven't changed a bit.' Sion stepped back to look at his friend. At fifty, Sonny had filled out, was losing his hair and looked prosperous.

'We're all getting older, Sion. Is that grey I see?'

Sion self consciously pushed the hair off his ears and replied, 'Nothing a hair cut won't cure. Come on, we'd better follow the Senator.'

They left O'Donnell with the plane while they went after Evan. The welcoming committee was already beginning to pile into cars. Sion had a quick word with his father and returned to the plane.

In the car, Sonny got down to business. 'Right, Senator, all the arrangements have been made, just like you instructed. When we get to the edge of town we'll stop and take down the roof. It's cold but you can wave to the crowds and we'll be going slowly. I've given the staff time off so there'll be at least a few dozen waving and cheering.' He grinned, pleased beyond words to be with them again. He owed his fortune to the Griffiths' and though nobody ever reminded him of the fact it was always in the back of his mind. His loyalty was unquestionable and unstinting. Evan grinned back, pleased to see his old friend once again.

Evan made an imposing figure, standing on the steps of the city hall. The tall, granite faced building was an impressive backdrop. He wore a fur lined jacket as protection against the cold wind sweeping down from the mountains and, at David's insistence, on his head he had a Stetson hat. At first he had felt self conscious but then, seeing that the majority of the men wore one, he knew he would have looked out of place to have done otherwise. David was bareheaded and wishing he had a Stetson, too.

Evan's farming and ranching speech went down well, especially when he compared the price of a steer to that of a steak in a Washington restaurant. His message was that there needed to be a fairer distribution of wealth and income. Cleverly he did not suggest between rich landowner and worker but between east and west. This bone of contention always found favour out west.

The highlights of Evan's speech were carefully edited by David before he wired them back to the eastern seaboard newspapers.

So far during their gruelling tour the two reporters Garfield and Tyburn had joined them by train for the weekly party and what had become known as policy speeches. This was when Evan talked about the big issues, including foreign policy, that he hoped to bring to the Presidency. The remainder of his speeches were carefully crafted to reflect local issues and problems, giving the impression that the man they voted into the White House knew what was happening in their particular neck of the woods. It was a masterly performance, enhanced by the brilliant speech-writing of David and of James Hay.

The reception in City Hall was attended by most of the local dignitaries and had only just begun when Evan received a message telling him that Meg and the girls had arrived and were waiting for them at the hotel. Thanks to Sonny, the party planned for Saturday night was no longer a problem and a suitable venue had somehow materialised.

Back at the hotel Evan sprawled on the bed. Meg sat next to him and asked, 'Is it really worth all this?'

'Is what worth what?' Evan opened his eyes and looked blearily at her.

'The Presidency. Is it worth all this effort? You look exhausted. It's been a tough campaign and at the end you might not get it. What then?'

Evan grinned. 'Then I'll get a high profile job in the Party and be Chairman of a few select committees. Then I'll wield power behind the throne instead of on it.'

'Who says?'

'David. He's had reports in from all over the country. Rutherford's going down a storm, using the speeches David and Jim are writing. The papers are making a lot about us having a black man on the team and that it's time blacks in this country exercised their democratic rights by voting. So that gamble has probably paid off. If I lose I still win. I won't be President but I'll have a hell of a lot to say in the Senate. Now, my sweet, let me get a few minutes sleep.'

He slept all evening and all night, waking up just after dawn. He looked at Meg lying alongside him and a surge of joy flowed through his body. He took his time waking and arousing her. Later, they dozed in each others arms, still in love, young at heart again.

At breakfast they joined their sons and daughters-in-law. It was a happy occasion, unspoilt by politics. Jim Hay and Mike O'Donnell sat with them and were on the point of leaving when two men approached their table. They were Indians. Although dressed in white shirts and business suits, they had pony tails and a quiet dignity that impressed Evan.

'Senator,' said the older of the two, 'my name is Billy Two Hats and this is my son, Joe. I am from the Crow nation . . .'

Joe interrupted. 'My father is the Chief of the Crow.

Evan stood and offered his hand. He indicated that the other men should stand too. He introduced them, nodding at David and Sion and saying, 'My sons also.'

'Fine men. Fine men,' said the Chief.

'Sion, move round and make room for the Chief and his son.'

As they were doing so, a small, fat, bustling man rushed up. 'You, Indians! You can't stay here. You know the rules. No Indians in the hotel. Now git!'

The Indians showed no emotion but began to stand, resignation and resentment showing in their postures.

'Please remain seated, Chief Billy Two Hats. You are my honoured guest.' Evan looked at his sons and gave a jerk of his head. Both of them unhesitatingly stood up and hustled the hotel manager away. The remainder at the table heard David say something about the Senator wanting peace and quiet. Meg smiled at their new guests and offered them coffee. Both men declined.

'What can I do for you, Chief Billy Two Hats?' Evan asked, respectfully.

'Just call me Billy,' the Chief said.

'And I'm Evan.'

Billy Two Hats looked horrified, if that was possible on the features of an "inscrutable" Indian. 'You're a Senator and about to be President of the United States. If you don't mind, I'll call you Senator.'

'If I may say so, Billy, you speak excellent English.'

'The Crow have been on the side of the white man for hundreds of years. We've worked at being American. The dime store Indian is – what do you call it? – a myth. We haven't lived in tepees for many years but have log cabins, fully plumbed. We have a school house and many of us are Christians.'

Evan nodded, surprised but not showing it. 'So why have you come to see me?'

'We need your help,' said the Chief. 'Oil has been found on our reservation and they are going to move us off. Already there's been a lot of trouble. Two of my young men have been hurt. Nobody's been killed so far but it's not far away. The hotheads of my tribe want to arm and fight. I've told them no! We must do it properly. Go to the courts. Stop our land being stolen from us.'

'So why don't you?' asked Evan.

'There's something called the Cherokee Nation versus Georgia. I don't understand it but . . .,' Billy Two Hats shrugged and paused.

James Hay interrupted. 'I can tell you about that, sir. It was a High Court decision on 18 March 1831. Gold was found on land in

Georgia but unfortunately the land belonged to the Cherokee Nation. The Cherokees filed a suit to protect their land and keep prospectors off it. Unfortunately, the judge at the time, name of,' Hay paused and thought a second, 'name of Chief Justice John Marshall, well he ruled that the tribe is a domestic dependent nation and, something else. Oh, I know. A distinct political society able to manage its own affairs. And here's the rub. He went on to say that because Indians are not bound by the law of the Constitution they don't have the right to sue. It's still the law.'

Both Indians nodded and Billy Two Hats continued. 'That's true. We are all known as Nations. The Cherokee Nation, the Sioux Nation, the Cheyenne Nation, the Chickasaws and so on.'

'And the Crow Nation,' said the Chief's son, 'and that's our problem.' Both men exchanged a few words in a language nobody else understood.

Billy Two Hats then continued. 'So we are not able to use the courts to protect us and yet we obey your laws. If we obey your laws then surely we are entitled to protection?'

'Sir, can I explain?' Hay asked. Evan pursed his lips but was aware that he was totally out of his depth and needed help, so he nodded.

'Within the reservations the laws are those of the tribes. Our laws stop at the boundaries of the Nations. There are no judges and no lawyers in the Nations and hence the ruling that the Constitution does not apply to the Indian Tribes. It would take an act of Congress to change it.'

'But surely it also means that these people are entitled to our protection? They own the land and nobody can take it from them.'

Hay shook his head. 'That's not the way it's been, Senator. They've just been moved off under one pretext or another. Usually it's been for gold and oil but on one occasion it was for water rights. I think.'

'That is correct,' said the Chief. 'Pawnee water. A lot of men died that time. And I fear a lot of men will die this time. Unless they can be stopped.'

'Who's doing it?' asked Evan.

'Standard Oil,' said Joe. 'They've formed a local militia to get us off the land. They're arming and making threats.'

'They can't do that,' said Meg, horrified.

'They're doing it. There's only gunlaw around here,' replied Joe.

'But that's ridiculous,' Meg protested. 'This is the nineteen twenties. They can't do that,' she repeated.

'Mrs Griffiths,' said James Hay, 'my people are too scared to vote, are still treated like slaves and, in some parts of the country, have to remove their hats if a white man enters a room. Hanging is common all across the south and the Ku Klux Klan are getting stronger all the time. So please don't be surprised by what the Chief is saying.'

'So how can we stop it?' Meg asked.

'You can't,' was the considered reply from Hay.

'Chief, can you give me a day or two to think about it? I need some help,' said Evan.

The two Indians spoke in their own language for a few moments and then Billy Two Hats nodded, resignedly. 'We have a few days. Until you leave, at least.'

'What do you mean?' asked Meg.

'They were going to come for us today. But we heard that nothing would happen until after you'd left. That is why we came to speak to you. If you had so much power that you could stop them just by being here then I'd hoped you could do more. You're our only hope.'

The two Indians stood and shook hands and, with a great deal of dignity, walked from the room.

Evan felt swamped. The awesomeness of being President of such a vast and diverse country suddenly frightened him. How on earth was he supposed to cope, should he win the election? How had past Presidents managed? The job was too big for one man!

He mentally shrugged off his fears. 'What can we do?'

Nobody said anything.

'We have to do something!' said Madelaine. 'We can't just leave them to their fate.'

'Any ideas?' asked Evan.

'Call out the National Guard,' said Sion. 'Tell them that the Crow need protecting.'

'I expect a lot of this so-called militia are National Guardsmen. Or are known to each other, at least,' said David. 'And let's not forget, folks, there's no votes in it. The Indians haven't got the vote.'

'David,' said Meg, aghast, 'how cynical!'

'Not cynical, Mam, realistic.'

'The problem is,' said James Hay, 'that oil means jobs and prosperity.'

'Only to the companies,' said Sion. 'They get richer by the minute.'

'No, wait a minute, Sion,' said Sonny. 'Jim's got a point. Listen. The real wealth does go to the companies and shareholders. Hell, we know that Rockefeller and J.P.Morgan couldn't count all their money if they started now and did nothing else until the day they died. But jobs are something else. High paying jobs mean a lot around here. New restaurants, auto dealers, other shops. More business for us.'

'So what are you saying, Sonny?' asked Meg. 'That we should just let the Indians be thrown off their land because we can make a profit?'

'Good Lord, Meg, you know me better than that! Of course not! We get a deal for the Indians to develop the oil. Under licence, maybe.' Sonny shrugged and lapsed into silence.

'Now that, Sonny, is about the best idea I've heard all week,' said Evan.

'How do you go about it?' asked Kirsty, fascinated to watch her father-in-law in action.

'First,' said David, 'we get more information. Then we see Billy Two Hats and put a proposal to them.'

'What sort of information?' asked Kirsty.

'We need to see the terms under which the land was given to them,' replied Hay. 'Who has the mineral rights? It could be the Government. If it is then we could have a real battle. If not, then the Crow can, in theory, exploit the oil and any other minerals they might have.'

'And if the mineral rights belong to the Government?' Madelaine asked.

'Then the highest bidder will get those rights. In this case Standard Oil because nobody could outbid them.'

'Yes, they could,' said David. 'The people of Denver could. Why not form a company with the majority shareholding in the name of the Crow Nation and the rest sold to the people of Colorado? That way, not only will jobs come to this area but so will real wealth. Now, there's votes in that!' he grinned, earning a glare from his mother.

'Do we have time?' asked James Hay.

'It's time, I think,' said Evan, 'to wield some of this political power

I'm supposed to have. David, get me the Governor. This is a problem for him. Sonny, what's the biggest bank in town?'

'The Continental Bank of Colorado.'

'Do you know them, David?'

His son thought for a moment and then replied. 'Not offhand. But I can look them up in my black book.'

Evan nodded approval. David's "black book" was a goldmine of information and contacts and had become invaluable over the years.

'What do you want them for?' asked Meg.

'We'll use Griffiths and Buchanan & Co Bank to underwrite the issue. We do it with the Continental acting as our local agents,' said David, in his element.

'Aren't you all forgetting something?' asked Meg. Her men looked at her, puzzled. 'Nothing important,' she added. 'Just that Billy Two Hats might not agree, the Governor might not help and a small war could start at any time. Like I said, nothing important.'

36

THE GOVERNOR WAS a Republican and when he arrived at the hotel he had four other men with him.

The handshake was perfunctory, the meeting did not start in an atmosphere of cordiality and the Governor's first statement was, in fact, rude. 'I wanted to meet you Griffiths. I wanted to see THE WELSH WIZARD OF ST. LOUIS and hear what he had to say. So what do you want?'

'If you want to hear what I have to say then read the press cuttings. My son here can supply you with them. Alternatively come to one of my speeches.'

'National politics bore me. Me, I like state politics best. That's where the real power lies.' The Governor was a florid faced, heavily built, tall man with bushy eyebrows and a shock of grey hair. 'And I'm the power in this state Griffiths, believe me.'

'I believe you, Governor. However, this morning representation was made to me for help from . . .'

'I know. Billy Two Hats. He'll be off the reservation an hour after you're gone. Is there anything else?'

'Governor,' said Evan, icily, 'you're making a big mistake. Don't cross me and I can help you. Are you going to listen?'

The Governor looked at the faces of the men he'd brought with him and stood up. 'I don't think so, Griffiths, there's not a thing you can do for me. Enjoy the rest of your stay in my state.'

'Your state, Stanstead? I don't think so. I think it belongs to the voters. I think you've been given a sacred trust to look after the men, women and children who live in this state. Everybody, regardless of their ethnic origin or the colour of their skin.'

'Is that so, Griffiths?' The Governor leaned heavily on the table and stared at Evan. It was the Governor who broke contact first. 'I don't like you, Griffiths and I don't like your bleeding heart politics. I run this state my way. Not the voters, me. They do what I tell them. I want them Indians off the reservation and I want them off fast. They'll be gone when I say so.' The Governor and his henchmen stalked from the room, laughing amongst themselves.

'Well, that went off just as we didn't plan,' said David. 'What now?'

'Now we get moving,' said Evan. 'I wanted to give him an opportunity to help. Did you write down what he said?'

David nodded. 'Pretty damning stuff if we could use it.'

'We can. Sion, can you and Mike go and find Billy Two Hats and ask him to spare me some time? We need his permission to continue. Sonny, can you find out how many men are going against the Indians? I shouldn't imagine it's more than a hundred or two. I also want to know what weapons they've got and what the Indians have to defend themselves with.'

'That's easy to answer,' said James Hay. 'Indians'll have nothing. Rocks and maybe bows and arrows.'

Evan looked puzzled. 'What do you mean? Surely they've got guns?'

James Hay shook his head. 'Maybe the odd carbine or two for hunting, but that's all. It's part of the agreement for living in safety on a reservation. No guns. Anybody caught supplying guns to Indians goes to prison for a very long time. I know because the Indian Reservations and ghettos of urban America were part of my university thesis.'

'Hmm, that makes it more difficult. We need help. It's time to call in some heavy favours. David, I want to speak to Matt Kapowski. He's at the St. Louis Army Barracks. I,' Evan smiled, 'have an idea.'

Evan's next speech was a damning indictment of the Governor of the State of Colorado. It was well received by some of the populace of the state and castigated by others. The balance of opinion was on a knife-edge.

Evan met with Chief Billy Two Hats in a small office on the outskirts of the city. He explained to the Chief what he proposed. Afterwards, the Indian sat in thought for a few minutes. Questions were asked and answered until finally the Chief nodded. The two men shook hands and left the room.

Back at the hotel Evan spoke to Kapowski by telephone. It was a cryptic conversation aimed at confusing any eavesdropping telephone operator. Evan was sure that the Governor would be listening in – figuratively speaking.

'Matt?'

'Evan, is that you? Should I call you Mr President yet or Senator?'

'Evan will do, Matt. Now listen. I've got a favour to ask. You'll receive a long and detailed missive from Stan Ogilvie. He works for me. When you get the report I'll need to speak to you. Matt, it's of the utmost importance. Please, don't treat it lightly.'

General Kapowski laughed. 'Would I do that knowing it was from you?'

'Thanks. He'll be with you in about three hours.'

'I'll tell the guard to let him in.'

The General put the receiver down while Evan listened a little longer and was gratified to hear a click as the operator stopped listening. Gently he replaced the receiver and turned to his sons.

'It's all set up with the Chief. He agrees. Have you checked the Constitution?'

David nodded. 'Yes. It's a bit grey but in a nutshell it's as you hoped. The law was changed to allow American forces to operate in a foreign country provided they were invited in by the host country. I should clarify that and say the legitimate Government of the host country. That enabled us to take part in the war in Europe. Since then we haven't changed things back again. It also explains why, in 1918, we didn't go into Germany. We're expressly forbidden from doing so as obviously the Germans wouldn't have been inviting us in. Anyway, that's history. We are open to invitation. Now, the Nations haven't been designated as foreign countries but the way the agreements have been made it could be argued that they are. Certainly, there's enough to obfuscate matters long enough for our objectives.'

'Good. Jim, do you agree?'

'I went through it with David. Like he just said, Senator, it's a grey area and a moot point. But we don't care because we only need cover for a few weeks at most.'

'Okay. Sonny, have you finished coding that information?'

'Give me two minutes, Senator, and I will have.'

'As soon as you're done, get down to the telegraph office. I want a response within the next three hours at the most. David, have you drawn up the agreement?'

'Yes, Dad. It's ready. You buy the total mineral and oil rights for one dollar.'

'And the other agreement?'

'You sell it back for a profit of one hundred percent,' David grinned. 'A whole dollar.'

'Money isn't the issue this time, son. Principle is.'

'I agree, Dad. How did the Chief take it?'

'He recognised that he's got no choice other than to trust us. He doesn't know it but we won't let him down. He just hopes we won't. Finished?' Evan looked at Sonny.

'I'm on my way, Senator.' Sonny left the room.

'What's next?' asked Evan.

'Next we contact our bank in New York. Tell them what we want,' said David. 'In the meantime you need to talk to a few people on the select committee for oil and finance.'

'I need a phone that doesn't have an operator. Or at least, not one reporting back to the Governor.'

'That's practically impossible,' said James Hay. 'He's got this state well and truly sewn up.'

'Jim, I like having you on the staff,' said Evan, 'but I want a solution to my query, not a statement of the obvious.'

Seeing for the first time the iron fist in the velvet glove, Hay suddenly realised how and why Evan had been so successful. Compassion wasn't to be mistaken for weakness or softness. The man in front of him was granite hard in his convictions, a contradiction in terms, a misnomer – an honest politician.

'No, sorry, sir. I think the answer is you leave it to me.'

'What are you going to do?' asked Evan.

'It's better I didn't tell you.' With that Hay left the room. He went downstairs and found the small cubby-hole where the telephone operator was situated.

'Do you know,' he smiled at the middle aged woman who looked askance at him when he opened the door, 'that it's illegal to listen in on the Senator's telephone conversations? Furthermore, it can be punished by a heavy fine or a term of incarceration in the local penal colony. Which would you prefer?'

The poor woman was frightened out of her wits and stammered confused words that meant nothing. Hay held up his hand and she stopped speaking. 'We have evidence that you've been listening in and reporting the conversations to the Governor's office.'

The woman blanched, terror making her hands shake.

'It's all right,' Hay was suddenly very friendly, 'don't be so worried. We knew what was going on. How much did he pay you?'

The woman was so terrified that she stammered when she replied, 'T . . . t . . . ten dollars a . . . a . . . a time.'

'Good. Now, we want your help. I want a copy of your roster when you're going to be on duty and whenever the Senator makes a call I'll come down and we can make sure you aren't listening.'

'But . . . but . . . the Governor. He'll know.'

'No, he won't because we'll supply you with a false report.'

'I . . . I couldn't do that,' the woman said. 'It . . . it's dishonest.'

Hay almost laughed out loud. 'No, what you're doing now is dishonest. It's against the Telegram Act of 1889. When you trained to be a telephonist you must have been told that you weren't allowed to listen to other people's conversations under any circumstances.'

The woman nodded her head miserably. 'I didn't want to. It was . . . was just that the Governor threatened me if I didn't tell his office what was going on.'

'I can understand why you acted like you did. However, you've now broken the law. Work with us and I'll pay you for your help. Twenty dollars a time for every report you put to the Governor.'

'I . . . I couldn't do that. It wouldn't be honest.'

Hay shrugged. 'I'll be here to make sure you don't listen in. The Governor won't like it if you don't tell him something . . . anything. So collect the ten dollars from him and the twenty from me and you're laughing. Do nothing and he may get really upset with you. And then what?'

Her voice was a whisper when she said, 'I don't know,' and tears rolled down her cheeks.

A short while later, her duty roster in his pocket, Hay returned to Evan's suite. 'Okay, Senator, whenever you make a telephone call let me know and try and make them during these times only.' He handed the piece of paper to Evan. 'Don't ask, sir, you don't want to know. You only need to know that the operator will co-operate with us.'

Two hours later the phone rang and Evan took the call. It was Matt Kapowski.

'Matt? Give me a couple of seconds, will you?' Evan jerked his head at the door and Jim Hay went downstairs to the telephone operator's room.

'Okay, Senator,' you can go ahead.' Hay's voice came over the line.

'Okay, Matt, we can talk.'

'Understood, phone lines have many ears, big ones. I've got your request. It's comprehensive and clear. Is it legal?'

'We think so.'

'You think so?' Kapowski repeated. 'I'd need more than that before I put my career on the line.'

'Matt, where are you going from there? You're not a West Pointer nor an easterner. I've been in Washington long enough to know that you've got nowhere to go. Another year, maybe two and you're out to pasture on a small pension.'

There was an embarrassed silence on the line before Kapowski said, 'Senator, you always called it in a brutally honest way.'

'Sorry, Matt, but we don't have time for niceties. You know what's going on here. I know you're a decent man, so what's your opinion?'

'I think it stinks. My blood pressure went through the roof. I'd like to rip the head off the Governor and stuff it up his fundamental orifice. Hell, Evan, I'm sixty three and I helped put a lot of those people onto their reservations. I missed the Little Big Horn by months when I was a bugler boy in 1876. Even so I think the Indians have had a raw deal. But, I don't know, Evan, I really don't.'

'Listen, Matt, the Chief here is going to fight. Bows and arrows against repeating rifles and machine guns. It'll be a slaughter. Men, women and children will die and then the whole sorry and disgusting episode will be swept under the carpet. We've checked the law as far as we can without going before a Supreme Court Judge. I'm prepared to gamble everything because if I'm wrong they can hang me out to dry. Hell, you've only got an army career and pension to lose while I've got the Presidency,' Evan quipped.

There was a long silence. 'Evan, I've tried to do my best, obeying orders while at the same time squaring things with my conscience. It's not always been easy. Okay, I'm in. One thing, though. I run a regimental fund. We use it mainly to support men who've retired on inadequate pensions, especially those who've been hurt – damaged by war is probably a better description. I could use a donation.'

Evan knew about the fund and wasn't surprised at the request. 'I thought I'd donate $5,000.'

'I think ten is a much nicer, more rounded figure,' said the General.

'Actually, Matt, I've got a better idea.' Evan told him what he had in mind. The General took little convincing.

'I'll tell my officers we're going on an exercise which includes a rapid deployment to test our ability to work under pressure and at short notice. I'll tell them we've been invited to Colorado, as it's nearly six hundred miles away and a good test of our mobility and organisation. I won't tell them where exactly we're going or why until we get there. I don't want any nasty surprises on the way, and soldiers have big mouths.'

'Matt, that's to balance their big feet,' said Evan, relieved.

Kapowski laughed. 'That's for sure. Okay, we'll meet you at the reservation in three days.'

'Good. I forgot to add one little detail, Matt, when this is over and you want to resign from the army there's a job in our new defence contracting company. We build and sell planes to the military and we need somebody to head up the sales department. The salary is double what you earn now.'

'Evan, that's mighty nice of you. But I've got a better idea. When you're President you can make me Chief of Defence Staff and a four star, to boot.'

'Okay, Matt, it's a deal. If I become President you get four stars and a job back east, if I don't you get a bigger salary, a lot of big company benefits and a job back east.'

Kapowski laughed. 'Sounds like I can't lose. See you in three days.'

Evan replaced the receiver and stood in thought for a few seconds.

What if it wasn't legal? Could he continue? Damn legal, he thought, moral was the guiding principle. If he became President he'd do his damnedest to look after the weak and vulnerable in society.

Jim Hay returned to the room.

'Well done, Jim. What's she telling the Governor?'

'That she overheard you talking to an assistant in Washington about the rest of your trip. That you'd be here for an extra couple of days because you thought the state was too important not to have a bit more time spent here.'

'Was that all?'

Hay grinned and shook his head. 'No, Senator. I also told her to say that you'd been sucked into a situation with local Indians but it wasn't any of your business so long as nothing happened while you were here that would force you to interfere.'

'Good. That might buy us some time.'

David entered and Evan asked, 'Have you done your bit, son?'

'I think so, Dad. Jim and I have finished drafting the contract for you to read. I've wired the bank. They're arranging matters now. Our trust department will have everything sewn up by tonight. Underwriting the issue will take about three days. We're using our own money for that.'

'Okay. Anything else we need to do?'

'Plenty,' replied David. The three men got down to work. David drafted and redrafted a press release. He intended making political capital from the affair. He wanted the headline to read something like "A CARING PRESIDENT FOR THE WHITE HOUSE".

It had been agreed that no further meetings could take place in public between Evan's party and the Indians. They needed one final piece of information to complete their plans when David received a message to meet Joe.

When David returned, he had the information they wanted. Evan phoned General Kapowski and Jim Hay went down to the telephonist's cubby hole. 'Matt? On the eastern side of the reservation,' said Evan, when the General came to the phone, 'is a high butte. Apparently it can't be missed as there's a river running round most of it. We'll have a party there to meet you.' He listened for a few seconds. 'Yes, I'll be there. I wouldn't miss it for the world.'

'Right, Dad, we still have an itinerary to follow,' said David, when

Evan hung up the receiver. 'There are two meetings today and we need to go over one last time what you're saying in each.'

The problems of the Crow Nation were put on the back burner for a while as they plunged themselves into the minutiae of the election campaign.

At the first meeting there was a little more heckling than usual but at the second there was what David called "Rent a Mob". Evan managed to finish his speech but it was the most difficult time he'd had so far in the campaign.

'The Governor's doing, do you reckon?' David asked his father as they climbed into the car to return to Denver.

'Bound to be. He's been told I'm going to be around for a few more days and he doesn't like it. He wants to get the situation on the reservation dealt with as quickly as possible so that he can pocket his money and let the fuss die down. Actually, David, is that a trick we've missed? Can we find out how much he's going to make once Standard Oil's taken the place over?'

'I'm trying at the moment, Dad. I'm pulling in every contact I've got to get the information. I know somebody who's a fund manager at the Prudential and he's got a chunk of Standard's shares. He tried to weasel out from doing me the favour but I reminded him of one or two I've done him. I'll know by tomorrow what the deal is, how it's set up and who's making the payments. We can use factual ammunition which the Governor won't be able to deny.'

'When you know, arrange another meeting for me. I'll make it a private one, so as not to embarrass the man.'

'Why do you want to do that?' David asked.

'Son, you know a great deal about a lot. Your organisational skills are about the best I've seen but you know nothing about politics. I want him in my debt. One day I may need to call in the favour and political debts are always paid off. It's the only way the system can work. So I'll deal with it in private.'

They were approaching the outskirts of the city when a figure rose from the side of the road and waved. Hay stopped the car, relieved to see that it was Joe.

'Senator, my father asks that you do him the honour of coming to his tepee. He is ready to sign the papers.'

'Good. If you get in the car you can show us the way.'

They drove into the dusk, the road soon deteriorating into a track. After about an hour Evan asked, 'When do we get to the reservation?'

Joe's reply was a great surprise to all three men. 'We've been on Crow land for the last thirty of forty minutes.'

'I thought we'd have to go through a gate and a fence, or something,' said David.

'No, they were done away with many years ago. After all, our boundaries aren't there to keep us in, they're there to keep others out.'

It was dark when they arrived at the village. Again there was a surprise in store. The tepee was a large wooden hut with smaller huts laid out in a series of streets. They could see half a dozen tepees and David asked about them.

'Some of the older villagers like the old ways and refuse to change. I like my comfort, as does my father. Believe me, there's nothing comfortable about living in a tent, not in the twentieth century.'

He led the way into the Chief's house. At the table in the kitchen sat half a dozen men, elders of the tribe. Introductions were made. A stool was ready for Evan and he sat, leaving the others to stand.

Discussions lasted an hour. At the end, Billy Two Hats said, 'I have asked many people about you. They all say that you can be trusted. You are unlike other politicians.'

Evan nodded, unsure how to respond.

'They tell me that you're an honest man. I will sign your papers now.'

'Chief, you do understand that it's not a condition. I'll get the army here anyway. But that only buys us time while we sort things out through the courts and with the government. My agents back east are progressing matters on my behalf. With this paper I can force matters on your behalf. If you have the people of Colorado on your side the Governor will have to leave you alone. It's a no lose situation but you have to trust me.'

'We do, Senator.' The Chief exchanged words with the other men and there were nods all round. 'Let me have the papers, Senator.'

David handed two sheets of paper to his father who signed and handed them to the Chief. Laboriously Billy Two Hats spelt out his name. Three others, elders of the community, did the same and finally the papers were handed back.

Evan felt around in his pockets. 'Damn, I've got no money on me. David, have you got a dollar?'

David felt through his pockets. Nothing. He found fifty cents in his trouser pocket, Jim found forty cents, but neither man had another cent.

'Heck, we need the dollar to make it all legal and above board,' said Evan, beginning to search his pockets again, looking for ten cents.

The Chief leaned down and pretended to pick up a ten cents piece off the floor. 'You dropped this, Senator,' and solemnly placed the coin on the table.

'Thank you, Chief, I believe I did.' He went on, 'Here you are, one dollar for the mineral rights on the reservation. This is another contract, Chief, which sells back the total rights back to you, whenever you wish, for two dollars. We'll get this filed at the courthouse after the army gets here. In the meantime, I'll get a royalty agreement drawn up with the Government. It'll be the first time it's ever been done but as well as their taxes they'll get five percent on the barrel. I think this is one we can win, Chief.'

A short while later Evan, David and Jim Hay left. They were shown the way back to the road and returned to the hotel. Over dinner that night they learnt that the new engines had arrived and that Sion and O'Donnell would expect to have the plane ready to go within twenty-four hours. Evan told them they could take their time.

The following day David received the details of the Governor's involvement and bribe to oust the Indians from their land. Sonny also discovered that on the day that Evan left a hundred and eighty men would descend on the Indians. Many of the mob were looking forward to killing, burning and raping. It was a sickening thought.

It was dawn, two days later, when Evan and his party met at the airfield. Meg and the others had already left by train the previous day after tearful farewells. The night before the Governor had appeared, all smiles and said that he was there to make sure Evan was really leaving. Evan assured him that he was leaving Denver the following morning. There was a small contingent of the Governor's men to make sure they did leave, confirming the telephone conversations that had been reported to the Governor's office by the hotel telephonist.

Once the luggage was strapped in and engines started, the plane took off, flew over the city and headed east. Twenty minutes later they landed next to the butte on a long straight trail covered with green lorries and jeeps.

Evan quickly climbed out and went over to meet the grey haired, grizzled looking Matt Kapowski. They shook hands warmly and Evan told the General what had been happening.

'We had confirmation yesterday that my company's claim to the mineral and oil rights had been registered in Washington and that I had also accepted an offer of five percent royalties for the Government on top of normal taxes. The five percent is for ten years only thereafter the money is kept by the Crow Nation. A company trust has been established and provided certain conditions are met people in the area can have a stake in the business as well as jobs. Sonny McCabe will be delivering a copy of the agreement to the court in Denver at nine o'clock.' Evan looked at his watch. 'An hour from now. We know that the attack is coming at twelve o'clock midday. Can we be ready by then?'

Kapowski grinned, sheer joy lighting up his face. 'That'll be no problem. Are any of the men coming National Guard or are they all so-called militia?'

'They're all militia but a lot of them also belong to the Guard,' replied David. 'At least, so Sonny thinks.'

'Okay, that gives us a better idea of what we're dealing with. I think they're in for the shock of their lives. How many are coming?'

Evan supplied the figure and cast an eye almost as far as he could see down the track where men were lounging in the strengthening sunlight, ready to go.

'Nearly two thousand men, Evan. I didn't intend doing things by half. Outnumbering them ten to one is odds I like.'

'Do they know why they're here?'

'They do now. I told them last night. A few made the usual noises you'd expect but, hell, on the whole they're a good bunch of men and don't like to see people hurt. Not even Indians.'

It was a statement of fact accepted by all of them. Racism was alive and well in America, the recipients being ethnic Indians and blacks, closely followed by the Chinese and other Asian minorities.

The convoy moved out with the General, Evan and the Chief in the front jeep. Sion and O'Donnell were told to stay behind to look after the plane, much to their disgust.

The army was fully deployed and in hiding when the militia appeared at the village.

37

Some came in old automobiles, dilapidated lorries and riding clapped-out motorbikes. Others came in modern vehicles, all carried weapons and all acted as though they were going on a picnic. There were loud cheers and some were singing as the village came into sight. The vehicles opened out into a straggling line and now the occupants fell silent. Tension mounted and an ominous silence settled across the plain.

Rifles and guns were cocked, breeches opened and slammed shut. Nothing moved before them and when they were less than a hundred yards from the first of the huts the convoy came to a halt. The men looked nervously from one to another, unsure what to do next. If there was nobody to see there was nobody to shoot. The fun seemed to be over before it even started.

'Fire at the huts,' yelled a voice. 'On my command.'

'Ready! . . .'

Two red flares mushroomed into the sky, distracting the men, making then look up, wonderingly. Three shots were fired and the attention of the men was brought back to earth. Standing along the front of the huts was a long line of soldiers, each with guns pointed at them. Vehicles came racing out from behind the huts and behind came a long line of other army vehicles, machine guns cocked and ready. The militia were terrified. A day of fun had turned into a day of terror – for them.

Evan and the General drove close to the leading vehicle. Evan recognised one of the men who had been with the Governor at an earlier meeting.

'You!' gasped the man. 'You left! I saw you!'

'I came back, obviously. What are you doing on the reservation?'

'That's none of your . . .'

Evan had a rifle in his hands. He fired it close enough to the man to make him duck and exclaim in fear. Evan jacked another round into the chamber and aimed at the man's head. 'If you don't tell me, I'll shoot you.'

The calm, matter of fact way Evan spoke was more frightening than any ranting or raving. The man knew he was looking at death. He wet himself.

'I . . . I . . .,' he croaked, and then fell silent.

'You came to kill innocent men women and children, to run these people off their land. On whose orders? Whose?' Evan barked the last word and the man jumped.

'The . . . the Governor's.'

'Speak up, we didn't all hear you.'

'The Governor's,' the man said, loudly. 'He said it was legal. He'd signed the documents clearing this land of Indians.'

'He doesn't have the authority,' said Evan. 'That's why the army is here. These reservations were given to the Indians by the national government and you've no right to be here.'

The man licked his lips. He was a thug and a bully, used to having the upper hand, the hand of the strong over the weak. He knew that he was walking a tightrope; between life and death. He started shaking, he couldn't help it. First his hands and arms and then his legs and then his whole body shook as though he had the ague. The man suddenly collapsed, curled up in a ball and didn't move. It was a shocking sight to watch; this complete collapse of a man.

Evan was the first to recover. 'Right, you men, listen to me. First of all drop your weapons.'

All along the line guns were lowered and put down, some in vehicles, others on the ground. 'You thought it was going to be a turkey shoot, didn't you?' Evan yelled. 'Well it is, only you're the turkeys. Climb down from your vehicles and stand with your hands in the air.' The soldiers waited, nervously fingering their weapons, ready for any false move. It took a few moments but finally all the men stood on the ground. 'Now walk out front and don't make a false move.' The latter was a superfluous order as nearly two thousand guns were aimed directly at them.

Once the men were clear of their vehicles they stopped. 'Right, take your boots off and your trousers.'

For the first time there were protests from the militia. General Kapowski stepped down from his jeep and walked towards the men. The General was a tough man in charge of tough soldiers. He picked on the biggest man in the militia, who was refusing to do as he had been told, and continuing to protest when Kapowski stopped in front of this bear of a man, the loudest protester. The General hit him in the stomach with the butt of his carbine. As the man dropped to his knees Kapowski brought the rifle down on the back of the man's head and effectively pole-axed him. The others stopped protesting.

'Do as the Senator says, or the next time I won't be so gentle. You're all scum and I want an excuse. Any excuse will do,' he yelled.

The men fumbled with belts, boots and shoes, as they hurriedly divested themselves of their trousers and footwear.

'Right, start walking, that way,' Evan pointed the way they'd come. There were more outbursts of protest, particularly about their vehicles and the long walk back.

The General fired a shot and silence fell again. 'Major, escort these men off the reservation!'

'Yes, sir,' the Major saluted, relieved and yet strangely disappointed that there hadn't been more trouble.

The men were herded away, and in a long straggling line began to trudge back to Denver. The Governor's aid was helped along, barely shuffling, almost catatonic. The soldiers lined up their vehicles on both sides of the men and herded them away in a long convoy.

One man was brave enough to look back and yell, 'What about my car?'

'It's confiscated,' replied Evan, to the anguished groans of the sorry-looking militia as they shuffled slowly along. It was going to be a long day and an even longer walk.

'What will you do, Evan?' asked the General.

'My instinct is to keep them but my commonsense says let them have them back. We want these men punished but not vengeful. I think it makes more sense to walk them for two hours and then tell them that if they'd like to come back they can have their boots, britches and cars. The guns stay here.'

The General nodded. 'I agree. A steel fist in a velvet glove is a good combination. I think you'll make a good President.'

Evan looked in surprise at his friend and colleague. 'Why, thank you! I'll do my best. Right, we've a bit more paperwork to complete and we can be on our way.'

'Where are you going from here?'

'Back to Denver. I'm going to drop in on the Governor.'

On this occasion Evan went to the Governor's mansion. He was stopped at the reception desk and asked his business.

'Tell Governor Stanstead that Senator Griffiths is here to see him.'

The female receptionist looked surprised and then scuttled through a nearby door. There was a roar of surprise and the door was flung open and Stanstead stood there, his face mottled with rage. He was spluttering in indignation.

'Wait here,' Evan told David and Jim Hay and marched into the Governor's office, shouldering his way past the man. 'I suggest you close the door, unless you want everybody to hear what I've got to say.'

The door banged shut.

'You left. I had a report that you'd gone. What are you doing back? By God, Griffiths, I told you before and I'm telling you again, get out of my state.'

'Stanstead, you're a corrupt, loud-mouthed bully. Now sit down before I knock you down.'

'What! You can't talk to me like that. Get out before I have you thrown out!'

'You mean like you were going to do to the Crow?'

'What? What?' The Governor was spluttering with indignation now tinged with caution. 'What are you talking about?'

'Stanstead, I've known all along what you were up to. I've come to tell you to stop. Leave the Indians alone, or else it'll be the worse for you.'

'You can't threaten me, Griffiths. Anyway, it's too late. Them redskins are history. My boys have seen to that.'

Evan's smile sent a shiver of unease down the Governor's spine. Evan shook his head, slowly. 'No, they haven't. Your thugs are currently walking off the reservation, without boots, with their tails between their legs. I was going to send them back like that but I've allowed the army to escort them back after a couple of hours to pick up their britches and boots and drive out the way they'd driven in.'

The Governor looked stunned. 'No boots? No britches? The army?' Then he seemed to rally himself. 'What in tarnation have you done Griffiths? I'll . . . I'll kill you.' The man stormed to his feet and lunged at Evan.

They were of a similar age and height but there the similarity ended. The Governor was overweight and flabby, Evan wasn't. As the man lumbered at him, in a blind rage, Evan stepped to one side, hit his attacker in the side and as Stanstead doubled over Evan used his foot to send him sprawling onto the floor. The Governor turned over onto his back and was gasping out threats when Evan picked up the straight-backed chair from in front of the desk. He placed it on the floor, a rung pinning the Governor's neck down forcing the man to stay still.

'Don't struggle and you won't choke. Now listen Stanstead. You might survive this whole matter or you might not. Quite frankly, I couldn't care less. However, I do care about the Crow and what you could try and do once I've left. I have bought the mineral and oil rights to the reservation and I will exploit them.'

'You, Griffiths?' The Governor sneered. 'So under all the pious, sanctimonious claptrap you're no better than the rest of us.'

'Don't ever,' said Evan, in a cold fury, 'compare me to a slimeball like yourself. I shall make sure the Crow Nation reap the benefits. We've set up a trust for local people to buy shares at a dollar a time, up to a maximum of one hundred dollars worth. Locals can then enjoy jobs as well as sharing in the wealth that will undoubtedly be created. Other trusts will take care of the rest.'

'You can't do that. I've got a deal,' said Stanstead, beginning to struggle but stopped when he realised that all he was doing was half strangling himself.

'I can do it, because I have. The full details will be in the newspapers tomorrow. I also know all about your deal.' Evan proceeded to give chapter and verse of the bribe, naming those involved and how it had been arranged.

'You can't prove a thing,' The Governor blustered.

Evan shrugged. 'Stanstead, don't add stupidity to your list of traits. If I know all this, how difficult do you think it'll be for a Federal Prosecutor to come up with the same answers? It's over Stanstead and tomorrow everybody will know about it. Except about the bribes. That's just for you and me and a few select people to know about. Bluster you're way out of this one if you can. If you do, you'll owe me. One day I might want to collect on the debt. By the way, the army is staying for a week on exercise. After that they'll be returning to barracks.'

Evan stood up and swung the chair off the Governor who climbed laboriously to his feet, rubbing his neck. The man glowered at Evan. 'One day, Griffiths, I'll get you for this.'

'I don't think so, Stanstead, otherwise I'll have to use the documented evidence I have proving your corruption. Now, I suggest you think about trying some form of, shall we say – damage limitation – if you want to remain as Governor?'

Evan nodded to the man and left the room.

They returned to the plane, where Sion and O'Donnell were waiting for them. A short while later they were in the air, heading for Salt Lake City in Utah, the 45th State of the Union since 1896.

'I've been checking these figures, Dad,' said David. 'The Crow keep 50.1%, the St. Louis Regiment gets 0.1%, a deal that the General seems to like, and the trust for the people of Colorado gets 49%. I'm sure I'm right.' He checked again. 'Yes, that's 0.8% still missing.'

Evan pursed his lips and nodded. 'I'm glad you can still add up son. You didn't think I was really going to do all that for one dollar, did you? The press believe it and like it. I'll have made a lot of people happy and rich. But I'm not so philanthropic not to take reasonable advantage.'

David and Jim Hay looked at Evan in surprise and then David burst out laughing. 'Dad, I'm so glad. I was beginning to worry in case your judgement was slipping.'

'Never, son, don't you worry about that. Jim, there's a bonus of a thousand dollars in it for you. I like to show my appreciation of my staff. A satisfactory outcome, all in all. So what do we have for Utah?'

'The usual whistle-stop tour I'm afraid, Dad. I got a report in from Rutherford who seems to think everything is going well. He's using only three speeches, as and when he needs them. He said he'll meet us in St. Louis in a fortnight. Right now he's on his way to Oregon. I've warned him what to expect in the papers over the next few days.'

Sion came back into the cabin, leaving O'Donnell to fly the plane. He went into the rest-room and then sat down with the others. 'We're going to be flying a few rough legs on this journey,' he said. 'We can't go straight over the Rockies, they're too high. We need to go around some of the range and so we'll be flying along the odd canyon or two. Don't be alarmed when you see cliffs on both sides of the plane and don't worry if we suddenly rise and fall, it'll just be the air currents grabbing us. I've done this before and believe me it's more alarming than dangerous. How are you holding out, Dad?'

Evan smiled at his son. 'Couldn't be better. Mam's going to St. Louis to open up the house. She's not coming to Salt Lake City. She thought it would be better to have everything ready for when we get there. You know how she likes to make things just so.'

Sion nodded. 'It's probably for the best. Not long now, Dad. In two weeks I could be the son of the President of the United States of America.'

Evan gave his son a friendly pat on the shoulder and said, 'Ah, but I'll be the President of the United States of America.' At which they all chuckled.

The plane lurched to port and Sion stood up. 'I'd better get back to the cockpit. So don't worry, all right? The engines are running as sweet as nuts, we've plenty of fuel and the weather ahead looks fine.' Sion climbed into the cockpit and closed the door.

The plane did swoop and twist and the three passengers were forced to stop working and concentrate on not being ill. Evan found that by looking out at the passing landscape he could forget about feeling ill and just wonder at the beauty of it all. The vastness of the country was daunting. Yet again he was assailed by doubts about his ability to run such a huge, diverse and rich culture. He shook his head. He might not be the best man for the job but right then there was nobody better in politics. That was a thought he had to cling to if he was to be an effective President.

For an hour the plane droned on. Although they came close on a number of occasions, none of the men were physically sick. Suddenly the flight became smooth and they were no longer surrounded by towering rock faces. In front they could see a huge expanse of water which gave the name to the city, the Great Salt Lake. David let loose the banner, they flew around a field crowded with people and then they were landing. They heaved a great sigh of relief when the plane finally came to a halt, though none admitted how happy they were to have landed safely.

As usual there were bands playing, flags waving and a cheering, happy crowd. Unknown to Evan and the astute David there had been an unexpected spin-off to what had happened in Denver. Stories were already circulating and many reporters had more than an inkling of what had happened. The wonders of modern communications meant that a garbled version of events had preceded them. The bonus was the support given to Evan by another threatened minority – The Mormons of Utah.

Evan's speech was listened to with respectful impatience. When at last he finished and was about to leave the rostrum, a voice called out, stopping him.

'Senator! Senator! Can you comment on what happened in Colorado?'

Evan looked at David and raised an eyebrow. David shrugged and said, 'It's probably not a bad idea. We can keep feeding the truth to the press to counter anything Stanstead might say.'

Evan turned back to the crowd. 'Ask anything you like,' he said, 'and I'll answer it truthfully.'

'Is it true you hit the Governor?' Was the first startling question, taking Evan by surprise.

'Do you know the Governor?' Evan countered.

'Yes, sir,' replied the reporter. 'I've met him a few times.'

'Do you think he deserves a good thump from time to time?' The laughter drowned out the reply and Evan quickly turned to another questioner.

'Sir, is it true you used the army to protect the Indians even though they have no vote?'

'Yes, it's true and what has votes got to do with it? They're at least neutral. Are you saying that when I become President I should only look after the interests of Democrats? After all, Republican voters are against me! No, as President, my job is to look after everybody and that includes the disenfranchised as well as everybody else. Next!'

'Sir, was it appropriate to use the army?'

'What have you heard?' Evan asked.

'That the army fired on American citizens.'

'Not true. Nobody was hurt. If the American army fired on anybody I'd hope they'd hit somebody, don't you?' Again, laughter greeted his words. It was clear to the reporters that the crowd was on Evan's side and wanted to hear the story from him. Evan obliged them and spent the next few minutes clarifying what had actually happened. He also explained the anti-trust laws that Presidents Roosevelt and Taft had fought for over many years. He reminded them that Teddy Roosevelt had called Rockefeller the personification of industrial evil and Standard Oil the vehicle of that evil. 'It is only ten or twelve years,' Evan said, 'since Standard Oil was forced to limit its activities. And it seems to me that they were back at their old tricks in Colorado. They had to be stopped not only for the good of the people but for business across all of America.'

At the end something unprecedented happened.

A member of the crowd suddenly yelled, 'Three cheers for Senator Griffiths, hip, hip . . . hurrah.' The cheer rang out three times along with a rendition of "For he's a jolly good fellow." Flowers were presented to him by a small Mormon girl who curtseyed prettily and three men wearing the black garb of the Mormons approached him.

'Senator, since statehood we have been reluctant to get involved in national politics. We feel the outside world had little if anything, to do with us. However, that is not to say that we aren't entitled to vote. We are and we will. We came here today to listen to what you had to say. I will recommend that my people vote for you.'

'Thank you, sir, that's very kind of you.'

The elderly Mormon smiled. 'Kind? I think not, Senator. Pragmatic is a better word. As the uncertainties of this decade open up I think it would be judicious of us to have, if not a friend in the White House, at least an honourable and honest man. I think you're both. Good day to you, sir.' The three men left before Evan could say anymore.

Their journey into the city was interesting. For Evan it was like stepping back thirty years, as pony and traps outnumbered cars four or five to one. It meant that there was a much gentler feel to the place. The slower pace was somehow peaceful, soporific almost, a reminder of a bygone, less frantic age. As he sat in the car Evan was conscious of a feeling of regret for what had gone forever. He had relished the twentieth century with its fantastic rate of change, innovation and prosperity. Suddenly he wasn't so sure that it was all so wonderful. Change needed to be managed, controlled, stopped from getting out of hand before too much damage resulted. He shook his head, he was being fanciful, silly. He could no more slow change than he could stop the sea from ebbing and flooding. He could, somehow, help to manage it, though. With these thoughts disturbing his equanimity they checked into a hotel in the City.

Their stay was dominated by the events that had taken place in Colorado. Press coverage was prolific and continuous, with Evan on the front pages of newspapers all over the country for days. One caricature of Evan showed him holding a gun, holding the bullies at bay while cowering behind him were the poor, the needy and the disadvantaged. The drawing was meant as an insult, instead it became a rallying cry for all those who had felt excluded from the political process of America. In spite of universal suffrage both major parties had been seen as bastions of white, wealthy privilege. Evan was now appealing to the down-trodden across America.

The use of the army was questioned endlessly and political writers across the land frequently answered their own questions. If the army was not to protect us from foreign invasion – nobody was going to invade America in the nineteen twenties – then what was it for if not to protect its own people within its borders? The Republican argument that the Nations were autonomous and outside the protection of the American army didn't wash, the Crow would be paying handsomely for the help received in the form of the 5% oil royalty Evan had negotiated.

When the plane took off for Oklahoma City, over a thousand miles to the south east, Evan left behind a great deal of good will and a popular press that, nationally, was calling him the next President of the United States of America.

'Dad, this is the longest leg. We couldn't follow the plan without one journey like this but after here we go to St. Louis for a rest.'

'A rest?' Evan asked.

'Well, perhaps not quite that. But an easier schedule than the one we've had so far.' David paused and then added, 'We need to work on the next speech. Jim says you've got a few ideas.'

'Yes, I have. I've got a report from Professor Kluttermann of

Harvard University that I think warrants attention.' Evan took out the thin document and put it on the table. 'This is a précis of what he has to say and I think it makes frightening reading. I know that so far we've told people what they want to hear, well this time I think we need to say a few words that they might not like.'

'Such as?' asked David, frowning, picking up the document and scanning it. Just then the plane swooped upwards, carried by the first of the updrafts that they had to endure to return across the Rockies.

'Such as, I think we'll leave it until we're through the mountains. I'm going to sit here and think while you two can read that report.' So saying, Evan sat in silence as the plane flew through the valleys and ravines. For the first time he allowed himself to contemplate winning; to actually being President. He frowned. Try as he might he could not see beyond the race. His plans once he was in the White House eluded him. He mentally shrugged. They would come once he had been sworn in.

They landed at Pueblo in Colorado to refuel and buy some food. Their arrival was a low key affair as nobody had been told that they would be arriving. They stretched their legs for half an hour, had a hot meal served at a small restaurant on the edge of the airfield and took off into clear blue skies with light winds from the north. Behind them, high over the mountains, clouds were gathering. Snow was predicted but they hoped that they were leaving it behind.

Pueblo is a city situated on the slopes of the Rockies and on the edge of the Great Plains that stretch the length of the country from north to south. As Evan's party flew east by south east the wind picked up and the occasional snow flurry struck the plane although there was nothing to worry about; not at first. Half an hour after take off the plane was enveloped in cloud and was bucking and swooping but flying steadily. They suddenly passed through the cloud and into clear sky. Looking back Sion could see that they were now safe from any more snow.

They were down at three thousand feet, flying across flat grasslands and as far as the eye could see were scattered herds of horses and cattle.

First the port engine spluttered and stopped and a few seconds later so did the starboard engine.

38

EVAN SAID, 'Stay where you are, both of you. There's nothing we can do.' Jim and David had both leapt to their feet. 'Sion needs to be left alone.' He paused as they men sank back into their seats. 'I suppose we could pray.'

'I don't think I'll bother,' said David, gripping the arms of the seat, his knuckles showing white.

The hatch opened and Sion said, 'It's not as bad as it looks.'

'Son, I don't know how it can get any worse. We're about to crash, we've no engines but you say it's not as bad as it looks?'

'Dad, we're over a plain, I can see a building to the left and there's a track we can come down on. We're gliding, just, but we are gliding, so we ought to be able to put down without smashing up. Stand by, we'll be on the ground in about five minutes.' He closed the hatch and the three men were left to their thoughts.

Looking out they could see the ground approaching quickly. The hatch flew open again and Sion yelled, 'Stand by. We're going in now, now . . . NOW!'

The plane landed with barely a bump and rolled and bounced along the dirt track. Luckily, no animals had strayed onto the track and they came to a gentle stop without mishap. There were smiles all round and the three men in the cabin exchanged handshakes, relief flooding their faces.

Sion and O'Donnell climbed down from the cockpit and Evan, David and Jim Hay jumped down from the cabin. A few hundred yards away a substantial house and barn stood and Evan began to walk towards the front door. Unexpectedly it opened and a woman appeared, holding a rifle.

'Stay where you are,' she called. 'What do you want?'

'Sorry, ma'am,' said Evan, taking off his hat and standing still. 'Something went wrong and we had to land. We didn't mean to startle you. If we can telephone for help we can get the plane repaired and be on our way.'

'We've got no telephone. It's a hundred miles to the nearest town and it's a long way to walk. It's that way.' She jerked her rifle down the track. 'Now git.'

'Hold on a minute,' said David, coming up beside his father. 'Do you know who this is?'

'Why should I care? Get your plane fixed, walk to town, do what you like. Just stay away from here.'

The woman's wrinkled face made her appear in her late sixties, her pursed lips giving the impression she was sucking on a particularly bitter lemon. She looked exactly like a dried-out old hag.

'Drop it, son. Let's go back to the plane and see what we need to do.'

Sion and Mike already had the carburettors off the port engine and were in a deep discussion.

'Can you fix it?' asked David.

'Sure,' said Sion, 'no problem. When both engines stopped like that it could only be one thing.' He saw the puzzled looks on the faces of his father and brother and hastened to explain. 'Oh, sorry. It's water in the petrol. We did check it but somehow too much water got in. I think there was some in the supply but also some seeped in when we went through that snow storm. It was enough to prove our undoing.'

'So what do we do?' asked Evan.

'We carry spare pipes, so we'll decant the petrol from the tanks and pour it into the pipes. The petrol floats on the water so we let it separate and refill the tanks. It's easy.'

'How long will it take?' asked David.

O'Donnell and Sion exchanged glances and shrugs and O'Donnell said, 'Ten, twelve hours?'

Sion nodded.

'Ten or twelve hours?' David was aghast. 'But we've got a schedule to keep.'

'David, apart from sprouting wings and flying out from here there's nothing we can do,' said Evan. 'Except maybe help.'

Sion shook his head. 'Leave it to us. We know what we're doing. It just takes time and there's no way we can hurry the process. Sit in the sun and enjoy a quiet few minutes. Actually, a cup of hot coffee would go down well.'

'The old biddy at the house isn't exactly the welcoming kind,' said David, dryly.

'Light a fire, Bro, light a fire.'

A short while later they had a fire going and water was on the boil. In spite of the fact that the sun was shining there was a distinct chill in the air and they were glad of the warmth from the fire. With a cup of strong, sweet coffee in his hand Evan wandered along the track and onto an adjoining field. It was fenced off, keeping the animals and the crops separated.

He looked along the ploughed furrows, as straight as arrows and stretching away as far as he could see. A slight breeze sprung up and he shivered and looked at the dust picked up by the wind. Thoughtfully, he went back to the plane to take another look at the report he had read about American farming methods. He found it depressingly true when he compared what was written to what he saw around him. Surely others could see it too?

In the meantime, Sion and Mike had siphoned all the fuel from one tank into the other and turned off the cross over valves, isolating the tanks. They had erected the spare pipes, each an inch in diameter, which now stood in a bowl of petrol. They poured the petrol down the pipes and when the volume of petrol in the bowl was sufficient, it held a column of petrol nearly four feet in height. They left the petrol and water to sit there, slowly separating. From time to time they'd tap the pipe, nudging the droplets apart.

'What now?' asked an impatient David.

'Now, we wait. We give it twenty minutes, lift out the pipe and pour the petrol into the clean tank. That's why it takes so long. Sorry and all that,' said Sion, 'but there's no other way to do it. Luckily, it's fairly cold today. Actually, it's a shame it's not way below freezing then we could speed up the process.'

'How?' asked Jim Hay.

'By pouring the water and petrol into the bowls and letting it freeze. The water separates out and the petrol is left. If it was a lot warmer, we'd be losing a lot of petrol because of evaporation. As it is, we're losing some, but not enough to matter. All we need do is go on with what we're doing. I think we should plan to be here overnight.'

'We'll get more wood for the fire,' said Evan.

'Good,' replied Sion. 'We'll be all right. There's plenty of blankets and food in the cabin. It's a pity the old woman won't help.'

'Leave her be,' said Evan. 'She's probably alone in the house and, truth to tell, scared of five men descending on her like we did.' All five grinned at the unintended pun.

'We'll sleep in the barn,' said David. 'That way she might not get too hot and bothered about us. I'll tell her what we're doing.' With that, David walked towards the house. He was fifty yards away when a rifle appeared in an upstairs window.

'That's far enough,' came the old woman's voice.

David halted and yelled, 'I don't know what your problem is and frankly I don't care. Tonight we're going to sleep in your barn. We won't trouble you if you don't trouble us. Do I make myself clear?'

There were a few moments silence. 'Why should I let you use my barn?'

'Because we'll freeze otherwise. We aren't asking much. We don't want any trouble and neither do you. So just leave us alone.'

'How do I know I can trust you?'

'Because the man you're refusing to help is Senator Griffiths, the next President of the United States. He gives his word nobody will harm you.'

'Just make sure you stay away from my front door. Senator! Huh! A likely story!'

David went back to the others. 'Well, at least she may not shoot us. How's it coming, Sion?'

'Not bad. I've done some calculating and I think we can get there with the tanks just a quarter full and still have fuel to spare. With luck we can be finished by nightfall.'

Evan, David and Jim left the two pilots to carry on with their task while they walked across to the barn carrying blankets with them. As they neared the doors the rifle appeared again in the window of the house but they deliberately ignored it and, to their relief, nothing happened. They went into the barn and found it was full of corn and hay, winter feed for the cattle and horses. There was no indication of any mechanised vehicles, not a car nor a tractor for ploughing. They moved some of the hay and made up what would be comfortable beds for later. Out of the wind it was relatively warm, and with the blankets and hay wrapped round them they'd have a comfortable night. Jim found a couple of kerosene lamps and, as night fell, lit one.

Evan hoped that there were not too many people worrying where they were. He wanted to get a message to Meg, to reassure her that they were all right.

When Sion and O'Donnell joined them they had washed the petrol off their hands and changed their clothes.

Sion had some cold meat and bread with him as well as a bottle of malt whisky. The five men settled down for the night, the blankets wrapped around their shoulders and some of the hay over their feet and legs. The talk was all about politics to begin with, ranging from America to Europe and the rest of the world. The politics of Ireland were discussed and dismissed. They concluded that the Irish problems were too difficult and complex for anyone to understand, let alone discuss.

Around midnight, O'Donnell and Jim Hay turned in, leaving Evan and his two sons to talk quietly together. Very soon they got on to family memories, starting as far back as Llanbeddas and the death of Sian, Sion's twin sister. It was a long and pleasant night, filled with sad and happy memories. Evan told his sons about his escape on the train with Uncle James after James had killed the mine owner, and about how they had got started in St. Louis after crossing the Atlantic aboard John Buchanan's ship.

They remembered the time Sion had been shot and Evan going after the man who did it. Sonny and Uncle James had gone with him.

'Do you know,' said Sion, 'it was about this time of year that you saved me from those breeds, when you two and that Indian found me, fighting for my life.'

'I remember,' said David, ' but we were lucky to find you when we did.'

Evan looked at his two sons and a feeling of well being and happiness surged through him. They had come a long way in their lives, and he had little doubt that they yet had a long way to go.

It was nearly dawn when they finally fell asleep. When they awoke the sun was high in the sky and the heavy frost that had fallen during the night had begun to melt. They collected their gear and returned to the plane.

'Dad,' said David, 'I'll boil some water for coffee and a shave. You find a clean suit and shirt. We don't want you arriving in Oklahoma looking like something the cat dragged in.'

After a poor breakfast but a welcome cup of coffee they climbed aboard the plane. O'Donnell and Sion carefully primed an engine and when Sion gave the signal O'Donnell swung the first propeller. There was a loud bang, a belch of smoke and the engine started, settling to its usual throaty roar. He did the same with the other one and after the third try it too banged, belched and started.

They were facing into the wind and Sion quickly accelerated over the frost hardened track. A few minutes later they were in the air and turning smoothly towards Oklahoma City. Evan looked down on the farm and was actually glad that the old woman had been so rude and inhospitable. The night with his sons had been priceless, more valuable, he thought, than all the tea in China.

They overflew the airfield on the outskirts of Oklahoma City, but there was nobody there to greet them. They had been expected on the previous day and now the crowds had long since gone home.

'What shall we do?' asked Sion, turning round to speak through the hatch.

'Fly low over the city while I stream out the banner. Stay around, flying in circles to give them time to get back out to the airfield.'

There were no regulations as to how low he could fly and so Sion took the instruction at its face value. He swept along streets and over roofs at a height that startled people, made dogs bark and horses skittery. However, when the banner was seen, many people waved and cheered and began to leave the city for the airfield.

After a while Sion said, 'We'll need to go in now. We're low on petrol.'

'Do so, son. One landing like the last is enough for a life time.'

Sion made a pass over the airfield and then took the plane down to a gentle landing and stopped. When Evan stepped out there was wild cheering and flag waving. He shook hands with a number of local dignitaries and ascended the platform.

He began his speech. 'The reason we're late is, on the way here, our plane broke down and we had to land out on the Great Plains.

I can tell you that it's no fun flying along one second and having no engines the next. Luckily, we were in the capable hands of two skilful pilots, who brought us down safely. Mind you, I am biased in my assessment of the two men as one is my son.' He paused to let the crowd laugh, yell and whistle.

'I want to talk about a serious matter. When we landed I stood at the edge of a huge field and watched the wind blowing at the top soil.' There was complete silence now. The problem of soil erosion was known to them all and was just beginning to be thought of as a potential catastrophe. 'I'd like to say that it doesn't matter, that the blowing away of the soil didn't affect us, couldn't affect us, but I can't stand here and lie. A report was produced recently for the Senate by Professor Kluttermann of Harvard. He spent two months travelling through Minnesota, Iowa, Kansas, Oklahoma and Texas. He's coined a new word for the twentieth century. Agri-Business. It's his description of farming and ranching – agriculture – as a huge business. The ripping up of hedges and the deforestation of our land is leaving it open to the elements. Harsh cold winters leave the soil dry and long hot, windy summers leave it vulnerable. He has estimated that in ten or twelve years we shall have turned the lush, green prairies into dust bowls.' His audience was uneasy, murmuring amongst themselves, not wanting to hear what Evan was saying.

'This vast region is the bread basket of America. It feeds the nation. Without it we'll go hungry, all of us. The number of people who work and live off the land exceeds those working in all other industries, including those working in our towns and cities, by three to one. If we don't protect the land . . .' Evan continued even when he knew he'd lost his audience. When he finished there was a splattering of applause and he left the rostrum.

The bands played, children walked past and a few unenthusiastic flags were waved. They rode into the city in gloomy silence.

'Come on, you two,' Evan said to David and Jim Hay, 'cheer up. You're so used to the cheering and adulation you forget that there's a lot of people who don't like to hear the truth. We can't win them all. And in politics we only need to win about half.'

'I know that, Dad, but it's a salutary lesson. If we always tell the truth we ought to be thanked for it. People should appreciate the warning and do something before it's too late. I read the conclusions in that report and if we don't start replanting hedgerows and building fences we will have an environmental disaster.'

'Son, over half the Senators in Washington don't believe that report. They all represent states that have huge farm . . . agri-businesses . . . who think that bigger is better. To plough in straight lines for a mile or more is the most efficient way to produce cereals. Well, it's an argument that's correct. The problem is, it's at a huge long term expense. Maybe. And that's the word. Maybe. I stood and watched a few particles of dust blowing in the wind, but presumably they'll land and others will come and fill where they left. I don't want to believe the report and if this was my land perhaps I wouldn't.'

'Presumably, sir,' said Jim Hay, 'you do believe it.'

Evan nodded. 'Unfortunately, Jim, I do. But apart from speaking out and warning the people, what can I do? If the country's leaders refuse to see the potential for disaster why should we expect the ordinary man and woman to believe it? It's an interesting problem. If we're right, and we *know* we're right, should we compel people to act for what is ultimately their own good? Or do we say, living in a democracy, get on with it and we'll sort the mess out later. After all, we might be wrong! One thing I have learned, although if the truth were told I knew it anyway, and it's that you simply can't tell the people everything. The leaders must make the decisions, no matter how unpalatable they are. That's what we're paid for. And in a democracy, if we're right we get re-elected and if we're wrong we lose our seats. That's the price we have to pay.'

Evan lapsed into silence and watched as the city unfolded around them. Oklahoma was booming. It was the agricultural centre for a huge area where millions of cattle were reared, and millions of tons of wheat, corn and cotton were grown. Huge reserves of oil had been found to the north of the city, with a spin-off of associated industries.

In the hotel there was a delay of two hours for phone calls and so Evan sent a telegram to Meg telling her that they were all safe and well. There had already been some press speculation as to Evan's whereabouts but so far it had not developed into full blown hysteria.

In Oklahoma State, ninety percent of the population worked on the land, and Evan's speech was not well received by the people nor by the newspapers. The most favourable headline in the *Oklahoma Gazette* was "A JEREMIAH COMES AMONGST US – ENROUTE TO THE WHITE HOUSE".

David gloomily showed the article to his father, but then smiled. 'Still, look on the bright side,' he said. 'The headline still claims you're going to the White House.'

Evan laughed. 'True, son.' He held up his glass of milk and said, 'What do you see?'

'A glass of milk,' David replied, puzzled.

'No, I mean how would you describe it?'

David thought for a second, 'As a glass half full of milk.'

'Exactly, that proves my point. You're the eternal optimist – it's half full. A lot of people, too many, would describe the glass as half empty. It's the difference between the positive thinkers and the negative, between those who do and those who have to be told what to do.' Evan shrugged. 'It's interesting.'

'You got all that because I said the glass was half full and not half empty?'

Evan grinned. 'Sure and from my study of human nature. Oh, and from reading "*The Thoughts and Times of a Psychologist*".'

'You read that?' David asked in awe. He'd picked up the book but had given up after less than twenty pages. It was too heavy going even for a legally trained mind like his.

'Sure,' Evan let David think so for a few more seconds. 'Of course not, son. I read a summary of the book that condensed eight hundred pages into twenty. What I just said about the glass of milk took Professor Friedman about fifty pages to explain.'

They both laughed but even so, David was impressed. There was a depth to his father that he had not been aware of. An uneducated coal miner from the valleys of South Wales was erudite, not educated but better than educated – knowledgeable – and he seemed able to absorb information like a sponge. David, was now more convinced than ever that Evan would be a remarkable, possibly even a great President.

For three days they travelled across the state. As usual, at the weekend they were joined by Peter Garfield of the *St Louis Times* and Wilt Tyburn of the *Washington Post*. Both men had filed some of the best stories of Evan's campaign and were staunch supporters. At first they had reported everything, warts and all, but as the weeks had passed both men had come under the Griffiths' spell, and from neutral allies had become combative campaigners. They were now writing in a manner that, frankly, Evan found disconcerting. He was being put on a pedestal that he did not believe he deserved and he said so.

'Senator,' said Wilt Tyburn, 'the people need to believe. Since the war and then the flu when hundreds of thousands died we've been in trouble. We've got strikes and disunity across the country that's frightening. Socialists and communists are springing up all over the place as the rich get richer and the poor get poorer. You're giving hope to millions, sir, and we're with you all the way.'

'But Wilt,' Evan protested, aghast, 'I can't deliver all that! It's impossible! You know Washington as well as I do. It'll take years to put things right. What happens when the people find that their leader has failed them? What then?'

'Sir,' said Peter Garfield, 'we don't think you will fail them. The system might fail you which in turn will fail the people but we have to report that, to try and help people to understand.'

Evan nodded slowly, unconvinced but still prepared to go along with the idea. His ambition to be President was now burning white hot in him. He wanted to have his name remembered in history – he could taste the power.

The Saturday night party was well attended but by the end of the evening Evan was convinced that there were more Republicans than Democrats there. He knew that he would not win the state but, as he told David time and again, he could not win them all. Although America was dry, Washington and its laws were far away and so drink was openly served at the hotel. Evan enjoyed a glass or two of wine with his steak and potatoes and afterwards, talking to men and women around the packed room, and even an occasional whisky.

One man collared him and said, 'Senator, how do you do?' Evan shook the proffered hand. 'Can I top up that glass?' The man held up a bottle of Wild Turkey bourbon and poured some for Evan.

'Thank you kindly, sir,' said Evan and raised the glass to his lips in salute.

The man grinned back and, seeing Wilt Tyburn approaching, vanished into the crowd.

'What did he want?' Tyburn asked.

'Oh, just being friendly. Gave me a glass of bourbon,' Evan showed him.

Tyburn said, 'Oh, Hell. Where's David?'

'Why? What's wrong?'

'That was Lew Hapsgood of the *Oklahoma Gazette*. He doesn't give anybody a drink without good reason and I can guess what that'll be. Watch out for the headlines tomorrow, Senator.'

Evan could picture them and the damage they could cause. 'Damnation. I shouldn't have let my guard down like that. Fool that I am,' he castigated himself.

'Never mind. Let's find David and see if we can't work something out.'

David was talking to a group of businessmen in a corner of the room. They were discussing oil and Evan's involvement with the Crow Nation. None of the men there had any sympathy for the Standard Oil Company; many had felt its power before the anti-trust laws had come into effect. Tyburn got David away and the three men went upstairs to Evan's room.

After Evan explained what had happened he asked, 'Any ideas, son?'

David sat down, his mind whirling, ideas flashing into his head and being instantly discarded. 'I suppose strong-arming him isn't on? You know, take him for a plane ride and drop him from five thousand feet?'

'Good God,' said Tyburn. 'You are kidding, aren't you?'

David laughed, 'Of course I am. Partly. Okay, so what else can we do? Deny Dad took a drink? That's not possible. Too many people saw him do it.'

'Yes, but they had one as well,' said Evan, protesting.

'Dad, none of them are running for President.' David got up and helped himself to a malt whisky and offered one to the others. They accepted.

'Right, we need some damage limitation. The question is, how? Have you got any ideas, Wilt?'

Tyburn took an appreciative mouthful of the Perthshire whisky and looked pensively into the glass. 'David, I'm sorry, I can't think of anything. I can report events but I'm lousy at instigating them.'

'Okay, what about this? suggested David. 'His story has to appear first in the Gazette, right?'

Evan and Tyburn nodded. 'So?' asked Evan.

'So we aren't going to win this state no matter what happens, are we?' Both men agreed with him. 'Therefore, there's no damage done to the race in Oklahoma, no matter what he writes.'

'Agreed, David,' said Evan with some exasperation, 'so where does that lead us?'

'Wilt, you may not be an instigator but you're a damn fine reporter. So we need to write the story and get it on the news wires before Hapsgood gets his story out. Only we put our own slant on it. Let me think, what can that be?' David was speaking to himself. 'Got it!' he exclaimed, snapping his fingers. 'Wilt, we want something along the lines that following his night in the cold air on the Great Plains, Senator Evan Griffiths resorted to a glass of bourbon to fight the cold and cough he'd picked up during his ordeal. When asked about drinking the liquor he said to this reporter and I quote "Young man, at my age" – no, we can't say that. We want the public to think you're a young sixty something.'

'Thanks, David, I really appreciate that,' said Evan, his voice dripping sarcasm.

David grinned. 'You're welcome, Dad. Now, let me see. "When this reporter asked him, Senator Griffiths replied, "Young man, if you know of a better remedy for a cold and cough then I'll be glad to hear it. In the meantime medicinal use of liquor is still legal in Oklahoma State." How's that?'

'Pretty good,' said Tyburn. 'I can work something along those lines. Is it, by the way?'

'Is what?' asked David.

'Is liquor still legal for medicinal purposes in Oklahoma state?'

'Who knows? Who cares? And why worry? By the time anybody corrects the statement it'll be last week's news and the election will be over.'

Tyburn laughed. 'That's truly, cynically inspirational, David.'

'Why, Wilt, how very kind of you to say so.' David raised his glass in salute and took a sip of the amber liquid.

'How quickly can you get the story out?' asked Evan.

Tyburn looked at his watch. 'An hour at the most. I'll have it on all the wires before midnight.'

'Brilliant, Wilt, thanks very much. Hell, what a load of trouble I've caused by a few unthinking moments.'

'Moments, Dad?'

'Hell, son, hours, but you know what I mean. I knew I wasn't amongst friends but at least I thought I was amongst men who fight fairly. I forgot how dirty and brutal politics really is. It's a lesson I've learnt well. It's one of very many lessons I've learnt on this trip. If you two don't mind I'd like to be left alone for a while, I've got some work to do.'

When they'd gone, Evan took out a journal, sat at the desk in the corner and dipped his pen into the inkwell. He began to write. He wrote steadily and quickly, his thoughts tumbling over themselves, in a hurry to be free. He felt a driving compulsion to get his impressions down on paper so that when he became President he wouldn't forget the lessons he'd learnt.

He wrote long into the night.

39

THEIR WELCOME, WHEN they landed at St. Louis, was the biggest yet. Their Senator was back with them and the people of Missouri wanted to show their appreciation. The state capital was Jefferson City, a hundred miles to the west, but St. Louis was Evan's home town. Here he had started his business and watched it grow into a significant company that stretched across America. Many of the people who started with him now had stock in the company that had made them affluent, and a few, like Sonny McCabe, rich.

Evan had represented the territory, first in the House and then in the Senate, for nearly thirteen years. In this territory he was the undisputed king. Now that he was the front runner for the Presidency, his welcome was the sort that is reserved for conquering heroes and emperors returning home. Bands played, flags waved by the thousands and people yelled themselves hoarse. Every sentence he spoke was met with cheering and his speech had to be cut significantly, otherwise he'd have been there all day. Meg was by his side, waving to the crowd, enjoying every moment.

Eventually they got away. Their house on the edge of town had been bedecked with flags and banners and people lined the streets dozens deep, just to get a short glimpse of them. Evan walked along the street, his family around him. The crowd, though tumultuous in its welcome, kept at a respectful distance and nobody tried to hinder their progress, only to cheer it on.

Finally they arrived at the house, Evan gave one last wave and went indoors. As soon as he'd gone a chant began.

Evan frowned and looked at Meg and then the others. 'What on earth . . . ?

David suddenly laughed. 'Can't you hear it? THE WIZARD, THE WIZARD, WE WANT THE WIZARD! It worked! We've picked your nickname and it's stuck! My God, the power of this sort of persuasion is enormous. There's potential in this I need to think about. Dad, you should go back out. Take an encore.'

'I'm not an actor,' Evan protested.

'Today you are. Tomorrow you can be presidential again,' replied David.

Evan took Meg's hand and walked out on to the porch. The cheering became louder while Evan waved his hands trying to quieten them down. He waited patiently and gradually silence fell.

'Listen folks, we really appreciate your welcome . . .' Cheers drowned his voice. When they fell silent he went on, 'But now I need some rest and time with Meg. So please! Please go home and I'll see you all tomorrow!'

He waved, the crowd cheered and he and Meg went back indoors. The crowd waited outside but as the minutes dragged past and Evan didn't reappear they began to disperse. Finally, apart from a few loafers, the street emptied.

In the house there were sighs of relief. 'Thank goodness that's over,' said Meg. 'I hope that's the worst of it.'

'It should be,' said David. 'Once everybody's used to having Dad around they'll leave him alone. At least this is one state where we don't have to bust a gut campaigning.'

'What do you plan to do?' asked Madelaine, delighted that David was there with her.

'Now we write articles about his policies and send out clever missives on what Dad plans to do when he's President. Wilt Tyburn and Peter Garfield will be along later to help with all this. We blitz the newspapers in every city and town in America. I've had people working on compiling a list of every paper in every town and believe me there's an awful lot. Now, my sweet, has a box has come for me?'

'What? Oh, yes! It's in the back room. What is it?'

'Follow me and you'll see.'

Intrigued, they went together through the house behind him. David used a jemmy to pry open the lid of the box and knock out the sides. 'Voilà! One small but highly serviceable printing press.'

'What on earth do we want that for?' asked Meg.

'Mam, there are over thirty-five thousand newspapers across America. We've been in touch regularly with the most important of them, less than a hundred and fifty. Many people don't read the main city papers such as the *Washington Post* although it claims to be a national paper. What really happens is the regional and town papers get a copy of the *New York Times*, the *Post* and so on and rewrite their stories. But that's always late news, often a week or two late. Normally that doesn't matter but now, with only a week to go till the election, it does. So we want to get our news and articles to the regions in the next three days. Their papers, many of them weeklies, will hit the newstands just before the election. We write new articles, revamp some old speeches and put them onto this press. We then send them out either by Pony Express or by telegraph to all the addresses I have.'

'You'll need an army for that,' Kirsty protested.

'Spot on, Kirsty. Sonny, what have you managed?'

Sonny grinned. 'I rented the old warehouse on Union Street. It's already staffed, David, and raring to go.'

'How many do we have?'

'Helpers?' Sonny asked and David nodded. 'A hundred and seven so far with more signing up each day. I organised them the way you said, in teams of ten with one leader. The leaders report to a manager by the name of Mrs Murray – a battle-axe, but she knows her stuff. She's got everything organised and is ready to go. Free food and drink has been provided and we're paying them a dollar a day.'

'Is that all?' asked Meg.

'That and a personal introduction to the Senator,' Sonny grinned.

Evan grinned back. 'That I'll be delighted to do. Also, we should hold a party as a thank you when we finish. When do we stop sending out the articles?'

'Two days before the election,' replied David. 'Dad, I need to get to grips with this thing. Why don't you have a rest and later on go down and talk to the people. That'll buck them up.'

Evan nodded, his arm around Meg. Weariness washing over him.

Meg caught his tiredness and said, 'It's all well and good you sitting up all night in a cold and draughty barn talking to our sons but it's taken it out of you, of that there's no doubt.'

'I'll help,' said Madelaine.

'So will I,' added Kirsty.

The men looked at them in surprise. 'Why not leave the printing to us,' said Madelaine. 'You can get on with other things.'

'That's right,' Kirsty nodded. 'I'd like to contribute more than I have. You two,' she smiled at Evan and Meg, 'can play at grand-parents.'

They all laughed, Meg in particular was delighted at the notion of playing with Alexander. Nobody, except David, noticed the spasm of pain on Madelaine's face. Madelaine was desperate to become pregnant.

Evan and Meg retired to their bedroom, to chat and hug and eventually make love. For them it was a long, slow process, savoured for its anticipation rather than enjoyed for its hungry climax.

In the late afternoon Evan went down to the offices with David and Sion. When they walked through the door, they were greeted by spontaneous clapping and shouts of joy. Evan spent two hours talking to and thanking the women and the few men who were there. David had already produced an article of a single page, and Madelaine and Kirsty had printed off ten thousand copies. Now the teams began work, preparing envelopes addressed to newspapers and arranging which newspapers were to receive the article by wire. Some were phoned in to other offices, mainly along the eastern seaboard, where further dissemination of the information would take place.

David had organised an election campaign the like of which America had never seen before. In fact, no democratic country had ever seen one like it. His father came up beside him and placed a hand on his shoulder. 'Son, you're a miracle worker. If we lose it won't be for the want of trying.'

'Thanks, Dad, but we won't lose. And I'm not saying that out of arrogance. A new science, if I can call it that, is being applied to this election. It's got something to do with mathematics and trends and statistics. I'm not a mathematician so I don't pretend to understand it. It seems if you ask 1056 people how they're going to vote you can extrapolate that number to the whole of the population in that state and it'll give you an idea of how well you're doing.'

'Why an odd number like that?' Evan asked, intrigued as always by something new and innovative.

David shrugged. 'I'm not sure that's the right figure but it's something like that. If you ask too many or too few you get a distorted picture. I received a telegram just now, saying that in six of the swing states you're ahead. If you are and that trend is repeated across the country you'll win by a landslide. Even if we then say, no that's too optimistic, let's cut all the figures back, let's be pessimists,' David smiled, 'you still win.'

'Let's not count our chickens, son,' Evan gave a word of caution.

'I'm not, Dad. That's why we're doing all this. Nothing will be left to chance if I can help it. You know, it's been a fascinating few months. If it's done properly I think it's possible to wield huge power and influence. What we need to do now is to look into the question of national radio. That'll be very interesting.'

Evan laughed, 'Son, you never cease to amaze me.' He broke off and took a proffered cup of coffee. 'Thank you, Maisie.' The girl simpered, blushed and scuttled away, her joy at Evan remembering her name evident in her smile.

'How did you do that?' asked David in a whisper.

'Do what?' Evan asked, puzzled.

'Remember her name. You met dozens of people today. You can't just remember a name like that.'

'Sure I can, son. It's easy. It was a trick taught to me many years ago when I started in politics. When you get the name associate it with something ludicrous about the person. For instance, see that woman over there?'

David looked in the direction his father had indicated and said, 'Quite pretty but with a fat bottom.'

Evan nodded and smiled. 'Exactly. Her name is Astrid.' Evan slowed the word down and pronounced it again, 'Arse-strid. Verbal and visual association. It's easy after a while but you need to practise it.'

'And Maisie?'

'Look at her. A nice, simple girl, fair haired and in awe of all that's going on around here. She's amazed by it.' He slowed the word down and then added, 'And her hair is the colour of maize.'

'It's also the colour of wheat.'

'Yes, but when you're good at association you add to the idea, hence the amazed air about her. You should practice it. It's a very useful skill in business and politics.'

'I doubt I'll be going into politics, Dad.'

'We'll see, David. We'll see,' his father repeated, enigmatically.

They worked non-stop, although Evan was able to leave it to the others and he and Meg spent some time together with their two grandchildren. As predicted, after a few days, the novelty of having a future President amongst them wore off the people of St. Louis and Evan was able to walk about the town in much the same way as he had before. The only difference was that now instead of being wished good day by the passers-by, he was wished good luck.

The day of the election was bright and cold. Evan and Meg walked down to the City Hall to cast their votes, the first to do so. There were loud cheers from the crowds and soon all the polling booths were busy with men and some women casting their votes.

The day dragged by interminably. Counting wouldn't start until eight o'clock and would take all night. The results would trickle in but the final count, state on state, would take two days.

The following afternoon Sonny stopped by to have a few words with Evan, in private. He found Evan in his study, busily writing in his journal. Upset by what Sonny told him, Evan sent for David.

'What is it, Dad?'

'You tell him, Sonny.'

'David, it's none of my business,' Sonny began, but Evan interrupted him.

'Yes it is. You're the one who's gone out there to give them money and ask after her. David hasn't!' Evan spoke more harshly than he intended.

'What are you talking about, Dad?'

'Susan, is what I'm talking about. Sonny's being going there off and on for years. Giving Susan presents and Gunhild money. So he does have a right to say something. Tell him,' Evan ordered.

'Sorry, David. It's just that I saw her about half an hour ago.'

'Who? Susan?'

'Yes. And Gunhild. They came in to vote. Kallenberg had his three loutish sons with him and their wives. David, I saw Kallenberg hit Susan so hard she fell over.'

David sat down, shock and horror showing on his face. 'The bastard. The bloody, filthy bastard. She's only a kid.'

'She's almost a woman,' corrected Sonny. 'She's a tall, skinny girl who's, I don't know, who's not living in the here and now. She just takes everything her stepfather hands out and does nothing in return.'

'What about Gunhild?'

'She's as bad. There's no will to fight back. It's like . . . it's like it's been beaten out of them. David, you have to do something.'

Anger welled up like bile in David's throat. It was tainted with guilt and anguish and threatened to overwhelm him. He gripped the table to steady himself and get himself under control.

'You're right. I've ignored the problem for too long. I've made excuses to myself that I see now are just pathetic. I need to rescue my daughter before it's too late. I can't do anything to help Gunhild but I can help Susan. She won't stay another night under that man's roof. Sonny, where are they now?'

'I saw them leave town. I guess they've gone back to the farm. David, I also saw scars and a splattering of blood on her arms and legs. She's got no shoes and is wearing rags. You have to save her.'

David stood up. 'I'm on my way.'

As he spoke Sion entered the room. 'On your way where, bro'?'

In a few succinct words David told him.

'I'm coming with you,' Sion did not hesitate. 'There's three sons as well as the old man. I don't think they'll let you just walk in and take them.'

'Them?' David repeated. 'I was only going to fetch Susan.'

'You can't. What'll happen to Gunhild then? Life will be intolerable for her and it's bad enough now. She'll end up killing herself.'

'No, she won't,' said David, bitterly. 'Her religion won't allow her to. She'll be committing a mortal sin if she did. And what do I say to Madelaine if I bring Gunhild back here as well? Look dearest, let me introduce you to my old, and my first, sweetheart and my daughter?' David's voice dripped with sarcasm.

'That's a problem you'll need to solve,' said Evan. 'But I agree with

Sion. Believe me, son, Madelaine won't feel in any way threatened by Gunhild. The last time I saw her she looked like an old woman.'

'That's true, David,' said Sonny. 'If anything she looks even worse now. If ever there was a woman just waiting to die, it's her. She looks sixty, like a tragic shrivelled up old woman.'

'We can get them both,' said Sion, 'and put Gunhild in a small house somewhere. Away from here where she can live out her life in peace. Let her have her God and her priest and her rosary or whatever she needs, while you have Susan.'

David thought for a moment or two and then nodded. 'Okay, you're right. I've ignored this problem for so long I'm ashamed. Are you sure you want to come?'

'Of course, somebody's got to cover your back.'

Evan opened a cabinet and started handing out rifles and guns. Sonny took one and so did Evan.

'She's my granddaughter, and I'm coming,' said Evan.

'But, Dad,' David began to protest.

'I told you before, son, but me no buts. You coming, Sonny?'

'Sure, Mr Griffiths. I'll cover all your backs.'

Evan nodded. 'All right. We've ridden together before. Remember Roybal?'

Sonny nodded, grinning at the memory of when he, Evan and Uncle James had gone after the man who had shot Sion and also tried to rob the warehouse.

'If you come there's one condition,' added Evan.

'What's that?' Sonny scowled.

'You call me Evan. It's taken long enough.'

'Sure, Mr . . . Evan.'

Sion laughed. 'We'll all have to call him Mr President soon so don't get too used to calling him Evan, Sonny.'

'I'll tell your mother where we're going,' said Evan. 'We'll take two cars. All ready?' The three men nodded and Evan went to find Meg.

He told her what they were about to do. 'Take care, my love,' Meg whispered. 'I'm glad this is happening. It was about time this matter was dealt with.'

'We'll be back in time for supper. Let Kirsty and Madelaine know where we've gone. Try and explain to Madelaine why we need to do it. I think she'll understand.'

‘I’m sure she will. She’s a sensible, loving woman. David’s done well for himself with her.’

Evan took Meg in his arms and gave her a hug and a kiss. ‘See you later.’

He strode out the front door, a Winchester repeating rifle in his hand. The two cars were parked out the front and Evan climbed in beside David. They started along the street, Sion and Sonny following.

When they went past the post office they noticed a small group of men standing by the door, talking animatedly together. Just as they passed one of the men looked at the two cars and recognised Evan and David. He yelled after them but the cars turned at the next inter-section and were gone.

The man ran up the street yelling, ‘Mr President! Mr President! You won!’

40

THE TWO CARS quickly left the city behind. There had been snow flurries earlier but now the sky was clear, though the fresh wind made it a cold day with the promise of more snow in the air.

'We should have done this a long time ago, son,' said Evan, quietly.

David sat with his bitter thoughts for a few moments and then said, 'I know, Dad.' He gave a heavy sigh, regret and self-disgust mixed up in the action.

His father patted his shoulder, 'Still, we may not be too late.'

'How do you mean, too late?' David asked, aghast, fearful his father knew something he didn't. 'You mean, she could be dead?'

'What? No! Of course not! I mean that after years of abuse we can't tell what mental scars she's carrying. Gunhild will be the same. I doubt she'll come away with us.'

'Why ever not? We can offer her financial security and, – oh, I don't know – physical safety.

'David, have you ever seen a whipped cur? One that's beaten and booted by its owner everyday? Take it away, feed it and give it a safe and warm place to sleep and as soon as it can the cur will return to the abusive owner. And do you know why?'

'No, I can't say I do.'

'The cur begins to think that a beating is the way it's loved. It wants the attention even if it hurts. It only understands one form of treatment. So it returns to an abusive master. I've seen it before and not just with dogs.'

'But surely Gunhild won't be . . .'

'I'm not talking about Gunhild. Since Hans died and the farm went to her brothers, Kallenberg has been even worse. He expected to inherit the farm as his payoff for marrying Gunhild when she was pregnant. Hans tried everything to get her to leave but it was no good. She's been punishing herself for years for what she has come to think of as a sin. No, the problem is Susan. She's never known anything except slaps and beatings. How she's survived so far is beyond me. But all I'm saying is that she could be seriously scarred in her mind. She might not understand love and kindness, and therefore reject it. We just don't know until we get there.'

There were tears in David's eyes as he thought of the life that he had abandoned his daughter to. 'Dad, I was a coward. I should have done something years ago.'

'If you expect me to say that you weren't then I'm sorry to disappoint you, son. But so were we . . . your mother and I, that is.'

'You?' David said, in a choked voice. 'How can you possibly say that?'

'Of course we were. She's family, and we turned our backs on her.'

'But you sent money, things!' David paused. 'You sent clothes and toys. If Susan didn't get them that was hardly your fault.'

'Son, we didn't give her the one thing she needed most.'

David glanced at his father quizzically.

'We should have given her love and help. I wield more power in this state than anybody. I could have got a court order and had her out in no time. Sure, we thought about Susan, your Mam and me. But not enough. I broke my first rule – always look after the family. At the end of the day that's all we've got.' Evan lapsed into silence and for a few seconds forgot about the presidential race but thought about his granddaughter. 'It was convenient to us to salve our consciences by sending things. It's not enough, David. It can never be enough. It's . . . it's the other things that are important in our lives. Love and support, caring and helping. I'm not saying that money isn't a part of that, it is, but it's not the important part.'

'Doesn't the Bible say,' Davis spoke dryly, 'that money is the root of all evil?'

Evan laughed gently. 'No, but it's the most commonly misquoted biblical saying of all time. It actually says that the love of money is the root of all evil.' Evan paused and then added, 'I think.'

David laughed. 'Good old Dad. Never lets lack of knowledge interfere with a helpful quote even if he doesn't know it.'

'Less of the old,' Evan chuckled, 'but otherwise you're right.'

'I think we're about a mile away now. There should be a turning up ahead. Yes . . . That's it. Just over that brow and we'll be there.'

David stopped the car just before the brow of the hill and climbed out. He had been in many tight situations in his time and he wasn't about to go galloping into something he could not handle.

Evan and Sonny stayed back by the cars, leaving the reconnaissance to the younger men. Sion crouched alongside his brother, a pair of binoculars in his hands. After a few seconds of scanning the house and the surrounding fields he handed them to David.

As the dilapidated house sprang into focus the memories washed over David again. So many years ago he'd tried to persuade Gunhild to leave with him. The world, as he had learnt, was a big place – big enough to lose themselves in. Instead she had wanted to stay because of her meaningless vows to an unforgiving and cruel God. David shook his head, pushing the memories away. After a few minutes he saw an old woman walk from the barn carrying a bucket. A few seconds later he realised with a shock that it was Gunhild.

Two men came out behind her and David guessed that they were Kallenberg's sons. One of them gave Gunhild a shove, making her stumble. The liquid slopping over the bucket looked to be milk. The door opened and a small figure appeared and David knew that it was his daughter, Susan Sian, named after his dead sister. One of the men, a blonde-haired lout, took a swing at her but she avoided it and went to help her mother. David's knuckles gleamed white with the intensity of his grip on the glasses.

Sion looked at his brother and said, 'You'll crush them if you squeeze any harder.'

'What? Oh, yes,' David relaxed his grip. There was one man who would need hospitalisation later on, he thought. They returned to the cars.

'What did you see?' asked Evan.

David explained the situation.

'What's the plan, Bro? Do we go charging in like the cavalry or do we sneak in like Indians?'

'If we charge in they'll get their guns and we could have problems.

Big problems. They could harm Gunhild or Susan before we can do anything about it.'

'Why not let me go in and talk to him. After all, I'm a Senator and that must count for something.'

'I don't know, Dad. From what I've heard about Kallenberg, I don't think it'll count for much,' said David.

'I agree with David,' said Sonny. 'He's a vicious man and I wouldn't trust him an inch. He could shoot you and swear it was self defence. I'm not saying he would, mind, but I wouldn't trust him.'

'It's Gunhild's and Susan's safety we have to worry about,' said David. 'I think the safest thing to do is to try and sneak them away. Get to our own territory and let the Kallenbergs come after us. In town we'll definitely be safer.'

Evan nodded. 'That makes sense. What do you suggest?'

'I'm going over the hills and down the side. I'll get into the barn and wait there until either Gunhild or Susan comes. I'll take it from there.'

'How do we know when we should do anything? And what?' asked Sonny. 'Do you want us to approach the house? Cause a diversion? What?'

'I just don't know,' was the honest reply. 'I'm better at playing it by ear than making plans in advance. Don't forget that I've done this sort of thing before. Let's see what happens. Have you all got your guns?'

They nodded, even Evan was armed. 'Let's try not to shoot anybody,' he said. 'I'm not sure it'll do the image of my Presidency any good if the first thing that happens is that I'm indicted for murder.'

David ginned. 'Ironically, it would probably have increased your support with the Republicans, but it's too late now,' he quipped. 'Okay, a couple of useful signals. If I wave both hands in the air everything is all right and you can come down in the cars. If I lift and drop my fist, like this, then I want you in a hurry and come loaded for bear. If I put my hand on my head like this, then I want you nice and gently. All right?'

David left them watching while he sneaked through the cover towards the barn. Luckily, in common with the buildings, the land was poorly tended and there were plenty of rocks and bushes to hide behind. Sion kept his binoculars trained on the house, looking for trouble. He saw a movement out of the corner of his eye and recognised David as he reached the barn.

'He's inside. Now all we can do is wait.'

The two older men sat in one of the cars, talking business, keeping an eye on Sion. Clouds were beginning to gather in the north and it looked as though snow was on its way. Sion was getting cold, in spite of the extra clothes he had put on. Dusk was falling fast now and the visibility was rapidly getting worse. Suddenly, light appeared in the doorway of the house. He focused the binoculars and after a few seconds of straining saw that Susan was walking towards the barn. He watched her go inside.

Nothing happened for some minutes and then there was movement behind the barn. Two blurred and unrecognisable figures briefly appeared. A few minutes later David and Susan appeared and breathlessly climbed into the car with Evan and Sonny. Sion continued watching the house. He'd been in too many dangerous situations not to stay on guard until they had got away.

'I knew you'd come. I knew it. I knew that one day you'd come,' Susan was gripping David's arm tightly, frightened to let go. 'I'm not dreaming, am I? Oh, tell me I'm not dreaming. Please, don't let this be another dream.'

David put his arm around her, giving her thin body a hug, tears in his eyes. 'No, sweetheart, it's no dream. This is your grandfather and our friend, Sonny.'

Susan smiled tremulously. 'I know who it is. The next President of America.'

Evan's heart was breaking. Susan's likeness to Sian was uncanny. It was as though she'd come back to him. To them. He needed to get Susan home to Meg as quickly as possible. Surely his eyes weren't deceiving him? Damn it, he thought, she's getting blurred. He wiped the tears from his eyes and tried to speak. It came out as a croak and he cleared his throat.

'Susan, dear Susan,' Evan put his hand on his granddaughter's hand and held it tightly. 'We should have been here a long time ago. Well, it's not too late. We can go now and you'll be safe for as long as you live. Nobody will ever beat you again, I promise.'

Susan shied away, cowering into the seat, pulling her hand from her grandfather and letting go of David's arm. 'But . . . but we can't. We need to get mother. We can't go without her.'

The men were stunned. 'Of course we can,' said David. 'It's too dangerous to go back for her now we've got you.'

'But we can't. You don't understand,' Susan was pleading with them. 'He said that if I ever left he'd kill mother. That's why I've never ran away. I've tried to persuade her to come but she's always argued that we had nowhere to go. I know he means it. I won't go without her. I can't! Please! You must help her too! I can't . . . I won't go without her!'

They could see that her mind was made up, and anyway none of them wanted Gunhild's death on their conscience if, what Susan had said, was true. 'All right, Susan,' said Evan, 'we'll go and get your mother.'

Sion appeared at the side of the car and climbed in beside David. 'It's freezing out there. The snow's started and I can't see the house any longer. Hullo, Susan,' he smiled. 'I'm your Uncle Sion. What's happening?'

'We're going to get mother,' Susan said, happily. 'Oh, I knew it, I knew it.' Her happiness was contagious and the four men smiled with her.

'You knew what?' Sion asked.

'That one day you'd come. I just knew that my dreams and my prayers would come true. And now they have and we can live happily ever after.'

'I wouldn't go quite as far as that,' said David, 'but . . .'

'Sure we will, poppet,' said Evan, interrupting his son. 'You can be as happy as you want to be. Now, what do we do?'

'What'll happen if you don't return to the house?' asked her father. 'Will Gun . . . I mean, will your mother go looking for you?'

'No. She'd want to but they won't let her. I expect it'll be Herbert. He'll come looking for me, trying to touch me.'

'Touch you?' said Evan, aghast.

'Yes. He tries to put his hands on my, you know, my special parts. But I won't let him and I've always been able to dodge out of his way.'

'Is he the oaf who tried to catch you earlier on?' asked David.

'What? Oh, yes. By the house. Yes, that's Herbert.'

'Okay,' said David, 'this is what we'll do.' He outlined a plan of sorts to the others and climbed out of the car. 'You, young lady, stay here. Promise?'

'I promise,' she paused and then said, breathlessly, 'father.'

David smiled at her. 'Call me Dad. That's what I call my father. And you'd better call him Gramps.'

Evan grinned, delighted.

David returned to the barn. By now it was snowing steadily and the dusk had turned to darkness. Evan, Sonny and Sion slipped through the night and went towards the house. Evan and Sion hid on either side of the porch, while Sonny covered the back. With the arrival of the snow, the wind dropped and the landscape gradually took on a silent mantle of white. They had only been hidden for a few minutes when the door opened and a man appeared, carrying a lantern. He hurried over to the barn. A few seconds later they heard a faint noise, barely discernible in the night and somebody, carrying the lantern, reappeared. It was David.

He went straight to the porch and the others joined him.

'All right?' whispered Evan.

'Herbert won't be hitting on little girls for a very long time,' was the reply. 'Now let's go in.'

They shucked their guns and followed David. As everyone inside had been expecting the return of Herbert there was no warning given when the three entered. A few moments later there was an exclamation and an oath from one of the men sitting at the table when he saw that it wasn't his brother who had come through the door.

'Don't move!' said David. 'Nice and easy and nobody gets hurt.'

They were standing in a large kitchen come living room. At one end was the sink and stove and near them a large, old and scarred table. At the other was a fireplace, lit because of the cold, with chairs and stools either side. The room reeked of poverty, slovenliness and mangy dog.

Old Man Kallenberg hardly blinked. 'So, you've come at last for the bitches. I've been expecting you for years.' As an opening statement it surprised the three intruders. 'Sic 'em,' he said harshly and grinned.

Two dogs rose from the corner and charged, growling. David kneeled and fired twice all in one fluid movement and both dogs died before they had crossed half the room. What was also a shock to Kallenberg was the fact that, though Evan had looked at the dogs, Sion hadn't moved a muscle in their direction.

As the old man reached for his gun Sion fired his into the table top and said, 'Leave it, Kallenberg. The same goes for you two as well. Believe me, I just want an excuse.'

Apart from the three men sitting at the table an unknown girl was standing at the sink, washing dishes and Gunhild stood with a pot of food, halfway from the stove to the table. Kallenberg looked at the door.

'He isn't coming,' said Evan. 'David's already taken care of him. Gunhild, if there's anything you want, bring it now. You're coming with us.'

'No, she isn't,' said Kallenberg, 'she's staying here. She belongs to me. She does what I tell her. It is the law.' His harsh, Germanic accent was a menacing sound.

'Nobody belongs to anybody anymore,' said Evan. 'Slavery was abolished a long time ago. Is there anything you want? If so get it and come on. Susan is waiting in the car for you.'

Gunhild suddenly made up her mind. 'There's nothing I want from him. I . . . I'll come.'

She hurried towards the door, wincing in pain. David stopped her and looked at the marks on her shoulders, under the loose, thin rags she wore as a dress. He could see the welts of previous beatings and when he looked closer he saw that her legs and arms were covered with old scars.

'You bastard, you filthy scum,' he said, his voice hardly more than a whisper.

Kallenberg sneered though the tobacco stained few teeth he still had. 'I enjoyed every moment of her and when I come for her and bring her back I'll do it again. I will do it every day to remind her of this night and the death of my two favourite dogs.'

'Cover those two,' said David. He walked around the table, grabbed Kallenberg by the throat and lifted him to his feet. The old man was suddenly afraid but before he could do anything David hit him in the side in a blur of movement, accompanied by the sound of ribs cracking. Kallenberg was still conscious when David snarled at him, 'Come near her and I'll kill you. I should have done this a long time ago. You're scum, woman beating, child molesting, cowardly scum.

You two,' David turned to Kallenberg's sons, 'if I see you in St. Louis I'll have the law on you and I'll make it stick.' The two sullen faces scowled at him, hate written across their faces.

The Griffithses moved carefully towards the door. Sion was first through, Gunhild and Evan next. David paused and looked back. It saved his life. The woman at the sink had lifted down a rifle from the wall and was levering a bullet into the chamber.

With a yell David flung himself out of the door and to one side. 'Look out, the girl's got a gun.' A bullet passed harmlessly into the night. They heard chairs overturning and yells from inside. Above the noise they could hear the old man. Whatever Kallenberg was, he was as tough as they come.

'Get the guns and get them. I want them dead.'

A side door opened and the girl came out. She yelled, 'Gunhild, I hate you.' Gunhild looked back and the girl fired. The bullet hit Gunhild in the chest and she fell, the snow falling on her sightless eyes and turning pink. Evan had been nearest to Gunhild and he stopped to help her. The girl fired again and this time the bullet hit Evan knocking him off his feet.

The three Kallenbergs were out of the door and aiming guns at them. David and Sion had halted, David yelled, 'Sonny, shoot the bastards.'

Sonny had appeared from around the corner, seen what had happened and with his first shot, killed the girl. David and Sion opened fire in a fusillade of shooting, many of the bullets finding their marks. Old man Kallenberg fired three more shots, all at Evan, before he died. Suddenly the sound of gunfire stopped and an eerie silence descended over the farm. David rushed to his father, Sion with him. To their relief they saw that Evan was still breathing.

'Dad, Dad, take it easy. We'll get you home,' said David. He was appalled at the blood seeping into the snow and over his hands. He cradled his father, tears in his eyes.

'It's all right, son,' said Evan, in a hoarse whisper. 'I know it's over. I never could see beyond winning. I never could see the presidency itself. Listen, listen both of you.' He gripped his sons' arms, coughed blood and after a few seconds he rallied his strength. 'Remember, it's always . . . always the family first. You must always look after the family. Promise me . . .' Evan's head sank back, the last breath a faint rattle.

David and Sion knelt there, horror stricken, sad beyond words.

'What do we tell Mam?' Sion whispered.

BOOK 5

David's Story

41

Spring 1924

SHE WAS A sixty foot motor sailor built by William Osborne of Deal, Kent. The oak ribs were nine inches apart and the hull and deck was half inch Canadian Rock Pine. She was an incredibly strong boat and had become my pride and joy, hence the name, *My Joy.*

She carried a foresail, mainsail and a mizzen. Her single screw was driven by the new Perkins S6 diesel engine and she could cruise at 8 knots. Her draft was only four feet six inches, even though her gross tonnage was 32 tons, so she needed the engine. Without it, as she had no keel, she would have slid over the water and been almost impossible to hold to a steady course. With the screw biting and the sails in full use she could attain speeds of 10 or 11 knots.

The wheelhouse was situated a third of the way back from the bow and could seat six people in comfort. The engine room was directly below and I could lift a hatch and drop down into it if I needed to. From the wheelhouse was a short set of steps led into a corridor. On the port side was the chart house and on the starboard side a cabin with two bunks. Aft of that, the corridor ended and the door opened onto a stateroom with a galley in the furthest corner. A door at the back of the stateroom led to another short corridor on either side of which were two cabins and another flight of steps up through the dog hatch – a sliding hatch with a set of ladders – and onto the small, aft deck.

Forward of the wheelhouse was the crews quarters and storage cupboards. I never carried a crew as I enjoyed the challenge of sailing her myself. She was a beautiful little ship.

That day we were sailing from Dover to Calais with a fair wind on our starboard beam and looking forward to dinner at one of the French restaurants situated around the harbour.

As I stood with the wheel in my hands I thought about the last two and a half years following Gunhild's and my father's death. He had won the Presidency by a landslide but, because he hadn't been sworn in, another election was called and this time, without us, the Republicans scraped through. Warren Gamaliel Harding was President and Calvin Coolidge, the Vice-President.

At the time we didn't give a damn one way or another. We had our own problems to contend with. Mam was amazing. She wept, railed against fate and appeared on the verge of collapsing. Then, just a day after the funeral, she pulled herself together and took charge of her affairs, albeit a shadow of her former self. We agreed that she should move back to Britain and I persuaded her not to go to Wales but to join us in London.

We began to unbundle our business interests in America and started by selling the warehouses to Sonny. Our own bank put up the cash and now held a twenty percent stake in the business. Sonny took the rest of the shares along with a substantial loan. I hadn't realised how many businesses my father had involved himself in over the years but there were over twenty to dispose of, although mostly he had been a minority shareholder. The house in St Louis was sold quickly and Mam moved all her possessions to Washington before shipping them back to England.

It had taken nearly two years to dispose of the accumulated assets but finally it was done. Mam was a multi-millionaire who would have given away every penny to return to Llanbeddas and their first house if she could have had Dad with her.

For most of that time Susan was a problem. She was prone to tantrums, petulant moods and open hostility. She blamed us for Gunhild's death, started wetting the bed at night and often couldn't be found as she wandered around Washington on her own. She was a very disturbed and lonely child who did her best to spoil my relationship with Madelaine. It was exactly a year before all that changed.

I don't know the full details because neither Mam nor Susan would talk about it. All I know is that on the anniversary of the death of Dad and Gunhild, Mam and Susan became inseparable. It seems that Mam had heard Susan crying in her room and had joined her, Mam shedding her own tears and sharing her own heartache. From then on there was understanding between them, and a permanent bond was forged. They were good for each other and came to terms with their mutual loss by sharing their grief.

By now, Susan's physical scars had healed and, thanks to Mam, the mental scars were beginning to fade as well. Susan stopped being so difficult and my relationship with Madelaine was once more back on an even keel. Although we continued to try, Madelaine did not become pregnant and so we gave up trying quite so hard. Accepting the inevitable I think was a relief to both of us.

When we had finally left America we had sailed aboard the *SS Plymouth*, the latest liner in the Buchanan Shipping Line.

Mam and I stood at the stern watching the lights of New York fade in the gloom of the autumn night, a feeling of melancholy becoming a cloak about our shoulders.

Mam put her hand on my arm, tears in her eyes. 'Oh, David, I can't believe it. Where's the time gone? It was only a short while ago that we arrived with so much to look forward to; so much excitement and adventure ahead of us. Now I can only look back and wonder where the time went.'

'But you achieved so much, Mam. You've had a wonderful life and there's still years ahead of you to enjoy.'

Mam looked up at me, sadly, 'That's spoken with the optimism of, shall we say, relative youth?' Mam suddenly smiled. 'It all goes past so quickly. Just as the preacher said at your father's funeral. What were his words again?'

'Man who is born of woman has such a short time to live?' I paraphrased.

'Something like that. Anyway, sad but apt. We had a wonderful life, David, and apart from Sian's death I regret none of it. However, it's forward we have to look. We need to get Susan educated properly and I'm not sure how we should do that.'

'Private school?' I suggested.

'My granddaughter isn't going away from home, David Griffiths, and don't you forget it.'

I smiled, pleased that Mam was showing some of her legendary spirit. She shivered. 'Come, let's go down to the bar and enjoy a large brandy. It will be nice to take a legal drink after all this time.'

We strolled along the deck, Mam with her hand under my arm. 'I think we need private tutors for Susan,' said Mam. 'To begin with, anyway.'

'You've obviously given this a lot of thought. What does Susan say?'

Mam smiled. 'I wasn't a school teacher for nothing, David. I've spent months getting the idea of an education into her head. She wants it now. She can read and write in English and German but any other knowledge is sadly lacking. Will you let me make what I think are the right arrangements for her?'

I was relieved at the suggestion and agreed with alacrity. In the bar we were joined by Madelaine and a short while later, by Susan. She had been on a guided tour with one of the ship's officers who appeared to pay her more attention than I appreciated. It was at that moment that I realised Susan was becoming a young woman and was hardly a child any longer.

I looked at Madelaine who appeared to be reading my thoughts, judging by the look that she gave me. That evening my wife was looking radiant. Madelaine wore a low cut, floor length gown the wine red colour of which suited her beautifully. Thankfully, John Buchanan joined us at that moment and Susan's young officer vanished.

'Did you enjoy the tour?' he asked Susan.

'Oh, yes, thank you Mr Buchanan,' Susan replied.

John smiled at her and said, 'Susan, please call me John.'

'I think,' said Mam to Susan, 'Uncle John would be more appropriate. John's as close as anybody in the family and closer than most.'

'I'd like that,' said John, smiling at Susan, who nodded and smiled back. I caught Mam's wistful glance at her and I could see that Mam was thinking about Sian. Whenever she did, that same look appeared on her face. I was no longer certain about the resemblance between my dead sister and my daughter; Susan was changing while Sian was frozen in time.

We sat with the Captain for dinner that night and John and Mam regaled us with stories of the crossing during which they had first met. They had us in fits of laughter, especially over the catty remarks that had been made about Mam and Dad. John looked debonair that evening and paid particular attention to Mam which pleased me. It was all very enjoyable and lasted until after midnight, when we finally went to our cabins.

In our stateroom I poured a night-cap and began to undo the buttons on Madelaine's dress.

'Do you know,' she said, smiling, 'I think John's in love with Meg.'

I laughed. 'Don't be ridiculous. That's impossible. They're just friends.' I was scandalised at the idea.

'Wait a second, darling, think about it. Your mother is still a very good looking woman and John is certainly a handsome man. Evan has been dead for two years and your mother deserves all the happiness she can get. No, I think it's time for those two to be more than friends.'

Madelaine had to encourage me back into the mood I'd been feeling only moments earlier.

As I put the wheel over and *My Joy* turned a few points to starboard I brought my mind back to the present. John came into the wheel house with a cup of coffee and sat on the bench over the hatch to the engine room.

Because my head had been full of the memories of that last Atlantic crossing I said, 'John, can I ask you something?'

'Sure, David. Ask anything you like.'

I took a deep breath and said, 'What are your intentions towards my mother?'

'What? Why, you young whippersnapper,' John sat bolt upright and glared at me. 'You can't ask me questions like that!'

'Why not? You do love her, don't you?'

'Don't be ridiculous,' he denied the allegation. 'She's a friend, that's all. Always has been and always will be.'

I looked at John and much to my surprise I could have sworn that he blushed, something I would have thought impossible.

I laughed. 'John, you do love her,' I spoke with wonder and then I surprised myself. 'Go for it, John. I know she's fond of you, and perhaps there's even more to it than that, I don't know. But she deserves all the happiness she can get and if you're the one to give it to her then you should.'

John was silent for a few seconds. 'You wouldn't mind? I mean, you know.'

'Of course I'll mind . . . but not much. You think of your parents, particularly your mother, as a . . . a Madonna. You don't think about IT. Then as we get older we realise that love and love-making goes on from Susan's age to well, Mam's.

John laughed with delight. 'Thanks, David. I'm going to woo your Mam like she's never been errm . . .'

'Yet,' I suggested.

'Yet,' he agreed and we both laughed. At that moment Mam joined us and wanted to know what the joke was but we side-stepped the question.

We had a full house on the cruise that weekend. Apart from the three of us Madelaine, Susan, Angus and his wife of three months, Catriona were aboard. Angus had finally seen the sense of moving to London with Catriona and marrying her. He was now once again working with me in the bank and enjoying his life as a doting husband and soon-to-be father. Thankfully, Catriona and Madelaine had become friends and it seemed that my wife was looking forward to Catriona's baby almost as much as Catriona herself was.

'Susan,' I yelled below, 'do you want to take the wheel?'

The words were hardly out of my mouth when her black, curly head appeared from below and she nimbly climbed the steps.

'Move over, Dad,' she said, 'and let an expert have a go!'

I smiled. 'Here you are. Now, there's five ships out there, none on a steady bearing.' I pointed them out to her. 'That white smidgen you can see over there,' I pointed, 'is the lighthouse we're heading for. Keep her steady. I'll be sitting outside, enjoying the sun.'

'Aye, aye, sir,' she gave a mock salute and I grinned at her. She was, as far as I could tell, a normal, happy young lady. I was grateful for that and grateful to my mother for all that she had done to help her.

While the women prepared a light lunch, John, Frazer and I sat behind the wheel house and discussed international politics in general and banking in particular.

'Germany is bankrupt,' said John. 'A two-kilo loaf of bread was selling for 34,000,000 marks one day and the next it was 480,000,000. It costs more to buy the paper and print the money than the money is worth. It's a nonsense which will end in real tragedy.'

'What sort of tragedy?' I asked.

'The rise of Hitler is inevitable,' said Frazer, 'and if he comes to power I think war will follow. In fact, if not Hitler, it will be someone like him. Don't forget that Lloyd George predicted another war five years ago.'

'You can't be sure of that,' I argued, 'and neither can Lloyd George.'

'No, of course not,' said John, 'but I agree with Angus and, though I hate to admit it, the Welsh Windbag himself, Lloyd George. The affair in the beer hall last year was a start. Hitler's prison sentence is a joke and he'll be out in a few months. The Nazis are fascists and anti-Semitic and have received huge encouragement from Mussolini's win in the Italian general election. Europe is going to hell in a basket and there seems little we can do about it.'

'Except make a profit,' I said.

John suddenly grinned. 'Except, as you so rightly say, make a profit. Thank God for the Channel. It keeps us apart and relatively safe. Right, what's been happening at the bank?'

Angus and I brought John up to date about our latest activities, including the details on the substantial loan we'd made to Germany. Along with the American government, in the form of a banker named Charles Dawes, we'd underwritten ten percent of the £45 million loan to the Germans. It was secured by a lien on German taxes, the railways and certain industries. The interest charged was 4.8%. Our Sovereign Trust paid 4.5% and we made 0.3% from the transaction. Altogether it was a highly satisfactory state of affairs.

'How are we placed with the radio contract?' John asked.

'Following the King's broadcast when he opened the British Empire Exhibition, we're able to invest in the new independent wireless company without any difficulties,' said Frazer. 'There's a report back at the office for you to read. Did you know that the King's message to himself went from London to Canada, New Zealand, Australia, South Africa, India, Aden, Egypt and Gibraltar before coming back to London, all in one minute twenty seconds? Overnight, the world has shrunk. Live music from the Savoy Hotel was clearly heard in John O'Groats and now people are rushing to invest. It's an exciting time for radio and we're right at the heart of it.'

'Good. What about the newspaper?' John asked.

'We can take a ten percent stake in the Chronicle. The money will be used for new presses and a new method of setting type which is faster and cleaner,' I replied. 'Based on what I've seen I don't think we can lose.'

'Good. And finally what about Imperial Airways?'

'Sion is rubbing his hands with glee. The government issued a statement yesterday promising to subsidise the new company. The four companies involved will amalgamate in about ten days. We'll put it all together, thanks to Sion, and will charge a substantial fee for doing so,' I replied. 'There will be thirteen aircraft flying from Croydon within three weeks.'

'That's an unlucky number,' said Frazer.

'Only for some,' I said, 'but not for us. Sion's contracted to supply another three planes, each carrying twelve passengers. He's started building them already.'

'How many engines?' John asked.

'Two, I think. We'll visit him when we get back and see how he's progressing.'

Mam appeared and called us down to lunch. Susan was happy on the wheel and we left her to it, going down below into the saloon.

Halfway through lunch the *My Joy* heeled hard to starboard, the crockery and food went flying and I leapt through the door and the stairs to the wheel house, my heart in my mouth.

42

SUSAN HAD THE engine in reverse and we were turned into the wind, stopped.

'What's wrong?' I asked.

She pointed out of the window and I followed her finger.

'Good grief!' I ejaculated. There, less than twenty yards away was a submarine.

'I saw the top of the thing sticking out right in front of me. I didn't know what it was so I turned hard away and stopped the engines.' Her lower lip trembled and I could see that she was on the verge of tears.

I put my arms around her and for a second she tensed as though she expected to be hit. For all the improvements there had been there was still the residue of fear left, and she still half-expected any error to be punished. I gave her a tight hug, listening as the others came up from below to find out what was going on.

'You did exactly the right thing,' I kissed her forehead. 'We could have had a very serious accident if you hadn't been so alert. Thanks, Susan.' She hugged me back, a tremulous smile hovering on her mouth.

'I was scared. That horrible black thing scared me to death.'

I nodded, not at all surprised. It had taken very fast reactions to see the danger, assess the problem and avoid an accident.

'Where did that come from?' Mam asked, staring at the black tower.

'Under the sea,' I said, dryly.

'No, I mean, silly,' Mam poked me in the ribs with a finger and winked at Susan who giggled, 'which country does it belong to?'

We exchanged shrugs. As was normal with submarines there was no name showing and no flag flying. Suddenly we saw movement on the top of the tower and a number of bodies appeared. An upper-crust English voice yelled across to us. 'I say, old chap, can you tell us the way to Portsmouth? We appear to be a little bit lost.'

We laughed uproariously and I pointed in the opposite direction to the one they were going. 'It's a hundred miles that way.'

'Damn it! I thought we'd come too far!' With that they vanished from sight and a few seconds later there was a blowing and snorting from around the submarine and it sank beneath the waves.

'That was great,' said Susan, excited now that the incident was past.

'It certainly was,' said Mam, 'but lunch is ruined.'

'Oh! I'm really sorry,' Susan said. 'But there wasn't anything else I could have done.'

I was pleased to see her stick up for herself. Perhaps she had healed faster and better than we had thought.

'I'm sure there wasn't,' said Madelaine. 'Come on, let's clean up and make a few sandwiches. That'll do for now. David, are you staying here to keep watch?'

I looked at Madelaine, and was on the verge of saying yes, when out of the corner of my eye I saw Susan's face. 'Of course not,' I said. 'Susan's showed what a great job she can do. If she's happy then she can continue on the wheel. Let's get the boat on track and moving again and the sails positioned.'

Susan nodded, relieved. A few minutes later we went below to clean up the mess, which wasn't too bad, and we left Susan once more in charge. I managed to stay away for nearly fifteen minutes before rejoining her in the wheel house. My excuse was to offer her a sandwich.

We reached port an hour before sunset. Once we were safely secured alongside John and Frazer went ashore to buy some wine and a few bottles of Cognac while the ladies took a saunter to find a restaurant for later. I busied myself about the boat, filling the water tanks and checking the diesel. The *My Joy* could cruise for upwards of a thousand miles without refuelling but I liked to check in case we'd lost diesel somehow, like through a leaking tank or pipe connection. As the diesel would accumulate in the bilges and get pumped out when the new electric bilge pumps were switched on, I had no way of telling how much diesel we still carried unless I physically dipped the tanks.

I sat down on a deck chair to enjoy the setting sun, a warm coat on and a small glass of malt whisky in my hand. At that precise moment I felt that life was pretty good and couldn't get much better.

I was wrong.

The following day, when we returned to Brighton, we were sitting around in the saloon enjoying a glass of wine. It was raining but we were warm and snug where we were. That was when life got better.

Madelaine was sitting next to me and nobody was taking any notice of us and she whispered, 'I'd better not have a drink.'

'Why not?' I whispered back.

She looked radiant, her eyes sparkling, her mouth stretched in a wide smile. 'Because I'm going to have a baby.'

I sat there stunned, my mouth agape, happiness welling within me, threatening to choke me. 'What! What? How?' I spluttered.

She burst out laughing, 'The usual way, you ninny.'

Mam looked at us and surprised me by saying, 'Good. You've told him at last! Congratulations to you both.'

'What? You knew?'

'Yes, Madelaine and I have been aware for a few weeks, only she just wanted to make certain before she told you, not to risk disappointing you.'

The evening became a party.

At first I was apprehensive about Susan's reaction to the news but she seemed delighted, hoping she'd have a baby brother to boss around. Now I felt that life was really complete.

The following morning we returned to London. There was the usual chaos in the office after we'd been away for a few days but everything was soon under control. Life settled down and I began to think seriously about leaving London to live in the country.

What finally made up my mind for me was the fourth pea-souper of a fog in as many days. With a million and a half chimneys belching out smoke, along with the exhaust fumes of thousands of vehicles, London had been prone to thick fogs ever since the 1890s. It usually happened when we had a spell of calm weather with no wind to blow the smoke away. We had a new name for the phenomenon and called it smog.

Whenever it struck, Frazer would have a fit of coughing which was not good for him and I began to worry whether it was the right place to bring up a baby. Madelaine agreed with me and so I began buying a copy of the magazine *Country Homes* looking for a suitable house. In fact, I was looking for an estate. I found one at a place called Ovingdean, a few miles east of Brighton.

I took Mam, Madelaine and Susan with me to see it. Most of the land had been sold but the house still had fifty acres, stables and various outhouses and sheds. There was also a dowerhouse and I gave Mam the option of living in it or living in the main house with us. She opted for the main house, much to our pleasure.

'Isn't it a bit big?' Madelaine asked.

'Nonsense,' I replied. 'We need servants, a nursery, a room or two for the baby's nanny . . .' I didn't get any further. There was an explosion of disagreement and I was told in no uncertain terms that there would be no nanny. With a mother, grandmother and older sister, my son or daughter wouldn't need anybody else. Three women to one seemed a bit unfair already! I made the mistake of telling them that and was severely reprimanded.

It was settled. Although a great deal of refurbishment was needed, it was still a beautiful house with magnificent grounds. In the distance I could see the sparkling water of the Channel. I felt at peace with the place – somehow I felt it fitted me like a worn and favoured coat.

I haggled over the price as a matter of form. In the end I had to pay fifteen thousand pounds for the property, but it was worth it. An army of workmen was hired and I spent as much time supervising the renovations as I did at the bank. Sion came down and spent a few hours deciding where we were to put the runway. When he left us to return to Biggin Hill we had decided on the exact location and I made the necessary arrangements. When he next returned, it was by the Griffin.

'Dad, can I start learning to drive?' asked Susan, taking me by surprise one day.

'What? No, of course you can't. What brought this on?'

'In the papers was the fact that the House of Lords is discussing a driving test to reduce accidents. I wanted to learn before I have to sit a test. That was all.'

'Young lady, I think age twenty will be early enough for you to learn to drive a car. Don't you?'

'No, I don't! That's ancient, Dad. I can learn now.'

'Sweetheart,' I said, 'you can't even reach the pedals properly. So no, you can't learn to drive yet.'

She flounced out of the room. Mam watched her go. 'Well, there's no doubt whose daughter she is.'

'What do you mean?'

'David, she is so like you, it's uncanny.'

'Me?' I was surprised.

'Exactly like you. Oscar Wilde was wrong.'

'Mam, what on earth are you talking about now?'

'We've just been reading an Oscar Wilde play, The Importance of being Earnest. In it, Algernon says all women become like their mothers. That is their tragedy. No man does. That's his. Luckily, that isn't the case with Susan. She's the spit and image of you.'

I was wondering whether that was a good thing or not when I heard an engine revving. I looked out the window and saw Susan behind the wheel of my sports car. I ran for the door, threw it open and was in time to watch the back wheels of the car spin, grip and send the car flying down the drive. I yelled at her to stop.

She did when she smashed into the pillar at the end of the drive.

43

I RAN DOWN THE drive. The front of the car was buckled in, the engine had stopped and Susan's head was on the horn. The raucous noise blasted the air apart and filled me with dread. As I reached the car I heard a low moan and I gently lifted her head from the steering wheel. There was blood on her face from a gash across her forehead and she moaned again as her eyes fluttered open.

Susan looked at me and said, 'Sorry, Dad,' and closed her eyes.

I was relieved to learn she was alive and almost conscious, and lifted her from the car. Mam and two of the servants arrived and between us we carried her back to the house. We put her to bed and waited impatiently for the doctor to arrive.

When he did, he didn't take long to reach his conclusion. 'She's got concussion. She needs rest, but she should be all right in a day or two. When she wakes up give her one of these Aspirin. They're ideal for a headache. She'll be up and about soon enough.' With that he left.

I was relieved and angry at the same time. I wanted her to wake up right then so that I could give her a piece of my mind. Luckily for her by the time she was well enough to take a telling-off my anger had cooled from boiling hot to barely tepid. She was either a consummate actress or genuinely upset, but either way I didn't have the heart to scold her too much. I did lecture her and she agreed that I could teach her to drive, she also agreed not to go off the estate. After all, we had the driveway and the runway so she had plenty of room to practice.

I also agreed that Sion could teach her to fly. How in the world she got me to agree to that I still don't know, but agree I did.

When she recovered she had a reminder of the incident in the form of a thin scar across her forehead. It would be many years before it faded away entirely. I spent a number of hours with her, showing her the rudiments of driving and was pleasantly surprised that she picked up the skill so quickly.

Sion arrived a fortnight later in the Griffin.

'I've brought the new tri-motor design for the passenger plane,' he said, walking into my study, a sheath of papers rolled under his arm. 'I thought you'd like to see it.' He unrolled them on my desk and showed me the drawings. 'I've decided to put an engine on each wing as well as on the nose. I reckon it'll cruise with two engines and land with only one. Most importantly, I think we'll have a speed of about 180 mph which will make it one of the fastest passenger planes in the world.'

'How many passengers will it carry?'

'Sixteen. There's a galley just here,' he pointed at the rear, 'and a toilet here.' He broke off as the door opened. 'Hullo, Susan.'

'Uncle Sion,' she skipped in, excitedly, 'has Dad told you?'

'Told me what?' Sion frowned at me.

'About me learning to fly. He said you'd teach me. He promised.'

'Huh?' Sion looked at me aghast. I mentally pleaded with him to go along with it and hoped my thoughts had reached him. They had not. 'I can't do that! It's impossible!'

'Why not?' Susan pouted. 'Dad said you would. Why can't you?'

Sion looked from her to me and back to Susan. 'Because, errm, because,' then he said the most stupid thing he could, 'you're a girl.'

That led to an argument. Ten minutes later Susan smiled and left the room. Sion looked at me, shell-shocked. 'Did I just promise what I think I just promised?' he asked.

I grinned. 'Yes, bro', you did. I don't know how she does it. She doesn't take no for an answer and wears you down. She did it to me after she smashed up the car. I've been teaching her to drive.'

'Driving is one thing,' said Sion, 'flying is another.'

I shrugged. I couldn't agree with him more. We spent another hour going over the plans. 'I think this could be a winner,' I said. 'Imperial gets the first three. Any other markets?'

Sion scowled. 'Only in America, right now. The trouble is there's real competition there, with Boeing and Douglas. Still, airlines are popping up all over the place so I might sell some. I think a lot will depend on how Imperial find the planes.'

The door opened and Susan came in wearing jodhpurs and a warm jacket. 'I'm ready, Uncle Sion.'

'What? Oh, errm, yes. Well, I wasn't thinking we'd be able to start today. I'm in a hurry . . .'

He may as well have saved his breath.

I watched them take off. They came round and landed and took off again. They did that six times, running circuits, Sion called it. When the plane finally came to a stop Susan climbed out and ran and skipped towards me, quivering with excitement.

'It's wonderful,' she yelled. 'I'm off to tell grandma.'

Sion sauntered up, a thoughtful look on his face.

'How did she do?' I asked.

He frowned and then surprised me. 'Amazingly well. She's a natural. David, I've taught a lot of men how to fly and few, if any, have her . . . what should I call it? Flair? Feel for it? I don't know. I only know she's a natural. When we touched down that last time I hadn't realised that we were on the ground for a second or two.'

'That was Susan?' I asked, shocked and pleased at the same time.

'She did three of the take-offs and two landings. Now she needs to learn how to navigate. You can teach her that. Or, better still, John can.'

'Hang on, Bro, I'm not so sure. I don't want to encourage her too much.'

'You aren't going to stop her, David. She's got the bug. She'll fly with or without your blessing. With it, she'll learn properly. Without it,' he shrugged, leaving the sentence hanging between us.

Susan took every opportunity to fly. Throughout the spring and into the summer she was to be found reading about flying or navigation and took every opportunity to take a flight with Sion. Mam encouraged her and John taught her a great deal about navigation.

Mam and John were getting on well and spent a considerable amount of time with each other. I was pleased for them both. Madelaine was getting bigger by the day and grumpier by the minute. It didn't help that we had a heat wave that summer but at least we were near the coast and out of the city and so the sea breezes helped to cool things down.

The baby was due in early January and, as far as I was concerned, couldn't come soon enough. I had the distinct feeling that Madelaine thought so too!

In late June I had a summons to the House of Commons. Stanley Baldwin wanted to talk to me. As he was the Tory leader I was intrigued enough to go. Also the fact that the invitation was couched in such polite terms made me highly curious. At that time the Labour Party was in power, led by the Scotsman, Ramsay MacDonald. It was a coalition government and was kept in power by the Liberals. MacDonald had stated back in January, when he originally formed the government, that he didn't expect to be in power for long. Since then the newspapers had been rife with rumours about the government's immediate fall.

I met Baldwin in the hall of the Commons. To look at he was fairly non-descript, of medium height, clean shaven with greased hair sporting a centre parting. However, he was currently considered the most astute politician in Britain.

'Ah, Griffiths, good of you to come,' we shook hands and I followed him along the corridors to his office. There I found Winston Churchill and John Buchanan. Baldwin went on, 'You know both these gentlemen, I believe. Take a seat while I pour a drink. Winnie, what will you have?'

'A whisky,' was the gravel-voiced reply.

John and I also settled for whiskies. By now my curiosity was burning and white-hot but I endeavoured to show no sign of it.

'Sir John, perhaps you'll explain to Griffiths why I asked him to come.'

John nodded. 'You know the Government's in a mess. We think the PM will have to call a general election before Christmas.'

I nodded, that was also my assessment.

'We want to be ready. Two days ago we had a meeting to discuss the fortunes of the Tory party and how we can best position ourselves should MacDonald call a snap election.'

'That makes sense,' I frowned. 'But what's that to do with me?'

'I was telling Winnie about the campaign you masterminded for Evan,' said John.

I looked at Churchill who was nodding slowly, a fat cigar in one hand and a whisky in the other. 'Quite so, David. I was very impressed.

Although I shall be standing as a Constitutionalist I will be offered a job in the Cabinet. But first, we have to win.'

'Exactly,' said Baldwin, leaning forward in his chair. 'And we want you to run our campaign. What do you say?'

I wasn't surprised by the question but needed time to think about it. 'I'm not sure. I'm very busy with the renovations to the house and I'm up to my neck in work. I need to go to Germany soon to see things for myself and I was also planning a trip to Spain to visit family friends. It takes organisation and dedication to run an election campaign. Oh, and a great deal of money as well.'

Baldwin made a dismissive gesture with his hand, spilling a few drops of whisky. 'Money we've plenty of. Willing helpers and a supportive press, the same. What we lack is organisation. With the Labour Party it's completely the other way. Their organisation is first class but they don't own the presses and have very little money. What do you say, Griffiths?'

My immediate thought was what was in it for me? Not in financial terms. After all, I had more money than I could spend in a lifetime, provided I didn't go mad and gamble it all away. And, in spite of the high taxes that the Labour Government demanded, the fact of the matter was I thought it was money well spent. We needed an educated and trained working class if we were to compete in the world.

'A baronetcy,' Churchill said.

'Huh?' I looked at him in surprise and guilt.

'You were wondering what your reward would be. You've plenty of money and no direct interest in politics so I take it you don't want a seat, so we'll give you a baronetcy in the King's Birthday Honour's List next year. If we win,' he added with a smirk and a self satisfied pull on his cigar.

I mentally squirmed, wondering if my avarice was so obvious. Luckily, John put me out of my misery.

'I suggested it, David. A hereditary baronetcy for you and an Earldom for me.'

'For you?'

'Yes. I'd work with you to get the Tories elected. The hereditary title of Earl is meaningless as I have nobody to leave it to. No siblings, sons or nephews. But it'll be nice to be an Earl.' John grinned at me.

Knowing John the way I did I figured there was more to it than that. He had something up his sleeve but at that moment I didn't know what.

'When do you want to know?' I asked.

'Today. Now,' said Churchill glowering.

'How much of a free hand do I get?'

'What do you mean?' asked Baldwin.

'In America I controlled the finances and made all the decisions. Money was no object and although I didn't spend it willy-nilly I also did not need to refer to anybody about what I was doing.'

'That can't happen here. We have committees and procedures,' said Baldwin. 'The former has to approve the latter and there's no way around it.'

I drained my glass and stood up. 'Thank you, gentlemen, for your time. I thought you wanted to win, not play games. Good day to you.'

'Sit down, sir,' Churchill growled at me, 'and stop being a prima donna. You just heard the Party line and it's the one for consumption outside this office. You will have access to one hundred thousand pounds to spend as you see fit. You will account for the money in the usual way but you will be the only signatory to the account.'

Instead of sitting I wandered across to a sideboard and poured myself another drink. I needed a few moments to think. One hundred thousand pounds was a fortune and they weren't playing at politics. They wanted power and, more importantly, they wanted to stop Labour. For a second I couldn't understand why they wanted it so badly and then it came to me. Labour's new inheritance tax would crucify Tory landowners from John O'Groats to Lands End. One hundred thousand was a flea bite by comparison. So that was it. They needed to stop the finance bill Labour had proposed. The Liberals would not be supporting it and hence there would be a need for another election. If Labour won an outright majority nothing would stop the bill's passage, not even the House of Lords.

I told the three men what I thought. Baldwin looked stunned, Churchill chuckled and John laughed out loud.

'I told you he was smart,' said John. 'And you didn't let me down, David. You've got it in one. The hundred thousand was my idea. I told them they wouldn't get you if there were strings to the campaign. Or at least, too many strings. You won't get carte blanche but you'll have a pretty free hand.'

I nodded. 'All right. It's a deal.' I shook hands with the three men and a short while later John and I left.

We went to the United Services Club where John ordered a bottle of champagne.

'What's the occasion?' I asked, taking a sip of the finest Krug.

'I want to marry your mother,' he said, causing me to choke on the wine.

44

WHEN I GOT my breath back I asked, 'What does Mam say about it?'

John looked shocked. 'Good Grief, I haven't asked her yet! I wanted to speak to you first.'

'I think you may have things the wrong way around,' I said, dryly.

He looked at me in puzzlement. 'What do you mean?'

'Mam makes her own mind up. I don't do it for her.'

'David, don't you know that as far as she is concerned you're the head of the house now? I need to get your, what shall I call it? Blessing? Yes, blessing, before I talk to her. That way I may have a chance of getting her to accept.'

'Where would you live?' I asked, playing for time, my mind seething in thought.

John shrugged. 'I want to retire. I'll do so and live with your mother in the dowerhouse. Or we could live in London. Or we could take a ship around the world and not come back. Who the hell cares where we live? As long as it's where your mother wants to be.'

'Calm down, John. I didn't mean anything by it. It's just that Mam's looking forward to the baby, wants to be around Susan, sees a lot of Sion and Kirsty and the kids. The dowerhouse would suit me but so would the main house. It all depends on what you both want.'

'You mean . . . ?' he smiled at me.

'Of course, I mean. I just hope she accepts you. If she doesn't I'll give her a severe talking to,' I grinned. 'There's one proviso.'

'Anything. Just name it.'

'You don't expect me to call you Father or Dad.' We both laughed uproariously.

John accompanied me to the house, now named "Fairweather", the next day. I wished him luck, shook his hand and walked with him into the library. Mam was there with Susan. I collared my daughter, dragging her away and left the two of them to it.

I hovered around outside the door, waiting to find out what Mam would do. I didn't have long to wait. The door slammed open and John stalked out, his face like thunder. He brushed past me and went through the front door before I could ask him what she had said, although it did not take much imagination.

I stormed the other way, into the library, ready to remonstrate with her. Instead I found Mam in tears and the words I had been about to use froze on my lips.

'Mam, what is it? Why are you crying?' I knelt beside her chair.

'Oh, David. I feel such a fool. So ashamed. John asked . . .'

'I know. He asked my permission before hand.'

'You knew?' she was aghast. 'You knew and said nothing? Didn't warn me? Prepared me for . . . for the humiliation?'

'Humiliation? What on earth are you talking about? He's just done you the honour of asking you to marry him. He's been in love with you for years. He's a fine man, a gentleman of whom you can be proud to call husband. And you feel humiliated? Good God, Mam, I don't believe it.'

'Oh, David. It's your father. He was the only man for me. I've never loved anyone else.'

'Mam, we know that. Dad was a big man with a big heart. He'd want you to be happy for the remainder of your life, and who better to share your life with than John? He knows all about the family, the history, the little jokes and anecdotes that make up our lives. He fits in a way that nobody else could.'

'But I don't want anybody else. Don't you understand? I'm perfectly happy the way I am. I've got Susan, and there's you and Madelaine. And Sion and Kirsty and the children come over regularly or I go there. David, what more could I want?'

'A man,' I said, more harshly than I had intended, which brought more tears to her eyes. 'Mam, Susan is growing up. She wants to do her own thing and though she loves you she won't want you hanging around all the time. John wants to share it all with you. He doesn't want to be an appendage to this family, he wants to be a part of it.' I shrugged, unsure what more to say.

'But David, what about you? Surely, you don't want me to destroy the memory of your father?'

'Huh?' I wondered if my mother knew what she was saying. 'How can your marriage to John affect my memory of Dad?'

Neither of us had heard the door open. 'Marriage? You Gran?' When I whirled round Susan stood there. I was about to make an angry retort when I saw the opportunity for an ally. I stepped back, away from Mam and glowered at Susan, nodding my head. She had been about to speak when she noticed my gesture. She tripped over her words for a second but quickly recovered.

'Gran,' after all the variations on a name for Mam, Susan had finally settled on Gran, 'I think that's wonderful. Oh, how lovely.' She crossed the room, knelt by Mam and put her arms around her. 'I'm so happy for you. Now, we must plan the wedding. When shall it be? What shall you wear?'

'Hush, child. I'm not marrying anybody. Especially not John.'

Susan rocked back on her heels and looked in astonishment at her grandmother. 'But why not? It's wonderful. A fairy tale come true. After all this time of unrequited love. It's like Romeo and Juliet.'

'Don't talk nonsense, Susan. Romeo and Juliet were children. John and I are in the twilight of our lives. It's not a fairy tale. This is real life and I'm too old to marry and that's final. Marrying John would be . . . would be like marrying my brother. He's been a friend for far too long.'

'Oh,' said Susan, tartly, 'so you'd rather marry a stranger, is that it Gran?'

'Of course not. I'd rather not marry anybody.'

'Then you're mad, Gran. It would be wonderful to have John with you everyday. Sharing all those things that enhance one's life. He won't be taking anything away, he'll be adding to it.'

I looked at my young daughter in astonishment. She never failed to surprise me. She had an old head on young shoulders and I suddenly realised that all those years with Kallenberg, all the dreams and introspection, had left her with a depth of understanding normally only possessed by those far older.

'I'm going to find John,' I announced.

'David,' Mam's voice stopped me in the doorway. 'I . . . I can't face him right now. Tell him, tell him I'm sorry. Tell him I want to think about his offer.' Mam suddenly sat up straight. 'I need a cup of tea. Tell him I'm honoured and it was such a surprise. Tell him he can have my answer one week from today.'

I looked at her in exasperation. Mothers!

I found John in the conservatory, pacing up and down, angrily puffing on a cigar. He calmed down when I told him what Mam had said.

'What are my chances do you think?'

I shrugged. I had no idea. 'John, you didn't give her much of a hint did you? I think it came as a complete shock to her when you asked. It's not as if you've been wooing her, buying her flowers, chocolates, taking her to the theatre.'

'David, it never even occurred to me! Except that when we have gone to the theatre I've always escorted your Mam. Or to the Hunt Ball, or to a restaurant. Anywhere.'

'That's precisely my point. You've been with us as a family friend. Not as Mam's . . . Mam's . . .' I hesitated, unable to use the word lover. 'Mam's special friend. You've not taken her out alone. Mam said she'll think about it for a week. If she does the answer will be no.'

John looked at me stricken and for the first time I realised how much he really did love her. He sank into a chair, his elbows on his knees, the cigar smouldering, forgotten, between his fingers.

'Help me, David, please. What should I do?'

'Go back and tell her that you won't wait a week.' He was about to interrupt me but I forestalled him. 'You'll give her three months. In the meantime, start courting her. Take her to the new flicks in Leicester Square. Buy her dinner, just the two of you. Get her away from the family and use your charm on her. What little you've got,' I added with a grin.

He looked up at me, saw my smile and smiled back. 'Cheeky devil. I'll show you little charm! Do you think it'll work?'

I shrugged. 'God alone knows. I can't tell with Mam. She's buried herself down here with us and while that was probably the right thing to do for a while, now it's time she got a life of her own. Dad was fanatical about the family but not claustrophobic. He knew that we knew he was always there for us. But at the same time he let us live our own lives. That's the secret of happy families. I suppose,' I sat down, thinking this through for the first time, 'that a gentle hand on the tiller is one thing, a tyrannical, despotic captain another. That's why we're all such friends. We get on with our own lives but are always there for each other. Mam needs to get on with her own life. And you,' I pointed a finger at John, 'need to make sure she enjoys it. Right, you'd better go and talk to her.'

Susan found us and said, 'Gran wants you, Uncle John.'

He heaved himself to his feet, mashed out his cigar and straightened his waistcoat and jacket. 'Wish me luck. Now I know how Daniel must have felt before entering the lions' den.'

'Come on, Susan,' I said, 'let's saddle a couple of horses and go for a ride.'

Much to the amusement of the local hunt and other riders, Susan and I always used the big American saddles, not the English type and what was more, Susan refused to ride side-saddle much to the horror of some of the older gentry in the area. However, amongst the younger set she already seemed to have a small group of followers, largely of young ladies who admired her daring and strong will.

The stable lad I had hired a few weeks earlier helped get the horses saddled and Susan and I rode across the fields towards the sea. We walked the horses to begin with and chatted.

'What will Gran do?'

'I don't know. It's up to John to show her what she's missing.'

'Missing? What on earth is she missing?'

I smiled at her. For all her insights and remarkable instincts she was still a child. 'She doesn't know it yet but she needs company of her own age. Somebody to talk about a time we know nothing about. I've only the vaguest memories of thirty years ago, but for Mam and John I suspect they're vivid and strong. They understand one another in a way that we can't.' I lent over and patted her arm. 'A great deal of Mam's life is filled by us but the part that Dad left behind is empty. It needs filling. And John is the man to do it. Come on, last one to the hedge is a baby.'

I dug my heels into the horse and broke into a gallop.

'Hey, that's not fair. You didn't give me any warning,' Susan yelled after me.

Within seconds I could hear her mount galloping close by and her shrieks as she urged him on. I eased up a little, wanting her to win but not by much. Instead, we declared a deadheat when we arrived at the hedge.

'How's your schooling coming along?'

'Fine. I'm conjugating verbs in Latin and French, I can quote Shakespeare and Marlowe and I know how to do logarithms. It's all tedious and boring.'

'I thought you were enjoying it.'

Susan shrugged. 'I am, sort of. I'd just like to see more people my own age,' she paused. 'A bit like what you were saying about Gran.'

That made sense to me. Susan had turned into a reasonably well adjusted young lady who was able to look after herself in most situations. 'What did you have in mind?'

'There's a school near here. It's called Brighton College for Young Ladies. I met two girls from there who were telling me how great it is. Could I try it? Please?'

I frowned, surprised by the request. 'What do you want to do? I mean, do you board there or travel in every day?'

Susan shrugged. 'I thought I'd give it a try first. You know, travel back and forth. If I like the place I could arrange to board later.'

'You'd really like to go there?'

'Sure, Dad. That's what I'm telling you. I'd really like to go.'

'Actually,' I said, thoughtfully, 'this could help your grandmother make up her mind about John. If you're not around so much she might see the sense of marrying John.' I nodded. 'Yep, that makes good sense.'

We climbed down from the horses and walked them across the road and down the steep path to the beach. We remounted and raced back and forth, Susan's squeals of delight making me smile.

When we returned to the house peace reigned once more. John and Mam acted as though nothing had happened and I didn't enquire. Instead of having dinner with us that evening they were going to the Grand Hotel in Brighton. Both seemed happy at the prospect and normally I would have said good, we'd come too. Instead, I nodded and made arrangements for our own meal.

After dinner Madelaine and I sat in the study, listening to the radio, a music revue from the Savoy Hotel in London.

I poured myself a whisky and a cup of tea for Madelaine. Once we were settled I told her about the meeting in the House of Commons and what I had been offered.

'Merely a baronet, darling?' she smiled at me.

'You'd still be Lady Griffiths,' I smiled back, 'even if it was an earldom.'

She laughed. 'True. Why not? You'll enjoy all the intrigue and to have a whole Government indebted to you must count for something.'

'I somehow don't think they'll think that,' I replied. 'All debts will be paid with the baronetcy. I don't know,' I looked thoughtfully at my glass, the amber liquid reflecting the fire light. 'I'm not sure I want all the memories. I'm not sure I want to do it anymore.'

'What? Oh, of course. Your father.'

I nodded. 'It was fun, marvellous. It was the most exciting time imaginable. Hell, you remember.'

Madelaine nodded.

'Still, it could be fun, I suppose,' I added.

'Fun?' Madelaine burst out laughing. 'David Griffiths, only you would think that a challenge to get a party elected to government was fun! Will you ask Sion to help?'

I shook my head. 'He's up to his neck in work. Anyway, in England we can travel from north to south in a day. And this isn't a presidential race about one man. This is about a party of hundreds. The problems are different but I think the solutions are the same.'

'That doesn't make sense,' Madelaine frowned.

'Yes, it does,' and I commenced to explain why. When I had finished I had made up my mind.

I intended to do the job, painful memories or not.

45

WHILE I BEGAN planning the political campaign John was busy mounting his own campaign to win Mam. He wined her, dined her and entertained her continuously. On one occasion three weeks later he appeared at Fairweather full of apologies.

'Meg, I tried to get tickets for the new Noel Coward play, Blithe Spirit. It's showing for one week here in Brighton but I couldn't get any. They were sold out. So, sorry my dear, but I've nothing planned.'

'John, thank goodness for that,' Mam replied.

'What? I thought you'd like to go.'

Mam smiled and said, 'Sit down, John dearest. I'm quite content to sit at home for one evening. A nice, quiet dinner with the family suits me.' She handed John a large malt whisky with a dash of soda. 'Plain food, a game of cards afterwards and an early night is just right.'

John looked crestfallen.

Mam put a hand on his arm, leaned down and kissed his cheek, 'John, I do love you. You've been wonderful to me. Give me more time, that's all I ask.'

John perked up immediately. 'You do? Love me, I mean?'

'Yes, of course. I have for as long as I can remember. But marrying you is another thing. So don't rush me.'

'You hear that, David? Your mother loves me after all.'

I smiled. 'I never doubted it for a moment. As long as she makes an honest man of you.'

John and I laughed and Madelaine threw a cushion at me. Mam smiled and I could see that she was looking and feeling genuinely happy. Susan came in at that moment, wearing jodhpurs and covered in what looked like oil.

'What on earth have you been up to?' I asked.

'Oh, this?' She looked at her clothes as though seeing the state they were in for the first time. 'I got oil on them.'

'Oil?' Mam asked. 'How on earth did you get oil all over your clothes?'

'I started the engine without securing a rocker arm properly. Oil squirted everywhere.'

We all looked at her in varying degrees of surprise and horror.

'Will you, young lady,' I said, 'kindly explain what you've been up to?'

'Working on an engine. If I'm going to be a pilot I need to know how it all works. So I figured the best way was to take an engine apart and put it back together again.'

'Is that what you've been doing out in the back shed?' Mam asked.

'Sure, Gran, what else?' Susan sounded surprised.

We exchanged helpless looks and I said, 'Okay, young lady. Go and bath and get changed. Dinner will be ready in half an hour.'

'Sure, Dad. To hear is to obey.' She gave a flowery salute and a bow and left the room.

'What on earth are we going to do with her?' Mam asked.

'Let her grow out of it,' said Madelaine.

I was not so sure Susan would, but at the same time I did not mind. I'd met enough vacuous daughters of rich parents not to be grateful that she was really interested in something. Even if it was flying!

The next few weeks I spent travelling between London and Fairweather. The Brighton to Waterloo express only took an hour and I found I could get a lot of work done. I arranged for an assistant manager from the bank to stay in a Brighton lodging house and travel with me. I dealt with any urgent business, gave instructions and sorted out any correspondence during the journey up to town. He then went to the bank and carried out those instructions and was ready, by the time I met Angus for lunch, to deal with any matters arising in the afternoon. On the journey back to Brighton we dealt with anything else that needed my attention. On the first day I arrived at Waterloo Station I went straight to Brook Street where I had set up my headquarters for the campaign to get the Tory Party elected.

I had a staff of twenty, most of whom were absolutely useless. Willing amateurs were one thing; stupid, arrogant amateurs, another. It took me two days to find the pearls amongst the swine.

I called each of them into my office in turn and issued my instructions. Fifteen were sent packing, two were under threat of dismissal and three I made section leaders. There were many threats and a lot of muttering from the fifteen I had dismissed and it was only a short time later that my phone rang and I answered it to an angry parent.

'You can't do this, Griffiths,' was the way I was greeted.

'I can't do what, to whom, why and who the hell are you?' I countered, in no mood for this sort of nonsense.

'This is James Fortescue Smythe, the Earl of Critchley to you.' The voice had a thousand years of breeding behind it, which gave it an arrogant, petulant sound.

'Well Smythe,' I said, not to be outdone in the rudeness stakes, 'if you're phoning about your son I'm not interested. I'm here to win an election and he's not only of no help, he is, quite frankly, a hindrance. Now, if there is nothing else, I've work to do.'

There was a spluttering noise down the receiver as though the good Earl was getting to grips with somebody speaking back to him, speaking for the first time in the same manner as he himself spoke, when I replaced the receiver.

'Now listen,' I said to the five people sitting in front of me, mouths agape, having heard some of the conversation, 'if you aren't prepared to work hard and do as I say then please leave. This isn't a game I intend losing. We're here to win and we have to do the impossible.'

'What's that?' asked one of them.

'Get the unelectable elected,' I replied, tartly.

Of the five, two were young ladies just out of Cheltenham Ladies' College and three were young men who had come down from Oxford. All were from good families – the moneyed classes, as Sion called them. I knew better. They were from the ruling class, and money had very little to do with it.

'I'm meeting the Party hierarchy after lunch. In the meantime I want you to trawl through the manifesto and highlight those things that will appeal to the most people, and then mark those which are of limited interest. I mean, to be more precise, those items which are evidently supportive of, shall we say, the upper classes?'

'Why?' asked one bright spark.

'Because this election will not be won on issues that are obviously for the benefit of people who are considered rich and privileged. It'll be won in a clear fight between the working class voting Labour and the middle class voting Tory.'

'What about the upper class?'

'There aren't enough of them to affect the voting patterns in this country.'

'So how do they get what they want?'

'With money,' I replied dryly. 'They pay for the result they want. The middle class can vote for it and, with luck, we can deliver it.'

The irony of supporting a Democratic Senator, my father, for President in one country and the party of the ruling classes in the other, was not lost on me.

'What good will it do to highlight the different aims in the manifesto?'

'We need to make a great deal of fuss about those ideas that appeal to the most people. We need to broaden the voting base of the Tory party otherwise they won't be elected. We play down those items that are obviously in favour of the very rich.'

'Such as?'

'Such as the way inheritance tax is to be treated. There are currently matters of trust law that Labour plan to change which will cost fortunes in taxes to the wealthiest landowners in the country. They are playing to one of the most powerful emotions we have,' I said. 'Any idea what that is?'

'Fear.'

'Love.'

'Hate.'

'Greed.'

'Envy.'

'That's the one. Envy. If he's got it, I want it. I can't get it for myself so I'll take it. It's the difference between America and England.'

'What is?'

'Over there everybody thinks that if they want it they can earn it.

Over here, I don't know, there's a defeatism about the ordinary worker which says I want it and I need to take it. It's communism, but wearing different clothes. So, we need to stop them. We need to beat Labour and right now it doesn't look as if we can.'

'So what do we do?'

'Rise to the challenge,' I grinned and got tentative smiles back.

I left them to carry out my instructions while I phoned a dozen businessmen I knew well. To each of them I gave the same message. I needed intelligent, hardworking individuals to help. I pointed out it was in their own interest to supply me with what I needed and with one exception they all promised to send me some workers.

By the time I left for my meeting I had a promise of thirty-five helpers and carried with me a breakdown of the Tory Party Manifesto.

The meeting was packed with the Tory hierarchy and started badly. It was, ludicrously, all about the men and few women I'd sacked that morning. When I was finally able to make myself heard I told individuals to be honest in their answer and asked if they would have hired them. It was amazing how the blunt answer was frequently, "No but" . . . And the but was the fact that it would have done their sons, daughters and siblings good to work as volunteers. Taught them to go to bed early and get up to go to work, some discipline etc., etc.

I let them have their say and gradually, once their spleen was vented, I had mine.

'Do you want to win the election or play at politics?' I asked, anger seething through me. 'If your children are problems, send the boys to the army and the girls to do charity work. Don't send them to me. I'm here to win. If you want the same thing, then you do as I tell you. I'm not a prima donna but I've done this before. None of you have. If you want somebody else to get you elected, then I'll leave you to it. I've got better things to do.' There was a lot of head shaking, muttering and thoughtful sucking on cigars and cigarettes. The room was a blue fugue of smoke and I wanted some fresh air. I enjoyed the occasional cigar but not somebody else's smoke!

'Right, can we now get down to business?' This time there were nods and calls of "aye" and "yes". 'Right, let me make something clear. Right now there's very little chance of the Tory Party winning the election, in spite of the fact that it's only been six months since the last one and people are fed up with elections and politicians. I think Labour will win with an outright majority.' There were outcries of dissent but Churchill quickly got the noise under control.

'It's a fact,' he said. 'Don't bury your heads in the sand or you'll get your backsides kicked.' That got a few chuckles and the atmosphere relaxed a little. 'If we go to the country with this as the agenda,' I waved the papers in the air, 'we'll be crucified.' This was the first time I'd identified myself with the Party. 'So we need two agendas, the public one and the private one.' There were a few protests but not many. 'If the public agenda is seen to be fair then it's possible we can widen our voting base and bring in more lower income families. If we don't and can't then we'll be out of power for a very long time. Think what Labour will do to the wealthy land and farm owner in this country.' From their bleak expressions and the looks that they exchanged I could see that it didn't take much imagination.

'Right, here's the first of the rules we need to work with. They are,' I almost choked on the words as the memories flooded back, 'the same rules that I imposed when my father was elected President of the United States of America.' I felt at that point it would not do any harm to remind them of what I had already achieved. 'And don't forget, he came from behind the field in his race to the White House. All press releases will be agreed by me and arranged through my office.' That caused a huge argument that lasted the rest of the afternoon.

By the time I got to the United Services Club with Baldwin and John, I was exhausted.

Over a drink, Baldwin said, 'They didn't like it much but, by God, they'll go along with it. Well done, Griffiths.' He raised his glass in salute.

I raised mine in turn. 'Thank you, Baldwin.'

'Call me Stanley,' he smiled.

'Then you should call me David.' I reached into my pocket and handed him a sheet of paper. 'This is the first story I want to run. I'm going to give it to the *Daily Herald* and the *Mirror*.'

'What on earth for?'

'I want to see what slant they put on it. We need a better understanding of the newspapers read by middle-income households. We need to target them and get them on our side. It was easier when I was aiming one man at them, but with a whole party it's a lot more difficult. We need to make it clear that we're a broad church, able to accept lots of views under one roof. We need to stop Labour and the Inheritance Tax Bill. Ergo, we need to frighten a lot more people about where it will end – the wealthy today, the middle classes tomorrow. Get a quote from a Labour supporter in Scotland and another in Northern England stating what they think is a high wage, what they consider is a big estate and how much inheritance tax should be paid. Frighten the life out of the small house owner in Sussex, Essex and Kent and motivate them into voting for us.'

There were nods from the other two as I warmed to my theme.

After Baldwin had left I asked John, 'How's the campaign going?'

He looked at me, startled and then said, 'You know how . . .'

He stopped as I shook my head. 'No. The real campaign. To wed Mam.'

He smiled. 'Slowly but surely.' He then didn't sound so sure when he added, 'I think.'

'You'll get there in the end,' I prophesied. 'Do you know,' I looked around the room to make sure nobody could overhear the heresy I was about to spout. 'I have never met such a load of self-seeking, self-important, arrogant buffoons in my life as the men who supposedly run this country. I found American politicians bad enough, but this lot really take the biscuit.'

'Shush, don't let them hear you say that. It might upset their delicate egos.'

I laughed. 'Delicate? They have the ego of an elephant; large, ungainly and once set in motion practically unstoppable. I've got to know men from all the Parties and apart from the leaders they're,' I floundered as I searched for a suitable word, 'useless,' was the best I could come up with.

John nodded. 'Which is precisely why we need you in Parliament.'

I choked on my drink, coughing. When I finally got myself under control I managed to say, 'Me? Forget it. This one election and then I take my baronetcy and bow out.'

'David, the real power is in the Lords. That's where the wealth and the privilege is vested. The Commons cannot get a bill through unless it's supported by the Lords. The real battle that will be fought over the next few decades will be about curbing the power of the House of Lords and Labour will work tirelessly to achieve that end. Look at Ireland. Every bill that's been proposed, every reform, has been stonewalled by the Upper House. That's why Ireland's in the mess it is. You need to get into the Lords and wield some of that power to help to modernise Britain.'

'John, you may not have noticed but I shall get a baronetcy, hardly more than a knighthood. That doesn't entitle me to sit in the Lords. So there's nothing I can do.'

'I know. But I have an hereditary earldom.'

'So? How does that help me to get into the Lords?'

'I marry your mother and adopt you. You inherit the title.'

46

I WAS SPLUTTERING again. John sat back in his seat, a smile on his face.

'Are you serious?'

'Never more so. Okay, it means it'll be some years before you get the title but you're still relatively a young man. You could go into the Commons in the meantime. Get a feel for the politics of the country and then get in amongst the real power. I can guarantee you a safe seat.'

'You've worked all this out, have you?' I was beginning to get angry. 'I don't want to be involved with politics. I loathe politicians. A necessary evil about sums them up.'

John shook his head. 'That's too harsh, David. They aren't evil, but they are certainly necessary. Many are incompetent and on the whole, useless. But the men at the top would have risen high in whatever they chose to do. They chose politics. Many have second and third jobs and nearly all of them have half a dozen directorships or more which pays them handsomely.'

'I don't need paying handsomely. I have more than enough money.'

'Precisely my point.'

'What? How do you mean, precisely your point?'

'You'd have no vested interests to support.'

'Yes, I would. Banking, shipping and a few others I can think of.'

'What's good for banking and shipping is good for the country,' John said, sounding really serious.

I laughed. 'So my vested interests are good for the country while those of other members aren't?'John wasn't embarrassed by the absurdity of his statement or upset by my tone. He merely nodded.

'Anyway, we're forgetting two important details in all this. I don't need adopting, and Mam hasn't agreed to marry you.'

'She will, though, won't she? If I tell her what I intend.'

I looked at John for a few seconds as the thought trickled through my mind. He went on, 'Your mother is an incredible woman who has discovered ambition. At first it was for Evan who achieved the impossible and became President of the United States of America. Now, it's for you. Money has no meaning for her as she has more than enough. Her only real ambition now is power and that's in politics. I think she'll marry me to satisfy her ambitions. If she were younger she'd do it for herself. As it is now, she needs to do it for her sons.'

I looked at John in shocked surprise. He was right! Mam would marry him to get me a seat in the Lords.

'That's appalling,' I finally said. 'That's tantamount to blackmail.'

John nodded, contentedly. 'I know.'

Anger welled up in me but then I suddenly saw the funny side of things. It had been a near thing. But instead of ruining our friendship and exploding at the disgraceful way he was planning to behave I exploded with laughter.

He suddenly relaxed, and I realised that he knew how close he had come to spoiling everything.

'You'd have risked it all? For Mam?' I was forced to believe this was true.

'I love her,' he said. 'So, yes. If you'd taken great exception to what I proposed and we'd fallen out, then that would have been that. I can't think what else to do.'

'What if I refuse to allow you to adopt me? After all, I don't need a father. I'm about to become one, again.'

His shrewd eyes looked piercingly at me. 'You will, my boy. You will. I'm offering you something that's almost impossible to attain. If you have a son he'll be able to inherit. You'll be established in the highest ranks of the nation. Wealth, combined with power, is a heady aphrodisiac, you'll agree.'

I was about to argue with him when I sat back and thought about it for a few more seconds, staring at my glass. He was right, of course. Money with power. I could, in my lifetime, establish a dynasty to compare with the Rothschilds and the other great houses. The power behind the throne. The real power.

John knew me better than I knew myself. I wanted it so badly I could taste it. Slowly I nodded. 'We have to win the election first,' I pointed out.

He stretched forward and held out his hand, which I shook, and said, 'We can't fail.'

His words were prophetic. On 6th. November 1924 Stanley Baldwin became Prime Minister with a massive majority. Winston Churchill was returned to Parliament as a Constitutionalist and Baldwin made him Chancellor of the Exchequer.

I was invited to Downing Street for a party, to celebrate our victory. When I arrived, with Madelaine on my arm – she was heavily pregnant but looking radiant – I was introduced as the man who had made it all possible.

Churchill took me to one side and said, 'David, I want to thank you personally for what you did.' He smiled around the cigar, a large whisky in his hand. 'When I become Prime Minister I'd like you in my Cabinet. I suggest you enter politics, my boy.'

His naked ambition repelled and yet attracted me. He was completely honest in his objectives and did not care who knew what they were. I knew he was a wonderful speaker, able to stir the blood with his rasping, gravely voice. I wondered how good an administrator he was, which was really what was needed in any post below that of PM.

'I'm thinking about it,' I replied. 'John has suggested one or two seats that will become available in the next year or two. But, to be frank, I'm willing to wait until I can get one in my area. I don't relish the thought of moving house into a constituency I don't know.'

'Not necessary, my boy,' he replied. 'Buy a small flat as your pied-a-terre and leave it at that.'

'But I won't get to know the area and its problems, its people,' I protested. 'How can I represent them if I don't know what they need?'

Churchill shook his head. 'You don't. You have to work to the big picture. The national picture. Leave the county councillors to deal with local politics.'

I hadn't thought of that and it made excellent sense. Perhaps I would take another look at some of the seats John was suggesting. I thanked Churchill for his suggestion.

'There's a lot of goodwill for you in the Party, so capitalise on it as quickly as you can. Take it from me, it doesn't last for long. I know.'

I nodded. In his lifetime he had experienced every sort of success and just as many setbacks. He was, I believed, a man of great principle . . . except when it came to his lust for power. Then he would stop at nothing. It was said he had changed parties more often than he'd changed his socks. It wasn't true, of course. He had only changed sides three or four times.

I thanked him for the advice and moved on.

Madelaine asked, 'Well? Are you going to run for parliament?'

I smiled at her. 'What do you think I should do?' Like my father, I enjoyed discussing matters with my wife. She was incisive and intelligent and had the uncanny knack of putting her finger exactly where it needed to go.

'I think you should. You'll enjoy it. Business is boring you now you've achieved so much. Politics could be new and exciting. For a while, anyway.'

I nodded in agreement. I had not told her about John's plans for me yet. I did so over the Christmas holiday.

Boxing Day was my favourite time with the whole family there. In the morning Sion, Angus, John, Susan and I rode to hounds with the local hunt, while Madelaine and the others rested. We had a superb late lunch which went on into the evening. After the meal, while Madelaine and I walked arm-in-arm around the terrace, letting our food digest before the party games started, I told Madelaine about John's idea.

'You're joking! My goodness, you aren't!' she exclaimed, her hands around her extended stomach as she started to laugh. Tears rolled down her cheeks as the merriment continued for a few minutes. 'Will there be a ceremony?' she finally gasped.

'What ceremony?'

'To adopt you,' she managed to say before she began laughing again. 'Oh! I must stop. The baby'll be coming out any second to find out what's so funny. Oh, David. It's priceless. What does Meg say?'

'John hasn't told her yet. What we thought was that we could, you know, the three of us, tell her what a wonderful idea it is. It may persuade her to marry John. That's what he hopes.'

Madelaine nodded. 'Yes, I think it will. But is that fair?'

'That's precisely what I said to John but his reply was that all was fair in love and war.' I shrugged. 'I can't say that I blame him. He's been chasing her long and hard. Playing hard to get is one thing but it's quite another to keep John dangling on a string.'

'David, that's a terrible thing to say about your mother!'

'Maybe, but its true. And don't forget that John's a close and intimate friend of the family. So it's time she made up her mind.'

'Who should make up her mind about what?' Mam asked from behind and I spun round to see her standing in the doorway.

'Errm, eh, nothing,' I spluttered.

'If you were talking about John and me then I agree. I wanted you to be the first to know.' Mam gave a tentative smile. 'David, I hope you don't mind, but, well, I'd like to accept.'

I hurried to her and put my arms around her, planting kisses on her cheeks. 'Mam, that's wonderful news. I really am glad and happy for you. John will be over the moon.'

Madelaine added her congratulations and the three of us went back inside to tell the others. Pretty soon the only person not to know the good news was John himself as he was out for a walk in the crisp, night air around the grounds.

When he returned we were sitting in the library, champagne in glasses, waiting for him. When he came in Mam was standing next to the door. We all raised our glasses and yelled congratulations and best of luck and so on while he stood perplexed for a moment until Mam slipped an arm around his waist and smiled up at him.

'What the? Does this mean what I think it means?' he asked, as comprehension dawned.

Mam nodded. 'Yes, dearest John. It does.'

He kissed her, to which action we cheered, though I exchanged an uncomfortable glance with Sion. It was followed by wry grins and shrugs. We were truly happy for both of them.

'Listen! Listen!' I rapped a spoon on my glass to gain attention. 'What none of you know is that,' I paused, wondering about my next words, 'John is going to adopt me!'

I can only describe the scene that followed as uproarious. Finally, we managed to tell the family what it was all about, and that gave further cause for celebration. Mam was aghast, pleased, excited, nervous but above all, happy. It was a truly memorable Christmas holiday.

* * *

I received my baronetcy in the New Year's honours list.

Madelaine had a baby boy we named Richard Evan John Griffiths on 11 January 1925. He was the cutest, blue eyed, dark haired little bundle I'd ever seen. I had an overwhelming desire to protect and love him. A feeling I hadn't had with Susan, although I'd done my best to make up for the shortcomings I'd shown during her early life.

Much to my delight, Susan took to her little brother and was often to be found giving him a cuddle; she even learned to change his nappy. Madelaine's routine now revolved around him, although she did have the help of a maid during the day. The question of a nanny was raised again but no decision was taken. I pointed out that with Mam's marriage to John and with Susan going to school help might be needed sooner rather than later. However, Madelaine and Mam protested that they could manage and I left it at that. I knew my place!

'What about choosing a school for him?' Mam asked me, a few months after Richard was born.

'What about it?' I asked.

'According to John, if you want Richard to go to a good school, you need to get his name down now.'

I frowned. The fact of the matter was I had not given it any thought. 'I need to discuss it with Madelaine,' I procrastinated.

Mam nodded. 'Naturally. Only you need to make some decisions soon. John suggests Eton or Harrow. He has influence at Eton, being an old boy.'

'That'll mean Richard going away from home,' I protested.

'Apparently they taken children as young as six,' said Mam.

'What!' I was aghast. 'Six? That's ludicrous! He's far too young. I want him here, with me. I want to influence him, mould him.'

'You make him sound like a piece of plasticine,' said Mam. 'If you must know I agree with you. However, he could go from the age of eleven to the upper school. It's a compromise; he'll spend the early years here and his later childhood years at the school. According to John it's imperative that he goes to forge the right contacts. Contacts that will help him all of his life. From there he'll go to Oxford.'

'So until he's about twenty-four his life is already mapped out for him and he's not yet two months old!' I joked.

'David, dearest, this is the way the aristocracy behave. They plan their lives and work to retain their wealth and privileges. They close ranks, belong to the same clubs, go to the same schools and universities and marry each other.'

'It sounds incestuous.'

'It is. It's also the reason the aristocracy of Britain has survived the upheavals of the last three hundred years. No other has. Not one, anywhere in the world.'

'How do you know so much about it?'

Mam smiled. 'John explained it all to me. It's a fascinating insight into the history of the world.'

I smiled at her words. 'Be that as it may, I ought to remind you that I've read *Tom Brown's Schooldays* and can't say I like the idea of a son of mine going to a school like that.'

'It's all changed. Or so I'm told,' she added. 'Anyway, I thought I'd mention it, as something needs to be arranged.'

I nodded. I would need to discuss it with Madelaine and possibly John, too. I needed some advice.

The telephone in the hall was ringing and I went to answer it. It was Churchill.

'Griffiths? That you?' he rasped down the line.

'Yes. What can I do for you?'

'I'm putting together an advisory committee, a group of men who know commerce and banking. Buchanan suggested I ask you.'

'I'm flattered. Let me think about it.'

'Don't think too long. I want to put Britain back on the gold standard. I've some ideas that I need to discuss with one or two experts before I announce my new budget.'

'Who else is invited to this brains trust?' I was intrigued. Power without responsibility had its own appeal.

'The Governor of the Bank of England, of course. Philip Steinway and Solomon Goodman. You know them?'

'By repute only.'

'All three are Jews. Does that present a problem to you?'

Th observation and question took me by surprise. I hadn't given it a thought. 'No. Should it?'

'Anti-Semitism is rife, and its growing. Look at the hysteria building up in Germany and Italy. It's rubbish of course. However,' he paused, cleared his throat and added, 'the committee will be secret. No public acknowledgement of what it does. No need to cause more trouble than necessary.'

I smiled. Typical Winston. 'All right. You can count me in. When are we to meet?'

'Good. Tomorrow at 7 pm sharp in a private dining room at the United Services Club. You're a member, I understand.'

'Yes. See you then.' I hung up, thoughtful. This was an unexpected turnup for the books.I was the first to arrive, quickly followed by the Governor of the Bank of England, Saul Goldsmith. He was the first Jew to hold the post and was considered a genius. He was short, fat and jolly. If he'd dressed in a red suit and white beard he would have been the idealised version of Father Christmas. The other two arrived together. Both were tall, slim and wore grey suits that matched their grey hair. I guessed they were in their late fifties, perhaps early sixties.

'Is Winston coming?' I asked.

'No, Sir David, he isn't,' replied Goldsmith. 'He has a late sitting in the House. Now gentlemen, to business.'

It was after midnight when we finished. I was excited and perturbed at the same time. Surely the decisions we had made that evening weren't to be government policy?

'Thank you for your time,' said Goldsmith. 'I'll leave you three to a night-cap. I'm going to Downing Street to see Winston.' He gathered up his papers and quickly left.

The three of us relaxed in our chairs for the first time that evening and I asked, 'Can I get either of you a drink?'

Both men nodded and a short while later we were served large malt whiskies from the Perthshire distillery.

We began to exchange views and stories. I learned that both men had extensive holdings in some of the companies we invested in, and that both of them used our bank. Soon the conversation turned to international matters and Germany.

'What's happening is a travesty,' said Steinway. 'That lout Hitler is a madman. A mad dog. Unless he's stopped there'll be another war. The anti-Jew hysteria currently being fanned will lead to more trouble. Already, I am being forced to sell my shares in Hamburg Steel to von Ludwig for a fraction of their worth.'

I froze with the glass half way to my lips. I hadn't expected to hear that name again, ever. I cleared my throat before asking, 'von Ludwig? I thought he was dead.'

Steinway looked at me in surprise. 'No. He may be old but he's as sharp as ever.'

I was confused for a moment and then I had the answer. The father; Karl von Ludwig's father. I asked a few more pertinent questions and established it was indeed my enemy's father and that they were now prospering as supporters of Hitler's ridiculous Brown Shirts – members of the Sturmabteilung; the Nazi Party.

'I'll buy your shares,' I said, drawing a surprised look from both men.

'I can't do that, Sir David. It wouldn't be right. The Germans have no intention of honouring their value to anybody who isn't German. No dividends are paid and there are no directors on the board who are not German. They aren't worth the paper they're printed on.'

I nodded. 'Thank you for warning me. But I'll still buy them. I have some unsettled business with the von Ludwig family which I intend to finish.'

Steinway looked piercingly at me for a few seconds and then said, 'It will be a pleasure to sell them to you, Sir David. May I suggest at fifty percent of their face value?'

'You just said that you had been offered ten percent,' I protested.

'That was before I learned that there was a market in the shares outside of Germany,' was the mild reply.

We began to haggle. We settled at twenty one percent of market value. I was about to be the proud owner of eighteen percent of Hamburg Steel. After we shook hands on the deal I learned that a further thirty six percent was in the hands of other Europeans, mostly Jewish, all of whom had been offered the same deal.

'Can you get the shares for me?' I asked.

'I should think so. Will you pay the same amount?'

'No. I would like a controlling interest but it's not necessary for what I have in mind. I'll pay fifteen percent of the market value to the owners and one percent to you for arranging the deals.'

'That is still a great deal of money,' was the reply.

'I can afford it. Is it a deal?'

'Yes, I believe it is.' We shook hands and then Steinway added,

'I cannot guarantee success of course. Some of our shareholders may not sell.'

'I'm sure you can persuade them. Can I get you gentlemen a refill?' I indicated their empty glasses.

'No, thank you. I have to go,' replied Goodman. Both men stood, reached for their overcoats and turned to leave. In the doorway Goodman turned back to me and said, 'Sir David, I suspect you're a good friend and a dangerous enemy. Good luck in whatever it is you're planning.'

I nodded, smiled and wished them goodnight. I sat down to think through the strategy that was half formed in my mind.

An hour later I sent telegrams to Sion, Angus and Jake. A personal Council of War was being called.

47

CHURCHILL ANNOUNCED HIS budget a few days later. It followed precisely what we had recommended at the meeting at the United Services Club. Britain was back on the gold standard, six pence was being cut from income tax and there was a new national insurance scheme to fund state pensions from the age of sixty-five. During his speech in the House of Commons, Churchill said that restoration to the gold standard was proof that Britain was recovering from the war and that prosperity was here for all. Within fifteen minutes of his speech the pound rose forty cents to the dollar to four dollars 83 cents. I had already sold one million pounds worth of dollars, all I'd had time to achieve. When I'd bought them back I'd made a profit of $400,000 for the bank. I bought gold with the dollars and arranged to ship it to Britain to be kept in our vaults. We were now one of the highest capitalised banks in Europe, although still tiny compared to many of the American banks.

Jake was the last to arrive. He had travelled by rail to Lisbon and fast ship to Southampton. He had taken five days from the time I had sent the telegram.

When he stalked through the door and saw me, Sion and Angus he said, 'What's this? A Council of War?'

My nod took him by surprise. 'That's precisely what it is.' We exchanged handshakes and I poured coffee. We were in the study at Fairweather, it was a sunny, spring day and lunch would be ready in an hour. I handed a file to each of them. I could see that they were intrigued and I left them to read it while I made a phone call. When

I returned they were sitting in contemplative silence, each busy with his own thoughts.

Sion looked up at me, leaned back in his chair, crossed his feet and arms and nodded. Frazer caught the movement, shrugged and nodded while Jake continued to look pensive.

I waited patiently, letting him make up his own mind. Finally, he said, 'The fascists are causing trouble in Spain. They've got connections with Hitler's mobs and I think it all means trouble in the future. Any little thing to stop them is a thing we should do. What does John say?'

I shook my head. 'Nothing. I haven't told him. He's got enough on his plate right now and I didn't see any point in troubling him.'

'I don't agree,' said Sion. 'You're involving the bank. His name is on it as well. John needs to know.'

The others nodded. 'Okay. He's getting here this evening. I'll put it to him then. In the meantime can we discuss the plan?'

We spent the day refining my ideas. The objective was simple – to wipe out, financially, the von Ludwig family once and for all.

'Why are you so determined to break them?' asked Sion. 'I know,' he held up his hand to forestall me, 'revenge for Emily. We all helped. But why this . . . this hatred of the family?'

I was about to lose my temper but got it under control before replying, icily. 'You need to ask?'

'Yes, bro', I do,' Sion said, softly. 'There's a great deal at risk, including our lives.'

'Von Ludwig's father masterminded the whole thing. Unfortunately, I never managed to get at him, though I tried. I overheard him when he told his son that an enemy of one was an enemy of all. I thought if that was good enough for them it would be good enough for me. I lost track of the von Ludwigs after the war but a chance remark led me to them again. I've had agents putting together the information you now have in your hands. Their greed makes them vulnerable. Von Ludwig's ambition makes them doubly so.'

Sion nodded. 'What's the time scale?'

'We start two weeks tomorrow. Jake needs to return to Spain to get the ball rolling. Do you see any problems, Jake?'

He shook his head. 'None. It'll be a pleasure. Like I told you, something needs to be done to stop Franco and his mad dogs. Any little thing will help, even if it only discredits them in the eyes of their allies in Germany.'

'Do you see problems in Spain?' Frazer asked.

'Yes. It'll come in the next few years. Franco's fascists are getting stronger and democracy's getting weaker. I think there'll be civil war sometime, though I pray I'm wrong.'

'When?' I asked.

'I don't know. It's a while away yet, but already the hotheads are gathering.'

'Who's Franco?' asked Sion.

Jake spent the next ten minutes explaining what was happening in Spain. It was all rather minor but becoming significant. Major Franco was becoming a nuisance. I was beginning to wonder what we needed to do for the future of our investments on the Iberian Peninsula.

John arrived in time for a cocktail at six o'clock. He was there to take Mam to the theatre and to discuss their wedding plans. The wedding would be in six weeks time. The ceremony would be a civil wedding in a registry office followed by dinner in the Dorchester Hotel, Park Lane. So far the guest list to the Dorchester Hotel included more than five hundred people!

I briefed John about our Council of War and what we planned.

'What will this cost?' he asked.

'Half a million,' I replied.

'Dollars or Sterling?'

'Dollars. Just over a hundred thousand in Sterling.'

'Profit potential?'

I shrugged. 'I don't want to line up any purchasers until the deal is done. Secrecy is vital.'

'What's your best guess?'

'Half a million.'

'Dollars?' he asked, puzzled.

'Sterling,' I replied, at which he smiled. He said, 'We can't use bank money, it's too risky. We can use the bank's name, though. I'll go along with that. The money needs to come from us, privately.'

I nodded. I wasn't surprised by the suggestion. 'Okay. Are any of you in or do I do it all?'

'What, and keep all the profit?' said Frazer, with a grin.

'Certainly not,' said Jake. 'We're in this together. 'Twenty thousand pounds each.'

The others nodded. 'I think this calls for a celebration,' I said. I went over to the bar, tucked away in a corner of the room and found a bottle of Premier Krug Champagne. I opened the superb wine and poured. When I'd done so I lifted my glass and said, 'Here's to a successful operation.'

All the arrangements were made and the train of events I had planned began to unfold like a story, chapter by chapter. I bought 50.1% of the shares in Hamburg Steel using nominee companies in Luxembourg and Switzerland. It cost me nearly £200,000, not the original £100,000 I had estimated. I didn't tell the others but funded the difference myself. This was a personal matter, and although they were in it with me, I didn't feel that I could let them risk so much money. The profits would still be split as agreed. I was not in it for the profit.

Jake, using code, reported back three weeks later. Von Ludwig wanted a meeting.

When Jake had returned to Spain, he had spent his time talking to his friends and colleagues, planting a simple idea in their heads. He had heard from his rich English friends he said, that a small company had discovered a new, cheap process for producing steel. The process was top secret but the market had been assessed as huge. Fortunes were to be made. It didn't take long for the message to reach the right ears and he was approached by two men, one a German who proved to be a member of the Nazi Party and also an employee of Hamburg Steel. Jake was paid a substantial sum to provide documents that proved his claim. The coincidence that Hamburg Steel was involved was not very surprising. As a shareholder, I had managed to plant information with the board of directors, pointing them at Jake. I wanted von Ludwig to receive the information from different sources. It helped to establish the "facts" . . . the facts I wanted him to believe.

The shareholding I now controlled in Hamburg Steel was held in different names, mainly those of nominee companies whose ultimate ownership was virtually impossible to establish. However, I had the letters of authorisation stating that I had the voting rights to the shares. The name on the letters was David Griffin. David Griffiths might be a name von Ludwig remembered.

I called a Board meeting to introduce myself to the directors of Hamburg Steel for 31st. May. As I was the majority shareholder, it was the equivalent of a Royal Command.

I had learned that fraud was easy to commit if you knew what you were doing. In this case, I knew.

My Joy was sailed by Jake, Frazer and John to Hamburg. Two days later I flew with Sion and Mike O'Donnell. We had two escape routes out of Germany, should we need to use either. I hoped we would not, but then, living in hope was not my way of ensuring a safe and happy future. We went armed to the teeth, not trusting anybody we would be dealing with in Germany. After all, I was still at war with some of them.

We flew, without mishap, to Germany and landed at the small airfield near Hamburg. Customs were perfunctory and immigration control virtually non-existent.

The meeting was in the headquarters of Hamburg Steel, near the port. The works were huge, sprawling over thousands of acres of land. It was noisy, dirty and dangerous. Smoke and soot belched from the chimneys and the yards were criss-crossed with railway tracks where an unwary foot could easily cause a twisted ankle or worse. Long lines of trucks laden with iron ore clanked along for a few yards and jarred to a halt, each cannoning into the one in front, all adding to the bedlam. Loud German voices shouted in the morning din, orders passed and repeated, a harsh sound in a harsh world.

Frazer and I picked our way from the car to the door of the main building, across and around dirty pools of water and pot-holes. In the reception hall we were met by an austere looking elderly lady who greeted us in German. As we had done in the past, we pretended not to understand and she switched smoothly to flawless English.

We were led up two flights of stairs, covered with threadbare linoleum and through a heavy door. We entered another world. Here, shareholders' money had not been saved. The floors were covered with deep pile carpets, the walls were panelled in oak and decorated with paintings of sailing ships. The noise and bustle from outside were background whispers, audible only if you listened hard.

Frazer was with me, Sion was at the airport making sure that we were ready for a rapid escape if we needed one, and Jake was aboard *My Joy*. John and Mike were outside the gates in a fast Mercedes car.

I had no idea what to expect and had done my best to cover every eventuality.

The greetings were brief. The woman who had shown us the way announced that neither of us spoke German and sly smirks were exchanged by the five men standing in the room. I recognised von Ludwig as an older version of his dead son. Two others were inconsequential directors but the last two were introduced as directors representing the interests of the Nazi Party. Already, I was feeling out of my depth. Crossing an old man was one thing, double-crossing the Nazis was another. However, we had come too far to back down.

Coffees were poured and we sat down around a huge, heavy table that could have seated twenty people with ease.

'Let us get straight to the point,' said von Ludwig. 'You have sent certain information here that suggests you have a controlling interest in this company – my company. I wish to know how this came about.' He spoke harshly, his accent gratingly Germanic and over-bearing. He must have been nearer seventy than sixty, slim, grey haired and with a duelling scar on his cheek. A supporter of the Kaiser, he was now backing a dark horse in the pursuit of power – Adolf Hitler.

I unlocked my briefcase and slid documents across the desk to him. He picked them up and scanned them briefly.

'These are copies. Where are the originals?' He passed the papers to the man on his right. He was a heavy set, thuggish looking brute whom I suddenly realised held the real power in the room. His name was Herman Goering; von Ludwig was merely a mouthpiece. The suspicion that I had blundered into an area far out of my depth suddenly became a certainty.

'I chose not to bring them,' I replied.

'Why was that? Herr Griffin, isn't it?' asked the other Nazi on von Ludwig's left.

'I didn't know what I was coming to. I have a proposition for you which can make us all fortunes. I have the upper hand in that I own over fifty percent of the shares of this company.'

'Own? I thought you represented a number of owners?' said von Ludwig.

I mentally cursed myself for the slip and said, 'Effectively, it's the same thing.'

'What are you proposing?' von Ludwig asked.

'I have here details of a manufacturing process that has been developed in a small English steel works in Rotherham. The company is seriously short of cash and, let me, errm, suggest, is probably the right word, that I can arrange a foreclosure on the plant. The lot can be picked up for £200,000.'

'Why should we be interested?' asked Goering.

'Because this company can buy the process and bring the technology to Germany.'

'Why do you want to bring the technology here? Why not use it for yourself in England?'

'Because we need a large plant to handle the new process, which does not exist, and because I have the shares in this, not in any other, company.'

Goering threw back his head and laughed. When he finished, he said, 'What makes you think these pieces of paper are of any use to you? We,' and he smashed his fat hand on his chest, 'the future rulers of Germany own this factory. Not a man with pieces of paper.'

I nodded and smiled before replying. 'However, you aren't the rulers – yet. And, until you are, the law of the land will dictate what is to happen. I can leave here and call in the receivers and close this place down if I wish. It may cause mayhem and chaos, but I can do it. Your government is desperate to be seen by the rest of the world as law-abiding. I'll get support for what I do, whether you like it or not.'

The hostile glares from the men across the table confirmed that I had hit home with my assessment of the power I controlled.

The other Nazi, named Goebbels, leant across the table and pointed a thin finger at me. 'I will have you shot for such a remark.'

I looked at him through slitted eyes, unsure how to react. My inclination was to laugh but I kept my face deadpan. He was an absurd little man. He spoke to the others in German, his eyes not wavering from mine. I showed no reaction to his statement that as soon as we left he would arrange to have us killed.

Von Ludwig told him to do no such thing until the deal could be examined in detail. He then switched back to English.

'What do you propose, Herr Griffin?'

'This business raises the money to buy out the English company and £300,000 to buy me out. You get the new process and I get a profit of £100,000.'

'Why are you asking so little if this process is worth a fortune?' asked von Ludwig.

'That's a good question and deserves answering,' I said. 'I make money. I don't own companies. I was in a position to put this whole deal together because of certain events that needn't concern you. If I conclude the deal my way I make a vast profit for a few days work. That suits me.'

I was treated to a tirade by Goebbels, in German, that I feigned not to understand. In essence he was calling me a blood-sucking leech, grinding down the workers. At that moment I could see no difference between the Nazis and the Russian Communists. Perhaps one did not exist.

When the tirade stopped, von Ludwig spoke. 'That is a great deal of money to buy a process we do not know will work.'

I extracted forged copies of patents and reports and handed them over. I sat back while von Ludwig read them and passed them around the table. He then spoke in German.

'I've heard all about this. Information came to me via another source in Spain, from a supporter of our ideals. If half of what I heard is true then this would put us years ahead of the world in the production of steel.'

'Yes, but why does he come here?' asked one of the regular board members whose name I'd forgotten.

'Perhaps it is as he says. He controls the situation and will make a fortune, quickly,' replied von Ludwig. '£100,000 is more than a thousand men make in a year and this man will do it in weeks.' He glared at me and I smiled back.

'Can we raise the money?' asked the other board member.

'The Rothschild Jews in Berlin will give it to us.'

'Give?' Goebbels joked.

'Lend,' von Ludwig corrected himself. 'But they will extract a heavy price.'

'It will not be for long,' said Goering. 'All Jews will be exterminated when we come to power and their wealth confiscated. They are carrion on the backs of the German people.'

I was shocked to hear such naked venom but, thanks to the training Frazer and I had undergone, before and during the war, neither of us showed any reaction.

'Yes,' said von Ludwig. 'We should ask for a long term loan, knowing it will be of a short term duration.' The men laughed.

'Would you care to share the joke?' I asked, politely.

'Ah, it is, how do you say? In-house. Yes, it is an in-house joke you cannot possibly understand,' said von Ludwig. 'I am interested in this proposal, Herr Griffin. But I need to consider it further.'

I shook my head. 'No, you don't. You still don't get it, do you?' I stood up, leant over the table and smashed my fist down. 'I've been reasonable so far, trying to win you over to this proposal. I can make it happen with or without your help. I can go to the bank right now and take over the accounts and stop you trading and there is nothing you can do to stop me. Get this clear, I control this company as of last week. You should have prevented me by buying up your stock but you did nothing. You sat and watched it happen. Now, I am not going to sit idly by and watch this opportunity be squandered. I can call a shareholders meeting and have you all sacked from the board and you can't stop me. I can have a Court Order in force before the end of today that will force the police to evict you. Now, I hope all this is clear. So let us proceed. Incidentally,' I sat back down and spoke in a more reasonable tone, 'it isn't necessary to use company money. You can buy the shares personally. I am sure the Jews will lend you the money.'

There was more chatter in German, the gist of which was that they saw the opportunity to make personal fortunes, not merely profits for the company.

'You will have no objection if we buy the shares?' asked von Ludwig.

'None.'

There was another burst of German which convinced me that we had them where we wanted them. They could taste the profits.

'I have heard all about this process and this company,' said von Ludwig. 'Which means that I do not need to make any further enquiries.'

'How did you learn about it?' I asked, pretending to be appalled.

'Let us say that we have certain contacts who are looking out for our interests.'

'But this is awful.' I stood up and collected in the papers.

'Where are you going?' asked a surprised von Ludwig.

'If you've heard all about it then so must others. I must conclude the deals in England before it's too late.'

'But I thought you said that it was straightforward.'

'It is,' I replied, looking up from what I was doing. 'But that's the point. Others may have heard of it and already be taking action. The deal could be lost. I have to move quickly. I can buy the shares with one of my consortiums and come back later. Nothing here will change,' I paused. 'Except, of course, that the price will go up. Come, Felix,' I said to Frazer, 'we need to go.'

'Wait,' thundered von Ludwig. 'What do you mean the price will go up? What are you doing? Let us finish this and get matters concluded. Please,' he suddenly smiled in an attempt to be friendly. 'What do we need to do?'

'I have first option on the shares of the English company that will last another five days. There is nothing to stop me taking a hundred percent of the company and doing as I wish. But I must ensure I exercise my position within the time limit. When I've done so, I can finish the deal here. After all, I own the controlling interest,' I reminded them. 'But of course the price will be much higher.'

The pressure I was bringing to bear caused von Ludwig to break out into a fine sweat, which spread across his brow. He was desperate for the deal; he did not understand it but in his arrogance did not want to admit the fact. Luckily, it was evident that the other men around the table were equally clueless. If this was German industry, no wonder it was in such a mess – a mess I was going to make worse!

'Can you give us three days?' von Ludwig asked.

'Two,' I replied.

'That is little enough time,' protested von Ludwig.

'I haven't set the timetable,' I replied. 'The fact that others now know about this means we have to move fast.' I was now identifying myself with them. I had come through the door as their enemy and now I was on their side. The real enemy was the other vultures circling the rich pickings.

'Let me see those figures again,' he held out his hand while I hesitated.

'You may as well show them to him,' said Frazer. 'We've come this far. Another half an hour won't matter.'

Von Ludwig nodded his thanks at such a reasonable statement and

I reluctantly handed the papers over. After a few minutes he said, 'This is a fortune.'

I shrugged, nonchalantly. 'I know. Which is why I'm doing it. I intend keeping five percent of Hamburg Steel as additional, shall we say, profit?'

After that it was plain sailing. We arranged to return to the factory in two days and Frazer and I departed. As we closed the door behind us I heard Goebbels saying, 'I will have them watched. Report everything they do. At the earliest opportunity I shall have them killed.'

Frazer and I exchanged glances. Somehow, it came as no surprise.

48

WHEN WE DROVE through the gates neither of us looked in the direction of the car opposite, manned by O'Donnell and John. We turned right and headed towards the city centre and our hotel.

Trouble came that night.

We did not acknowledge O'Donnell and John who were sitting at a nearby table while we had dinner. And we ignored them when we left the hotel for a breath of fresh air, strolling through the Rathaus Markt. It was a large square with the Rathaus – Town Hall – on one side and the Bourse – the German Stock Exchange – on the other. We were near the canal when the attack happened.

A dozen men in brown shirts suddenly appeared in front of us, carrying staves and heavy handles. They spread out and we faced them with our backs to the water. Each of us had a hand in a pocket, holding a gun.

'Ja, it is them,' said one of the men. They advanced towards us and he added, 'Remember, do not kill them. We frighten them only. Make them more reasonable in their negotiations.'

They were only a few yards away when there was a shout and a flurry behind them and four of the men suddenly dropped to the pavement. Two others went flying into the canal and we pointed our pistols at the remaining six. Jake, John, Sion and Mike stood behind them, wielding handles of their own. The attack had been so unexpected that the Brownshirts had been taken by surprise. It was rare in those days for anybody to stand up to them.

I pulled back the hammer on the gun and said, 'You want something?'

The men began to back away, fear alive in their faces. 'Halt!' I said harshly, aiming at the forehead of the ring leader.

They stopped.

I looked at them with loathing. These were thugs of the worst order. They had been hurting and maiming men, women and children for years as they gradually took over the power base of Germany.

'Do you speak English?' Nobody answered. '*Sprechen Sie Englisch?*' I repeated.

'*Nein*,' came a sullen reply.

I turned to my partners. 'Throw them in the canal,' I ordered. Before any of them could move Sion hit one on the head with a glancing blow and barged into another. The latter went flying into the canal and, as the other staggered off balance Sion caught hold of him by the arm and swung him over the edge. I had not noticed what happened with the others because all of a sudden there was only the ringleader standing in front of me. I walked slowly up to him, the gun pointed at the middle of his forehead. He backed into the arms of John and Jake who stopped him going any further. I put the gun to his forehead and pulled the trigger.

There was a loud empty click. I never carried a gun with the first chamber loaded as accidents can happen and it is possible to fire an automatic by dropping it. There was the sound of water and a low moan from the fat thug in front of me.

I stepped back, looked at the puddle at his feet and said, 'He needs a bath. Throw him in.' They frog-marched him to the edge and with a boot up the behind from John the man went flying into the filthy canal. The others were floundering, calling for help and starting to make a racket. I pocketed the gun and spun around, surprised by the sound of clapping.

I had not realised that a small crowd had gathered in the dusk, watching us. A number of voices yelled thanks and well done and all of them applauded. One small, bespectacled, elderly gentleman said, 'You should go now. Before more of them come along. Thank you. It was a pleasure to watch.'

We heard yells and whistles and suddenly the small crowd vanished. We accepted the hint and quickly lost ourselves in the back streets as we made our way to the *My Joy*. We had decided that the hotel would not be a safe place to stay any longer.

We moved the boat to a mooring in the middle of the outer harbour. It took very little time and we were soon ensconced in the main saloon with large malt whiskies before us.

'Any thoughts?' I asked the subdued group before me.

'My initial thought is that I'm too old for this,' said John. 'And too respectable. I'm an Earl for goodness sake. What am I doing here?'

'Enjoying yourself,' Sion said, laconically, raising a laugh. The dam was burst and the fright and adrenaline seeped from us. We swapped stories as we tried to make sense of it all.

'Did von Ludwig put them up to it, do you think?' asked Mike O'Donnell.

'I don't know. If he didn't then I think it was Goebbels. He seemed to me to be the really vicious rat at that table,' said Angus. 'David, I have to say I enjoyed that.' He lifted his glass and added, 'Cheers. Though God along knows what Catriona would say if she ever found out.'

'Or Madelaine,' I said. 'Cheers.'

'Or Meg,' said John. 'Cheerio.'

'Or Kirsty,' said Sion. 'Here's mud in your eye.'

'Or Estella,' said Jake. 'Skol.'

'Or my mum,' said Mike. 'Cheers.' At which we fell about laughing.

We worked out a roster to keep watch during the night. The few belongings we had left at the hotel we decided to abandon. We had left nothing important and the papers were only copies, of which I had more. In fact, if von Ludwig did get his hands on them he would find additional information that would further whet his appetite for the deal. I had come expecting to be robbed, although I had not expected the violence.

The next day, Sion and Jake went into the city while we stayed aboard, out of sight. When they returned, we sat in the saloon and over coffees made our plans

'There are Brown Shirts all over the place,' said Sion. 'They seem to be asking the same question, which in a nutshell is where the hell are you two?'

Jake nodded. 'We met a few of them who tried asking us.'

'No real trouble?' I asked, surprised.

'None. They're bullies and cowards. They have vague descriptions of you and seem to think that if they bluster and bully loud enough they'll get what they want. They soon left us alone when I showed them my membership card to the International Fascist Society along with my Spanish Passport.'

'What's the International Fascist Society?' John asked.

Jake shrugged. 'I don't know, it was Sion's idea. We were talking about the problems in Spain and what Franco was up to and comparing them to what we see here. We know that Hitler is a supporter of Mussolini and of Franco – it's common knowledge. Sion had the idea of suggesting we were a part of it all by coming up with the International Fascist Society. It worked.'

We roared with laughter.

'I still don't see how we're going to get away with this, you know,' said Sion. 'I mean, it's all very well, but we're here to pull off a criminal act and then escape. I don't see how we can.' He paused and sipped his coffee. 'Also, I can't see how we're going to win. And you might not like this, but I don't see the point.'

The others exchanged glances and I felt that Sion had spoken for them all. I knew I could count on their support but I wanted them to give it wholeheartedly. I felt Frazer was the only one to really understand.

'All right, let me explain something. I have a controlling interest in Hamburg Steel, right?' They nodded. 'Of itself, it's meaningless.'

'Why?' Mike asked, frowning. 'If you've got most of the shares surely you can do what you like?'

'In theory, yes. In practice, no,' I replied. 'What can I do with bits of paper? Sack the board? Replace them with whom? What if they won't leave? How do we get the Nazis out if they decide not to go? Go to court and get some sort of injunction? And then what? Who'll support me?' I shook my head. 'Having the shares is a tenuous advantage which has enabled me to get this far.'

'How far is that?' asked Sion.

'Far enough to sow the seeds of greed,' I replied. 'We have two objectives. To make a profit and to bankrupt von Ludwig. Agreed?'

There were nods around the table.

'We make a profit by selling the shares we have in Hamburg Steel back to the company. They'll be bought using what is technically our own money – the cash in the company's bank account. Except we wouldn't be able to get our hands on that cash unless the board of directors agree to the purchase. They'll agree because they want to control the company and own the other shares. The net result is they'll own all the shares. Okay so far?' There were more nods. 'The deal to buy our dummy company will go ahead because von Ludwig and the Nazis will use their own money to buy us out and then sell it to Hamburg Steel, taking a huge and legitimate profit. Except, of course, there won't be one, as there's nothing to buy.'

'Look,' said Mike, 'I've been a bit slow in all this. I still don't see how you're going to get away with it. If I was spending a load of money to buy a factory I'd want to make damn sure it was there in the first place, and that everything was above board.'

'Naturally. But that's exactly what they have been doing for days if not weeks,' I said.

'So how will you get away with it?' Mike asked.

'In cases like this you rarely go and look for yourself. You amass all the information you can, check it out and, if you're still unsure, walk away from the deal, no matter how tempting it seems. Now, we've put together a vast amount of material and sent out hundreds of snippets of information to the right people. You forget, Frazer and I were expert at this sort of thing during the war. So much information has come back to them from so many different directions that they know it's true, even when it isn't. And don't forget, they want it to be true. That's important as well. Von Ludwig and his cronies will buy the shares and by the time they find out that they've been duped it'll be too late.'

'When are you due to see them again?' asked John.

'Tomorrow,' Angus replied. 'At noon.'

'How will you get in?' Jake asked. 'Assuming that the Brown Shirts are looking for you, an obvious place to look will be at the gates of the factory.'

'We half expected something like this to happen,' I replied. 'After all, if we vanished, as far as they're concerned there's nothing to stop von Ludwig and his thugs from buying the English company without us. Angus and I will be leaving first thing in the morning to go to the factory. We'll get in all right. Getting out could be more difficult. That's what we need to discuss.'

* * *

The hooter sounded at six o'clock and we drifted with the hundreds of other workers towards the factory gates. As we expected, there was nobody keeping a lookout for us at that time in the morning. We were dressed as ordinary workmen, scarves around our throats and shabby coats covering our suits. Frazer carried a canvas grip in one hand while the other was thrust in his pocket. Like me, he kept a grip on his pistol, just in case. Nobody spoke to us and we said nothing, keeping our eyes cast down, watching for the potholes.

Inside the gate we ambled towards the administration buildings which, as we expected, were still locked. I quickly looked around, saw that nobody was taking any interest in us, and while Angus stood with his back to me and the door, I picked the lock. It took less than twenty seconds. I was pleased I still had the old skill.

Inside, I relocked the door and we climbed the stairs. In the board room there were two other doors, one of which we knew led to the secretary's office. The second we guessed led to a WC. I opened the door and, sure enough, there was a toilet and wash hand basin. There was also a lock on the inside.

We spent the next two hours searching the offices and discovered a gold mine of information. It became obvious that Hamburg Steel was not only highly profitable but the profits were not being fully declared. As a shareholder I was being cheated! Secondly, there was more in the company bank account than I had expected and as a result I decided to play out my hand to get more money. Thirdly, there was a letter signed by Rudolph Hess, secretary of the Nationalist Party, in which he had written that Herr Hitler expected the deal to be concluded to the satisfaction of the Party. I showed it to Angus and pointed at the paragraph which spelt out what was to happen to us. He shrugged and grinned at me.

'It's what we expected,' he said. 'Hush! Someone's coming!'

We hurried into the boardroom and closed the door behind us. We heard footsteps pass by and the door to the secretary's room open and close. We went into the WC and locked the door, composing ourselves to wait. It was something we had had plenty of practice at in the past. I looked at my friend and he smiled back.

'Just like old times,' I said.

'That's exactly what I was thinking. Do you remember when . . .'

The next two hours passed quickly as we reminisced about the adventures we had shared together. I was in the middle of one story when Frazer held up his hand for silence. We heard voices, a laugh and somebody rattled the door. Von Ludwig said something and there was further laughter. Whoever had tried to open the door let go the handle. We breathed sighs of relief. I looked at my watch; it was ten forty-five.

There were no further attempts to open the door. We tried listening but could hear nothing above a murmur. Finally, at five minutes to twelve, we unlocked the door and stepped into the board room.

'Good day to you, gentlemen,' I said.

Startled heads turned, oaths were ejaculated and anger and hate were directed at us.

'Herr Griffin, where have you come from?' von Ludwig was the quickest to recover his poise.

I nodded at the door. 'We were taking advantage of the facilities,' I smiled. 'And as I own this company I saw no reason why we shouldn't.' I reminded them of my status, not wishing to discuss the matter further. 'Now, shall we get down to business?'

Goebbels glared at us whilst Goering sat back and rubbed a fat finger along the side of his collar.

'I'm afraid the deal has changed a little. The price for the shares, to be purchased by the company and paid by banker's draft is now increased by twenty thousand pounds.'

There was an explosion of anger and protest from the men at the table. I held my hand up for quiet. I knew they would agree because they did not expect us to leave Germany alive and so any agreement was academic.

'I assume that you will be purchasing the shares in the English company personally?' I asked.

There was a moment's silence before von Ludwig replied. 'That is correct. I have the necessary bank drafts here. Do you have the paperwork that will conclude the purchase?'

I nodded and handed over a sheaf of Bearer Bonds, beautifully engraved, in the name of Manchester Iron and Steel.

Von Ludwig nodded. 'It is as I expected. However, how do we know that this represents the fully issued and paid up shares of the company?'

I handed over another sheet of paper, apparently proving the point.

There were other matters to discuss to conclude our business, which took very little time.

'So, to conclude,' said von Ludwig, 'Hamburg Steel has bought back its own shares for three hundred and twenty thousand pounds and we have bought the shares in the Manchester Iron and Steel Company.' He looked at me, malevolence glowing in his eyes. 'On the table are the banker's drafts to conclude the business and there,' he nodded at the bonds and papers, 'is the paperwork to transfer ownership. Is that correct? Herr Griffiths?'

It took a second or two to register what von Ludwig had said.

'You didn't really think that you'd get away with this . . . this charade, did you?'

'When did you know?' I asked.

'I would like to say from the very beginning,' von Ludwig smiled, evilly. 'Unfortunately, that was not the case. You were seen at the wrong time in the wrong place.'

I frowned. 'What do you mean?'

'At the Rathaus Markt, when you fought with the Nationalist Party. You were recognised. I played along with you this morning because I want the shares in Hamburg Steel. I wanted your signatures on the correct documents, concluding the business. Now I have them. I also have the money.' He put out his hand to take the bankers drafts but stopped when Frazer pointed a pistol at his head and pulled back the hammer, making a loud and distinctive click.

I had to hand it to von Ludwig, he had plenty of courage. 'Do not be so silly. If you kill me you will never get out of Germany alive.'

'True, but then you don't intend to let us escape anyway,' I said, taking my own gun from my pocket. 'Don't move,' I said, pointing the barrel at Goebbles nose. He suddenly broke out into a sweat. 'Now, this is cosy. Sit perfectly still and you may just live for the next hour or two. Angus.'

Frazer stood, removed rope from his canvas grip and walked around the table. He tied the arms and legs of each of the men to their chairs and stuffed gags in their mouths, pausing at von Ludwig.

'You won't get away with this, Griffiths,' said von Ludwig. 'I shall hunt you down for what you've done.'

I shook my head in mock despair. 'No, you won't. Your son tried and he's dead.'

Von Ludwig's mouth dropped open in shock. 'You! You're him! The man who killed my son?'

I had assumed that von Ludwig knew precisely who I was and so his reaction came as a surprise. He began to squirm, fighting the ropes. 'I'll kill you! Kill you!' He spoke with anguish and despair in his voice. Suddenly he stopped and opened his mouth to yell. Before he made a sound, Angus hit him across the head with the butt of his gun and he slumped unconscious. Quickly, Angus tied a gag across von Ludwig's mouth. Blood dripped steadily from the wound on the old man's head and onto the plush carpet. For a few moments I felt sorry for him.

I picked up the banker's drafts and put them in my pocket. Next, I locked the door to the secretary's room and pocketed the key. I turned to leave when I thought of more mischief that I could do. I threw the documents relating to the transactions we had concluded into the fire place where they burnt brightly before dying to ash. I stood watching the flames until Angus prodded me out of my reverie.

'Come on, David. It's time to go.'

I locked the door to the boardroom behind me. We walked calmly down the stairs and out through the front door. We nodded greetings to half a dozen people as we passed, but did not pause. Outside, the weather had turned nasty, the wind had picked up and the rain had started. We were both grateful for the change. We turned up our collars, pulled down the brims of our hats and hurried across the yard. We had reached the gates when there was a yell from behind us and I looked back.

In the poor light I saw a window was open and Goebbels was leaning out, yelling. Suddenly, a regular series of whistle blasts could be heard, answered by others ahead of us. We took to our heels and ran.

49

OUTSIDE THE GATES we saw a gang of men running towards us. They were carrying sticks and wore brown shirts. They were headed straight for us. The nearest man was less than ten paces away when I pulled my gun and shot him. This was no time for niceties; survival and escape were the order of the day.

The gang scattered and I fired another shot over their heads. They left their comrade where he had fallen. A car screeched to a halt next to us and we piled in . Sion gunned the engine and we careered down the street. John grinned a sickly smile and looked ahead. I looked back in time to see two cars leave the curb side and chase after us.

'We've got company,' I yelled. A gun fired and missed.

'This is another fine mess you've got us into, Bro,' said Sion. 'Any ideas?'

'Keep going. They'll be stopped in a few moments.'

'How?' Sion yelled. 'Hell, that was close! He was referring to the bullet that had smashed into the wing mirror.

'Keep going and you'll see.' I leant out the window and fired a shot at the nearest car closing behind us. I missed. 'Turn right!'

Sion turned the car into the narrow street, it half spun, on the point of going out of control and then we shot into the narrow opening.

'Stop!' I yelled and Sion slammed on the brakes.

As we ground to a halt we all looked back, in time to see Mike emerge from a nearby doorway and scatter small pieces of wood with nails hammered in them across the road. He ran towards us just as the nearest car turned the corner. Its tyres blew and it spun out of control, smashing into the wall, blocking the street. Mike dived in and we drove away. This time, Sion kept the speed down. Our biggest problem right then would have been to have an accident.

It only took a few minutes and we were at the docks; nobody was following us. They didn't need to; they were waiting.

We stopped on the jetty, the *My Joy* a hundred yards away at a buoy. I could see Jake in the wheelhouse. He waved to us, darted outside and threw away the bow rope. Even as the boat turned towards us a hail of gunfire opened up and smashed into the foredeck. Miraculously, the bullets missed both the wheelhouse and Jake.

'Over there,' yelled John, pointing.

I looked towards a four storey warehouse two hundred yards away. In the windows were a dozen or more guns firing at us and the boat. If we did not do something soon, we would die. It was Mike who acted first.

'Mike! Wait!' I yelled, but he was already moving. Sion was alongside him. 'Sod it!' I said and ran after them. Angus followed. 'John! Cover us!'

John knelt behind an empty oil drum and opened fire with his shotgun. The cartridges were seven shot, the type used when hunting deer. The gun held ten rounds in a tube lying along the barrel, and John fired as quickly as he could pump the action. It was a long distance for a shotgun but John was an expert.

Each shot smashed through a window or went through an opening. There were screams and loud curses and the hail of fire suddenly stopped. I looked back. Jake had manoeuvred the boat alongside the wall and only the masts could now be seen, the hull and superstructure were completely hidden. There were more shouts from our attackers but by now I had reached the relative safety of the doorway into the warehouse. Shots were fired down at us but the angle was too acute for our enemies to get a proper bearing. Suddenly a shot rang out and came within inches of my shoulder. I looked up and saw a man holding a rifle, leaning out of the window and aiming directly at me. There was another shot and he lurched forward, teetered for a second and crashed to the ground alongside me. I looked across at John who held up his thumb.

Rapid fire erupted as Jake began shooting with a Lee-Enfield rifle, working the bolt as quickly as possible. The odds were shifting, and I now estimated we had a fifty percent chance of survival.

We worked our way through the door and into the warehouse, moving carefully. The hall was empty. Doors led off to the left and right and a stairway faced us. Mike darted forward with Sion at his shoulder while I covered them. A door on the next floor faced down the stairs. It opened and a man holding a gun appeared. Sion and I both fired and the man died instantly.

Mike, his back to the wall, was slowly moving up the stairs, Sion was behind him while I provided cover. We alternated, each covering the other. I was in the lead when we reached a corner of the stairwell. I knelt down and looked round the corner at floor level. I found I was looking at a pair of legs, striding towards me, just one pace away. Startled I looked up, the man was brandishing a rifle and had not seen me. I shot him in the stomach, the noise of the gun sounding deafening. He flew backwards, into another man, sending him flying. Before I could aim, Sion, who had been standing behind me, stepped forward and fired at the second figure now climbing to his feet. The bullet got the man in the head and he was dead before his body hid the floor. I held up my hand. We realised that silence had descended and no more shots could be heard from outside. Suddenly there were yells and the sound of feet running on the floor above us. The sounds receded into the distance. Mindful of a trap, we continued our slow progress. We heard nothing and ten minutes later we were satisfied that the building was empty. We hurried down the stairs and back into the sunlight. We found John where we had left him, but Jake was nowhere in sight.

'Jake's run to the end of the basin to see if the lock gate is open,' said John. 'We saw a few of them escaping down the road.'

'They could be back at any time with reinforcements,' said Mike. 'I suggest we get away from here as fast as possible.'

'What's the quickest way?' Sion asked.

'In the car, out of the city and to the airport,' I replied.

'What about *My Joy*. Are we just abandoning her?' Mike asked.

'It's only a boat,' I replied. 'I can get another one. Let's go as soon as Jake returns.'

We did not have long to wait. He came running back as though the hounds of hell were on his heels. Panting, he said, 'The lock gate's open. It's a clear run to the river.'

'We're leaving the boat,' I said. 'It'll be quicker to get to the airport.

Germany's too hot to hold us and the sooner we get out the better. We'd have miles of canal and river to travel along before we reach the open sea. And we've no way of knowing what could happen if the authorities got involved. What if they've gone for the police? The last thing I want is to have to explain what we've been up to.'

'This,' said John, heavily, 'has been a monumental cock-up from beginning to end. We should never have started it. Revenge isn't worth it.'

They all looked at me and after a few moments I nodded. 'All right. I know you're right and I'm wrong. I'm sorry. I was, I don't know, obsessed with it all. But what we need to do now is to extricate ourselves from this mess. We'd better go.' I looked up at the sky, realising that it was well into the afternoon and that dusk was only an hour away. The weather had cleared and there was a promise of a fine night ahead.

'Mike, run to the lockgates while we get a few things from the boat. Get the car ready, Sion.'

John and I ran to the *My Joy* while Angus and Jake took up defensive positions nearby. We threw the most important papers and possessions into a couple of holdalls and clambered back up to the dockside. We piled into the car and picked up Angus and Mike near the gates. 'Where's Jake?' I looked around but could not see him.

'He went down the street to see if it's clear. We don't want to drive into another ambush. We've been lucky,' said Angus, then added, 'so far.'

With that I had to agree. Our luck had been monumental but then we were facing thugs and louts. It could easily have been a different story if we'd been up against trained men.

Mike said, 'Jake went left a few minutes ago.'

'Nice and slow, Sion,' I said. 'We don't want to miss him and we don't know what's around the next corner.'

We slowed down and approached the cross-roads. Suddenly, Jake appeared in the road and waved. We stopped before we got to the turning and he climbed in. 'Don't go any further. There's a roadblock around the corner and I saw at least a dozen rifles being waved in the air. We need to go the other way.'

Sion turned the car and we headed in the direction opposite to the one we needed. We turned left and left again and found ourselves on the street behind the roadblock. I looked back to see at least twenty armed men, maybe more, hidden behind the makeshift barricade.

'That was a lucky escape,' said Mike.

'We aren't out of the woods yet,' said John. 'Not by a long chalk. Do you know the way, Sion?'

'I think so. Down to the bottom of the road and then right. We skirt the city and head east. I reckon it's about ten or twelve miles to the airport.'

'I hope you're right,' said John. 'Because I don't have a clue.'

That raised a few half-hearted chuckles.

'The streets are strangely deserted,' said Angus. 'I would have expected more people around than this.'

'Been warned away, most likely,' said Mike. 'These Nazis seem to have a lot of influence for a group that aren't in power. There's something ominous about them, frightening even.'

'That's just imagination,' scoffed Sion. 'Hold on, it looks like we've got company.'

'I see them,' said Jake. 'Two cars. Yes. They're definitely chasing us. Hell! Look out!'

I looked behind and saw the nearest car, still three or four hundred yards away but coming up fast, spouting the barrels of rifles. Jake was aiming his gun out of the rear window. He fired three rapid shots at the car. He missed but it caused the driver to swerve left and right, spoiling their aim.

'Here!' I thrust a handful of small, wooden blocks bristling with nails to Jake. He scattered them across the road behind us.

A shot was fired but it didn't appear to come near us. I looked back in time to see the leading car drive over the nails. As tyres were punctured, the car swerved, there was a screech and a loud crash as the car smashed into a shop window. The car behind missed the nails and closed up on us. A hail of bullets thudded into the back of our car as Sion twisted the steering wheel back and forth, trying to put them off their aim. Luckily, no one was hurt and the car continued with nothing vital damaged.

'Persistent swine, aren't they?' Mike yelled.

'Jake, John, Mike, get ready. A fusillade when I give the word.' They steadied their guns and I yelled, 'Fire!'

They opened up through the rear window and I fired from the side.

Angus was sitting between Sion and I in the front and could do nothing. The car behind swerved, slowed and burst into flame.

'Got it!' John shouted.

'Right, get the guns out of sight but be ready, just in case. I've seen a few people running for cover and I don't want the police to stop us. Sion, how much further?'

'The signpost said Glinde 12 kilometres, that's 7 or 8 miles, I think. We've plenty of petrol and the car's behaving so we should be there in ten or twelve minutes. I can't see anybody behind us, can you?'

'No,' answered Jake.

The next few minutes passed in tense silence. We left the city and were now in the countryside with only an occasional house to remind us of civilisation. Our nerves were strung as tight as banjo strings but as we neared the airport we began to relax slightly. Too soon, as it turned out.

'Ahead!' Sion called and swerved the car to the right, onto a dirt track. Only his superb reflexes, honed while flying, saved us. From behind trees sixty or seventy yards ahead three men had appeared and opened fire. None of the bullets hit and we shot down the narrow track, which wound through dense woods. The car bucked and bounced and after only a few hundred yards came down with a thump and stopped.

'The camshaft's gone,' said Sion. 'All out. Let's get the hell away from here.'

We clambered out, sorted out our few bags and weapons and headed towards the airport. We had less than a mile to go, darkness was falling, the night was dry and the going firm. Our only problem was the Nazis.

'They'll be ready for us,' said John.

We were walking in single file, Mike was twenty yards ahead and Jake about the same distance behind. We did not plan to walk into another ambush and if we did, Jake was the cavalry.

'I think you're right,' I answered. 'Any ideas?'

'Right now, none,' said John. 'I thought that as you got us into this, you could get us out.'

'Thanks, John. Your optimism instils me with confidence.'

'Quiet, you two,' Angus said, in a loud whisper. 'This isn't a Sunday afternoon's picnic. We can't make any plans until we get to the airport and see what's happening. We need Sion to tell us what's what.'

We stopped at the edge of the woods. Mike went left, Angus right and Jake stayed back, to cover us.

'Over there,' Sion pointed, 'is where the plane is. See those buildings? You can just make them out against the skyline. That's offices and there's a large hangar behind.' He looked at his watch. 'I shouldn't think that there's any airport staff here at this time. Ergo, anybody we see is probably a Brown Shirt.'

I could barely make Sion out in the gloom and the others were ghostly, dark spectres in the night.

'Okay. We move slowly and quietly,' I said. 'No shooting unless we've no choice. Angus and I will speak in German if we're challenged. See if we can get close enough to knock out any of them, rather than shoot them.'

'It's a bit late for such niceties,' said John dryly.

'I was thinking more about not being fired at, rather than any damage we might do. By all means, hit them as hard as you like,' I replied. 'Hey, Jake, close up,' I called in a loud whisper. A few seconds later, Jake crept silently into view. 'Before we go, check your guns. We want them cocked and ready.' There was the reassuring sound of bolts being worked and magazines checked. 'Right! Let's go.'

We started away from the woods. The scuffling of feet, clothes and bags seemed loud to my hypersensitive ears but commonsense told me nothing could be heard a few yards away. We were crouched over, moving quickly. I was in the front, Sion at my shoulder, the remainder strung out behind us. I heard a cough followed by a guttural German voice and stopped. A few seconds later I identified the source of the sound. It came from a position only yards in front of us. I indicated that the others should stay where they were, and Sion and I wormed forwards on our bellies. The ground suddenly dipped and slightly to the right I could make out two men, complaining to each other. They were lying behind the trunk of a fallen tree and if they had not been making such a noise we would have walked over them. I pointed to one side and Sion went in that direction. I went in the other. As I slowly crawled along my hand touched a fist sized rock and I picked it up.

'*Achtung! Was ist das?*' I heard one ask. His whisper carrying clearly in the still air.

'*Was?*' asked the other.

And then I saw Sion rise up beside him and wield his gun like a club. I did the same and smashed the rock down on the other man's head as it turned to look in Sion's direction. There was a solid thump and his body collapsed. I gave a low whistle and the others quickly joined us.

'Where's the Griffin?' I asked Sion.

'Just the other side of the hangar. I'll need five minutes to get ready.'

'What about warming the engines?' Mike asked. 'We need time for that too. '

'No, we don't,' Sion replied. 'The runway is long enough for us to rev the engine and take a longer than usual run to takeoff. We need to be on the move as soon as the engines start. Otherwise we could be in trouble.'

'That's an understatement,' said John. 'Come on, let's keep going.'

'We can't. I need to set a light at the end of the runway. Something I can aim at. Otherwise I won't be able to head in a straight line. If we come off the runway we'll slew round and probably tip over onto a wing. I know, I've seen it happen.'

'Any ideas?' I asked.

'I've got a small lantern in my bag,' said Jake, 'but you won't see it more than a few yards away.'

'I've got a detonator and timer,' said Angus, reaching into a side pocket of his jacket. He grinned. 'No well dressed man goes out without one.'

'Especially,' said John, 'if he's in the company of David Griffiths.'

There were chuckles all round.

'How long is the timer set for?' I asked.

'It's about twenty minutes. It can be as long as twenty-five but no more. It's the same type as we used once in France. I've been trying to improve its accuracy but I haven't managed it yet.'

'Can you and Jake set it to go off, using the lamp to create a fire?' I asked.

'Sure. That's easy,' was the laconic reply.

'We'll wait here,' I said.

'Don't rush it,' said Sion. 'You need to set the fire at the end of the runway so that I can aim directly at it. Okay?'

'Don't worry,' said Angus as he and Jake set off.

We waited impatiently for their return. Twenty minutes later we heard the rustling of branches and the shuffling of feet and they were back with us.

'We've got about fifteen minutes,' said Angus.

We crept nearer to our objective. This time it was the smell of cigarette smoke that warned us of danger. Thank God for amateurs, I thought.

Jake and Mike were already moving quickly and steadily to the source of the smell. There was an exclamation, a yell cut off before it amounted to much and then the low whistle. We sneaked forward, past two prone bodies.

We reached the building identified by Sion as offices. So far it had been easy and we had been lucky. At that point, our luck ran out. The place was crawling with Brown Shirts.

'Where did they all come from?' John asked, aghast.

Around the corner we could see men moving, some were entering and leaving the building, others were restlessly fiddling with their guns and others were cupping cigarettes in their hands to hide the glow.

'There's at least fifty of them,' said Angus. 'Maybe more.'

'Christ, they really want us badly,' said John. 'Now what?' he looked at me.

'Now we create a diversion, run like hell for the plane and pray,' I replied.

50

I'D BEEN CARRYING a grenade in my pocket, as a last resort. I took it out and hefted it in my hand. 'Where's the petrol kept?' I asked Sion.

'Over there,' he indicated the other side of the building. 'A large tank.'

'Right! I'm going to blow it up and when I do I want you all to make a dash for the plane. Shoot as many of them as possible. In the confusion we might get away. Give me a few minutes. All right?'

'Good luck, Bro,' said Sion, clapping me on the shoulder.

I darted along the building and stopped at the next corner carefully looking around it. I was aware of a presence behind me and did not need to look to know who was there.

'Too many scrapes, too many fights, David,' said Angus.

I grinned. Somehow, I was not surprised to hear him. 'Thanks. Damn! There's a group of them coming this way. Three, no four. All carrying guns. Ready?'

I kneeled down and Angus stood over me. 'Me left, you right,' I said.

'Got it,' he replied.

We fired, reloaded and fired in a swift, smooth action. The four men were dead before they hit the ground. There were yells and curses, loud orders shouted and general chaos amongst the other Brown Shirts. To add to the confusion I stood up, yelled and pointed.

'*Da. Sie sind da. Schnell.* – There. There they are. Quick'. I ran towards the woods on the further side and pointed. Men streamed after me. In the confusion I stopped and ran back to the petrol tank. I opened the tap to let the liquid pour onto the ground, unscrewed the lid at the top, pulled the pin on the grenade and dropped it in. I ran like hell back to the corner. As I dived round it there was an almighty explosion behind me and a huge ball of flame shot into the air. Angus opened fire and I could hear the others at the other side of the building doing likewise.

'Time to go,' I shouted. Angus nodded and we ran back the way we had come. The others had already run for the plane and we followed.

Behind us was a scene like Dante's Inferno. Some men were trying to put out the fire, using water which only spread the flames further, others were firing at imaginary targets, and near the woods a fight had broken out between two groups of Brown Shirts. We could not have asked for more chaos.

Sion had already got one engine started and just as I scrambled onboard the other fired up. The noise of the engines was drowned in the cacophony of sounds around us. The plane lurched, stopped, lurched again and began to move smoothly. We picked up speed and were soon racing along the runway.

I looked out of the cockpit window, over Sion's shoulder, and saw a fire burning brightly ahead of us. Angus and Jake had done a good job. No one took any notice of us – at first.

'Two cars are chasing us. Coming from the starboard side,' yelled John.

There was nothing we could do about it except hope that we could take off unscathed. There was an increase in the roar coming from the engines and we began to move faster.

'They're shooting!' Jake shouted. 'Missing by a mile!'

We seemed to have been racing down the runway for an age. The cars had stopped and the men began to shoot more accurately and then the rumble beneath us ceased and we were flying. The plane banked to port and within moments the airfield was merely a dim glow of fire behind us.

I sat back in my seat with a sigh of relief. 'Thank God that's all over,' I said, with feeling.

'David,' said John, 'any more of your hair-brained ideas – keep to yourself.'

'You mean you didn't enjoy it?' Angus asked, with a grin.

'I mean I'm too old for this sort of thing,' John retorted. 'I want a quiet life where the most adventurous event is taking the dog for a walk in the rain.'

'Fat chance of that,' said Jake, 'with David as a stepson.'

The flight was uneventful and when we were twenty miles out from Biggin Hill Sion began to radio ahead to get hold of Peter Cazorla. We needed lights to land by.

It took a few minutes but eventually Sion looked over his shoulder and shouted, 'Peter's lighting the runway for us. We'll need to circle for a while until he tells us we can land.'

I waved a hand in acknowledgement, too tired to worry. A short while later I could see the runway lights and we lined up to land. We came down with a heavy thump, a bounce and then the Griffin settled down. Sion brought the plane quickly to a halt and turned off the engines. We sat, savouring the peace and the feeling of safety it brought. After a few minutes we stirred ourselves and opened the door. It was a wonderful feeling to step down onto English soil again.

At Sion's house large drinks were quickly dispensed and soon we were sitting around the kitchen table talking about the events of the night.

'I hope you learned your lesson, David,' said John. 'Revenge isn't worth it.'

I nodded. 'I've learned my lesson,' I replied. 'Only it was worth it.' I took out the proceeds of our ill gotten gains and laid them on the table.

There was an embarrassed silence as we looked at the banker's drafts. 'I'll cash them first thing in the morning. We can meet in town and share the proceeds.'

'How much . . .' began Mike, who then cleared his throat and tried again. 'How much do I get?' He paused and then added. 'I mean, I just went along for the ride. I didn't expect,' he paused again and waved a hand over the table, 'any of this.'

John laughed. 'Welcome to the land of the Griffiths family.'

'What do you mean?' asked Mike.

'I mean that the Griffithses look after their own,' said John.

'That's £520,000,' I said. 'Deduct expenses, the price of *My Joy* and a few incidentals and we have £320,000 to share seven ways.'

'Seven?' Mike queried. 'There was only six of us.'

'One share goes to the capital,' I replied.

'In this case,' said John, 'we will share one share between those of us who put up the money. That's the way we do things,' he shrugged.

Mike grinned. 'That means I'm rich. How much . . . ?'

'Your share,' said Sion, working on the back of an envelope, 'comes to £45,714 and some change.'

'You can keep the change,' said Mike and burst out laughing.

'I must get back to London,' said John, getting ponderously to his feet. 'Anyone else coming with me?'

I stood up. 'I will, on one condition,' I said.

'What's that?'

'That you don't nag me all the way. I was wrong, we shouldn't have done it. We were lucky.'

John grinned. 'It sounds as though you've learned your lesson at last, so I won't say another word.'

A few days later John and I were sitting in the library at "Fairweather", a coffee in our hands, watching the rain lash the windows.

'I hope it clears up for Saturday,' said John.

I nodded. Saturday was the big day – the wedding.

'The adoption papers are ready,' said John. 'They're simple enough. According to my solicitor it's unprecedented.'

Suddenly I was not so sure that I could go through with it. It sounded ludicrous. I was too old to be adopted, even if it was for a potential benefit. It must have shown on my face because John picked up his coffee, sipped and sighed.

'Stupid, isn't it?' he said. 'It seemed like a good idea at the time but now, seeing it in writing and looking at you, I'm not so sure. We've discussed the matter endlessly but . . .,' he shook his head. 'I'm just not sure. It seems like cheating, somehow. You should become an hereditary peer by your own merits, not by some sort of sleight of hand.'

I shrugged; the same thoughts had been in my mind for some time. I voiced them. 'The argument against that, of course, is the fact that peerages are inherited by undeserving men who happen to be the sons of peers. And some of the history of those peerages doesn't bear close scrutiny. Many were given for services to the Crown that were murderous, larcenous and, in some cases, treasonous. The history of the Peers of the Realm is fascinating but should be left hidden, in many cases, to the mists of time. So, I don't know what to do. There's also the potential for embarrassment once the facts are known.'

'Nobody would know before my death,' said John. 'Your mother would, because she likes the idea but nobody else. I know we had a laugh about it with the others but it's all but forgotten. We needn't talk about it. The title could even pass quietly down to Richard, many years from now. The mantle could slip quietly over his shoulders and nobody need be any the wiser.'

I was not so sure about that. If I did become a Member of Parliament I would not want to be saddled with a Peerage. In fact, I would have to renounce the title to sit in the House of Commons, so it would all have been for nothing. For the first time in my life I was in a quandary that I could not extricate myself from. My dilemma was simple. If I accepted then, I would lay the foundation for the family's position in society to be one in the highest ranks. If I refused, to save myself potential embarrassment and possible ridicule, I would be denying future generations positions of influence and power. But would they deserve it? Damn, I was back on the same mental merry-go-round as before. I needed to talk to somebody who would be passionately interested and intelligent enough to help. And who would be directly involved. Madelaine, of course.

The wedding was the next day and Madelaine and I were lingering over breakfast. Motherhood suited her. She had bloomed with Richard's birth; she had an inner contentment that somehow showed in her smile and her actions. She was, by her own admission, very happy.

I explained my dilemma about the adoption and peerage and said, 'So, what do you think? Should I accept and put up with the ridicule or should I refuse? For the first time in my life, I can't make a decision. I just don't know what to do!'

'It's difficult, darling. My instinct as a mother is to say accept it for Richard's sake but on the other hand he won't exactly be wanting for anything during his life.'

I nodded. I wanted my son to strive for success, building on what we had already achieved. The only difference was that he would be starting from a much higher platform than the one Dad and, later, I had started from; I never forgot my roots were in the Welsh mining valleys.

'Compromise,' Madelaine said after a few moments silence.

'How?'

'See John's solicitor and ask if it would be possible for an adoption to take place just before John's death. With any luck he'll live a long time yet but one thing is certain, he will die in due course. If, somehow, you could then be adopted and inherit, well,' she smiled, 'you'll be the oldest person in history to do so. One thing puzzles me, though. How can this happen to a grown-up? Surely adoption is only for children?'

I shook my head, helping myself to another cup of coffee. 'Apparently not. When the legislation went through Parliament nobody thought to put an age limit on it. After all, who in their right mind would want to be adopted once they're past maturity?'

Madelaine's smile widened, 'Apart from you, you mean?'

I smiled back. 'Apart from me. What you say makes sense. Perhaps we can have all the paperwork in place and somehow have it triggered just prior to John's death. I'll talk to John about it. It'd be a compromise I can live with. In the meantime, perhaps I will stand for Parliament.'

'That's a bit blasé, isn't it?' Madelaine asked.

'I suppose so. It's just that Winston has promised me a safe seat and I understand one will be available shortly.'

'Where?' Madelaine sipped at her usual breakfast cup of Earl Grey tea.

'In Kent. It's not far and I can arrange a flat in the constituency, near Sion. We'll see. In the meantime I'll have a word with John about your suggestion. It might be possible.'

'Good,' she stood up. 'Susan is taking Richard for a walk but I need to change his clothes. Just one small irony,' she added. 'What's happened to your assertion that you'd rather make money than be a politician?' With that she gave me a peck on the cheek and left the room. I smiled, reflecting on how lucky I had been to end up with Madelaine. I dialled the operator to place a call to Brighton, to the hotel where John was staying. Apparently it was bad luck for a bridegroom to see his bride on the day before his wedding; even if they were no longer spring chickens, as we used to say in Wales. I grinned. More like grandmother hen and old rooster, I thought.

'John? I want to talk to you about my plans to stand for Parliament and em, the adoption. I wondered if I could meet you this afternoon. Good, thanks. At the hotel.' I hung up.

We sat in the quiet of the deserted lounge. 'Can it be done? I become adopted effectively at your deathbed, in effect, and hence I inherit the title.'

John nodded. 'When I spoke about this with my solicitor he stated that I can adopt a child right up to the point at which I die, provided the papers were completed and could be registered at a court.'

'I'm hardly a child,' I retorted.

'I know, that was when I clarified the question of the age of the person being adopted. There's no limit. Common sense prevails in a court of law. Or it's supposed to, at least. So I see no reason why we can't arrange matters to suit us. Let me telephone my solicitor and check on one or two things.' He heaved himself up out of his chair and added, 'You know, I'm getting really nervous about tomorrow.' With that he strode away. If he was nervous, he was doing a good job of hiding it.

The following day dawned bright and fair. I lay next to Madelaine, thinking about what the next few hours would bring. I was suddenly overcome with grief when I though of my father and the injustice of it all. The lottery of life was as unfair as it was sometimes kind. I wondered what Mam was thinking and whether or not she still wanted to go through with it, or was she having second thoughts, as I was?

I slipped out of bed, not to disturb Madelaine, put on a dressing gown and went down to the kitchen to make a cup of tea.

I was surprised to see Mam sitting there, a cup of tea at her side, staring into space. When she looked up at me I could see the tears in her eyes. Neither of us spoke for a few moments as I crossed the room and put my arms around her, holding her head to my side.

She patted my hand and said, 'It's all right, bach. I'm all right now.'

There was a lump in my throat which prevented me from speaking for a few seconds. Mam always said that tears were for the pillow, not public display. I cleared my throat.

'It's not too late, Mam. John will understand, I'm sure.'

She smiled, looking up at me. 'I've come too far to back out now. Anyway, the fact is that I want to marry John. I'll never love him as much as I loved your father but I do love him. He's kind, considerate and we're good companions. I hope for a long life yet and I don't want to spend it alone.'

'But you wouldn't be,' I argued, pouring tea from the pot into a cup. 'You've got us.'

She shook her head. 'David, much as I love you all, it's not the same. I need to talk to somebody who understands me and my generation. And that's somebody who is of my age and, thankfully, knows just about all there is to know about me and, by extension, my family. John fits the bill nicely and I know that he loves me.' Mam shook her head, 'No, I want today to happen but I needed to indulge myself a little with my memories; some sad but many wonderfully happy. I've sat here the past hour playing it all through my head. Now it's done with. The past is locked away in my memory, available to me to take out, dust down and think about whenever I wish. The future starts today and I'm looking forward to it. Now, tell me, what's happening with this adoption thing?'

I smiled, pleased that she was happy. 'John telephoned last night. His solicitor had already taken advice from a leading barrister. John is going to set up a unique, interest in possession, discretionary trust which will only be triggered on his death. The trust will contain all the paperwork relating to the adoption and my inheritance of the title.' I shrugged and added, 'So I'll remain a commoner until John dies, which hopefully will be a very long time from now. Nobody else will ever know about it and even after I get the title nobody will know that it was by adoption. So we achieve our objective and everyone is happy.'

Mam placed her hand on mine and smiled warmly. 'I'm delighted for you and the family. From a small mining village in Wales to become pillars of society in one generation is an unbelievable achievement. The price we've paid on the whole, has been too high, but then there's always a price to pay. And, young man, on that philosophical note I'm going upstairs to bathe and dress.'

She walked out, carrying her cup of tea while I sat immersed in my own introspection. As always, I thought back to Llanbeddas and my sister, Sian. The time of the terrible accident. In my mind it was the day when it all changed for us, when we started the great adventure which had led us up to where we were. I would never forget the day a million tears had been shed.

Epilogue

THREE WEEKS HAD passed since the boat trip when Tim Hunter had first met the family. He was sitting in the room Sir David called his den. They had just returned from Sion's funeral. The family and friends were milling about the grounds and house, chatting, smiling and drinking. The reporter sat with his feet on the corner of the desk, a large malt whisky in his hand. He reflected on the vicar's sermon which had been apt. Sion, like the others in the family, had indeed lived a charmed life. It was a word that summed it up for them all: *charmed*. He smiled to himself and raised the glass in salute.

'To you, Sion Griffiths, wherever you are,' he said out loud, and took a sip.

'I agree with that,' said a voice behind him which sent the reporter lurching to his feet, causing him to spill his drink. 'Relax,' said Sir David. 'I won't bite you. It's the end of an era. The last of my lot.' Sir David walked across the room to the fireplace, a glass of malt whisky in his hand.

'Except for you,' said the reporter. 'Sir, the mess in Germany . . .'

'What about it?' Sir David asked with a certain amount of amusement in his voice.

'Well, it was such a mess. So, I don't know, out of character, perhaps?'

'Maybe. I'm not sure about that. What it did do was teach me a hell of a lot. A lesson I never forgot.'

'What sort of lesson?'

'In particular I learnt that revenge is not a good reason to do anything. In fact, the reverse. It was also a salutary lesson in arrogance. I had begun to think that I was invincible. I could do anything and get away with it. Of course, it wasn't true and I nearly learned the hard way. In my defence I can say that I never forgot the lesson. It was a complete and utter mess, one we were lucky to survive. If we'd been up against a trained force the outcome would have been entirely different. It took years for the Brown Shirts to understand that but when they did they became very formidable. Do you know, I can think of at least two occasions over the next twelve years when history could have been different. But you'll come to that later on, as you work through the papers. Now, I'm the last one,' he paused.

'Along with the wives,' the reporter added.

Sir David nodded. 'Except for Kirsty and Madelaine, though in reality they don't count. What I mean,' he hastened to add, seeing the look of astonishment on the reporter's face, 'they weren't there from the beginning. I mean,' he was confusing himself now, 'they didn't know the whole story. We kept a lot of the facts away from them, so that they wouldn't be needlessly upset. Like the time in Spain. We kept that away from the women.'

'You tried, you mean'. Both men looked towards the door. Unknown to them Madelaine had been standing in the doorway for the last few minutes, listening. 'Of course, we knew what had happened. We put two and two together and usually came up with the right answer.'

'Four?' Sir David suggested with a wry smile and a lift of his eyebrows.

'In your case,' Madelaine stepped into the room and tucked her arm through his, 'at least five. We never let on,' she smiled at the reporter, 'that we knew what was going on. The lot of them were in one scrape after another. If it wasn't one, it was another, leading them astray.'

Sir David patted his wife's hand. 'I often wondered whether you knew more than was good for you.'

Madelaine gave a girlish giggle that, somehow, was not out of place. 'Jake told Estelle most of it, Kirsty learned some from Sion and Angus would tell Catriona bits and pieces. We would write down what we'd learnt and share it, by letter, with each other. We had a better network of intelligence than the Secret Service. Oh, don't look so surprised, darling, you all married intelligent women, so what did you expect?'

Sir David laughed. 'You see, young man, why they say that the female of the species is more deadly than the male? Conniving, clever and, in this case, beautiful.' He shook his head in mock sorrow. 'We don't stand a chance.'

'Come, my dear, we need to go back and see the others. This is, after all, a wake.'

Sir David nodded agreement. It was also the celebration of a wonderful life, that of his brother's.

When the old couple had left, the reporter sat a little longer. Yet again his thoughts were interrupted, but this time, to his pleasure, it was Sian. She closed the door behind her, stepped across the room and planted a kiss firmly on his upturned face.

'I think you've been patient long enough,' she said.

'I have?' he pretended to be surprised, knowing precisely what she was alluding to.

'Tonight I'm supposed to be staying at a friend's house in Brighton. I gave up my room to one of the visitors.'

'I know, so have I. I'm staying in a hotel in the town.'

'No, you aren't. You're staying with me.'

'I am?' he asked, surprise and delight chasing themselves across his face. 'What about your friend?'

'She's gone to France for the weekend,' Sian smiled, coquettishly. 'Here's the address. You can spend the evening telling me how the new book is coming along.'

'And the nights?' he asked.

'The nights are for something else,' Sian replied.

The third book in the series about the Griffiths family is called *A Million Tears III, The Tears of Darkness and Light* and will be published by Good Read Publishing Limited in the autumn of 2000.

A Million Tears

A Million Tears is a mighty epic, the first of four books chronicling the life of the Griffiths family.

This is a tale of love and hate, murder and suicide, poverty and wealth – the story of a family whose devotion for each other helps them to succeed where others fail.

Dai's world was confined to the close-knit South Wales mining community where the most exciting event in his 10 years of life was a trip to the market town of Pontypridd. But he has his atlas and he has his dreams . . .

'A Million Tears' is the realisation of those dreams. From the hardship and poverty of Wales in 1890 to the optimism and wealth of America, the Griffiths family strive for success. Follow Evan, the head of the family, as he fights his way from coal-miner to businessman to politician. Dai, whose search for adventure takes him to the exotic corruption of the West Indies and Sion, who has to grow up fast to survive the brutality of the west. There's Uncle James who will stop at nothing to save the family and finally Meg, the rock of the family, the constant in all their lives.

This is a compelling story of adventure and love, tragedy and survival. A wonderful story by a master story teller.

ISBN 1-902483-00-6

Débâcle

TIFAT File I

A Nick Hunter Adventure

Following a summit meeting in Paris an alliance of interested countries form an elite fighting force to combat terrorism throughout the world. Based in Britain and under the command of a British General, the team is made up of Western, Russian and other non-aligned countries' special forces.

Without warning the terrorists strike. A group of bankers, politicians and industrialists are taken prisoner off the coast of Scotland and the new, untried force is sent to search for them.

The Scene of Action Commander is Nick Hunter, Lieutenant Commander, Royal Navy, an underwater mine and bomb clearance expert with experience in clandestine operations.

The enemy is one of the world's most ruthless and wanted terrorists – Aziz Habib! Hunter leads the team against Habib, backed up by two computer experts: Sarah from GCHQ and Isobel, hired by the General to run the IT for the new force.

While stock markets take a pounding and exchange rates go mad, the state sponsoring the terrorism is making a fortune. It has to stop. At all costs.

This is non-stop adventure from beginning to end. A riveting story told by a master story teller. You are guaranteed not to want to put it down!

Débâcle mixes fact with fiction which will cause you to wonder, how true is this story? Did it really happen?

ISBN 1-902483-01-4

Mayhem

TIFAT File II

A Nick Hunter Adventure

The Nick Hunter adventures continue faster and greater than ever. TIFAT is now an established organisation in the old Royal Naval base at *HMS Cochrane*, Rosyth in Scotland. When Israel is threatened by an overwhelming force from the countries that surround it Macnair has to take action. As terrorist incident follows terrorist incident a pattern emerges. The usual suspects when it comes to sponsoring terrorist activities are closely examined but the evidence makes no sense.

Only when David Golightly, Deputy Prime Minister of Israel, contacts Macnair does the jigsaw begin to take shape. The perpetrator is a powerful and rich Israeli whose ambition it is to create a Greater Israel at any cost. Millions will die unless he is stopped; innocent men, women and children who are pawns in the hands of their Middle Eastern leaders.

From the Highlands of Scotland, across the Alps, into Italy and south to Israel the action is a non-stop rollercoaster. Fact and fiction mingle to make a breathtaking story you won't want to end. The twists and turns are as ingenious as ever as Hunter races across the bleak landscape of Northern Israel pursued by enemies who will stop at nothing to kill him. If he doesn't succeed, mayhem will engulf the whole of the region.

Mayhem will be published in the spring of 2000.

ISBN 1-902483-02-2